Song of the Shank

Also by Jeffery Renard Allen

FICTION
Holding Pattern (stories)
Rails Under My Back

POETRY
Harbors and Spirits
Stellar Places

Song of the Shank

A Novel

❋ ❋ ❋

Jeffery Renard Allen

GRAYWOLF PRESS

This publication is made possible, in part, by the voters of Minnesota through a Minnesota State Arts Board Operating Support grant, thanks to a legislative appropriation from the arts and cultural heritage fund, and through grants from the National Endowment for the Arts and the Wells Fargo Foundation Minnesota. Significant support has also been provided by Target, the McKnight Foundation, Amazon.com, and other generous contributions from foundations, corporations, and individuals. To these organizations and individuals we offer our heartfelt thanks.

Song of the Shank is a project of Creative Capital.

Creative Capital

Published by Graywolf Press
250 Third Avenue North, Suite 600
Minneapolis, Minnesota 55401

www.graywolfpress.org

Published in the United States of America

ISBN 978-1-55597-680-4

2 4 6 8 9 7 5 3

Library of Congress Control Number: 2013958011

Cover design: Kimberly Glyder Design

Cover photos: *Blind Tom*, circa 1880, photoprint by Golder & Robinson, New York; copyrighted by John G. Bethune. From the Library of Congress Prints and Photographs Division. Piano keyboard and photo border used with permission from Shutterstock.

Map design and illustration: Matt Kania, Map Hero, Inc.

for Zawadi,
my wife, heart and gift, gift and heart

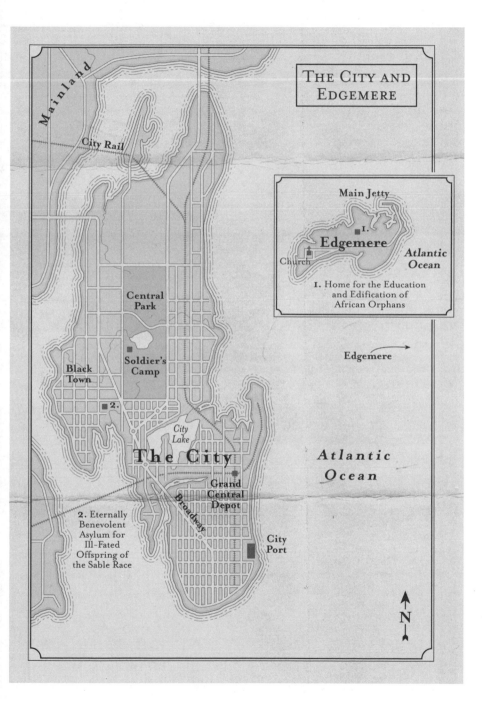

THE CITY AND
EDGEMERE

Mainland

City Rail

Central
Park

Black
Town

Soldier's
Camp

2.

City
Lake

The City

Broadway

Grand
Central
Depot

2. Eternally
Benevolent
Asylum for
Ill-Fated
Offspring of
the Sable Race

City
Port

Atlantic
Ocean

Main Jetty

1.

Edgemere

Church

Atlantic
Ocean

1. Home for the Education
and Edification of
African Orphans

Edgemere

N

Contents

Traveling Underground (1866) 3

Moving House: Three Views of the City (1867) 99

Bird That Never Alights on the Trees (1849–1856) 157

Rain Storm (1854–1856) 217

Voice of the Waves (1856–1862) 349

The Celebration of the Living
     Who Reflect upon the Dead (1867) 365

Gold and Rose (1868–1869) 481

Song of the Shank (1869) 503

Underground (Return) (1869) 541

Song of the Shank

Traveling Underground
(1866)

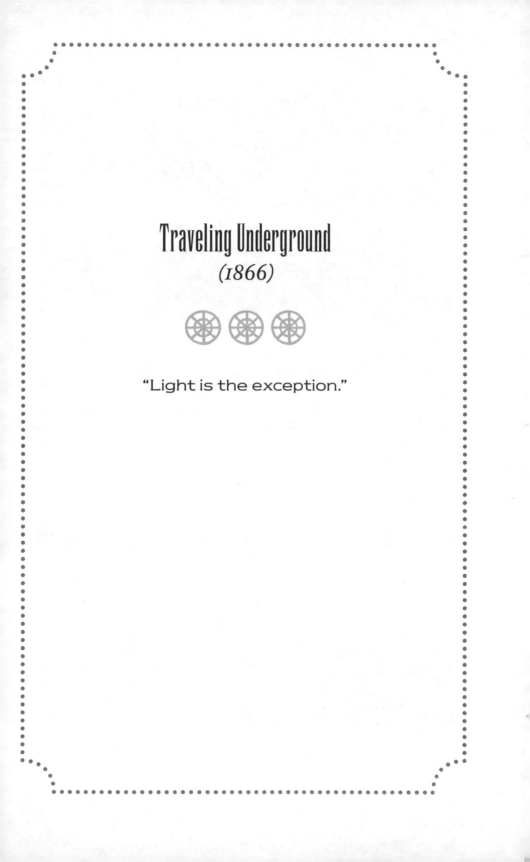

"Light is the exception."

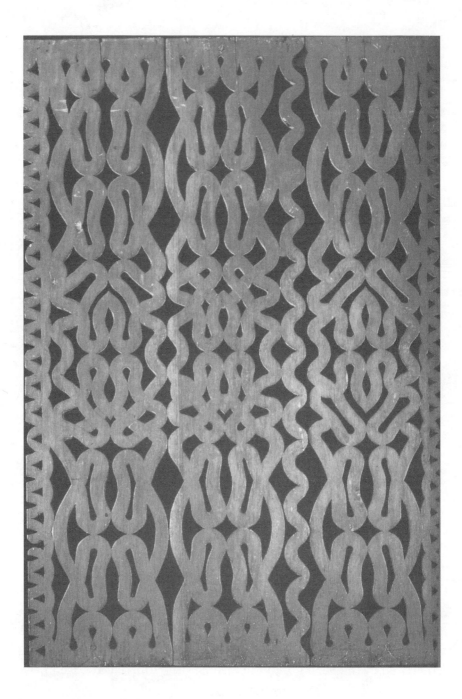

SHE COMES OUT OF THE HOUSE AND SEES FRESH SHAPES IN the grass, a geometrical warning she does not understand. Blades mashed down under a foot, half-digested clots of earth where shoe heels have bitten in, mutilated worms spiking up through regurgitated blackness—piecemeal configurations, suggesting a man's shoe, two, large, like Tom's but not Tom's since Tom never wears shoes in the country. A clear track, left foot and right, running the circumference of the house, evidence that someone has been spying through the windows, trespassing at the doors. Had she been back in the city, the idea would already have occurred to her that the journalists were to blame, those men of paper determined in their unstoppable quest to unearth the long lost—three years? four?—"Blind Tom"—*Half Man, Half Amazing*—to reproduce the person, return him to public consumption, his name new again, a photograph (ideally) to go along with it, the shutter snapping (a thousand words). She has grown accustomed to such intrusion, knows how to navigate around pointed questions and accusations. (Ignore the bell. Deny any insistent knock on the door and that voice on the other side, tongue and fist filled with demands. Speak calmly through the wood, polite but brief. Use any excuse to thwart their facts and assumptions. No matter what, don't open the door.) Yet no one has called upon them their entire summer here in the country, those many months up until now, summer's end. This can only mean that the journalists have changed their strategy, resorted to underhanded tactics and methods, sly games, snooping and spying, hoping to catch Tom (her) out in the open, guard down, unaware, a thought that eases her worry some until it strikes her that no newspaperman has ever come here before in all the years—four? five?—that they've had this summer home. Alarm breaks the surface of her body, astonished late afternoon skin, all the muscles waking up. Where is Tom? Someone has stolen him, taken him away from her at last. She calls out to him. Tom! Her voice trails off. She stands there, all eyes, peering into the distance, the limb-laced edge of the afternoon, seeing nothing except Nature, untamed land without visible limits. The sky arches cleanly overhead, day pouring out in brightness across the lawn, this glittering world, glareless comfort in the sole circle of shade formed by her straw hat. Tom! She turns left, right, her neck at all angles. The house pleasantly still behind her, tall (two stories and an attic) and white, long and wide, a structure that seems neither exalted nor neglected, cheerful disregard, its sun-beaten doll's house gable and clear-cut timber boards long in need of a thick coat of wash, the veranda sunken forward like an open jaw, the stairs a stripped and worn tongue. Nevertheless, a (summer) home. To hold her and Tom. It stands isolate in a clearing surrounded by hundreds of acres of woods. Taken altogether it promises plenty, luxury without pretense, prominence without arrogance, privacy and isolation. Inviting. Homey. Lace curtains blowing in at the windows, white tears draining back into a face. The trees accept the invitation. Take two steps forward, light sparkling on every leaf. The nearest a dozen yards, a distance she knows by heart. Deep green with elusive shadings. Green holding her gaze. Green masking possible intruders (thieves). She must move, have a look around. No way out of it. Takes up a stout branch and holds it in front of her in defense, uselessly fierce. Even with her makeshift weapon she doubts her own capacities. Look at her tiny hands, her small frame, the heavy upholstery of her dress. But the light changes, seems to bend to the will of her instincts, lessening in intensity. (Swears she hears it buzz and snap.) She starts out through the grass—Tom keeps the lawn low and neat, never permitting the grass to rise higher than the ankles—her feet unexpectedly alert and flexible across the soft ground under her stabbing heels, no earthly sense of body. Winded and dizzy, she finds herself right in the middle of the oval turnaround between the house and the long macadam road that divides the lawn. Charming really, her effort, she thinks. In her search just now had she even ventured as far as the straggly bushes, let alone into the woods? It is later than she realized, darkness slowly advancing through the trees, red light hemorrhaging out, a gentle radiance reddening her hair and hands.

Still enough illumination for a more thorough search. No timepiece on her person—her heavy silver watch left behind on the bedroom bureau—but she's certain that it's already well past Tom's customary hour of return, sundown, when Tom grows hurried and fearful, quick to make it indoors, as if he knows that the encroaching dark seeks to swallow him up, dark skin, dark eyes.

Had she missed the signs earlier? What has she done the entire day other than get some shut-eye? (A catalog of absent hours.) Imagine a woman of a mere twenty-five years sleeping the day away. (She is the oldest twenty-five-year-old in the world.) After Tom quit the house, she spent the morning putting away the breakfast dishes, gathering up this and that, packing luggage, orbiting through a single constellation of activities—labor sets its own schedule and pace—only to return to her room and seat herself on the bed, shod feet planted against the floor, palms folded over knees, watching the minute lines of green veins flowing along the back of her hands, Eliza contemplating what else she might do about the estate, lost in meditation so that she would not have to think about returning to the city, a longing and a fear. She dreaded telling Tom that this would be their last week in the country but knowing from experience that she must tell him, slow and somber, letting the words take, upon his return to the house for lunch; only fair that she give him a full week to digest the news, vent his feelings—in whatever shape and form—and yield.

It takes considerable focus for her to summon up sufficient will and guilt to start out on a second search. Where should she begin? A thousand acres or more. Why not examine the adjoining structures—a toolshed, outhouse, and smokehouse lingering like afterthoughts behind the house, and a barn that looks exactly like the house, only in miniature, like some architect's model, early draft. She comes around the barn—the horse breathing behind the stall in hay-filled darkness, like a nervous actor waiting to take the stage—dress hem swaying against her ankles, only to realize that she has lost her straw hat. A brief survey pinpoints it a good distance away, nesting in a ten-foot-high branch. She starts for it—how will she reach that high?—when she feels a hand suddenly on her shoulder, Tom's warm hand—Miss Eliza?—turning her back toward the house, erasing (marking?) her body, her skin unnaturally pale despite a summer of steady exposure, his the darkest of browns. (His skin has a deeper appetite for light than most.) He has been having his fun with her, playing possum—he moves from tree to tree—his lips quivering with excitement, smiling white teeth popping out of pink mouth. Tom easy to spot really, rising well over six feet, his bulky torso looming insect-like, out of proportion to his head, arms, and legs—what the three years' absence from the stage has given him: weight; each month brings five pounds here, another five pounds there, symmetrical growth; somewhere the remembered slim figure of a boy now locked inside this seventeen-year-old (her estimation) portly body of a man—his clothes shoddy after hours of roughing it in the country—an agent of Nature—his white shirt green- and brown-smeared with bark and leaf stains.

He turns her fingers palm up like a palmist reading her hand. Pulls and leads her back to the front door of the house, bypassing the back entrance. Because his eyes are lidded over, all the energy in his face is in mouth and jaw. (Eyes are globes that map the feelings of the face.) He grasps the door handle as if it is a butterfly—delicately, barely touching it with his fingers—pushes the door open, and with a great show of strength turns to carry her inside, lifting her high above the ground, overestimating, throwing her face momentarily into his black cap of kinky hair. She hooks both arms around his thick neck, ringed with sweat, for the ride. Her body against his, she can feel his heart beating rapidly beneath his damp shirt. In fact, he's exhausted, struggling for breath. Something vulnerable about his features, a child's earnestness in his unknowing blind face, which gives to his obesity the suggestion of exposure rather than strength, more unaware flesh available for ambush. He takes time to wipe the bottom of his feet against the hemp doormat, one foot after the other, again and again, Eliza stilled in air. They flutter in. He almost drops her when he is setting her down. In the act of balancing she detects a faint scent in the room, the smell of tobacco. Someone has been in the house. Might still be in the house. She latches the door while Tom, sensing nothing, dizzy with the scent of pollen on his hands, grass on his feet, whistling—always a tune buried under his breath—hurries over to the piano—his feet slide like dry leaves over the carpeted floor—which squats like a large black toad in the sitting room. He takes a seat on the bench, removes his hankie from his back pocket, and cleans his face. Returns the hankie and brings his hands to the keyboard, his long fingers fanning out in excitement. Begins playing, his routine, discipline of pleasure. She sets off to inspect potential hiding places, twenty rooms of ample size, upper and lower, sets off, charged by fear she doesn't dare feel. How quietly she goes above the music rising up from downstairs; she feels lighthearted, competent, in a situation she knows she can handle. Could be a burglar sneaking through some unsuspecting person's house, increasingly confident and safe, her pendular breathing causing her to believe that she is only moments behind the intruder, just short of reckoning. A feeling quickly dispelled. Expecting everything, finding nothing. Looking through glass, she scans the jagged red-lit landscape impressed upon her mind with the sudden violence of a dream, all those yellows greens and browns separate parts of something, no longer the stable signs of summer sanctuary but disjointed hostile eruptions. She feels even more the need to leave the country at the earliest opportunity, tomorrow or the next day at the latest. Hard to imagine putting off their return to the city. Something real ahead.

Downstairs again, satisfied with her search—check the latches, front and back—safe and sound for now, she settles down on the settee, Tom twenty feet away from her at the piano, his face directed at the ceiling with the height-bound music, his hands chasing one another squirrel-like over the keyboard, Eliza turning speculations about the unknown intruder, mind spinning down to concentrate on her own slowing pulse, buried sense, the music relegated to the edge of awareness as she sits face to face with the fact of herself in this red-bright room filled with handsome well-crafted furniture and plump well-stitched upholstery, light making the objects look incongruous and absurd, lurching in and out of focus like this countryside that lurches in and out of her (their) life with the seasons. She wants to get back to the city, to her (their) apartment. A strong drive to part with this place for good, sever all seasonal ties. Easier now for her to entertain the thought of year-round residence in the city. Everything in between their apartment and this house a mistake. Torn (her) from the city each summer, they holiday here because there is little risk of entanglement, danger from others, the house far beyond the usual hunting grounds. Not that she is not trying to keep them hidden, keep Tom underground.

The facts trip her up. (What she does not say is clearest.) Forced to admit, the city is ideal for her, but not for Tom. Would she dare live here in the country? A city girl her entire life, she's not sure she's cut out for the countryside. All that harmony and light. Greenness pulling through the leaves. And flowers blooming out in the heavy humidity of the air, growing things too colorful to look at but nevertheless created beautiful for the delight of man. Scents and nectars and fruits that act as attractive guides for insects. She cannot get her mind around the idea of Nature, Barmecidal feast. Too much to take in. The promised primal power and purity of the elements—fresh air to clear the head, space for the body, rest and reclamation—rarefied to a degree that eludes her senses. There is nothing she desires to map, mount, or measure. So who she is in the country is unclear. Tom's safety is not reason enough to stay. End of story.

Or is it? The morality is ever changing. (At cross-purposes with herself.) She gets caught in all the choices. What's bound to happen? What might happen? What should happen? The questions cast long shadows that do not disappear.

She watches as if from a watery distance, a red-tinted vista, dusk besetting the edges of body and piano, profile opening, redefining the boundaries between ivory and skin, muscle and wood. Tom is signaling her, white and black flags moving under his brown fingers, as if he can sense her rigid unresponsiveness—is she holding her breath?—and is determined to break her out of it. This bounteous act, premature calls floating around her. She casts out—what precedes what—to meet them, drawing to herself many points of sound, many others lost, breath held to slow down the reeling in, that which is brought back heard singly (as should be?). What a pleasant feeling to find (sense) her person in an upright position, rebodied, flesh again in a distinct sort of way, no longer just a sleeping form, but a working one, thinking, planning, and organizing, fields clearing in her mind. The sound growing there says too much. She feels it—pinching the keys—in her mouth, teeth, tongue, and gums. She wants to curtail it. Can't. Her mood rising with each minute. Uplifted. All this music he gives only to her. She's no expert, but he seems to play better than ever, no part of the force lost, his three-year hiatus from the stage hurting him none. He could step back under the spotlight tomorrow and simply pick up where he left off and then some, his past performance mere dress rehearsal for his prime. All that music still, "Blind Tom" preserved. Words prepared, she wants to tell him right then that they will be leaving tomorrow, but the music chases the idea of departure from her head for the moment. (After dinner, tell him after dinner.)

The splintered edges of a voice. Is Tom singing? No. Speaking her name—Miss Eliza—clearly and cleanly in a way pleasant to hear, the play of a smile around his mouth.

Yes, Tom?

Lait, please.

She gets up from the settee to honor his request, walks down the long tunnel of hall to the kitchen filled with the odor of meat—

blood congealed in the cracks and the lined spaces where the floor joins—music following her. Pulls the pantry open (hinges creaking) and enters the cool sound-muffled dark. Bends at the waist and lets her hands search through black air for the bottle of milk kept curdle-free in a bucket of water.

In the light, she fills a slender cylindrical glass to the high rim and makes her return—music drawing her back—steady hand, careful of tilts and spills. But Tom, planted on his bench, fingers skipping like grasshoppers across the keys, doesn't seem to notice her standing there right next to him. She nudges his shoulder with the glass, and his right hand springs up to seize it while the left continues to pattern chords, arpeggios, bass lines. He throws his head back and takes a deep draft, throat working, until the glass is empty. Pivots his face ninety degrees in her direction and holds the glass— face, neck, Adam's apple—out toward her at the end of his fully extended arm. Miss Eliza, he says. *Lait,* please. She knows where this is headed, her feet fated to flux between kitchen and tongue. (Been there.) Might as well bring the whole bottle and preempt any need for orbiting.

So why doesn't she? He takes more time with the second glass, drinking and blowing melodies into the liquid at the same time. Drains the third—see, you should have brought the bottle, or made a fuss—then bites the rim in place between his teeth, the glass attached to his face like a transparent beak, both hands free to roam over the keyboard. Tom drinking milk, making an event of it.

Milk seeping from the corners of his mouth, Tom sits quietly on the bench—buttocks seesawing over the narrow mahogany edge—facing her (twenty feet—more—away), practicing gestures on his pliant face, each expression holding the burden of a moment—what is he pondering? feeling?—and not for the first time the thought occurs to her that his face is not unattractive, the skin smooth and unblemished, the hidden eyes protruding against the lids to give them a pleasant bell shape, the ears large and relaxed at the sides of his head, close and tight, the nose spread wide and clinging, a bat hanging upside down in sleep. All in all, a look of still calm that he can never fully eradicate from his face.

He's forgotten all about the piano—the music sleeps between his fingers, which are joined together and resting atop his paunch—and is ready for something else. His arms moving in circles now, hands trawling through the air, like someone swimming. What is it that he wants? She pushes her thoughts (speculations) into his body and face. He wants her to choose a song for him to play. (Yes, that's it.) She calls out a selection—*Waltz in A-flat*—but he continues to gesture. She shouts out more guesses, the two of them partnered once again in this dance of communication. He won't simply come out with it. A game for him, having fun at her expense. Lured (roped) in, she'll just have to play along, abet him. What choice does she have? Looking at these arms and hands moving even quicker now in strange uneven arcs, frantic, annoyed.

Perhaps what he wants involves some act where words can't go. She relinquishes her place on the settee, rising up to meet what? And answers with a dance that moves her feet forward, two steps, three, which succeeds (at last) in eliciting a change in Tom. He hears her move away from the couch, hands waving her on. (Advance.) She stays put, and he begins a hauling motion, as if she is attached to an invisible rope. And when she still doesn't move he leaps up from the bench and charges, face forward, body behind, Eliza startled (confess), not knowing what will happen, knowing nothing ever. Comes and takes her by the hand (left), palm up, and starts to lead her back—now she understands: he wants her to sing while he plays, though she can barely carry a tune—to the bench, where he begins to wedge her down before the piano, bending her fingers back, stretching the seams of her palms, testing the durability of the hem that is her wrist. She sits and he settles into his space right beside her, close enough for her to feel the heat come off him. Sings. (What tongue, mouth, and throat don't know.)

Sometime later, she salts, cuts, plucks, soaks, scrubs, rinses, chops, grinds, dices, pounds, oil sizzling in the skillet, pots bubbling and boiling, her mind working over tomorrow's departure, while Tom stands listening at her side (touching distance), swaying slightly—his body can't keep still—mouth watering, strings of drool webbing his chest, a sticky obstruction between now and tomorrow.

She readies her knife while he hovers over the cutting stand, poking and playing with the dead thing, exhibiting the straightforward curiosity of some innocent—a puppy or toddler—unburdened by any evident capacity for prejudice or appraisal. Her hand claims the handle, blade venturing out to discover the difference between air and flesh. The pleasant rhythm, slice and clack, of the knife, hitting the butcher's board, traveling from gullet to gut.

When she is done, Tom seizes the knife and begins running it back and forth over the butcher's board, sharpening silence, his mouth moving, some song just beyond the ear. A short time later he rinses the knife in the sink, strokes it dry, and puts it quietly away in the cutlery drawer. Circles back to the sink to wash his hands and face, water and skin splashed and slapped. Dries himself firmly with a clean towel. She spreads a fresh cloth over the table and sets two places, and they take seats, he on one side and she on the other. He is quite capable of serving himself, his fingers drawn to steam, and already his plate is full, spongy biscuits pushed to the edge, like shipwreck survivors overcrowded into a single emergency craft. Tom bent over his plate, lips quivering—is he saying grace? a new activity for him if so—the same angle he assumes at the piano, one hand rising to his mouth.

Eliza enjoys watching him eat, the physical manifestation of a fact. But she can't take in much, too much room in her stomach for remorse.

The darkness that comes on them is startling (her momentary blindness, her fear) and complete. She lights the lamps, releasing the smell of kerosene. Tom floats against thin white curtains hanging straight in still air, the shadows concealing, revealing nothing of his color, his or hers.

His skin is ready. He holds his arms closely to his chest as if determined to guard this limited (torso) part of his nakedness—flabby mounds not unlike (almost) a woman's breasts, belly button in layers of abdomen suggesting the bird's-eye view of a volcano—and wobbles toward the tub. Hauls his legs up one after the other over the high porcelain side and joins her neck deep in high islands of foam. It's the only way she can get him to bathe, the two of them together—*He never has taken much to water, Sharpe said*—two huddled forms stationed at either end of the tub, face to face, an archipelago of suds between them. Two bodies peeling away, layer by layer, soap the substance that obscures when it is smeared across cheek and brow, nose and chin, before running white fingers over muscle, bone, soft places, hard places—knows them all—making it hard to tell which leg or elbow, one outside, one inside, belongs where, to whom. She reaches to slow down his wild hurried hands. Rebuffed, cut short, they go moving like dark fish through the water, swimming to another world.

She grows considerate. Guides him back, hands that work as hard returning as running away. Stroking her face. Down-stroking her shoulders. Drawing warmth across her breasts until he takes tight hold of her silent back. She lets his touch linger, feeling the power of his fingers, this body embracing her reminding her that she is not alone. He reaches up and fists a hank of her hair, letting the strands sieve through his splayed fingers. Hairs pushing against each other, flickering back and forth, a mass of flowers set afire under his water-warm touch.

Two washed bodies, light and clean—she dries Tom then herself, using the same towel made from Georgia cotton—smelling of lavender soap and talcum powder. He dresses her, she him, her form preserved under the wide heavy folds of her nightgown, Tom exotic in his white sleeping caftan and peaked nightcap like something out of an Oriental tale, *Arabian Nights*.

Back in the parlor she takes a seat on the settee, and he kneels at her feet, rests his head on the altar of her lap. Lets her (needs her to) massage his scalp, harvesting the naps, black buds blooming open. Unexpectedly, he pulls himself up midtouch—short season—and ambles off to the piano, where he sits on the bench, hands positioned above the keys. And he stays that way, still, withdrawn, music withheld, leaving her to measure the distance between them. It's as if he knows that something is up. (No, she hasn't told him.) She feels a deep sense of gnawing discomfort but refuses to let it take hold. No use trying to draw him in. He'll find his way to bed. In fact, she should allow him to savor this hour, his final night here. She rises—heavy filled skin—and snuffs the lamps.

I'm going to bed now, Tom.

As might be expected.

With no light to guide her, she starts her ascent up the imposing mahogany staircase—a body wound through space—reaching out for the inclined railing to steady and direct her. Pain sets off in her hand. She realizes that she has actually grabbed the blade-like finial, which is carved in the form of a fiery torch (Sharpe's idea), with pointed top and sharp spiraling edges, rather than the customary polished globe. Soon finds herself sitting upright on the bed, its circular shape (Sharpe, ever the iconoclast)—a beached sea creature trapped inside the pink and blue and gray squares and diamonds of the crocheted bedspread—so familiar to her bottom and the soles of her feet, yet she feels like an exile in an unknown space, her fears scrawled into words on the unmade sheets. Lets her head fall back into the pillows, her turn to be quiet.

She awakens the next morning in a semi-trance-like state. Shudders loose. Scrambles out of bed. If she slept at all last night she does not remember doing so. (What actual and what the engine of dreaming?) Opens one drawer after another, moves into the closet and dresses for the day ahead. Finds Tom downstairs—he is always up at the first fluttering of color in the sky—seated at the kitchen table, an empty plate before him, utensils set, fully clothed, a napkin tucked into his collar.

Miss Eliza. Sleep well?

Yes, Tom. Thanks for asking.

And how are you today, Miss Eliza?

Fine, Tom.

I am fine today too. The smile on his face is meant for her. No trace of last night's glumness. (Forgotten? Denied?) The old Tom in full effect. How faithfully he assists her. Pumps bucket after bucket of water from the well out back—the motions come naturally, the trajectory of handle and shoulder—and hauls them to the door. Grinds her coffee. Beats eggs in a bowl, his hands circling faster and faster, while she slices some strips of salt pork and sets them popping in the hot lard-lathered skillet.

The discarded bread crumbs, the empty coffeepot, the quiet sink, the cups, plates, and utensils cleaned and put away—only now does he pick up on it (again), the smell of moving, uprooting, as present and pervasive as the odor of their long-finished and satisfying breakfast. Tom seated across from her, fingers locked on the table, head bowed, like someone saying grace. It's not easy for her, his silent pleas cutting through defenses. The best recourse is just to get on with it, Eliza dumbfounded once again at how poorly she has understood his feelings.

In the parlor, he calls himself to order. Fits his bell-shaped bowler hat onto his head, a pristine object she hasn't seen all summer, since their arrival here. Picks up his portmanteau—when had he readied it?—in one hand and his malacca cane with the gold knob, a gift from a former stage manager, in the other, his actions weighing everything with a solemn expectancy. She ties her bonnet in place and pulls the door open, but he remains standing, wavering slightly, rocked shut. She takes him by the arm and leads him out.

An hour later at the rental stable, Tom begins to unload their luggage in neat even stacks directly behind the buckboard, quicker than she can count, a tumultuous rush, nothing she can do to stop him; her admonitions go unheeded. Must be that he insists on believing they've already arrived at the train station, the first leg of their journey complete. Stands waiting, leaning on his walking cane, the horse one place he another, as if each, Tom and horse, understands the other is off-limits, the rules and restrictions reestablished. She steps down from the driver's platform and situates herself midpoint—equal distance—between Tom and the horse, throwing in for show a few demure adjustments of her bonnet to offset the way her hands move into confident position before her waist. The owner smiling politely in the doorway less than fifty feet away, tallying up Eliza's transgressions and calculating their severity and trying to decide what chastisement or punishment is warranted before finally seeing fit to leave his post and amble over to her. She settles her account with a one-pound sack of sugar, a luxury she's sure the owner's never seen by the look on his face. (More where that came from—despite a summer of ounces weighed and measured—all those unused sacks she must lug back to their apartment in the city.)

He places the sack on the running board, then looks at Eliza, looks at their muscled-over luggage, looks at Tom, back at Eliza. You must be after the early train? he asks.

Yes, the early.

And could do with means of transport. He palms his neck and rubs it. Well, miss, it grieves me to inform you that I can't carry you.

He pinches some rheumy annoyance from its lodging place between the corner of his eye and the bridge of his nose then takes a fresh look at Eliza to find out how much damage his report has caused.

She can't say a word in response.

I'm constricted. You see, my boy is out sick, leaving me short-handed for the day as is. And I am beholden here, to my livelihood. No getting away. He nods at the road fifty paces off. Try the first able body that comes along. Already he is bending over and grabbing one slender leg, anxious to see what the stallion has dragged in with its hooves. Finding nothing out of the ordinary, he unhitches the animal from the buckboard and man and beast disappear behind the closed door of the stable. (The last snort of the nameless horse.)

So be it. She feels cheap and stupid, feelings in no way lessened by her knowing that the owner is of that variety of white man who believes she and Tom hardly deserve his professional courtesy. But he is willing to extend it anyway, clear evidence of his patient and generous nature, his time and words bordering on abundant acts of chivalry where Eliza and Tom are concerned. (Lucky them.) Whatever her true feelings, a proper lady would, at the least, openly thank him while privately counting her blessings and expressing gratitude to the forces that govern the universe. She stands, studying the sound and quality of the air. Small creatures clicking in her ear, the clatter of the leaves, a crow caught in a hot gust of wind somewhere above. She's reminded how close the South is. How recent the war. (Time comes flying back. What has changed? What will change? What can change?)

The road encroaches upon her like a tightening band, squeezing into view a single solitary figure who strolls along it, shoes thumping in the dirt. Eliza watches the shape with almost scornful incredulity, fearing that she has given physical form to some mad hope filling her heart, and wont perhaps to admit that the stable owner's predictions (promises?) might be fulfilled so quickly. Notions and motives that seem reasonable enough until she sees a head spin in her direction, a quick look of recognition before looking away, and only then does she believe that the figure is real, Eliza witnessing this brown face catching sight even as it is caught, catching then confirming her presence and Tom's with additional discreet glances. The Negro seems wary, content to carry on. So why is it that she can't call out to him, can't lift her tongue to the roof of her mouth and press a single word out, or at least signal him over?

Sees him curve off the road and begin to make his way toward them, brisk and definite. What strikes her is how the Negro takes the initiative. No way she could have expected that. Surely, he has caught wind of her situation and looks to gain some improper price. And she will have to pay it. She shuts her eyes tight for a second to prepare herself. Finds him standing with his eyes open in apparent expectation only feet away from her. He's an imposing man, several inches taller than Tom and twice Tom in years and almost double his weight, but there's nothing slack about him. Statuesque, chiseled. And perfectly groomed—shirt ironed, collar starched, sideburns trimmed—like somebody for Sunday service but in a manner that seems natural, unobtrusive, as if he had done little more than slip into a fresh set of skin.

Day, ma'm. He lifts his derby then lets it settle back onto the shelf of his forehead, a certain pause in his gestures and a smile poised on his face, deliberate contrivances meant to give her ample time to return the greeting. But her voice is still trapped somewhere inside her body. I can tote them bags for you, he says. His eyes are white and quiet, staring at her. The derby softens his appearance and makes his head look like an egg lodged inside a bowl.

She looks between Tom and the other Negro in a kind of agony. Her faltering now, at this moment, can't be a good thing.

Lend a hand, Tom says.

The Negro looks at Tom then back at her. What time's your train, ma'm?

How can such a quiet voice come from so large a man? Perhaps he is dropping it so as not to be discourteous. She tells him the scheduled departure time.

The luggage, Tom says. He makes a pseudogeometric move with his walking stick, part circle and part directive. If the Negro feels insulted he refuses to show it. Only picks up the lightest suitcase and closes the fingers of Tom's stick-free hand around the handle, performing this apportioning of labor with such diligence and ease that Tom makes an impatient sound—breathes deep once—but does not resist. Then in an acrobatic display, he takes up every piece of the remaining luggage, muscled out in both fists, wedged between his elbows and his rib cage, and—the largest trunk, heavy even when empty—mashed up against his chest and stomach. Leaves not a single bag for her to carry. (She's paying after all.)

The Negro handles the luggage with assurance—moving matter— like one used to it, although it takes all of his focus to walk in a straight line, trying hard not to display any strain. She can't remember the last time she's seen a Negro in this county, certainly not since the days when she and Sharpe and Tom first came here together to spend their summers. Little clouds of dust rise from their shoes, reaching a maximum height three or four feet above the road, slow and lingering dust, hanging in air. Easily another two miles to the train station, and Eliza becomes aware of curious sounds spilling out from the Negro's body—wheezes and belches, grunts and snaps. Soon—a quarter mile—he is panting furiously, his arms, legs, and back wearying down, giving way to exhaustion. The remainder of the trek is one of constant upset, Eliza fearing at every step that the Negro will lose his balance.

They have come a good piece, and the three of them show signs of it. She can hardly stand, quick to collapse on the settle right outside the door that leads into the ticket office. Tom finds the settle with his cane and takes a seat beside her, still clutching the single bag the Negro had assigned him, arm crooked at his side to keep the bag from touching the floor. The Negro lets all the bags he is carrying fall into the dirt three paces short of the porch. Leans against a vertical post to catch his breath, so tall that he has to lower his head to avoid touching the wood roof under which he shelters from the sun. In all this not a word has been spoken among the three of them. Three people walking and sitting and standing while abiding by a hard bright silence that she did not find disconcerting. (It would hardly have been fitting for her to strike up any conversation with the Negro. Knows well how to play her part.)

He looks at Eliza from under his hat—Ma'm, just giving my arms a rest—before he starts loading the luggage onto a handcart. Takes the last bag from Tom—tugs once twice before Tom relinquishes it—and stacks it neatly on top of the others. Stands there under the roof, head hanging like a horse's above her and Tom, his face glistening with sweat of the earned type, like a polished badge proudly announcing its achievement. He wants to be paid.

Of course, the Negro will prefer banknotes to sugar. (Common sense.) Thinking such, she removes the three lowest denominations of bills from the drawstring purse she keeps on her person (dress pocket) and holds them up to him.

He throws her a hard disapproving look. No'm, he says. You ain't got to pay me.

Hearing confounds sense. Had she understood every word, Eliza asking herself although she knows that she has, knowing bringing change. All of this is quite different from the way she has been conceiving it. He simply wants to help her (them). She continues to sit, staring up at him with an amazed and incredulous question. *Why?*

I'll tote them on for you.

Sir, Eliza says, I must not detain you any longer. What she says, although she would be happy enough to accept his offer, even let him do it all again, right down to his clumsy performance at the end (luggage dropped in dirt), a mishap that she is willing to forgive, seeing that in these three or four or five seconds they have established something noteworthy between them, formed an alliance to make the best of the worst.

Ma'm, you ain't got to worry bout that. I'll just tote them then—

Sir, she says, I must decline. You've gone out of your way, her refusal almost lost between whines of gratitude. Let us manage henceforth.

His eyes dart at Tom, as if to read the meaning of what she is saying. As you see fit, ma'm. Beneath his hat he looks disappointed. I should take my leave. He seems reluctant to move. Safe passage. He lifts his hat and tilts his head.

I bid you a very good day, Tom says.

Eliza watches the Negro disappear around the corner of the station, and she continues to watch, not knowing where he has gone any more than she knows where he came from, and debating whether anyone had ever bestowed upon her a greater act of charity. She gets up from the settle, leaves Tom—The tickets, Tom, I'm off for the tickets—and walks with brisk purpose inside the station to the ticket booth, where she sucks in the dense air of the room and coughs a wave of gagging unstoppable coughs (heaves). Greets a small naked face crossed by three black iron bars. A face with too narrow a forehead; the eyes seem to be starting out of the sockets. The face sees only the one standing before him requesting two tickets, but this face does not question her purchase, bestowing the tickets on her with a courtly motion.

She returns to find Tom standing up, on the verge of panic, his cane waving about in the air like a confused insect feeler. She touches his arm and they sit down together on the settle and wait for the train. Plenty of time to kill. More than an hour. The journey here by foot had seemed slow, their own dust getting ahead of them, but it had not been, only seemed that way because (perhaps) of moving through country without another soul around.

The train is just a sound at first. Then it comes all at once, punctual to the minute, great iron wheels and rods slowing beneath the tossing ringing bell, black smoke flaring out of the stack and steam wailing through the whistle, the station full of cloud and noise, Tom moving beside her, his mouth urgent and wide.

The conductor is standing on the steps of the dining car, directly behind the engine, a heavy-built man with a red strong-boned face, bodied like someone better suited to hard labor, laying tracks rather than riding on them. For a brief moment, more a gesture than an act, he glances from his perch toward Eliza, travels on to Tom and sees all there is to see of him, then directs his gaze elsewhere, a dismissal. Steps down hurriedly to the platform and starts a slow walk down the length of the station, but there is nothing to supervise, conduct, since she and Tom are the only boarding passengers.

All aboard!

Never acknowledges her. Never collects their tickets. His dismissal multiplied by heads framed in windows, faces pressed to glass, peering out in judgment. Determined not to let the insult inside her, Eliza takes the time (seconds) to study everything that is grotesque about the conductor, irritated by her powerlessness to force the issue. She gets up easy, like she has no weight to herself, and touches Tom in such a way as to let him know she is not going far and she will not be long. Makes her way over to the handcart and takes down the first item of luggage from the mound, aware that the conductor has already reached the end of the station and started the walk back. Seeing too something else that beggars belief, the Negro emerging from around the station corner, a black mass of speed, moving determinedly with head forward and a fixed from-under stare like a charging bull's. This entity that shoulders right past the conductor, who, startled, understanding, stops dead still for a moment, looking at the Negro, the Negro continuing on, coming straight for her.

Ma'm. He lifts his hat, and before she can react he takes (snatches?) the bag from her hand, gets another bag and a third, then climbs onto the first passenger car and deposits them into the carrying space, loading and reloading two bags at a time, working with a kind of furious patience, a calmness and authority that surprise Eliza after his deferential antics earlier on. The conductor assumes his perch and hangs there in frozen immobility, his gaze calmly following the Negro, the conductor looking (trying to) more unconcerned than perturbed. (Just for a moment, she catches the fire of anger in his eyes.)

All aboard!

After he loads the heavy trunk, the Negro sees to it that she and Tom assume a berth on the train—moving single file down the narrow aisle, the Negro, Tom, Eliza—one (his decision) all the way at the rear of the car, meaning that they must pass row after row of their fellow passengers—the car half full—proper ladies and gentlemen who are nevertheless shocked and alarmed at this occurrence, drawing back in disgust and (even more) willing to express their feelings through faint cries of protest and indignation and (probably) derision and scorn. Tom takes the inside seat, near the window, passing his malacca cane off to Eliza for safekeeping. Eliza relieved that at least this much is settled. Duty fulfilled, the Negro stands poised in the aisle, waiting quietly—loud breath, silent sweat—looking down at them, eyes bright, as if the lifting and carrying and conducting had been a form of play. She takes it that he is waiting for her to discharge him.

Sir, I'm both sorry and thankful, she says.

Much obliged, ma'm.

Please allow me to compensate you something for your time and effort.

No, ma'm.

Are you certain?

Yes'm.

Iron scrape and drag, the train begins its sluggish pull out of the station.

Well, I best be leaving. The Negro bows slightly and lifts his hat. Ma'm. He shifts his attention to Tom. Mister. Tom neither moves nor speaks. The Negro stands, watching and waiting, the great iron wheels slowly rotating in hope of greater momentum, and succeeding somewhat, a beat or two. Mister. Momentarily he leans all the way over her and touches Tom's shoulder. Tom turns his unseeing face at the contact. Only then does she notice that the Negro is staring at Tom with a marveling smile. Now she gets it. One poor son of Ham helping out another. Kindness, generosity—it was more than that with the Negro. It was Race and blood, shared suffering and circumstance. But wait—watching him watch—is that the true sum of it? She feels privy to an even greater, deeper, emotion. Apart from anything else, what—she sees in his gaze—can only be described as admiration and devotion, sentiments fully evident—unmistakable— from something in his manner and posture that had nothing to do with strength or height or poise or clothes or their cut and fit.

You can help us again, Tom says.

Much obliged. The Negro tilts his head-hat. Safe passage. Turns and starts down the aisle, swinging his shoulders lazily as he walks, unconcerned about what *they* think and at the same time very much concerned that they get a good look so as to recognize and remember this man, this Negro, moved by his own words, his own thoughts, made significant and present in the world because he has accomplished something of value for none other than the one and only Blind Tom.

It makes Eliza smile to herself as she watches.

And then he is gone, out there in the steam and smoke. She eases back and relaxes in her seat. Glances at Tom beside her, almost indistinct in bright light blaring through the window, a smile on his face, enjoying the movement of the train as it follows the curve of a hill, leaving the edges of the town to their left, scattered farms and homesteads hugging hurtling earth. A gradual thickening of brown and green until soon nothing but vegetation is visible through the windows (left right). The thought that they are finally leaving the country for the city becomes irresistible.

Mile after mile the other passengers maintain an illusion of civility and pay her and Tom no mind. Only shifting corner-eyed glances. Tensely hissed whispers. Words drifting between words. Diction strikingly precise. A general sense of touchiness all around. She has the greatest desire to start a discussion with these people. To confront them. (Something of the defiant Negro rubbing off on her.) So why doesn't she?

The conductor enters the coach at the far end with a smile-commissioned face, squat and out of proportion to the visible rest of him under his short-brimmed cap. Starts his way down the narrow aisle, cumbersome and bulky, dodging knees and elbows, exchanging greetings (automatic discourse) and collecting tickets with a supplicating nod of his gray cap. At the appropriate time, Eliza holds her tickets up, and, shoe-leather hands, the conductor makes as if to take them, actually lowers and targets his brim, only to move on to the passengers seated in the row behind. A crude deliberate formula in his treatment.

Sometime later—the next station, the one after that—a soldier boards their car, brass buttons bright against the dark blue cloth of his tunic, varicolored medals splayed across his chest, mapping for the world the war he has returned from (that has returned him). The field saber holstered in its scabbard alongside him an awkward appendage, a rudder steering him this way and that down the aisle. And the hat he's wearing, the biggest she's ever seen, looming large on his small head, some powerful ocean-crossing ship bouncing on the peaked waves of his ears. (Does she even see his face?) Taken by glory, another passenger relinquishes a seat at coach front so that the soldier need not suffer the slight indignity of sitting in the rear where Eliza and Tom sit. (Does the soldier thank him?) Before he has comfortably put himself between the cushions—saber removed—even before the train has pulled out of the station, the conductor enters the car and speaks to the soldier with a catch in his voice and a smile hung on the end of his words. Takes his ticket. Nods his thanks and good wishes. Then he brings himself before Eliza and asks for her tickets with triumphant malice, his eyes lit sharply with exactly what he thinks about her. She produces them and he accepts them, satisfied with having the power to diminish and delay, even if he must capitulate and perform his job.

He slides away down the glistening aisle. They are speeding through space, tracks catapulting them toward the low sun, the city, toward home. Her bones jerking and shaking. She feels no more solid than the disparate streams of smoke swimming past the window, kicking their skinny black legs, bringing (now) the smell of fire with them.

Traveling north through a continual cascade of trees, moving between dialects and regions, a rise rich in territorial overtones. Unclear to her the national claims, where (before the war) what federation begins or ends, no line of demarcation, no sharp defining difference—they cross the river—separating one state from another, between there and here, only this river curving them into a view (window) of a halo of motion on the horizon, then, an hour later, sun sinking into the dark waist and a flaming flower rising up, the glass glistening with its fuzzy light, the city's brooding skyline, growing across the distance with each closing mile, waving its petals of roofs and towers, domes and belfries, factories surmounted by smokestacks and churches surmounted by the cross.

The conductor jams his body in the door to keep it open, wind rushing in and something inside the coach emptying out, all speech and sound snatched free into the world. Eliza actually feels her insides suck; drowning in the air. But the conductor only stands there smiling (back) at them, features distorted under the rushing wind. After a gradual easing off of speed, they pull into the iron-vaulted shed of Grand Central Depot, a structure as big as a cathedral and possessing many of the same Gothic affectations.

The entire production of leaving the train, walking through the station, and passing out of its wide portals takes only a few minutes. Panic and anger and the beginnings of elation all in an instant. The point is to hide right out in the open, put up a front of normalcy and routine. Nothing out of the ordinary here. No crossing of boundaries that should not be crossed. But suspicion permeates every syllable and glance. They think he is dead. "Blind Tom," the eighth wonder of the world, the Negro Music Box, for her eyes only. His three-year absence from the stage having produced tenfold theories about his death. Strung up during the draft riots. Frozen in Alaska. Drowned in a Pennsylvania flood. Consumed by fire in a London hotel. Caught under the wheels of a railcar in Canada. The victim of a soldier's bullet in Birmingham. Felled by his own heart in Paris. Felled by his own hand in Berlin.

Tom gives her hand a little tug, meaning, Let's move a little faster, Miss Eliza. Distracted by their return to the city, she only now notices his distress. A timid destitution has closed over him, a folding in on self (collapsible flesh), which forces him to walk in a slouch, Tom conscious of being watched. Wisps of panic begin to flicker through her brain.

Eliza is already searching for a taxi among the many lined up one after another curbside, horses parked head to behind, their drivers outfitted in ragged and ill-fitting frock coats and stovepipe hats, attending to their carriages cheerfully, dancing around the wet slap of dung hitting hard ground. If only their good mood could work in her favor. The first just looks at her in a dull unresponsive way, her request left stinging in her throat. The next waggles his head from side to side. It gets worse after that—shouts and curses, faces turning away, glares that promise pain. She approaches the final driver in the queue, thinking that this may be the occasion when they will have to walk home. But why give him a chance to refuse? But the driver only smiles back at her delightedly from his perch as if he has never seen anything funnier. She calls out to Tom. Tom passes her his cane then heaves his considerable bulk into the cab next to her, leaving the porter to attend to their luggage. The taxi does just hold it all.

They ride out into the strange wonders of the city, trundling across dry bridges and wet streets rivering up out of twelve canals, a city stitched together by water. Houses and buildings pushing against each other like contentious waves. The glow and hum of the gaslights clinging silt-like to their frames. Their windows crawling with lurid light. Shadows of people moving behind them as if performing (for her). The factories and mills burning even at this hour. The shops still open for business, many hundreds of objects arranged so as to arouse desire. People tumbling out from restaurants and saloons or leaning against the crossed telegraph poles from which black bodies had hung during the draft riots. The entire city welcoming her back. How happy she is that they are safely hidden within the hooded cab. They took something away from Tom, and he'll never get it back.

As they drive deeper into the city, it seems to her that hundreds and thousands of facts crowd into memory. The reek of feces and urine, lime and kerosene. The air stinging her skin with some invisible but definite spray. This crisscrossing of the senses too much and achingly familiar. The tiniest details recognizable. (Seeing them now?) Before long she can feel her whole body revive. Strange how altered the city seems after a summer away. Unreal. The wagon moving faster than warranted, bouncing them into the unmistakable dimensions of Broadway, a wide well-lit boulevard running like a river of whiteness from one end of the city to the other. (The boundaries stay clear.)

Tom's ears perk up. They have only to take the next corner, follow this last street, empty and mute and dark (dim lamps stationed far apart), which presses in on them like the walls of a narrowing tunnel. Tom relishing (smiles, grins) these bumps and declensions. Under inspection, the corners and lanes scramble to order, form a neat row of identical nondescript five-story residences reflecting the crude elemental law of symmetry, which has directed much of the layout of the city. She tells the driver where to stop. The facade pleases the observer (the broader view) because it looks so gray in keeping with its actual age, but sturdy, able to withstand. The brick—she wants to believe she has memorized each one—honeycombed with bullet holes. Every window is open, except theirs—a sultry night despite the time of year.

The driver will take the luggage into the vestibule and no farther.

Tom gets out of the cab unassisted and, golden-headed cane in hand, hops shifts and hobbles along the sidewalk up to the building entrance, his hat flying away from his head, Eliza behind him struggling to keep up, walking deeper into the darkness, away from the gaslights. They walk through the heavy door, pull moonlight in, and start the five-flight climb, Tom wheezing fitfully from the effort of lifting his ample bulk, voices from the street following them up, loud, night-singers, and frenzied laughter and shouts, mixed with the erratic barking of neighborhood dogs.

She rattles keys at their door. The one that should won't turn the lock. Tom clings to the banister, alert and listening.

I'll need to go fetch Mr. Hub.

Tom makes a slow sound of assent. As might be expected.

Forcing himself to immobility, remaining at the banister while she descends five floors—six?—to the basement in search of Mr. Hub. The Hubs inhabit the smallest dwelling in the building, the sort of place you see all at once upon entering. (And she has, once or twice over the years.) They have a bell and a knocker at their door. She tries both. For quite a long time nothing happens. Mr. Hub is someone who usually rushes to answer a bell. She knocks and rings again. That sensation that has to do with a shut door. Mr. Hub answers, a ripple of surprise passing over his face, that shapeless lump jammed into the angle of opening, little circles where the eyes should be as if thumbs have gouged in. (How he always looks or only the pallor of the late hour on his cheeks?) He smiles, nods—Mrs. Bethune—trying to hide his discomfort. Hovers anxiously in the doorway, looking leaner than usual, perhaps because of the bedclothes. Eliza used to seeing him in denim overalls, a rag fraying away in his hand.

Now his wife, a gaunt woman with stern pale features, is standing behind him, holding her dressing gown at the collar, flanked by their children. Eliza cannot recall a single instance when she has heard the woman speak, even in greeting or to chastise one of her offspring.

I'm sorry to draw you from your bed. She tells him succinctly about the key and asks him to look into the matter.

Yes, Mrs. Bethune. Of course.

They hasten along, Mr. Hub rising before her with a three-foot candle, which he carries like a sword at his side. He is low and stout but lunges his body up the stairs with long strides as if someone is pushing him from behind.

A most peculiar thing, she says, the key.

It ain't the key, Mr. Hub says. A lock can shrink and swell. Like most things.

She sees the logic of that.

Mr. Hub reaches the landing where Tom is standing against the banister. He barely acknowledges, a peep, a nod. Puts his whole body before the door, hands working, and the door springs open. There. He lights the candle, stops at the threshold of their inviolate privacy before passing off the candle to her.

That tallow's still got some life. The wife will be wanting it back.

She looks at him dubiously. This small matter. Burning wax. Will the morn be soon enough?

Certainly, missus. Make as much use as you need.

She informs Mr. Hub about their luggage waiting down in the vestibule. Okay squeezes out of his eyes faster than his mouth. He holds out a new key to her. You'll be needing this, he says.

She takes the shiny new key, wondering how it confirms or contradicts his theory of contraction and expansion.

He starts back down the stairs, Tom still, waiting. Only when Mr. Hub's footsteps have died away does he move, half-stumbles half-dances into the apartment. Continues on, the fingers of one hand touching the wall, a map to orient him, the carpet muting the sound of his and her feet.

They gain the sitting room. Using the candle, she lights a lamp and steps to the center of the chamber, surprised to find that the entire space has been dramatically transformed into a cube of dazzling white. In their absence someone—Mr. Hub?—had entered the apartment and liberally coated the walls in several layers of fresh wash. The room seems otherwise undisturbed, furniture and lamps collecting dust and spiderwebs. Tom's piano is the dominating object, black and shining (had Mr. Hub polished it?), rising like some rocky formation—a butte or cliff—out of the carpeted floor. Overall, the room produces (the long view) a strange impression, spacious (airy) but subdued, because of the limited light, the shadows, black vectors. The first thing she'll have to do is to open all the windows, for the apartment has not been allowed to breathe for months now.

We have returned, she thinks. Feels her body subsiding to the calm thrill at being home.

Tom gives her a sudden and delighted embrace, squeezing her to his steeping softness, her body crushed against his. The back of his jacket is wet with sweat, and his body reeks of coal and exhaustion. He speaks into her neck.

Lait, please.

A clean form in her line of sight: Tom seated on the piano stool, arms crossed at his waist, clutching the corners of his body (elbows), guarding his borders, trying to remember where he is. He is in a bad fix, dejected, has been for days, since their return. Has seen reason to do little more than position his slack pounds on the stool, head bowed, the piano blankly waiting for him. No music has broken from his fingers for hours, having long since moved away from the morning's mazurkas, inventions, and variations. The only sound that of her struggling to remain upright on the thickly upholstered settee, along whose velvety seat she has been sliding all afternoon. All of the furniture feels wet—the room filled with the pungent smell of salt, scales, and sand—as if deep in the insides of something living. Sitting with her feet in water hour after hour, that dark expanse of carpeted floor beneath her, she could not have gauged with any accuracy the duration of the silence. (What is it she wants to say?) Sunlight expanding and contracting with passing clouds, creating the feeling that the room is a great bellows, opening and closing around them. The whole while her own quiet voice carrying across this fluidity of space, nothing to answer to, its sound coming back at her again and again, never failing to make her feel useless and alone, at fault, as if they have both failed. A gradual falling away of words until no words at all. This is just how he is, mute and inaccessible, he looks flat and unreal, like a silhouette cut from paper, the resident shadow flickering in and out of vision, lips folded, biting something back, and she must suffer the effort of watching him. She smiles to comfort him, an instinctive but utterly useless response. Strange how she still slips up even after so many years. Of course, he can't see the smile, can't even guess at her expression, since all he knows is confined within the reach of his fingers. Other acts of kindness surface in her mind but she knows better than to try. (Her claim on honesty.) Only Time will put everything to rights.

He shifts his bulk on the stool, and she bobs slow passage across the room, trawling past the piano's oblong front to windows that cut the sky into four sparkling pieces. Where sea and boats can be had. Why this feeling of out of placeness? She lifts one window as high as it will go and props her elbows on the sill, upper body on the other side, head lowered. What is it that she hopes to see? Edgemere perhaps, but the dazzling light hides the island from view although she knows it is out there only a few miles away. Is Edgemere where Tom belongs? Would he find life on the island with other black people more suitable? The urge to take him there sometimes comes over her. (Admit it.) However, the world below her window (the city) is absolute in both its certainties and its dangers.

She thinks of her life with Tom as necessary, pressed on her. Not that her situation is all bad since there is the music to console and comfort her. (When he plays.) And when she gets her fill of his company, when she needs to put some distance between herself and Tom, she can put her head outside like this. She compels her aching chest to hold in lungfuls of pure ocean air and lose them quietly, breath rattling along her ribs. Her unbound hair drops, thick, flying, far short of the street five stories below. Empty distance. Nothing touching. Nothing close. (Is that what this is about, things falling short?) Perhaps it is best that way. Birds dive close to the water, too close, catch the currents, carried under. (This detail strikes her as excessive, pure invention.) The boats—white triangles, tiny pillars of black smoke—going backward now, like retracted thoughts, half-told secrets.

❀ ❀ ❀

She remembers it this way, how she came to on the settee, faint moonlight floating in the air, unsure what had awakened her, unwilling to believe that she had actually dosed off. In truth she could not tell, having lost track of time, a terrible lightness to her body. Deprived of sleep over the past crush of days, maintaining a pitch of vigilance at the windows for hours at a time, mornings/nights curling around her like smoke, taking in shouts screams gunshots hurled obscenities sobbing pleads hurried prayers spit-laced laughter rollicking applause invading her apartment from the streets below. Heard urgencies that sounded completely different, depending on whether her eyes were open or closed. Which brought pictures upon entering the brain, her attempt to map the featureless surround, for what she could actually see—flickers of fire shooting upward—was limited since her apartment offered no view of the street, only the usual, the sea.

The more she watched the sea, the more it proved it could hold: a dozen crashing colors, schools of Negroes gone fish—fleeing the city was not a thought that had crossed her mind; her husband was out there—in the dhows that made their livelihood possible (fishing, ferrying, the transportation of cargo), in other small crafts, or with nothing but their bodies, a kind of oceanic monster of faces and limbs, sails and oars, tossed around in the rough exhaustive currents. Lights shining far across the water from the island of Edgemere—how else could it be seen?—were uncertain and distant. She supposed the island was within reach, even for those with only their bodies to carry them. In reach but far away. Some would not make make it, would drown. If only these Negroes had some Moses who could part the water. If only—not to put too fine a point on it—they could walk on water.

Had she already put an end to any form of hoping? How many days had it been since Tom had left the apartment in the company of Sharpe and the manager? Close to a week? Even as chaos was breaking loose in the city neither her husband nor the manager had considered canceling the concert. Days of waiting and wondering—Sharpe?—spreading in her head, on the verge of shattering it. Sleep was compensatory. Stripping her of consciousness.

What had she missed sliding in and out of sleep? The room sounded soft and hollow. The world seemed to have quieted down outside her windows. Was it over? That question in her mind, she shifted her gaze to the shadow cast by moonlight striking a lamp shade when she sensed a new kind of darkness, different from the darkness she had been experiencing until that moment, bleeding into the edgy air, beginning to burrow into her consciousness. She sat up and looked around. At first she thought she was hearing the outside, a resumption of the chaos, the violence. Then in the illuminated darkness she could make out a form curled up under the piano. She went over for a closer look and found Tom wedged in the cave of space formed by the piano's spindly legs and heavy chassis, knees tucked to his chin. She gave herself time for two deep breaths. She had not heard him enter the apartment. Back without a sound. (She had fallen asleep.) How had he found his way back? How had he gotten in? No key of his own that she was aware of. Sharpe's key? And what about the others? Where were they?

When she spoke his name, he shuddered, stirring up the dust floating in the darkness. He raised his head in her direction, his face in the shape of a snarl.

She took in the brutal aspect of his person. She dared not strike a lamp. Only this light to prove that he was actually there. He was still outfitted in recital dress. One jacket sleeve had been almost completely ripped away. The front of his shirt had a large black stain shaped like a butterfly. And his pants legs looked as if they had been singed, one cuff nothing more than straggly ash. His head and face had been spared, except for missing hat and one ear that was aglow with dried blood.

You found your way home.

Tom remained perfectly still.

Where are they? Sharpe? Your manager? Thinking, Tom has the answers.

He let out a breath she didn't know he was holding.

Dawn came, a tiny crack separating one world from the next. A new day began to take shape. An unbroken covering of white clouds—clouds few enough to count—hung in the sky, clear and precise, textured as never before. From somewhere smoke funneling black and back on the wind. A single gull lent its monotonous cries to the scene.

The sun angled high and struck the surface of the piano, day giving her her first clear view of Tom, throwing too much light on his form. The boy holding himself, clutching the sum of his life. Then his arm lifted, a long shadow cutting across the emptiness and venturing out toward her—*Miss Eliza* (did he actually say it, or is she only remembering?)—and she stepped back, out of reach, a body reaction. He opened his mouth and the sound escaping it was all Negroes in one mouth.

No, Tom. They'll hear. It's not safe.

Trying to quiet that sound twisting through her head. (What the human mouth can bring into being.) After a time, it weakened and finally gave out altogether, only a few clumps of noise that still hummed in his body. In the stairwell outside, someone was passing by, speaking in a loud voice. She couldn't catch the words. She had to wait, too soon to try Tom again. So for a while he stayed put and she stayed, only three feet—maybe four—separating them, Tom hanging in her eyes, an intrusive speck that couldn't be blinked out.

Miss Eliza, he said, almost as if he realized she was waiting for him to speak, give her a full report.

She tried her questions again.

That sound tolling a response. Enough with the questions for now. Is it that she sensed more than the tongue could say? Coated his mutters and groans with emotion, hearing them as her own?

The piano seemed to assume Tom's shape, the flesh hiding underneath it, covering it. So it was, he believed that she couldn't see him nestled inside the hard black excess of his containment. Tom (indeed) in a place far removed from the bounds of her consciousness. She felt both pity and frustration for this boy, hiding, with or without her, innocent of outcome. Could not recall a single instance of being alone with him, always a trio with her husband or the manager, a quartet with her husband and the manager. How to breach the divide? Sharpe had given Tom much patience and correct words. He spoke to Tom in a quiet voice that he made stern when he had to, and tolerated her awkwardness around the boy.

Before she knew what was happening, something wet streamed down Tom's face, one long spill. On closer inspection she saw water puddling at the concave of his shut eyelids, a drop slowly separating from the lash and speeding to the floor. A discovery: the blind can actually cry. (How had she escaped noticing this among the blind children at the Asylum those many years ago?) Might it be that the images she needed, the unsayable truths—where is Sharpe, where is my husband?—were trapped inside the salty liquid, dripping to the floor, lost forever?

With her eyes closed, she saw Sharpe, the manager, and Tom leaving the apartment, their coats cut generously to accommodate them, three attitudes of self-assurance. Stacks of programs—under whose arm? in whose hand?—still smelling of the printer's ink. Everything connected with their departure remarkably fresh and distinct to her.

Time wound around her. All right, then, she thought: here I am with Tom. Backed up on all fours under the piano, like some animal in hibernation. Still for hours at a time but for fevered motion that quaked through his shoulders and teeth. Now bent over, a praying Mohammedan, driving his face into the floor. Crawling on his bloody knees to one corner, and crawling back to his cave. Or twisting and turning like a troubled dreamer, the backs of his hands shining with bruises. Whole days of this, Eliza hovering in clear orbit above him, afraid to sleep, for without constant attention her floating body would be carried off to another world. Tethered directly overhead while the boy's torso swelled and his limbs cramped, while his skin grew gray, his body giving off waves of stench, a sour orange-yellow smell, and the air in the room (she felt) thinning out little by little.

Then she heard something snag, and the boy let loose with a flood of urine. She watched, poured into a strange heaviness. Only the sound of Tom's heart fluttering around inside the empty birdcage of his chest. Then nothing. Not a twitch or twinge. Bereft of sound, of movement, he seemed so far away. She knew he was dying.

She had to move her body, begin working toward some goal. She went over and touched him. (Touch is the body's sense.) He was cold to her hand. She lifted his forearm and it flopped back to the floor. She shook it vigorously once or twice like a dog with a branch between its teeth, but even then he didn't stir. Nothing. But she was sure she felt a current just under the skin. A stuttered beat. Which could only mean that she had to do more. Kneel now into that puddle of urine and get wet, her petticoats gathering in the warm scent of his shadow, her knees squishing, her ear pressed close to his chest—she bent so easily—a thorough examination. (How else?) In an instant, he began to warm, as if something of her was seeping into his skin. Her hands bearing down on his back. And this body that had been holding its shape unfolded, extended into the room. The heavy down-directed sun seemed to aid her, pressed his mouth open, the black inside punctuated with teeth, a heavy expression of breathing and hunger.

Before long, the first sip of water, the first nibble of bread, the first bite of an apple. Then utterances, words or parts of words, language springing back. Food and liquid reviving his tongue. Why was she so entirely agreeable to the task? And why did he accept her comfort so easily, trust in her voice and her touch?

With his damp nose nudged deep into the crook of her elbow, she began to run through ways she might gain more, what she might resurrect, bring forth from the blood, stink, and sorrow. He was and was not like what she was. (A young Negro of the male sex. A musician. A Southerner.) Before anything else, she had to draw him out from under the piano. But he wanted her to sit beside him on the floor, his insistent hands stretching up to her own, and when she was there, he pressed her and touched her as if she had just returned after a long absence. He wouldn't tolerate any separation. (This body holding her.) Came upon her like a shadow, forever hovering around, getting in her way. Whenever she was seated on the settee, he settled near her on the floor, trying to get comfortable, with his head propped against her knees. The need, attention, filled her with a strange elation.

His hands came flickering up through the light, like dark moths, as if they would tell her something. They didn't.

She told him, If I could have a word.

Put one question after the next to him. He told her nothing. But she had better say the words while she could. No intention to speak them ever again. (Too hard with words.) Truth to tell, weren't the questions a form of avoidance? What she had been moving along to in her mind was this: What will I do with the boy? But she was too balled up with comforting him—mothering?—to think past this moment. (The future sensed beneath the present.) What would come later she could think about later. The last thing she wanted to do was think, acknowledge the sum of what was, Sharpe, her marriage. Could she have changed the outcome had she accompanied them to the concert?

Separate from Tom, the piano looked like something foreign, something that didn't belong, a sea creature washed up onto a beach. She remembered herself. Thought about the trapped bones of her own body. In the months to come, she would have plenty of time to weigh both her suffering and her hatred, for wishing damnation upon the sea. (There to remind her, the city's sins resurfacing in the water, never under for long.) Right here, right now, she was content, taken with the strangely tangible impression that something had come to an end. She could feel it in her face. Knew that she and Tom were either at the start or finish of a life. Eliza and Tom, new to each other.

❋ ❋ ❋

Tom sits at the piano in postsupper stupor amid long shadows in the gathering dusk, tugging at his belt, trying to wrestle his waist in place, a body slumping at the edges, slowly losing the pattern of its own dimensions.

The windows glitter with faint fluorescent shapes, lines of fading sunlight shimmering on the walls like the red strings of a guitar. The piano holds the sunset's color. She hears light drumming on the keys now, like shells rattling in a boiling pot. Thousands of tiny tinkling hollow echoes. The boats seem to move in time to the music, at the mercy of the rise and fall of Tom's hands. They continue their forward advance, moving farther and farther away until they are about to fade from view, an ever-widening wake, but they will never arrive, reach their destination, caught, under Tom's control. Must slumber a new course. That sonata he is playing, each controlling finger made to lift alone. She listens with inward breath to the way he pushes deeper into the keys, so many notes overlapping in this room, so that no note ever sounds alone.

For a long time she goes on listening. He will play the entire night. (Let him, as long as Mr. Hub brings her no complaints from the neighbors.) Watching him, she feels as if the flow of Time is slowing down little by little. She strikes a match, igniting wet wicks, the lamps humming, coating the room with their expected flush.

Toward the end of one afternoon a week later, Mr. Hub comes for the return of his tallow candle. *The missus sends me.* How had she forgotten, even with his almost daily appearances at her door? The bell pulls and she opens it to find two fresh bottles of goat's milk sitting outside the door, like mushrooms that have sprouted up through the floorboards. In his darned coat and scuffed shoes, and bearing about him a smell of lye and ammonia, Mr. Hub runs errands, sees that her deliveries are sent, and receives her mail, what little there is, from the postmaster. He has a real talent for the execution of such practical duties, never complains and will consent to any request without argument, grateful for the small fees he receives, these supplements to his meager caretaker's salary. Standing in her doorway with a happy face, the gay animated expression of someone with fascinating things to relate, although he never reports matters of consequence. She listens with keen indifference, in no hurry to deepen her relationship with him. In fact, she senses a kind of uncertainty in him. Exactly what she can't say, but it comes every now and then in his words or actions. She might ask him something (I don't believe I thanked you for touching up) and a single breath will intervene before he answers (I'm not deserving), just the slightest hesitation, but in that split-second interval she senses a kind of shadow of menace or distrust.

So kind of you to do it while we were away, sparing us the inconvenience.

It wasn't up to me, Mr. Hub says, no change in expression. A man was in your apartment.

She heard him. Had she heard him?

I was making my rounds. And I saw that the door was open. Just a pinch. You could have missed it. He was sitting on the couch like the most natural thing in the world. Gave me the scare of my life.

She waits for him to speak, waits to hear his words.

I supposed him an apparition or God knows what. But he was nothing as terrible as that. Just a colored. All dandyed up. Imagine.

She tries to.

Never thought I would set eyes on another one. *Here,* at least. Not in this city.

Already she is flipping through a mental index of her past acquaintances, remembered and forgotten. Could he—*a colored*—be someone from her past life, from the Asylum?

He didn't bother to hide. Just sitting there, like the most natural thing in the world.

She wonders what kind of man this is who would brave the dangers of the city alone. What did he want?

Mr. Hub draws his lips slightly to one side. Your guess is as good as mine. But you can bet money, he would have robbed you blind had I not chased him away. I keep my hammer on my person. He shows it to her then returns it to his coat pocket.

Did he say anything?

Just some gibberish, trying to talk his way free. He asked for you.

For me?

He asked your whereabouts. I'm sure he took your name from the bell. He knows his alphabet, that's for sure.

And nothing else?

He tried to hand me something, but I didn't let the wool slip. Mr. Hub shows his hammer. Yes, he was a slick one.

What was it?

I barely looked. I figure, why stand for more lies? Given an ear, he might claim your relation. The king of England. God knows what.

The same intruder, she thinks. From the country. What can she do besides listen? A foreign body had entered their home, their space. What if anything left behind? What if anything changed?

A lot of courage that one. Mr. Hub shakes his head in disbelief, a rush of wind streaming between his teeth. You have to admit. To come here. He deserves a medal. Or maybe he's just plain stupid, or simple. Touched.

She hears herself utter some reply.

Would you believe, there was a second one out front waiting for him? The driver. Not dressed up like the first, but I didn't get such a good look.

Eliza has no words.

Sorry to upset you, ma'm. I had hoped to save you the trouble of worrying over it. Nothing is missing?

No.

He had mud on his feet. I thought to take every precaution. So the lock was changed, Mr. Hub says, as if this were all logically consistent. One of those gestures perhaps offered in the sure expectation that she would take comfort in it.

After mutual good wishes, Mr. Hub strides away, leaving her with the weight of words, her ears retaining their living sound. Two men, colored, her name in the mouth of one, the thing offered, mud on the feet: she had heard it all, and now comes the realization: Mr. Hub had talked his way around her question. She still doesn't know what prompted him to paint her apartment.

Each thing accounted for—checks again—but Mr. Hub has unsettled what she thought was settled, shaken her belief in anonymity, that there's no one in the city with a passing thought for her. The building big enough that no neighbor is near and all acquaintances are vague. Eliza a familiar face in the hallway or on the stairwell or on the street (those rare occasions), passing under a street sign, already gone, a woman without name or connections, or a woman who was only a name. Mrs. Bethune. Apartment 5B. Where the piano music comes from. As far as she knows, they assume that she is the pianist. Whatever their assumptions, she is uneasily conscious of her neighbors. More so now. (Yes, on Monday—think about it—there was someone leaning in the shadows, watching.) Who has she seen this week other than Mr. Hub? And how many of her neighbors have caught a glimpse of Tom in the past three years? Before the violence, every resident in the building knew Tom; half of them were Negro and for that reason took pride in the proximity; but who among the present neighbors—white, all of them white—can place him here, in apartment 5B?

❈ ❈ ❈

When Sharpe was here, working with Tom and the manager, the neighbors found any excuse to knock on her door—I thought the young master might like some custard—some with punctilious regularity. Pulling the bell, but not without a certain guilty sense of invading someone's privacy—blurting out explanations and regrets, even as others were less polite, ventured to make forcible entry. She would screen the visitors when she could—

Tom, this is little Sally from the second floor.

Some little girl lifting herself out of memory, wearing a short dress of white satin, a black-buckled pink belt around her waist.

Hello, Mr. Tom.

Hello, girl. Hello, Sally. Tom took the girl's hand. She's a nigger, he said.

—but Tom was often quick to answer the bell before she or Sharpe or the manager could refuse or turn away the caller, resolved to present "Blind Tom" to one and all.

I am Blind Tom, one of the greatest humans to walk the earth. Syllables paced out one breath at a time.

Nice of you to visit, Tom said. You don't know me, and I don't know you.

Names circling names.

This was all they wanted to know about their neighbors. Indeed, Mr. and Mrs. Bethune maintained close relations with only one other family in the building, the McCunes, Dr. and Mrs., who were further along in years than Sharpe and Eliza, but not significantly so, and whose offspring, boy and girl, were deeply attentive to Tom. *They're niggers, Tom said.* Once a week, the older couple would extend a supper invitation to the younger—never the other way around—so that the Bethunes became a regular presence in their home, a sumptuously furnished apartment (third floor, 3A), the chairs and couches tattered and antique, proud of period detail, the walls hung with tapestry and bedecked with a great number of spirited modern paintings, landscapes and seascapes, in frames of rich golden arabesque set against walls papered in an expanse of white flowers. The McCunes themselves smacked of careful cultivation, presentation pieces with their own form and meaning. Their tastes ran to art, theater, geography (places traveled, destinations to come), and politics—

I won't support a losing cause. Sharpe passed the decanter of wine across the table to the Doctor.

I take that to mean you are perfectly comfortable supporting the winner?

Hardly.

At least you have no doubts about who will win.

I have no doubts.

The children ran through the room, set forth in their own wonder.

How can I? They will destroy the South just so they can rebuild it in their own image.

The causes are deeper.

I'm not saying they aren't.

So why then do you aid the rebels?

Sharpe stretched his body, easing into an answer. Look, Doctor, I'm still a Southerner. A man can't simply cut off his family. He sat back in his chair, arms spread wide in a request for pardon. I won't leap to their defense, but why not throw a few bills at the battle-scarred and the war widows?

The Doctor poured the last of the wine into Sharpe's glass. Does it matter what the boy thinks?

Obviously you're saying it should.

The Doctor continued to look at him, shoulders curved forward, head hanging over the table.

A benefit concert or two. Is that taking advantage? Besides, do you know how much money we've given the Abos over the years? More money than I can count.

Ah.

Not openly, of course. Under the table.

That's unfortunate. You will never get the recognition. The boy will—

Doctor, I stopped wondering long ago about what people think of my doing this or that.

Useful hours for both men, even when they disagreed. These visits revealed a side of the Doctor that Eliza had not been privy to during the many years she had known and worked with him at the Eternally Benevolent Asylum for Ill-Fated Offspring of the Sable Race, something beyond what was contained in the structure of his medical duties. (And it was her own duties in the charitable wings and halls of the establishment that by either providence or happenstance she would come into contact with Sharpe—and Tom.) Though he insisted on a limited schedule, working no more than four hours a day, four days a week, so that his private practice and research should not suffer, he was charged by his work, bright with it, padding through the wards in his white coat, the legs of his binaural stethoscope clamped around his neck. There was a practicality about his body, a man built to a purpose—the total opposite of Sharpe, the tallest man she has ever seen, even today, all angles, juxtaposition, jagged elbows jutting out, forward-pointing hatchet-like knees, and square blocky forehead and temple, aspects of person defying the uniformity of line that is supposed to define a body—moving with tireless fluidity along beds lined up like boats in a dockyard, attending to as many as 160 children at a given time. (A massive four-story building of fine recent construction, the Asylum could accommodate up to 200 orphaned children, providing them with the luxury of modern facilities—indoor toilets, sinks, and baths, gaslights—that only the city's wealthy had access to.) But he sought to do more than heal and see to the good health of the Negro children under his care. He was determined—the greater goal—to refine their artistic and intellectual tastes through regular attendance at museums, concerts, and dramaturgical stagings. (He took all 160 children to a production of *Uncle Tom's Cabin* at his own expense.) *We should endeavor to expose the most unfortunate of the Race to the better class of general culture.* It was clear from the atmosphere he projected that he was no ordinary person. Mrs. Shotwell and Mrs. Murray hoped that the Doctor, in his professionalism, the way he spoke and handled himself, would serve as a masculine exemplar who could illuminate the orphans' own conditions and inspire them (the boys) to aim high and achieve.

Doctor, should we hire a music teacher? Mrs. Shotwell asked. Do you believe the reports that music can reform a bad disposition?

Eliza could not help feeling a certain strange joy whenever she had assisted the Doctor, frantically eager to carry wash pan, thread, scissors, knife, to boil the surgical instruments, prepare the opium paste, or stanch bleeding. As house matron she had earned nine dollars a month, a decent wage, but the work was exhausting even if fulfilling, the hours immense. She saw to the stocks and supplies and took daily inventory, the large brass storeroom keys kept on a five-pound iron ring; she tallied up donations, engaged the domestics, and supervised all of the other employees to ensure that they weren't making light of their duties. Her work with Dr. McCune made up for certain agreed-upon reductions of self, for the Doctor, in his ministrations, showed an emotion deep enough to confirm her own power—*They need me, irreplaceable me*—a fact that made it easy for her to bend to her other labors with a quiet mind. She had spent so much time with him—month after month, one year after the next—she felt his duties had become part of her. No exaggeration to say that it was she who drummed up patients.

Once a week, she left the Asylum and went in search of fresh orphans, venturing away from their Midtown locale to explore the narrow twisting streets of the Black Town, the city's most densely populated district, where surfaces (sidewalks, roofs, shutters, corners, walls) pressed together in unexpected ways, noisily in place, life here chambered inside a ramshackle accumulation of tenements leaning over the sidewalks, as if bent against a winter wind. Eliza advancing softly with a sense of mysterious invitation, feeling the uneasy force of all those lives hived within, families (four or more) jammed up against each other inside a single room, unable to confine respective kin to respective corner, assorted limbs jutting out of slanted windows and crooked doorways, Eliza dizzy with forms all about her. Clusters of Negro men toting pyramids of firewood and Negro women dangling strings of fowl, and men and women and children alike in slow drift with satchels of sweat strapped to their backs, or water pots or baskets (fruit, herbs) positioned on their heads. Faces staring accusations at her, bitter in an undirected way. She would stare right back—hopeful tension—pushing against refuse and waste thick and abstract at her feet, and ask the simple questions that brought such satisfying replies from the two or three or four that she extended invitations to, willing to give themselves up to her then and there. Candidates collected, she would then taxi on to the Municipal Almshouse and spend hours cycling through a maze of warrens where monstrous forms—albinos, pinheads, she-hes, worm-like legless and armless torsos stationed on wooden carts, pig-child hybrids with snouts and curly tails, deer-children (fauns? satyrs?) with horns and hooves, mermaids swimming in their own urine, Cyclops, Blemmyae, three- and four-eyed Nisicathae and Nisitae, a boy with an underdeveloped twin hanging out of his abdomen, as if the hidden head was only momentarily absent, mischievously peeking into the keyhole of his stomach, a girl with a second canine-toothed and lizard-tongued mouth chewing its way out of her left jaw, and rarer creatures shackled and chained—huddled in dim light against the smell of sawdust, some folded monk-like in cloaks and hoods, others completely nude. Eliza careful to appear curious and concerned, a desperate devotion undercutting her probing looks, her riddle-solving, translating texts of skin and eyes.

Back at the Asylum, she saw to it that the new arrivals were thoroughly washed and comfortably dressed, each child's hair combed free of lice, each body put to bed under folds of fresh linen in the Inspection Ward, awaiting Dr. McCune's examination. The admissions were naturally reluctant to undergo examination, poking and prodding, but before Dr. McCune all their defenses vanished. They gave in with trustful surrender, the ready-made quality about the way he spoke. *Disrobe, please. Including shoes and undergarments. Miss Viel here will take care of your belongings.* At times she found herself speaking the diagnosis even before he had. The cleared would be taken immediately to the appropriate ward housing their peers, Whole Orphans or Half Orphans, and the wing therein specific to their sex—the wards could amalgamate during meals, boys on one side of the dining hall, girls on the other—where they would be *ghosts* for several days, invisible, suffering at arm's length a brief trial of discretionary exclusion before they were accepted into the fold. The eye-sick were afforded the opportunity of surgery to remove the diseased orbs. (One darkness defining another. *Now the eyes of Israel were dim for age, so that he could not see.*) To aid in healing and lessen the chances of inflammation, Dr. McCune would apply a thick paste made from crushed peanuts and water—*peanut butter* he called it—over the empty eye sockets, two six-inch-high brown mounds that would remain in place for up to a week. Eliza was there to fan flies away and pluck ants and cockroaches from the paste. To wet fever with cold compresses and diminish pain with warm opium. Once the paste was removed, Dr. McCune had to judge that no part of the infection had escaped to another region of the body, before the patient could be assigned his/her own bed in the Eye Ward. Dr. McCune put a high practical value on his work at the Asylum, believing that it aided and enhanced his research and his private practice in the homes of the city's wealthy Negroes and in his own home, those packs of proper Negroes who made daily pilgrimages to his apartment (3A) in their well-cut clothes, depending on his dogged efforts to keep them in top form.

Was it this blood commitment, the bond and obligation of Race, that laid the unspoken rule that the Bethunes would only enter his home as friends, never as patients—had he offered? had she or Sharpe?—however much the Bethunes were in perfect accord with his moral and professional life? Bound up with the Asylum, the circumstances of that life first established between Eliza and the Doctor passed on to Sharpe. Tracing back, she recognizes now that it was through her that the two men met and that she had a hand in the friendship they forged, unaware that in serving as this instrument of connection she was sealing the fate of each and forever linking her and Tom. (True, but one should beware of such judgments.) Not that the pattern is completely clear to her, the where what why and when, the x that preceded y and z, only that she is at the center of the likeliest sequence of events. Sharpe is gone now, forever, no coming back, but she distinctly recalls the morning, a few days after Tom's benefit recital, when Sharpe called at the Asylum, his face smooth and smiling—yes—and without a word took her hand where it rested at her side and shook it gratefully. His uncalendared appearance—a new intake of feeling—the moment she pinpoints as the start of their enthusiastic days together. Sitting over tea in the matron's office, he expressed his hope that *they* should again entertain the children at some point in the not too distant future. He had no sooner finished his cup than he rose to leave. *Their* stay in the city would be short; there were places to be. Something in his tone of voice, a glimmer beneath the words—*We welcome another opportunity*—in his posture and manner and excitement—partly observed, remembered, partly dreamed—occasioned in her a feeling that his linen-dressed body was a conspiratorial screen designed to mask the true intentions of his visit. He seemed to want to talk to her. (The screen too easy to see through.) A hope belief powerful enough to pluck up her courage to ask him, the caller—*Mr. Bethune* he was to her then—if one afternoon he might desire to leave the side of Tom and the manager for a few hours and accompany her for a walk about town so that he might embrace the good weather and see—*Allow me to show you;* was that it?—if not visit—yes, that was it—a few of the city's most impressive sights, just the thing he might need to feel fortified and refreshed before carrying on with the many duties—the boy needed to be outfitted for the approaching concert season less than a month away—and blur of appointments awaiting him. Of course, for her to extend such an offer was to overstep the boundaries of acceptable behavior, action made even more brash and bold given the many speculations and rumors circulating in the journals at the time concerning the reasons why Sharpe's father, General Bethune, several months earlier, had removed Tom's longstanding manager and replaced him with a new one, Warhurst, and given that the General's scheduled visit to the city in a few weeks as a stop on his national tour (Save the South!) to raise funds and supporters for the Confederacy was the talk of the town. (The stories always seemed to be accompanied by that now familiar photo of the General, posed behind the seated pianist, one hand in paternal rest upon the boy's shoulders, the boy's fingers—those cherished objects—fitted together in two fists of knuckles inside his lap.) For his part, Mr. Bethune readily accepted. In view of the (his) circumstances, he suggested the sooner the better. Why not tomorrow? Why not.

They rendezvoused on an unusually fine day, one of those summer afternoons that commanded the populace out of their homes. Wherever one looked, people were pouring out of open doors. On the street, everything was rushing and physical, a light gaiety in the air. Men touching theirs hats in mute greeting, women tilting their faces forward to smile. At her suggestion, they began walking toward Central Park, the nearest lawn only a few blocks away. What better way to impress him on their first outing than with the city's most impressive location? (He was a foreigner after all, a Southerner.)

Once they reached the park, they started down the wide central lane, which wound five miles from one end to the other. The park was only a few years old at that point; Seneca Village, the northernmost section of Black Town, had been razed and the park constructed in its place as part of a municipal beautification project. But the Negroes had never completely relinquished their hold, sanctioning the park as their communal site. This day dozens of celebrants strolled about, a flash of unrestrained smiles and theatrical bodies done up in lavish and gaudy costumes, a hundred colors and cloths heating the holiday—John Canoe? Pinkster? Emancipation (state) Day? some Union victory?—air. Again and again Eliza and Mr. Bethune met by whistles, drums, gyrating hips and feet. Some of the celebrants made a fearsome impression with mock guns and swords, more comic the paltry contingents of horsemen with their sorrow-worn almost-dancing steeds. Then too something neither noble nor humorous about the knot of boys huddled into guards, ribbons of tree-circling summer-maiden girls, or the deputation of deer-skinned and eagle-feathered elders seated in ceremonial poses like some rare delegation of the most venerated and powerful Red Indian chiefs. All told, the holidaymakers, whether in couples or family groups, produced a kind of pressure of presence of which everyone was a part, an insider's air of intimate entitlement that caused them to cast exclusionary looks at Eliza and Mr. Bethune. What's your business here? Eliza and her guest did not allow themselves to be put out in the slightest by sucked teeth and jeers. Still, since the park had been seized by the Negroes, she wondered if she ought to have made other arrangements. Through her work at the Asylum, she had come to know a less-traveled section of the park, just down this path. Far away, not easy to see, but well worth the effort of getting there.

Eliza and Mr. Bethune continued on, enjoying the walk and the view, letting the features gather. Things had been arranged to be gazed on. Endless brilliances planned, tidied up, and straightened out to the last square corner. She drew his attention to one sight after another. Slim rippling trees with heavy bunches of flowers. Sparkling lagoons. Gardens with birdbaths, fountains, and paved watercourses. A three-mile-long central lawn. Gazebos with mosque-like domes. A marble pavilion stretching almost four city blocks. A paved path, climbing in four or five levels to a shelf of pale crags. A hilltop edged with a castle, a modern structure trying to create an element of medieval intrigue, add something old to the new. This place returning to them a sense of their own motion through it, their limbs growing progressively warmer from the movement. He seemed interested in what he saw, awed even at times—was he really, or is she supplying this impression years after the fact?—but had nothing to say, at least about *this*. Words were bound to come. (Of course, he must take the lead, draw her into conversation, Eliza showing restraint, holding true tongue back, determined—however difficult—to move within the parameters of convention lest she give him the wrong introductory impression.) What would it take?

They walked another mile or two before he responded to her with something more than a barely perceivable nod of the head. He asked her about the orphanage. Getting on all right there?

Yes.

I take it you enjoy your position?

As much as one might.

It's not too much for you? It would be for me.

It's too much.

So why do it? he asked. Why work there? His question was so quiet she had to watch his lips to understand. He did not wait for an answer but carried on talking. It's too much to bear, but you stay on because of what you can produce in the children.

She explained that the best children—those clever enough—would take up positions of indenture, mostly on farms in the city's (four) outer boroughs, where skin prejudice held less sway. What better way for independence than through entry to a trade.

He nodded slightly, approvingly.

They walked over the narrow spine of a bridge. The sun shone so warm that Mr. Bethune chose to remove his hat and carry it beside him. It seemed to her of particular significance that he showed an interest in her life. Her life at the Asylum against his life abroad: the South, Britain, the Continent. Her years (twenty) against his (thirty-five, her estimation). Her innocence against his experience.

A figure shot from the brush two yards ahead and stopped dead center in the path observing them. Jolted, they stopped too, registering the danger. A cur, mangy, unwashed, cut and bitten, obscene. Showing worth, it opened its mouth, flashing yellow teeth, only to sit back on its hind legs, exposing two egg-red testicles, this display of maleness portending that a violent attack might be the least of their concerns. Indeed, the animal began trembling from tongue to toe as if fully anticipating what was to come next. The muscles went still. The frame shuddered. A lengthy turd began squeezing out the rump. Eliza turned her body 180 degrees away from the sight. Only when she heard the animal lope off, panting, a sure indication that it was done, did she turn around. They stepped around the small steaming volcano, at once cautious and oblivious—cancel height, stench, texture, color—and resumed their walk.

Mr. Bethune looked unashamedly at her and uttered something, Eliza numbed by guilt, helpless to compel an order to the rush of sounds. Took another sentence or two for her to realize that he—his sharp bright eyes restlessly on the lookout—was now talking about his vocation. The forthcoming season would carry them east for the first time. Prague and Belgrade, Kraków and Bucharest, Oulu and Ekaterinburg, Turku and Split, Tirana and Trieste, Skopje and Saint Petersburg, Ljubljana and Riga, Tartar and Tallinn, Helsinki and Kiev, Warsaw and Pristina, Gdańsk, Tbilisi, Dubrovnik, Heart, Bukhara, Sarajevo, Uzbeki, Kirgisi, and Sofia. Places on the edge of imagination. (Last year, a Mediterranean circuit—Bastia, Calvi, Cagliari, Alassio, Sartène, and Sassari—streaks of color—pastel-colored stone houses, whitewashed stone buildings, blackened stone forts—dancing on waves.)

This sudden leap to a new topic—where had they left off?—was its own explanation, for she recognized with shamed certainty his effort to allay her embarrassment. How noble, his at-the-ready responsiveness to her feelings gaining him favor in her eyes. Such luck, she said. Excitement. To be sped from town to town, city to city, adventure to adventure. (The concerts in fashionable metropolises, before fashionable audiences, including the private commissions and gatherings for city burghers; Russian czars and nobility; landed earls, ladies, and dukes; and the Continent's kings, princes, and queens.) And the music, night after night.

He maintained his gaze on the path before them, but his face grew active with thought, trying out one idea after another, only for him to nod his head in affirmation, giving up all hope of constructing a reply.

Will you give me a full report? I need to see something of life.

He smiled. Perhaps you will get your request sooner than you imagine. You might find us as your neighbors.

Eliza made a soft incredulous noise, tagging the idea with melodramatic amazement. You don't expect me to believe that could actually happen?

It could. He went on to explain. Since home was now in the heart of the war zone, the family—his father, mother, sisters—had already left the main estate for another property. But what was the difference really? Commerce and culture have already vanished in the South—his sentiments not exactly in those words but something like them.

You plan to resettle?

Yes, we do. Tom, myself, and Warhurst, the manager.

Was he implying some divide within the Bethune family?

My father has his own direction.

She felt embarrassed for bringing forth this secret. Here she was leading him to places he would not have ventured to on his own. How had she gotten so ahead of herself?

But perhaps this is not about my father, he said, taking any accusation out of his voice. All of the traveling can make you feel something different.

She did not understand.

There are other things.

When she glanced at him, she found that his face was transformed. Was he about to take her in confidence? If so, she would be careful not to accuse, to judge.

He expressed that yesterday at the orphanage she had picked up perfectly on his desperation. How satisfied he was to abandon his affairs for a few hours, to detach himself from Tom and Warhurst, to get clear of promoters and agents and schedules and journalists and reports and wires, and join her.

I understand something of what you're going through, she said. It was a lie put out there to bait him. Where had she found the strength to act this way? And how so quickly, so spontaneously? Would it cost her in the end?

Yes, you would understand, he said, given the responsibilities and directions of your work.

Already you know me so well. Her eyes slanted upward toward him in that accepted female way considered both coy and inviting. *Go further. Try more.*

He smiled. Are you telling me that I'm wrong?

No, I cannot call you wrong. Indeed, in my position at the Asylum, there might be the chance occasion when I experience feelings identical to yours.

But you make it seem wonderful, your work.

Do I?

Yes. That and more.

Nothing is special about my condition. This is simply where life has found me.

I would put it down to more than that. Your affairs are positive and important but fraught with worry and complication, as is any career completely devoted to either maintaining or uplifting a weaker party.

Ah, so she had not lied. What luck. They seemed in a way to belong to the same thing, a brotherhood/sisterhood of sorts. So, is that what it is with Blind Tom?

Thomas. We call him Thomas.

Thomas. Of course. Tom. Of course.

Tom is constant wonder. And trouble too, much of the time. But wonder. Charm. Magic. To be there in his presence each and every day and witness it firsthand. Those gifts. *Blind Tom. Come and get your miracle.* To see that. It's everything else that turns you inside out. Spectacular disasters. Mundane upsets.

He took some time to explain.

Earlier that day, he had suffered through a "brunch" with the boy's publisher. A game of extraction, he called it. The numbers never add up the way they should. One would think that Tom's fame would be reflected in thousands of sales of his songs. But we seem to sell fewer and fewer songs each year, even as the list of publications gets longer and longer. Can you imagine the bother of trying to keep that in order, under your thumb? In fact, you don't press for payment. You feel rather happy to be cheated. A strange trade-off.

From what I'm hearing, much of the daily business goes through your hands.

Yes.

So what does Warhurst do? What is he around for?

Sharpe said, He takes care of the performance. I take care of Tom—said, staring straight in her eyes as though expecting a response since the distinction was perfectly clear.

She did not know what to say in return.

Then his eyes brightened as if charged by her confusion. (He'd gotten that much from her.) You will hold this against me, he said. He turned his face away. I look after my family's most profitable investment.

How solicitous and civilized those words sounded despite their meaning. Until then she had never thought of him as a slave owner.

But what am I really telling you that is news? It's rather simple. I look after Tom.

She could not make herself utter the words burning inside her mind. *It is wrong, an evil.*

Then again I'm being unfair. *They* own him. My father, my mother, my sisters. Where am I in any of it? I was born into this wound.

She was surprised at the intensity of his dismissal, dislike.

At least that's what I tell myself. Of course, I can reel off another half dozen ways of looking at it, all equally valid.

Did he expect her to supply those ways?

Perhaps I'm just a coward. A useless one at that.

She saw the way he tightened his lips, the way words fell from his mouth.

There is an even worse possibility. Perhaps I have the nature for it.

Grudgingly, she took in this admission, trying to determine to what extent it mattered, how it would shape whatever it was that was developing between them. She wondered if he thought his confession somehow legitimized everything. Wondered, too, if he felt entitled to her empathy, automatically expected her to forgive him his shortcomings because he was smart, rich, powerful. She asked, Where are his parents?

He is alone.

Wanted to ask him what exactly had happened to the boy's parents, but she did not. What was the point of thinking about it all if the most it did was raise ugly fact or speculation? She was already considering the least hurtful way of untangling herself from the topic, not because he had won her over—too soon to say—only that what he had already said was a beginning.

The first appearance of water halted their conversation. They had reached the man-dug and -filled lake at the park's center and now decided they'd walked enough. (The spot she originally had in mind was still some way off.) They sat down beside each other on the grassy ground at the very edge of the water, verges churned by the feet of animals, paw impressions—trails with no beginning or end—set and hardened in evidence. (Hopefully no droppings or urine.) A good mile in circumference, the lake glistened like a gigantic silver coin, sun lying on the water in manifold glittering, water trembling soft impossible light, composed silence, no sound but for furtive cracks (trees) and urgent scurrying (animals), the smell of fish strong, leaping out at them—all told, a scene marked by expectation. Nature making itself powerfully felt.

Now a dhow was on the lake, its triangular sail slanting forward like an oversized shark tooth cutting through water. She was disappointed—why?—to see a second then a third sleek brown-white form on the lake. Watched the sharp sails drifting by and thought how fragile they were, not in the least knowing if this were true.

Some yards off, an animal came to the water to drink.

I expect to be anywhere but here when my father arrives, another state, another country, circling the rings of Jupiter—anywhere other than here when he starts making a fool of himself with his war talk. One should know how to behave in another's house.

So there was a rift. Was she ahead of herself again? Pardon my mentioning him, she said. Of course, his reputation is so often put before us. The entire city is awaiting his arrival.

You are innocent of any wrong. I would be suspicious if you had said nothing. He dropped his head and stared at the ground with an expression of immense satisfaction. She was only now noticing the strangeness of it, how awkward he looked sitting there, his collarbones jutting out like mountain peaks. For as long as I can remember, my father has sought secession, separation. Five years ago, before anyone was talking war, talking seriously about the possibility, he raised the first regiment in our state out of his own pocket.

So you've heard much more than we have.

Yes, and for far longer.

The lake was bringing a change, making them lower their voices with the feeling its sight and presence stirred in them.

Had he wanted, he could have formed an army before I was born. Does that sound so impossible?

She watched a smile pull his mouth up at one end, a derisive look.

Well, it isn't. My fellow countrymen suffer the pathology of ignorance. How easy it is to pull the wool over their eyes. All it takes is some savior or devil cleverly done up as a man of the people, an otherwise average man of learning and consequence who has been unjustly wronged and has no choice other than to fight for self, family, and country. If such a man told them the pope was an Israelite, they would believe it.

She didn't know what to say. Could only imagine how hard it must be for him. Although she could not recall ever having seen his name or image in print—he remained ghost, operated from behind the curtain—the name Bethune surely fitted him like trouble, given his father's celebrity and notoriety.

The hand (troubled) in closest proximity had found his hat, one finger flick flick flicking at the brim, as if testing if the hat were alive or dead. She wanted to reach out and touch it, to lift it off the grass and position it in place, then draw her hands away and let it settle onto the shelf of his forehead.

Where will you go? she asked.

Good question. Better near or far? What do you recommend?

She thought about it for a while, pretended to.

Perhaps I shouldn't be so eager to run. After all, his stay will be short, three days. That's really not so long, is it? I might simply hide away, go underground. This city is vast.

She smiled. Well, if you do you can gain some practice in being my neighbor.

Yes I could.

They sat looking out at the lake, lost between sentences. Yet another vessel had taken to the water, a gondola, its driver aiming and sinking the long skinny oar, gliding gradually forward to join the other vessels, the lone canoe and compounded dhows. Almost as if the five vessels were competing, three totally distinct forms pitted against one another.

She wondered, where was the boy Thomas, Tom, in all of this? From what she had gathered Sharpe saw the boy as an entity that existed only in relation to the family. What did the boy pianist think about it all? What does Tom think about it all? Does he know his value, worth?

Will the boy come with you or stay behind with your father?

He comes. No two ways about it. He has come so to rely on me.

Ah, so that was it. Sharpe weighed down with dependence. Another life. (Was that it?) He was in charge of Tom's life.

Of course, Warhurst could assume primary responsibility. He would, gladly. But I can't fathom the rightness or wrongness of such an arrangement.

She worried; if the boy was so delicate, who was looking after him at that very moment? Your concern is perfectly understandable, with such a special case.

Another animal had come to drink. A bird had taken to the sky, branch vibrating. And what were the vessels doing now, moving into some sort of authoritative formation?

She said, His blindness, that's always been the great cause of debate. As I remember from the reports, he was without sight at birth. She tried to make it sound more like an assumption than a question. Whichever, she saw nervousness on his face—she was asking him to uncover a secret; no, another source of discomfort—and something else she was not sure of.

That lie has served the interests of publicity. In fact, he was born with sight, and he had sight when my family purchased him. He quit his fussing (energy, trouble) over the hat. He was the cause of it.

It was not what she expected to hear. If he hoped to shock her, he had succeeded. How so?

He gave her a report.

We were not planters. We had no fields to plant, no crops to harvest. In fact, we kept in minimal communication with planters and farmers, did not buy from them or barter or trade or hold or engage in any significant transactions with them that I am aware of. So, at Hundred Gates by age three or four when a servant—*slave*, she thought, *slave*—should assume the responsibility of labor, Tom should have settled into a quotidian life involving random chores about the estate or a more active assignment in town at my father's office or his press. But when he achieved that age (four? five?)—he was less than a year old when my family acquired him, a babe of six or seven months—he still had not gained the ordinary abilities, talking and walking. (*Speech*, she thought. *Does that include all speech? All movement?*) In fact, he showed no signs that he understood the purpose of either. He could not follow instructions. But my parents decided to keep him on rather than abandon him, having little either to lose or to gain by his presence— his absence would have devastated his family, mother, father, siblings (sisters); *Ah, so he has had a family,* she thought—since our commerce did not depend on free labor. He was given each day to use as he pleased. Let me tell you how he spent his time. Sharpe measured what he was saying, as if trying to remember whether anything had been left out. He passed most of each day sitting out in the open, under the sky, with his face upturned at the sun, and with his eyes fully open. He screamed, kicked, and punched if you tried to pull him away, into the shade. He crawled after the sun as its position shifted in the sky. Then in the evening, when there was no more sun to be had—the moon did not seem to interest him—he would sit before the hearth all the while passing his hand rapidly before his face.

And this is how he went blind? She could ask.

We believe it was the cause of origin. Greater damage came. He began forking his fingers into his sockets.

My God, Eliza said.

That's not all. He began digging into the sockets with sticks and stones and anything else he could find.

That was worse, hearing it, seeing it. And nobody stopped him? she asked. (She had the right.) No one stopped him. Why did no one stop him?

I would have, had I been there. And my father would have, my mother. Would have. Anyone there. Would have. None of them. None of us. We are not cruel people, whatever their faults or our vices. But Tom largely saw after himself, as I understand it. I was not there. To stop him.

Where were you? She could ask this.

Even then I was circling the globe, pursuing stories for my father's journal, doing my part to see that it remained a vital publication, among the best in our country—the South, he meant, *his* country—if not the best. She heard his explanation as best she could, her mind pushing out, exploring, formulating, but he kept speaking, speaking before she had a chance to locate her words—a few brief illuminated thoughts—without giving her an opening to surge forth in response, overtake.

You must understand, the family doctor determined all of this many days after the fact, weeks even. For quite some time the mutilation went on daily without our notice. Then one evening the boy's mother came crying into the parlor before my father, carrying him in her arms, the boy, carrying the boy, and the boy trying to fight his way free, and the father trying to keep him still. Fresh blood covered his face, so much of it that they could not locate the source. All thought he had only then injured himself. Dr. Hollister, our doctor, was sent for. The eyes could not be saved.

She took this to mean that the sockets were empty—in fact, as she discovered several months later, the orbs were (are) very much present, intact, although useless. How it all might have gone otherwise if this Dr. Hollister possessed talent equaling Dr. McCune's. More often than not in his examinations, Dr. McCune found that the orbs—afflicted, damaged—could be saved, and he made every effort to achieve such preservation, the question of whether or not vision could be restored in whole or part notwithstanding, for he knew—she knew too—that the presence of orbs makes all the difference to the structure of the face, rounding it out rather than flattening it, and thereby maintaining a deep inner structure, those few ounces providing (proving) by their mass and weight an addition amid the loss, a measure of hope, however false.

Dr. Hollister speculated that the boy had acted out of curiosity, a curiosity brought on by mental incapacitations, or vice versa. Whichever the first.

Eliza lifted her hand so that she could feel the breath inhaled and exhaled by her nostrils. If only she possessed the ability to breathe out of every pore.

And given the severity of these injuries, the Doctor estimated that the mutilation had been going on for quite some time, for days, or weeks, months even. Right under our noses. Tom had outwitted all of us.

The lake crawled in the direction of the drinking animal.

We were able to draw much after the fact, although little good it did us. One sister—*his?*—had observed the poking, while another sister—*his?*—had chanced upon the prodding. The parents too had noticed some minor cuts and scrapes, which they chalked up to normal roughhousing and mischief. Innocence cannot be expected to save innocence.

Word-done, Sharpe returned to toying with his hat's stiff brim. They sat lost between sentences, Eliza trying to follow the features of Sharpe's face, bushes cooing and whispering behind her. What was clear, he had not seen it for himself. What was lacking: music. Music had to figure in there somewhere. (Stories await the telling.) Where was music? She could ask him. The mother, no, *mistress*, that was the word; the mistress, Mrs. Bethune, had been a music instructor, information she had gleaned some time ago from reading a racy exposé about the family. (True, not true.) Of the many stories she could construct, the easiest has Tom drawn to the piano after the world goes black. Who can stand vacancies? Tom gives himself up to Music. (How close is this to the official account? She tries to remember.) The world for him now no wider or taller than a piano. What it takes to get through the dark succession of constricting years. The story she invents, imagines. As good as any. Why not simply ask? She could ask. But the questions would have to take different form.

She adjusted her legs—numb, sleeping—to be sure that they were still functioning. Her knee brushed against his shin—no memory of the feel of his skin—but they were both quick to recover.

Dr. Hollister has him on a regular schedule.

He's still not done talking. She will have to say something.

But if there's no hope—

Tom seems to derive pleasure from the visits. Is that why we carry on with it? And the Doctor. Is that why he carries on with it?

Your Dr. Hollister sounds like a thorough and exhaustive type. Yes, he is.

He puts me in mind of someone. I wonder if he has ever crossed paths with Dr. McCune. Here she was again, wading out of her depth.

He keeps active company with the living and the dead. Sharpe released the hat. Healing would be their sole affiliation?

Yes. He is another eye man. Perhaps he could examine the boy. The words took a long time coming from her mouth. A voice her own but outside her, speaking something that she was only thinking. She was still watching the distant shore, certain that Sharpe was watching her. Her offer not so surprising really. For—understanding everything—she felt an unspecified sense of duty—sight slowly fading from memory, images dissolving one by one, like wafers in water—although she didn't know the boy and she hardly knew Sharpe. (Was just getting to know.)

What good would it do?

None. But what harm? The doctors one and the other will have much to talk about.

Who is he?

Eyes, hands, she gave up water—the lake is still there unchanged—and trained her attention on him. A colored man of distinction that I work under at the Asylum.

He turned, leaving water, looking at her—what we do to resolve blur and disbelief—so she could see her words reshape his face. How she had phrased it—*work under*—was that it or instead the meaning of what phrased?

Said (asked), A Negro doctor? A nigger doctor. And shook his head as if to empty it of her suggestion. Imagine how that would fly with the family.

They needn't know.

They wouldn't know.

A difference. A quiet disdain in the way he stared back. He was taking her offer as an insult. She knew that he wanted to rise and walk away, but he had the grace to continue sitting quietly (keeping quiet). Easier in fact if he showed his anger, but it is as though he thinks her unworthy of even that. For whatever reason, his stifled passion doesn't sit well with her, doesn't settle on her stomach but rises. (Jesus.) For a brief irrational moment, she wishes she could (rise) walk away from him. Need grants him power without his trying, deserving it. The color of his statement has moved something in her long forgotten. The weight felt.

How would this play out in the South—give hate a proper home—that land decimated by the plague of slavery, all those black skins caught, actively trying either to run away or to stay put? She's never been there, but even here in the city she has witnessed certain Negroes, decent people, with money in their hands and pockets and purses and minds, has seen the way these dignified types, of unquestionable repute, shirts buttoned to the throat, shoes polished and glistening like fish, will drop their heads in the presence of a white person, or cross to the other side of the street to avoid direct contact, staying away (this corner, that street, those wards), or give up a place in line and let the white person behind move ahead, use the side entrance/exit to circumvent unnecessary attention, thank the clerk who cheats them out of a few coins, that mortuary stiffness and fear, which make them smile peace at their disappointments, smile and forget everything else.

Over the lake, the wind rises—a commotion rising in the water, a current—and catches a bird by surprise, shaking it, tossing it. Somehow its song gets out.

You only want to help, Sharpe said.

A bee tried to pull nectar from a flower, petals swaying, drunk.

That was horrible of me. I'm sorry.

You think so? I wouldn't accuse you of any disrespect. Those words. The offers that come pouring in, all the time, from every corner. He looked at her in a way that softened his eyes.

She recognized at once what he was putting forward, no denying the source of the tongue—the South, a Southerner—that made it. What had she done to earn the dramatic reappraisal? Nothing really. No, he was showing her another dimension of self. This is me too. Generous. Ready. No closing off. Now, in the strain of the moment, she feels as if she has been found out in a weakness beyond remedy. He has opened up the chance for her to make amends, to win back his attention, make a full return. What to do? She needs help understanding exactly where it is she can't go. Eliza, matron of the Asylum, as used to throwing things away—baby, bathwater—as she is to salvaging.

But in this short time I've gained enough of you to understand that you place trust in the expense, he said, his tone gently teasing.

Those words. She felt grateful that his bluntness gave her no space for self-pity, gave her nothing to hide behind. But she said nothing, knowing that she would sound stilted. Looked and discovered that he was at the hat again. Actually had picked it up and fitted it on his head and remained there hunched forward, rocking with some indecision—the doubt of shoulders—near to panic. He seemed to be looking beyond her to some private trouble of his own. And he was including her in his worry. She could speak now.

I shouldn't be volunteering his services. He keeps his own calendar.

Kindly arrange it if you can. He rises to his feet, uprooted, making ready to go. She comes up too, light with relief, their past dispute put out to sea (so to speak), oared along until it falls over, out of view. (Water and its ways.) They reach the (closest) park exit without having said a word. So much in so short a time. Enticed by what she barely understands. Tom—the words used on his behalf—lurking vaguely in her mind in the days to come. What was so terrible about the world that he stopped himself from seeing it?

Sharpe signals a taxi in the queue. Look at the hour.

Time well spent.

Indeed. Horse harness hooves arriving. So you'll let me know?

She has to tilt her head to look at his face. The sun has shifted position, shining from behind him, right into her eyes. Yes.

❀ ❀ ❀

Edgemere. A mile or two out in the ocean—waves lengthen and shorten, the lull and pull of distance, water that finds a way—nothing beyond it, horizon's fuzzy edge. Sister isles—Hart's, Hunt's, Tipping Point, Nanatucka, Fool's Favorite, Shoisfine, Wanstaten, and others whose names she can't recall, words hard to pronounce even if she could, that fuse with the tongue—certain but hard to make out, a bump here, a lump there, positioned with the proximity of knuckles on the hand. Or is it that vision has grown so weary it cannot hold anything more? Sea caught in glass. Framed. (What's kept in, what's kept out.) The window she stands by a clean rectangle of light overlooking shimmering blue, lines of white waves sliding along surface in rhythm, like a stitch traveling to its proper place in patchworked cloth. Appearing and disappearing. Weaving a bright thread of constancy through their lives. Even as the island shrinks daily. Dwindles. Something eternal at work. Something forever undone. Gaps where the water can't come together, can't rise high enough to submerge that row of hard buttons, black islands knotted into position. Her unfastened blouse exposing a triangular channel of hot skin as she stands on display, propped at the window, mounted on land, bust flaps waving against five-storied sky. This sea ruthless, empty of witnesses. Years since she's seen a dhow on the waters. (So she believes.) The lateen sails. Can she even remember what one looks like?

The notes lower to a comfortable audibility, reviving the light, that stub of redness reaching through the glass, sea burned by setting sun. Eliza hears the song breaking in his hands. Two-fisted snatching at the keys, rebel green thumb ripping up roots from earth. Elbows sliding along horizontal, a straight track from left to right, right to left, the arms agile, the fingers quick. Skipping from short rows of black to long rows of white. Pulling air to the bottom of himself before letting it go. Mouth opening and closing, counting so that nothing is left out, inhaling and exhaling his little triumphs. Bench sagging some—yes—but bearing the full weight of his efforts. The shape appropriate to what comes out of him. That sound. (Making.) Arms, hands, fingers sensing the weight of water. An invitation. Anything you want. Anyplace you want to go. The sea closer by every step on land. But silence marks a stopping point. The pleasure in looking ruined. Horizon gone. Vanished. Edgemere where the world ends, every time.

The island demands contemplation. Extra. More. A bright world lost at sea. Each day, year after year, the surface strikes Eliza as new and she is refreshed by it. Could it be that ocean flows from isle, from this rocky flipped-over bowl spilling out flow, wet nourishment for all the world? Should it flip in reverse, hollow side up, the world will run dry, drained water pooled at inexhaustible island bottom. How big, how deep. Edgemere a world deeper and ampler than anything here on the mainland. City and anti-city, island and anti-island, place and anti-place, water and its negation. Once again she wonders (in her best moments, on the verge of logic, a humming coming from the corners of consciousness) if she and Tom should venture there. Across the watery wilderness. A clean start. *(Get clean of him.)* Escape on (in) her mind—she observes from a distance, images more so than words playing across a black screen at the front of her skull—if not on her tongue. Thinks the action, sees it even. Edgemere the city's great unknown, dark space of silent speculation set between her and any magical possibility of relocation. Eliza thinking about flight again as she used to in the concert days, Sharpe off freely roaming the world with Tom and Warhurst—*tour* means *gone, see you later, my heart, my love*—and she left alone, here, with herself, feeling like an outsider in her (their) own apartment. (Room and its evident lack.)

❋ ❋ ❋

As the one who had stayed put, stayed at home, excluded from the joys and sadnesses abroad, whatever they were, only fair that she somehow be part, one of the sojourning band (birds of a feather) from a distance, so that the word *overseas* could appear in her vocabulary as it did in Sharpe's. Rumor the method of passage, the Blind Tom Exhibition surfacing out of anything anyone had to tell from flat paper. Not that those distant reports ever satisfied her for long. Words slipping away, a sentence breaking, at a dead end, and Eliza feeling short-changed, starting to taste extinction, words working against her. To come out seeming solid even if empty, she found it necessary to console herself with communications put down in a clear hand—the store of fine blue-colored lavender-scented paper Sharpe had brought her from Provence, the gold stylus with the silver nib he had brought her from Marathon, the marble well filled with deep blue ink he had brought her from the Adriatic—

> *Dearest Husband,*
> *What shall I do with Monte Cristo? I've abridged my reading*
> *of it until it resembles someone suffering from typhus. The*
> *first part—until the Count becomes rich—is very interesting*
> *and well written, but the second, with few exceptions, is*
> *unbearable since Monte Cristo performs and speaks inflated*
> *nonsense. But on the whole the novel is quite effective. Please*
> *send your recommendations.*

—blue ink staining her fingers whenever the need arose (whatever the time of day), when she thought it would do the most good, transport her. Fingers, wrists, eyes, back straining to yield justification. Counted on, his missives told her little, a short blocky paragraph or two that it behooved him to say and that provided nothing useful, that left her dispirited—counted out—even if she was grateful for any little crumb, not having voyaged herself.

Until the day Sharpe would come bounding through the door, bright as an actor onstage, still enjoying his free range of the world. He, Warhurst, Tom each in a suspicious state of freshness, despite months of travel. Sharpe would pull her forcefully into his chest and kiss her, her body pressed so tightly to his that she would have difficulty breathing. Would hold her at arm's distance—Eliza (always) conscious of their difference in height—look her over, but her eyes would stay firm, looking dead at him, for to trust him implicitly would have been a mistake. (The tour was never finished. Years coming and going.)

And so Sharpe would start putting down on the table the first of many gifts. Sugar and spice. (Curry, cardamom, cinnamon.) Coffee from Arabia. (Plentiful in Paris.) And he would be talking, as if she had been waiting there weeks months in suspense for him to bring back a report from his travels. In the parlor—she sees it now—he sits down, stretches his legs out, long narrow boots crossed at the ankles, laughs. He seems content, at home with himself. He is. The liberties he takes, allows his person. She looks up, looks down, looks at him and looks away. Warhurst a far better study in avoidance, fixed in place beside Tom at the piano, down-turned eyes, hair combed into obedience. Coachman brings in the first of the luggage, a trunk as tall as short as he is and too heavy for him to lift. Why he drags it behind him like a corpse. He gives off the edible smell of fresh-turned dirt.

Missus. He smiles, gone in the teeth. Bows, the top hat spilling forward like a toppled tower.

Offering to assist the midget, Warhurst leaves when the midget leaves. With only Tom there, Eliza takes the opportunity to ask Sharpe why he has been away for so long, and walks right past him without waiting for an answer.

Alone in the bedroom she takes a few moments to collect herself before she returns, returns only to find Sharpe gone.

Testing Tom, she touches him on the shoulder. Who knows if he misses her in the least. Nothing from him. Not a handshake or hello.

How about a hug, Tom?

Any reason he should press his thin arm against hers? Chomping at the bit, ready to sit on the bench. Any reason she should stop him?

Doesn't. Already he is in position. Already his face is glassed over with music.

Coachman, Warhurst, and Sharpe come in with the last of the luggage. (Who actually says it?) Sharpe needs to go out again. After all the traveling (ships), he has to take his legs for a walk.

A turn or two in the park, a lazy float in a gondola along the canals. Eliza wrapped in a layer of self-consciousness, refusing to let herself be carried away from any impulse of happiness. She doesn't let his name pass her lips. No words in fact. Just nods her head yes or no without further elaboration. Means to have no intimate talk. Must keep her pride and not cross certain lines. For his part, Sharpe refrains from pressing her. Doesn't ask "How've you been?" or "How have you kept busy?"—concerns best left alone. A wound he understands he must smile through.

Hambone Hambone where you been?
Around the world and back again

Presents her with more gifts from abroad—ivory combs, ebony bangles, pearl necklaces, mahogany bracelets—but neither his words nor his hands touch her, Eliza determined not to let herself slide into nostalgia and forget the real man in front of her. But nothing really goes away. Every return is just that. Feeling much more than she was able to feel while he was away. What she can do with her back facing him: tear up, spill over, wipe her face with the new lace handkerchief just given her. What she can do afterward: for the first time look directly into his face. Quick to look away, but he's seen her, though, in that one brief moment, has seen her face change. Starts moving with all the confidence of a man who has triumphed, her resistance not an issue.

Why slip into bedclothes only to slip out of them? (The force of routine.) Is it that a gown seals Hope in—*Stay. He will stay*—just like those silk lamp shades (overdressed paramours) that bowl as much light as they release? He bends to take off socks and shoes, while recounting the story of Tom and Morphy. (Who knew that Tom could play chess?) It sounds so good and perfect when he tells it, smooth and ideal.

She settles between white sheets and quilts. Does not stir, afraid of what she might set loose. When he closes in, she evades him by fingering the ruffled collar of her gown. His mouth stuffed still with Tom and Morphy. The small senseless words she can offer in reply, not at hand (lack) the full range she needs to speak to him. (Who knew that Morphy could play the piano?) He bends his reaches around her and she orders herself to wait. If he is the ladder to pleasure, she should not climb. She takes his tongue, putting an end to denial. Holding herself before he enters her with a tenderness she could not expect. Fitting in, his *I love you*s, trying to fill the hole created by absence, distance, separation. Shaking the two of them, some of the sweat on her body his and some of the sweat on his body hers, the best part of marriage, warming up a foot of air above and beneath them, fucking when what they need is sleep, arms and legs moving through it, since what divides her from him will never close.

For weeks after she bears him, unbears him. Two minds to leave, one to stay. His being here a time of plenty that she knows will end. A month or two. Squirrel-like, hoarding away words and pictures behind her eyes before she feels him from behind placing the softest line of kisses down her back, a wet trail over her spine. And out the door again. Gone.

❀ ❀ ❀

Each key has its say. Notes rising in three dimensions around and about her. Reflections rattling against glass where moon bends through. The hours swaying above water. Edgemere rocks as never before, drawing closer to shore. The air, the light, the sounds different.

She draws back her gaze, looking away from so much water, satisfied to let the disrupting tumult of Tom's notes throw her head clear, free her from wandering in that space between memory and Mr. Hub's report about the two intruders. *A man here. A Negro.* Something at the edge of all this. Layers/levels of sound sliding together like stacked plates. Tom, spine arched, face tilted up at her, muddy with feeling. Sweat popping from his pores as if from some inner struggle he is going through, organs caught in the open. Reddish sediment collecting around the legs of the piano. Rising. Not a speck of kindness in his face for her.

Seeing the grievance in his face, thoughts that would have shamed her on other days come with surprising ease. Get clean of Tom—why not? Edgemere looming, expectant, glistening beneath a layer of moonlight—correct this disharmony of fate, a black possibility that gushes into bright night sky. (Night can find color.) Hasn't she already done enough? Keeping him safe, protecting him from the city, keeping him nourished and clean, shutting herself up like this, watching hands for three years. (How long?) Is this what she deserves? Is this what she'll do, watch hands for the rest of her life? Hands cooking cleaning playing praying fanning patting slapping rubbing or caressing her whole life. Tom her inheritance, with her perpetually in this city, this apartment. Consider other avenues, compromises that might be struck. Deliver him to Edgemere where he can be with his own kind. Letting herself think it for the first time. Afraid of being discovered in her feelings. But he can't survive another upset—she's sure—another relocation. Besides, he has earned the right to stay. Something to be said for dying quietly, for disappearing, a victory of a kind that has earned Tom the right to be here, in the city, for as long as the hours, the days permit. Them *here* until she can tell herself different.

She does not think of Tom as having desires other than those demanded by the way they live. How might Tom describe himself? (Occurs to her to wonder.) Is she promising something not hers to keep? They live reasonably well—she gets something half-right at least—their life neither complicated nor tragic. But what does Tom want? Narrow choices seem natural. Certain patterns of thought so simple and one-sided they become irresistible. You imagine you are

Tom and ascribe your own thoughts to him. What does Tom think about her? How does he feel? (Wishes known and unknown. Where the heart is. Hidden beneath ribs curving around stomach and chest.) Clearly much affection but something else too, as if he is holding her up to something. She worries that she comes out lacking in his estimation.

The melody winds down. Sparser range. Softer scales. She tries to speak. Voice catches and the song ends. She knows exactly what Tom has in mind. (Why does a body want to be entered or embraced?) Getting him to bed will be torture. No point in insisting. She sneaks away from the chords, leaving Tom where he sits, in the shimmering distance behind her, his gold-headed cane hissing at her from its place in the corner when she passes.

She wakes some mornings, mouth gummy, eyes filmed over with sleep, legs feeling weary and leaden, a drug-like sluggishness throughout her body, and expects to find Sharpe in the parlor. But only in death is he completely available to her—as he was not in life—moving (contained) in a certain part of her mind. Eliza free to forget or to remember, thinking about him sometimes merely for the purpose of distraction, a buzz or dim ache that seems to carry toward the past.

What exactly has kept her from feeling more about her loss? (What plunges in the heart and is gone.) Her anger to help this thing (longing, grief) along. The passage of time putting an edge on her remorse, making her sense of independence, freedom, sharper. His broken appearances, migratory passings to and fro, rehearsals preparing her for the final sending off. So once she decided he was gone for good—three months? four?—she packed up his entire wardrobe, along with Warhurst's—ten crates filled—and had Mr. Hub transport them to the Municipal Almshouse and the city's other poorhouses and hospitals. She allowed Dr. Hollister to rummage through piles of souvenirs and mementos that had collected over the years and decide as he saw fit what should be put up for auction and what should be saved for posterity, these few items stored away in a single trunk that History will (might) want to know about the "Blind Tom Exhibition."

Loaves of bread line the counter like closed coffins. Heavy pitchers filled with water and milk rising like mausoleums from the table. Basins covered over with big towels. Five ripe apples on a clean plate. Twelve porgies fried on a platter, mouths open, awed by air. She examines the blade of the knife and at that exact moment Tom enters the kitchen.

Miss Eliza, he says. Might I suggest we—then the words go wrong in midsentence.

He talks nonstop for more than an hour, words flying from his mouth like directionless bats, a mishmash of centerless verbiage, bottomless sound taking over her skin. Recitations from his stage days—*Half Man, Half Amazing*—voices within voices, a second, low and calm, that rises and separates itself from the main, then a higher third. Entire passages of one oration, snatches of another, the words lilting, sentences curling up and breaking off at the ends. Mouthed so rapidly at times that the words lose all sense.

What's driving him into language? What is it exactly that comes back to find a tongue?

He stops as suddenly as he started and stands quietly before her, expecting her to say something—ah, she knows what he is thinking: she must be impressed, she must be astonished—his hands open in front of him as if he wants to be ready to catch her first words should she decide to speak, but she is feeling vague inside, not knowing what to say and wondering whether she has any moisture left in her mouth for framing it.

He takes her hand in his—the right palm, wet and greasy with fish—and leads her to the piano. (Not the objects themselves but the way to arrive at them.) Sits down, fingers flexing and finding themselves. (Idle hands, the devil's playthings.) *His notes are so thrilling, and his execution so perfect and so startling as to amuse every listener. The piano itself seems gifted, and sends forth in reverberation, praises, as it were, to Blind Tom. Blind Tom is the Temple wherein music dwells.*

He jerks her sideways with his always-perfect timing. Pulls her into his chest, close enough for his hammering heart to break her resistance. Pieces their forms back together in a harsh rhythm. A dance. (What he wants.) Tom free and light, enjoying his own movements.

And that's only the beginning. He spends the next day, sunup to sundown, running frantically about the apartment, throwing his legs out with aggressive confidence, his arms in the air, providing the gravity needed for country to gutter out of him in two flowing streams of sweat. And the day after that, he pursues her from one chamber to the next.

Run, Miss Eliza. I got you, Miss Eliza. These are some fast legs, Miss Eliza. Speeding along like an afternoon breeze. Room emptying into room. And Tom on her heels. How remarkable it is to be able to do that. Whether he catches her or whether she wins.

So it is. Back to his old self. All of his previous (summer) vigor regained. Joyful. Small chuckles converted into big laughs. Ridiculously happy. A long string of fabulous happenings. Eliza at first unable to appreciate the value of these new pleasures—the laughter has a cruel strain of its own—but with what predictability she eventually gives in.

Tom is quick to notice her change.

Time for our bath.

No better time to.

He stands quietly before her while she undresses him. Holds her hand in a tight grasp during the short walk to the tub, open and waiting and poised to pounce on four lion's-paw feet balanced against the floor. The whole of him bending into the tub once the water is ready. They hunker down like two passengers setting out on a long journey, two soaking in the soft sounds of liquid prosperity, little concern for where they are headed.

From somewhere indistinct the moon begins to shine, red light thick and slow-moving on the water like wax. In a rapid sinking action Tom disappears beneath the surface, some time before he comes up again—she starts to count—choking and spitting.

They are digging a canal in Egypt, he says, water still in his mouth, shining against his teeth.

Here is the soap. Her breasts give in to the buoyancy of water, two pointed canoes riding the surface.

> *Two pounds of powder*
> *Two pounds of soap*
> *If you ain't ready*
> *Holla billy goat*
> *Billy goat!*

Seems to spill out of him, uncontrolled, the soap sliding over his body with a kind of furious impatience.

My mouth is closed, my ears are open, he says.

The cloth, she says.

He commandeers the cloth and proceeds to rinse the soap from his body. After a long thoughtful pause, he puts all his fingers deep into her hair and holds her head then leans forward in order to deliver his instructions, doing his best to be gentle, reassuring, his fingers moving with a bargaining touch that indicates that this natural familiarity will take nothing from her.

They stamp upon the mat to get rid of excess water. She whitens his entire body with lemon-scented talcum powder that Sharpe once brought back from Spain. Tom in her world again and she in his. Calm, helplessly so. How does it all become so familiar?

Perfectly content in the skin he calls home, Tom lives inside his body like a turtle, his world limited to the extremities of his skin. He can never escape his own head through the distractions the world offers sighted people. *Perhaps he suffers from some mental deficiencies, Sharpe said. Still, I wonder how much of his mental state can be attributed to my father's neglect. Because of Tom's genius my father was reluctant to apply the correcting hand.* But he gains much more in compensation, fortunate that his lack of sight, lack of mind does not permit him to know that he is of the despised Negro race, a former slave. *Hellfire, Sharpe said. Maybe he even thinks he's a white man.*

For a time she is able to forget everything as she looks at the watery light, this sensation that the building has unmoored itself from the earth and set sail, Eliza captain at her window station, rocking between lower and higher joys of journey. Still, after days, after weeks, why is she not able to get completely used to this thing in Tom, in herself?

Tom gives a whole clear utterance, holding neither promise nor blame.

In the ashen noontime Dr. Hollister enters the parlor, dressed too heavily for the weather in an outer coat hanging over a fine woolen jacket and creased black trousers, his legs stocky, like sawed-off trunks, his feet shod in half-shoes half-boots that rise above his ankles. His white shirt seems to supply a soft light of its own, and Eliza wonders who has pressed and ironed it, since the Doctor as far as she knows travels without servants. Indeed, he is well dressed but needs some touches to be added, matters that fall under the purview of a good servant.

She hears his words but she feels nothing for the Doctor. Always this pretense once a month that he is only dropping in to visit on his way up to Saratoga Springs, where he keeps a stable of racing horses, his supposed reason for venturing here, even during the off-season. She allows that she is glad to see him. He brings her a bundle of two or three books. Lets himself express natural affection for Tom, certain in his touch that Tom can understand him.

How long was it after Sharpe's disappearance (death) that he turned up one day, unexpected? She heard the knock, put one eye to the cold glass of the peephole, and discovered Dr. Hollister put before vision. Half a mind not to open the door since the Doctor was

General Bethune's man, and she had no way of gauging his intentions. But to deny him, she risked his return.

He walked in that first time, mouth tight, eyes cold, took her hand and kissed it, barely greeting her before he made his way across the room to Tom. The emotion brought on at the sight of Tom occupied his face for a full minute or more. He began the examination, but Tom's skin was selfish, hugging to his frame, making it necessary for Dr. Hollister to use certain instruments again and again.

Dr. Hollister looked at her then looked past her, which she thought boded ill for Tom. He treated Tom with substances contained inside a dozen or more small glass-stoppered bottles. Tom moaned with the relief at these ministrations. He drank green liquid from a tiny urn, draining the vial. Slowly color began to come back to his skin. At the end of it all Dr. Hollister prepared Tom a bath with salt from Saratoga Springs.

Is the comfort the same, what the good doctor offers Tom and what she offers? Her arms and his, her bath and his?

Dr. Hollister pats Tom on the head. Don't I know what you hate by this time? he says.

His leather bag is open just enough to allow her a glimpse of a caliper, pincers up. Why is it that he chooses to perform his examination, take measurements, in front of her? Why does she watch?

He furiously registers his findings—"data" he calls it, part of Tom's ongoing "medical history"—in a vellum ledger, after writing his notes, then writing them again on cleaner paper in a cleaner hand, careful strokes, more beautiful lettering, not a single smudge.

He continues to eat well, beyond what he needs?

Eliza throws up her hands. He always has.

Well, do what you can to regulate him.

I will make much effort. How is his water?

Dr. Hollister takes a seat on the settee, the fingers of both hands laced on his head. Looking like a hot mess, overcoat still in place, blanketing his body. Sweat outlining his cleanly barbered hairline.

The moisture has decreased some, but fortunately there's still a valuable surplus. The orbs have not deformed any and are effectively preserved inside the chambers.

So there's still a chance for sight?

Very much so.

Dr. Hollister's diagnosis—Tom's pickled eyes biding time—was opposite that of Dr. McCune's. *He can detect some light, Dr. McCune said. But expect no improvement in his condition. The orbs will slowly putrefy.* However the experts differed, upon first meeting she impressed Dr. Hollister with her interest in and understanding of the facts and details of ophthalmology, all she had gleaned from Dr. McCune in their rounds at the Asylum.

Continue to keep the orbs moist.

I should by all means. His seriousness imposes a silence on her, on Tom, and she senses that if anything important is to get said it will have to be said quickly. Someone was here.

Dr. Hollister ceases to move, sits rigid for a few moments, as though making any motion at all might be of unintended and dangerous consequence. She sees the way age has set into his skin, a map crumpled and creased, folded too often, overhandled. When?

I'm not sure.

You're not sure?

I received a report.

The Doctor does not appear startled, as if in the common ease of these surroundings nothing can put danger in the front of his mind. And when was this report received?

It takes her a bit of calculating to arrive at an approximate date.

Yes, the Doctor says. I see. So then you were actually away?

We were away. Foremost in her thoughts facts she decides to withhold: A Negro. Two.

Yes, the Doctor says. Yes. Who could it have been? He cracks for her benefit a small understanding smile. Why shouldn't he? At this late time the watching eye and listening ear know better than to expect any upheaval that would end up leaving things radically different from the way they are. Well, send word if you have to.

Certainly, Doctor.

I should say my good-bye. He gets to his feet, puts away his instruments, shuts his bag, touches Tom, bows his farewell. Remember his appetite.

Certainly, Doctor. Certainly.

A door open and shut, and already the strong smell of damask roses is taking over the apartment. Each breath brings with it a smell of flowers. The smell lifts the corners of Eliza's mouth.

Tom moves the vase one inch to the right in obvious irritation. That inch won't do so he moves it another.

She sits down on the settee, trying to conceal her uneasiness, hands clasped together in front of her.

Tom tries the vase an inch or two more, in one direction or the other. And she searches his face for something she didn't know was lost until then.

We can place them elsewhere, Tom.

You, Miss Eliza, you keep them there. This is my piano.

Wasn't that nice of Mr. Hub? Mr. Hub was only trying to be nice. The roses. And fish, too.

I'm Blind Tom, he says. I'm one of the greatest men to walk the earth. Nostrils flared, he goes about in the shadowed cool sniffing the room, from corner to corner, length to length. Dressed by his own hands today, a finely tailored suit, the wale in his pants close together as if stitched by miniature fingers.

He removes his jacket, revealing the harness of his suspenders. Folds the jacket across the settee at the end opposite her and resumes his walk, moving quickly and lightly about the room, with his hands wrapped around the shoulder-looped straps of his suspenders, navigational tools directing him this way and that.

Tom—

I have dominion over my life.

Tom, if you will—

Now he begins to parrot every word that comes from her mouth, having an easy time of it, an exact reproduction of all the nuances of diction and tone of voice. Strange to hear yourself coming out of another person's mouth, that person of the opposite sex, and a full-blooded Negro.

She gives up trying to engage and distract him. Later he will be all softness and apology, but she'll make him pay. All she can do for now to maintain a fruitless distance, sound cutting the air in half. Rose petals shudder with the piano's vibrations. Move like little knives in the air, trying to cut free.

Vexed, Tom measuring her wants against his, showing and giving her a sampling of his worst, but not the worst he is capable of, the store of inflictions he directed at the manager Warhurst. Tom readily accepted Sharpe's authority but was every bit the disobedient child with Warhurst. A terrible irony since the manager, unbeknownst to Sharpe, indulged Tom in ways that would never have met with Sharpe's approval, honoring every demand, only for Tom to repay this gluttonous generosity with resistance and outright refusal—in the end the reasons for Tom's recalcitrance are unclear, stemming from more than the mere consequence of age, Tom's youth—until Sharpe, shouting, shoving, stepped in to exercise the restraining hand.

He thinks you're a nigger, Sharpe said.

A nigger? Warhurst said. He has Coachman for that.

You work like a nigger. And you worry like a nigger.

I do my job.

Yes, you do your job, but you take everything for a sign.

She wakes up feeling tired and at fault. Feet aching as if she had spent the night walking sleep. Tom had done the walking. Roving about the apartment all night. (What she heard.) Why the sudden restlessness?

He drinks his milk after it cools to the right temperature. Replaces the stagnant fluid in the vase with fresh water. Despite the dominant scent the roses are already wilting, becoming less noticeable, like a flag receding in size and color with distance. The vase (glass) seems to be decreasing in size too. Losing to the piano's black shine, hard-set radiance.

The piano is growing, subtracting the world around them. A little more each day. She fears that it will soon take over the parlor. Dead center in the room now, so that you can't help but see it, have to walk around it to get from one side of the room to the other. The furniture redefined, going miniature, one object crowded up against the next, some actually forced out into the hall.

Little by little. The universe constricting in front of her eyes.

Tom is seated on the bench with his legs spread wide apart, the expansive globe of his belly propped on black wood, hands serving a supportive role at his sides, some upset nesting in the hollows of his abdomen. He sits that way for a time, a pattern of dying light stretching across the ceiling.

An owl night, he announces. Sitting on a tree.

Having enough of the dark, she strikes a lamp, the smell of kerosene weighing down upon them. Tom's mouth cannons open and before long his entire body is erupting into convulsions, retching up a stomach-warm lump stillborn inside an orange-yellow puddle.

Takes her some time to move, since she is in no great hurry to clean the floor. Fears that any movement will touch off his belly again. And even after she performs the task she takes the precaution of preparing a tablespoon of cod liver oil to help settle his stomach.

Heavy with the oil he sits for a time before joining her on the settee, stomach noisy. Twists his fingers into hers, her smooth pink hands and his smooth brown hands forming a single fist. His face stunned and drained, yellow flecks of vomit in the corners of his mouth. She has of necessity to clean his face too. Already pitched beyond her limit. (Isn't it enough?)

Dr. Hollister arranges his gauges and instruments on top of the piano.

Here you are at last, Tom says.

Yes, I am here.

You came because of me.

I shall not pretend. I came because of you.

Dr. Hollister makes quick work of his examination. Records his findings.

Perhaps you can give him something for his belly, Eliza says. He suffered a bad stomach last week. Tom touches his abdomen in verification.

He has too much flesh, Dr. Hollister says. He's gained more than ten pounds since my last visit. He looks at her, making sure she understands.

She does. For the good doctor how one looks is of first importance.

He mixes Tom a tonic with medicines drawn from several vials.

He closes his bag in less time than it takes to tell. He will require a daily constitutional. Facing her again while he talks.

Where will we walk? Where would they walk? Of course, Dr. Hollister can imagine (knows) only too well the life they live here.

He will do well to walk. And you would do well to give him relief from his person whenever possible. His continuance depends on these conditions.

What exactly does he mean by that?

Did you hear that, Tom? Dr. Hollister asks.

Good doctor.

Dr. Hollister takes the time to fasten every button on his overcoat. He grips the handle of his bag. Already she is wondering about his instructions.

Tom turns toward the Doctor. What kind of time is this to leave, to go home?

I'm all done here. You've made my stay light.

I have. I hope you're not too tired. Tom gets up from the bench. You're dropping with sleep.

Am I now? The Doctor touches Tom's head.

Even your hand. I ask you, where's the sense in your leaving?

You wish to delay my going? Dr. Hollister takes a seat on the bench with his bag at his feet. Who will look in on the horses?

Tom sits down beside him.

Yes. I see. I see.

It's good you do. So we'll sit for a time. My afternoon is totally dependent on you.

Is Dr. Hollister offering her an opportunity to escape as he had on that mad afternoon three years ago during the violence?

We can travel at nightfall, Dr. Hollister said, drawing himself up in his seat.

No, she said.

Do your best not to worry. I have agents here in the city who will see to our safe passage.

I've suffered a shock. I need to consider my options.

Her words temporarily shunted Dr. Hollister into a disbelieving silence. Yes, you've suffered a shock, he said. Now you must let it end.

No, she said.

Madame, if you entertain thoughts of a respite—

No I do not. But I do entertain other thoughts.

He gave her a woebegone look.

I will go out for a short time and you will remain here with Tom and see after him until I return.

I cannot honor that arrangement.

So Tom must accompany me.

Madame.

Doctor.

You don't want to see what's out there, he said.

I can quite believe it. But I will go all the same. She wouldn't have him coming in her home telling her what's dangerous and what's safe.

Accepting that he had no voice in the matter, Dr. Hollister looked at Tom again and again, as if trying to read the saving solution in the boy's expression.

She walked out into a maddeningly sunny afternoon, some underworld creature slinking into light, into air, after a long hibernation. Blinking off the shock of sudden glare. Then taking the light inside her, blazing from inside out like a dream. She walked awkwardly, her feet unreal, feeling exposed beneath a dress falling in stiff folds. Even with the sun scouring everything, drops of water were hanging from the trees, reminding her that it had indeed rained last night. Either that or the trees were sweating.

In any direction she looked she saw long ropes of smoke rising in gray-black rebellion against the sun. The sidewalks and streets paved in shards of glass—hop, skip, jump—like some sparkling but reckless carpet, her passage across it accentuating her amazement that the city was still in place, the houses and buildings standing. Telegraph wires had been cut. Along the shore lay scattered the rusting remains of rifles and cannons, tools and field equipment, canteens, shovels, picks, and axes. The ocean drowned in a frantic proliferation of debris— hats, blouses, scarves, shoes and boots, staves and paddles—along with bloated cow-like forms bobbing in the surf. Avenues clogged with streams of rioters spilling out from smashed-in doorways, with booty floating on their shoulders: cumbersome lengths of carpet, heavy iron bedsteads, finely crafted desks and tables, leather-topped stools and chairs, and porcelain basins and commodes. Hands pushed through broken windows burdened with bulging sacks that they quickly dropped to other hands raised greedily in wait at street level below. This was what she saw. *This was what I saw.*

Was she any more than they?

Perhaps why she hurried on, kept on her way, seeing nothing at all, unless it was the glass under her feet. Why break her eyes with all the sights? Why when she was already fully weighted with words of apology, words of guilt?

Is she any more than they?

Walking now, she wonders how long it has been. Too long. Stiff legs, crotchety arms, and rusty joints. (What she has lived to know.) Testing the waters. Indeed, motion brings the better. Footsteps with nothing physical in them. Just out and about. Seeing what can be gained from an aimless stroll, a brief separation from Tom.

The first leaves to change stop her. Now all the trees pop into bright color one after the next. Autumn in an instant. Leaves in free fall. Falling about her shoulders. The colors look elegant on her sleeves. And loose leaves carpeting the ground. (Which leaf belongs to which tree?) One color giving shape to another. Twirling on the sidewalk like scraps of another world dropped from the sky. And she stumbling forward, the world beautiful again. Remembering what this feels like.

Why has she left this pleasure until now? How easily she could have done this before, take her feet on casual stroll around the neighborhood. Take in some fresh air.

Evening arranges itself around the fallen leaves. And then the sky blooms. She watches the stars pop out, one by one. Now here is something she has forgotten, that you can see stars here in the city. There they are, like—looking at them closely—holes punched in dark cloth so light underneath bleeds through.

Of course she has already stayed out longer than she should have, but the harbor is just over there. All the big ships sailing to Britain and the Continent and the West Indies and Africa and South America and the Pacific. Just over there.

Something goes skimming by her in the air. Ship blowing its

horn. Much has changed, much between her and Tom. So why is she scanning ahead in her mind to find an excuse for why she has stayed away so long? What is holding her in this world?

What if she returns home and finds Dr. Hollister no longer there? No, she will find him there—and Tom—giving her some last words of advice as useless as all the others he has given her.

Mr. Hub calls, Tom says. He calls when you are away.

When am I away? she says. I am never away, she says, except that one time—yesterday or the day before that, two, three days ago, four—when Dr. Hollister came. And she is thinking, Could he really have missed me for those few hours when I stepped out?

He calls with thoughts of flowers and fish.

And where am I when this happens? Just where do you suppose?

Mr. Hub wishes to drive you to the country. Our house in the country. With flowers and fish.

He is slouched all the way forward on the bench, with his face turned sideways in flat repose against the strings, the piano's cantilevered lid raised guillotine-like above him.

But where have I been?

So come here and sit and let's figure it out.

Tom must be confused, thinking her gone, thinking that she has left the apartment when she has only been spending a few necessary moments elsewhere. (Could she have missed Mr. Hub's call?) And why shouldn't he have such thoughts? Hasn't she been avoiding him? Indeed she has. As of late, she finds she can't remain in the same room with him for more than a few minutes at a time. She sees only the outline of his body or his back hunched over food when she enters a room and just as quickly leaves it. Whenever he leans for her, she leans away, until with each passing day he becomes more and more remote, disappearing into the crevices of forgetting until he squeezes through again to remind her. Who would think that he should miss her so for a few unimportant hours taken on the fly?

Now Tom is standing firm in the middle of the room, hurting her in his way, all impatience to have her sit beside him on the bench and listen to a new song. She gives in to his excitement, not unbearably at first, pours herself into being another person since this is what he will accept as compromise, conscious to make no open display of her need for distance.

His an expression of the most steady attention. Smiles, the shine of teeth, strong urges to burrow into her whenever she is comfortably seated on cushions and pillows. He occupies the apartment completely, from the lines of the walls to the edges of the doors to the joints in the floors. Tom brimming in the doorways. Tom stationed on the chairs. Tom framed in the windows, venetian blinds sectioning both him and Time into lit rectangular hours.

Turning on the movements of his face, the motion of his limbs, her life repeats itself every time Tom takes her by the hand and insists that she follow where he pulls her. Agitated breaths. Bumps and bruises. Sleight-of-hand reflections that go skimming over solid surfaces and disappear. Anything to keep him still.

Why not here at the piano, where one can enjoy the firm feel of wood while watching one's image trembling in clear particular silence, a dark glaze of laminate? Where one may study the deep hollow with strings cast in tight suspension like a fisherman's net. More than three years now since the correcting fingers of the tuner have paid a visit, but each key sounds the pitch it should. What keeps them in tune? Some memory of the tuner's hands caught in the layered depths of shine? Or is the piano itself the tuner's petrified shadow (soul), severed from the flesh where it rightfully belongs and (caught) forever here?

Slow heavy notes and stalled chords hold in the air somewhere above her head and hang bat-like from the ceiling, teaching her longing and loathing in equal measure.

Even the music has turned against her. (No, *he* has turned it against her.)

How ugly it makes her feel to be simply sitting here, doing nothing, day after day, like an anchor rusting in water. Easy to drift from one room to the next. Space before her, space to her left and right, space behind her. Her life a muddle in this way. Easy to turn a familiar corner only to lose your grasp on the known world and collide with another body coming into the room you are leaving and see your twin sitting on the floor trying to clear her head.

Is she any less alone with Tom? How meagerly she opens her heart to him. For his own good, she must set some boundaries, limit contact to mere glimpses of his grumpy silhouette. She feels angry, capable of causing pain. Just the other day, she was sullen and spoke too quickly at him, her tone harsh, thinking it might cause some change in his manner, ease his demands and contentions, bring an end to his finding her wherever she is. He seized her by the hand, as is his custom, and generated a deep pressure on her flesh. Began touching and pulling her, and when she resisted—No, Tom—took her neck in the crook of his heavy arm and tried to wrestle her out of herself, drag her down to the floor to sit with him. She shoved her palm in his face with something more than annoyance, something closer to hatred, and freed herself, rising up from the floor, gaining the settee and hastening to the other side of the room. Then he was on her again, his hands quick and warm. She pried them from her dress, one finger at a time.

She doesn't want his ugly touches. So much else she doesn't want anymore, some point of definition in the past from which she is receding, some point of embarkation in the future where she is or isn't heading, Eliza glowing distinctly in her own lessening light, sparklingly aware of that world cut off from her. Never so alone.

Tired of always being cooped up with her thoughts, she opens a window and sticks her head out into the open. Takes in air that brings a welcome fragrance and taste into her nose and mouth. She'll take it, this air, take it for what it's worth, even if it gives her trouble. Undoes what's done. Her hair shifting sideways from the full-on breeze blowing at her. She catches up the shiny-dart strands with both hands, wind so hard she can't see a thing, can't keep her eyes open, hair, eyes giving her trouble. Using both hands she scoops hair forward from the sides of her face, head tilted downward. Is it that she is leaning out the window, her untended hair hanging like rope? If she extends her tresses full length she can climb down them to the street.

Her mind furling, rolling on its own into some unchartable dark sanctum. Hair, eyes, mind—what are they telling her? She has taken her ease long enough. If she is to be any good to Tom, good to herself, she will have to step for a spell (again) beyond the confines of walls, no farther than the street below, into the air.

Taking up her shawl, she quits the apartment, her desperation no less deep for its suddenness. Color is noticeably absent. Only the same brown of barren trees and gray of empty sidewalks and streets. (Autumn over already?) Still, standing here is good. Under open sky. The day overcast. Secondhand light. Dusty and old.

Is she to trust her eyes? Since starting out, not another person has crossed her sight. Can it be that they've all gone away and left the city to her? Worse, some destruction has reached each and every one of them in their homes? She will continue on to the first canal.

Advancing at a quicker pace fails to ease the sourness of her suspicion. The thought of them all dead. Hardly a satisfying outcome even if a just one given what she has endured, changes enough for several lifetimes. (The body never forgets.) Just like that the world chooses to end but not before spoiling her with a short taste of normalcy. She is like anyone else: a satisfying taste creates expectations for more. Has she not already begun forecasting, making plans? (Before the weather changes, winter arrives, each day she will have her walk, two or three or four modest hours at a time. Stroll along the canals. Through the park. Take in the museums. Where's the harm? What trouble can Tom come to while she is away?) So what is she to do now?

She reaches the fourth canal and still no sign of people. (Dogs yes. Cats yes. Birds yes. Squirrels and the lesser forms.) She senses the air standing out against the cloth of her shawl. What's the point in venturing farther? Something futile. Something nostalgic. Something stupid. But she can neither stop nor turn around. In fact, the impulse to advance, push ahead all the way downtown, to the harbor, comes over her. When had she last seen the harbor, the beautiful waters and ships there?

Soon she crosses the sixth canal, takes a corner, and chances upon a fantastic sight: a Great Wall of backs, elbows, napes, formed along the boulevard less than a hundred paces ahead. A scene that overpowers her as much for its unexpectedness as for the total unaccompaniment of sound. Thousands of people standing in complete silence, straining calves and necks to see over the heads in front of them some display of public celebration. Has her grip on time become so lax that she has forgotten this holiday?

She has trouble making her way through the crush of bodies, four or five rows deep, but polite requests, dexterity, and force eventually gain her the front and access to an even more impressive spectacle, a slow river of color flowing southbound down the boulevard. Negro soldiers on parade. Black, brown, and yellow skin enlivened by blue uniforms, the best blues embellished with white gloves and white leggings. They step bravely, heads high, bodies stiff, displaying a dignity of purpose even when a sleeve is torn, a cap mended, a cuff tattered, or a collar worn away. Their regimental flags (colors) swaying wildly above although there is no wind that Eliza can feel, the previous breeze stilled. Some soldiers ride high on horses. Counted among the hooves that carry men those that pull along cannons mounted on wheels. And the men to a one are fully armed with muskets, bayonets in place, holstered pistols visible in the belts of a few. Altogether enough firepower to set ablaze acres of white skin.

Her ears awaken in an explosive instant at the sound of a rifle, the first bullet fired. Surely a volley will follow. But no body falls dead. No one runs for sanctuary. And she realizes that what at first struck her as the absence of sound was only its denial, a vain effort by that white wall of bodies to cut off any and all evidence of these Negro soldiers to the listening ear and the observing eye. Only now can she hear the thud of boots, the smacking of hooves and the creaking of wheels, the straining of leather, the swishing of cloth and clanking of metal, the clatter of drums and calls of bugles and shrill of flutes.

The last soldier reaches the end of the boulevard and slips from sight around the corner with his compatriots, and the crowd moves as one body in curious pursuit of the Negro soldiers when they should be fleeing in the opposite direction. She simply stands and looks into one face after another, trying to read the emotions stirring there, their faces radiant with panic. Charmed by the piper, the entire city tags along to its doom. Is she fated to perish along with them? For surely the soldiers are here to enact their revenge against the city.

With no loss of speed or obvious sign of tiring, the soldiers make the many miles back to the harbor, where the big metal ships that had carried them hulk like resting whales, their guns the size of houses. The soldiers march the half circle of the harbor then start to travel north again, along Broadway, passing one canal after the next until they reach the southernmost entrance to Central Park. They enter the park and continue on to the Great Lawn, and only cease to move when someone shouts a command. A second shouted command brings them at ease.

Now the city beholds the third astonishing sight of the day. Tents pitched across the Great Lawn. Dozens if not hundreds of them. Flapping in the breeze, they seem perfectly at home. Even their canopies were a familiar shade of seasonal green. Not hard to believe that these tents have sprouted up through the earth of their own accord.

Then the sense of unease. She feels it, but she can't be alone in her feeling, glad that they are feeling it too. (She sees it on them, hears it inside them, even for those who can only manage a murmur.) But it also feels good for some reason she cannot fathom to be standing as part of the crowd, as if she is one of them still. She mingles her surprise with theirs—why not?—even as she recognizes with new intensity just how alone she is, just how far the world has left her behind.

Her arms shiver in the coolness of the evening. Bare limbs bearing their loss. She adjusts her shawl and continues up the street, shadows gathering behind her, planning ambush. All along the avenue the gas lamps come on one by one. No cause to worry.

How will Tom greet the news? An invading army of Negroes. Victorious in one war and readying for another.

So much around her is untried or different that it takes her almost a half block to realize that she has passed the building where she lives. Making hasty return, she finds a man sitting on the front steps, wrapped in his overcoat. A Negro. She decides in an instant to simply make her way around his person as quickly as she can.

He takes to his feet at the sight of her. Mrs. Bethune? Eliza Bethune?

Who are you looking for?

Madame, I believe you are the reason for my call.

She stands watching.

My presence must be a surprise. Tabbs Gross. The Negro holds his hand straight out. She reaches and takes it, and he shakes her hand with the minimum of movement and force, like a bird alighting on the thinnest of branches. Mrs. Bethune, I'm pleased to make your acquaintance. The Negro eases his features into a relaxed smile. He is tall and very correctly dressed. He is calm and dignified, a man who makes himself felt at once.

I don't mean to excite you.

You haven't. She rubs her hands up and down both arms under her shawl.

It pleases me to know that. I should make haste and explain.

You called once before? You were here back during the summer?

Well, I have expended considerable time and debt to find you.

She senses that he is pleased, he is delighted, he is glad, but he allows nothing of his feelings to appear on his face. Does he expect her to make apology for his troubles in locating her?

I'm sure you will find the purpose of my business most satisfactory to yourself.

Yes, Mr. Gross. I feel certain of that too. Kindly inform me.

Madame. You see, I've come for Tom. I've come to return him to his mother.

What could have prepared her for this response? Far easier to draw upon certain acceptable assumptions that might make quick work of explaining his presence here. A journalist. A soldier even.

You would have me believe that this mother is alive? *He has no one, Sharpe said.*

Yes, madame. Even as we speak she is resident on Edgemere, awaiting reunion with her son.

And she has been resident there for how long? Why is she not here instead of you? She can barely get her voice to work.

Madame, I fully understand your concern. You see—

She can see colors when the Negro speaks, this Tabbs Gross, colors, as if the seasons are moving in reverse and autumn is returning again. The circle ending where it began.

She takes two steps back and falls on the curb. Sits there looking up at the man, Tabbs Gross, afraid to talk, afraid of what might happen if her words hit air.

Moving House:
Three Views of the City
(1867)

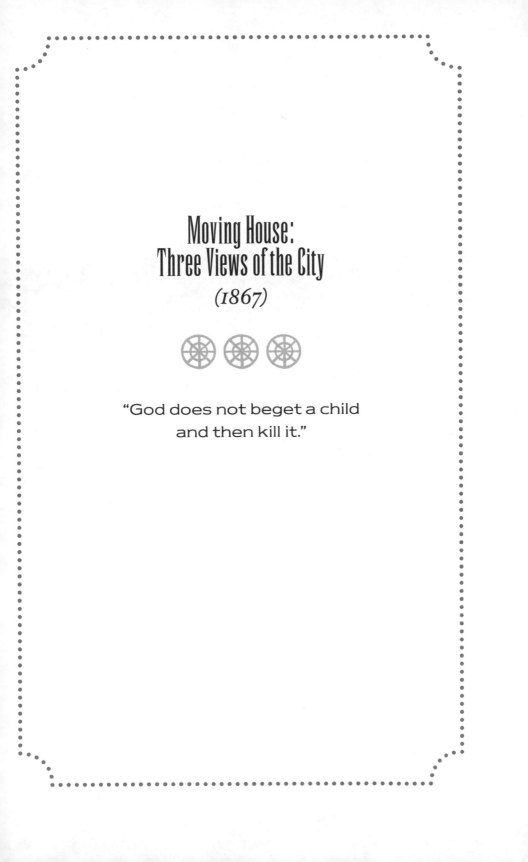

"God does not beget a child
and then kill it."

SHALLOW-BREATHING BODIES SHUFFLE ABOUT, FEET MAK-
ing a way, making way. Some feet shod, others routinely naked.
Ankles made raw, skin white with calluses. Dim shapes, both fact
and becoming, who feel more in control, more hopeful than their
eyes suggest, eyes bright and empty, the sockets weak, the orbs so
frighteningly clear that they look completely disembodied, hovering
in midair, that wild unsteady look of bewilderment and doubt offset
by the intentionality of their presence, tangibly here and here for a
reason, for the long haul. Tabbs sees the agitation in their faces, faces
heavy with an expectation that cannot be put down. So assured, so
much purpose, so determined—promised (a plot so wide so long; a
beast of burden so young so strong), thought capable of, expected
to—To your tents, O Israel!—bringing their hands tightly together
in prayer to defeat Doubt, beseeching in bodies that are designed for
activity far more vigorous than this, waiting, passing time, ready
for the next thing although that next thing is uncertain, so they must
keep holding on to God's unchanging hand (for now) in a world that
refuses to stay still. They move with the weight and speed of their
own expectations, confidence (new) in the quick movement of their
legs. Their once slow tongues up the pace too, stumbling into strange
conjoinings of consonants and vowels, a metamorphosis that Tabbs
has heard seen with his own skeptical ears and eyes—Tom's mother
speaks at double the speed he recalls her speaking in the South—even
as he gets stuck in the thick speech of fresh arrivals, those just off
the boat as it were, struggles to understand their muddy English, the
thick drawn-out syllables, and the way certain words sink beneath
sense altogether. Listen to them. The one the many. Here those who
were not now are. Strays who have drifted up from the peculiar lands,
customs, and institutions of the South, otherwise know as Freedmen,
the freed who feel free and think free and talk free. Ripening so fast.
Even the sun seems to lighten the color of their skin—however dark
their eyes—new skin for a new race.

But, as Tabbs knows (present, a witness), they were not the first

··· 101 ···

to make (find) their way here to the city from wretched Southern climes. Many months earlier the soldiers had returned, unexpected, uninvited, war's contraband, men who at the very start of the war had sworn an oath of patriotic commitment and duty and enlisted into an all-Negro regiment so as to take up arms and forcibly bring slavery to an end—granted, some found a secondary motivation: to keep a republic that was both in conflict with itself and unsure of its future from a sundering into two separate nations forever conflicted, forever divided—and thus enlisted had shed blood and allowed their own blood to be shed. Entrusted with the task of taking lives, taking towns and cities, on the one hand drawing the last breath from the enemy, and on the other shepherding to safety their emancipated brethren and sistren. Embedded in battle perhaps at the very moment when their kinsmen, neighbors, and friends came under attack, when they were being shot, strung up, and struck down, when they were being burned out of their homes in Black Town and every other precinct in the city, only to be chased from and otherwise expelled and expunged from the city's municipal boundaries altogether.

Tabbs wonders, when did word of the violence and the expulsion reach them? And—having given their all in battle, maiming and killing (the skirmishes that memory would—will—never let them relinquish), only to learn that they were now all exiled from the destroyed and crumbling houses of a previous life—what thoughts curled around them at that critical juncture in time? (Standing at the crossroad.) What forces of will, upbringing, counsel, morality, or law urged restraint and kept them from shooting or impaling every alabaster on sight? (Try to feel it now.) Moreover, how were they able to throw themselves back into the fray for the remainder of the war under the auspices of a country, an authority that had if not outright betrayed them, had at the least done nothing to secure and protect the person and property of those they had left behind? Not to mention (to say nothing of) the entire matter of punishment and retribution, what those white men who were duly appointed in the appropriate and austere offices of power would do to see that those of the city's alabasters (of whatever sex, of whatever age, of whatever standing in society) who had committed unpardonable wrongs against the city's Negroes would be held accountable and brought to justice to the fullest extent of the law and with all deliberate speed.

Perhaps it was this wounded sense of weighing and waiting—never forget, never forgive—that sustained them through all of the fallen bodies and sacked cities, however scant and remote (distant) their hopes of return and reckoning. And when the Surrender finally came, to their surprise it did not give them the immediate release from active duty that they had expected, but only further deferred the dream, for they were issued a new assignment: keep the peace, maintain order, provision and protect the Freedmen. For months on end they were summoned to one contentious Southern location or another to put down a last stand by random elements of the enemy's collapsed army and to deter, detain, or otherwise do away with sporadic groups of bizarrely dressed (faces hidden inside triangular-peaked hoods, bodies concealed under bulbous bedsheets or robes) irregulars and stop them from committing the most brutal retaliatory and fear-instilling acts of sabotage, assassination, rape, kidnapping, hanging, and immolation.

It took well over a year for the opposition to trickle down and thin away to a point where it either no longer caught the attention of the generals and their counselors or caught their attention but was not deemed worthy of action. At that point the regiment was officially dissolved. The men pooled their wages, commandeered a vessel, subscribed their names to a man in the ship's manifest, more than seventy-five in all, and set sail for home, each and every one looking all the way to the end of his gaze, determined to return no matter where he had been and what he had done. So the same water that took them away brought them back, as if the ocean too was homesick. The ship's arrival in the harbor drew no particular notice. Just another ship, one of the many daily, transporting cargo. Then in the sky reddening remains of the day the men started scrambling down the gangplank under a burden of personal belongings (the memories they had carried around in leather satchels and gunnysacks) and military-issued (stolen?) rifles, tents, crates, and barrels, and wheelbarrows that they carried, pushed, or tugged ashore, and stood there before the ship, loosely assembled, stretching their arms, time breaking over their skin, shaking the journey off. The sudden and unexpected image of soldiers, black men in blue, awoke a quiver of sudden alarm and fright inside the alabasters, and drew them to the city's streets from inside the comfort and safety of their houses and apartments.

In a voice clean as polished steel, one of the soldiers issued a call and the men fell into parade formation, their flags (colors) holding sky and time, their rifles slanted against the wind. The voice rang out again and the men began marching up Broadway—move as a team, never move alone—waves of clamor radiating from their synchronized boots; light catching and gleaming off metal—rifles, medals of merit, and wheelbarrows stacked high with crates of projectiles and grenades and barrels of kerosene and gunpowder—while the city's alabasters looked on still, silent, and wide-eyed like grazing cows. Home again. (All the rest now a falling back.) Their sonorous bodies and the keening whine and groan of their wheelbarrows halting the movement of the many buggies, cabriolets, carriages, buckboards, and horse-drawn streetcars crisscrossing the city's most fabled avenue, stillness staking the alabasters in place like the stately lampposts and sturdy telegraph poles lining the avenue.

As the light thinned and evening gathered, the regiment continued at its own pace mile after mile, every man sweating and straining for their collective destination, some (see it) indefinable substance or feeling pumping through them—this much: they have a firm understanding of victory and defeat—shunting aside their proven capacity for patience and postponement, driving them all the way to the other end of Broadway, at which point they turned in one sinuous line and passed through the high wrought iron gates of Central Park, where they lit lamps and struck torches and began to set up camp on the Great Lawn, assembling tents, digging trenches, their movements both separate and coordinated, their shadows long and dark, black shapes moving in a silent ballet, their legs partly obscured in the high uncut grass as if they had all been amputated below the knee. They cut down dead trees for firewood. Fire and light. The only blaze in the dark, radiance visible for miles. (Tabbs saw it himself.) Then they retired for the night on pallets inside their tents or slept out in the open on the half moons of hammocks slung between trees. Morning brought a butchery of park creatures—deer, squirrels, and rock doves—that they skinned, cleaned, cooked, and feasted on. The next day the same. And more still in subsequent days. And so on. A standing army sprawling in their camp on the Great Lawn for longer than anyone could have known or expected, waiting through both good and inclement weather to be recognized.

And there they remain, even while the city accelerates around them, a fast new geography. In a matter of hours a goat path becomes a turnpike a turnpike a road a road a street and the street a name. New Place. New Here. New There. New House. New Water. New Well. New Creek. New Yonder. New Street. More Street. Street Street. New New. Each street breeds an architecture, neat perfect rows of houses. Skinny blocks of wood on a mud alley. Fat blocks of wood lined up before a gutter like men relieving themselves. Active space, men hard at work, no shortage of hands and backs, colored and alabaster (city locals), earning a good wage, some able for the first time to afford pants that button. They work wood with axes, saws, planes, and other (carpentry) tools, ankle-deep in soft wood refuse, while army surveyors scuttle about insect-like with instruments of planning and measurement. The city expands, corners and lots and blocks, Freedmen settlements spreading in all directions, even in neighbor-hoods that were off-limits to colored citizens only a few years ago, before the riots. Righting wrongs, the city issues a call of welcome to the Freedman (as well as the Uprooted, those who were driven out of their homes and forced into exile on Edgemere)—*Everything that had to happen has already happened. Danger and tension are past. It's a new day. Come and become a citizen, become one of us*—seeing miles over the present into a high and limitless democratic future. The sky whitens with justice. The city's promise pulls smiles out of worried faces, one after the next, not unlike a many-colored sash of infinite length drawn from a magician's sleeve.

A new life in a new land among a new set of people in a new united republic where autumn leaves scuttle across the ground like papery crabs. Stubbornly, the arrivals retain time, dragging their feet along, lengthening every moment to pull their histories forward, even as they venture a new soil, bodies covered with dirt. You would think the earth grows on their backs. You would think the earth is trying to bury them.

Tabbs takes slow almost ashamed steps to maintain a solid distance between himself and them, finds it hard to engineer his body into a vessel of mercy, to set aside the instinct, drive, and industry he has always had and bring his own head and heart into their plight. No small matter to serve a nation. When last was it that he comforted someone? They (the city) want to root him when he wants to stretch. Just how deep does his sense of independence go? He has recently caught himself in a new trend, letting the dutiful language of racial uplift slip into his transactions.

> *The boundary lines have fallen for*
> *Me in pleasant places;*
> *I have a goodly heritage.*

But he is like nothing they have known. They don't know what to do with his words. They raise their hats in apology, a rush to please on their faces, mouths snapping open and closed, straining to speak. They never look him in the face, don't see him at all, his odd ways.

Everything seems to happen from a distance. Hard to witness, hard to believe. He looks at them with all angles in his eyes. Truncated forms missing hands, feet, and limbs. Ruffled figures with broken

backs, bent impossibly at the waist, wrists touching ankles, like malfunctioning bridges unable to either lower or raise. Wobbly creatures
with wasted bones knocking out of rhythm under sagging skin. One to
the next. The hard lines of their hunger sketch a blueprint of possibility against the faded backdrop of recent history. No language for this.
Slavery is a puncture—have you ever picked cotton?—the hole (hold)
that can never close. The hole that still bleeds cotton, rice, sugarcane,
tobacco. How do they lift their feet without becoming undone?

> *I would never have believed*
> *That Death could have undone so many*

Bless them their trying, their displaced elbows, disjointed knees,
sturdy necks, assured fingers. They hold their hands up to the sky with
joy and look God in the face. Delivered.

With heavy rusted teeth they fashion new names. Emerson,
Garrison, Brown. Adams, Douglass, Turner. Jackson, Lincoln, Jefferson.
Johnson, Grant, Washington. Tubman, Phillips, Hamilton. Strong.
Freeman. North. (Looking at God.) They practice saying their names
and practice them on each other, words slipping in and out, too busy
with the speed of speak to think more.

Having withstood hardships that would destroy most, they can
now remold themselves into something greater here in the city, even
if they don't see much of their history in the wood and brick here
and have trouble getting their bearings, tracing a course from one
corner to the next. Tabbs hears a thousand hearts turn inside desperate chests, a song that cuts through bone and muscle, kept hidden
until now. What gesture of commitment can he send out to them?
His past stands right before him, judging. How can he be both more
and less himself?

He starts for the ferry to Edgemere, a long line of bodies following him, bringing their uncertainties and contradictions along.
So it is. They lift their faces expectantly toward the heavens. Their
eyes seem to look through and beyond everything they see for some
visitation of blessing or warning.

He sits with his back doubled to them, hearing their chatter. Tries to listen past their voices and pushes his shoulders against the darkness, breathing the salt air, Edgemere, the black island, pressing upon him in slow continuity, a drop of ink spreading in the ocean. Disembarks from the ferry and under a white hook of moon takes a circuitous route home, full of false stops and starts, diversions, stalkers (freed, free) behind—who can say how close?—throwing shadows of alarm across the street and high on alley walls, Tabbs moving with an intense sense of direction through Edgemere's little streets winding in upon each other like a basket of eels. After some time he arrives at his place of residence confident that nobody has followed him, steals up the outside steps careful of his footing in the dark, the stairs narrow, shaking under him, the three-story house starkly rectangular in the dark. He leans his guilt into his room.

Already he can feel the city dropping off his back. He takes a seat in the darkness, hard black light passing through the window. Darkness upon darkness. Here he is with nothing that matters to him in his room. Only that single window looking out and looking in, and the thick box of his days. He thinks of all those hands out there moving around in the dark, dragging the night forward. And his room starts to move, as if the entire house—the walls, beams, roof—will up and shift to an anywhere anytime place like nothing he has known.

He sees the dawn rise three feet. Blackbirds arrow across autumn sky. Comes out of his room to find the morning waiting for him with too much clarity, the sun casting its best clean light, allowing him to see the city in distant outline across the water. The city wants him to see and remember. He tries to walk off the urge, but so much crosses his consciousness amid the rush, sweep, and crisscross of bodies. Things left behind or discarded, things he didn't know he had absorbed or that he'd forgotten, time and distance no barrier in a place that is all water and sound, sound carrying across water, snapping him (elastic) in and out of the present, Edgemere city, city Edgemere.

Does the city really expect men like him to accept its promises? The time away has pushed him into another existence here on Edgemere, out beyond his old life before the war, afar from the city's field of influence, the space between him and it changed. (Something holds, something stays in place.) He will break back into the world of the alabasters on his own terms, through the boy. *Blind Tom.* Having worked the details—the mother and Tom together here on Edgemere—in full and determined preparation, Tabbs is ready to take advantage. (One follows the other.) Go about his life with a familiar concentration. Do the things he needs to do. The Freedmen are immediate in the face of his nostalgia.

Pushing his drained body along, he can't locate the kinship he feels for the Freedmen, he cannot look at them without thinking about what is to come. They put their song in the air, a sound not easily separable from their bodies and what moves within their bodies, usually kept under wraps, but not so now, skin curving back like windblown curtains to expose auction blocks, swinging gates, the whips, hounds, chains, crops, violations, and vulgarity. Tabbs seeing it all so clearly, body looking. It should unsettle him. It doesn't. In fact, he starts to see himself in it all, he Tabbs selected, singled out, belonging, living it too. In a manner of speaking, he is one of the Freedmen.

So engaged that when he stumbles, the force of it does not register at once. Sitting on his haunches, knees up, hands down, confused, catching a breath, waiting for something to happen. He regains his feet, wondering what brought him down. Almost immediately he sees someone come slouching out of the crowd, arms folded across chest, hands inside armpits, lessening the distance, putting himself a yard away from Tabbs, his arms uncrossing and moving into Tabbs's face, a complete cut in upward vision, two threatening nubs round and smooth at the ends like whittled branches only inches from Tabbs's nose and mouth. Tabbs can smell them, could kiss or lick them if he wants. The man brings one missing hand to his mouth in a gesture of eating. Please, master. A thin man with a terrible face, he stands with his head twisted to one side, a look of half smile half supplication. Now repeats that ladling motion, compounding the minuses, missing hand feeding air to empty mouth. Please, master. God demands. Talking into Tabbs's silence. *How will you fathers give your son a stone if he asks you for bread?* Then the silent head-twisted supplication. Please, master. Stiff and vacant, Tabbs neither moves nor speaks.

Do you have anything for me, master?

Does he?

What effort it takes to see what is there, Freedmen trying on their new houses, their faces small, almost unnoticeable in windows not made to their shape.

❀ ❀ ❀

He isn't talking. He isn't playing. He isn't even moving. Her Thomas. *My Tom.* Hunkered down in high stiff silence at the piano on the stage above her, face bowed, body slanted forward, his hands in his lap, black skin and black wood glistening with wet light pouring in through the chapel's four windows, so high up (twenty feet or more) that she can see the sky and little else, a sky swept clean of everything except for a few infrequent tatters—birds? bats?—streaking in and out of vision, cutting across the blue living hand of the Almighty, He who lifted her up from that peculiar country where her blood was harvested along with cotton, sorghum, tobacco, coffee, and carried her across land and water and set her down on this island, Edgemere, then carried her across the threshold into this broad sturdy white-stoned edifice, the Home for the Education and Edification of African Orphans, tucked away at the far end of one of Edgemere's ancient and narrow streets, where she can be (reunited) with Thomas, her Thomas, *My Tom—Didn't I take care of my Hebrew children?*—at the far point of their lives, mother and son on the verge of great joy after an existence of great sorrow, granted the means to pick up from where they left off eleven years ago when Thomas was so rudely and wrongly taken from her at Hundred Gates, a moment that her mind holds on to and will hold on to, so help her God, for as long as she lives. *Never forget, never forgive.* Thomas, I am here. Your mother is here. Here we are, together again. (Words she might have even spoken once or twice to him since her arrival here on Edgemere.) Waiting for light (or food or drink) to make a difference and brighten his mood, raise his spirits and pull words out of him and save her from another lost afternoon, another lost day inside this chapel where her thoughts are a little less each day, the small parts of herself that she has retained (what is felt in the heart and felt in the blood) among the many lost through both the coming of age—is fifty old for a woman?—and through stolen time, everything that was taken away from them when they were taken from each other eleven years ago, those small parts that remain that she wants to give back to him, needs to give back—the debt she owes, the dues she must pay—breaking away from her little by little each day like the specks of late afternoon dust carried along high above her in the light streaming in through the chapel's four windows, until (soon, in the course of time) nothing will be left. Crucial not only that they establish and maintain whatever they can, moment by moment, but also that they regain (recover) anything he remembers from their past lives at Hundred Gates, the twenty feet separating them a telescopic space that can slide back in time eleven years (and more), Thomas up there onstage at the piano and she down here on a pew, perfect quiet sealed on the piano's shiny wooden surface as it is on his burnished skin, his silent tongue hidden inside his mouth, the black and white keys hidden under the lacquered lid. The names of the many places that worked her ragged bright inside her. Athens, Leland, Rome. And the names she has forgotten. Where she had day after day staggered through fields and kitchens and bedrooms and outhouses, sold or traded or bartered or rented out or shuttled about from one plantation or estate or farm to another in her long career as a slave, a contagious song picked up by other presences rising up around her in the room, the dozen or more niggers planted inside glass-fronted frames who assert themselves in song, their proud and heroic countenances sprouting flower-like from high stiff collars, their voices falling through her from where they hang ghostly from walls painted the color of everything and nothing combined—colors are the deeds of light—this choir (Champions of the Race, Reverend Wire calls them) whose identities are a mystery to her, although she recognizes (remembers) two or three faces from years ago in the pages of the *Columbus Observer*. They sing in a foreign tongue, voices ascending in a long climb that might go on all the way to heaven, up to a listening God but for the plastered ceiling, a ceiling strong and sturdy in its construction like all the others on Edgemere, fortified both lengthwise and sidewise with the slim black hard branches of the bleem tree, a crisscrossed network of wood not unlike a railway depot in appearance. (A hundred places to go. A hundred people to be.) The voices hold in orbit a little longer before they start a slow slide down the walls and large (man-high, man-wide) wood (bleem) cross nailed to the wall behind the stage (black serpent on the cross) pooling around the bottom of the altar, which ripples with the reflection of gold carved letters: WHEN SHALL WE LIVE IF NOT NOW. Now the voices spill over the edge of the stage onto the floor, which is made from irregular and rather broad planks of bleem wood, and tide forward to flood this entire sparse chapel that offers nothing pleasing to the eye other than rows of pews worn smooth with age, each sculpted from an entire trunk of a bleem tree solid and thick to withstand the destructive force of a child, enough of them to seat a hundred orphans or more. All the day the song will hum inside her. She should speak up, say something, say anything and put an end to it, but she doesn't want to ruin any hours she and Thomas spend together. Enough simply to spend them, together. It is always toward him that her longings turn, a moment followed by a lesser moment and a hunger to return. They are from each other. *I am you.* (What are the roots that clutch, that bind?) Entangled in the soul and knotted in the flesh, the spirit of union is uppermost in her. She tells herself as she did yesterday and the day before and probably will do tomorrow that she is on free ground. It is from here that everything can come. It is here, right here in this chapel that everything begins. No matter how late in life, she is not immune to fresh experience. Ask her where she's been, she'll tell you where she's going. (See there, up above: not dust carried in the light pouring in through the windows but seeds following the most direct path to growth, impossible to stop them.) Her life was lived way from here in that (unchanged) country that the Almighty told her she had to abandon, He who decided that she should make a life elsewhere, because she had found favor in His sight and He sent her an angel (Mr. Tabbs) who brought her here to Edgemere and reunited her with Thomas and bestowed His blessings upon her (them, *us*) in succulent abundance: delicious food and drink, beautiful garments, spacious and comfortable quarters where she can settle into soft sleep each night and awaken anew each morning. *O Lord I wait in my room at your mercy.* Each day runs its course simply enough. Break of dawn, a rooster will cock-a-doodle-do and set all the roosters to crowing to bring the ocean awake, cause it to close its waters around the island. (Listen and hear it.) As the island gropes toward wakefulness—that which takes its color with the locals turning on their beds—she will hear the bedsheets snap when Thomas jumps from his bed, and she'll fall to—the floorboard creaking under her feet like rusty hinges flying open—and get everything in readiness for the day ahead—choose an outfit for him from his closet, lay it out on the divan, then draw his bath. He will shed his sleeping tunic, hunker down in the tub, and make the water sing, his forming hands lending shapes to the suds. She will kneel before the tub and help him with soap and rag, his bones dancing under her fingers, the only time in the course of a day when he allows her to touch him.

Are you her? he will ask her.

Yes, she says. But his interest in her soon disappears. (He casually pushes away the arms that try to embrace him.) He will dress himself then take his place at the table, the sun spilling its copper glow into and across the room, Thomas lathered in golden light, honey, amber, stuck inside his silence with deliberation. (Why should the sunlight care?) Dressing, she will be heartily uncertain (afraid?) about who she has become and who he is and what he has become and what he recalls. Does he remember or has he forgotten who she is? After all it has been eleven years, eleven long years. Or perhaps something about her has changed? Smell? Sound of her voice? The way she walks? Sound of her footsteps? Or could it be, might it be, that this is somebody else in the supposed form of her son, a somebody who bears her son's name? Three brief knocks on the door summon her to open it, and an orphan (always a boy) standing there on the other side hugging a large silver serving tray, his smile reaching out to her through the open door. Ma'm, I have been instructed to bring the morning's repast. The orphan's voice causes Thomas's body to move. She knows the hunger behind his face, but throughout the day he limits what he consumes, the brooding taste of a glass of goat's milk (still his favorite) to move each morning along, and some morsels of bread perhaps with a dollop of jam or a sprinkling of sugar, then for dinner a fistful or two of meat (hen, guinea fowl, goat) and a few forks of potato or vegetable (the utensils' bright clatter and chime), and not much more than that for supper, every part of his body unsatisfied.

She studies the creases edging his eyes, the bones pressing up from under the cheeks—he needs to eat, he must eat—the places (temple, forehead) where the skull turns outward, revealed, and his clothes sagging from his bones. His face, his whole bony frame—he looks like he might dissolve. (The body through time.) He must eat because she wants to see him looking like a man, the way he looked when she first saw him again after eleven years, all thickened and broadened into man skin and man muscles, but in her presence he eats almost nothing and drinks almost nothing and never goes to the (indoor) toilet. (When does he go?) Something in him has turned, settled, quieted down, something essential. (The chapel is lonely-still just like Thomas.)

When she knew him, when he was still hers, eleven years ago, it took two or three hours of him roaming through the countryside to tire him out sufficiently to keep him seated long enough to have his supper. She, Mingo, and the girls had grown used to Little Thomas wandering off from the cabin into fields (white to the very door of the mansion with cotton and green to the wraparound porch with coffee) and meadows, up the tall rock (the way he sat on top of it)—down by the sides of the deep river and lonely streams, bounding over the hills or rolling like a log across the plain, headstrong into the deep and gloomy woods. Like a kitten playing through the falling leaves. Wherever Nature led. No fear of a world he couldn't see, since his sense of smell and taste missed nothing—see his hands reaching to bring leaf and flower and insect and bird and fish to his mouth, an entire afternoon in the shape of that touch. She remembers the fluid fascination that every thing and person exercised upon him. Trees pushing at sky. Maggots churning inside the cold corpse of an opossum rotting in the grass where worms gather in testament. The way birds let loose their three-toed grip on the earth. Something moving through air, moving through him. Life changed to landscape and landscape life. Thomas made sleepy by the expanse. She would call his name in that long dragging way, extending the syllables accordion-like. Then his face would poke out into the tunnel of her seeing from some hiding place (brush, bush, or briar patch; trough, kennel, or pen; outhouse, cave, or coop), a child's grin pushing up through his drowsy features, and she would take him, Little Thomas dirt-faced and barefoot, her hand firm in his hand, and start back to the cabin in the failing light of sunset, a red river of ribbons above them. (How many times had she and Little Thomas strolled, hand in hand, in the murmuring shade of the water oak trees?) His voice would flood the evening with stories he couldn't tell fast enough. (Feeling the language run over her body, a garbled stream, so she had to listen closely and sort through the flow, fishing out a word here and there and stringing them together in meaning.) Figures homebound at sundown, flashing past—he forces her breathing to catch up—a constellation of niggers (men, women, and children alike) still crouched in the fields under wide-brimmed hats, coursing in and out of smoke- and steam-fueled factories and mills with an infinite supply of materials (lumber, textiles, leathers, metals) in constant circulation through doors and windows, she and Little Thomas zipping past vistas such as these and other scenes of normal life. His frenzied uneven way of walking—each uneven step took an ambitious piece of ground—threatened several times to steal her balance, but she held fast until they reached the entrance to Hundred Gates, where they followed the long gravel road lined with cottonwood trees on either side up to the white house, only to go around the house and off into the deep recesses of the estate to their cabin, which commanded its own modest place in the world. And when they bounded through their cabin door—the flutter of moths in the waning light of the lantern—Mingo and the girls could see that Little Thomas was different, could tell him from the restless boy who couldn't keep still even when he was sitting down, fidgeting, fussing with his clothes and limbs and face, blowing on his hands or knees or feet as if trying to extinguish flames nested in his flesh. The boy would be innocent off in a corner of the yard imitating the twittering sounds of birds, each chirp small, clear, and sharp. (The sound comes to her unexpectedly every so often. She can hear it even now.) In a pitched assault he would ram himself into a wall over and over again—like the ocean out there smashing into the island of Edgemere, and slapping up against the dhows, calling them back to water—until someone managed to tackle or trip him to the ground. Those aggravated presences from earlier in the day would still be lingering in the cabin in diminished form, force, and capacity, echoes that would hum and snap back into Little Thomas shortly upon his stepping across the threshold. Quiet and steady, he would sit down to a heavy supper—

fatback sandwiches, black apples, two or three helpings of sweet root lathered in lard and corn cakes glazed with molasses, two or three Seminole potatoes, some red grass, and a pitcher or two of lemonade or iced tea—that proved to be no challenge for him. *Feed me bushels of light.* At the first sign of any agitation, the girls would remove every article of his clothing until he was butt naked and quiet, stripped of music and words. Supper done, with the slightest roll of the tongue Charity could sing him to sleep. And she too could now bed down for the night after a long day of labor and the exhaustive challenge of Little Thomas. (Asleep, his body hummed with the expectation of sunrise—*Let us cast off deeds of darkness and put on the armor of light*—the yearning outside world anxious to have him return, the impatient moon nosing about the window, trying to peek through.) Daylight would set him ablaze with some song—if he had one he had a thousand—that he would be bellowing at the top of his small voice. He would take his station at the table, the fingers of both hands moving in every direction in the air until they settled down onto the splintered surface, where they would glide along the wood thirsting for music. And he would eat and drink whatever they put before him, songing through a mouth filled with food. Even before he had had his fill, he would say to her, Please leave me now, repeating the words ever and again until she stood up from the table and selected from one of the few garments she owned. She would sling the dress over her shoulders and comb her hair back into a ponytail, cover her head with a scarf tightened in a knot at her nape, and take him up from the table and quit their cabin for their yard. There she would hold him close. (The only image she can see now, in the silence, the only image of herself that she likes, in which she can recognize herself, in which she delights.) After a few stumbling steps, they would start hand in hand for the house, past the flower garden that Miss Toon tended with all the loving care that a green thumb is capable of and on to the house itself, where she would turn the copper doorknob and fling the door wide. They would make their entry into the foyer on the Oriental carpet. Miss Toon was never long to meet them. Standing there in her flounces and high collar that came all the way up to her chin, Miss Toon would smile at Little Thomas with keen interest and longing. Then she would take him into her company and they would slip behind the French doors into the parlor, shutting the doors behind them, the two glass doorknobs like big diamonds, and Charity's breath would catch for a small expectant moment. Charity wanted nothing more than to stay in the parlor and hear what Little Thomas would play and what he and Miss Toon might play together. (Charity forgave them their inclination toward companionship, their wanting to be alone with Music, this blameless act, for she had seen the way their hands moved across the keys, the impossible made possible.) However, without an excuse to linger, she soon went about her employment, her body emptying through the house and the reaches of the estate. Little Thomas—my Thomas, *my Tom*—moored at the piano with Miss Toon at his side for a period of instruction whereby the spirit flowing between them had a chance to reveal itself, as each had it in her or his person to test the mettle and endurance of the other with melodies, ditties, and songs, for each seemed to know where the other was strong or weak, she carrying the first verse and he either repeating it or carrying the next. And so on. Music would fill in the hours, would come to Charity through walls and shut doors. A line of melody would sit on the laundry lines like a flock of birds, would gush out of the well with every pump of the handle. How untroubled she felt. Indeed, it would have been a double burden to fulfill her duties and also keep Little Thomas entertained. With the arrival of noon, she knew then that he was sharing in repast with the Bethunes at their long mahogany table, even as she headed back to the cabin for dinner with Mingo and the girls. She saw Little Thomas lick the music off his fingers in preparation for food. And after an hour, dinner done, chores resumed, she was brought back to herself. Recoiled from afternoon sun, light and heat wearing her out, her body opened. (The body is made up of things that grow stiff and accumulate pain.) Was it actually weariness that had overtaken her or simply the idea of going back to Little Thomas? For soon the moment would come (an hour or two later) when the General would put an end to the time he had granted Little Thomas and his wife for instruction that day and summon Charity to the parlor. Take this boy from my house. Easier said than done, for even then Little Thomas would be playing at the piano and it would seem that nothing could deter him in the effort. On a fortunate day, a sugarplum or two could lull his hands still, lure him away from the piano and lead him out of the house. And there she and Thomas would be, brightening in the colors—petunia, zinnia, chicory, four-o'clock—of Miss Toon's garden, with her chores to get back to.

I am the one, he would say. (Even now she has no idea what he meant, not the slightest clue, despite the many times she heard him say it.) And he would wander off into the woods. No—try again—she would allow him to wander off while she stood watching. If only he could spend—had she the power—all of his waking hours at the piano. It was this alone that could pull the wildness out of him. Had he been so allowed—had she the power—he would have played until his fingers bled. (And bled they had on two or three occasions.) Of course, the General never would have granted permission—no way— generous (for a woogie) of him to allow what time he did.

Let's bear the burden of this life
We haven't far to go

So, day in and day out, she took that little he gave and made do. Nothing to occupy her hours, other than work. All the time in the world on her hands and no time. The rigidity of her station in life. The lack of options. No true leisure time to speak of. She would let her imagination loose on any sights that crossed her vision. Look up and remark on the shape of the clouds. Going from herself to herself as far as her feet could carry her, to the very edge of the estate's grounds, or to another town or city within walking distance (ten miles or twenty) when the Bethunes sent her on errands. No matter how hard she tried she couldn't succeed in desiring non-places whose existence she couldn't verify with her own eyes, although she had heard about people (woogies) and even knew certain people (woogies) who had supposedly sojourned to or taken up residence in some of those places that had names such as Atlanta, Oxford, London, Paris, Zanzibar. In fact, she had doubts that another world existed—what Union? what North? Washington? what White House?—right up to the moment that the steamship whose deck she and Mr. Tabbs stood on pulled into the city's harbor. It took little convincing to get her on board that ship. Mr. Tabbs made her his offer and she gladly accepted it. She was ready for adventure. The prospect filled her with joy. She and Thomas would be reunited. A thousand miles between them (ten thousand), a moment that perhaps she and her son both dreamed of, she from Hundred Gates and he from wherever he was on this earth. So—tell the truth about it—she told herself that she would voyage in order to see—things belong to those who look at them—voyage to prove this other world did indeed exist—that was the real reason why she accepted Mr. Tabbs's offer, was so willing to believe in his promises— and, also, believe that Thomas was alive somewhere in this other world.

At Hundred Gates, everything brought her back to herself and her small world. Surely Hundred Gates (or some other estate, plantation, farm, kitchen) would be the last sight her eyes would register for all eternity. She felt a stranger to herself. Talking little if at all because she had no say. Indeed, she was happy to go through her labors if it meant limited contact with other people. People were obstacles to be avoided (diverted looks), never approached, and rarely spoken to. And when someone did speak to her, she would put on the appropriate face and say nothing true, nothing false, in an effort to hurry on her way. Night never returned what the day had taken, for she would awaken with aches and pains, sore, stiff, puffy and swollen. So it was that she would pass each and every day, moving slowly but surely toward disappearance, toward extinction, knowing that her disappearance would have no impact on the world.

That life of nothing she had thought was a permanent part of her, branded in her skin. (That small darkened kitchen, that other small darkened bedroom, that tiny cabin.) Then the Almighty brought her to Edgemere by His beneficent hand so that she could repose her body and have peace of mind with time at her disposal to get reacquainted with Thomas, her Thomas, her first reprieve from industry (labor, work)—shake the rug into the fire—in her many many years (fifty, more) of residence on this earth. Now, she feels parts of herself that she never felt before, muscles she never knew she had.

She repositions her feet on the floor of the chapel (well-seasoned bleem wood) without the old agility and grinds her teeth in annoyance. Thomas moves his head ever so slightly at the noise. Could it be (she wonders) that hard labor, constant work, the daily routine of toil, enabled her to bear up better than this present inactivity, for at Hundred Gates, where the hour and the minute ruled her, she perceived the flow of time less? Released (cut loose) from her time-constrained body, there is no longer anything that can distract her from herself. Memory won't leave her alone, won't let her escape this body she has inhabited for so long. Eager with possibility, the self she might (can) become is held hostage—what other word is there for it?—fights tooth and nail against a past that would conquer and claim every inch of her, all of her glands and organs contested.

She plants herself deeper into the pew. But is she really here? No. She is still there, at Hundred Gates, watching the carriage wobble off down the tree-lined gravel road. Everything grows up around that image. Where she is now, this Home, sprouts up right through tufts of grass on the estate. The floor is shrinking beneath her feet. She looks up and sees the dust motes above floating and swaying in reverse out through the windows, taking the years back from her, eleven years. (Count them.) *I can't keep no numbers.* She looks at Thomas. His face is disappearing, particles of skin pulling away into a tiny cloud. The ceiling is lifting. And she starts to rise too. Her new life here on Edgemere, her new life here with Thomas is only something she has dreamed up—

I woke up this morning
Where I was I didn't have a clue

—a dream that began the moment she and Mingo stood in broad afternoon light watching in outraged resignation as the carriage left the way it had come down the tree-lined gravel road and gradually dissolved from sight—corrosives of sunlight—the sound of its wheels turning in their torn ears. Nothing she or he could do to stop it. (What could a nigger do?) She almost speaks those words to Thomas now. *Nothing we could do to stop it.* (How doubt that now?) It matters somehow that he knows. But the time to speak of it hasn't come. She has retained a fixed image of Little Thomas in the carriage, an image that lasted all the way across to this island of Edgemere and is with her still. As she rises, higher and higher, she closes her eyes to visualize the moment better, the entire scene in perfect focus. The sunset blazing as if pumped up with blood. The woogie's finely tailored trousers of an indeterminate color. The driver's crumpled hat. Some carefully phrased farewell—*Safe travels,* was that it? *May the Lord be with you,* was that it? *We bid you Godspeed,* was that it?—that the General or Miss Toon muttered into the hot air, while she and Mingo kept silent without a word to anyone who had a say in the matter, Mingo's face broad and smooth and full of astonished disbelief. The trees swaying, the green world turning on its machinery. Little Thomas's white teeth brilliant in his open mouth. The sound of her asking herself, What had she done, they done, for the General to enact this punishment on them? These living pictures from another country, another time, unsettle her.

She pours words, all of the words she saved up from the moment she set out on her journey with Mr. Tabbs and all that she had accumulated since Little Thomas's departure (eleven years' worth), that she planned to speak to Thomas, she pours them into the bottommost parts of her heart, reinforcing her plans and projects, a weighty (unshakable?) foundation. Slowly, she feels and hears herself start to descend back to earth, drawn down. She opens her eyes— she doesn't want to see anymore—as soon as her backside resumes its place on the pew, heavy, beaten (spent), and pain-ridden like the rest of her. And still she feels weight, causing her to wonder if she will sink right through the floor, but with the question she feels an answer rise in her chest, which draws her gaze toward Thomas, and she looks at him now, the two of them sitting here in the chapel breathing the same hungry calm. She takes his face apart, dissects his motionless hands, frail body, and fixed well-cobbled feet, the all of him, trying to find any indication that he remembers his abduction. For her part, the recollection of her final seconds with Little Thomas is what stood upright in her mind for all these years, her body what subsides, Thomas growing, taking on flesh, while she decays, loses substance, life rushing out of her lungs with every breath. As year followed year, she grew to hate more and more the General and Miss Toon and their rotten shat-out seed, hated them with all the thought and feeling her body could hold, hated every single nasty-ass wet-chicken-smelling woogie living or dead who had ever stank up the earth. Strangely easy to hate them, to intone chants and curses— *Further on up the road, someone gon hurt you like you hurt me*—that would bring boiling plagues and flesh-eating locusts on their generations to the end of time.

She wants him—her Thomas, *my Tom*—to know that if she gets angry at him, if she voices any displeasure, he must know that it is only her past attacking him. Forgive her. *Forgive me.* Her resentments, her disappointments, her feelings of isolation, indifference, and resignation followed her here. (The weather doesn't help, a miserable day, humid and muggy, reminding her of home, the way it always seems in her dreams.) But she has crossed over—*Mr. Tabbs, do we really have to cross all that water?*—so how can she allow herself to think that way? She should be rejoicing. *Wade in the water.* There is life and abundance for future years. (They both know it. They feel it in their throat and lungs.) A white devil in fancy trousers took Thomas away from her and a nigger angel in fancier pants brought her back to him. That old life is gone. That life shouldn't (doesn't) mean anything to her anymore. (The point at which memory softens.) So she must give up thinking, must empty her body of the past and let the future draw her forward, even if Thomas just sits up there at the piano hour after hour, day after day like a lump on a log, treating her to copious silence, nonspeaking and nonmoving no matter how hard she stares across the distance at him, stares until her eyes throb. (It is now later than it was awhile ago and still he hasn't moved, no way to tell if he is awake or asleep.) She has crossed over, thus it is enough for her to just sit here with him this way, sit and contemplate their past and their prospects, while the closely scheduled activities (instructions, lessons, learning) of the orphans and their teachers go on around them. Indeed—she sees it now— that wise someone—Mr. Tabbs? Reverend Wire? Deacon Double?— had the presence of mind to realize that she and Thomas *need* to be alone together in the chapel each day, this is just the place for them to trade their silences, for they know, have always known how to answer each other without speaking, without questions. What they share as mother and son, they share alone. Between them sleeps the words they never exchanged, were forced to leave behind. Each day she feels his silence more keenly. (*Silence* is not a word she associates with Little Thomas, even at his most innocent.) She is apprenticing herself to hush, which withdraws on occasion—she hears chalk clacking and squeaking against blackboards, counting beads colliding, orphans asking about the words that surprise them most during their spelling lessons, orphans at their looms, pottery wheels, and knitting and sewing machines, everything in the Home talking to itself; and beyond that faint distant sounds in the distance: tinkling cowbells, the braying of donkeys, rattling carts, and sea currents muscling into the shore—giving place to the echo of her secret thoughts that surprise even her. Tears stanched behind her shut eyelids, she cried all down inside herself that first night and many nights after. (The ache still even though he is here.) Never the full outpouring of grief because she knew that such letting go would unravel her, turn the spindle of her self until nothing was left. But from time to time she could feel it rise inside her and threaten release, threaten to leak (seep) or spill out of her closed mouth, especially when she unknotted and removed her head scarf before bed. (A body responds differently in the dark when it knows that other people are not around to observe it.) Perhaps Mingo heard it, that soft wet sound dammed inside her. Perhaps Thomas is listening too. Before coming here to Edgemere, when was the last time she had slept without dreaming he was dead? (And longing to return the favor, kill each and every woogie in revenge, man, woman, and child. Wanted to resurrect the ones that were already dead and buried, murder them again, then incinerate all trace of them.) She turned her thoughts toward forgetting, but to her surprise, thinking Thomas dead did not help her any, for death does not sever the ties with the living but pulls the worlds of the living and the dead closer together and braids them in eternal alliance (allegiance). Thomas was the afterlife, pieces of him everywhere. (The cupboard drawer startled open, the cup that moved of its own volition across the table, the sudden chill on a hot day, curtains swaying in a room where all the windows were shut, a shadow glimpsed from the corner of her eye.) How could she gather up what was left of him in this world and move it permanently to the other side? *I am poured out like water.* As year followed year, she searched for a reason not to long for him. And why should he be the one to claim her attention? *I am the only one.* Of course there had been others, the ones taken away from her; Thomas was not the first. To say her world is shot through with loss like a moth-eaten garment is to say nothing since every gap in the cloth opens into possibility, what the eye sees when it peers through the holes, what the fingers find when they poke through. She believes in the ability (the will) of mothers to make right—she assumes blame; a need builds inside her—to weave patterns of past and present (fashioning) into a cocoon that can keep her offspring's name intact, Thomas (never Tom), confident (now) that their suffering, Mingo's, her daughters', her own—*I am the mother*—cannot touch him anymore. This Thomas is moving toward being *her* Thomas again.

She retraces the stages of her journey and comes to remember that port (two white ladies under two white parasols) from where she and Mr. Tabbs set sail on a small steamship tossed by the large sea. Distinctly recalls the urgency in which the ship slid out into open water and how the horizon exploded out of the lovely expanse of blue before the deckhands had completely raised the gangplank, the harbor quickly thinning from view, everything hurrying along with all deliberate speed to afford her no chance to change her mind and turn back. Having never confronted the sea, she stood on the deck for a while, wondering at passage over water, at buoyancy, power, and weight, at the salt in the air, the movement of the craft keeping her body occupied as it sought balance, her shadow floating alone on top of waves brimming with scooting fish, more ornate sea creatures submerged beneath, their scales sparkling like the shards of a broken mirror, and mermaids and mermen surfacing now and again to chew the thirsty air, their transparent lungs shining through their exposed rib cages. The many ports they entered, passengers boarding or disembarking, and the many sights, sounds, and smells revealed to her even as she stood on deck and looked back at her past, all that she was flashing from the flashing water, her tragedies like sunken vessels with an angle of hull rising up out of the water.

At last—two weeks? two months? two years?—they approached the city's harbor, and as if to give her maximum time to take in what she was seeing, the ship came almost to a standstill, the lulled water tossing it (and her) gently like a body turning out of sleep. A swarm of vessels (dark-sailed dhows and the bulky overcrowded ferries, body braided to body on deck) with their high massive hulls came into her line of sight out of the resounding vastness, some approaching the harbor, others heading out to sea, one vessel alive in another's movement. Nothing like this had ever happened to her before. A waking dream. (Light asks no questions.) Every breath of air made her face shudder. The engine cut off altogether and the ship bobbed into the pier, moored in perfect alignment between two posts like a horse inside its stall. She and Mr. Tabbs were among the first passengers to descend the gangplank onto the pier—she was wobbly at first, a necessary weight (more of the world than we think); with all that water under her for days and weeks she had forgotten that she weighed anything; for his part, Mr. Tabbs took a moment to accustom himself to land, shaking each leg energetically—where the land moved with mariners studying their travel charts and maps, muscled crews hauling crates into and out of blockhouses and stores, drivers fixed on buckboards behind packhorses idle in anticipation. They did not leave the pier to enter the magnificent city surging with legions of people—had she wanted to?—but made haste, ascended another gangplank and boarded a ferry for the final crossing to Edgemere. In less than an hour she heard the call for landing. Edgemere floated into sight. Seen from board at a distance this expanse of sea seemed a thing totally distinct from the small outspread island that emerged from it. These were special waters. Perhaps this was the very sea where the Almighty had drowned old Pharaoh's army to save Mr. Moses and those Hebrew children.

Wade in the water
God's gon trouble the water
(Yes, she had these thoughts.)

Once on land, she and Mr. Tabbs set off by foot for their destination, the Home for the Education and Edification of African Orphans. She walked the black length of her mind under a dark overcast day, tall curtains of fog hanging beneath dense low-hanging clouds that burned faintly red and black above as no sky she had seen before, the ocean a long flat cloth connecting the island to the horizon. Through the fog (inland) she saw the faint outline of houses silhouetted in the distance. She watched as the ocean started to pull its waters away from the island and restore several feet of borrowed shore, the dhows bobbing slowly back to land. In a counter cadence a thronging of fishermen started hauling in their nets, bright streams of wetness running over them as they pulled fist on water-logged fist. She kept closely in step with Mr. Tabbs as he took a path that turned into one tight street after another, each sidewalk part of a little valley pierced with pinpoints of light from the many candles that were already starting to be lit in the windows of two-story stone houses rising up on either side of them. Soon she caught her first glimpse of a donkey, the beast approaching her from the opposite direction, crates stacked on its small but powerful back and its head curled into its own shadow, but the animal still certain in its course. That donkey followed by a second then a third, each donkey raising its face to the others, breath passed from mouth to mouth, owner behind. Ah, the wonder of it all: ocean, island, dhow, donkeys, fishermen. *But you're free now, Mr. Tabbs said.* She had tasted the sound of her new identity on her tongue and liked it so much she would call herself nothing else. Free. Emancipated.

The curtains of fog parted and the sun broke its chains and drifted from behind the clouds and found its place, a little bright island floating in the sky. For the first time she saw in full clarity the little green and yellow and pink and orange stone houses of Edgemere, and beyond in the middle distance a tower-like structure that she took to be—Mr. Tabbs pointed, There, he said—the Home set a good mile inland from the ocean in its own alien (an aloneness) terrain, a vast grassy plot, against a blurred background of trees (bleem). The Home hung (floated?) before her eyes, even as she flowed (floated?) toward it. So here she was—*Here I am*—plugged into this brave new world—where she is now, who she is now—her mind throbbing beyond language, beyond meaning. Thomas. Little Thomas. *My Tom.* Her eleven-year wait would soon be over thanks to the Almighty—all praise due—who had decided to make the impossible possible through His mysterious means.

Voices reached her even before she and Mr. Tabbs reached the stone fence that rose up from the ground ten feet into the air above them. Passing through the gate, she saw a wild constellation of orphans roaming in playful circles across the wet grass of the main lawn, boys and girls alike dressed in cheerful uniforms (black pants, white shirt or blouse with a length of red tie extending down the front), their voices singing through her skin.

Down, down, baby
Down, down, baby
Down by the riverside

Grandma, grandma sick in bed
She called the doctor and the doctor said
Let's get the rhythm of the head, ding dong (Heads rock
    bell-like side to side)
Let's get the rhythm of the head, ding dong (Heads rock)

Let's get the rhythm of the hands (Two claps)
Let's get the rhythm of the hands (Two claps)

She relished this dance that she had seen many times before. Would it be too much to say that she wanted to join them with her old arms, legs, and hips? She pushed to know. They scattered away from the macadam walkway on her approach.

Hey, Mr. Tabbs, sir, they said in one voice from both sides of the lawn. Did you bring us anything from the city?

He got some chocolate.

Some wine candy.

Turtles.

You eat that? That's nasty.

Nawl. Some cracklin.

Nawl. Some Jumpin Jacks.

Candy cane.

It ain't Christmas.

He brought the lady.

Who she?

Who you?

She a teacher.

Nawl.

Uh huh.

She his wife.

Nawl.

Uh huh.

No way.

Is that yo wife?

She his wife.

Shut up.

You shut up.

Their next words like their last. A calm sharpened her as she looked at the face of each child. Carried by memory, she wanted to hear all their voices at once, even if she had to close her eyes to hear them. (What the heart believes it needs.) And even if some (many? most?) of the orphans did not speak the way she was used to hearing niggers speak, but instead, like Mr. Tabbs, vocalized their say with that new city (Edgemere?) way of saying, a tongue that was already starting to sound familiar to her ears. (Mapping language.) She could feel the movement of shared blood, theirs and hers. Why could they not remain one body? They were niggers after all, and every nigger was a slave—so she had been told for as long as she could remember— Africa a whole country full of slaves where woogies could go shop and take their pick. Blood was blood, even if, as she was to learn, Mr. Tabbs and some of the orphans had been born here, on Edgemere or in the city.

All of their humility drained away as they drifted around her, the ground saturated with their dance. Come on inside, Mamma.

They wanted to look at her, touch her, get the closest look and feel that they could, eyes in their fingertips. She did not object; she was in thrall to all of them. She and Mr. Tabbs continued up the macadam walk toward the Home accompanied by dozens of rejoicing orphans, their dancing bodies bumping into her. A few minutes later they all moved as one through the dimness of a long wide corridor, the last rays of sunlight persevering in stained glass windows that she would later come to find in every room of the Home except for the chapel. Light shining through biblical scenes—Christ multiplying one dhow into a thousand, Elijah carried into heaven on a chariot of fire, and so on—in variegated pigments, a kind of red-yellow-blue combination (light interwoven) that stood out as the only color through the stained glass. (What Thomas cannot see you look at.) Little that she could make out amid the loose shadows on the rise (three flights of stairs? four?) to an upper floor, but she could tell that the Home was a formidable structure, sturdy and well built with the same thick stones that the other houses on the island were constructed from.

They stopped before a room on a floor of many rooms, the line of children behind Mr. Tabbs and her. Mr. Tabbs slipped one hand into his waistcoat and removed an iron ring that encircled a well-notched key, then slid the key into the door and unlocked it for her to enter, which she did, a little dazed by the speed of things.

This is your room, he said. I will bring your son. The look in his eyes made her feel strange. He took his leave, and the orphans followed him, mostly without complaint, waving their good-byes, feeling exactly the way they wanted to feel, the older children pulling the reluctant younger children along.

Not long after an orphan brought her supper, three fish sleeping side by side on a plate. She ate. Then the night came to shut her in anxious waiting. She felt the walls contract as most of the air in the room swirled around her. Could feel the walls pressing on her skin. She sank off to sleep. Little did she know, it would be one week before she would see Thomas.

Early the next (second) day, Mr. Tabbs called upon her with six or seven orphans in tow, carrying the dresses, blouses, skirts, gowns, stockings and undergarments, and shoes that constituted her new wardrobe. They filled her closets with the clothes and set her table for breakfast, then went away without a word. And Mr. Tabbs repeated what he had said the evening before, that he would bring Thomas to her.

There in her quarters the world dropped away. Morning light so heavy that it almost shattered the stained glass windows as it fell into the room, so heavy that it hurt when it dropped onto her—bearing up in that light, bearing that light—every familiar object in the room (table, chair, bed, closet, lamp, bowl, basin) atremble (quivering), fragile, brittle in the face of such breakage. Like the clouds the walls changed color. She tried to keep very still in the fantastic temperatures of the room and make her way to the fires in her mind where Thomas might be, a place she could never hold for long, light distracting her, as she should be distracted, the sound (hearing) of light searing her flesh. (Light has many names.) Would lean out the window as far as she could, looking down into the ocean's hush and hurry. And so time would wear on, each frame of the day free and clear in the unclenched light down to the dhows (mechanisms of wind) with their jagged sails, coming and going each hour, their giant hooks—gaffs they were called—coils of fishing line, and baskets visible even from her window. She would take her supper and settle into bed, until the moon appeared (at last) in the night sky, her shutters open and window swallowing a mouthful of stars.

Rooted thus in her quarters, each day passed pretty much the same her first week on the island of Edgemere. The orphans would arrive in triplicate to bring her breakfast, her dinner, and her supper—eventually, she and they came to acknowledge one another without astonishment—and, supper done, she would have to get out of bed to receive a new visitor each evening. On the third supper-curtained day, a giant stooped under the lintel and lengthened his body into the room—the wonder of it, all her life happened long before this—then stood there in all of his tall broad majesty in his billowing robe, a wild mangle of folds. The curious circumstances of his height, which elicited feelings of attraction and repulsion, protection and terror, placed him beyond the physical confines of handsome and ugly. (His face hardly registered.) He introduced himself as Reverend Wire. Even his voice made a powerful impression on her. *Sometimes God chooses not to explain. Sister Wiggins, if you need answers I would encourage you to sojourn to that place where only the Holy Ghost can take us through prayers.* Whenever he delivered his weekly sermon to the seated assemblage in the chapel, it was the word of the Almighty writing Himself on her flesh. *Many of us believe that God gives us too little. Oh, how wrong we are. Let me tell you, my children, that when God gives He gives in excess. Make no mistake about that. It is for each of us to take full advantage of His plentiful quantities. The five senses exist for more than five reasons. He who listens too hard does not see. And he who looks too hard does not hear.* To all appearances he was completely at ease sermonizing from his lofty position at the pulpit, his long arms fully extended beneath him on either side of the podium to support his long body, which jutted all the way forward over the podium at a precarious angle as if he were about to make an acrobatic effort to jacknife his lower extremities into the air and stand (balance) on his hands.

Each Sunday the orphans make a spirited march into the chapel as one organized body, more than two hundred of them—how many lives can go on at once?—only to break into playful frenzy: bodies planted between the furrows of pews, hiding-and-seeking, hands scooping up coins of sunlight scattered across the floor, lips drumming rhymed banter—the Dozens they called it—all of their endeavors bright and hopeful. Talking, playing, laughing, until they realize that she is there in the chapel with them and they surge forward—the aspect of delight insists upon a closer look—welcoming her with daisied smiles. They want to hold, to be held. Perhaps she gives one or two of them a hug. The watching faces swoop down from the wall in a swarm of armed appearances so that the service can begin. *We give thanks for the young ones among us, who remind us how much we need to do to create with them a better world. We should not indict our children with our deeds and ambitions. So what must we say?* The orphans all hold her hand—what else means anything to them?—or the dense folds of her pleats. *While we look not at the things which are seen, but at the things which are not seen, for the things which are seen are temporal but the things which are not seen are eternal.* There's a fullness here, some surplus, that she won't respond to. (Is that it?) She can only empty herself with prayer. *I was reading the Book of Corinthians the other day and I came across this strange verse. Let me read it to you: 1 Corinthians 12:17 says, "If the whole body were an eye, where would the sense of hearing be?" The rest of the verse is also strange: "If the whole body were an ear, where would the sense of smell be?"* She takes a good hard look at the children, her hesitations blurred. Each Sunday she brings herself to the chapel, but she knows she is not enough. For all of their dawdling, their moping and whining, their store of groans and paroxysms of wails and howls that accompany the sorrow of her leaving the chapel after Sunday service, Reverend Wire is reluctant to take the whip or rod to their backsides. They give reason for cruelty, but he has opted for accommodation. (Quiet feelings come to suffice.) *God makes us good, but it is our duty and responsibility as Africans and as Christians to be better. Think about it. Turn it over in your heart.*

The fourth day, a figured shaft of air spiraled in the doorway, Deacon Double bringing the scent of earth and flowers. Awkwardly smiling, awkwardly received. He inclined his posture toward her—this impulse to lean forward, to lean across—nodded, and took her hand but took it too hard. A quaver, a fumbling, a missed beat, a smile held too long. His head rested egg-like softly on his shoulders, and his narrow eyes and broad forehead reminded her of a statue with its fixed sculpted eyes, an ancient granite face (his skin gray). He moved buoyantly around the candlelit room but with almost hoofed (goat, horse, deer) precision, stepping slowly and carefully as if on dangerous terrain. While circulating he looked around with curious insistence, intoning words as if he were singing in the voice of someone twice his size. *Sister,* he said, *be patient, and keep your head high, for the one you are waiting for will soon be here. I believe that the time is at hand when the sons of God shall be revealed*—stopping every now and again for a lingering look, that sconce on the wall, those porcelain knobs on the cupboard doors, the ill-fitting drawers, his skin changing color depending on where he stood in the room, now yellow like the bedsheets, now red like the clay pitcher, as she had heard that certain magical lizards could do in Africa. *I saw a door standing open in heaven, and the same voice I had heard before spoke to me with the sun of a mighty trumpet blast. The voice said, Come up here, and I will show you what must happen after these things. So I went up and I saw.* She tries to understand the riot of his words—*I marvel at the sun which is not afraid to repeat itself and at the seasons that come again and again, or the bee returning to the flower, and at new things repeating the old*—for he has a thousand proverbs and verses to hand, one for every occasion. *Those are hurt who want to be hurt. Agony does not only belong to the heart. And thus do the innocent suffer. Not because God is punishing them but because they have very little power to stop what is causing their suffering. But power with others can change the world. The spirit bears the body forward.* Charity pleased to learn something new and useful, although she said nothing to him about her gratification. Each glass-globed and sconced flame burning on the wall bent toward him as he passed. (He bent the light toward him.)

After some time he stopped walking, light collecting around him. (She bedazzled, swayed by movement, words, light.) He lost the sense of inexhaustible and energetic joy and gained a certain mundane solemnity and rigidity, but even as he stood in place directly before her he kept touching himself—his shirt pockets, his trouser pockets, his hair—as if he were searching for something. Talking always, holding counsel. From all evidence he was a man who had lived and still lives a God-fearing and God-directed prayer-stained life. *All of the schemes and deceptions of the past are past. You are with us now, you are among us now, you are one of us now. Here you have found sanctuary. This is your resting place. So be patient, sister. The hour of our redemption is soon near.* Once he ceased to speak, he stood for a time in silence until she observed his right hand cross his body, disappear into the cavernous sleeve of his robe, and withdraw to her astonishment a weathered copy of the Good Book. He brought the tome to his lips, kissed it, allowed his book-heavy hand to fall to his side, then remained silent and completely still as if in preparation for more. A strong possibility that he had a second heavy book up the other sleeve. For all she knew this man full of words had an entire library hidden in the recesses of his garments or his body. He opened the book, the smell of an earlier time (Bible days) leaking out of the pages, and read some passage—*. . . an old battleground* (limbs strewn around)—the pages whispering as he turned them. He touched her arm. Spread his fingers on her back. *Sister, I hope you are ready. Time is waiting. We—you, Tom, the church—we have much work to do. Multitudes will sing his name once again. But this time he will sing for us.*

Would it be that a dozen or more of the brightest orphans with their teachers (light shining through their dresses) paid her a brief visit the next morning, her fifth day? Not that they meant to tell her anything or take anything away from her. (Unlike her other visitors.) She was still an other, but they had decided to take her in with compassion and trust. How tender of them. After all she was somebody's mother, somebody's wife. Later she sat in the foreign evening thinking about the deacon's words from the day before, seeing this place the way he saw it, as a getting-away place. And just as her thoughts began to settle, she heard the door. Found a man in his prime neatly tucked into his blue uniform, with his little cup of cap above his uneven eyes, his hair in glossy slicked-back waves, and a brass-buckled belt encircling his waist, with a revolver sheathed inside a polished leather holster, a braided cord looped in its handle. Lieutenant Drinkwater. His hand moved in swift short strokes, and their blood neared in a quick clasp, a brisk intensity. Wire brought word of your arrival, he said. He was so excited. I don't think I have ever seen him so excited. So I was dandering by and thought I might as well call. The line of his thin brown lips eluding his words. What was there for her to say? (She brings little to the scene.) These simple facts closed an evening.

Although she often wondered that week why Mr. Tabbs was taking so long to return with Thomas, truth be told, she was also happy to remain confined in her quarters, looking at dhows fixed on the sea, lapping waves, and the sun bobbing weightless on the horizon. (Where is the earth? Nowhere.) She knew nothing worth knowing, for the walls silenced all trace of the world, could keep any voices in earshot out of her, the small floating lives of all those orphans. (Some excitement puddling into laughter.) Nothing slowed or sped her. For her time was not divided into seconds and hours but into light and sound. (Hold sound and light apart.) So she assumed small guilts and was content to eat her meals, tolerate her visitors, retire to bed, enjoy a night of unbroken sleep, and wake at daylight looking at the floor.

She was among people far too eager to have her, to receive her. Their admiration, their enthusiasm. (If only she could feel incredible to herself.) Only her last caller seemed to express any reluctance, that small-hours visitant on the sixth day. As the door opened, he was slightly turned as if ready to go away, sensing he had disturbed her. Perhaps the candor of the light dismayed him. Then he turned to face her and her throat dried quicker than a match put to a kerosene-wet wick. He was well groomed and slim with a muscular elegance— how would you have him?—his medium-height frame encased in a perfectly tailored suit. She immediately felt underdressed in her new clothes and her old scarf on the sweat-wet nest of her hair. He made his sign, spoke his greeting. His well-shaved face did not know what expression to hold. She was happy to feel him take her hand, touch that convinces the hand. (Let's see how she felt that day.) His voice rose up thick and comforting. You can take me or leave me. At her invitation he sat down easily in a chair at the table. The story is his thick hands holding a glass of water in the unruly afternoon light. So much is misunderstood about your presence here, he said. And your son. Especially him. His left hand pressed the loose fabric of his waistcoat to his chest. It is my sincere hope that both you and he come out the better for it. And that was the start of it, this Mr. Ruggles putting words together for her purpose.

With him hunkered into his angle at the table she came to know his seasoned intelligence. I've had some dealings with the planters, I've been there, I've seen. (Who can prove one place more than another?) Surely there must be something they share beyond that? And then he said something else to her, and she spoke back, the table becoming conversation where nothing had been. She felt grateful and grounded as they lived against each other, their talk widening and widening. Indeed, she did what she could to hold him at the table as long as she could. He gentled the long afternoon by sitting with her. Her feet twitched. And her hands. They took the evening as it came. Darkness moving under the table and along the walls. Aware of the smell of burning wax, the heat of the flames, the cool night air. She ate her supper, and he watched her. (The orphan pleaded with him to sup too, but he would not.) They sat in the dark until she got up to light the candles. What was the conversation about for three hours, for all evening?

Her head cleared in the hard morning light. She watched the wind fall back across the water and birds caught in midair by her own wonderment. Watched them drift through layered currents like white lace torn away from a dress. And rake their claws into the ocean. She had to bend and twist—oh her aching back—to register these clear occurrences of Nature. A few notes from a piano floated across the water—she heard it—a flat sound on the waves, music that suggested some gathering in the distance, and she seemed to remember something that she thought long forgotten.

But before memory could resurface, yet another orphan called upon her. Ma'm, you are wanted in the chapel. The orphan's voice joyous in telling her this. He gave her his brightest smile. So she followed him, her footsteps attached to those of this boy who preceded her, her gaze held by the narrow openings into the classrooms and workshops side by side with one another—none of the rooms connect—crammed full with children and piled high with books, tools, and materials (leather, brick, iron), orphans at their desks working on their letters and numbers. (She likes the sound of words doing what they do.) At their workbenches and anvils, sewing machines and looms, side-glancing her as she passes them. (Mamma, she could hear them whisper. Mamma.)

When they entered the chapel she saw that the vast open stage was crowded with Mr. Tabbs and the men she had come to know over the previous days as Mr. Ruggles, Lieutenant Drinkwater, Deacon Double (a tight smile on his face), and Reverend Wire, along with other men she had not met and did not recognize against the big wooden cross, the Bible (bound in animal hide) open on the podium at the center of a stage and the humiliating glare and polish of other objects she could not name on the altar. And there he was (the ocean air and light found his form), a man-boy clearly outlined against the piano shaped like a spreading stain (puddle). She saw him and thought, That can't be him. That can't be my Thomas. *My Tom.* Long white tunic with buttons big as medals and gold fringe on the chest. White trousers with black stripes down the sides. His shoulders as broad as Mingo's. And a string of other features she can no longer remember. (What she saw.) She opened her mouth to speak, but only muddled sound stumbled out. So she moved toward him to feel what remained, but at her touch, he peeled his bulky frame away from her skin.

Are you her? he said.

Seeing the trouble, Reverend Wire laid his hands firmly on Thomas's head in the same steady manner that she was to see time and time again.

Finding speech, she thanked the Reverend for his intervention, although inside she was locked up in a curious double mood: angry (would that be the word?) that her reunion with Thomas had assumed this public form, the anger even more so, even more acute after she had been forced (no other way to put it) to live in pause for a week waiting for this reunion, no reason given, no apologies offered.

And all of this was true. Still, that first day back in their chambers she was delighted. She had her Thomas back with her at last. (Praise be His name.) But as time went on—the next day and the day after that and the others that followed—he remained detached from her in the guessing silence. Not that it troubled her. She told herself that if Tom remained deaf (to her) that was only because she had not tried hard enough, spoken loud enough. So those first weeks, she tried so hard, would say whatever words drifted onto her tongue. But still he said nothing and kept her firmly at a distance. Silence on the tongue on the eyes on the ears in the nose in the palms of her hands. In fact, he gave no indication that he could even hear the sound of her voice— had he become deaf?—continued to shrink and shrivel away, only a little bread each day to keep the taste of the world on his tongue. *Feed me banks of light.* Perhaps he was sick. Perhaps he needed a doctor.

Meeting her concern, Reverend Wire, a man of the cloth and a healer (two hats, two-heads), examined him. Dr. Wire watched Thomas's chest rise and fall, put his ear to Thomas's chest and listened as if to a broken watch, held down his tongue with two fingers and looked into his throat, picked up each hand by the wrist, counted the pulse of his blood.

His body is perfectly fine, the two-headed preacher-doctor said. But this business of reunification is too much for him, too upsetting, a shock to what he knows and expects. You must give him time. The return to himself will take time.

A return she is still waiting for. *In this life I have heard your promise and I am ready to serve.* Waiting for Thomas her Thomas to emerge from this *man.* She spends each day looking for ways to fill in the hours, to stretch them out so that they can run into each other. *How bout we play our game now?* Waiting is one thing a nigger knows how to do. So she can wait a little longer. Time on her hands. All the time in the world. She reserves all of patience and tolerance for Thomas as she did at Hundred Gates so many years ago. *I am the only one.* She feels justified in her determination, thinking only about the person he can become, she can become. But each day rebuilds itself like the one before. Tomorrow he will install himself there onstage before the piano at his body's insistence and so will she on this same pew. So have all the days been and perhaps they shall be for a long time to come. How deeply must he be touched to enter?

Now she hears it, a breath breaking open, almost like a strangled cry that comes again and again—listen to it—huh, huh, huh. His mouth causing the shape of his face to change, some new face trying to be born. She falls under the spell of the cadences of her son's breathing, the two of them sounding as one, until his breath quiets after a final whistle.

The bell rings, signaling the end of instruction for the day, the orphans released from learning and labor. Time now for an orphan to escort them back to their quarters—as if they don't know their way by now, as if they will get lost in the halls—and for her and Thomas to retire their troubled skin until tomorrow. The strangeness of light between Thomas and his piano, the fine edge gleaming around his body. He is touched with heat, flushed—could it be?—a little red even. She sees the reflections of his hands in the piano's laminated shine, hands that are useless on Edgemere. *Thomas, leave that piano be.* What will put them back into motion?

Let us join hands in prayer, Reverend Wire said.

Your hand hot, Thomas said. Fire. A faggot of fire.

Now she hears it, her breath a flat tune limping its way out of her mouth. She cannot trust what even her own body tells her. The thing she is feeling now fits nothing she knows. Pain but she can't say where. Now she understands that this is a new hurt, an all-over hurt happening beneath the skin, the grinding friction caused by two bodies, past and present, moving up against each other inside one skin. (That accounts for why she feels so heavy all of the time.) Or is his silence taking her apart nervewise? (No, that can't be it.) So she starts to say what she has actually wanted to say but had put off saying because it had seemed premature, begins to remind him (again?) about the blackberry patch that grew wild off the road to Hundred Gates, the crooked tree with its white peeling bark, the horse behind the rock quarry, the hills like beached whales, all the rises and curves of the land, the sloping riverbank, the minnows wheeling in the shallows—even now there's something she keeps trying to say that never comes out right; what is the language that will keep their past as it should be?—the earth odors and rock odors and plant odors and animal odors. (His spirit lives for her in such odors.) The light on Sunday mornings, *those* Sunday mornings. She sees his face move, sees it go sideways on his neck, tracing a movement from one end of the keyboard to the other then back again, and so on, as if he were reading a book. But nothing manifests. She feels blocked about saying anything else. Perhaps her words come too late. She can admit the letdown to herself.

She looks at his face, his lidded-over eyes, and something in her unhouses itself. Now she understands. He does not remember because he cannot remember. What the eyes see is preserved in the orbs themselves, where sight is stored in the seeing. Tom cannot see; hence, he cannot remember, has nothing to see to remember. Something opens between them. Who is she to want to hang back there? None of that matters anymore. It is less a question of *where* and *when*—the hills that go doubling back, the bedding straw piled to one side—and more of *how* and *what*—she knows the *why*—her useless nostalgia draining away. She must create the right conditions. Unless she does something now, right now, tomorrow will be the same, him up there and her down here. Is it possible for her to learn to do what he does? (What better way?) The space for it exists in her, now that she has been freed from Hundred Gates, freed from labor, her time and body her own. (If you have a song to sing then sing it right this minute.) Not that she could ever get music the way he got it, from the getting place. Called. Marked. Sounds planted deep inside him. (Why he moves the way he moves, walks the way he walks). A story foretold.

She can pinpoint the day when music claimed him. The day when in the haze of a rainy afternoon a wet wind, with him still unborn in her womb, she stumbled into the center of town, Broad Street, more relaxed than she should have been for someone expecting a child. She might have been six months belly-round then. She had been sent on some errand—sweep the floor into the fire, shake the dust into the wind—but she can no longer recall who sent her or for what reason. The first thing she remembers seeing: niggers bent over or kneeling cleaning up a wagonload of apples that had burst open on the road. The wind brought the sound of whistles, drums, and fifes. She let her gaze float in the direction of the sound just as a brigade of woogies and niggers in plumed regalia came marching into view at the other end of the street. She stopped walking and stood facing fixedly this disturbance. Eight musicians in all—if memory serves—two whistles and two fifes and two bass drums and two kettledrums that kept them in stride. What was the occasion, the reason for the jubilation? The nodding accepting crowd granted the band passage. Wagons and carriages halted to let them through. For some reason she remembers more about the woogies and niggers who were walking on the sidewalk and in the street that day than she can about the individuals who made up the brigade, can actually picture one bent woogie head after another concealing a grim gaze, heavy heads under bright parasols—so was it some sad occasion? a mourning?—and a nigger herdsman (all the herdsmen were niggers) driving his bell-tinkling flock—cows? goats? sheep?—down the street. High-stepping, the brigade paraded their bannering sounds from one end of Broad Street to the other, then circled back again. Then the fife players called out a line, and the drummers whooped and moaned in response, and they all began to dance and sway. And so did she.

The air smells faintly of burning—leaves, refuse, and shit (donkey), never the smell of kerosene or coal since Edgemere has neither—is sweet with the pugency of wood fires. Will she get to go out into the open today? She lifts her eyes, frets to see through the high high windows. Maybe if they actually leave the chapel, leave the Home—she has hardly gone out of the asylum the two or three months she's been here on Edgemere—to knock along the shore. They will walk and sing—singing shortens the road, lessens the distance—his hand with its heat and bones just so around her, the measure of the sweetest promise, as the dhows drift inland. What a good idea. So they will get up and go now.

She leans back and hears (feels) her bones crack. The sound severs whatever it is that anchors the stage in place and yanks it free of its moorings. The stage begins to drift about the room. Thomas panics, afraid of drowning. Reaches out with both hands and grabs the rim of the piano in the gap between the soundboard and the cantilevered lid and he sits there with the piano fastened to his long outstretched arms.

What has she done? Then something clatters into the air. She turns at the sound. Can barely make out slow-moving figures crawling along the floor, tunneling between pews, row after row, and coming up for space and air, the hide and seek of laughing faces, one boy almost connected caterpillar-like to the boy in front or behind him, their shadows sealed together.

Yall better get up from there.

. . .

You heard me.

Ah, Mamma. We ain't doing nothing.

We jus come to see.

Ain't nothing to see, she says.

. . .

You ain't hear me?

Faces and bodies sprout up from between the benches. Four, five, six.

Look at that blind nigger.

He yo son?

Yall get. Gon now.

Hey, Mamma. We jus lookin.

Is he gon play that pianer?

When he gon play it?

I bet you he don't even know how to play it.

Yah had better gone.

We jus want to see him play that pianer.

Yeah. Ain't nobody botherin you.

I ain't gon tell you again.

What?

I ain't gon tell you again.

Mother, ain't nobody scared of you.

Wit yo old ass. The boy's lips draw down in a sickly sneer.

She grabs her bowie knife by its bone handle and gets up from her chair. The boys scatter, their eyes bright with terror. They had better. Let them tremble and beware. Where she comes from *stab* is another word for *knife*. *Slit* another word for *throat*. *Shank* another word for *dead*.

Get up on I the one.

What? she asks. Thomas has slurred something. Thomas—*my Tom*—what did you say? And the more she doesn't say. Go ahead. Don't stop now. Cat got your tongue? Speak to her as if he is the past. Thomas, please tell me—

Then, as if this is the sign (word) he has been waiting for, he breaks into movement, starts fingering the ivories hard and with purpose, and just like that he is Little Thomas again, the Blind Tom that the world knew. A three-headed song—how many melodies can the air hold?—that pulls him this way and that, and that pulls her into the circle of melodies. See, silence could not hold him forever, because he is who he is, a Wiggins (not a Bethune), her and him both, one, same blood, like to like.

Then his fingers stop making sense. Why has he stopped playing?

Why you stop?

The ox is on my tongue.

What? What did you say? Willing herself futilely to be calm. In fact, she can hear the calmness of her own voice as if from a distance. Thomas, please tell me—

Take me. The only one.

Thomas?

But the words wilt right there. He turns wordlessly back to the piano. Holds up his big hands and shows her them, front then back, knuckles on display. She has no idea what this gesture means. Tom gathered in his own arms.

❀ ❀ ❀

Wire thinks back to last night when the ocean claimed so many, passengers busy underwater, their mouths and throats full like overflowing chalices even as their eyes were burning, red. Not that he could see them in full detail really since he could only make out the contours of bodies trying to keep above the waves and the ferry hanging on the horizon as if pinned to the sky before it was carried under. And then he was being drawn down too and could hear his fellow passengers, the wet groaning language of his brethren and sistren through his soaked skin, the ocean wild around him with foam and glitter and swarming colors. In unison they upped and downed and scissored their arms and legs. Then as the light began to fan out and open up and land and sky began to assemble themselves around him, he realized with astonishment that he was as much excited by what he had dreamed as he was terrified. Why?

Defined against the sky, the dhows consume him with their

overwhelming presence, teetering and tottering under the constant force of water and wind, bewitched currents that dance light and wood to their own needs. Only yesterday he had blessed the boats to start the fishing season. *May you open your eyes to water and may the creatures of the sea open their mouths to hooks.* The serenity and calm in the ocean, in the land, and in the heavens, even in the straight still trees, is almost enough to distract him as he makes his rounds through the camps, but once inside an encampment with its dark little tents and stooped figures in rags, misery in drabness is thrown back to him, tells him where he is. The tents turn around to look at him and the refugees mutter suitable thanks and praises, their attention commanded (he tells himself) through his simple unadorned presence rather than his height, his learning, his profession, his verses and prescriptions and treatments and medicines. The refugees line up in a long queue, as if they have come to present their lives—well, in a sense they have, haven't they?—his hands active and his eyes full. One by one he takes the measure of them. Each person he examines tenses up and assumes odd angles like a model sitting for a portrait (study). The human body dazzles the imagination with existence from crown to heel bone, from the brain riding in the head to the winding provinces of the intestines and the heart that branches with its wild arteries and the muscles of the back that somehow remain steady and strong under stress and strain. These Freedmen suffer in silence, try to hide their hurt (sorrow just sits and rocks), although here in the camps heartache and sorrow have nowhere to hide.

How are you feeling? Which part is paining you? Are you able to eat?

They kill his ears with their barely audible words. So he composes habits for the camps so that these Freedmen's expectations will be neither gluttonous nor starved. Liniments and elixirs that can bring the blood back to the cheeks and heat to numb digits and limbs. His method of strengthening and enlarging the circulatory and respiratory systems by diet, rigor, and breathing. (See Avicenna.)

The refugees burrow their bodies under damp blankets, settling in for the night. (The thought of them that evening in the camp.)

Now the song calls him.

Oh for three words of honey, and two strips of fatback
that I might tell but one wonder of thy wedding night

That seems to be the song of the moment in the camps, can't miss it, it is everywhere, and he makes a record of it in his head for future reference, no telling how the information may prove useful down the line—words you say to show that you are one of them, words to put in a sermon. So let them sing. (Sing yourself to where the song comes from.) Whenever he is lost deep within himself their songs call him out. The children follow him around the well, singing. *Dear water, clear water, playful in all your streams.*

Who does not love to hear them and see them, perfect in music and movement? With his listening funnel, he hears the way history sounds in a chest—*Into the air, as breath into the wind*—the lungs taking up their work. Judges the force of circulation with just the lightest touch along the wrist, feeling the sequence of intervals—loud and soft, regular or irregular—as they abide in the pulse, the blood banging in the body. He finds the true extension of himself in them, in all of the refugees, these Freedmen, but the landscape (what he sees) is inexact in its slant of figures, facts of the flesh suggesting fewer souls than are actually here. The city still has nowhere to place them all despite the makeshift and quickly constructed houses put up on new streets. And so much is in short supply. Victuals, medicine, clothing, soap, tents, blankets and bedding, lamps, kerosene. The provisions of food and other necessities made available to them through the Bureau and through the Christian goodwill of the Red Cross, Action Now, and the League of Churches dwell in awkward distribution inside their silos. The body is owned by hunger. So the body says. But not even these shortages can spoil the children. Take this as proof: a group of boys have made glassless spectacles from orange rinds. *It is your own self you hunger for.* How clever.

In the last camp on his rounds—each day this human coming and going into the camps—the refugees are busy with grief. They carry a coffin high above their heads and move in equal pace, swaying from side to side. They believe in giving the coffin a dance, action that is not work, but matter itself through which the work navigates, the commandments of metal and wood. Once the coffin is comfortably tucked into the freshly dug grave, he says his say then they pour their libations. (All in man that mourns and seeks.) And he trembles inside himself, undone for a moment by the three or four things that can happen to a man in the camps. He and the mourners turn away.

For whatever reason, he looks back to see bored children leaping over the grave.

Ah, that dead nigger is going off to glory.

Around their wood fires the refugees melt into light, but there is nothing luminous about this. (In the fading light does the sound of the water also darken?) Holy is that dark which will neither promise nor explain. He is no fool. Knows that their bodies, as the bodies of us all, are promised to something more certain than Emancipation or Liberty or Happiness: Death. However, the trouble with them— his people, *us*—is that we are always preparing to die.

> *Body, ain't you lonesome?*
> *Lay down a little while*
> *Body, ain't you tired?*
> *Lay down a little while*

The challenge (always) is to win their hearts and their minds and change the way they view themselves and their situation. He has to both kill the nigger (slave) inside and bring the African out. Such are the selves they struggle with and are struggling out of.

What pains have we not felt? What suffering have we not known? (The thoughts of a wise man in the language of common African folk.)

Who understands better than he does their hunger and desperation? Slavery taught them the ways of doubt so that they may believe. Life knows no time or limits. Even death makes life.

Take my yoke upon you and learn from me, for I am gentle and humble of heart, and you will find rest for your souls. For my yoke is easy and my burden is light.

Jehovah has double blessed him with the gift of gab (mouth) and the gift of healing (hands), talking and touching his way into the truths these professions require. *Once more he put his hands upon the man's eyes, and his sight was restored and he saw everything clearly.* So illuminate he can and illuminate he will until every single person in the camps, until each refugee in the cell of himself is convinced of his freedom.

Brothers and sisters, the darkness and the light are both alike to thee. But behold, I tell you that we stand at the edge of centuries facing a new era of ten thousand years, and He, Almighty Jehovah, stands with us. It all comes together *here,* all there ever was is *now.* Soon you will rise and walk away from this life. You and I both, together, will rise and enter a holy house, on this earth, not in the heaven above. Until then hold on.

His heart beyond both worry and anguish: *Light breaks where no light was before, where no eye was prepared to see, and animals rise up to walk.*

These ideas have their satisfaction. They turn a rambling and brutal chronicle of bondage and pain and abuse and injustice into a neatly structured story of triumph where the African (black sheep) awakens to the fullness of his strength and inherits a plentiful earth, some forty thousand acres along with a million mules.

Bright stars fixed in thick light in the black night sky beckon. Jehovah willing, he can now go home and take a moment to grieve, catch some shut-eye, then rise fresh and resume work on Sunday's sermon, "God Has a Hand in It." *Holding on to God's unchanging hand. My people—*

My people? People don't belong to you. You belong to them, but only if they let you. *So let me.* Whatever it takes, he will do, he is willing. By any means necessary.

Doctor Reverend. Mr. Reverend. Pastor, Doctor, sir. Reverend Doctor. Pastor, sir.

I'm listening, he says. Tell me what you have to say. He can't help thinking that there is something mysterious about the way the boy accosts him.

The boy speaks his piece. Them soldiers paid me this quarter, the boy says. The boy holds it up so he can see it, as if he needs convincing.

He wishes he could pay the boy two quarters or a dollar, bargain some sum that will relieve him of the obligation to travel to the soldiers' camp in Central Park. He can't. The hour of his seeming quiet has passed. So he dismisses the boy and simply stands there waiting for his second wind—is he struggling for breath?—and diligently gauging his own mood, not proud about what he is thinking. God means to impose impossible tasks on him and others like him until they breathe their last.

Central Park is a distance he can cross by foot, and he will cross it by foot no matter how tired he is, moving hesitantly as if he fears stepping into a hole. He sees big gashes in the sidewalk, unusual colors showing through, and has the distinct impression that the buildings are sinking into their foundations, dwellings freighted with the city's past, year upon year. His eyes seek out something else. (The city does not tell its past.) Outside of him—way back, beyond— are others of unknown number. He knows that they are watching him even if the city to him is his own tongue. Is it possible for him to forget the rank and rancid odors that wafted across the ocean into Edgemere after he had taken up exile there? Most terrible of all in those first months were the rumors, yet to be proven these many years later, circulating among the fellow exiles on Edgemere (and even a few of the natives) about profitable new industries on the mainland, hats and ties and vests and chaps and belts and shoes made from African skin, which, for a time at least, surpassed the same products made from chupacabra leather; vials filled with the semen of hanged men—sales surpassing (supply and demand) gourds filled with morning dew and wineskins filled with Italian, French, or Spanish water—and tea made from weeds that had sprouted up where men had pissed themselves moments before death. Is memory (the facts and rumors and the speculations created by the facts and rumors) what spurs him on?

Trees at a wet and dripping distance mark his progress across the Main Lawn of Central Park. Grass sprouting from the ground underfoot. (The landscape is something he moves across.) What is that large feeling he notices spreading in the air even before he reaches the guard-(gate)-house? The entire bivouac gripped by an apprehensive energy. The blocky house is stark, self-announcing, and though the room is austere and cramped inside, it is oddly partitioned into two distinct apartments with rifles and bayonets and trunks of ammunition in the first, and a table-dominated sitting area in the second, where the men, veterans of the war to free the Negro, are engaged in voluble discourse, gazing into each other's eyes as they talk. Aggression holds everything together: room, arms and ammunition, table, the light coming from kerosene lamps that casts murals on the walls from the shadows of the animated men, the afterimages of light. He has long been curious. They have killed. They have killed white men. But he has never said anything to them about it and they have said nothing to him. Still, they are part of something, and he is part of it with them, a simple allegiance.

With cognition of his presence the room plunges into complete silence. He walks briskly to his usual place at the table, although he knows that there is no reason for him to hurry. *Why are you hurrying?* And before he has even gotten fully comfortable in his seat he is wholly given over to their troubles—it would seem that the city has demanded that they relinquish their arms—all talking at once—in their urgency they forget to thank him for coming—voicing ideas that strike him as unacceptable.

He feels a little dizzy with the cacophony and also because the table has been wiped down (polished) with kerosene to keep the flies away. (This act performed much earlier in the day, for surely they know that flies don't fly at night.) The entire room smells like fuel, like burning, smoke, fire.

Wait, someone says. God damn it. I said wait. Have you loss your hearing or something? Well, shut your goddamn mouth.

Around the table all of the men in uniform follow Drinkwater's lead, hands gathered together on the white surface of the table along with the bottles and glasses. Although he is a lieutenant, Drinkwater is a man of silence who is happier listening to others than leading the conversation himself. He accepts a glass of whiskey—emancipated from some dead Confederate's pantry *(the planters are all dead)*—and seeks the face of the soldier who puts it in his hands.

You think I want to sit here listening to all that jawing and whining? Sound like a bunch of women. I want to hear what Reverend Wire has to say. But yall carry on if you like.

Drinkwater is an intense young man but pleasant usually, easy to see how he became a lieutenant.

Now that Drinkwater has commanded silence, the veterans are all waiting on him, Wire, so he says, Do I have to be the one to say it? then frowns noncommittally.

Yes, Reverend, you do. Deacon Double looks him in the eye. Several of the soldiers nod their heads in approval. Until that moment the Deacon had escaped his notice, just another shadow blending in with the other shadows on the wall, but sitting there now—his sun-touched skin and his hair close and curling as if he has all he can take. Is there any reason why you should not?

In the expression on Drinkwater's face Wire detects a hint of unease, as if Double's question conceals some other question, both provocative and wounding.

He wants to give wise advice without forcing it on anyone. Be that as it may, he says, because they have already inked it into law. They did not deliberate. They did not survey our thoughts and recommendations. Because they know full well that we can put up no challenge to their laws since they hold suzerainty over all articles and declarations and ordinances and codes and decrees.

With his impassive face Double looks like he has nothing better to do than to sit there and listen to him say what he already knew he would say. Does any man here care about their laws?

God damn they law.

Spit on every one of they laws.

Piss.

Shit.

What law?

I got they law. I got they law right here.

And they are all talking at once again. He tries to think above their shouts to and at each other. He goes deep into himself for a visit to his own knowable connections to them. (Move in memory.) Even in later years he will encounter by chance some man of the Race who will stop him on the street and remind him that it was he, Wire, who had recruited him to the war cause so many decades ago. The campaign to put men of color in uniform and on the battlefield had required herculean efforts, a crusade sown with false starts and sidesteps and humiliations and betrayals and failures.

> *Mr. President, in order to prevent enrollment of Negroes in the rebel services, and induce them to run to, instead of from, the Union forces, the government, you, Sir, must undertake the commissioning and promotion of Negro men now in the army, according to merit. How, you might wonder, can you overcome the inevitable objections of white officers and conscripts to the commissioning of Negro officers? I have the remedy, Mr. President. It is my most important suggestion to you. And I think it is just what is required to complete the prestige of the Union army to penetrate through the heart of the South, and make conquests, with the banner of Emancipation unfurled, proclaiming freedom as they go, sustaining and protecting the freed men, leaving a few veterans among them*

when occasion requires, and keeping this banner unfurled
until every slave is free, according to the letter of your proc-
lamation. I would also take from those men already in the
service all who are competent for commissioned officers, and
establish at once in the South a camp for instructions. By
this we could have in about three months an army of forty
thousand Negroes in motion, the presence of which any-
where would itself be a power irresistible. Mr. President,
you should have an army of Negroes commanded entirely by
Negroes, the sight of which is required to give confidence to
the slaves, and retain them in the Union, stop foreign inter-
vention, and speedily bring the war to a close . . .

    Yours, subscribed,

Penning and talking the flashy errands of his dreams into existence. (Word anything into being.) A thousand bodies he made active by one slogan or another—*White people must learn to listen. Africans must learn to talk*—although, truth to tell, the men he had approached required little persuading. In the future when he encounters a man that he had recruited, he and the former soldier will exchange the usual kind of polite talk before the latter begins to interrogate Wire about his present life—a doctor still? a man of the cloth? the name of his church? wife? seed? grandseed? names, ages, and number?- at which point Wire will find some reason to excuse himself. Not that he will feel either guilty or ashamed about his past actions and deeds. Indeed, he will still be able to hold his head high about the things he had tried to do.

So how can he back away, back out of this now? Up to his eyes in it. I have heard a lot of talk, he says, plenty of talk, although in theory he has nothing against talking for the sake of talking. You have to know how to look even if you don't know what you are looking for.

Go tell them no, we won't give up our arms.

Yes, Reverend. Put it to them.

I ain't givin up what's mine. I don't care what their law say.

Yeah. They want my rifle, let them come here and take it from me.

He notices a murky exchange of glances between Drinkwater and one of his men, his second-in-command.

What about my house? Drinkwater says. I haven't heard them say one word about that. They want my rifle, they give me back my house.

Our day is our loss, Double says.

I understand how you feel, Wire says. I know what you feel. You don't think that I feel the same way? I feel the same way. Am I not one of you? I am one of you. But you know these people. I don't need to tell you, I don't need to tell any man seated at this table. You know these people. They will invoke some statute or decree and demand notarized deeds. He can see his gloomy words move like black slugs over the bodies of the men seated around the table.

So we invoke, Double says. We demand. We bargain, exchange.

The right to return.

What they took from us. What they owe us.

You put it to them, Reverend.

Eyes bright, Double is looking with a question, a challenge, as it seems he was born to do. Always both for you and against you at the same time. A contradiction.

Wire hears in the silence that follows their desire for his approval and thus his support, advocacy, agency, his willingness to author acts on their behalf. Who will speak for them (*us*) if he doesn't? He belongs to them.

Although the hour is late, the first thing he does when he arrives at the Home is to go visit with the boy Tom and his reserved mother in the rustle of fine fabric that Tabbs has provided her (at considerable expense).

Preacher, Tom says, you smell like dirt.

Bird That Never Alights on the Trees
(1849–1856)

"...gossiping with two hands."

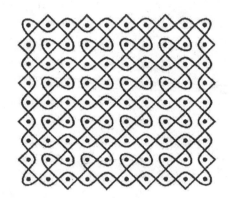

HE CAN'T SEE IT, CAN ONLY FEEL ITS WARMTH ON HIS SKIN, feathers of light and shadow. Steady light. Everything waits to be seen, wants to be seen, and remembered. The world taunts him with its sights. But touch is his primary means of witnessing the world. Taking stock. Fingers the patterned ridges of tree bark, which reveal less of what is actually there—weight, density—offering only the skeletal outline of some longing.

Sound too. Birds warbling in motionless air. A barking dog. Snakes in tree branches that repeat the same songs. And frogs that croak slowly in day and crickets that chirp quickly in night. And ants that dance a frenzy over a meal. And the crackling noise of a flame.

Animation surprises him. (What lives leans into the sun.) Flies hovering about his nose, a mingling of pleasure and suspense. He does not drive them away. The world rushes at him alarmingly from every side. How do his fingers measure and remember?

In vibrations of grass earth records the sound and intensity of falling shafts of sun. And things man-made too: the peanut-shelling machine's gyrations forever imprinted in the soil below. Arms and legs moving at the same time. Big circles and small circles. Tiny rituals (ceremonies). Accidents of air.

Nothing strange about sound pressing in, showing a sense of mission. Place. Names rise from locations. Hundred Gates. These few sounds, segments of breath, he rehearses. The syllables of his name skip across his tongue. Thomas. *Where do you live? Whose boy are you? Boy, where do you live?* Even if there is tangible distance between saying and meaning, a distance that keeps enlarging in breadth and range.

The sun drifts back inside, hidden behind a curtain of clouds, already damp, beginning to swell. Stars penetrate along with the smell of the fields, the stable, the shed and the gardens, paths and roads. Freshness, a shift in the way he feels.

His legs hold him upright, his head floating off where birds fly past. This body isn't his (he doesn't own it) but moves when he moves, takes him traveling. Easy-gaiting. The long way round. Knows it, knows it all the way.

He can hear the sound of his own breathing. (Does he own it?) His feet working harder now on the earth.

Home. (What else would he call it?) The keys line up like hogs in a pen. They are cool when he touches them, as if he is submerging his hands in a cold stream. Trees bend toward earth in strong wind, the longest leaning touch, each a shadow of the other.

Is it any wonder he sang like that? Why he played like that?

A pail of water remains near the stovepipe in case of fire. Its cousin, a larger wooden tub, positioned a few yards in front of their cabin. When the door is open it frames a tree-occluded sky. Dirt, the solitary chair, the rough table—all that is sparse here makes it enough to see this wooden tub, set off in a grass-free area of the yard, where they often wash in the morning. It is here that what she remembers happened.

No one missed his shadow moving before the house. Nothing unusual there. Familiar in fact. Little Thomas quick and secretive that way—some shadow scurrying across your shoulder beyond vision. It is a struggle even to hold him, to cuddle him, Little Thomas, all vigor and resistance. So easy to lose the chain of connection. His form appears clearly among the leaves, and just as quickly, in a surge of color and motion, you see two brown legs sticking out of the wooden tub like ladles, your eyes surprised, well before understanding catches up. (And this part she has either reconstructed or invented: his head disappearing, one arm thrust out of the water and then nothing more.) Words of panic. She runs to the tub and sees him splashing beads of light. An onrush of angry swells, all of the world's seas lashing at the baby. Remembers lifting him from the tub, hugging his chill limbs to warm them as she carried him to the cabin. Heads and bodies rising in guilt and alarm—you must keep up with Little Thomas—everyone (her daughters) except her husband,

Domingo, who continues to slouch, a bony-shouldered hump. He is a small slim man, quietly sensitive about both his height and his weight, refusing to allow things of denser body or stronger elements to torment him. (No sun or heat is enough. No spiraling rainstorm.) He even resists the ease of a man-made chair, preferring the uneven planks of the floor. She hugs the baby against her chest, his breathing infinitely far from his heart. She closes her eyes. Whispers a prayer in the dark. Her body is cautious and will not ask too much, just this one thing. Let him live.

She opens her eyes to find herself looking through the open doorway. Sees herself taking a clean rag to wipe down the baby's body. Her hands lifting him like a plant destined for a pot and plunging him into the wood tub. A sound slips out of the corner of her mouth.

Mingo gets to his feet, shaking off tension and fret. Casually—do not get caught up in the uproar of the moment—takes the baby from her and holds him up and out for inspection, rough assurance. Kisses the baby and hands him back over to her. But he doesn't have quite the skill to pull it off, to calm and convince. (Which comes first?)

In the days that follow, the near tragedy works on and into all of them, even the girls, everyone silent and uncomfortable, nervy and on edge, muted and mutual disgust at their failings, although Little Thomas's injuries are few. This will not be the last mishap, his last escape from serious harm in the formative years. Her unusual son. (She prefers the term *curious*. He seems receptive to things that usually escape our notice or that notice tries to escape: shit, piss, spews of dirt, foul odors such as the smell of stagnant water or boiling chitlins, what crawls or flies, buzzes or hisses. Seems to imbibe as much pleasure from the sound of sucking sap from the stalk as from the taste of the sap itself.) So she devises this method of keeping an eye on the baby as she goes about her work. She puts him in a cotton-bale box that she can carry around with her. But he soon masters the ability to crawl over its high sides and scramble away, on the prowl, the border between him and the world thin. (He can't observe the universe so the universe is without boundaries.) In this way rusty nails puncture his knees. (She is convinced to this day that the metal found its way to his skin less by accident than by choice. Put simply: he had unearthed them. Recall the dirt under his fingers and impacted in the map-like creases of his palms.) Splinters embed themselves under his fingernails and make wood claws out of both hands. His injuries become a discernible point of reference, crawling and walking one continuous thing to her. For the first fifteen months of life he either lies or sits, shaking in his own noise. Then the helpless scatterings that typified his first attempts to push and pull himself. He never seemed to get better at it. Never seemed to move forward or back, but remained, immobile, confined to his belly, like a worm. (Forgive her for thinking this about her own child. *Forgive me*.) Almost never saw him sitting in an upright position unless he was propped up against a leg of the piano while Mary Bethune or one of the Bethune girls sat prim and proper playing above him. Even took his food while prone on the floor on his belly.

But all that changed when he learned how to crawl. She remembers it this way: she was sitting on a stack of logs a few yards behind the mansion, where she usually took her break under the shade of a tree, a block of time that belonged to her, short as it was, a few minutes after she had finished serving supper to the family and before she had to begin the tasks that would carry her through dinner and beyond.

She enjoyed that spot, her husband's handiwork all about, wood he had neatly cut and stacked. Almost like an unfinished house (hers), the laying down of some promised future. Not that she ever really thought about it that way. Her break afforded her the opportunity to go slow with a coffee, provided a chance to be starkly alone with Thomas, belly down on the ground beside her, her thoughts soft, faint, and faraway. She remembers the silence of this day, just the sound of her sipping coffee, turning her little spoon in her big cup, and the usual curious noises of the boy, harsh and moist. The Bethune residence an amazing sight, as light was actually pushing up from the ground so that the mansion seemed to be floating on a blanket of illumination. She lowered her head and brought the cup to her mouth and the next thing she knew Thomas had somehow managed to climb up an inclined stump of wood to perch at the top of a pile, a deliberate elevation of self.

That was the start of it. Crawling brought a striking transformation, a living thing changing before your eyes, some lowly creature confined to dirt, his hands directly under his chest and his knees bent outward at odd angles, allowing him the sideways motion of a lizard weaving between legs and chairs. By this means achieving ambulation, however odd. And then, once more, he became unhinged from time. No slow progression from crawling to standing to the first stumbling steps with hands balanced against the wall. Instead the crawling went on for years, his legs refusing to allow him to stand upright let alone step a foot forward.

After a frustrating year or two, he somehow upped his crawl and acquired speed and lift, so that he was able to actually lope catlike above the ground.

But the miracle of walking brought new challenges. (The lineage of a thing in its later stages.) He never mastered the ability to go up or down stairs unaided, or to sit down or get up from a chair. Trying to perform one action or the other he would totter backward and forward, and from side to side, his otherwise strong legs brittle and uncertain. (Not unlike General Toon attached to his black canes.) And rarely could he put one foot in front of the other with natural recognizable rhythm and ease, his gait either so heavy that he seemed to be sinking into the ground, or so light (in Miss Toon's presence) that there seemed nothing solid about his person.

He squeezes the pale shell until it cracks open, rubs off the crackly brown skin with a set rhythmic motion of thumb and forefinger, and tosses the nut into his mouth. The husk remains on the ground, collecting water and sound, one among many, humming gourds. A numbing buzz in his hands and feet—there is a nerve that stimulates, another that slows down—music entering him as far from the voices and fingers that made it.

The sun appears as to one looking through smoked glass.
Where is Little Thomas?
Smoke rises in shafts of pure black illumination.
Where is Little Thomas? You must keep up with your brother.
Glass glints, half smoke, half sun.
Thomas?
Why doesn't he respond to the sound of his chanted name? Truth be told—she knows it, her whole family knows it—he is caught in the grip of a habit to flee the restraints of their scrutinizing presence—his conspirators, pigs and chickens rush to greet him—and find his way into the mansion. In fact, he can find his way all over, seemingly no place or thing he can't pry his way into. Rambling. Has even wandered miles to trespass on neighboring farms and estates and march into people's homes and lives. His escapes, invasions, necessitate new secrets and new lies. No one can check his ability to go sightless wherever his feet will take him. Quick and fearless like a carriage hurtling along in the darkness.

After dinner each day Mary Bethune plays the piano like a medical regime. She returns to the piano to give her daughters lessons in the long deep lull after supper and before retiring to bed. Tom leans out from between the lower levels, the legs of the furniture, the side of a cabinet. He sidles up to the piano while the daughters practice, his body writhing to the tones.
It's okay, Charity. Leave him be.
One day like any other after she has completed the lessons, put an end to her daughters' complaints and hesitations, and called for Charity to see them off to bed, one day like this as she is walking off, she hears the music that had just ended begin again, the same piece. She turns and sees Tom with his chin at the keyboard, his hands in

their mischief toying with the keys. Struck by the moment, they all stand and look, her, Charity, and the girls.

Charity gives her an expression, half-amused, half-apologetic, unable to invent some excuse. No, Thomas, she says. I'm sorry, ma'm.

He certainly takes to the instrument, Mary Bethune says. I've never seen anything like it. Thinking, They surprise you this way every so often. (One day he is crawling behind her as was his habit and the next day he is walking behind her. Skips a stage in his evolution.) She picks up the blind boy, his bare feet kicking the piano keys as she hands him over to Charity.

Anything else, ma'm? Charity shifts her gaze. I best be getting these girls off.

Although the other tries to veil it she detects a bit of admiration in this event. More than a little. No doubt about it. Charity seems pleased by the look on her mistress's face.

One afternoon not long after, she hears music rising from the room and enters it expecting to see one of her daughters at the piano. (Any excuse to avoid their other studies.) Can't believe what she sees. What she hears. Before the moment can overwhelm her he hits another chord, tinkles out another melody. Hands flashing everywhere.

She sends for the mother, her other, who is not sure she sees things clearly. Eyeballs humming. Ears spinning. A feeling in her body, light, tilting over, all link lost to her surroundings. *Ah that's it. I've finally gone off the deep end. Jumped the plank.*

She sets out to retrieve him.

Little Thomas drops down to the floor and embraces a piano leg. A small target of conflict. Refusing to let go. She has to pry his hands away, finger by finger. Another time he actually crawls under the piano itself, slides and burrows into the cramped space between mahogany above and pine below. Stays a long time, calm and happy.

General Bethune stares at his oldest daughter indifferently, taking in her report. It is a disagreeable feature of her character that she always seems to enjoy revealing secrets in her possession. But he hears what she has to say, half believing, and dismisses her with instructions for Charity and Mingo to appear before him immediately. Not later, now. His daughter skips off in excitement. While he waits for them he tries to reassemble the essential facts from his daughter's garbled telling. This much he knows: if what she said is true, his wife hasn't told him about it. Why hasn't she told me? Not a question really, but a rumination, a reflection. How well he knows the sentimental attachments of the weaker sex.

While he is busy with one thing or another he will hear music drifting through the house. This is not listening, a conscious effort on his part, far from it, only the music's lurking presence following him from room to room. No way he will ever sit and watch the girls and the women—his wife, his daughters, his servant—and the boy at the piano, an act of spectating that is as much vulgar as it is awkward, like spying on someone engaged in an intimate act.

He gets to his feet with a certain effort before they enter the room. (Best to be on your feet in situations like this, assume a stance of authority and command.) On first sighting he fixes them with a ferocious glance before they can avert their eyes. *He means business. General Toon means business.* They come in cautiously, as if the house might collapse under their footsteps. Come before him slowly and quietly with heads bowed.

Suh, you wanna see us? The woman, Charity, saying it, not her husband.

He doesn't even bother to reply, to speak at all and ferret out their account, but waits for a lifting of their gaze before he casts his eyes first upon Charity then upon Mingo—he knows they can see him, even if they pretend not to—his look itself demanding a full and factual explanation.

If he wants to play, play he will. She will see to that. Any right-minded person should be ready to do the same, be willing to afford a pitiful soul this much. The crude but touching expression that bares his innocence and devotion. Little more than simple curiosity perhaps, explainable by some of Nature's extraordinary aberrations. What matter the source? The motive? (Could you call it that?) Let him play. Under her guidance. Not training exactly. (What would you call it?) She sees his face go bright. He is enjoying this immensely and she begins to enjoy it too.

At the piano he is strong and loose, no matter how awkward and ungainly he is at other times. Mary Bethune is quite careful in her instruction. Everything is shown in motion and in harmony. Whenever he plays a lesson correctly—well, truth to tell, he plays everything correctly; he shows himself capable of great technical variety; demonstrate a scale and he will play it; show him a melody and he will bounce it back, working the pedals as she worked them; she can only fault his playing for being excessive, too forceful; all that frantic passion (on one occasion he embraces her, laughing into her neck); then too there are times when he duplicates her exactly in volume and intonation, the original inflection—she rewards him with, Admirable! An odd calm completes each lesson, as if he is waiting for her to say the word. Admirable! She comes out of the room exhausted after she finishes her lessons with him, for she can never show him too much, his desire an insurmountable force, hands having made a hundred exertions, ready for a hundred more. Given an attentive pupil—no, that is not the word; given a faithful pupil, timing, and technique—his left hand may even be better than the right, the Negro's natural sense of rhythm—are easy enough to demonstrate, familiar ground under our feet. But the finer things—a definite feeling for order, a communicable clarity, an accurate sense of form, the lucky finds and the discovered refinements, the ascendance of beauty—are untranslatable, locked away in the farthest and darkest corner of the soul. No instructor or academy can teach that. And what can't be shown can't be mimicked. A long way of saying that these lessons are headed nowhere, are the proverbial dead end.

Nothing gained. For the Negro race can never produce a Mozart. The world has never known and will never know a Negro genius. Still she feels inclined to continue the lessons as she notes some change in his playing—she wouldn't exactly call it growth, development, more a polishing, the mastery of repetition until something shines—as each day he performs some little note or phrase that causes her to look at him with renewed interest and surprise. And when they are done for the day, he sits with his dark hands on the ivory keys, fingers spread wide, a settled pleasure.

So it goes. Then one day several months into their lessons, she rises from the piano at the close of a session, ready to summon Charity—*Take the boy and tidy up a bit*—when Tom's voice springs up. He is singing. What she sees and hears tells her that he is transplanting the foreign lyrics to the unrelated melody she just taught him. She knows the words to the song. He gets some of them right, some of them wrong. No. Something else. In fact, he is mixing the verses of three different songs her daughters are quite fond of singing away from the piano. Somehow the phrasing and timing are just right, perfect.

He bites into the pink skin of the boiled pig snout. Admirable! he shouts. He drains his glass of lemonade and places it back on the table. Admirable! He tastes his potatoes. Admirable! He gets up from the table and walks around the cabin touching things. Admirable!

Or this: Standing still, taking pleasure in the idle noises his shoes make. Steps can form whole words. But the words do not move his feet forward. In the shed a cow with a large belly standing as cows do, standing and staring stubbornly. He stretches out his arms to caress her muzzle, saliva collecting on his fingers, tongue lolling in its mouth. Admirable!

General Toon beckons her to sit. Her legs will not move at first, fearing they have misunderstood his command. He points at a chair. She sits down.

Your boy, General Toon says.

Thomas?

Her glance briefly meets his steady gaze. Her eyes fall.

Your boy, Thomas. *Grant her this.* Can you explain it?

Thomas knows what he has to do, suh, she says. He is smart, she thinks. He clacks a little, she says.

You call that clacking?

Here comes trouble, she thinks. Thomas is out to expose them. No, suh. Some of my other ones had it, she says. What she doesn't say: she even stammers herself sometime. Certain words drawled strangely. So she's been told.

You call that clacking?

Yes, suh. I mean, no, suh.

Little Thomas's body is renouncing speech while amplifying every other sound that enters him. Unusual—she will admit that.

Miss Toon wants answers, too—of course, Miss Toon also gives advice; she is anxious about Little Thomas—her interest and concern amounting to a challenge. But the questions don't annoy or anger Charity—they are decent enough questions—for the light in her mistress's eyes, the other woman's pure excitement, is enough consolation. Tom issued from her body. No denying it, no changing it.

But more and more in the days and weeks that follow her meeting with the Toons, Thomas deserts them to spend all his days in the mansion. *Tom, where you at?* They summon her again.

The culminating structure of the house, set in this landscape, a natural part of it, no other place it can or should be, rising white out of the ground like a mushroom. She stands wincing in the light. Takes a deep breath, fills her lungs. Call it a gathering of courage. She hesitates to go in. General Toon looks bad-tempered, the room otherwise cool and pleasant. Only an accident of timing has allowed her to get here now, late as it is.

No one to blame but herself if she is here standing before him yet again, if she hasn't already figured out a way to tell him once and for all what he wants to hear and in so telling put an end to the accusations. Not that she is eager to aid him. Of course, she has thought it over, she is prepared, armed with excuses, ready to count the hours and the days, sketch in what only exists for him for them in shadow outline. Easier said than done. Already her story starts to lose coherence.

He looks sourly at her. Instructs her to bring Tom to the house in the morning to begin daily obedience lessons. As well, he details a list of chores he expects the boy to perform. Starting tomorrow. Bright and early.

Sit, Tom. Good.
Stand, Tom. Good boy.
Be quiet, Tom. Quiet down now, Tom. No blubbering.
Good.

They are walking briskly now, a constitutional, under the elms at the edge of the garden. A walk seems to help settle him, make him easier to cope with for the day. Mary Bethune always takes the lead, with him behind her, though they take turns at varying the pace, a shifting distance. A hot day, and the air so still that it seems to absorb all sound of their footfalls. Then something changes. She isn't sure who first steps up the pace, only knows that she turns to see him following her as fast as he can, arms pumping, head bouncing, a charging bull. She picks up speed, and so does he, matching her pace. It is not unlike watching your shadow following you. And she will admit that this unsettles her. For she has reason to believe that the skin of another is no barrier against his advances. In fact, there are times when she swears—has seen it with her own eyes—that he assumes the *look* of other persons, their stances, their gestures, their posture, his face a mask of theirs, changing expression when theirs did, their bodies and identities like clothes he can hang on his person, a total embodiment. Where some see the presence of the supernatural in his feats of imitation, feel a foreboding, the first elements of some danger to come, she seeks a physical cause that will—she is sure of it—eventually reveal itself. (Although she is a believer in both the Man Above and the Man Below, she is not inclined toward either fundamentalism or superstition.) Granted, she will admit that his behavior on occasion unnerves her, but these occasions are rare. She is perfectly at ease around the boy and finds a certain comfort in his presence. They leave the shade of the trees, bright light now, sun in every step. Perhaps you don't need to see a thing to be it. (Can she help it if she thinks this?) After all, this boy is bonded to sound. There must be some way that his ears are able to register and measure the exact rhythm of her footfalls and his. An interesting notion, even moving in a way. She turns her head to look back at him and sees him take one step, two, before he also turns his head and looks back over his shoulder.

Steeple. Church. People. The congregation is in step with the church and the church is in step with time. After service ends the lead deacon comes out front to give poor farmers and such unlikely beings to understand that the pastor does not converse with ordinary mortals. They must put everything in writing—ask the impossible—and hand him a note the moment he leaves the church. He never leaves through the front but goes through the back. Where Negroes push and shove each other amid a hubbub of noise and gossip while they wait for the pastor to appear before them and lend an ear to their secrets and complaints and mouth opinions and advice, usually in the form of biblical scripture but sometimes in plain English if you are lucky. When he appears in the doorway, the world draws to a hush. Ritual perfection. He holds up the bottom of his black gown to avoid tripping over it as he comes down the stairs. One after the next they begin to pour out their sufferings. She hears him say to one man, But after all, who is your father? Moves on to the next person. She thinks she is going to faint, everything whirling around her. Does her best to breathe the air at calculated intervals. Deeply moved, he squeezes one woman's slender bony hands. As the solemn moment draws near she quiets her breathing. He puts a hand on her shoulder, leans forward some, and turns his ear toward her face to hear what she has to say. Saying done, he draws back and looks at her with a stern expression. You ought to be ashamed to ask me such a question. How is it possible for a mother to pray for the peace of a living soul? It's a great sin, I tell you, and it is forgiven only because of your ignorance. Your son is alive, is he not?

The Doctor has an inkling. Once, not many years ago, he successfully treated a three-year-old Negro for this same incurable and often terminal affliction. The boy had poked himself in the eye with a twig, what at first seemed a minor injury, a scratch, a doctor's poor diagnosis setting the stage for greater injury. A week later the eye became infected. After a second week the other eye became infected, both eyes causing the onset of brain fever. Then he was called in. Upon a careful review of the case, he decided to remove both eyes, and remove them he did and in so doing he not only saved the boy's life but also prevented any further physical and mental deterioration. A paper detailing the case had been published in a British medical journal.

Now he has the opportunity to study the effects of the illness in its later and perhaps even final stages. (This Bethune boy promises much. He senses it and trembles at the possibilities.) Does the fever seep down to the most profound layer of the mind, rooted, biding its time, never to rise again until the terminal moment? He can see another paper on the horizon. How he would love to deliver it in Paris, or at some other open and welcome gathering on the Continent, before the most distinguished men of his profession who are attuned to the latest advances in science and medicine. How slow the progress here. How thick the ignorance. A matter of endless frustration for him. So good to have an ally like James in the scientific cause. But he is as much struggling to comprehend James's uncharacteristic stealth—why had James kept silent about the boy, kept him hidden, and for all these many years?—as much as the strange case of this boy Tom. So unlike James to keep secrets from him. They are old friends, best friends perhaps, although he doesn't always agree with James's national and ethnological policies and prophecies.

He is moving briskly but not urgently, headed toward the Bethune mansion. Although he is preoccupied he makes it a point to tip his hat to all he meets, regardless of their position in life. He has yet to reach the height of his fame, but he has already developed something of a reputation as a man of science bent on ridding the men and women of their region, their country, of their faulty and dangerous notions and traditions. In particular, he sees no way of holding his tongue against the planter's wasteful practice of forcing expectant mothers to work in the fields down to the period of delivery. No way to prove it, but he is convinced that either maternal anxieties or industry itself cause crippling and irreversible effects on the brain of the unborn. Hence, a mentally weakened infant enters the world, fulfilling the prejudiced hypotheses about the Negro's limited intelligence. Indeed, he is convinced that the planters can do away with many of their numerous complaints against the Negroes if only they take it upon themselves to rear a better crop of workers.

Some of his beliefs rub his fellow citizens the wrong way, but his authority is too great for them to disregard his opinions.

How quickly he arrives at the mansion and how gracefully he steps down from his carriage without the assistance of his Negro driver. He arrives on the porch, out of breath, out of words. The Bethunes' Negress Charity opens the door, and he removes his hat and bows a little, lets his hat return and says a few casual words to her, the way one makes polite conversation, before she takes him in and shows him to the library, him on guard, observing and evaluating, beginning his inquiry as soon as he is one foot inside the mansion, looking for the signs.

She wonders if she should thank the General for bringing the Doctor. (The vague hope that the Doctor may reveal something useful.) That is, she wonders if she should feel thankful. Even if she decides that the General's action warrants her appreciation—she is only beginning to mull that over, hasn't had long to think about it, all so unexpected and sudden, in a rush of minutes—how can she voice the words? Not her place to. And even if it were, she doesn't think she could bring her tongue to do so.

No, it doesn't surprise him, for the Negro, like his Anglo-Saxon superior, is an imitative being. How wrong of them to sneer at any act of simulation, no matter how peculiar or extreme. Might imitation be proof of buried intelligence, the first stirrings of coherent function and knowledge that, when thought and deed come together in noble agreement, form the basis of culture? The question warrants further investigation.

His thoughts on medicine mingle with the voices of fellow doctors and surgeons he has reviewed the case with, all rank outsiders in matters of research. So easy for common eyes to refuse to see what they should see because they don't wish to see it, for common mouths to parrot the same reductive beliefs in the same old weighted language. *Freaks of nature. Oversights or accidents of God.* He longs to get the examination under way. He has never been so upset by waiting. The thought hardly out of his mind before he feels something shift around him. It takes him a moment to locate the subject, sitting still and quiet on the sofa, blending in. How had he missed the boy's entry? Might he have been here the whole time? As impossible as it seems, he senses that the boy had deliberately tried to catch his attention only moments earlier, for he sees a definite alertness in the face. (Later, he will recall having heard a noise—a cough or a clearing of the throat—a sound coming before the sight. This addition.) No doubt about it. The boy is listening and smelling.

That's when it hits him. *This is the boy.* The other's dark complexion glows before him, mingling with the light and odor of candles, body and face causing him to draw back as before a vision of rare life. What difficulties an artist would have in painting his portrait. His physical advancement, certain aspects of his appearance—the bulging forehead, his ample mouth and cheeks, the wide neck, his broad shoulders, the height and strength—evidence of the vital spirit within. In the struggle to survive his illness the strong thing within has stripped him of all unessential thoughts, hindrances to living. Confined as he is to his world of darkness, is he even capable of detecting the ailment present but hidden within his person? How difficult to get to the ordinary life behind a thing.

He can scarcely sit on his chair. The skin is not that different from any other he has touched. He runs his fingers across the ridge over the brow—a feature common to the African species—testing the strength of the skull. The eyelids are impossible to lift, dead weight, even against maximum force of the fingers. The ears show no sign of under- or overdevelopment. (Some wax inside.) Two rows of shining teeth—he has never seen such clean teeth on either Negro or Caucasian—well enameled and formed. The spine seems somewhat soft to the touch, like a plant's lacy skeleton. He lifts one arm by the wrist—he can both hear and feel the patient's breathing change. The lips move. Is it a strange wild smile or a silent conversation? He puts a hand on the knee and feels a softening then opens his bag and takes measurements with the latest instruments. Takes in his entire form and structure.

James enters the room, working his noisy canes, a smile spreading slowly over his goateed face. He holds back on reporting his findings, asks that the boy be removed from the room and the parents brought forth. A short time later, they appear before him—ah, so she was the Negress who had answered the door—heads bowed, hands cupped. Both before he begins and after he finishes interviewing them, he and James talk in low tones and try not to look at Charity and Mingo. (Those are their names. So James informs him.) He does not rush his questions. Had he fallen into some calamitous illness? Suh? A calamity? They look at one another. Yes, suh. Thomas did indeed suffer a serious injury in childhood. A fever? They look at one another. Was he weaned on a cow's tiddy? Did they bathe him in homegrown wine? (Both are practices he has observed firsthand.) Did he crave the thick taste of goat's milk? He awaits each answer, looking at them, openly evaluating. Their awkwardness causes him to feel embarrassed. (He considers himself a quiet champion of the Negro cause.) He can see plainly enough how hard it is for them to respond to his unusual inquiries and suggestions. His feelings of sympathy offset by a certain anger as he senses that they seem determined to keep the full facts from him. (How foolish his fellow white men to trust every word and smile and expression of glad thanks and plea of innocence or ignorance from their slaves.) If only they could understand that a full confession might aid him in a precise diagnosis and an effective course of treatment and possible remedy for their son.

Satisfied that he has elicited the best answers he will ever get, he dismisses the parents. He returns to his original place on the couch, while James remains standing, leaning forward over his canes. He drinks in all of James's concerns, matters more troubling for Mary, he suspects, than for James himself. Tom might wander into serious harm in a barn or under the wheels of a speeding carriage, stumble into a well, or come to accident by fire. He sits passively and digests the information. From James's lengthy report, it is clear that this matter has been troubling them for some time. (They already have enough trouble with their son Sharpe, who is constantly on the go, running here and there. Away. Always away. Cooking up reports for the newspaper. Brought him up the best they could, although he had been a handful and still is. Trouble spares none of us.)

The end of obedience is protection, James says.

How poorly his good friend understands that the dangers within are the ones he must fear most.

Would this have been the moment when Mary entered the room?

Dr. Hollister.

Still formal after all these years. Her hands spilling from the sleeves of her dress, pale against the cloth's dark shine. Her skin toneless, almost gray, the color of stone, a heavy contradiction given her slight figure. She still looks young if you catch her in the right light. (The wrong light now.) He recalls the one time he saw her with her hair down—what circumstance made that possible?—black strands falling freely to both sides of her face. The novelty of that sensation as she stands before him now hair fixed in place and dressed as he usually sees her in plain unassuming garments. Despite her noble stature and bearing she is not a vain woman; nor will she allow James to be carried away by exaggerated feelings of self-importance.

James, he says, why don't I have a look at your legs while I'm here? His offer is an excuse to push Mary out of the room. They all know it. She won't stay around and watch her husband with his trousers down around his ankles before a third party. No fool, she knows that the men want to be alone with the boy, and she will concede, as a woman of discretion and taste should.

Without a backward glance she reaches the door and goes out. James begins again, but he holds up his hand in a gesture of silence. I've seen this many times before, he says. My own person has treated many a case. You should have spared yourself any feared embarrassment. *Where had they kept the boy hidden these many years?* Why didn't you call me sooner?

James does not answer.

He drops a knowing smile. Don't vex yourself, James. He has already formulated some very precise ideas about the nature of Tom's improbable condition. Through research and meditation had sought out and outlined the etiology of a vicious disease and discovered that it is numbed here but not quelled completely, and that it still roams free in the jungles and deserts and savannas of Africa. If I were a man who had not been out in the world, he says, you would find yourself hard put for answers.

James looks at him, measuring the words. What can you tell me?

The organs learn to adapt themselves to an existence that at first sight would appear to be utterly impossible, he says. My own eyes have seen it. My own hands have examined it.

What? What have you seen?

Brain fever, a cruel malady that lasts for a cruel length of time: a lifetime. A debilitating sickness that began long ago, before the invention of medicine.

James stands and listens, eyes alive and searching.

I'm not talking about this religious foolishness that so many of our people spout from bench and pulpit. That black people are children of the devil and such nonsense.

No one here is questioning your knowledge or experience, James says.

I trust you would.

So we've said that.

Yes.

And you will tell me more?

Yes. It's a simple matter, really. Africa is the chief stronghold of the real Devil, those reactionary forces of Nature most hostile to the uprise of humanity.

Go on, James says. He will take it all standing. He refuses to sit down.

Here Beelzebub, King of the Flies, marshals his vermiform and arthropod hosts, insects, ticks, and nematode worms, which, more than on any other continent, convey to skin, veins, intestines, and spinal marrow of men and other vertebrates the microorganisms that cause deadly, disfiguring, or debilitating diseases, or themselves create the morbid condition of both the persecuted human being and lesser forms—beast, bird, reptile, frog, or fish. The inhabitants of this land have had a sheer fight for physical survival comparable with that found on no other great continent, and this must not be forgotten when we consider their history.

His good friend remains silent. Looks at him as if he hasn't understood a word of it. Or was it something else completely? Perhaps James gets nothing, accepts nothing except by instinct. Or maybe it is simply hard for him to define exactly what he wants, both what he had hoped or expected to hear and what results he expected.

I suppose that's more than you care to I know. I've laid out the pertinent *facts*.

Indeed you have.

James, we've known each other a long time. You trust me completely, just as I trust you. So why your delay in contacting me? If only you had called for me sooner. Much sooner. Years ago.

Years.

The best I can do is to provide you with a powder that might restore the use of his tongue. Otherwise he might lose his voice forever.

Once he is outside, he angles his hat on his head to let his hair breathe some. How different was the former age of healing. Jesus cured the blind with his own spittle. *In the beginning was the deed.* If only the methods of modern medicine were equally effective. Unfortunately, the body is holy no longer but a thing of Nature. Every day, knowledge of how to put the constitution in such a state that it will have no disease, or that it can recover from disease, takes a higher place. Thus, it is most annoying to have to deal with facts that cannot be completely or adequately grasped, and only right to expect a doctor to hate the things he cannot explain. Invisible and unknowable things.

Such are his musings and meditations, the line of inquiry and examination, as he leaves the house on approach to his carriage. His horse raises its face at the sound of his shoes on crunching gravel. Neighs and lifts one hoof then another, all four in turn. It is only then that a simple fact registers. He can't see me. The thought strikes him again. He can't see *us*.

Listen, Tom says. Rain fall and not a drop fall on me.
    But, Tom, your clothes are all wet.
    My clothes is all wet, but my skin is dry as can be. He lifts his arms outward from his body shoulder-high and cranes back his head like a bird in flight.

The thought of the lives and houses embedded in her skin. The stresses on head, legs, feet, and hands. Still, she holds together well after all these years. (The testimony of the mirror.) She awakens with all her past hardened into the blue of morning. Perhaps it is for this reason that her first activity of the day is to sit alone at the table, with her palms flat against the wood. She stares down and sees light breaking through between the fingers, light that is nailing her to this place, fixing her in the moment. She turns her hands over, palms up to the light, either a morning offering or a morning collection. Dues paid, debts settled. Let's be plain about it. Her head is full of so many pressing memories. While she is safely lost in one thing or another, in an instant and without provocation, all the dingy rooms and dusty cabins of her past pass through her mind. Friends long vanished, their words and prayers now hers, part of her. (Belonging. By one name or another she has always known him. *His silence is mine. His eyes, mine. His hands and feet, mine.*) How many times has she entered a new house and parted from it? (Count them.) A parting that lingers, no way (what way?) to transfer the bitterness. There is this: not a single day, not an hour passes that she does not tell herself, I have four left and four is better than nothing.
    Look, she says. I see three of you, and only two of us. Do what we ask. Keep Thomas outta the house.

Although the girls are caught between waking and sleep, they are quick to speak; their apologies seem already formed on their lips, calculated in advance.

There three of you, she says. Girls. She has long held the belief that the female sex are the most capable of managing the world. Three of you can keep him out of the house.

The girls raise a chorus of excuses.

I tried to.

He too fast.

I was doing my choirs.

She feels an irrepressible rage building up inside of her. Far from learning from their blunders the girls, her three daughters, continue to heap more errors on top of the existing ones. Little by little, they are destroying everything that she has been trying to build, this cooperating workforce—call it family—she and Mingo have both longed for all these years and have tried to nurture since their arrival here at Hundred Gates.

Take your brother out and bathe him.

The girls raise a chorus of refusal.

We did.

He won't stay in the water.

He bit my hand.

Do it every day, she says. You must. Can't you smell him? Smell him. Do it when you do it, she says. The girls are also creatures that hate water. And don't let your brother waste himself in the house.

He just went.

He always smell like that.

I can't smell.

Find a rag and clean it up. You help her. And, *you,* come and help me wash him.

They prepare the tub. Get his clothes off with minimal damage. He will not step into the water. She has to lift him into the air, and when she does, he spreads his arms wide, believing he can fly.

Although he is far larger than the tub, he steadies himself inside it, careful to remain completely still, water silent under him. She and her daughter wash him while making sideways glances at each other. Soap and water and dirt are easy enough to understand. Plain facts her girls can't deny or disown. But how can they know the tremendous effort required to build this union? A whole history lost to them. Unaware of the many who've come already. (Once again back in her mind. How much easier to roll through the day under a stray tumble of thoughts.) Can't recall the last time she counted all twenty on her fingers, one by one, a way of remembering their names. The sixteen she will recall although even in recollection she no longer speaks their names. *Gal, you've set a record. How many loaves can you bake in that there oven?* When was the last time? A ritual she used to often perform. Certain things she never speaks aloud—some days how painful it is simply to open her mouth—even to a husband, especially to a husband—Domingo. The silences, the distances. (How can she hear the void?) So much the eyes don't see when they examine another.

She imagined (defined) her history (theirs) as a single rush of air sweeping all their past days toward the Bethune mansion and their own cabin of logs hacked sloppily and fitted together in haphazard hurry. (They did not build it. Have built many others but not this one. The smell of the previous occupants, a thousand men and women, all that remains.) You are born where you are born, but a person's true soil is not the place of birth. You bide your time, you continue to make all the small improvements you can—more food, more clothing, less toil and torment—with quiet hopes for the future. But more than hoping and waiting. More a matter of scheming and planning—although you are at the mercy of chance—of figuring out a way to position yourself so that the next shuffle will land you a few inches higher than your present state, and knowing the right thing to say or do when you are so positioned for such a move. All of this contingent upon life lasting and things holding out, for how quickly the world can change in an hour.

How well she remembers that moment when Domingo first spoke to General Bethune, a man whom she (they) had no knowledge of, save the name she heard spoken only moments earlier—

Why yes, General Bethune. It's an honor, sir. Glad to have you with us today. I was just down at the printing office.

—as the trader began positioning them in a horizontal line before his buyers. The words trickled down her body with the sweat. At first she misunderstood the nature of the General's physical condition. She realized that he walked with a limp. No, that was not the word. (Even now she can't describe the moment properly.) He did a little wobble to throw one leg forward then the other, as if each weighed a ton.

A number of men began circling them at top speed, their wives remaining behind in their buggies and carriages. A constellation of white faces shooting past her eyes, orbiting this band of eight or nine niggers, of old-marrieds and their unsightly children, standing— some just barely—tattered in the wind, heads slumped, feet swollen, drowsy and cold in bright clean heat.

Sorry, the trader said. Wish I could be of service to you. These the last I got.

The trader was a tall husky man—a few inches taller and a few pounds heavier than the General—well into his thirties but who tried to mask his age behind a light youthful mustache and adolescent glasses. A loud man, no force in this world capable of shutting his mouth. She stood absorbing the noise and movement, every few seconds his announcements bouncing off her body. Already woozy from the long day's drive march to this clearing in the woods, she didn't have the strength to correct him when he got her name wrong. On the silent march here, their feet built a common language. Some started to come undone, some already undone even before her family joined the little band. She heard someone murmuring pleas to Jesus. And words whispered in consolation. But she was not caught up in this, prayer the last thing on her mind. What was happening before her now, around her, neither awed nor moved her, for it was more tremendous than religion or church. Days of blind faith and belief behind her. She was past the point of crying. Important to her to know that there were others who felt worse than she did.

She pondered these men swarming around her, something hungry and desperate in their speed. Some stopped to look and listen, getting the drift of the trader's pitch and seeing if their eyes could verify his words. Someone leaned forward hoping to catch a glimpse of the baby she held in her arms, mummified in blankets. She pulled the baby closer to her bosom. Still they came, a flurry of white hands (and feet), poking, prodding, tugging and testing, opening mouths and closing them.

Careful now, the trader said. You break it, you own it.

The details of contact. She watched in a spell, unable to speak even if she wanted to. Her voice would be too small.

No, ma'm. They are not rejects. What in God's earth would possess you to say such a thing?

This General Bethune did not rush, but moved slowly with a composed eagerness, his hands folded behind his back. From what she had overheard he made no attempt to conceal either his intelligence or his eloquence. (In the years to come she will see and hear both often.) *The essence of high breeding, of intelligence itself is to be perfectly natural under the most artificial circumstances.* And the trader chose to cling to this general's presence even as he argued and bargained with his other customers, engaging them in plenty of hassling and haggling, mostly for show. Who was this sprawling elastic creature so capable of being everywhere at the same time, his smile here but somehow also over there? The General seemed to resent the trader for some personal reason unknown to her, a man unworthy of sight, looking at him only casually and briefly, perhaps wanting to be done with the introductions and advertisements and ready for concrete terms, negotiations. She would be happy to be rid of him as well. Had known him only a day or two—depending on how you counted the hours, where you began—insufficient time to make a studied judgment, but she had come to the conclusion that he had crippling doubts, was unsure of himself.

Sir, Domingo said. Just that one word. It was the greatest thing anyone had ever said in the history of the world. She felt something leaping under her skin. His strength in these matters, turns of mind, made her want to join him. He was a smallish man, and she was a woman of average height, which made it possible for them to look each other face to face without any lifting or lowering of heads or adjustments of feet. They were both slight as well, and she liked to imagine them as two units conjoining to form one substantial body. People (a person) of few words, able to set the silence against each other's doubts.

Sir, Domingo said. He never called any white man master. Look at us standing here, he said. He held his palms out at his sides, like a Bible-mouth pausing midsermon to hook his congregation.

The trader gave Domingo a look expressing silent betrayal. He stuck his hands in his pockets, nothing better to do with them. But from the look in the General's eyes and the smile on his lips she could tell that he already knew what Domingo was asking. Seemed to expect it in fact. Had he not lingered before them? Had he not passed them by on several occasions only to return again? His gaze sliding over all of them—her, Mingo, the baby blanketed in her arms, their three girls, who stared hard at this funny-legged white man.

Then Domingo did the impossible. Took two steps forward. Sir, we been put out cause a white man couldn't keep up with his affairs.

She saw the trader's fisted pockets go heavy. The trader made some clever remark, trying to draw a laugh from the General, but the other man said nothing, acting like he hadn't heard. Sir, could I interest you—

No, the General said. He looked at the trader. Tell me about this.

They are foreclosures, the trader said.

From where?

Out by Thirty Wells. A little run-down habitat called Solitary.

Solitude?

Yes, I believe that's the name.

And what is the other name?

That would be a Johnson. Should I get the papers?

You mean Jones?

Yes.

A Wiley?

Yes, the trader said. A Wiley Jones. He had to say something.

Now how hard was that? the General asked.

Sir?

Then Domingo cut in. Sir, maybe I don't look it, but I'm two niggers in one. I can work like you ain't never befo seen a man or any two men work.

The trader pulled his hands from inside his pockets. The General seemed to take pleasure in his anger and discomfort. I can assure you, the trader said.

Is that something you wish to spend your time doing? the General asked.

This gave the trader reason to pause. Sir, I am deeply disturbed. I really need to get these off my hands. I'm getting wed in two days.

The General looked at him. That's pressing business. And here you are, he said. I commend you on your locomotion, with so much else before you.

I could be convinced to give it all up.

The General didn't look at him. How much for this bunch?

The trader worked some numbers.

That's not what I'm asking, the General said.

Sir, I'm deeply sorry if you misunderstood me. The trader started on his numbers again, like a drunk man who couldn't stop himself. Then he said, I'll even throw that uncle over there in at a five-dollar discount.

I don't need an uncle.

Okay. Perhaps—

What would I do with an uncle?

The trader said nothing.

Now, what am I asking?

I'm sure we can arrive at a fair sum, the trader said.

Or I could go rob the treasury.

And so it went. While the men worked figures, she and Mingo looked at one another, exchanging unspoken thoughts. They did not hold hands. They did not hug. They did not kiss.

It did not take long to finish the negotiations. The trader seemed satisfied, happy even. That is a price I can live with, he said. I'll throw in the blanket warmer for free. Eyeglasses glinting in the sun, he shook the General's hand in farewell. I'm forever in your debt, he said. You really learned me a thing or two about a bargain.

Despite his casual disposition, General Bethune took the discovery of Tom's talents with more than a grain of salt. Within a month of learning (seeing) what the toddler (crawler) could do, witnessing with his own eyes and ears, he instituted a new routine. At least once a week, he would instruct her to bundle Little Thomas up in a carry-all and bring him out to the carriage, where she would hand him up to the General's wife, already seated there. Then the driver would help the General take his place beside his wife, the toddler cooing in her arms, and she (they) would assume charge of Thomas, the couple partnered in some secret cause—never revealed to her, even now, though she has her suspicions—lasting from that moment until Miss Toon returned Thomas to her later that evening, comfortably asleep. She would stand at the gate and watch the carriage pull away, escape vision, leaving her to imagine, without forming detailed images—that would be too much—Miss Toon accompanying her husband to the printing office and aiding him in whatever activity transpired there. (Either openly or clandestinely, she never heard them discuss what went on.) An odd calm would set in. Indeed, if called to judgment, she would admit that she met these weekly separations with an uneasy mixture of fear and relief. For during this period of her life Thomas dominated and consumed all her mental energy even when he was not directly present. If nothing else, the weekly separation gave her, both physically and mentally (what could she do about it? Out of her hands, beyond her control), a safe and justifiable withdrawal from her son for that short spell of hours, during which, in matters of child rearing only the Bethune daughters, and her own, were left to her care. They were proud girls, arrogant, and bashful only among themselves. Twelve frenzied limbs that made daily chaos of the mansion.

The good thing, she always knew that Thomas would be returned to her that same evening. (She is not making excuses.) She understands that her separation from him was always temporary, could never be anything more (glad to have him with her, back where he belongs), and not something that she either wanted or willed. But suppose that she in fact secretly desired longer periods of separation, that she wished somehow to prolong the displacement? Could anyone blame her? Knowing as we do that in the course of normal activity, on those days when the transfer didn't occur, the Bethune girls and Thomas formed part of the weight of her day. She and Domingo would dress quickly at first light, bright and clear-headed to do their sweat-drenched work. Their paths would rarely if ever cross during the day. Her husband—tending to the acres of gardens and lawns, tending to the stable of horses, sharpening the axes and knives, varnishing the General's spare (backup) canes, blacking boots and shoes, drawing water, cutting wood, making repairs to or fixing up the house (every week, Miss Toon or Sharpe wanted one room or another completely altered), leading a cow to the shed and butchering it. *I feel like eating meat.* (It fell to her to knife chickens and the hogs and to shape the meat.) Then curing the leather. Hides hung up and drying like linen. Service the carriage and when called to, take it and drive on an errand to town or a neighbor or up-country. It often fell to Domingo to drive the General and his wife and bundled-up Thomas to the town hall, where he would wait outside with the carriage, while Thomas performed on the stage inside—an old piano, a rotting splintery thing, badly tuned—for some unidentified strangers Domingo had spied arriving in his carriage and entering the hall, always well-dressed travelers.

And herself: open out the curtains in every room of the mansion so light falls clean over and brightens objects (an array of familiar shapes) and skin, prepare the bathwater, prepare the stove, set the table, cook breakfast, clear the table and wash the dishes, polish the piano (rubbed shine), scrub and hang the laundry *(they will dry quickly in the sun)*, scrub the floors, prepare the stove, set the table, cook dinner, clean the table and wash the dishes, tend to the mistress, remove the bright laundry from the line *(they dried quickly in the sun)*, iron the next day's clothes, fold the clothes and put them into their proper drawers, prepare supper for the family, clear the table and wash the dishes, and see the family off—*Anything else, ma'm?*—to the evening, sometimes even to bed, tucking and kissing. Time finally to go to your cabin, barren of those things (possessions) most people surround themselves with, attachments to the past, sentimental items endowed with emotional richness. Your lopsided door resistant to shutting, especially on humid days. Feed your family. (Food makes you happy for a time.) Get your children off to sleep then settle into your small bed next to your husband. A man is some comfort. Then the steady rise and fall of his chest beside you, two nestled under the mess of blankets sharing sleep, his head heavy beside yours in the low space—their bed stunted, no right to rise far from the floor—a ripe full day coming to term followed by an appalling night—in the dark where do all the painful noises, sighs, and creaks come from?—to look forward to after the day's exertions. Wake at the line of light glowing up at the bottom of the misshapen door and dawn entering through cracks between the poorly fitted planks of the walls and floor. Rise, touching ground gently like a migratory bird landing after a long pauseless flight. One day just like the next. Come Sunday, you have to remind your body to keep to the bed. *Hey, fool, it's Sunday, the day God rested.* She and Mingo would drowse for as long as they chose, relegating the breakfast, laundry, dinner, and such, the usual maintenances of family, to her oldest daughter, she allowing Mingo to be the first to rise, her husband off to trap, hunt, or fish—cage, rifle, cane pole—always cleaning and cooking (supper) catch and kill himself.

So it was. When the Bethunes purchased a second girl, Antoinette, to assume her chores, while assigning her a new single duty—she was to accompany the General on his daily visits to the printing office and attend to whatever needs he had there—she welcomed the purchase and transfer of responsibility with a sort of silent celebration, as it brought a fundamental change to what had been a life of unvarying routine. Her time at the office freed her of constant responsibility for Little Thomas. (It was not a question of renunciation, of love, that permanent resident in her heart.) And it brought something else she might not have expected. It raised her in the eyes of others. At the office or in the street, woogies rich or poor greeted her as Miss Charity—some even slipped up and called her Miss Bethune—according her a position of respect, finding something admirable in her constant service to the General, her presence in his privileged company. And she had to admit that their acknowledgment made her feel favored and charmed, would encircle her in a bubble of light-headed pride that floated her through the next hours. The General often spent much of the day receiving visitors, prominent men, magnanimous men with loud voices who talked out their ideas and plans, devised plots and election schemes. He usually heard it all while seated behind his desk, one black cane unashamedly placed in full view along either side of the desk. He often seemed bored with it all, murmuring in irritation and making no attempt to disguise it. Men of lesser status called upon him too, an ant heap of travelers from all the regions round about, filling the office and rushing up to his desk, here to consult him, each one with his troubles. (White folks and their troubles.) General Toon seemed to take greater interest in these men, the desperate and needy, while she performed her duties—on call, standing off to the side or in a corner, observing, listening, or moving but keeping to the edges of the room as the men complained or conversed—feeling a measure of detachment from the matters at hand, her attention drifting along the factual edges, hearing but not really listening, seeing without really observing, other and apart from the General and his visitors but also miles and years removed from whatever might be happening back at Hundred Gates.

When can I get a look at that boy of yours? How come you stopped bringing him down to the office?

On occasion the General would send her down (belowdecks) to relay a message (an order) to the man in charge of the Negroes operating the big noisy machines, or upstairs (the nest) to one of the men cramped over a square of board with ink and pen, usually a notice to hire or fire. Quiet days too when it seemed he had no true reason to keep her around, no visitors calling upon him, nothing to do but sit reading a big book at his desk, rapidly flipping through the pages at times, she seated not far from him, in one of the chairs normally occupied by a guest. They took dinner at his favorite restaurant down the street, she waiting out back and eating her meal there while he stayed inside for as long as he wanted. (She could live with the waiting, although the food could have been better.)

This new life uneventful by comparison to the old one, so much so that she had to fight to keep Little Thomas in her thoughts. The one drawback, the office required her constant presence before the General and forced her to give up the one good thing labor at the mansion had rewarded her with: a few minutes of privacy thickening in the time it takes to drink a cup of coffee, big cup little spoon, or to slip undetected into an unoccupied room, the steadiest satisfaction of her day.

She whispers into his ear, Wait for me here.

He hears.

Cut that out. She squeezes his hand affectionately. Don't talk so loud.

He knows from experience that she will only be so long. So he stands and waits for her to return in the coolness of the shade, sunlight noisy around him. Heat transforms into hay under his feet. *Wait for me here.*

Despite the caution with which he advances—he has been learning to slow down, their soft voices aiding him in this—despite running a hesitant hand along the barn wall, not anticipating any obstacles, he sends a pail crashing to the floor. Hanging empty. But the cows hang full. He leans his head on her shoulder. He gently probes her udders— this is a word he does not know—with his fingers. Cows and trees have branches. He gets on all fours and crawls into the cave beneath the cow, the animal spreading her legs farther apart to facilitate him, his entire body fully under the belly now, letting the soft branches above trail along and across his face. He pulls and squeezes and sucks. In a low voice the cow encourages and supports him. *More.*

Milk spreads across the barnyard floor. *More.* He feels milk warm around his ankles. Hears it rising around him in the hall-filled barn.

Truth be told, General Bethune is neither the best nor the worst man to serve under. Many pluses in his favor. He maintains an unimpeachable position in the public mind, among his own kind, for his continuing service to country, his advocacy of their national cause, its voice both in print and at the platform, his flair for coming up with the right ideas in laymen's terms. Not just this—many think him a kind man, as he rarely speaks dark sentences to his wife, children, employees, or slaves. Rumors that it is enough for a man to express a desire and the General will take pity on him and help in whatever way he can. Has she not seen this herself? Perhaps this aspect of his personality, his shining and noble sentiments, feelings of generosity and altruism, might help her now. Knowing also—what is most important for her—he is a man from the outside who has neither understanding of nor affection for plantation life. But she must not feel tranquil standing before him as she is now. A white man—a master—has limits. Through experience she well knows that a good servant (nigger) must be able to cross both fire and water.

So when—yet again—the General confronted her about her little Thomas, she gave the answer she thought he wanted and waited for him to reply as she thought he would—he did—and dismiss her for the night. She started for her cabin, her bosom swollen and heavy. She remembers how her Little Thomas would nurse with unexpected pauses and interruptions, a herky-jerky rhythm. He would stop sucking every so often, quiet and still. Then it occurred to her—or it occurs to her now—that he was actually stopping to listen to the sounds of his nursing. And if she, Mingo, or one of the girls spoke or made any sound he would pull his lips from her breast altogether, leaving the uncomfortable impression that the family, her included, were intruding on his feeding.

By the time she entered the cabin she had recovered her outlook. Mingo was sitting on the bed, Little Thomas and the girls conspicuously absent. In his face she saw uneasiness and anticipation, but this time he did not ask her about the outcome. Her own nervousness and expectancy gave her a painful sensation in her chest. What if she were to tell him her feelings, namely, that she cannot think of any solution to gain time? How often noted the silent conversation between husband and wife, air itself projecting words that need no tongue to speak them. She was unable to acquaint her husband with the thoughts that had been passing through her mind for the last hour or more, so she sought to minister to his pleasures before the children returned.

With something of the feeling of the night before a decisive battle, she was unable to sleep. This night, and the next, and many upon many. She is part mother, part more.

Tell it fresh, she says to her oldest daughter. Not the same ole lies.

The three lined up before her, elbow to elbow, like links in a chain. The expressions the same, threatening and at the same time afraid. (Was the fear of one the fear of the other?) Was she being unfair? Her own eyes told her that only the voices of the Bethunes, master and mistress, for whatever reason seemed to give Thomas pause. She suspects that the girls are willing to engage in the lowest imaginable tactics to manage their brother, bring him under control. Then too the more painful thought, the possibility of vile means for vile intentions, anger, spite, and ill will pushing the girls to punish him for all of his trouble, transactions of skin—she has not spared the rod—repaying in kind all she has paid them. He is bruised, black areas in the skin. He draws back from her touch. He wiggles out of her arms when she tries to hug him, a frantic animal chewing off a limb to limp free of a trap. What punishment will suffice? Her daughters (or is Thomas to blame?) have suddenly returned her the thoughts, the feelings, and the black griefs, which from her earliest childhood she had permanently entrusted to her white owners.

She holds her most severe admonishments for her oldest daughter, whom she believes—she must believe something—is leading the other girls astray by the contagion of example.

The girl watches her, hard-eyed and defiant. *Don't know why they always blaming me.*

She gives her a bold and specific instruction. (What alternative does she have? Plans, chances, undertakings. Hard questions, harder choices.) Starting tomorrow, tether Thomas to a post or tree. She goes so far as to suggest a location. The order fails to surprise the girl.

Silently and with solemn slowness Mingo continues to eat his supper. Knife and spoon are instruments of wonder in his hands.

Which tree? her daughter asks.

In outrage Mingo allows the utensils to spill from his hands then pounds one fist on the table, the table splintering in the center, spreading an infectious silence, all in the room, all words, sound and language, caught in the web-like splinter. Startled too perhaps at this quiet man who rarely displays anger, who loses all of his powers of reasoning at the sight of violence. He gets up from the table and leaves the cabin.

She goes out to check on him, to comfort him. Finds him sitting in the grass a few feet from the tub. She takes the tub and flips it over to use the bottom as a stool. Facing one another across the night. The first thing she does is to take his hand gently in hers and check it for signs of injury. I should send for the Doctor to inspect you, she says.

Better you send fo God, Mingo says.

No appeasing him. What tone will first light assume?

The following day, she travels to the printing office with the General in customary fashion. Nothing different about this day except he doesn't speak a single word to her. Come evening, together they return to Hundred Gates, the General to his white mansion and she to her knotty cabin, and after she has finished feeding her family, the new girl, Antoinette, all speed and efficiency, shows up at her cabin door; she stretches out a hesitant hand and meets Charity's hand on the way; informs her that *the Bethune*—those exact words; what she always calls him, them—would have her up at the house.

She finds herself in a vast green drawing room. General Bethune speaks her name. Then he says something about his regrets at having to impose a better discipline. Instructs her to fix a pallet in the back pantry off the kitchen. Tom will live and sleep here from now on.

She stares directly into the face of her master.

I suppose my wife will have to look after him, he says. Count yourself lucky, he says. Note my generosity. What might another man, a lesser man, have done in this circumstance? Always remember that. And be thankful.

What a wild state he is in. Clattering, hissing, whistling, blowing off gauge cocks. Fire up the engine! Ringing his bell, thundering over bridges, whooping through tunnels. Fire up the engine! What muscles and what wind, dreadful hour after hour. Heavens, she thinks, will his devil never run his viewless express off the track and give her a rest? Fire up the engine!

Tom chases his own voice about the room from one corner to the next:

> *Tell him to come up*
>> *I'll do your Topley*
> *I met my mother in the morning*
>> *Poor thing*
>> *There there there*
>
> *Now comes the tutti*
>> *Don't be in a hurry*
> *Poor thing*
>> *You hurt your Topley last night*
> *There there there*
>
> *Now he has gone up*
>> *Into his mansion*
> *Poor thing*
> *Don't be uneasy*
>> *Until I see you*

Tom bites into the hard green apple. (Whale of an appetite.) The cold sweet grain against the roof of his mouth. Seeds perhaps. The shape of words enter and play at making sense. Leaves hover on the verge of speaking. Clutching at the air. Words rise to sky with the chickens but drop back to earth after a brief flight. Worms whisper marvelous things into his fingers and feet. And when others speak he can taste their language and thoughts in his mouth.

She taps the backs of his hands, just hard enough to hurt. No, Tom. Don't put that in your mouth.

No, Tom. A horse is not a big mouse.

Tom, don't eat standing up like a cow.

This is food, Tom. Feel its heat enter your teeth.

This is water, Tom. Feel the cool on your tongue. Note how it gives way like nothing else. And this is a flower. Put your nose right here and smell. Each color also has a smell. Both scent and touch allow us to distinguish one color from another.

He repeats what she says, word for word. Tries it again, doing her voice a little longer.

Tom punches the keys, pinches her awake.

Miss Antoinette, he says. Who your pappy? He lets out a little scream of delight. Miss Antoinette, who your pappy?

Tom makes a motion of swatting at the keys, as if warding off a swarm of flies. His arms are too short to span the entire ivory length, eighty-eight in all. (Proportions at work.) So he rocks from side to side on the stool to reach them. Music so foreign to the figure of the boy.

Tom is a delight. A happy rumble. A welcome change of pace from her previous students. Rarely has she had one worthy of her efforts. Most of the parents refuse to invest in a piano at home, and when they do, it is something secondhand and second-rate. Might she make a diligent effort to drum up a better breed of trainees, because taking up with the inhabitants of their town doesn't bear thinking about. She is in no mood to waste any more time at the pretense of instruction. Tom is a solid way to pass the time, seconds, hours, and minutes otherwise impoverished. Either in the town itself or on her estate how few entertainments or distractions. How similar it all seems after a while. A series of laboriously linked actions. Many affinities here. A sameness intensified by this uniform landscape and climate. No change in the weather really, no turning of the seasons, just an easing off of sun and heat twice each year, like the lowering and dimming of a lamp. (The female sex are said to be more tolerant and resistant.) And how deep the dark gets. The dim liquid lights of the lamps no match. How seldom have they gone on holiday in their many years of marriage. Such are the drawbacks of lifelong attachment to a man of importance, a Race man. And how seldom to spend sundry affairs with the man you love when he is rarely at the house, busy days and some nights, taken up with the dealings of his newspaper and politics. (Is she right in bemoaning her fate? After all she lives in a free city.) People's real home is where they lay their head. She prefers Culture, and for this reason she prefers big cities, the bigger the better. They live in a town offering a poor impersonation of a city, empty miles stretching left and right. She would love to relocate to New Orleans—she has expressed this to James one or twice—Charlotte, or Atlanta, but preferably somewhere up North. (Blasphemy! If James knew. She dare not confide in him, although he wants it too.) True, age brings the advantage of history, insight, and wisdom, but also the disadvantage of the exhaustion of experience. The mind is locked in the fortress of the skull as the soul is forced to join the congregation known as the temple of the body. And the tired mind, tired soul, requires a new stimulation.

Her pupils have repented. They are urging her to return, to take up their guidance and instruction again. They have drawn up a letter and taken the trouble of direct and immediate delivery through the quick medium of a servant's hand, having subscribed themselves on the best paper in the best ink. The missive assures her that they need her, that they are lost without her. They swear to listen. They swear to obey. They swear to practice. They swear hard work and deep sweat. They will look lovingly at sheets of sound during all of their free hours. But Tom is her judgment, the solid basis of all her hopes. It is not the miracle that makes a realist turn to religion. A true realist, if he is an unbeliever, will always find the strength and the ability to believe in a miracle, and, faced with a miracle as an undeniable fact, he will sooner disbelieve his own senses than admit the fact.

After the rain, the air is rinsed clean, the light precise, every line and edge firmly in sight, the farthest distance diminished, as near as your hand, lands across the oceans captured in a single glance.

The wood is dry. Who will saw it?

Tom.

The fireplace crackles and smokes. Smoke whistles and sings, rising its way through the chimney and out into the world where the pines run. Tom's arms rush forward at acute angles.

What is that you are playing?

The fire sounds like loud kisses.

I am playing the rain, he says.

She takes several clean sheets of paper with staffs already printed on them. Tom has already moved on to another piece, one she recognizes.

Tom, would you play it for me? she asks.

Tom does not answer.

Play the rain for me, she says.

He switches melodies without interruption. Once he finishes it, she has him repeat it, and once more after that, five times in all until she has completely scored the composition. At the top of the sheet where the first bars begin she writes "The Rain Storm."

James, look at this. She holds the pages of sheet music before his face. Good God. The woman has lost her mind. Trying to get him to read music was like trying to teach Sanskrit to a Choctaw.

Mary—

He wrote it, she says.

He looks at her distrustfully. Mary, now this too. He actually stands up, bad legs and all. What are you trying to tell me? Have me believe only so much.

No, James, she says. He *wrote* it.

Sound lending sense.

His first composition. (Could you call it that?)

She sits with her husband. We should have it published, she says.

He does not answer her right away, a good sign. Whenever she outlines some idea that he doesn't agree with, he interrupts her before she fully lays it out. But if he agrees he keeps quiet until she concludes, then closes his eyes as if searching his dark places only to discover that the words she had spoken were the same ones he had already formulated himself.

Nothing of that now. He gives her an odd look, one she has never seen before. Why? he asks. Suspicion in his look, watching her like a potential thief.

The following day he purchases an upright piano for his printing office.

Would you use the word *composer?*

Let us consider the possibilities.

Though she would not be so bold as to describe herself as a technician, let alone an expert—an artist? not even; never that word for herself, something shameful even in pronouncing it—she has known music all of her life and considers herself well versed on the subject, both in mind and in heart. Understands a thing or two about the complex and complicated (murky) process of inspiration and composition. Start here: all sounds are not the same in value even if they share external similarities. So much in what lies behind the utterance, the hidden life, and we must seek to recognize and identify this spirit, learn to distinguish one motion from another lest we confuse conscious intention with simplistic assertion (reaction). Would we accord the same musical weight to a nursery rhyme as to a sonata?

Countrymen and foreigners alike have noted the Negro's special gift for song. Melodies snap through their blood. Rhythms wholly specific to their skin ambulate their breath and limbs, animating their bodies in a perpetual eye-exhausting frenzy. These are facts we all agree on. But how little or how much does this really tell us? And how useful, she wonders, is it in helping us to understand this peculiar boy Tom, a full-blooded member of his race and also its singular contradiction? Tom's playing and preferences pose the most urgent questions. Granted, he has God-given and blood-driven talent. No lesson he can't master—she takes some credit for his achievements; she is a teacher, a director, fine at what she does—even when she applies the most advanced pedagogic methods. Surprised at the occasional error in his playing or singing. Has come to expect a flawless response; he seems to know what you want and gladly provides it. But can he do anything other than parrot what she does? Can any Negro be more than a parrot? True genius creates. A recital is more than a reproduction. The player must animate the preexisting piece with his own breath and in so doing put the idiosyncratic self on display, in all its glory but without hiding any of its imperfections. She has yet to witness—what she has been waiting for—the unexpected in Tom's playing, that something more that would tell her that Tom is doubly conscious. For no mind can engender until it is divided into two. (She has given some thought to this matter.) Creation in either composing or playing involves the vital interaction between opposing forces to bring forth an even more vital third.

Knowing thus, she concludes that Tom is fully of a piece with his race. Shut eyes and bulging forehead, he lacks the needed spirit. (He does not have the spirit. He does not have spirit.) Yes, his details are exact, his description is accurate, but his interpretation and conclusions are random. Where is the conscious breath? (Easy to let your lungs operate on their own, under the unconscious rhythms of habit.) He plays others, never himself. What we have to consider, Tom does not survey the world with the eyes of an explorer, adventurer, or builder. No. He never stirs from the field of the possible, however much he might like to enlarge it. (Assuming that he possesses such a lofty desire. Assuming much.) Should not a song disturb the ear, the senses, even as it pleases? Deformations are not foreign to a composer. In Tom's case the only thing disturbed is a certain order of whatever is already possible. If he has complex (divided) emotions, are they not entities he can neither locate nor name?

The name is a crucial point of entry. So much in the heading, the title of the composition, where a few words or numerals can convey an entire story. And the lack of a proper heading closes down the melody and brings a corresponding absence of involvement in the listener. Disregard at your own risk. *I am playing the rain.* On first hearing Tom you seem to detect the richness, the precision, and the balance of high classical manner, accomplished through an agreeable variety of techniques. Upon closer examination—have another listen; listen—you realize that a song, or composition (your call), is for Tom a mere means like any other. You hear the presence of imitation not far behind what at first strikes the ear as an original melody, the distillation of one or two eternal truths. The mundane veiled in a flourishing of riffs and rhythms. (After all, he is only a boy, only a nigger. And he suffers a malady, one or more.)

Art is expression, and for lowly forms expression is an impossible act. Would a sow show its love for mud and oats by means of a grunt, or a cow moo in appreciation of cud and grass?

His head sways on his shoulders, as if he has a hard time controlling it, is barely able to keep it upright.

An idiot and a nigger—lord have mercy—Tom is doubly short of self. (Perhaps triply short. She had not counted his blindness.) Though he cannot see and he hardly (rarely) speaks—or communicates at all for that matter; often he just sits or stands, doing nothing in particular, other than smiling or baring his teeth—his manner at the piano, his ambience, his bubbling over with happiness, suggests that his primary reason for playing is to please the family, especially the female sex, her and her daughters, and his mother and his sisters. But true expression is independent of occasion.

It seems impossible that he should ever do anything different from that which the best have done already. (The speed an accuracy of her reasoning. How logical she can be.) Would it not be impertinent to suggest that he wishes to? Can he wish, aspire, set goals? Other than in the bodily longing of a chicken desiring feed, a bird desiring a worm, a duck drawn to a pond? Other than in the set demands of Nature, essentials, such as the changing of the seasons or the earth's need for rain?

The evening is drawing in, the dim lamps seeming to gain strength.

Your colors sing, Tom says.

You can imagine her surprise when Dr. Hollister, after yet another examination—they have not digested his previous few visits, let alone got him out of their system completely—tells them that Tom can actually see large bright objects held up right before his eyes.

All would like to believe they have saved Tom from serious harm or irrevocable death more than once. Belief along the lines of a confession, as in, *I bit off more than I can chew,* as the saying goes. Count him among these confessors. Granted, Tom is enough to break down the courage and resolve of even those well accustomed to the Negro's frequent aggressions and outrages. (Imagine the dangerous consequences of all this seeing its way into print—a comic front-page headline: *A Scentoriferous Fight with a Blind Musical Nigger. See p. 18. Containing Adventures, Melodies and Scrapes.*) So what should one do now, install him in his room (pantry) for all eternity? Or leave him to his own devices, come what may?

This is what I've been saying, his wife says.

Let him, he says. The dim light from the lamp outlines his bent shoulders and twisted legs. I've never met or seen a nigger who can't get himself out of something he got himself into.

From then on she starts to leave Tom alone at the piano for hours at a time. Days and days of this. But what of those moments when no music comes? What does he do with himself? She can only assume.

Say what you want, his wanderings establish a routine, this element of habit that develops a muscular sense of place. He knows the land, this space called Hundred Gates. Breathes its air and absorbs its sun. Not that all of those invisible and silent hours are taken up with wandering. She learns as much when a neighbor, some planter, calls to inquire about their blind nigger. Only then does she discover that her daughters have been spending much of their free time secretly presenting Tom for impromptu performances for a handful of their neighbors, have been transporting him by foot to their parlors—ones with pianos—to demonstrate his peculiar talents. Of course, she is shocked, and the revelation causes her to question the why, what the girls stand to gain from these activities, holding out the possibility that they gain nothing at all, pride motivating them perhaps, vanity—showing off their possession—or some lesser transgression, such as pure childish indulgence. More than a bit of planning in all of this, for the next day, even before she has a chance to confront the girls, she unearths a new fact: her daughters—the oldest is behind it; she is sure of that much, proof not long in coming—had actually begun sending written notes, crude advertisements, to the other farms through the hands of the nigger girl, Antoinette—such insubordination; now they will need to purchase a new girl at the first opportunity; tell James—discovers this when she intercepts Antoinette, message in hand. But it doesn't end there. She is even more surprised to see how the note expounds glowingly upon Tom's abilities but also how it praises him far too lavishly, speaks of him in an almost reverent tone, like a superior being. *His mouth speaketh great swelling words. His hands bringeth forth great swelling sounds.* Her oldest had penned it, no doubt there: her language, her syntax, her wonderment, her high-sounding romanticism. She will outdo them. She will present Tom to the world.

With a roll of wheels and the tramp of horses' hooves, the guests arrive. Some stand looking wide-eyed at their surroundings, as if they have never seen a mansion before, while she stands outside the main door, evening air cooling her face, observing them. All smiles and courtesy she welcomes them into the house, and each guest greets her accordingly. *How are you this evening, Miss Charity?* Once they are comfortably inside the music room—the General receives them warmly, shakes hands, even mock salutes—she and Antoinette work diligently to bring out the prized vessels and begin serving the guests refreshments. Many of them have brought along their slaves, musical instruments attached. They strike up a tune. And the men turn jubilant, sharing circumstances, anecdotes, and memories as they share the smoke and embers of their cigarettes and pipes. The harsh sounds of their niggers' banjos and violins like so much distant backdrop, commanding about as much recognition and concern as a mosquito's irritable buzz. They inquire about Sharpe, who is never in attendance at these gatherings, his time consumed in speculative affairs on the General's behalf. (So the General says; *for all of us.*)

The General's parties are not exclusive to men. Sometimes wives accompany their husbands, all joining in conversation, the women taking dainty sips of water (no spirits) while the men imbibe brandy and whiskey. (Best savored in moderation.) But the men always find a reason to leave their wives and wander out to the garden—how well one breathes out there, she thinks while she remains inside to attend on the wives, fully hearing their chatter or demands (requests) but also half listening to the men, the private cadence of voices outside, the pungent trail of tobacco in the air, smoke trailing their gestures and words—each man buoyant when he returns to the room, as if he has just delivered the punch line of a joke. Antoinette goes out to the garden and sweeps up the ashes.

On one occasion, the boy Bible-mouth, H. D. Frye, came with his wife, who, for whatever reason, was the only white woman present besides Mrs. Bethune. Frye by some accounts was no older than fourteen—no telling, he keeps quiet on the subject—the wife twelve. Sharpe had discovered the boy, an itinerant or circuit rider—unclear the distinction—during his many travels, and after much discussion, convinced him to come back to their town and take over the church the Bethunes attended, as the cholera had recently put their pastor under the earth (en route to heaven). He dressed the same at the pulpit and in the street, assuming a single garment, a black robe fitted at the waist that flared out at the ankles like a woman's dress. He was rather tall, fresh-complexioned, with prominent cheekbones and clever observant eyes. Despite his youth his face wore an expression of absolute reverence, the skin reddish, burning with faith. He was thoughtful and seemingly abstracted. She never understood a word he said either from the pulpit or from the floor. *Providence moves through time as the Gods of Homer through space.* She suspected that his congregation was as much impressed by his impenetrable sermons as by his prodigious memory. Name any verse—Isaiah 2, verse 4— from the Good Book (of Trial, Affliction, Punishment, and Eventual Redemption) and he could recite it word for word. Even more, he could rearrange the words in any order you requested and seemed to take pleasure in delighting children and niggers alike by reciting verses backward, forward, upside down, and sideways.

He was otherwise a quiet boy, never talkative, saving his words for the pulpit. (The entire evening she never saw him once speak to his wife, equally quiet as her husband, the plain-faced girl speaking as much with her hands as her mouth.) With the exception of the General, all in the room seemed both highly impressed and highly honored by his presence. The visitors rose from their seats and greeted him with a bow. He did not bow in return, or greet them at all. No words or bodily contact, only a gesture resembling a slight forward tilting of the head, barely discernible. With a show of feeling, Miss

Toon went up to him and kissed his hand. But he only returned her a blankness of face suggesting that the kiss had never happened, a moment now excised from time, which caused her to doubt the doings of her own lips. She quietly disappeared from the room. Without pomp or ritual the General touched the boy between the shoulder blades as if he were any other youth. Maybe this was the way he had once touched his own son, Sharpe. (She thinks she recalls such scenes. Even forms a picture. But wasn't Sharpe already a man upon her arrival at Hundred Gates? Possibly. So whatever it is she sees now must have occurred before her arrival. No other way.) The two had come to know and like each other—only Dr. Hollister commanded equal time, attention, and respect from the General—and almost daily he would show up at the printing office for some coffee or cakes, the General fondly observing the boy while he ate. She also remembered how the boy cried out behind the church after he had preached his first sermon—power in his words, eyes glowing with administrative fire—a show of emotion that required a strategic response from General Toon, who went over and began patting the boy on the back, solemnly confirming him in his new function.

Just as things began to settle down and as the visitors were managing to elicit a few curt and reluctant sentences about church matters from the Bible-mouth, Miss Toon returned to the room, leading Thomas by the hand. Charity was as surprised as anyone to see him, and almost didn't recognize him. How much he had grown since she had last seen him several months ago and how well they had outfitted him in a little black suit. Miss Toon released his hand and faced the assembled. Where he stood Thomas was full of agitation, turning his head up and down, this way and that, his hands and arms and torso twisting about, like a wet dog shaking dry. Miss Toon made her announcement then concluded by asking them to take a seat and maintain silence during the performance.

The guests were clearly disenchanted at first, casting a glance over the wild nigger boy who would supposedly be entertaining them at the piano. In their faces they made no attempt to disguise their true feelings of disgust for the nigger. Some even trembled, fearful. The boy Bible-mouth stepped back in revulsion. They looked at General Bethune as if they were questioning his sanity—he was indifferent as always—for what man in his right mind would bring before them a wild untamed animal and even worse, a creature who was apparently feverish, rabid?

Undisturbed by their reaction Mary Bethune ushered Thomas over to the piano, where he sat down on the stool, positioned his hands above the keys, and moved his head around him with some curiosity.

That's when the men broke out in a chorus of laughter. (All but the Bible-mouth and his wife, two silent peas in a pod.) James, you are a prankster. Hands down the best. You have it in you after all? Whoever heard of a nigger playing the piano? Where's his violin? Someone please fetch his banjo. His spectacles. But they all saw that General Bethune (their James) was indeed serious. One and all, they seated themselves as Mary Bethune with great formality of voice instructed Tom to begin his recital.

Thomas teased out the opening notes, the men by turns startled or impressed—read their faces, record their gestures—at Tom's performance, not wanting to believe but enjoying it all the same. (And Charity watching and listening, but feeling nothing.) Not surprisingly, the Bible-mouth and his wife sat in solemn gratitude. By the end of his recital, the last crescendo of chords, their eyes and ears had grown accustomed to Tom's primitive condition, responding with smiles and laughter to his strange movements and gestures. Basking in the high revel of event, they all wanted to touch the nigger—and touch they did, the men almost fighting one another to get a sufficient number of feels and caresses—their previous discomfort dispelled, all acting and behaving as though they had known nothing else, at ease with this nigger like all the others they had known. The only holdout was the one planter among the group—how rare it is for General Bethune to even allow a planter in his house; but it was necessity, duty, a way of both keeping the peace and preparing for longed-for war—who deliberately did not change his expression to show his sophistication.

Brethren, the boy Bible-mouth said, it disappoints me that you find mirth in this remarkable display of the glories of the Almighty's unchanging hand.

One man spoke up. You said it, Pastor Frye. It's monstrous kind of our almighty father to send such likely niggers for our convenience and pleasure.

You should learn from this gift, the Bible-mouth said.

The men in the room eyed him one and all then gave each other slanted looks. *Did I hear correctly? What did he say? Does he mean it?*

Hold back on your words. Who among you can laugh and be elevated at the same time? The Bible-mouth looked at each man in turn. Do you question the Almighty's handiwork? For it is He alone who directly assigns to each nationality its definite task on earth and inspires it with a definite spirit in order to glorify Himself through each one in a peculiar manner. Every nation is destined through its designated organization and its place in the world to represent a certain side of the divine image.

He's starting early, Charity said to herself. Can't wait til Sunday.

The whole of mankind is a vast representation of the Deity. As the good book says, Behold, I have engraved you on the palms of my hands.

Frye's wife had pushed to the front of her seat in excitement, as if she were seeking a moment to applaud.

Therefore we cannot extinguish any race either by conflict or amalgamation without serious responsibility.

Charity thought she heard someone whisper, Save it for Sunday.

The merciful aspect of the Almighty's economy shines out in history as clearly as His justice and judgment. Who among you is chosen? Who among you is free?—for as every man here knows, submission to the Almighty turns out to be the only true freedom.

General Bethune squeezed the boy's shoulder. No harm done,

he said. He smiled at the boy and turned his inclusive face to the men before him. These intelligent gentlemen are kindred spirits, he said. How often have I had to relay to them these very same sentiments.

Sentiments are not facts, the Bible-mouth said.

Okay, General Bethune said. Facts.

I am prepared to believe you, another guest said, at least in principle.

On the contrary, the planter said.

He's the preacher.

I admit to minor moral stagnation.

Do you not have greater sins to acknowledge? the boy asked. Yes? Then admit to more. My aim is to win you over.

The men looked perplexed, at a loss for answers. General Bethune rushed to save them. So this means you enjoyed the performance?

A blessing, the boy said.

Indeed.

Very much.

What a find.

No, the Bible-mouth said. General—he always called General Bethune "General"—do you not feel some sabbatical obligation?

Sabbatical? one of the men said.

It means Sunday, someone else said.

I know that.

Yes, Sunday. I do not mean to confuse. I am here to humbly serve all of you. General, unbeknownst to your person, you find yourself in the honorable position of holding the power to save our Sabbath.

General Bethune just looked at him.

Would you assign this boy to play in our service this Sunday? As you are well aware our pianist is abhorrence.

General Bethune looked at his wife. I don't see what would prevent it, he said. You but ask.

I ask. Your boy would be a welcome respite. God willing.

For a single Sunday? Mary Bethune asked.

We might first begin with a Sunday service, then try another Sunday, and another, and by and by through the Sundays, for a long-standing tenure could not possibly exceed our needs. Not to exclude the nonsabbatical services during the week. At present these services present us with less need for musical accompaniment. This Sunday would be the trial for all else. The Almighty will see to it as He sees fit.

Thomas began fussing with his clothes. Mary Bethune went into action to quiet him down. His animation disappeared as quickly and as suddenly as it had appeared.

It would be an interesting experiment, General Bethune said.

Hardly, the Bible-mouth said. Our dilemma surely is real and constant. The boy is chosen.

Tom don't play no Sunday school music, Thomas said.

His affront registered on every face in the room, although no one voiced complaint.

Party over, guests gone—Charity goes so far as to kiss Antoinette on the cheek in farewell—she returns to her cabin surprised to discover that the three girls are still awake, fresh-faced and happily seated in a circle on the splintery floor where Mingo is indulging and tantalizing them with some sleight of hand involving forks and spoons. She offers her family a brief and censored report about the party, gone from her whatever element of detachment she felt earlier during the actual event, images developing clearly and cleanly now in her mind as she retells it and as she concludes with an emphatic paraphrasing of the boy-mouth's request-offer. (Does she pass on Thomas's demurral?) Only to herself, inside her own skull, does she sing the old melodies, religious or secular, she learned on other farms.

O massa take that bran new coat and hang it on the wall
Darky take that same ole coat and wear it to the ball

Has she not caught her girls, at work and in play, singing the tunes? Songs Thomas has never known in their isolation, their withdrawal from the world of the plantations at Hundred Gates.

One of her daughters asks, Is that preacher a man?

He ain't no preacher. He a Bible-mouth.
Same thing.
No.
Like water and rain.
Mud and dirt.
No.
Tell her, Mamma.
Tell her, Daddy.
It's the same thing, she says.
See. I told you.
That ain't what you said.
Did too.
Did not.
Is he really a preacher? her oldest daughter asks.
Yes, she says.
See.
But he my age. He a boy.
Yes.
Where his mamma?
He ain't got no mamma, cept God.
Can I go over to his house sometime?
Why?
So we can play.
He don't play.
How you know?
Cause I know.
What, he ain't got no toys?
He don't play with toys.
And he white, another daughter adds.
That's not the play he means, she says. He wants Thomas to play
the piano and sing in the church.
I wanna sing too.
Me too.

You can't sing.

This gets them singing.

I can see the coming—

—of the glory—

—of the lord. Hallelujah.

Amen.

Glory be.

She bustles the girls off to bed, where they go gently into good sleep with a few final words.

People don't dance no more.

All they do is this.

And this.

She lay down beside her husband, her mind astir with her daughters' chatter, with Thomas's sudden appearance and her family's lack of interest in it, and with the boy-mouth's show of interest and his offer. She thinks about his church.

The Bethunes and other prominent people of the city take up the first rows of pews, an empty row separating them from ladies and their daughters dressed in white cotton sunbonnets and long-sleeved dresses and their crude husbands and sons outfitted in coarse cloths and unraveling ties—their Sunday best, meaning some clothing other than their tattered work garments—hair and clothing glistening with fish grease. Niggers take up the last rows of pews if any are left—the small church has yet to construct a balcony for them—otherwise congregating about the open door outside, some leaning in to look, slipping in their Amens and Hallelujahs, humming responses between verses, and joining in on the hymns, these activities competing with, made all the more difficult given the discomforts of the sounds and the smells of the poor farmers' bony mules and skinny horses hitched to run-down buggies and wagons. (The better grade of horses and carriages are afforded a lot behind the church.)

I can't say I see nothing wrong wit it, Mingo says.

She turns her head and stares at him in the dark.

The thing you spend your time at is what you are, he says. A hewer of wood is a hewer of wood, even if he spends all day fancying he's some big-timer driving a carriage.

He continues to whisper to her. A man can spend all his day fancying he's laid up in bed with the queen of England while lil Sally is the only flesh he knows. You are what you live. Mighty fact, I can't see not a damn thing wrong wit it.

She is left to think. Yes, she wants to say, but will this be the last? How many Sundays? Thomas is chosen. The boy-mouth said that Thomas had been chosen. God had handpicked him. Like walking down a dark road, then somebody up and clobber you over the head. Chosen like that. How come nobody had chosen her?

A rapid gust of wind. Tom alone in the river tangled with fish, color washing across him. His mouth jumps and every few seconds his nostrils flare, breathing words and breeding air. How it is. See Tom leaning away. He scarcely disturbs the water.

Certain things even God can't repair. In hindsight, looking back to piece it all together, Charity will recall it this way. The image of Mrs. Bethune piled up on pillows in her bed, her bloodshot eyes glowing in the hollows of her withered face, Mrs. Bethune upset to the point of sickness over her husband's decision regarding Thomas. Go only so far, as Dr. Hollister has forbidden all to enter the bedroom, although no one can keep out Sharpe, who arrives from overseas even as others are trying to escape, hurrying along in poor light, cloaks wrapped around them, shifting shadows who seem to be whispering in foreign languages, even as General Bethune implores them to remain, because his wife is not long from the grave. Long legs, long boots, Sharpe will come up to Charity and ask for certain information with a penetrating glance, at once both skeptical and kindly—he stands up with real devotion when she enters the room—eyes and cheeks aflame, a little black mustache like a pencil balancing on his top lip. Days of this, sickness and questions.

Then, on an impulse, she heads down toward the river, and finds Thomas on the bank where the harsh water flows, a sight that both chills and excites her, just out of view herself, spying as Thomas piles up little stones to build structures that resemble towers. What she sees now before her she sees again. Had he not constructed such structures before? Had not her girls in fun or anger kicked them down?

She sees him rise and start up the bank. Sees him stop to embrace first one wet tree then another and still another. Embrace the air itself.

And then she sees her body embrace a new dress, a black garment that reveals her form, elongated in the sunlight. Her breasts sag and her stomach too. Holy sounds reverberate beneath her feet. True, this is another Sunday, but it is also a day like nothing else. Sun, heat, smell—she sheds these elements as they appear. Her family stands around, watching and waiting without seeming to look, masking their true intentions with lackadaisical ambling, taking advantage of the usual assumptions about their race, namely, that the observer will fail to see anything beyond a handful of niggers—one, two, three, four—on pause from their chores and activities, niggers lazing about as niggers are supposed to. Thomas emerges. Never before has she seen him so well dressed. The sight brings a clear sharp pause in her thinking, much like that day many years ago when she spied his legs sticking up like ladles from the tub. In one prolonged instant she sees the strange escort take Thomas's arm and guide him by the elbow toward the carriage. Thomas. Almost not wanting to believe. Thomas. His face is trained on the carriage. Thomas. He picks up speed and almost leaves his escort behind, the grass unbelonging to his feet. Heat shimmer on the horizon. How can the world shine from that far away? There is less fear in her now. She is upset. Why try to hide it? How tell about it later? All of the fragments of her life collect around this one afternoon, meet at the point right there in the grass where her sweating feet are planted.

Domingo and the girls move forward to help Thomas up into the carriage. No need now to draw back or to be timid. He wrestles his arms and hands away and lifts himself up into the carriage unaided. She can't understand. There is nothing to understand.

Get these niggers away from me, Thomas says. Pulls away as though he has never known them, carrying with him all the light and air.

Rain Storm
(1854–1856)

"Sure, I been ripped off. I been cheated.
But they gave me a name."

FROM THE START PERRY OLIVER WAS BOTH BEWILDERED and annoyed by the noise of the fiddles, the lamps in the trees, the chatter of smartly dressed men, the medley of gaily colored dresses— mostly white cottons and silks done up with floral patterns—the clink of bracelets, the gold crosses and lace, the niggers in white jackets and pants scurrying about serving hors d'oeuvres ordered specially from New Orleans. In this garden setting, all the women exchanged kisses in the European style—Perry Oliver had never been to Europe—while the men seemed to take pride in their provincial accents. A few guests had even brought along their niggers to fan them cool.

Perry Oliver walked the grass lawn up and down by the neat rows of flowers, hoping that the fragrances of soil and stem might drown out the powerful odors of the overly powdered women. He exchanged a few words here and there, practiced being sociable when he had to—he felt not so much antisocial or shy as careful and opportunistic—using his routine that he was a tobacco planter from Savannah. *I've heard that's a nasty business. Terrible stains on the fingers. You're much too young for it. Get out while you can. But perhaps it is wrong of me to criticize. I must admit, I do like a good smoke every now and then.* Even as he talked, he was careful to observe the going-ons of the party through a watery shimmer of heat and haze. Men and women alike, the guests gave their hosts, General James Bethune and his wife, Mrs. Mary Bethune, inquisitive welcoming looks, each considering it was her or his duty to make some pleasant polite remark. The couple was standing directly in front of a white trellis with several varieties of roses blooming out. In contrast to the commanding presence of her husband, Mary Bethune was small and slight, pale and thin, with protruding collarbones. She was very willing to raise the most casual remark—Are these Negroes on loan? They are quite delightful—into a conversation, while her husband was quite content to let his wife do most of the talking, smiling here and there and responding to statements directed at him with expressive movements of his mouth and eyes. Hands in his jacket pockets—he seemed to have the habit of keeping his hands in his pockets—he watched his guests with a strange glow in his face, as if he possessed a certain strength that he thought they all lacked. When he did speak—He is a soldier, his wife said, that's all he can say for himself—he expelled words in a deep voice like some stage performer as if he expected his booming words to knock the listener off his feet.

Mary Bethune was the first person to welcome Perry Oliver. She left her husband's side—pink, white, and red roses blooming up behind his shoulders and back—and came over to Perry Oliver and introduced herself, offering him a white-gloved hand. He didn't have one sentence ready in case she should ask him how he came to be invited to her party. (He had not been invited.) Taking evasive measures, he tried ingratiating himself, complimenting her on the house and the grounds and the servants and the food and wine. Well, she said. You are here to enjoy yourself. Let me know if it all meets your satisfaction. For now, I beg your leave, she said, but I must pay my respects to—she soon moved off to greet other guests.

Another guest, a pretty young woman, a bright vision of elegance in her flowing white gown—some fancy drape guarding a sculptor's prized creation—came over and started up a conversation. Somehow the talk got around to the Bethune children. The young woman raised a slender wrist sparkling with three silver bracelets of separate diameter and actually pointed out their son, Sharpe, who was standing in another segment of the garden with a circle of listeners. Is that so? He feigned interest. Took her hand into both of his own. What a pleasure this has been. She raised her chin to move her face closer to his. He let her hand fall. If you will excuse me. Freed himself of her company under the pretense that he was off to meet the son. And there she stood, smiling, while he hurried through waves of guests bustling about with cheerful faces. But he only walked far enough to observe and listen.

Sharpe was a handsome man of around twenty—some vague resemblance between him and his father, or mother for that matter, although there was more of her in his facial features—possessing that special self-consciousness that only actors have. (He was no professional actor, as far as Perry Oliver knew.) He wore a splendid shirt and tie, without a jacket. But the most striking thing about him was the exceptional length of his legs, which he displayed in well-polished knee-length black leather boots. The young women in attendance certainly seemed stirred by the style and quality of his dress, but he struck Perry Oliver as dull, colorless, and stupid, for the moment anyone started a discussion with him he would start talking about himself—what concerts he had attended, what paintings he had seen, what business he had conducted, where he hoped to travel. Otherwise he spoke about things that were common knowledge. He seemed most engaged with people of comparable age and tastes.

As though he had heard every silent word and wished to prove Perry Oliver wrong, Sharpe actually parted company with the circle and sought out a group of elderly guests to talk to. At one point Perry Oliver was engaged in conversation with another pretty young woman—about breeding expensive racehorses, a subject he cared little about—and since the lady's perfect lips were taking too long to form a word, he turned his head to discover that Sharpe was watching him. It was hard to say how long he had been looking. He did not come over. Instead he found a group of elderly women and started kissing hands and cheeks.

The party went on this way. Perry Oliver seemed to always catch the attention of some busybody who liked to rattle on. He sometimes smiled and sometimes sputtered at a loss for words. Even found himself repeating phrases in parrot fashion. He blamed himself. What kind of feeling, what motive had compelled him to linger in this city for a full week to attend a party of posers reeking of elitism, and at that, a party he had not been invited to?

A week earlier while he was on business at the orphanage—the director corrected him, *We are a Christian mission*—he had overheard the elderly director discussing the party with her young assistant, holding up the perfumed invitation to the other woman's nose. The orphanage had turned out to be of little use to him—he would have better luck finding an understudy a few days later in the next town he visited—but he did learn of this party being put on by perhaps the most powerful man in the county, General Bethune, a newspaper publisher and political player. He decided to hang around. So, here he was, thoroughly bored and wanting to leave. (He also worried at the thought of chancing upon the fragrance-awed orphanage director or her assistant. Why hadn't he thought about this sooner?) But leaving might be awkward. So he continued to make conversation mechanically, careful not to make the error of stretching the truth too little or too much or of supposing too soon or too late. And he went on this way until they were called into the mansion.

Barely a minute after all of the guests had taken their seats, Perry Oliver saw General Bethune struggling into the room, his fists gripped around the looped ends of two black canes. (So that was why General Bethune had remained standing in one place back in the garden.) The son Sharpe was at his side, walking at a measured pace with his hands behind his back and carrying on an ordinary conversation with his father. The other guests seemed to notice them as well, and their chatter started to die down, replaced by a gradual hush. Father and son seated themselves in two of the three mahogany chairs positioned under the mantelpiece of the marble fireplace. Then the Bethunes' three daughters entered the room, dressed in white gowns, each with a different shade of rose—red, white, yellow— pinned to her collar. All three girls wore their hair wound in a Grecian knot. Perry Oliver estimated that they ranged in age from seven to ten, which meant that the oldest of the three daughters was only half Sharpe's age.

Mary Bethune returned to the room, with a little nigger boy walking beside her, hand in hand. She led him over to the piano, where he sat down perfectly straight on the stool and positioned it under him with the legs turned at a slight angle toward the audience. He was no more than ten feet away from Perry Oliver, who would estimate that the boy was no older than five or six (although with a nigger age was never certain). His eyes bulged as if someone had fitted stones in the hollow sockets then sealed them over. They had outfitted him in a black suit with short sleeves and pants and a freshly pressed white shirt with a rounded collar. His hair was as glossy as his highly polished shoes. There on the angled stool he started twitching his shoulders and trembling as if he were feverish. He seemed to move his head in the direction of the daughters, who giggled when they saw his curious gesture.

This is our prized attraction for the evening, Mary Bethune said, our boy, Tom. Rather than prejudice the performance that you are about to see and hear, I will ask that Tom simply begin. Mary Bethune took a seat slotted between her husband and son.

Tom positioned his small hands over the ivory keys and began playing the piano so violently that the furniture rattled and the paintings on the wall trembled. Perry Oliver kept a mistrustful ear to a melody that ran along, then jerked at intervals.

While Tom played, the three daughters remained perfectly still, only the occasional movement of an eye, a twitching of a nose, or a trickle of sweat indicating that they were living and breathing creatures. Even as he played, two niggers dressed in white top hats, tails, and gloves went about serving the guests savories and dainty glasses of French wine from silver trays. (Hungry, Perry Oliver would have been satisfied with a main dish.)

Tom sounded the chord that closed his first song. His listeners gave him generous applause, a sound that sent him into long loud fits of laughter and handclapping. General Bethune and his wife looked at each other. They seemed equally delighted to see Tom receiving such a warm response. The wife was smiling openly, and her husband showed some easing up of his habitual reticence, only to quickly resume his old expression, perhaps thinking it an improper display of affection.

As the applause died down, Perry Oliver heard someone whisper behind him, Now that's my kind of nigger. He'll do what you tell him with his eyes closed.

Tom began his next song. In Perry Oliver's hearing and perception, the music broke off now and again, and the great glass over the mantelpiece, faced by the other great console glass at the opposing wall, increased and multiplied the image of Tom at the piano, until you saw the piano fading away in endless perspectives. The music knew no denial. Perry Oliver felt like a hunter being lured into ambush by some unidentified prey just up ahead beyond his field of vision. Music set the trail. Somehow in all of this he managed to study the faces of those seated around him. Their eyes were mocking, tender, clear. And perhaps their eyes showed something else that he had no name for and that they themselves would fail to name even if they knew it existed. (Best they didn't know, for awareness negated any possibility of acknowledgment and could only bring denial under the regulatory lens of social custom.)

It went on this way, Tom fingering one song after another. Perry Oliver could not recognize any of the melodies let alone the titles because he knew little about music. His entire life he had been uncomfortable with sounds. He knew this much: the disparate lines of the party—the chattering, the laughter, each guest's clever or stupid remark, every grace and gesture, the shoes and clothing made of the simplest materials or the most fancy, the attendees in all of their perfections and defects—took pattern and form in the melodies, chords, and rhythms of Tom's piano. The more Tom played, the more frenzied he became. He turned his blind eyes and face to the audience and shouted "Look at me!" or "How about this?" or "Let's see you do that!" or "Straight now!" or simply "Hey!" Perry Oliver might have been mistaken, but he would have bet money, and plenty of it, that Tom was expressing the comments for Perry Oliver's ears only.

With a great rising, waving, and falling of his hands, Tom closed a song and immediately stood up from his stool and took a stagy sort of bow. All of the objects in the room returned to their customary place, piece by piece, as did the various layers of Perry Oliver's skin. (A week later, two weeks, he could still hear the music buzzing softly at the back of his skull.) The audience greeted the finale with a standing ovation that caused Tom to begin bowing again and again, like some well-oiled or broken machine.

Guests began to leave their seats and gather around the performer and his master and mistress at the piano. It took some effort for Perry Oliver to take to his feet, but he worked his way around the gathering bodies to squeeze within touching distance of Tom, evening sun reflecting off the boy's black form. (While Tom played, Perry Oliver had felt, heard, and remembered nothing of the weather.) Perry Oliver was so agitated and exhausted he couldn't evaluate what he had heard—was it good or bad?—with a cool head. Closer up, he could see that Tom's hands were dirty, the nails rough as if he'd been scratching and gouging the earth.

One after another the guests praised General Bethune and his wife to the skies.

What a remarkable find.

I've seen nothing like it.

They were skilled appraisers, knowing when to pause to let a compliment sink in.

Did you really enjoy it? Mary Bethune asked.

Why of course.

Need you ask?

I'm so pleased, Mary Bethune said.

From their place behind the piano, the three daughters rose in unison and went to stand among themselves near the fireplace then seemed to decide against standing and took the seats formerly occupied by their brother and parents.

Tom is quite something, General Bethune said. He infuses our best melodies and harmonies with a barbaric element.

Yes.

And you should hear him sing, he said. My wife prefers his playing, but I'll take a good song any day.

Fascinating creature.

How do you explain it?

A conundrum of Nature.

God.

Or the devil.

How did you acquire him? someone asked.

Nothing in the Bethunes' manner of expression showed that they had heard. So Perry Oliver asked, How old is he?

Mary Bethune stopped one of the fancily dressed niggers and took some old porcelain cups from the silver serving tray he was holding, then personally poured each guest in the immediate vicinity a mouthful or two of steaming tea from a silver kettle. You must really try this tea, she said.

Tom? an elderly gentleman asked. I don't believe I recognize that last allemande. What's it from?

Tom rubbed his knuckles against his teeth.

You play delightfully.

Other guests set about paying their compliments to Tom and his master and mistress. Tom responded to the remarks with a faint tilt of the head, a raised jaw, and random nods and head shakes directed at no one in particular. Mary Bethune put her hands on the boy's shoulders and pulled him back into her body, hugged him as if she were protecting him from ghosts, while the daughters sat silently before the fireplace, snuggling close to each other like tiny animals feeling the cold, and watching this world of adults with amusement perhaps or terror.

A pretty young woman, earrings glinting like stars from the darkness of her tanned skin, stood smiling at the boy. His head rose as he caught her scent, and his hand rose too, reached out and touched her bare arm near the shoulder. She shivered.

Perry Oliver spoke at that moment. I really enjoyed your playing, Tom.

Tom spun around to face him. Mary Bethune looked at Perry Oliver.

Tom, she said, this is Mr. Perry Oliver from Savannah.

Her statement impressed Perry Oliver. She had remembered his name and an important particular, though they had spoken for only a few minutes.

Tom peered up, merry-looking. Hello, Mr. Perry Oliver. Tom reached out and took Perry Oliver's hand, his own still trembling from the music. Glad to meet you. He gave Perry Oliver's hand a painfully wild squeeze and pull. And just as suddenly threw the hand free.

The lines in Mary Bethune's face tightened. He seems to respond to you, she said. She studied Perry Oliver's face. Most unusual.

Whatever thoughts she was trying to puzzle together were interrupted when Tom walked off in the direction of the fireplace without warning. The blind boy moved—he walked with the same small quick steps of his mistress—without stumbling into objects or chairs over to where the daughters were seated. They stood up from their seats to greet him. The oldest girl hugged him, while the youngest rose up on her toes to kiss him on the cheek. Then one of the girls said something Perry Oliver couldn't hear. Shut up, Mary, Tom said, pushing her back. And he set off lumbering through the room, the little girls screaming with laughter as they pursued him and tried to catch him. When he neared the piano, he trotted over to it and leaned over the keys, where he did some violent hammering with one fist, as if he were trying to nail the keys in place. Mary Bethune retrieved the boy—the girls hurried off to their former seats at the fireplace—and returned him to his position beside her husband.

Once again, Tom reached out and took Perry Oliver's hand. It is a pleasure to meet you, Mr. Perry Oliver from Savannah. He pumped the hand in steady rhythm.

Tom, Mary Bethune said.

He released the hand. The girls tittered and giggled.

Tom broke away from his mistress and began moving through the crowd, firmly and impulsively grasping the hand of one guest after another, and squealing (singing?), Hi, sir. Hi, madame. Good day to you, sir. How's the weather, madame? Soon he was rushing about the room, bumping into both servants and guests and screaming, Comfort ye, comfort ye, my people. Mary Bethune's face quivered with embarrassment. Her husband lowered his eyes to hide his feelings. With her natural quickness, Mary managed to corner Tom and calm him with one touch of his elbow. He allowed her to lead him out of the room. The three girls got up from their chairs and followed.

Not long after, the party drew to an official close. General Bethune stood by the French doors leading out of the room and offered good wishes as each guest departed, many of the women kissing his hand, as if he were some sort of holy man. General Bethune was the only person Perry Oliver said good-bye to when he left. He had so much he wanted to say to the man about Tom, but the General stood before the opened door and seemed far away in his mind and somewhat put-upon. Once Perry Oliver was in the garden, he noticed some object—gray in color? He couldn't say with distance and the distorting light—on the lawn. He took it up, with an immediate lifting of scent. It was a perfumed invitation that one of the guests had left behind, with all of the necessary facts—date, time, location—printed in fine type on cream-colored paper—not gray—with a red border. He folded the invitation in half and placed it in his pocket.

On his way to the main road, he was surprised to discover that the Bethune estate actually had an abundance of gardens, sectioned off by wrought iron fences six feet in height, fences that were no doubt crafted by the finest nigger hands in the county. Pine trees grew by spiraling iron shafts. He wandered into one garden after another easing about, noticing but failing to truly observe the colorful flowers in fading evening light. Strolled all the way down to a pond where he sat on the bank and looked thoughtfully at the water. The gloomy pines with their shaggy roots stood motionless and dumb. After some time he crawled on all fours to the edge of the pond and dipped his face into the water and gulped the fresh liquid, his eyes open, seeing all the way down to the bottom into another better world.

❁ ❁ ❁

Two years later, Perry Oliver boarded a hot autumn train—cloth suitcase weighing down one hand, leather briefcase weightless in the other—with his young assistant, Seven, a boy not yet a teen, to make a journey of several hundred miles for a speculative sit-down business conference with General Bethune—a man he had met once and a man he had come to despise after all he had learned since that meeting—an interview that might provide him nothing and cost him everything. He suffered at the thought of travel, for he had a theory that each mile of travel shortened a man's life by months, even years. Distance ages us, not time.

These speculations were reason enough for Perry Oliver to remain homebound—he felt no disappointment for places he had not seen—and for him to, on a daily basis, sit and do nothing, as much as possible. He would admit that this habit of pondering disagreeable facts and suppositions—he estimated that he repeated his theory five or six times a day to an audience that was always the same, always interested: himself (curious how little the ideas of an individual vary)—always brought with it a measure of certainty and comfort, but he also believed himself savvy enough to recognize the possible limitations of his theory, to distinguish what was probable truth from what was improbable exaggeration. Any man who hoped to make his way in the world needed an ability to see both sides of an issue.

He was unsure to what extent this journey would either verify or invalidate his beliefs and principles regarding travel, but the risk of a train ride—how shocked he was to unveil the heroism that had been concealed within him for so long and that was pushing him forward into new ventures—was meager in comparison to all he stood to gain. So be it. He was in a state of becoming. In a word, Tom summed up everything he desired.

While he had made sure that both he and the boy dressed in light summer clothes—given the significantly cooler climates where they lived, this requirement entailed purchase of a new wardrobe, required his spending some tens of dollars of the six thousand or more that he had saved up over the years and that he carried on his person now—their fellow passengers were all starched and ironed. Some were red in the face from the heat and the weight and color of their dark garments. (The men had even refused to take off their hats. Perry Oliver never wore a hat and wouldn't pretend to now.) And the numbers of bodies in the car only made it worse. Although the car was a first-class compartment, it was crowded and had been so from the start—and so it would be to the finish—three to a side with small windows—he would have preferred double—a narrow aisle, and no corridor. He had paid top dollar in the mistaken belief that he and Seven would have a compartment to themselves. A few hours after setting out, the journey began to seem tiresome and absurd, the heat uncomfortable, the smell (sweat and steam) offensive, the method of transportation violent, and the results increasingly uncertain. Seven did not seem to enjoy it any better, following the world outside the window with a sad worried expression. Every now and then he would shut his eyes and breathe desperately. He was thin and anxious—Perry Oliver often had to remind the boy to keep his hands still—and had been from the very moment Perry Oliver brought him into his service those many months ago. (How long has it been? Yes, nearly two years and counting.) The traveling clothes Perry Oliver had purchased for him did little to improve his appearance, as the new tailored order of neat angles and patterns was disrupted by the old familiar chaos of the boy's sloppily manufactured cap. This matter of a ratty cap could easily be accounted for. The little traveling they did do by train always made Seven feel like someone important, although Perry Oliver's custom of keeping the boy in the dark, of failing to reveal to him where they were going or why—Perry Oliver had his reasons—never seemed to bother him. In fact, it brought a lifting of spirits, a ritualistic sending-off that necessitated the donning of this favorite cap, a cheap beaver skin that fit his head somewhat too snugly. Perry Oliver wondered, had he himself purchased the ugly cap—when? where?—or did the boy already own it when he came into his service?

Seven?

Sir?

Answer me this one question. Where did you get that godforsaken cap?

From the getting place.

It was not the answer he expected. Surprised (shocked?), one mind told him to challenge Seven's statement and press for the clarity of detail—when? where?—even if for no other reason than to instruct the boy in the proper method of answering a question—*Rule number one: Always answer in a complete sentence. Rule number two . . .*—while his other told him to let it stand, for the phrase had a certain enchantment that, momentarily at least, took his mind away from the drudgeries of travel and the mental worries of his scheduled meeting with General Bethune, as it hinted at some deeper penetration, made him ponder about what it held back. Seven's wide serious face seemed to suggest that he was almost afraid, forbidden, to pronounce the name. All the better if the boy had thoughts and projects he did not disclose. Up to now Perry Oliver suspected (feared?) that he might be, through either birth or upbringing—Perry Oliver had few pertinent facts about either—totally empty.

He rocked to and fro—was he moving his body or was the train directing it?—half dozing, his whole mind on the contract and cash in his briefcase until the city rose up out of the landscape, a black shapeless mass that air and sky began to mold into a recognizable form with each passing mile. Even at a distance of twenty miles it was little more than a church steeple rising up from and pinning down the horizon, but as they drew nearer he could see small houses huddled on its outskirts, placed down in patches of crops, then large farmlands radiating outward from white mansions, looking down on rows of cabins and shacks like badly aligned teeth, then the city itself with its town hall and three-story buildings and stone streets. Bell clanging and steam rising, the engine pulled them into the station. Hardly had they stopped before an army officer forced his way into the overflowing car, followed by a second soldier with a rifle mounted across his chest. They moved slowly from one end of the car to the other, row by row, staring down into the face of each passenger. Satisfied, they moved on to the next car. (Perhaps additional officers and soldiers were performing this very same duty on the other cars, serial repetition and imitation.) Only then could the passengers detrain.

Even with the shade awning overhanging the platform, the hard midday light stunned Perry Oliver quiet. Everyone's face had the longing for something cool and wet. A small group of soldiers stood posted along the stationhouse platform. Seven's eyes widened in admiration at the sight of them. He even stopped to look. What next? Would he ask for an autograph? Perry Oliver spoke his name to move him along. Miniature suitcase in hand, Seven resumed walking, turning his head for a final look or two and stepping on the heels of the person in front of him.

Mind your feet, Perry Oliver said. He might have said more. But he understood that little minds mistake strength and action for beauty, are crushed by pomp and spectacle. Why bother challenging such vulgar perceptions? Seven had many other annoying qualities that caused Perry Oliver greater distress.

For a respite from the heat (the sun at least) and the travel, Perry Oliver decided to take the boy for dinner inside the station diner. They had their choice of a table since few patrons were inside, mostly men traveling alone who would walk up to the bar and order a beer or whiskey before taking a stool and struggling out of their jackets and vests, which they threw across their laps. Perry Oliver ordered the special. The boy wanted hard-boiled eggs and lemonade. They took their time about eating. Trains came and went. They lowered their napkins and left them behind on the table, then returned to the platform, feeling all the better for it.

Nigger porters were busy, attending to luggage and freight, some carrying trunks, boxes, or crates on their backs and showing remarkable speed despite their top-heavy condition. (Many riders were returning from vacations, bearing magnificent purchases.) One older porter sidled over to take their bags. Seven glared angrily at the nigger when he reached for his suitcase. Perry Oliver had witnessed this struggle before. It was not so much that the boy believed the porter a thief but that the relinquishing of his bag lowered his own sense of self-importance, for he feared that his fellow citizens would observe his luggageless condition and label him as another anonymous urchin, a hanger-on awaiting a handout, or even worse, a conniving thief or troublemaker.

Allow him to perform his job, Perry Oliver said. Go fetch us a taxi.

The boy hurried off under his ill-fitting beaver cap, which looked like some mad animal that had seized his skull. He stopped to peer into one carriage only to pass it up and run up to the next, where he stopped and stared in. He approached every carriage one and all in such fashion. Then he returned to Perry Oliver with his head lowered.

Where is our taxi?

None were suitable, sir. They got niggers doing the driving.

He had to restrain himself from slapping the boy. (He had slapped the boy once or twice, always with good reason, a calculated chastisement, and never in anger.) They were in public. Don't be stupid, he said. Niggers are the best drivers.

Seven looked at him, surprised by the words. He did all their driving back home.

Please go and fetch us a taxi.

Moving at a much slower pace than before, the boy went to fetch a taxi.

Time and again, Perry Oliver reproached himself with the question, Why did I settle for this boy instead of another? And why do I continue to put up with him? He did not know the answer. True, the boy was a loyal and dependable driver. (Driving their old carriage was one of his few chores that Perry Oliver would gladly admit that the boy performed with remarkable skill, totally to Perry Oliver's satisfaction.) And the boy had one other good quality: he needed little beyond what he already possessed under Perry Oliver's service—food, shelter, and his beaver cap. However, he had continual reason to wonder if this boy could be left to supervise a peculiar nigger pianist (his eventual duty), since these past two years (three?), not one day had passed without some upset. *I'm sorry, sir* was a ritual habit. He certainly felt no pity for the boy—in fact, he had no feeling at all for the boy; well, perhaps he had to admit he had some—and he certainly felt no parental obligation or duty to keep him fed and employed. (Perry Oliver was almost thirty and still did not know if he liked children or if he would want to father and raise a son or daughter himself someday.) So it pained him, made him feel serious disgust for himself, that he tolerated this boy. Seven had no idea why he had come into this world, why he had been created. He could only visualize himself in the future as rich and important. What are your plans? Perry Oliver would ask him.

Be rich and handsome. And I will have a strong body to carry all of my riches.

Perry Oliver strongly believed that Seven was set for a life of repeated mistakes and constant suffering. Perhaps he should be looking to replace the boy? He told himself that he could do better. He had to do better. The boy's days were numbered.

These were his thoughts as the taxi driver helped him and the boy into the hooded space of the carriage. By the time he took his seat the fabric of his pants had gone wet against his skin, the cotton hot and sticky.

Without even remembering the how and when, Perry Oliver was awakened from a nap with several knocks on his door and a voice telling him that the innkeeper Mrs. Rudge was calling him down for supper. He pulled the door open to find her curious nigger servant standing there with his head wrapped in a bonnet and his body strapped in an apron, and with Seven at his side, looking rested.

The hand Mrs. Rudge gave him was plump but weightless. A fleshy petal, the red-painted nails like shiny beetles stuck to a flower. She was extremely thin and extremely ugly in both shape and face. Even her eyebrows looked deprived, like two thin columns of ants lined up on her pale and powdered skin, powder that helped her countenance none. She seated them at the largest table Perry Oliver had ever seen, one that could easily accommodate twenty people, already laid and glittering with linen and silver. Seven got up from the chair where Mrs. Rudge had placed him and hustled off to the end of the table farthest away from Perry Oliver.

Perry Oliver took his time about finishing his plate. If the food was not bad enough, his napkin—the cheap material stiffened with too much starch—was rough against his lips. Once he placed his napkin on the table, the nigger in the white bonnet and apron cleared away plates, bowls, cups, and utensils then made a pot of tea. Mrs. Rudge took the kettle and poured out three glasses. Standing, drinking her tea, she turned her talk to matters of the city, the estates and the harvests, the people of consequence, local men of great importance and the noticeable men of lesser importance. Perry Oliver was quick to realize that the conventional, definitive nature of her views and convictions was a barrier between him and the truth. Nonetheless, he tried to learn what he could about General Bethune—she had mentioned him time and again—without being obvious about it. The General had done a great deal of good in that city and the people loved him. He dispensed charity without stopping to consider whether he should or not. Paid poor schoolboys' fees. Took coffee, sugar, and molasses to widows and old ladies. Gave indigent brides dresses, and grooms tails. Found homes for niggers who had unexpectedly lost their owners. What she told him confirmed another one of Perry Oliver's theories: the city valued the part of General Bethune that he himself valued the least.

From what Mrs. Rudge related, in the final months of his wife's lengthy illness General Bethune had to hire a man to handle the daily operations of the newspaper, a task that would have fallen to his son Sharpe, who was away from the family for recognizable periods of time. And then too, General Bethune had the additional concern of his three daughters. After the loss of their mother, the girls spent their waking moments walking about the mansion and grounds, prayer books in hand. Mrs. Rudge went on to narrate a detailed account of the wake, funeral, and burial. *We are all saddened by his recent loss. Such a noble woman. I counted her among my oldest and dearest friends. From the time she was a child she had a heart of glass.* General Bethune gave permission for anyone who so desired to attend the funeral, even farmers and niggers, on condition that they did not wear mourning clothes. He himself came in uniform, his military outfit from twenty years earlier freshly tailored to account for new flesh and pounds. The girls were terribly overwrought at the loss of their mother, but Sharpe was hit especially hard. He had actually dropped to his knees at the gravesite. Otherwise it was a quiet and beautiful gathering, as an appreciative city had put forward the money to have the grave dug with silver spades, and to have the pallbearers lower the fine casket into the earth with golden chains.

As if to rest her voice for a moment before she continued her narration, Mrs. Rudge performed a casual turn of her head in Seven's direction, saw the boy, and trembled with a little shock of recognition. Dear, boy, she said. You must find this talk disagreeable. How could I have lost track? Please, join me in the parlor.

Perry Oliver declined. Mrs. Rudge and Seven retired to the parlor where she promised to entertain the boy on an upright piano, while Perry Oliver departed for his room highly satisfied with the conversation if not the supper. He was not displeased at having heard the most recent details about General Bethune's state of mind and health, for whatever he learned he could use. He was not unlike a general planning his strategy the night before a big battle. (So he viewed himself.) For this reason he couldn't help wondering why she had omitted Tom from her narration. He had wanted to ask, And what about their strange nigger boy? Any word about him?

A month earlier while he was enjoying his morning coffee, he saw a notice in the paper about the death of Mary Bethune. He set the paper aside, even as the black words he had perused remained in his mind like a bird perched on a high limb. Sunlight caught the glossy surface of his coffee cup, and he leaned forward and perched his chin on the metal rim. Peered down into the hollow interior, hoping to catch a glimpse of whatever might be hidden in the darkness feet or miles below.

He ordered Seven to ready the carriage. The speed with which he responded was astounding, as was the speed with which he drove. Their little house was a good thirty miles out from the edge of town, but they reached his lawyer's office in what seemed a single moment of action. He hurried through the door, Seven behind him, pulled up a chair, and put forth everything directly and boldly. With attentive calculation, his lawyer took up a pen and wasted no time in drawing up a contract registering nuances both foreseeable and unforeseen.

The settling of ink brought the first moment of pause. Perry Oliver tried to remember the appropriate code of conduct and obligation. By the time they left the office with the dried contract, he had decided that such code required his wiring a few words of condolence to General Bethune. That done he purchased two first-class train tickets, and it was only his realization that they had neither suitcase nor clothes that stopped him from actually boarding the train. While his first mind told him to strike while the iron was hot, meaning arrive in time for the funeral and the burial, after which he would seek the most opportune moment to take the widower aside and lay out his proposition and produce his contract, this deficiency in items of travel afforded his second mind to direct him to wait a week, even two. Certainly that man is greedy of life who should desire to live when all the world is at an end. Yes, he would have to hold back and wait a week or two. No purity of heart motivating his decision but clear cold awareness that he could not risk being so dangerously blunt.

He spent the next week drafting a letter to General Bethune, applied himself with extreme calm and single-mindedness—he didn't take to writing easily—to construct long studied sentences appealing to the widower's political sympathies. Bethune's newspaper, the *Columbus Observer*, made no pretense at hiding his nationalism; the General wanted freedom now, independence now: *Fellow citizens, ready our sharpshooters. The best army will be the army with the best eyes*—crafty calculated words that both concealed and revealed their true significance. He made himself wait another week before he mailed the letter, day after day sitting and glaring down at the contract glistening on the table before him. In the third week he got his response in the form of a one-word telegram: *Friday*.

General Bethune would sign. Little doubt there. Perry Oliver banked his success on a simple observation. Through his limited travels, he had come to believe that no one in the South knew what to expect or what was supposed to happen without a war. (One thing he was certain about: he would not be maimed or killed in battle since he had no plans to enlist, for he was no patriot.) These existing expectations would provide his means of winning over the General. But what would happen *after* General Bethune accepted his proposition? Management was an understood business, Perry Oliver's way of earning his bread, but a raw black feeling moved through his body—charcoal clunking through the blood—whenever he tried to picture in anticipatory outline managing a peculiar talent like Tom.

He undressed at the open window, the air on his body stiff and heavy, a second set of clothes. It came as no surprise that night here came suddenly, quick as a guillotine. Followed by a soft gradual blooming as people lit lamps in their houses and on the streets. Then a smell like dead cows clumped through the window. He guessed that niggers and women were boiling wax for candles. Hardly had he completed the thought when the sound of the piano came up through the floorboards and walls as in counterpoint or accompaniment to the smell, the light, the scene. The only good thing about Mrs. Rudge's playing was that the piano was in tune. If her hands were pedestrian, her voice was worse. She sang so loudly it was impossible to hear anything else. But without knowing why he listened so intensely it tired him out.

Perry Oliver awakened when he heard the door to the adjacent room open, then he hurried out of his room and caught Seven just as the boy sat down on his bed to remove his boots. He stood silently in front of the boy. In the lamplight the boy's eyes were large and black. Perry Oliver was trembling with anger.

Seven.

Yes, suh.

Sir.

Sir.

Must I remind you yet again to think before you speak?

I do think, sir.

If only you did. He went over and took the boy's face in one hand and studied it as if it were a gem. Seven.

Yes, sir.

Use this tool between your two shoulders.

Either reflection or confusion reshaped the muscles in Seven's face.

He returned to his room, put on his nightshirt, and got into bed. He waited fifteen minutes then knocked three times on the wall. The boy answered back with three knocks.

He was so tired that his eyes closed of their own accord. Far away a steam engine whistled its cry. His last waking thoughts were about Tom. In dream or reality he heard the boy signal three taps on the wall. He did not answer.

Even in sleep he shivered now and then despite the heat. At some point during the night the cold forced him to get up and shut the window. He returned to bed and pulled the covers over his body, one layer after another, these layers that brought a force of buoyancy and motion. He felt the bed drifting on waves of black water.

Perry Oliver did not begin to feel any better until the following morning when they were in the moving taxi, the carriage squeaking and trembling on the slow uneven approach to Hundred Gates, some ten miles south of the city. And the lifting of his spirits was either so sudden or so gradual he hadn't noticed it. He found himself reflecting on what Mrs. Rudge had said about General Bethune's acts of charity and found solace in the reflection. (Was it something in her gestures this morning, her acts of kindness toward Seven that brought it on?) As far as he knew, Bethune made his money solely from his newspaper. (Perhaps he had some investments. Only a fool would rule out that possibility.) His charitable acts caused Perry Oliver to suspect that General Bethune might have some personal debts that he would be too ashamed to tell anyone about and that caused him considerable distress, these facts demanding the necessary cover-up and temporary relief that certain public spectacles might provide.

Their horse was actually galloping, the hooves digging like spades into the dirt road, carrying them from city to countryside, a gain in nature. Speed and rushing air brought the feeling that the winds above were racing far ahead of him in warning. Heat broke into colors such that living creatures seemed to be moving against a painted backdrop. Niggers drying fish along the riverbank, their cane poles stuck into the mud in odd formations, like impoverished tents deprived of their canvas covers. In the distance niggers struggling up tree-covered hills, baskets balanced on their heads, or wedged across their backs. Poor farmers emerging from three-windowed little houses, working small plots of land. Bonfires of manure, straw, and other refuse crackling and smoldering—human heat adding to natural heat—and every now and then niggers drifting through the smoke like shadows. Perry Oliver found no vitality or beauty in people at work. What did these planters see in it all? Why this love of the land? The whole air smelled like hard labor. He did not dare to take a deep breath. Who knew what diseases and plagues lurked in this air?

The coachman halted the horse near the main lawn of a white, newly painted and plastered three-story mansion, the very same mansion that Perry Oliver had visited two years earlier and that to all appearances was unchanged beyond new paint and new plaster. The sprawling main lawn was freshly cut. They stepped out of the taxi onto the dirt road at the gates of Hundred Gates, no gate really, but two chest-high posts constructed from a motley collection of brick and stone. The cement walkway leading up to the porch was lined with a column of oaks on either side, each tree identical to the others in width and height, forming—for Perry Oliver—a monotonous picture.

It would take them a good five minutes to reach the porch. Perry Oliver held Seven at arm's length and took stock, noticing that the boy was already defiled since his morning wash, two white lines of dried saliva stretching across his mouth and lips. Matter-of-factly (without fuss, anger, or disgust), he retrieved his handkerchief and presented it to the boy. Nodded for him to clean his mouth. Made him remove the beaver cap and tuck it under his arm.

Do you know why we are here? he asked.

On the assumption of important business, Seven said.

Well put. Display your best behavior, as I will display mine.

Yes, sir.

Side by side, man and boy walked up the paved path toward the house, under late August light that somehow managed to find its way through the trees and slash at a low angle, almost horizontal, into their heads into their eyes. The scene presented the vacancy and hush that is often said to accompany an ambush. Of creatures human or animal, they saw but one: a little male nigger whom Perry Oliver placed in his early twenties, who was sitting under a tree outside the garden, quaking as if somebody had routed him from his warm bed and forced him out into the cold. He raised his head and looked at them wide-eyed, but he did not rise to either greet or stop them. Something in his gaze caused Perry Oliver to quicken his step and reach the porch, get out of the open and under cover. And there he stood, feeling vulnerable as he prepared to push the bell and knock on the door.

The door opened to reveal a Negro servant, roughly equivalent in age to the nigger sitting under the tree, with a black head covering knotted at the back of her neck. She gave Perry Oliver a look of recognition—he had never seen her before—and confusion. She turned her face to change her line of sight, as if she were deeply embarrassed.

Good morning, he said. She said nothing in response. I am Perry Oliver and have an audience before General Bethune.

She turned from the door without speaking to him, an action that clearly indicated she expected him to follow. And follow he and Seven did. She was slender, fine-boned, dark, but not as slender as she looked at first sight. Older perhaps too. From his vantage point behind her, Perry Oliver noted several rolls of fat on her neck, covered with the finest skin. In the rooms they passed he sought to detect any traces of grief—flowers, black ribbons or cloth, black draperies. Seven walked with difficulty on account of his effort to keep his head high in continuous observation, face turned first this way then that, only too easily distracted and impressed by every glorious adornment, almost stumbling over his own feet at times when he attempted repeated looks. In contrast Perry Oliver saw less with each step, as each movement brought an intensification of his nervousness and a decrease in his awareness so that by the time they finally stopped walking, the details of the house had barely impinged upon his thoughts.

The room she led them into was large and airy, teeming with furniture—sofas, spindly chairs and armchairs with curved backs, a chaise longue, little tables with spidery legs, and a stool tucked under a grand piano. Every surface except the piano top was crowded with objects: tall blue vases (porcelain from China, Perry Oliver assumed), Venetian mirrors with flowers, small porcelain plates with gold rims and floral designs, bowls filled with rose petals, fancy clocks, and silver-framed portraits and sweeping landscapes of ample dimensions. And there were golden cornices and polished wainscoting and mahogany chairs positioned before a large marble fireplace. Only then did he realize that this was the very same ballroom he had visited two years earlier.

You can wait in here. She walked away.

He had expected, *Please wait in here, suh. Kindly inform me if I may be of service.*

A general? Seven asked, rooted to the spot in amazement, his dream showing on his facc.

Perry Oliver looked at the boy but did not answer him.

A short time later, General Bethune limped into the room through one of the French doors aided by his two black canes, throwing out one and then the other to pull his body forward, less an image of oddity and weakness than of comfort and habit, for he moved with an ease that showed he had grown accustomed to his condition. (Most assumed that the General had suffered a battle wound during the Indian Wars, but Perry Oliver had read somewhere that he had fallen off an unruly horse here at home several years after the war he had served in ended.) The canes were weird instruments that amplified the man in Perry Oliver's vision, raising him up the way a scaffold might thrust one's face into the cracked details of a painting. He was untidily dressed and poorly groomed, as if he had been awakened from a nap. Perhaps the death of his wife had pushed him to a new stage of his malady. Indeed, Perry Oliver had expected as much, knowing that the General would be vulnerable, confused even, as his wife's death brought with it new burdens for a parent and an owner. But would it fall to his favor if the germ of infliction or grief spread victoriously to every part of the General's body, either killing or totally incapacitating him? This would leave Perry Oliver in the less certain position of having to negotiate with Sharpe the son for Tom.

As if to relieve Perry Oliver's worries, General Bethune looked at him quite calmly and held out his hand in greeting. Perry Oliver moved to take it, a simple action that required tremendous effort as his elbow and fingers were stiff with anxiety.

Which of them spoke first? During their meeting for the next hour, Perry Oliver would scrupulously note every detail of the room and the man, but it was such that over the course of the next few months, the field of vision and memory would draw in, so that when he walked into this very same room a year later, he would not remember it. In fact, he would have tremendous difficulty recognizing the man himself two or three years hence, upon General Bethune's visiting them backstage following a concert. He would hear the voice and voice would bring back the man.

I see you brought someone along with you?

Yes.

And what is your name?

My name is Seven, sir.

Seven. Hello, Seven.

Hello, sir.

And Seven would be your son?

Perry Oliver had anticipated this question. Had even played over the possibilities of lying—*yes, sir*—but decided against it, figuring that a man in General Bethune's position, a newspaperman, could easily investigate the facts and uncover the truth. The lie would cost him down the line. No, sir. He's my understudy.

Your understudy? General Bethune shook his head once or twice in mock astonishment. Is that the term they use for it now? He made a gesture with his hand as if he were presenting Perry Oliver to an audience. So that would make you his overstudy.

Finger at his chin, Perry Oliver pretended to give the comment serious consideration. Yes, he said. I suppose it does.

I already supposed for you, General Bethune said. He gave Perry Oliver a measuring look, checking to see if the words offended or disturbed. Working his canes he made for an armchair near the fireplace. You will have to supply me with all of the details at a later date. Please take a seat. General Bethune eased himself into the armchair and crossed the looped ends of his canes in his lap. Perry Oliver sat down in the closest armchair near the piano, a good distance away from the General. Seven moved to take a seat.

Not you, Seven, the General said.

Seven stood like a trapped animal, unsure where to run.

The General gave him a tender and curious glance. So, Mr. Seven, how old are you?

You must beg my pardon me, sir, but I never tell my experience without good reason.

General Bethune laughed openly. Perry Oliver could not force himself to smile—wished that he could—let alone laugh, finding no humor in the boy's ability to repeat a vulgar line used by every commoner in the street. (Pity Seven's spirit of imitation.) Well then, the General said, you've made yourself perfectly clear. I won't inquire any further. Your overstudy and I have some crucial matters to discuss. Why don't we send you off to the kitchen for some cool beverage. Would you like that?

Yes, sir.

Unless your overstudy objects. General Bethune looked at Perry Oliver, challenging him. You obviously had good reason for bringing your boy to my house. Does your understudy need to be present for our meeting?

Perry Oliver was sure that he saw a mocking smile part the General's lip. He judged himself from the same point of view as the General did. He said without hesitation—hesitation would kill his chances here and now—No.

As I thought. General Bethune raised his head and shouted, Charity! When the nigger didn't appear quickly enough he took up both canes and banged them loudly against the floor.

The servant in head rag who had answered the door appeared in the room. Yes, suh.

Take this boy to the kitchen for a cool drink.

Yes, suh. She summoned Seven with a hand signal. Right this way, young master. Seven followed her.

General Bethune watched them leave the room. Then he directed his gaze at Perry Oliver. Perhaps I sent her off too soon, he said. It didn't occur to me that you might require something from the kitchen.

No, sir.

Coffee? Tea? Lemon water?

No, sir. I am well replenished.

Of course. Mrs. Rudge. You are staying with Mrs. Rudge?

Yes.

He laughed a small laugh. How are you getting on with her? She is famously polite.

Indeed, Perry Oliver said. He noticed that shadows had collected in each depression of the man's white face. Beyond his unkempt appearance this was perhaps the only discernible physical change that Perry Oliver could detect in the man from his previous visit two years earlier, comparing what he saw now against what he remembered, drawing up the image of the General standing in the sun-drenched garden.

And how are you getting on in the town? General Bethune raised his hand. Don't answer. I apologize. This city is so boring. It must be murder for a man of your taste.

Perry Oliver sought some neutral response. General Bethune was hard to read. His words alone challenged, and to everything he said he added a facial expression that would have seemed more suitable for a different phrase. In the silence Perry Oliver breathed so hard he was sure the General could hear him. So to fill the void he blurted out, Thank you for taking the time to see me.

A transmutation took place in the General's face, some blend of astonishment and anger. You are here on business.

Yes, sir.

That is why I granted you a hearing. I'm not taking time. The General's eyes were mocking Perry Oliver, like a child seeing how far he could go. At once his presence in the house became clear like vision itself. This was stage, public performance. He had been here less than five (ten?) minutes and was already on display. Perhaps he had come all this way for nothing, thinking he had the upper hand when in actuality General Bethune controlled everything, had lured him into this trap, this elaborate joke. Here was the General Bethune that his reading and research hadn't (couldn't have) revealed.

He simply sat there, his back trembling before the danger of making another mistake.

Tell me, Mr. Oliver, what is your profession?

Until recently I worked tobacco in Savannah. He tried to conceal the trembling of his hand.

Tobacco?

Yes. His awkwardness filled him with disgust for his own body—heart, lungs, arms, and legs—which only made him feel more discomfort.

General Bethune shook his head in apparent (clear?) disdain. You count yourself among the common herd. Planters are a vile and filthy lot, totally uncultured. I have to deal with these types on a daily basis. That's why this town is the insufferable disappointment that it is.

Excuse my lack of clarity. Allow me a correction. I fought down in Mexico. And then I put myself in the service of the most important tobacco planters in Savannah.

Mexico?

Yes, sir. Perry Oliver had meticulously prepared a list of battles and two or three detailed anecdotes.

If you can imagine such a thing, those Mexicans are a more savage lot than the Indians, from what I've heard. I'm glad I never had to square off against one.

I suffered that misfortune.

Yes, the General said. But I guess one man is as good as the next.

Perry Oliver held his tongue, unsure what the General meant.

Perhaps you can tell me all about it sometime. I'm not one of those who relishes swapping war stories or showing off injuries and scars. Each day presents us with some fresh triviality. General Bethune looked down at the floor, as if he regretted having allowed himself to even think of such matters. So now you see a need to free yourself of these planters?

Yes, sir.

You are a smart man. They fail to understand a fundamental fact. A nigger never pulls his own weight. Far be it from me to put my means of survival in the hands of unpaid servants. General Bethune spoke with a rhythm of pure certainty that required silence as the only possible response. (Thematic closure, harmonic return.) Then he went on. You are not here by accident. We've met before, you and I?

Yes. Two or three years ago at a party for your daughters. This much was true. I came at the invitation of your wife. This part wasn't, but if the General caught the lie he didn't let on. Not taking any chances, Perry Oliver pulled the invitation he had saved—it had lost none of its scent over the years—walked across the room, unfolded it, and handed it over to the General for further verification.

General Bethune looked at one side of the paper, then the other, only to repeat the inspection, looking without seeing, validity in touch and scent. That's when you heard him play?

Yes, sir. He left quite an impression.

General Bethune looked up at Perry Oliver as if in seeing him so clearly now he couldn't doubt his presence two years earlier. He returned the invitation, and Perry Oliver returned to his seat. Then you met the family?

Yes, Perry Oliver said. It was strategic common sense for him to avoid inquiring about the son or daughters' well-being. Familial matters formed no part of their conversation. The two men were feeling each other out for worldly motives.

Cholera laid out half the porkers in this county dead, General Bethune said, and almost as many niggers. And my wife too.

Such misfortune, Perry Oliver said.

General Bethune frowned as if Perry Oliver had cast a deliberate slur against his family. Life would withhold no misfortune from any man. Perhaps you've been spared your due up to now. I'm convinced that defeat starts from inside. It has to first get inside you before you can be conquered.

I suppose that's why I'm here, Perry Oliver said. We both want the same end. War.

How often have I urged this very same thing.

When the day comes, you will have public duties to perform, even if they are not directly on the battlefield. You can do without needless distraction. As for your son, he being one of same blood and like mind and disposition, he will feel compelled to serve. In fact, we must all contribute to our cause. Our niggers should not be free of these obligations.

Go on, General Bethune said.

At the least they should earn their keep. Niggers are built for work, not charity. You expressed this very same sentiment only moments ago. As he spoke, Perry Oliver struggled with a somewhat comical sense of embarrassment and shame at such (his) obvious spectacle and manipulation, squeezing out the words with jerky constraint.

You have no idea what you're asking. Though we've been hard at training him, Tom is only a few degrees from the animal.

I understand fully, sir.

I doubt that you do.

Trust me, sir. I've given it deep thought. I have at my service expert men of music, Europeans, who will help to the extent that it is possible to polish and develop Tom's crude skills.

General Bethune was quiet for a moment, thinking it over. Let me ask you something.

Sir?

Even if all you say is true, what makes you think that *you* are the most capable man for the job? Do you not think that others have approached me with the same offer?

Perry Oliver could think of nothing to say at first. This General Bethune was sharp. Perhaps the injury or illness that hastens the aging and deterioration of the body retards and preserves the mind. Perhaps he had underestimated his opponent and left himself ill prepared. How many hours had he rehearsed this meeting in his head? Working under such difficult conditions he had experienced one hour's labor as two or three. Perhaps the hard work made him feel that he had put in more time than he had—reality remains reality, an hour is only an hour—as each task a man completes is like a whole lifetime and with each little life a man pieces together an entire history. So he sat in silence, half in desperation, half feeling like giving up.

I am putting myself at your service, he said. If you know of another who is both capable and willing to take on this task, I will respectfully withdraw my offer.

What are the terms? General Bethune asked.

The question took Perry Oliver with shock and surprise, coming as it did so quickly and so casually after the General's former hesitancy, these feelings thrusting outward into something else, excitement—

yes—as if the doors to a treasury were suddenly thrown wide open to him. He sought to ease his body and slowly withdraw the expectant look from his face—a tremendous undertaking. I will pay you fifteen thousand dollars over a period of three years, at the conclusion of which you will be fully expected to review my performance so that if my services have failed in any way you will be free to cancel our agreement.

With clear disbelief, General Bethune smiled into his face. Who was this far-fetched and shameless confidence man? Such nerve. Such gall. He would not have been surprised if this other demanded he produce two coins of silver as proof he was not a total pauper.

I am prepared to pay you five thousand dollars upon signing of the contract, even should that signing be today.

General Bethune seemed to study those words carefully. Perry Oliver felt triumphant, knowing fully well that only a fool would turn down five thousand dollars for a blind, crazy nigger.

You have done an excellent job in laying out your case, General Bethune said. It would be uncouth of me to refuse you. Come to the offices of the newspaper tomorrow. My lawyer will be present. We will sign and notarize whatever documents are necessary to put Tom at your disposal.

With those words some force in Perry Oliver's mind absorbed, reduced, and crystallized all that had preceded into a black reflection casting a single image, the only image he could see later whenever he gazed at it, always there in the dark of his memory: General Bethune struggling to position his black canes and raise himself out of the chair, like a fledgling bird leaving its comfortable nest to test flight for the first time. Sound came from far away like a lost language, nonhuman speech: *I will have Tom delivered to you in accordance with a mode of transportation you find suitable.*

With that General Bethune turned with a distracted air—perhaps this too was recorded for posterity—like one who suddenly remembered something that needed immediate attention, and left the room.

Perry Oliver stood up from his chair, unsure at first what had just happened. His visit was clearly at an end.

It would figure that he and Seven left the house and headed for their taxi, still waiting on the road. *We met a general.* Even under the high columns of oaks the sunlight fell so strongly that he narrowed his pupils and saw nothing but glare. Little did it trouble him. *We met a real general.* In fact, light and heat began to dissolve into fragments and sink into the ground. Seven entered the taxi but Perry Oliver did not, somehow forgetting that this was an action he should also perform. He continued on through the wooded area on the other side of the road, seeking an explanation from the trees. For he could not explain it, did not know how to explain it. What he had planned came to be. It was flatly inconceivable. Nothing like this had ever happened in the world before. He touched his body all over, sensing a new anatomy. Felt two hearts beating inside his chest. He took pleasure in the discovery. He went around the trunk of one tree, raised one foot—left or right?—to step over a log and found himself putting it back on a moving floor, seated as he was beside Seven in the taxi, experiencing pure joy as he traveled along the hard road in late autumn, in an uncomfortable bumpy carriage.

I met a general, Seven said. It's only the beginning. Just watch. He gazed off into the distance. One day I'm gonna come back and buy this city and stuff it in my shoe.

❀ ❀ ❀

Seven had been cutting marks into the table again. Only yesterday with tremendous effort of wrist and elbow Perry Oliver had managed to sand the previous marks away, and applied a touch of varnish to restore the original appearance, and now they were back, deeper, plainly visible from across the room where he stood. A long splinter of wood had actually come off from one corner. Despite what he saw before him now Perry Oliver was willing to give Seven the benefit of the doubt. Perhaps the lines (figures?) were accidental, the necessary product of Seven's daily cleaning and tidying up, like the smudges he often noted on the surface of the few other items of furniture they possessed. Perhaps he was not standing close enough to the table for an accurate assessment. He spit on his thumb and tried to rub the marks away. No doing. Incisions indeed. Permanent.

He had only just entered the apartment, greeted by the sound of Seven's excited voice reciting the latest newspaper dispatch humming with the distant and happy echo of Paul Morphy's victories from across the Atlantic. Seven and Tom remained seated at the table drinking hot chocolate, candle flickering—all things are born of a single fire—shadows booming up behind them, the boys lit less by the small candle than by the shimmering surfaces of cup, plate, and spoon. They did not acknowledge his arrival, although they must have heard him enter, heard lock opening and door closing. Seven partially hidden behind the open halves of his newspaper, and Tom plainly in sight next to him. Only when Perry Oliver reached the corner of the table, angling into Seven's line of vision, catty-cornered, no mistaking him, did Seven look up from the journal, long enough to pause in his reading, but he evidenced his employer without surprise or astonishment, observed him walk to one corner of the table to inspect it, and simply went on with his monologue, voice rising and falling, hurrying up or slowing down, in a haughtily adult tone to an apparently passive and indifferent (we assume) Tom—so still he could be asleep; in fact, he often fell asleep in this position, especially after a meal (usually a heavy supper, several helpings of meat and milk), fully dressed, and sitting erect at the table, head held up, until a telling flutter escaped his lips, and Seven roused him enough to lead him off to bed—who remained perfectly still, eyes closed and face free of expression, as unknowing as the objects before them on the table.

Perry Oliver listened to Seven, each word an unmooring, taking him further and further away from his own thoughts that he wanted, needed to hold on to. (Words would keep him.) Nothing he required more than some silence after a full day of planning and work. (In his dealings with the world the two were the same.) But every evening when he returned home Seven wouldn't afford him such escape, intent on sharing with the world (Tom) the latest news about the "New Orleans Sensation," in a voice that gave glory to a flesh-and-blood deity constructed out of black ink crowded onto cheap paper.

All in all, Seven took great delight in delivering news good or bad. He would have wrong news rather than no news at all. The afflicted had sought out Perry Oliver to inform him that Seven, upon reaching his destination to deliver a message, would draw out the pleasure by asking the recipient teasing questions or, to the recipient's considerable surprise, bowing his head in concentration, pretending that he had forgotten the message, or by searching his pockets, having (pretending that he had) misplaced or lost Perry Oliver's note. Once the maneuver took effect, he would finally get around to relaying the message. And at those times when he returned home with a reply to the original message, he tried to hold on to it for as long as possible, searching his pockets—now, where did I put it?—until finally turning over the note trembling in his hands.

He had to resign himself to Seven's quirks and concerns, and his occasional lapses in performance—the logs had been crudely hacked despite their deceptive arrangement into neat stacks; the outlines did not hold—and disturbances and delays. Even on the rare occasions when the house was noticeably untidy he voiced no complaint, for Seven tended Tom with expert care, with knowledge and command, perfectly present right down to the hands-on and messy task of regulating Tom's hygiene, not the easiest of jobs.

Seven wasted no time in offering his opinion of the improbability of Morphy's ever losing a match.

Fire, Tom said.

No, Seven said. Not that kind. A contest. A tournament. A series of games. He returns to his reading.

Though the ward where they lived was colorless and dull, for Seven the large bright world began only a few blocks away at the general store where he purchased the newspaper, the *Watchman*—cities of glittering words—each afternoon. It had taken him only a few minutes of reading to discover how Paul Morphy was connected to his life. In Morphy Seven discovered the model example of an intellectual and social development he admired, and given favorable circumstances, he himself might one day achieve. Paul Morphy the destiny he had assigned himself, the appointed end. He was always speechless at first after he completed his reading of the report and his patient inspection of the illustration. With somber authority he would place the journal flat on the table and raise his head and stare off into space. After some moments of this he would look down at the journal, studying it like a map. A prearranged and agreed upon action, clue (Perry Oliver suspected) that always set Tom's mouth moving, elicited a flat and spiritless recitation of the dispatch word for word. Then talk came more easily, Seven asking (demanding?) that Tom recite the report from the day before, and the one before that. Paul Morphy, Seven, and Tom—a drawn-out affair. Day in and day out, the boys under Morphy's spell.

It turned out, Perry Oliver felt strangely touched to see them together like this. At moments he observed them bent over laughing together at the table, laughing as only boys can. More than once he had seen them embrace like brothers, Seven taking the lead, leaning into the other under his charge. And he often spied them sitting conspiratorially, showing no regard for the man who fed them both. (It is one thing to provide food for another person and quite another to be faced with the sudden, complex, and increased responsibility of providing for two additional mouths.)

Why can't we get us a nigger? Seven said.

We can't bear it.

I want me a nigger.

Can you feed one? Clothe it?

But he took continual pleasure in Seven's development, his increased independence, the sharper differentiation of his mental apparatus into various agencies, the appearance of new needs (food, chess, Paul Morphy). Seven employed precisely the energy Tom had set free in him. (What those under our care bring out in us.) How to repay that?

My dear chess master Herr Löwenthal, Seven said to Tom, your play is very good, and worthy of a great master, but as to beating Morphy, don't dream of it.

Tom didn't seem to hear or notice.

You must have too much time on your hands, Perry Oliver said, if you can find nothing better to do than sit there babbling nonsense with Tom.

Seven didn't respond to the accusing observation, both of them aware that his hands held plenty, time included, that he put in a full day's work—Perry Oliver had made it clear that Tom must never aid him in any form with the household chores—and this form of play—whatever you might call it—was a necessary pause, a gathering of strength for the other chores to be done around the house today and the next day. With the exception of the three or four hours when Seven guided Tom down to Scaldy Bill's Drinkery and Eatery to play the piano—the nearest piano Perry Oliver could find, a fortunate arrangement as owner William Oakley charged him nothing, their patronage (breakfast, dinner, supper) of his establishment pay enough—Seven and Tom remained indoors. Perry Oliver insisted on it. (Assume that Seven followed his instructions to the letter. No evidence to the contrary.) As much as possible, Tom should stay within the confines of their apartment—confined? he couldn't call it that—so as not to offend the sensibility of other persons in their house or on the street. *Look at that misery. But by the grace of God, that could be me. Blind and a nigger. Count my blessings.* Perry Oliver was not insensitive to their misfortune, but this is the way it must be. (Soon enough the public would get to see as much of Tom as they could stomach.) Before he departed each morning, Perry Oliver reviewed the measures Seven should take in the event of his unexpected or prolonged absence or in circumstances of injury or illness. But even this review was grounded in the many months of thorough preparation that preceded Tom's arrival from Hundred Gates. Perry Oliver had put Seven through a rigorous apprenticeship. As a rule, each morning he would assign the boy a lengthy and detailed series of errands and tasks to train his memory, put it to good use. A test for the body too. (Fair to say that he was the first person to introduce Seven to axe and saw.) Put Seven out on a limb, to both measure and increase the level and range of his ingenuity and skill. Would he fly and survive or would he fall prey to either earth below or danger from above? Undeterred by his tough initiation, Seven never uttered a word of complaint about hard work—he still didn't—saving his back talk for other matters.

When we gon get us a nigger?

Seven, you make my head ache with your voice. Kindly close your mouth and let the hammer talk.

Perry Oliver seated himself at the table, sharp pulses from his lower regions making themselves felt. He removed some money from his purse—the exact amount, down to the penny—handed it over to Seven with instructions for him to run down to Scaldy Bill's to pick up their daily supper, a whole leghorn hen. (The killing of a fowl does not give in itself a positive or negative answer.) Seven set the table before he departed, light and rapid as a bird. At once Perry Oliver regretted his absence—too late to catch him—as he was now left alone with Tom, his black skin part of the darkness, so that Tom seemed knitted into place, black threads. Often Tom assumed a pose of absolute stillness and silence, his face like some dead object on display, two closed eyelids carved in stone. And you the observer were a mobile subject before an ideal artifact (object). (Did Tom feel the full weight of observation? The object in all of its unappeasibility.) This was how you might see him sitting at the piano, so straight and still before he began playing. (The stability and strength of the spine.) And that was how he sat now. Or perhaps not, because Tom seemed to lean back into the darkness, plenty of space behind him, and it was only then Perry Oliver noticed that the table had been beautifully laid, glass and silver sparkling in the candlelight, as if in leaning back Tom had somehow pushed these objects forward into vision. Pitcher, candle, blue enamel pot unadorned (the barest table, no cloth to cover it) but striking and noticeable in their arrangement. Peach, pear, and plum in a bowl, each shape and color distinct. Seven was organized, not subject to improvisation, but his newfound knack for table design was almost certainly a talent he had inherited from Mrs. Rudge, although their stay at her hotel had been short.

Perry Oliver leaned forward in his chair and studied the grain of the wooden floor. Oak. Each knot in the wood like a miniature island. Isolated and alone. Was it this visual promise of solitude—the altering eye—that caught his attention, attracted him, drew him in? His line of work didn't permit the possibility of severing oneself from the world. The fleshy cord never gets cut. The other's skin was always linked to yours. Stay connected or die. A necessary dependence.

How many more addresses must he visit? How many more people must he meet? How much more in his quest to bring Tom to the stage? Walking in the street, he did not love the questions of strangers.

Excuse me, sir. Your nigger looks just like my boy Ned who expired a decade ago.

Or he heard his name from afar. *Mr. Oliver.*

Black buggies beetling to and fro against his crossing. White sails snapping in silence where he strolled along the bank to follow his thoughts, breeze coming off the water. Dark bordered the light's collusive motion. What was clear in this complicated territory? (A handshake. A certain sigh.) What to guide him through the world other than his unfailing instincts?

What was keeping Seven? The mute life of an empty house. Perry Oliver whistled a tune he had picked up in the street earlier. Only his effort made the melody sweet. Tom whistled it back to him, sweeter. He leaned forward and ran his hand across Tom's knuckles. Surprised at the heat of the other's skin, each knuckle like a warm stone. Tom trembled at his unwanted touch but did not draw away. Perry Oliver cast a concerned glance at the child. So be it. (There is a time for picking up stones, but also a time for throwing them away.) Drew his hand back.

He tried another tune, humming this time, expecting its attenuated repetition. Once again the thought occurred to him that he would have to hire a knowledgeable musician to show Tom some tunes. A goal he was working on, little by little. (The correct words open, but the wrong words follow.) Nonetheless, he was intrigued at the ease with which he was able to enter an unfamiliar world and learn its customs and language—the random phrase, the odd word—learn who's who, and what's what, which authority to approach and which to skirt, this method allowing him to penetrate a little further each day. And even if he was mistaken in his evaluation, gave himself undue credit, it made no difference to the end result. A meeting was scheduled for tomorrow. Several in fact over the next few days. (Those who remain to listen. Those who remain to talk.) Though he could not rid his thoughts completely of the possibility of standstill or failure.

In this dispirited frame of mind he heard Tom's voice, no ordinary tone, no ordinary words.

Permit me to repeat what I have already said invariably in every professional community I have had the honor of entering, that I am not a professional player, that I never wished to make any skill I possess the means of pecuniary advancement, and that my earnest desire is never to play for any stake but honor.

He could hear every word with singular clarity, but some part of him refused to allow them to register in his mind, neither the sounds nor their meaning. The conflicting feelings began to fuse—the transformative heat of Tom's skin—causing his waking consciousness to ebb away. More than once he had lived in a house under the belief that it was the high price one paid for isolation, anonymity, and privacy, only to discover shortly after moving in that a stranger would knock on your door to welcome you or simply ring your doorbell out of casual curiosity—Who are you? What do you look like?—or wander up in practical desperation to inquire if he might water his limping horse or exhausted hounds at your well. In fact, a house is an invitation. So he had opted for this small apartment in a multi-unit dwelling, living space he leased from a landlord he never saw, an overdressed nigger, who arrived once a week at a determined time to collect the rent. His means permitted more, but this was all he allowed, all he needed. His entire wardrobe hung on pegs on a coatrack near the door, with hats, harnesses, and whips making a definite silhouette against the gray background of wall. And the few pictures he elected to hang—a watercolor depicting men and mules struggling up a mountain during the California Gold Rush, a vivid oil painting of a bloody war scene from the Mexican conflict, a sketch of George Washington crossing the Potomac—he did for Seven's amusement. Moving through these few rooms, he felt like a tourist walking through someone's private collection.

With practiced hands, Seven placed their simple but ample supper on the table. (The table was their base of operations.) Tom was already digging into it, all ten fingers going. Perry Oliver realized he must have dozed off—at what point?—missing Seven's return. Took him a minute to take in what he was seeing and to understand that he didn't like what he saw. Tom rarely received his criticism or chastisement. Why should he? By any measure, it is not fair that the mentally and physically incapacitated and therefore upright and innocent individual should pay for his capable but compromising counterpart.

Seven, Perry Oliver said, look at him.

Seven caught Tom's fingers to slow him down.

Often Perry Oliver disdained from joining the boys at the table for supper, taking his plate at the window or in his room. But since he was already here, in this firm chair positioned against the hard floor, he might as well. He picked up his fork, the metal shuddering in his fingers.

They ate their meal in absolute silence. For the third time that evening Perry Oliver put his poor voice into song, but Tom had ears only for the noise he made as he chewed his food, steady and advancing destruction, a greasy graveyard of bones on his plate. Ready for more.

What do you want, Tom?

Food.

Seven gave him more vegetables.

Perhaps Seven's appetite had not improved as much as Perry Oliver had supposed. He took slow gradual nourishment, picking at his food, tentative portions, close inspections, like a scientist on an archaeological expedition. Even before he had finished his first plate Tom was ready for a third.

Would you like some more food, Tom?

No.

What then?

Meat.

Seven gave Tom another helping of chicken. Tom smiled at the sound of the meat touching his plate. It seemed a happy smile, a deliberate expression of emotion, and perhaps it was. Soon came a request for milk, Tom's first request every morning, Seven pouring him half a glass, seeing if that would satisfy him, before he gave in and poured a full glass. A simple pattern of back and forth between the boys, of mock protest and playful negotiation. Catching sight of them like this, Perry Oliver remembered Tom's troubled entry into their apartment and their lives.

❊ ❊ ❊

As he had wanted to surprise the boy with their new charge, he had made Seven wait behind in the apartment when he went to retrieve Tom from the station, electing to hail a taxi and relieve Seven of his usual chauffeuring of their carriage drawn by a single black horse. An hour (two?) later, he stepped through the door guiding the blind boy by the hand. Seven was kneeling on the floor, busy with the waxing and polishing of it, his rag whirling over the surface, until all at once it drew still, less in response to Perry Oliver's return than at Seven's noticing of two human shadows cast against the shiny floor. He raised his head and turned to look.

You got your nigger, Perry Oliver said.

Seven shot back a wide-eyed look Perry Oliver had never witnessed before, as if he didn't know what to make of the blind nigger standing in their apartment. (Truth be told—yes, he will admit it—neither at first was sure what he was seeing.) Got to his feet and studied Tom with appropriating eyes in the dead silence. With minimum effort, Tom shook free of Perry Oliver's grip and ambled forward, hands out in front of him, more for the purpose of throwing path-clearing swipes in the air than for guiding touches to avoid potential obstructions. He bumped into the table and continued on, knocking it out of his path as he angled into the farthest corner of the room—why this corner as opposed to another? Perry Oliver still had no answer—next to the open window—the world blowing in, bits of their privacy blowing out—and spun around facing them, his body turned toward the door. Without instruction, Seven had immediately gone over to Tom and tried to take him by the arm. Tom swung. Tom kicked. Seven did not give up, persisted in his efforts, cautious creeping, like a trainer trying to bring a stallion or bull under control. Tom kicked. Tom swung. Perry Oliver didn't blame him, understanding as he did the economy of fear and self-preservation. (Two modes of fear: actual danger and the avoidance of it.) Tom's lungs were hard at work, breath after breath charging in and out.

Come on, Perry Oliver said. We'll leave him there until the morning.

Seven looked at him, doubtful.

He wondered: Would Tom sleep? Or would hunger and terror keep sleep at bay? And would morning bring an end to his battle? If not, how long could this condition last?

Over the next few days, Tom had remained in the corner, taking neither food nor water, and standing on two feet the entire time, no easing up, never once lowering his body to the floor, at least in their presence. (How many nights did it take for Tom to give in? Could Perry Oliver trust his memory?) Without warning or reason he would take a few steps forward, only to stop, as if he had suddenly lost all notion of the place where he had found himself. They maintained a careful distance from across the room, hearing Tom's body give off murmuring surges every now and then, low noises that gradually lengthened into a continual droning—on and on—that was a bit soothing once you fell under its repetitive spell, and observing—creatures at a further remove from man—gross disturbances of this same body, strange shivers of the neck and ear and head, and motor discharges of the shoulders and feet, at almost calculated intervals.

Be still, you dinge, Seven said.

Shut up, Perry Oliver said.

Were these the tactile and general sensations his muscles and skin had preserved in the long journey from Hundred Gates? Exactly how much of Hundred Gates remained in his memory, wherever memory is stored? (What does a nigger carry with him?) No easy answers, for whatever his concerns or protestations they were confined to the dumb machine of his flesh. Easy to be fooled by this fact. How well Perry Oliver knew that words are not the only way of expressing or distilling emotions.

Seven seemed to have his own questions, the distance, the resistance, the reservations all behavior he seemed both unaccustomed to and unprepared for. (The battle was taking its toll on them both.) Far be it from Seven to give an unwelcome impression, but Tom incurred his suspicions, his first doubt Tom's blindness. Within minutes of Tom's being in the apartment and firmly ensconced in the corner, he spoke his first words to him. Hey, don't look cross-eyed at me like that.

He's not cross-eyed, Perry Oliver had said. He's blind.

This explanation did not satisfy the boy. In those initial days and weeks, Seven would hold out two fingers before Tom's face or wave both hands at him from across the room as if to lure him into the light that way. (Indeed, Tom's blindness seemed to possess a particularity all its own. Something Perry Oliver couldn't put his finger on even as he became more and more accustomed to it. Eyes completely shut most of the time, but partially open on other occasions. Involuntarily turning in one direction or another. Or glistening with tears. Nothing like what Perry Oliver imagined blindness to be, nothing like the image of the affliction floating—two dark islands—for so long in his mind. Blindness is in the first place something felt, and as a feeling it is of most obviously unpleasurable character, not that this is a complete description of its quality. Though they have lived together and worked closely for this extended period of time—how long has it been? nine months? a year?—and he felt that he knew Tom as well as anyone might, he was far from in a position to explain the boy.) Seven also began to scrutinize Tom with a disapproving air, frowning, mumbling curses, crossing his eyes, once a foul odor began emanating from the corner that the chance breeze coming through the open window would carry to even the most remote areas of the apartment, the smell of sweat, urine, and feces collecting at Tom's feet where Seven's rag and polish usually fell.

It was asking much. The boy found himself obligated to clean up waste spilling from another whose name he still did not know. For his part, Perry Oliver had forgotten to pass on certain facts to the boy—*Tom. Seven, his name is Tom*—taken up as he was (no intention, no deliberation) with the immediate exigencies of Tom's physical presence, his being there, although it was also true that both before Tom's arrival and after, he and Seven had rarely breathed a word to each other unless some matter of Seven's duties or instruction needed addressing. Bottom line, Seven would wipe up the shit and piss, and he would do so grudgingly, his anger and disgust offset by the incontrovertible fact that they finally had a nigger in their possession.

You got your nigger. Perry Oliver feared that a far greater challenge would be his getting the boy to understand the true purpose Tom should (would) serve in their lives.

One evening, Tom had dropped into the waste he had created and remained seated there, Perry Oliver knowing that the boy could hold out no longer from food but also fearing he would not be able to eat, that after so many days, hunger had possibly settled like a weight that might permanently keep him to the floor. Seven prepared victuals and drink, and Tom, weakened, took his first meal there in the corner, Seven feeding it to him one bite at a time, taking care to keep safe distance between his fingers and Tom's teeth. (What did the repast consist of? Yams—yes—three or four miniature plump and naked women lying on his plate. And slimmer strips of bacon.) Several hours later, Perry Oliver instructed Seven to leave Tom's next meal on the table. Tom would have to come and take the plate if he wanted to eat. He did. Came and took it back to his corner. Then for the third meal Perry Oliver went even further. Tom would have to sit down and eat at the table. Another battle ensued, Tom resisting, even though his stubbornness meant that he would go hungry. But once he took his first meal seated at the table, Perry Oliver believed the full exercise of his control was soon to come, a matter of hours rather than days. Strategizing, he would allow Tom to carry a plate back to his corner for one meal, only to deny him this privilege at another. From his corner how eagerly Tom's face—nose—followed the steaming food, from the place where it was taken, to the exact spot where it was set down on the table. His mouth would open, his teeth and tongue would move, then a flash of white bone, a trickle of saliva, his muscles and organs rehearsing the act of consumption. Along with this anticipation, he would speak a single perplexing sentence, the only words Perry Oliver could recall hearing issue from his mouth in those first days and weeks. *My taste gets worse every day.* Perry Oliver has never been able to figure out if it was the table Tom was resisting or the food itself, or some combination of the two, refusing one on a given day and the other on another. And what exactly was the nature of this resistance, conscious revolt or some form of muscular denial? Which would be the easier of the two to defeat? Would body eventually overcome the obstinate resistance of his mind, or vice versa?

Seven seemed far more capable of winning Tom to the table. After the first taste of food and water, a slow and gradual erasing of distance, signs of increasing and mutual trust, Tom permitting Seven to come closer and even closer still, to take his hand, lead him to a chair, seat him and put a fork between his fingers, indicating that it was now okay for him to begin tackling his plate. What had been unusual only a few days earlier assumed the character of normality, Seven masking his mouth and nose with a handkerchief before kneeling down in the most rudimentary way to clean up Tom's waste, then thoroughly scrubbing his charge's arms up to the elbows until finally he felt obliged to happily seat himself beside Tom, a warmth that Tom seemed to return, the black contours of the one face not unlike the lighter contours of the other. Their eating a noisy and spirited ritual, a touching of elbows in the working of fork and knife, a knocking of knees beneath the wood.

Perry Oliver could scarcely believe Seven's generosity. He could remember precisely the moment following one meal when Seven, clearing away the soiled plates, carrying them over to the sink, was heard to mutter with back turned, Our Tom.

I didn't buy him for you, Perry Oliver said.

Seven stopped in the middle of the room and turned his head to look at Perry Oliver over his shoulder, his body seemingly paralyzed with an odd stiffness.

In fact, I didn't buy him at all.

Seven looked at Perry Oliver for a moment longer with blank attention then, changing up, began observing him with a relaxed astonishing ease that startled Perry Oliver. Composure recovered, Seven took a seat next to Tom at the table. (Perhaps they meant far more to each other than Perry Oliver had been—and is still?—

willing to admit.) Perry Oliver took some time to explain why Tom was here.

He's the General's nigger?

Yes.

We are serving under the General?

Perry Oliver had never thought about it that way. How had he thought about it? And had his feelings changed with the passage of time? In fact, as he looked at the table attempting to summon up the correct sequence of events that had brought Tom to his present station in their lives—of course, the larger *it*, the past, is never whole, never totally retrievable once the actual events solely exist in the reduced confines of memory; if only his cheap pocket watch could magically wind (skip) backward and return him to the far-off scene; the world awaits a capable invention—he realized that he had left out one important detail—that moment when water first touched Tom's skin. Logic if not the far less objective demands of comfort and decency had required that Seven bathe Tom right there in the corner before he escorted his charge to the first defining meal at the table, otherwise both Tom's appalling odor and equally appalling appearance—after days of neglect, the boy's hair was a piecemeal mess, resembling a hastily constructed bird's nest; as well, brown stains ran in stripe-like patterns down from the seat of his pants to both ankles—would have been too much of an affront. Indeed, Perry Oliver's timing was off—inevitable lapses and alterations, forgetting the B preceding C—but one thing he knew for certain was this. Once it had become clear to Seven that Tom was willing to take his meal at the table, he had taken it upon himself to forestall Tom's hunger until he could properly clean up. The usual industriousness opening out of him. He secured his handkerchief around his face and with both hands lugged a pail brimming with cold water over to the corner—he dare not drag it across the floor—set it down before Tom, then proceeded to remove and bundle up the soiled clothing, and scrub and clean him right there in the corner. (Surprisingly, Tom did not shudder at the first slap of cold water against his skin nor flinch at the abrasive knot of soap.) He toweled Tom dry and helped him into fresh clothes. His charge done over, Seven carefully secured the towel around the bundle of clothing, isolated these items from the other laundry, emptied the dirty water, and returned with a fresh pail of clean water to clean the corner. Wall and floor restored. He was now free to feed Tom, his frail pail having claimed both the filth darkening in the corner and the filth clinging to Tom's skin. Good details to forget.

After the battle over the table, the next struggle became one of getting Tom to sleep in his bed. He would fall asleep at the table like one slowly succumbing to poison. Seven would awaken him, but he would refuse to relinquish his chair, clutching it so firmly you might have believed that the wood had actually penetrated his skin and nailed him to the object. But once he became accustomed to sleeping in the bed—the room where the boys sleep is so narrow that they can actually extend their arms sideward from a prone position and reach across and touch one another up to the elbow—Perry Oliver decided that the moment had come for Tom to return to his music.

The very first time they had taken Tom out of the apartment, in the hallway he had leaned into nothing and went rolling and tumbling down the stairs. Three flights.

Seven?

Sir?

Did you see what just happened?

Yes, sir.

Do you fully understand your responsibilities?

Yes, sir.

After this exchange of words—he was hard toward Seven when it came to his wishes and expectations—he recalled Seven hurrying off while he made an effort to pull himself together. Recalled reaching the bottom of the staircase and seeing Tom all bloodied with scratches and scrapes, struggling to his feet, tottering and dizzy. He had to decide then and there if he should summon a doctor, a matter quickly resolved when the name (threat)—General Bethune—sparkled up out of his ponderings. He knew there could be no doctor.

Thankfully, their destination was close enough for Tom to reach it in his pitiful condition. (How fragile we are.) Perry Oliver, Seven, and Tom—three—entered the establishment under a rusty horseshoe nailed over the door, with a small hand-painted sign—NO ONE ENTERS THESE PORTALS BUT THE TRUE IN HEART—swinging from it, and to the murmur of conversation that immediately ceased at their entrance, as if they had let in a powerful wind that extinguished sound. All heads turned in Tom's direction.

Tom. An intimation. A signal. Every room was transformed when he entered it. (Perry Oliver recognized this fact for the second time, but only now truly acknowledged it. Tom's commanding presence bringing back the feeling from weeks earlier when he had gone to retrieve Tom from the station, faces turning, eyes zoning in, as he led Tom to a hansom taxi, heads cocked, eyes aimed, attracting the same unthinking reaction as now.) Everything got put into the background, relegated to the shade, while this ugly little blind imbecile nigger boy became a radiant presence. The exact opposite of Perry Oliver, who all his life had been retiring and modest, keeping himself to himself.

Stationed behind the bar, owner William Oakley saw them enter and nodded welcome at Perry Oliver. He looked at the nigger and looked some more, but he said not a word, nor allowed his face to express surprise, disapproval, or disappointment. However odd or transgressive his behavior appeared, Perry Oliver had no intentions of divulging to anyone, including the owner, why he had brought a nigger into this establishment or why this nigger looked the worse for wear. One and all, his dealings with Tom made him feel supremely indifferent to public opinion at this moment and fully justified in saying nothing. Besides, whatever might be ruined now could be set right later. Comfort in that thought.

Although he and the owner had a long-standing business relationship—he rented space for his horse and carriage in a stable, Spectacular Spurs, that the owner operated up the street—he rarely set foot inside the establishment, in distinct contrast to Seven, who was required to come here at least three times in a single day to pick up their meals.

He eased Seven in the direction of the upright piano, indicating that the boy should direct Tom over to it. Tom sat down on the unvarnished bench, raising all of Perry Oliver's expectations, and tapped out a few chords. Then he sat still, his hands folded in his lap. Like a puppeteer, Perry Oliver lifted the other's hands and moved them over the keys. No doing.

Perry Oliver threw a questioning glance at Seven. Seven shrugged his shoulders. In the other faces Perry Oliver saw ludicrous expressions of disbelief, not that he was expecting to gain their sympathy or understanding.

You can't blame him, Oakley said.

Why not?

It's out of tune.

Indeed, it was the only conclusion one could draw. No doubting it, Tom knows what he wants to hear and knows how it should sound. Perry Oliver laughed at himself—the silent movement went a long way in releasing many weeks of tension—having to concede that Tom's resistance went beyond his expectations. No, he had not foreseen in complete perspective the kinds of hesitation—five varieties?—the boy had put up, and could only assume that there might be more.

Two weeks later—three?—Seven had informed him over breakfast that the piano had been brought up to speed—the boy's exact words—and awaited Tom's use. The news made the food easier to digest. The moment was not far away when they could begin their work. Once breakfast was done, they hurried down to Scaldy Bill's and placed Tom before the piano, the instrument thoroughly made over, shining with a fresh polish, and smelling all the better for it.

Tom moved both hands over the ivories in a trial run. Then he picked his way through each key, first the black, then the white. Satisfied, he fingered out an entire song. And so it went. The patrons applauded after each number—*What a remarkable nigger*—and called out requests, but Tom seemed to play whatever came to mind. No one present was more impressed with Tom's abilities than Seven, who remained standing near his charge, seized by the sight, totally reluctant to part from his side.

❊ ❊ ❊

Seven heard their neighbor urinate into the same bottle the old man used to collect his milk. More than once he had considered going across the hall and telling the old man how to manage this action without making a noise. *Show proper consideration for others.* The neighbor's good fortune that Mr. Oliver had already finished his breakfast and left the apartment, that he had been spared this offensive sound. Heaven knows what he might do. Understand, Mr. Oliver was a civilized man, the most decent sort, but some things he would not tolerate, especially from a certain class of people.

Seated across from him on the opposite side of the table, Tom knocked his hands several times against the flat wood side. You are hungry, he said.

What would you have? Seven asked him. Tom had a good appetite.

A little milk. A little bread.

Seven poured Tom a glass of goat's milk, cut him a slice of bread. Despite his dexterity on the piano, Tom had difficulty bringing the glass to his lips without spilling the contents. One quick motion and the glass jerked up to his mouth, splashing milk across his face. Equal difficulty with bread. Less a matter of him biting the bread and more of him moving the bread sideways across his teeth until it all disappeared. A few archipelagoes of crumbs positioned above his milk-glistening upper lip.

Employ your napkin, Tom, Seven said.

··· 271 ···

Tom picked up his cheap cotton napkin and wiped his mouth.

Seven recognized that Tom was feeble-minded—is that how Mr. Oliver had put it?—and he tried to remember by what means he had brought Tom this far. He cast his mind back, hoping to recover an image of Tom as he was before. (Tom muffled in a worn black suit three sizes too large for him.) Yes, some progress, plenty, truth be told. Still, he had to get Tom to drop some of his ill manners, smooth out some of the rough edges, a goal he had set for himself. He had found common cause in the things Mr. Oliver required of him and those other things that he felt he should require of himself. (Principles and habits.) Only proper that he should give more, for Mr. Oliver had bequeathed him a tremendous responsibility, a laying out of trust, an investment of faith. One that posed a challenge from the first, but one he gladly stood up to since it filled him with new purpose and confidence.

Although Mr. Oliver had left the apartment physically, he was still present everywhere in the clearest way. He had moved this, had left that lying around, had not closed his window, forgotten to shut that drawer properly, left that slipper sticking out from under the bed and a half-empty glass of water at the window in his room. Seven didn't believe these were oversights, mental lapses, but intentional disorder to keep him on point, to see how capable he was of putting each object back in its proper location. Even if he believed Mr. Oliver had no good reason for testing him this way—his skills were far beyond the basics; had long since adapted to the role of Tom's protector and guardian, though he didn't know the exact number of days, had known Tom all this time but had never made the effort to keep count until a week ago; give these days back, a full accounting—Mr. Oliver felt it was worth the trouble. So be it. Who was he to complain, to ask more?

Cows keep the milk down, Tom said.

No, Seven said. Cows keep the milk in. Tom turned his face to Seven in his crooked way. Seven forked back Tom's eyelids with two fingers on his left hand, a slow revealing, like stage curtains being drawn up. The orbs were completely black and hard in appearance—should he touch them?—nothing soft about them, stone; you might believe that two objects had speeded down from the heavens above and come to a deep burial inside Tom's face. If our eyes are indeed windows into our soul, as he had so often heard, then Tom lacked windows. Hard blackness sealed off inward entry. God had deliberately put Tom's soul on his face.

Tom was seated in a chair identical to his—straight-backed wood, uncushioned—but Seven afforded Tom what he believed was the more comfortable of the two. His job to preserve order in the apartment's August emptiness. His duty, sure, but he also felt a quiet affection for Tom. Tom opening up new areas of feeling in him. He could not get over the fact of how much freedom the blind give us. The closest thing to being by oneself. You can do most anything before them undetected. Not that he chose to do so, took advantage. He was always correct in his bearing toward Tom.

Absently, he passed his gaze over the surface of Tom's face, unseeing eyes that made the aspect of him a particular delight. Sitting carefully upright in his chair during silent moments, he found himself staring into this face. Black calm. Blankness. The shiny smooth innocence of an unused stone. The most comforting person he had ever met, Tom was happy here with him (them) and he took considerable pleasure in the knowledge, as in his good handling of Tom he deserved primary credit for Tom's state of being. Whatever he said to Tom would be heard with sympathy, with kindness. And Tom had the additional advantage of Mr. Oliver's close and careful management.

Seven decided to leave the apartment as it was for later. Too much trouble. They should be able to depart and return with sufficient time left over for him to tidy up before Mr. Oliver returned. Time for all things.

Tom, he asked, where are you?

I'm on earth.

So you are. He stood up and stretched out the stiffness. Leaned across the table and fit Tom's hat onto his head, flattening the thick-rooted hair, low, mashing, right down to the ridge of Tom's brow and just above his blind bulging eyes.

Every day, Tom said, I put on a new head.

Hat, Seven said. Tom could well use a new hat. It would decidedly improve both his appearance and his existence. A good head covering—his beaver cap, Paul Morphy's panama—provides important relief from the heat. (Mr. Oliver somehow managed without one.) He tugged on the brim of Tom's hat, signaling that it was time for them to depart.

Tom rose up from the table, came around it, and embraced him so hard he thought he would choke in Tom's arms. Chest constricted, breath trickling out, he allowed Tom to hug him for a considerable length of time until it was clear that Tom had no intention of releasing him. He wiggled free by distracting Tom with a tune he whistled into his ear. (One trick he had learned.) His skin felt different, as if Tom had left some element of his body behind on Seven's. In fact, it seemed to have taken on a certain painful illumination, and he wondered now if he had wrongly sensed Tom's embrace, the stationary hug not stationary at all but a rough rubbing of skin against skin, a hard-worked polish.

Tom had been his shadow ever since he hit town. His Tom unique, a totally new person in human history as far as he could tell, and his singularity left him unable to exist without Seven. Height against height, he loomed above Seven, a fairly sizable nigger at seven years of age—his reputed age (Mr. Oliver's estimate), certainly (probably) far younger than Seven by several years, five at the least, possibly more, but niggers don't develop by the calendar or the clock—tall but not excessively so. Seven was small for his age, a full head shorter than Tom, and just as slim as his younger charge, spindly, boy-skinny—

Eat, Perry Oliver says. You need to eat more—but he was a force capable of imposing the necessary discipline. Easy when one was experienced in such matters. His job to keep Tom regulated, under a daily routine, an unavoidable necessity as Perry Oliver had made it clear that Tom lacked the internal clock that most of us, white people and niggers alike, are born with.

Tom unlatched the door, opened it, and made his way to the head of the stairs, then waited for Seven to help him down. They hurried out into late-morning light. The worst heat. Seven looked out at the world, a red line throbbing on the far horizon, his senses awakening, detecting. In the clear silence, Tom wordlessly clutched Seven's hand with both of his, and allowed Seven to lead him forward. But Seven's gaze was no longer directed upward at the much taller Tom but downward at the wobbly cobblestone road. The road seemed more even, your walk less steady if you concentrated on counting the individual stones as you stepped onto each one.

Tom sniffed the air like a hound. Raised his face—peered up; could he call it that?—as if something—a bird, a cloud—had passed overhead. The sky is so high, he said.

He often had much to say. Seven encouraged him to speak up, to talk loudly, even if he confounded sense, for he had found that much of our inability to understand Tom came from our inability to hear what he was actually saying. Hushed tones. Failed to speak at a high enough level for our ears to detect him. *Speak up, Tom.*

Caught in an unreal space. Heat and overlapping speech. Faces came out of the blackness to glare and shout. Bibulous types who downed hot drinks, the temperate fuel that allowed them to blow fiery words from the open furnaces of their mouths. For some reason they thought it amusing to offer Tom tobacco. Like a smoke, Tom?

Seven spoke kindly to the patrons, but he was quick to whisk Tom away, politely excusing them, removing his hat and tipping his head. He guided Tom toward the piano, scarcely registering the things around except in glimpses of single objects, as he (they) weaved between the tables, dodging a gauntlet of propositions, patrons offering Seven spirits, tobacco, and whatever else their tongues saw fit. Courteously he took the time to pause and decline to each and every one. Perhaps he and Tom were the only sane creatures within these four walls.

A man stepped in front of them, blocking their passage. His thin cheeks were badly shaven, here and there short little tufts of hair having escaped the razor. He stared over Seven's shoulder at Tom. What's the nigger's name?

Thomas, Seven said.

Thomas?

Yes, sir.

Are you sure?

Seven tried to subdue his irritation. Yes, sir.

That is too much of a name for a little nigger to carry around.

Sir?

Thomas, you said?

Yes, sir.

That means twin.

No, Tom said. It means Tom.

Taken aback, the man turned away noisily in a vibration of cloth, hobbling but decisive, a fantastic construction, his image changing and reforming, by turns good-natured, crazy, and threatening, like a passing cloud.

Seven and Tom continued on until they reached their destination. Tom sat down on the long stool (bench?) positioned before the piano. Seven noticed that he was trembling. Sat down on the bench beside him, slanted, facing Tom but also able to turn his head and take in the room if need be. Not that he wanted to. He was unconcerned with his surroundings, closing in on himself, pushing the saloon further into the back of his consciousness. Tom and Seven, two plotters ill at ease in the light. Here they could unite with angles and corners, make themselves invisible to the population.

The piano was an awkward piece of work, with its tall square back and massive elephant-like legs and its cracked and discolored keys. It seemed strangely out of place here, this saloon the last place on earth where one would expect to find a piano or any other brandishment of fancy. Seven saw great meaning in this fact, knowing as he did the troubles that Perry Oliver had experienced in trying to locate an instrument for Tom. Something almost magical in all of this, as it could be this piano and no other. As if the piano had awaited Tom's arrival, biding time, possibly for centuries. Had always been here, a natural formation like a rocky monolith, this roof this floor and these four walls constructed around it.

Where did you get that piano from? he asked.

I never got it, Mr. Oakley said. It was sitting right where it is when I accepted the deed.

The piano had become a cherished habit, the tool that would clear the way for him and Tom to develop an understanding. Seven distinctly recalled the very first time (second?) Tom touched the keys. His hands jerked back, as if the keys were some burning substance. (Seven had heard that electricity has the same hot effect.) Then again, minutes earlier Tom had fallen down three flights of stairs. Perhaps he had suffered an injury.

Seven was not sure that Tom was comfortable playing here. The tension of his posture betrayed him. His tongue came out of his mouth to moisten his lips. Then, all by themselves, without the help of human eyes, his hands began to find the complex track of chords and notes, the heart of melodies that kindled the desire to pat one's feet, to clap one's hands, to dance. A twist of flesh touched. Senses awakened, Seven felt his heart leap seeing this simple and wild display. Suspended. Sealed off. (Echoes and fragrances.) Impervious to time. Music glistened everywhere. Barely attuned to his surroundings, he noticed that someone had taken a seat at the table nearest them, a sun-darkened and slim man. (Thirty? forty? Age is no consequence for Seven, still new to the world.) A good-looking man, unlike the others here, a man of good standing, like Perry Oliver, very well dressed and groomed. He seemed unconscious of anything except a set purpose of staring at the table (smooth darkness) and grumbling to himself, lips silently moving. Perhaps he was drunk, though Seven saw no evidence that he had been imbibing alcohol. His only refreshment a half-drained glass of water, chunks of ice floating on the surface. Ah—looking closer—he was reading, reviewing a document spread flat across the table. Pen in hand, inkwell at the ready. He lifted his face up. Their eyes met, or so it seemed. No, he was wide-eyed as if staring at words in the air. Stared vacantly past Seven, his face relaxed and oblivious, before returning his eyes to his document, his reading and writing. A short while later he raised his face again. Yes, now he was looking right at Seven (them). Squared the corners of the sheet he was reading, then edged around the table to position himself in proximity to the piano. He said he was waiting for a friend, although Seven had no idea why he chose to relay this information. In one hand, he carried a musical score (black lines, black circles, white space)—yes, this was what he had been reading—and he had been humming it under his breath, tapping the accompaniment on the table with his fingers, even as he talked.

Tom's hands stopped moving. I like that song, Tom said.

Do you? the man said. He looked at them from behind an almost immobile face.

Yes.

He grinned. But it's a sad song.

No, Tom said. Niggers are sad.

Yes, the man said. They are. He introduced himself as W. P. Howard. Seven introduced them. *Seven and Thomas.* Is he your boy?

I'm his, Tom said. I'm his boy.

Tom resumed his playing. Shut eyes glazed. Hands moved over keys, feet worked pedals. Body rocked from side to side. Smooth steady movement. He looked less like a man playing an instrument than like a captain steering his ship. Transported.

Perry Oliver found the apartment pitch black—as well it should be, since he was late in returning, quite late, having missed both dinner and supper—with a peculiar stillness. Tried to get his bearings, half a thought ahead, half a thought behind. He lit a lamp, a flame that was not bright enough to illuminate the entire room, but he was accustomed to the parlor-kitchen lit at night by a single inconstant light, as he was reserved in the use of candle and oil. He could make out two figures dozing deliciously at the table. The pair seated side by side, a hand apart, slumped forward and face down. He stood and watched in this semidarkness favorable to spying and conspiracy, his emotions keeping him from speaking the words and thoughts that crowded into his head like a panicked herd. Such harsh language inside him that it might rip his throat apart should it come out.

He methodically went about inspecting the room.

Tea was on the table. Impossible to convey its color, its smell. Everything had been gathered up, the smaller objects placed inside the larger ones, the dirty items washed and dried, both litter and leftovers collected and disposed of. The supper—dinner?—basket was empty. Not a single remnant—shredded meat, greasy bone, bread crumb—of food.

Tom lifted his head. Come in, come in, he said. Everybody is a member. He returned to his sleep.

A trail of breath. A moan. He saw two little bodies moving forward in the hall toward the staircase. One put a foot out and stepped onto air, onto nothing. Pitched forward and disappeared as if sinking beneath water. The observer-listener shaking with fear at the sound of a body tumbling down and rattling against stairs.

Perry Oliver could feel the house shudder. The second body hurried after the first, but Perry Oliver hesitated, a quick gasp of astonishment in his mouth. His instinct had nudged him off course.

His consciousness in a state of alert. (Too far away, too far behind.) His vision blurred as if he had suddenly gone under water. Once he decided to (once he could), he moved feverishly as if in a hurry to assure himself that the situation was not as dire as it appeared.

He discovered a Tom-at-rest three flights below, propped up against the banister, Seven kneeling down before him, touching his charge at the wrist. A noise came from Tom's body. His lips moved although no words came out. At least, none they could hear. He would kneel too, but he was afraid to touch Tom. But he had gained enough courage not to deny reality, what he had just seen with his very own eyes. He did not lose his calm. He even had the presence of mind to realize that he could (should?) consider himself lucky, all things considered. Tom was alive and apparently only slightly injured. He screwed up his eyes and spoke to Seven without anger or panic.

The agonies of shame. This was why Perry Oliver didn't speak now, why he chose to let Seven and Tom sleep. (In the morning, he would hear, he would judge, he would forgive.) The burden of words and their sounds meant to awaken the past. He had to keep his suffering intact. Would follow painful memories but only so far, a past he tried his best to confine to the long forgotten. How else to keep a tight hold on what was closest, the immediate tasks stretching before him? His mind turned wholly to the menace of the moment, the struggle that each new day imposes. Who has not tried to read the beginnings of today's calamity—he had failed to find an instructor for Tom—in the memory of yesterday's error? For Perry Oliver, each error was an opportunity, a stepping-stone to somewhere else. Of course, no getting around that strange fringe of uneasiness among his thoughts, muted strands of uncertainty and foreboding that were always there, that he had to struggle against. Loss has a way of creeping back. With the future crossed out, the past will become an obsession. So he welcomed what life brought each day, good or bad, and constantly strove to bring himself into a new understanding of it. The old Perry Oliver had to disappear to make room for the new one.

Had to give up everything. Homes he had lived in. Books read. Places traveled. Previous sentiments and passions. Give it all up. Come from nowhere.

He groped forward, stopped to look inside the boys' room, which was after the parlor-kitchen the second largest room in the apartment. (His the smallest.) Handheld light revealed three images hanging on the wall above Seven's bed. A daguerreotype of Senator Douglas and one of Senator Calhoun. *Since our beloved, aged defender was unable to rise and take command of the floor, Senator Mason of Virginia stepped in as his voice.* And the portrait of Paul Morphy. The two beds positioned on either side of the room were exactly like his own, all three identical in shape and construction, none longer or wider than the others, and all consisting of the same make and grain of wood. Functional constructions built to last, and fully capable of supporting the plump unshapely mattresses that covered them, rough burlap amply filled with discarded peanut shells and skin (far cheaper than cotton).

Once he was in the tranquility of his own room, he barely took the trouble to undress, having survived another rough day. Tomorrow sure to be the same. He threw himself on his bed. He had a plan. In those towns and cities containing a preponderance of cultivated people, theaters do not flourish to the same extent as in locales where the reverse is true. Cultivated people have no reason to go out, already finding music at home. (The parlor piano.) Music halls in this city primarily catered crude spectacles for the lowly of life with the occasional special event or festivity that all may enjoy. His goal was to draw the cultivated out with music—Tom—they couldn't get at home. Kindle a desire for a form of serious (classical) entertainment they had never seen before.

Though his plan required the preponderance of his time, he got away from hard work to pay attention to other things—mainly the newspaper. He preferred the Negro journals published in the North—he said and thought *South* without attaching any importance to it; he took no particular pride in this land where he was born and where he still lived—even maintained a subscription to the best, despite the suspicious glances of the local postmaster. More actuality—truth—in the pages mixed in among all the propaganda of racial uplift. *Uplift the race.* In the reporting more words than not that actually fit the occasion, rather than adorn or preach.

> *Noble Reader, certainly the negro is not our equal in color—perhaps not in many other respects; still, in the right to put into his mouth the bread that his own hands have earned, he is the equal of every other man, white or black. In pointing out that more has been given you, you can not be justified in taking away the little which has been given him. All I ask for the negro is that if you don't like him, let him alone. If God gave him little, that little let him enjoy.*

He slowly and wearily put the newspaper down. Closed his eyes the better to see with his inward gaze those landscapes and horizons where printed words carried him. It amused him to come up with a subject to reflect on every now and then, an entertaining theme that could pull him away from the present. If only refuge in the self were that easy. Something had happened that his intelligence was wearing itself out trying to define. Willingly, he let himself slide into a kind of lethargy, waiting to better understand. (In the night we move forward.)

Noises reached Perry Oliver quite unmuffled by the thin walls. The least little sound he heard (or imagined?) impelled him to be on his guard, sometimes even pulling him out of bed. Despite the heat, he closed the thick damask curtain, reinforced with a white blind behind it, impenetrable fabric that prevented any light from entering the chamber. But no barring sound. He heard feet flutter in the room next to his where the boys slept, stopping here, stopping there. No discernible pattern in the movement. Took some listening to recognize it as Tom quick's tread. Was Tom entering the kitchen (parlor)?

Now he heard voices too, snatches of murmurings. Tom and Seven? Both boys moving about? Moving and talking?

Sometimes, on a good morning, in the clear silence, he could relive the triumphs of his life. Was this so today? He peered into the mirror but couldn't see his eyes. Gaped and gawked at his reflection, but the image didn't improve. The mirror—polished glass, reflective capacity, the power to throw back—swinging freely on its stand. A black screen interrupted by light. He splashed water on his face and watched it roll down his reflected cheeks and chin and drip down into the basin. His mind struggled to awaken.

From the window he could see the woodshed and everything that went on in the yard. Bare-chested and barefoot, the nigger who took care of the house was putting the shed in order. The nigger had a full day ahead, a hundred tasks to complete. Now beat out rugs and mattresses, now shovel the garbage into a pile and set it aflame. And once that was done, he would be ready to clean the lavatory on each floor.

Just at the outskirts, where vision ended, he could look—and he often did—at the black city under a heavy sky. His destination today.

He went into the kitchen (parlor). Seven was still half-asleep in his chair, eyes brimming with light, heavy and comical. (Where was Tom?) He waited patiently for the boy to recover himself, his heart quick to tremble and be touched. Why bother about the boy's feelings, about the fact that the boy worried about Tom, too, that he was perhaps three times more concerned than Perry Oliver was himself about Tom's cares and hurts.

Seven got up from his chair and stood before him, wobbly, in respectful expectation. Beneath the harsh reflection of his tired mouth and blank eyes, his real face appeared, the face of an adolescent.

Shadows slithered in and out. Mr. Oliver was waiting for Seven to speak. Seven wondered what he should do, what response might be the least detrimental to him: call out or remain quiet? His mind was too foggy, the conflicting thoughts inside his head unable to focus or affix themselves. He stammered, got tangled in his attempt to control his voice, master his emotion, and find the right words, the expression that would be convincing. Instead, he emitted a kind of mush, syllables jolting each other and running together.

Perry Oliver listened to capture every word and pause.

Overwhelmed, Seven lowered his head, clinging to the faint hope that Mr. Oliver would understand.

And still Tom fell down the stairs, Perry Oliver said.

Yes.

You must do better.

I must do better.

Mr. Oliver walked to the door and took silent leave.

Sometime later, Seven stood on the bed admiring the summer trees. What could he see? (Squirrels change branches.) He wanted to see the world. Break away from everything earthly and set out on a great adventure. For now, he held Tom fast in one place. (If you can't stand something, don't do it.) Tom had to do everything in full view while Seven watched him. A bed's width of silence separating them, between them, building a secret room. He got down from the bed and straightened the sheets. Tom popped up. More sheets to align. (Two diverging elements.) What it means to introduce another self into the equation.

What body was that, hunched and shaking at the kitchen table? He recalled (his wounded memory) a happy dinner, things as usual. He told himself that all had passed off smoothly for him and Tom until supper time arrived, when Mr. Oliver returned—he recognized footsteps then heard the door yank open—from his work and joined them at the table.

No, he couldn't twist the facts. Yesterday (afternoon and night) had not worked out to his greater glory. A warning unleashed inside him. He was glad just to stir again. He had suffered no ill effects. (If you can't handle the job, don't volunteer.) It was all in his hands now. (This boy has put himself entirely in my hands.)

He comforted the face confronting him. Gave Tom tender consideration. Playfully patted his other's cheeks, slapped him on the back of his neck. Soared aloft. Higher. And now out into the fresh air, which would make them both feel better.

Once they arrived (landed) at Scaldy Bill's, Mr. Oakley quickly installed the two of them at the piano. Seven sat and listened. Cherished habits. But what was this he heard? The same tunes from yesterday. (So he remembered.) Tom was reciting as if by rote. (Re-creation.) He had never known Tom to be negligent about playing (practicing?). As good a reason as any not to listen, to lock out his emotions.

While Tom played, not once did Seven turn around on the stool and he did not so much as glance at the other patrons in the saloon (restaurant), as was his custom. Established a boundary that no one dared cross. He and Tom must not be noticed by the outside world. He and Tom must not notice the outside world. He sensed and felt nothing; all of his thoughts were focused on one point: Tom. No matter how hard he might try, he couldn't hear the music now. He heard nothing. Locked out sight and sound.

So they remained for several hours, Tom playing. Then the attentive Negress barmaid came over and sat a pitcher of iced tea on top of the piano, the diversion Seven had been waiting for.

Time to go home now, Tom, he said. Time for food, he said, strategic. Long minutes had worn by; Tom would obey hunger and taste. Tom nestled against him. Tenderly close, the two of them got up from the piano and made their way to the bar. Seven received their dinner basket from the Negress. Handed Mr. Oakley the money due. The owner seemed to be giving serious thought to the changes in Seven's behavior, today's standoffishness, aloofness. (The mind twists and turns as it sees fit.) Seven was transgressing a simple rule of propriety with his silence. Even so, the owner didn't express his feelings, only issued Seven a message that he instructed him to pass on to Mr. Oliver. Then he enclosed the two boys in his arms like sons, with more of the family, a sparkling pair of green glasses, awaiting their kinship on the counter.

Discreetly, Seven made as if reaching for one of the glasses and by such deceptive means managed to rearrange his limbs and create some elbow room. Tom, his welcome accomplice, was not so discreet. Dropped right to the floor free of Mr. Oakley's skin. Seven hastily apologized—no telling what a nigger will do—then stooped down and helped Tom back to his feet in a nonclaimed space, three bar stools of distance between them and the owner. The owner showed no reaction beyond breathing. Seven mentally filed away the owner's message, but found an excuse to refuse the green liquid, quick to forestall any objection by saying that they were already late in meeting Mr. Oliver back at their residence.

Outside, they encountered the usual stares and disavowals. Pure fantasy to expect anything less. Seven was fully prepared. These petty figures underestimated his strength. Just by looking at them or refusing to look he could switch them on and off. Tom, his natural cohort, fluttering along behind him, leaving reflections in the store windows.

Perry Oliver dreams of walking in a deserted and silent street. But the city is overpopulated, swarming like flies on kill, no matter what the time of day or what the season. It resounds with their footsteps and voices. Buzzes with their wings and working tongues. He shrilly struggles for breath. With what joy he would like to send them all to hell.

Face it, he is living among barbarians. Nothing can change that fact, alter the immovable difference between him and them. How is it that of the many people he knows in this city only Tom and Seven and Oakley meet his expectations? So many frauds, failures, and incompetents. He has come to expect the worst. (Experience is fact.) Has to be overly cautious in his dealings because the local good citizens offer the world, but what they can actually provide is insufficient to help him get on with his work. To expect good craft, care, is an excessive demand. Nothing is done thoroughly enough, everything is rushed and imperfect.

He strikes out along a new road, trying to get his bearings so that he'll know how to behave once he arrives. Trying his best not to think about what may await him. All of his business may be there. Perhaps. Wouldn't bet on it one way or the other. So far this has been a ridiculous, hideous, preposterous day. He no longer knows where he is, where he stands. This sense of confusion disorientation is why—no other explanation—he feels surrender rising in his blood.

And why shouldn't he? What has he to show for his efforts? One after another he interviews those instructors whose names have been put forth. From each he gets the same response. No. Always looks so promising at first. Anxious to earn a fee, they hurry him inside their homes, but after he makes his request, they refuse him flatly, impatient for him to go. Turn down good money. So he must try another approach. If money can't persuade them, perhaps his words can. (His mouth the organ.) He puts forward his case. (Indeed, he has learned that he can make a fine fresh impression when he pushes ahead in order to be the first to say something out loud. No matter what he says.) But they don't care if Tom is an exception, a rare breed, a nigger like no other. You see, Tom's skin is definitive. His blindness is end of the road. His idiocy a mockery, an insult—the brutality of fact—to culture and civilization. Perry Oliver tries again, backing up rational speech with firm gestures, raising a finger here and there to underscore a point. A doomed approach. Those who listen and entertain the possibility of Tom's difference quickly decide this nigger boy is incapable of benefiting from instruction, and even go so far as to warn that *I will summon the authorities,* sensing a confidence scheme. Some don't even consider him worthy of formal address. No matter. He knows he has to be prepared for such reactions. Not his place to argue. Silly to worry one's head about something that can't be changed, something beyond one's control. Still, he is upset at this moment, tugging along, heavy with a thousand sensations. His thoughts muddled, only residual traces of the original motive. He needs to restore his confidence, faith.

When he returns to the apartment for dinner, angry nausea rising up the column of his body, he barely looks at Seven and Tom, who are seated at the table facing each other. He bypasses food (no appetite) and closes himself off inside his room, seeking ease (release) after a rough morning. Gives vent to his confusion, having lost his form, the door shut to Seven and Tom. (He will meet them across supper.) Starts to read his newspaper by candle—drapery shuts the light out—only to put the newspaper aside and reinforce his plans through the tedium of preparation. (Who will I see this afternoon? Who tomorrow morning?) The flat calm of Time that kills in silence. A silence where he is afraid that everything will remain as it is. Not that his fear alters his conviction. (Doesn't in the least.) To cloak his feelings, he tells himself that the word *no* is a beginning, not an end. The start of a new conversation. His opponents cannot block his way forever. The knowledge makes him feel strangely fortified, even though his quest is undeniably something of a guessing game. He feels that he is on the right track. His daily failures, stalled efforts, can't cancel out all that he has achieved up to this point in his life. So he must face the truth of what he hopes to accomplish through Tom, face the absolute nature of his work. In this way he can go out into the world again.

He makes his way into the parlor. An hour has passed.

From the table Seven turns his bright splotch of skin toward him and brings word that Mr. Oakley offers to sell *us* the piano outright, and charge nothing for its delivery.

Now there's a thought. (Tom reaches out and chokes Seven's beaver cap in one hand and starts caressing it with the other.) The price is fair. And perhaps it makes perfect sense to purchase the piano. The apartment has enough space for it. (Right over there.) And it would help to remove Tom from public view. But he has no desire to own a piano. Has sufficient possessions already. No, that is not quite what he has in mind.

Say nothing, he says. I will speak to him.

Yes, sir.

They have nothing more to tell each other. (Why waste words?) He leaves without saying good-bye.

Out in the street, he admits an important truth to himself. This city impresses him. That is, he is reluctantly impressed by the limits he pushes against in an attempt to expand beyond them. His mental mettle is sagging, although it hasn't broken yet. Tense to the point of pain, of his beginnings, he is incapable of deciding what to do next and incapable of holding on to whatever he might decide. He is open to suggestions, open to anything and everything, no matter where it comes from. Perhaps Oakley can help. The saloon owner dares to do what others merely promise. He must tell Oakley about the troubles he has been having. He will seek his advice.

He approaches the saloon. Comes through the door expecting the usual but doesn't immediately recognize the room. Has it changed, been done over? Patrons waver in one direction then another. He can't glimpse any pattern in their wavering. Oakley's nigger is kneeling by the bar stools, hammer in hand, nails between his teeth, installing brass cuspidors. Careful where he places his knees and feet to avoid the many pools of brown spit (tobacco juice) covering the floor around him. The owner is there too, behind the counter, talking to one of the regulars. The scar marring his face seems to have darkened in color, as black as the derby covering his head. Perry Oliver installs himself on a stool near the owner and barges his way into the discussion. (He does not go to extremes. Only right that the sober citizen should put himself before the drunk.) The regular issues no challenge—Perry Oliver has come to stake his claim—only gets up from his seat and ambles off into the smoky gloom.

He listens to the owner's offer. He says that it is a fair price, although he knows he has no intention of purchasing the piano. He improvises an excuse for putting off the purchase for a month. The owner accepts. They shake hands on the deal. (String him along for now.) Then he starts in on his difficulties finding a music instructor.

He is no crier. (Cry and the world will pity you. He wants no one's pity.) So how does he come to find himself seated at the bar before the owner, drink in hand, spilling liquid onto the counter? Oakley fixes his stare on Perry Oliver's face, and suddenly the latter feels, he doesn't know why, like placing himself in the saloon owner's hands. Perry Oliver goes on talking for a full half hour or more, deliberately throwing in all the details and nuances. He enjoys immensely talking about all this, with the owner seated regally on his stool, silent and motionless, and staring straight into his eyes, something aggressive and challenging in his gaze. At the most intimate passages, he notices that the owner looks a bit embarrassed.

There you have it. A fair shake is all I want.

Don't tease my brain any more on the subject, Oakley says. You allow people to treat you like that. But you do nothing about it.

Perry Oliver says nothing at first, surprised to see Oakley showing a different side of himself. Not the customary exchange of ideas, man to man. Perhaps the owner is only sounding him out. He proceeds to try to justify his actions, his doing nothing, his tolerance of injustice.

You're going about it all wrong. Don't be diplomatic. Remember that you are dealing with idiots. Diplomacy is beyond their understanding.

Perry Oliver listens, taking it all in.

You have to face them head-on. Confront and complain. That's the only way.

Later, Perry Oliver will ponder what he had actually heard the owner advise (demand). Was it "complain" or "come plain"?

Make it clear who's in charge. And if you have to, give them your boot to lick. To that, he gives Perry Oliver another round. Leaves Perry Oliver this example of everything and nothing.

But you will not have to go that far, Oakley says. I will save you the trouble. I know someone.

Seven sits at the table carefully examining every detail of the illustrations of Paul Morphy's exploits. He would like to be made utterly immobile. To sit forever.

Tom sits too, his hands moving, feet moving, now his head. Sits, time whizzing around his urge to move. He begins to speak, to recite, giving back word for word. Fourteen games were played in all, of which two were drawn, and three won by Herr Löwenthal. So great a disproportion evidently proves the practical superiority of the victor. How marvelous, the constant magic of Tom's memory. His tried-and-true companion. Too incredible for words. And no less grand and impressive after repeated display. Seven sags in his chair, catches his breath. At such moments, Tom belongs to him more completely than ever. A private kitchen (parlor) occurrence that compels him to project himself, safe and sound, into foreign streets and gardens (Hyde Park) and rooms—St. George's Chess Club, King Street, St. James's; London Chess Club, Cornhill—Tom and Mr. Oliver silently accompanying him. That's the way he pictures it. Maybe (his wish) he will travel to such places someday.

Tom rapidly taps his chin with two fingers. Seven perks up his ears, ready for more. Tom taps his chin again. Will he say more?

Game twenty-nine, Seven says, prodding him.

Paul Morphy, Tom said, the American, victorious in thirty-four moves!

Tom's voice rolls pleasurably across his thoughts. How relaxed he feels. He tries returning to his journal, to Paul Morphy, but can't see what's there. His eyes retain Tom's image. For now, Tom's sheer presence will suffice.

Or will it? Tom tugs, knocks, shakes. Utters monotonous sentences about heaven knows what. Agitated, he wants to leave this place. But not everyone can leave a room anytime he feels like it. Nothing happens unless Seven says so. And he isn't saying so now. Tom will simply have to wait.

For a good half hour, Seven tries everything conceivable—humming, whistling, helpings of water and tea, further excursions with Morphy—to quiet Tom but to no avail. Tom gets up from the table and makes his way around. Halts an arm's length away from Seven and stands there thrusting his head in the air like a bull. Seven won't budge. He lowers his gaze, hardly looking at Tom although Tom hovers around him, trying as hard as he can to attract Seven's attention. Seven caught in this downward act of looking, witness to Tom's stubborn demands, the harsh tangle of his speech. Dismayed, half fearing for himself, half wishing this odd distraction shut away. Can't avoid glancing (in his mind) sidelong at Tom and directly at himself sitting in this chair, beset with choices, weighing departing against staying. He can stand up and oppose his charge, but it is very hard to mold a nigger once he gets riled. So, with labored care, he gets to his feet and fits his beaver cap on his own head and Tom's furless black hat on Tom's head, even then determined that they will return before Mr. Oliver does. Restored, Tom hugs him and keeps hugging, as is his wont.

Soon they are out in the street—it couldn't have gone any differently—where Tom trustingly puts himself in Seven's hands. Late afternoon light finds them walking north on the cobblestone road, away from Scaldy Bill's, Seven hoping to avoid putting temptation in Tom's ears and mouth. Tom follows him silently. It is only as they are drawing close to the river that words start bursting out of him.

We are walking, Tom says.

Yes.

A constitutional.

Yes.

Does the body good.

Well.

Does the body well.

Tom picks up a short branch that has fallen from a tree. He throws it into the field. A few yards later he picks up a stone. He throws it into the field. More finding and chunking as they work their way across the meadows of the city, lack of destination and light-footed energy carrying Seven along, and some immeasurable energy driving Tom. Tom walks and walks and doesn't seem to be tiring any. In fact, Seven has to work hard to keep ahead of his charge, his ears filled with the unmistakable sound of someone carrying something. It is his own breath that he hears, his lungs struggling to bear and lug weighted air, and his already heavy chest all that heavier for his long solid ribs, like a bulky load of firewood permanently sealed up beneath his skin. If he has any say in the matter they will stop and rest soon.

Tom, he says, slow down.

Yes, suh.

I'm not a sir.

Yes, sir. But Tom doesn't slow down.

Seven stops at the side of the road. Tom keeps walking, right past him. Seven juts forward and catches him by the arm. Let's wait here a moment. He guides Tom roadside and proceeds to seat himself in the grass. Tom remains standing. So be it. Despite what it seems, Seven is not at odds with himself. Tom's candid face, his quietly breathing chest, the ease in his movements, all clearly indicate to Seven that no malice, spite, or guile dwells in his body. An unquestionable fact like the hard-packed dirt beneath his buttocks.

Since they've advanced this far, perhaps they should go for a swim. (Can the blind swim?) Or they can simply go and rest on the banks. Tom won't have to get wet.

Seven leads Tom through the grass toward the water, where they sit down together on a grassy little knoll, fully within the sprawling ragged shadow (shade) of a large tree, Seven a few feet above and behind Tom. He's got the best overview of the river. He's got the best overview of Tom. After he has rested for a while, he gets up and carries a hollowed-out branch down to the river, fills it with water, and drinks himself cool. Refills it and returns to Tom, who upends the branch sluice-like to allow the water to run into his mouth. Drinking done, Tom flings the branch into the water. So they sit. Seven often touches Tom's face without thought, running his fingers across his cheeks, around his jawline and mouth, and over his eyes, feeling the hardened lumps beneath. Tom remains undisturbed during the touching, as if these are fingers he can't feel. Seven looks at the water now, but his eyes alight on nothing. Nothing happens, and nothing happens in Seven.

Shrieks circle out from a small source of noise. Birds. He sits observing them—the circle closing in on those who watch—these airborne creatures grounded some distance off, venturing through the grass and pecking dirt near the base of the tree. So much to see. Sees, placing every stream every river every leaf every branch every tree every stone every bird every blade of glass in its proper place.

Tom remains unusually silent and still. No humming or singing or fidgeting. A person who doesn't speak could easily be thinking.

Do you like to swim, Tom?

The fish do, Tom says.

The pecking search for food brings the birds closer and closer to where they sit. Several of them rush Tom's exposed ankles. Tom kicks his feet, scaring them off, flapping back to the heaven.

There go the dead arisin, he says.

Now if that don't beat all. Seven thought that he had heard everything from Tom.

They sit for a spell in calm assurance.

Time to go, Seven says.

Time to go, Tom says. He hops to his feet. Nature is over, he says.

They return to the road with Seven in the lead, heading toward a shortcut home. He looks back over his shoulder and sees Tom hurrying off the opposite way.

Tom, where are you going? He remains there, holding his pose of entreating, thinking that Tom will come directly to him. Tom continues on. Seven rushes and overtakes him. Good lord, what has gotten into this nigger? All this time, time that he has lavished on tracking down some amusement that will keep Tom calm and content. (Approach the other with understanding.) All for naught. Is this a challenge that he detects and that he has to meet? If so, what has fallen to him is more than a decision about direction. He must exert driving force, supply a directive. They will go by the stable—their secret enterprise—even though it is quite a haul from where they've found themselves.

W. P. Howard—*the best music professor in the country, Oakley said*—lives in a clean quiet neighborhood on the outskirts of the city with houses tall and wide standing apart from squat servants' houses, and niggers all about busy with upkeep and work. Perry Oliver addresses the opportunity with a solemnity that suggests his very life is at stake. Even Oakley's introduction and recommendation may not be enough to guarantee Tom's selection. All he has is a name.

A name he would rather do without. Doesn't want to know it, doesn't need to. (In fact, later he will almost say, "Please, sir, don't speak your name in my presence." Holds his hands up, warding off knowledge. "I promise not to speak mine. Let us talk money.") The title, Professor of Music, is all he needs; in fact, it is far more appropriate than a name, for which holds the greater importance in the world, what we are called or what we do? True, a name can lift you up by the workings of social convention and ignorance. But Perry Oliver doesn't buy into the whole principle of name and ancestry, name as designation, the linguistic path back to flesh and blood lineage, noble or otherwise. (A thousand particular stories.) By luck and chance and enterprise any white man can succeed. W. P. Howard is a name he is already trying to forget.

He arrives at Howard's house with eagerness in his eyes, in his gait, a pretense that should provide him with the necessary deception of confidence. The decent aspect of the house—large but modest, nothing gaudy or ostentatious or overstated—brings with it the sense of a small promise renewed, revived. Still, he is leery of ringing the doorbell, leery of entering the house, but he must since he is unable to bear the tension of waiting. A nigger answers the door. Seeing the nigger is enough to awaken in Perry Oliver the value of himself as a person.

The nigger shows him into the house and they proceed down the hall to an open door, where the nigger pauses before entering, Perry Oliver behind him, looking, the open door a box of perspective, a transparent cage that illuminates a man standing in the middle of the room, man and room separating him from what is indistinct and undefined. Looking a visual purification, cleansing after the darkness outside. The man wears a jacket that is well made but long outdated, and the man stands with his feet wide apart and his head lowered. Perry Oliver thinks, is sure, that the man is muttering something under his breath. The nigger enters the room and calls out to the man. *Professor Howard.* As soon as the man sees Perry Oliver he literally leaps toward his visitor with his hand out in greeting, so that Perry Oliver involuntarily reels back. Howard takes Perry Oliver by the elbow and leads him over to a sofa covered with a green-gold draping, where he sits down himself, then pulls Perry Oliver into an armchair next to him, Perry Oliver easing into the unfolding dimensions of the room. Much smaller than he had at first thought, a full-sized piano taking up almost half the space. So this would be Howard's studio, small perhaps though certainly sufficient in size for the few students he takes in—according to Mr. Oakley, Howard largely makes his money working on an as-needed basis with the city's two schools of musical instruction for girls and with other local or county-wide organizations for the training and development of the female sex— and well designed to compensate for its extreme simplicity.

Sitting with one hand resting in the other, Howard is full of questions that alarm at first and amuse later. Perry Oliver goes with it. Easy. He hears himself say, Yes, a boy approximately seven years of age. Yes, more than a handful. Surprised that his voice carries any sound.

With deliberate ceremony the nigger serves them coffee. That is exactly what Perry Oliver needs, to be accommodated, to belong to this little world.

Professor Howard smiles at his servant. Roman, he says, I no longer require your services for the day. You may be excused.

The servant bows and leaves hurriedly, giving a backward glance as he flounces away, a glance that only Perry Oliver catches.

And what is his name?

Tom.

And how long has he been playing?

Professor Howard turns his ear toward Perry Oliver, as if he is listening all the way to the other side of the city, listening to Tom.

Perry Oliver will leave no question unanswered, will omit nothing even if he has to make it up. Gives something of Tom's history, scrambling in his mind to hold on to and remember what he is saying.

So I take it you don't play yourself?

No, Perry Oliver says. I listen.

I'm sure you know far more than you think, Howard says. Whoever can distinguish musical sounds from their reverse is a musician. At least to a degree.

Yes, to a degree. Perry Oliver sits with a touch of astonishment and gratefulness that he has gotten this far. He has come here freely on his own. Has come to yield up himself. Shaken, breathless, he sits regarding Howard with his own terror, wondering if he might have done things differently. He had considered bringing Tom along—and leaving Seven behind in the apartment—to allow the Professor to see firsthand the project he would be taking on. Still can't say why he decided against it.

Rest assured, Howard says. He gives Perry Oliver a little smile to put him at ease. You are doing the right thing. The South is no place for a pianist to develop. The air is too damp. It ruins the instrument and at the same time it ruins the pianist. The hands and head go soft in the shortest time.

Howard gives Perry Oliver a look, implying that they are conspirators united against a ridiculous world. However, Perry Oliver steers clear of responding, refusing to be drawn into a discussion that he knows could lead him on a tirade against their country.

See here. The instructor held up both hands palms outward, like a cornered victim going soft before a highwayman with a pistol aimed at his heart. Look closely, he said. See the ridges and grooves standing out from the skin. They help the fingers help the pianist along. They are as important for absorbing and recording our touch as they are for enhancing and tightening the grip. Music enters here through the tips of the fingers and travels up through the hands, arms, shoulders, neck, and makes its way all the way up to the brain.

Perry Oliver sat listening with bemusement at an enthusiasm he had never heard before, soaking in the instructor's words and gestures, so much so that he missed half of what Howard was actually saying to him, afraid to move, feeling that anything he did would disturb the mood, clues to what Howard was really thinking, the hidden behind the words, held up to eye to tongue to ear.

Is he equal with both hands?

Yes, Perry Oliver said, unclear what he was acknowledging. Both hands are equal.

Forthright instruction, Howard said, is a way to learn how to play two voices clearly but also after further progress to deal correctly and well with three obbligato parts not only to obtain good ideas but most of all to learn the process of invention that is necessary to any style of playing by which to acquire a strong foretaste of composition.

He composes, Perry Oliver said. However, he has a limited program. Perry Oliver looked right into Howard's eager eyes. Might you be able to demonstrate a full range of songs for him, as many as you know, as many as you can, and build up his repertoire? He tried to keep the pleading out of his voice, hoping to establish by his very intensity a stronger claim to the child than any could make.

Yes, Howard said, although I'm sure some exercises will be necessary. I can assure you that within a week Tom will have learned a new song.

That is quite generous, Perry Oliver said. However, I suspect that he might be capable of learning five songs in a given day.

Something in the other man's face startled Perry Oliver. It was a look that said Howard had nothing but scorn and contempt for the man who was hiring him.

You see, he possesses an iron memory. Whatever he hears he can play. Perry Oliver never wasted time pondering the origins of Tom's gift, wondering if Tom's powers were evidence of the mysterious workings of God's awful hand or some other supernatural force. Enough to accept a paradox for what it is. He is one to keep to what he knows and understands.

Yes, that is a special consideration. Howard's eyes flashing the secret of his excitement. We should start tomorrow.

The words surprised Perry Oliver, even more than he had hoped for. Delighted that the Music Professor had put forth the request.

Please bring him here after breakfast.

It was Howard's expectation that he see Tom as often as possible, three or four times a week—he asked double his usual fee, a sum amounting to almost two dollars per day—a proposal suggesting that both Perry Oliver and Tom would have to lift their own work to merit being in the same place with him.

A rigorous schedule should suit his nature, Perry Oliver said, for he never tires of playing.

Pianists have amazing endurance.

Perry Oliver looked at the piano, a black levitating mass.

A short time later, he emerged dreamily from the house. It's settled. Saying it to himself, to the other houses, to fading (red) sun and the wind and the trees. Not a moment to take lightly. Even though he had gotten what he wanted, he needed to feel bigger than this man, Howard. What is it that had brought the Music Professor into his life?

He walked faster in the stiff air, trying to calm his racing mind, his eyes filling with the distance that had already sprung between him and Howard. What is this he heard from a block away? Bone-white notes. Trailing behind him, intent on following him home. He found himself standing before a haberdashery window, hats perched bird-like on their stands. Without giving it much thought he decided to celebrate his victory by treating Seven to a gift, a Paul Morphy hat.

It took Howard a week to break Tom out of the habit of simply walking over to the piano and hooking his hat onto the cantilevered lid. Could it be that he truly believes a piano is a casual object of furniture like any other? Tom would step through the door, break away from his navigator, Seven, remove his hat, angle it on the piano, then sit down and begin playing whatever pleased him.

Now Tom has quickly fallen into the proper routine. The servant brings a bowl of water so that Howard and Tom may clean their hands. Holds out a fresh towel so that they may pat their skin dry. They are now ready to begin.

So much depends on where. Start with Tom's teeth and gums. Tom must learn to keep his mouth shut. When he plays he keeps it open like an oven waiting for unbaked food.

At first Tom gives in with no resistance. Simply goes along with Howard without his usual force of will. He is peaceful and composed before the piano. His face tilted slightly upward as he listens to Howard demonstrate a bar or melody. Mouth shut, eyes unseeing, both naive and enigmatic.

That afternoon when Howard first heard Tom has stayed with him, a sharpened echo in his memory. Clings to the present even as it ceases to make sense in terms of where they are now, of his (their) present goals. Easy enough to recall the many patrons sitting or standing in happy ignorance and a group of overseers seated together at a table with their coats off, their faces twisted out of shape with laughter. He made sure to seat himself as far as possible from them, all the way at the back of the saloon—the tables scarred with initials, the tables without tablecloths—near the decrepit piano.

That's when Seven and Tom wandered in and took the instrument. A great deal of what followed, the musical performance itself, is lost from memory. A single hearing allows us to retain only so much. Not that he was seeking to absorb anything as Tom touched and sounded the keys, as he tapped sharp glinting notes into a wall of air, the melody rising in pitch and excitement, the cadence increasing, Tom mouth open, hammering the keys, building the song into his body.

At the very first lesson in his home less than a week later Howard learned that Tom has a good ear in the sense that he can reproduce anything he hears, no matter how difficult. But copying is cheap. The hands must engender. And the ear must reign over the hands.

Attuning. Training the ear which is a way of training the mind to hear. Can't have one without the other. The two are inseparable, go hand in hand. That roughly is how he would (might) describe the process. The clear shape he listens for, the frame of the composition beneath the harmony, the melody, and the rhythm, the lower pattern or higher, as it were. To grow an ear for this hidden structure.

> In order to prove that Tom was possessed of ordinary
> common sense, I asked him if he knew what key in flats was
> synonymous to another key in sharps. He promptly answered,
> "No." I then played piece upon piece upon the piano in the key
> of C Major, at the same time informing Tom that by making
> the signature twelve sharps and playing precisely as I did

*before, there would be no difference in the music. I then
explained to him that the key of D double flat (twelve flats),
was synonymous to the keys which I had just used, when
played or sung, although appearing different on paper. Tom
seemed to comprehend this explanation perfectly, and when
told that there was a key formed by the use of flats precisely
like each key formed by the use of sharps, and vice versa,
I found that he soon had no difficulty whatever inputting
this theory into practice upon the piano in any key that I
mentioned.*

> *Subscribed, W. P. Howard*

The title of a composition should be purely functional, factual. The composition provides all you need to know, as the actual movement of sound contains. What it evokes in you. Where it takes you. What you find when you arrive. The many colors, tints, and shades.

How does that feel, Tom?

What do you think of this, Tom?

Get your hands around this little phrase, Tom.

Howard will play a phrase three or four different ways. Which one do you prefer, Tom?

Is this the correct way, Tom?

Listen to this, Tom, how Rubinstein might play it.

From Tom's astonished face and innocent answers, it's clear that he seems to think Howard's questions are a form of wit, clever riddles. Tom's not getting what he needs most from Howard. His voice can't get through. How to strike a responsive chord and free Tom of his ready-made notions. Help him to overcome himself. *Tom, you can't have heard that properly.* A painful but challenging and fascinating task. He is entitled to be impatient with Tom. *No, Tom. Listen.* For Tom must realize that he is a distinctive body with attitudes, memories, turns of mind, and habits of expression.

Any command is also a release. He tries to rouse Tom to indignation or astonishment. *Try it again. Slower this time.* Building him up bit by bit. Until he can do it on his own. His own choices and decisions, his own way. The subtleties and give-and-take of musical instruction, of study and performance.

Tom listens on, interested, smiling at everything new.

Howard has never found the knack for composing, so he has given his life over to the proper interpretation of the Great Masters, although he sees himself as only a competent player at his best. Competent and correct. The moment he thinks he has a hold on a work he's lost it. He is duty bound to devote himself absolutely to those composers who have brought the best music into the world. To respect the inviolable laws of the composition as penned by the composer's hand. This is the guiding principle of his life. And the key method behind his pedagogy. He is never so cheerful as when he is playing music, even if he is playing in the service of a dull pupil.

His favorite composers have designs on him. He can't escape their power. Their putting him on paper, what they have brought into the world. The composer speaks through your hands, lives through your hands. The performer can only be him, the composer. You create yourself so far as the composition dominates you. Obligated to the composition but free. Independent. Every note matters. Every note has meaning. No note can stand on its own. You enter the score and must find your way around. Each note is a station, a step. *This way.* So many bread crumbs leading you both away from and back to tonal center. Calculated coherence and balance. A unity of count. Numerical magic.

He places Tom's hands on top of his so that Tom may feel the proper way hands should move. He sits Tom on his lap with Tom's shoes on top of his shoes so that Tom may know how the feet properly work the pedals and how hands and feet complement one another. He has Tom touch his face—his brown hand nice and warm in its roughness—hoping that Tom may feel what he feels. (What changes underneath the skin no one sees.) Tom the shape of his own push and pull. (Bach for four hands. Four feet.) No matter how often he is put off he perseveres. He will work with Tom for as long as it takes.

Howard closes his eyes to keep from seeing Tom's hands move. Tom is getting a better focus on matters of importance. Loosening up the reins of his imagination. Howard finds himself nodding agreement when Tom plays something correctly, forgetting that Tom can't see him. He must speak in order for Tom to know. That he is advancing, going somewhere, although the direction is not clear. So much to glean and deduce. Glimpses through the gaps of what has been denied him, of what he has denied himself. But Howard must be careful not to say too much, to bring up everything that comes into his head without reckoning the consequences. Not to confuse Tom, tie him up. The more Tom holds on to Howard, the more Tom belongs to himself. Little by little Tom is getting hold of Howard's way of being so open. Little by little, he'll give up his idea that he has no life of his own, that he has never had a life of his own up until now.

The gleam of dollars, perfectly new coins. He takes the money from Seven without impatience. Seven pays him weekly, always on Friday. Mr. Oliver gains you this sum, he says. Howard has set eyes on Perry Oliver only once in his life, those many weeks ago, the sole encounter in person, in the flesh. Howard opened the door and was granted the sight of Perry Oliver's anxious face. This solicitor had dressed with serious intention, obviously with care, like someone attending the theater, although he wore no hat. Their conversation was private and enclosed. Very quietly and without having to consider his words Oliver spoke of the child as a beloved person, almost kin. Let himself express natural affection for the child as he hinted at the stunted surroundings in which the child had grown up, not so much reared by its parents as guarded by its owners, and explained his speculations about these parents and these owners and their relationship to the child by filling out the details of its present situation and environment with him, Oliver.

Who knew if anything he said was true. Howard listened with interest and respect. The hardest thing was to keep from laughing in his face. Damn fool. Speaking in his drawn-out, carefully articulated sentences. Little did he know, Howard had already witnessed the boy for himself less than a week earlier. Oliver hasn't the slightest clue about what he has on his hands here. Doesn't know and probably doesn't care. Without even thinking about it, Howard took two steps back—Oliver had been standing not farther than two feet from him—fearing contamination. Damn him and all his high-sounding words.

He cannot get used to the awe that, through no wish of his own, he inspires in certain people despite his quiet modest disposition. Even the planters are respectful in his presence, almost timid and fearful, shy. They speak little and do not say what they mean. Stare at him without blinking, as though expecting every minute that he will say something important, something infinitely significant. Their compliments bother him. He finds their unshakable convictions insulting. He believes their acts of charity are nothing more than bribes, methods of indenture. The planter will come down off his high horse and treat you with courtesy, pretend to stand equally before you all the while believing you are insignificant. They try to make the difference felt. They make it felt without trying. For they are used to dealing with plebeians who have so little that they look to the planters as the ones to serve and lead them. Damn them all. Howard thinks amicably of every kind of disaster that might befall them.

He gladly agrees to Oliver's offer, despite the weakness of this man's character. (Teach him all you can, Oliver says. He has money in him.) He smiles, having made a silent renewed resolution to remember his debts—the house, the servant, his publications, his books—and his commitment to the higher cause. It is (becomes) important to stand before this man with a straight face, free of anger, however difficult. Tragedy offers no consolation. No, he is not without twinges of doubt, and hatred, but he is mildly hard up and needs the money and needs this mission. He quietly accepts the banknotes that Perry Oliver hands him in advance of the first lesson. Money or no money, he can't refuse. The weakness of others demands a greater strength from him. Tells himself that he is not so much taking on a student as taking on a moral obligation, that he is serving as someone who can do for Tom what no other white man in this city can do. This is his conviction that he will repeat and reaffirm in the months and years to come.

Can he save Tom?

The patent of nobility is the color of the skin. To the watching world it sounds like the carefully thought out result and experience of reason. But it is all too cruelly untrue. The hurt to the Negro is the wound dealt to his reputation as a human being. Nothing is left. Nothing is sacred.

He has no reservations about race. Like music, race is a sturdy armature on which you can hang all types of feeling and sensation and behavior. Our society works the theme like no other subject. The very fabric of what we manufacture, export, and breed.

Tom sniffs the keys. An animal taking outer skin in. Something heavy and skeletal. Blocked from the fleshy insides that nourish and sustain. Howard has never seen anything like it, and doubts if he ever will again. He is moved. He is profoundly grateful.

So this is how Tom does it. This is what he is after. (Squeeze yourself into Tom's shoes.) Music slumbers in the shell, biding its time. The blind live in the world of time alone. The auditory hemisphere colonizes the visual hemisphere. And it is Howard's belief that this metamorphosis goes further still. The olfactory enacts hegemony over the auditory. Tom smells the notes. Why his head moves when he plays, probing around, sniffing out the melody. It is there already, waiting for him to find it. What could be better, more perfect? No need for imagination, speculation, or invention. No need for study, for planning the planting of the initial seed, or for fertilizing, tending, harvesting. No. For Tom the notes are already buried inside the composition. A composition without compost. A coming to position, a bringing forth of what is already there, like a fully grown potato hidden under the soil that pops to the surface when summoned. What is already there. What is always there. Self-plenishing. Self-generating. Self-contained.

The piano for Tom is a tool of reference, not an instrument of discovery. Any other could do, might at any time be called into service. Music is the most lasting touch, awaiting him. Howard can be little more than a steadying influence. Help him to sniff here as opposed to there.

Seven has never called him master after that first day. *I'm not a master. I'm no master, I don't master.* Seven small under his wide-brimmed field hat. He seemed unaware that you don't simply walk into a house with your hat on. Take a seat on the couch or in a chair with your hat on. Sit through a musical lesson or recital with your hat on.

Seven drives Tom from a far district of the city. They enter the house shaking the journey out of their limbs. Hold hands absent-mindedly but firmly. Sometimes both boys smell of the horse and the harness. Tom's clothes are slightly too small, cuffs and ankles (no socks or stockings) revealed, so he looks half tramp, half clown. Seven looks far more untidy and underslept. Both their shirts are buttoned to the neck, which give them the appearance of being in uniform.

Tom begins to wander about the room, but Seven stands, wordless, humble, stiff as a paper doll, seeming out of place among the cold heavy furniture. Even when he is spoken to he doesn't raise his head (hat) to talk to Howard. Directs his words at the floor. Good afternoon, Professor Howard.

Why don't you take a seat over there.

He doesn't seem able to take the first little step toward the couch.

And when he does, he sits down as people who feel guilty about something sit down, timidly looking about him, his legs dangling over the edge.

Howard begins the lesson. Uneasily conscious of Seven. Can't see him but knows that Seven is watching them, *him*. Can feel Seven's eyes gazing right through him. He turns and sees that Seven sits listening, his cheek on his hand. Trying to be brave, he will gaze without blinking at Howard, although it is obvious he feels a little apart from the musical lesson, feels left out. He seems unaware that he is creating a distraction. He stretches his neck like a snake out of young wheat and smiles unexpectedly, with no trace of enjoyment. Smiles, almost as if the sight of Howard and Tom at the piano amuses him. No, he lacks such pride. He thinks his goodwill is something he must establish. Smile always at the ready. Eyes cast down. Words like *master* in his mouth. Seeing his smile, Howard grows annoyed—He doesn't know, Howard thinks in amazement. He doesn't even know what I'm fighting for—and will send him into the kitchen or out of the house with instructions to feed or water himself or the horse. It takes Seven quite a while to get to his feet, to get his body to budge from one spot, moving slowly, lead shoes, heavy with shame. Then he will suddenly jerk forward and turn away as if he has been pushed, lurching through the doorway. The timid anxious glance he steals at Howard as he leaves the room. After a spell of an hour or more he returns from the horse or the kitchen and lets himself fall onto the couch. Sits, adequately nourished, quiet, indecently dressed.

Remarkable that Tom can play anything at all with his pudgy hands and fat fingers. He touches the piano as if he has lumpy pillows at the end of his fingertips. This explains why his playing is so forceful at times, during certain passages or movements, so forceful when it shouldn't be, or less than it should be. A music of regurgitation that expels—a grunt, a shout, a fart—after being bottled up too long.

But it is well possible for someone with an inferior touch, bad hands, to develop a warm tone. Tom's posture and hand position are far from good. (Start there.) The pianist must not allow his body to dominate his hands. (Among other things the professional recitalist must create the proper picture for his audience.) The pianist need first sit inclined decidedly toward the keyboard. (Tom sits straight up, except when he is sniffing notes.) The upper arm and forearm should be light, float in air, for maximum ease and freedom of movement. The fingers must remain near the surface of the keys so that the playing is delicate and uniform. The piano key must go all the way down. The finger, the hand, the wrist, the arm, the torso, the head (face bent forward, chest hovering two feet above the keys, a bearing that is graceful, lively, alert)—all operate in conjunction for this to happen. The whole body comes together in a rhythm that goes deep. Master the principle of moving the fingers only at the joint where they are connected with the body of the hand. Do not battle the keys, hammer them like some blacksmith. As large a surface of the fingertip as feasible must engage the key. The thicker the cushions of flesh upon the fingertips, the wider the range and variety of touch. The wrist must always be flexible, loose, sinking below the level of the keyboard. The more spring the less bump. This Rubinstein calls the pedal *the soul of the piano*. But a soul resides either in hell or in paradise. Fine pedaling is worthless without a sense of touch. Hand controls the foot. And brain controls the hand. Instructs hollow fingers to transmit feelings to the keys. So why this focus on the hands when so much of the body is involved? When all of the body is involved?

As little of the self as possible. The performer is a facilitator, a middleman for the—unpresent, often deceased—composer, bearing a tremendous responsibility of presenting the composer's music to the public while staying true to the composer's ideas and intentions, to his thoughts and feelings. But most pianists lack the faculty of actually hearing the composer, of hearing themselves as the composer, of hearing the text.

(*Unfortunately I have to reconcile myself to the thought that nobody will ever play my works to my liking as I had imagined them.* Chopin.) Sometimes it is necessary to go far then come back. Imagine the melody as heard from an instrument of different quality from the piano, say the oboe, trumpet, flute, or French horn. But how does one teach the blind, who have no way of first seeing the text on their own, but must always arrive at it secondhand, through another? *This way.*

Bach. All those voices crying out. Faint floating sadness. Music is a map of the world. A map of Time. The sense of release it (he) brings. Unless his thoughts are pinned down by musical business they tend to drift off to painful matters. Second-thinking. Strain and worry. Even more reason to give up his mundane students and give all his time to Tom. Assuming of course that Perry Oliver continues to pay.

Today, he starts Tom on the Chopin études. "Aeolian Harp" étude (op. 25, no. 1). Tom is looking positively cheerful while Seven sits on the couch legs dangling, reading his newspaper, the leaves pushed close to his face. He is no longer watching us, Howard thinks. He is not even listening. He is not afraid of me now. That Howard can stand. Howard can ignore him, efface him, act like he isn't there.

Howard and Tom, all thrill and trembling, the teaching a great source of pleasure for them both because they both welcome the unexpected, never know what will come next. Now he hears me, he thinks. He hears me. He places one round hand on Tom's shoulder to encourage him, praise him. His words do not belong to him any more than his body, his hands, his feet. Utter them back, claim them, or they will be lost. Tom takes on the glamour of something still to come.

The instructor draws the curtain and shutters.

Have a little sun, Tom says.

The instructor opens the curtains and shutters. Tom waves his hands as if directing light over to the piano. Then his fingers descend upon the keys, descend without touching, prepared, caught in space, awaiting orders.

Tom, let's give this a try.

Let us do the work of our hands, Tom says.

From his place on the couch twenty feet away, Seven notices how the instructor looms above Tom, closely observing Tom's posture and hands, the awkward sprawl of his knuckles, the elements of his movement and fingering. Sometimes the instructor keeps time with his feet, throwing his hands up high. Tom firmly on track. Only when his hands stop will the instructor sit down. Right there on the bench, beside Tom, the wood whining under their weight. Four hands now at the piano. Two of each color. A white man and a black boy seated side by side on the same polished wooden bench. Where Tom is concerned, perhaps he can do nothing right, the way the instructor wants it. Seven the unmoving witness. He must sit quietly. Not a squeak or a stir lest he be banished from the room. But he is perfectly capable of being silent, figures that he can even maintain silence for longer than Perry Oliver. In fact, put to the test, he can pass days on end in uninterrupted silence—no talking, no music.

He sits under the sun's invisible weight. Day slants through the window. But the atmosphere in this house, in this room, is still heavy. The instructor's face set and distant. All Seven can sense from him is his anger, his dissatisfaction with things. He recalls their first introduction to the house. The instructor saw them come in, but he didn't see how frightened Seven was. He gave Seven a little smile and tried to make small talk. But Seven could hardly hold up his end of the conversation.

Didn't know what to say. Nothing he could say. He said nothing, tongue-tied. He didn't want to say anything stupid. How do you converse with a music instructor? What do you say and what do you not say? So he simply stood there, praying that words would come. No wonder the instructor has not encouraged him to speak since.

That first day, he took in the dimensions of the room and its sparse furnishings and many books, his gaze relinquishing one space for the next. He made his first tactless remark. That's a shiny piano.

The instructor actually turned to look at the piano. Then turned back to Seven, his face a thousand words, none of which he cared to sound. The tilt of his head and his expression—a curious mixture of pride and spite—brought to mind the planters and the pose they assume when they speak to their overseers, although the instructor—Mr. Howard, kindly call me Mr. Howard—is far more modest and unassuming in appearance and dress. And for this reason, he was a rather plain man, Seven decided. If he seems on in years, it is only by comparison with Mr. Oliver.

You will find the couch directly over there.

Seven sits with uneasiness. Mutely, he looks at the bookcases, at the window, at the bare walls. If he gets up to move, say to glance out of the window, or to browse at the titles of the books on the instructor's shelves, he must do so on tiptoe. The strange sensation of knowing that he is the object of the instructor's secret glances. Who knew that sitting could be fraught with dangers?

One day the instructor leaves Tom at the piano in the middle of the lesson, comes over to Seven, and shows him into the small dim kitchen with orders to find himself something to eat. Seven makes no fuss. Thinks little about it. He doesn't want to be in the way. Although he is sick with shame and worry and can barely eat, no matter how hungry he might be. Soon the instructor goes a step further and suggests that Seven might prefer outside. Seven complies. The sense of ridicule that covers-uncovers him. What will he say should Mr. Oliver ask? His job to keep an eye on Tom at all times, even in the presence of this instructor. So how is it that he allowed Mr. Howard to banish him from the house? He waters and hays the horse's mouth again and again, reassuring himself with solutions he will come up with.

Perry Oliver had made his orders clear. A plain statement of intention. Seven was to escort Tom to and from Mr. Howard's residence, but he was also to remind Mr. Howard at every opportunity to show Tom as many new songs as possible and to keep the lessons, the training and exercises, to a minimum. Frighteningly simple. But now he doesn't have the slightest clue if this is what the instructor is doing. Nor does he know how to ask. He lacks the courage to confront Mr. Howard. His heart is too soft. That must change. Indeed, it comes to him that he will need to voice certain words one day. (Most words are kept.) For Seven wants what Mr. Oliver wants, even when he is not thinking about him. His feeling for Mr. Oliver stops short of love.

Couch, kitchen, horse—for nearly three weeks that's the way it goes until the day Seven enters the house with his newspaper under his arm. The newspaper (reading) appeases Mr. Howard's desire to banish him from the house, and the couch has been his since. Not that he had planned it that way. The paper was only an accident. (His usual seeking out of Morphy.) Even so, the dishonoring memory of his feeding the horse, his feeding himself, is overtaken by the consoling image of his sitting here on the couch reading his newspaper.

Seven feels himself returned to the road of his mission. A cause for celebration. Rightfully so, for the music lessons have become point and purpose of their day. *Teach Tom some tunes.* In fact, the lessons come with more, are benefiting him in ways he could never have imagined. Are giving him something he wasn't even looking for. The instructor will play four or five different notes, then a moment later play the same notes again, making them sound totally different. He plays them a third way and a fourth. The same notes for unalike ears. How is this possible? Hard to believe what he hears. Hard to believe.

Tom risks putting his hands on the keys. Fallen chances.

Wait, Tom, wait.

A discomfiting silence falls over the room. The instructor sits down at the piano, causing Tom's hands to fly up then come to rest comfortably in his lap. The instructor proceeds to demonstrate the melody that Tom bungled. Once, twice, three times. Again and again. He watches Tom try the melody with some determination in his movements.

Wait, Tom, wait.

Tom makes an odd little gesture of helplessness.

Set in his ways, Tom clutches at playing things in the manner he knows them. Can't seem to let go, pleasure and habit impeding his advance. Not clear if he even knows what the instructor is after. At times he doesn't seem to understand what the instructor is saying, what the instructor is going on about. *Sharps and flats. Keys and doors.* Seems unable to divide one thing from another. Doesn't even try, make the effort. He can be impatient, forever geared up to move on, to get into the next satisfying adventure, that sense of *now* when he is sitting at the table with his fork and spoon at the ready. No, these lessons are far from easy sailing. Quite rough at times. *(No, Tom!)* The first week or two Seven feared that Tom was proving to be too much for the instructor. In thought and deed Tom roamed uncontrollably, unable to halt once he got started at the piano, tearing on until the end of a tune, deaf to the instructor's orders and directions (pleas?), as if he owned the piano and would do anything he damned well pleased with it. The instructor shouts, but Tom simply ignores him. Seven breaks in, asking Tom to behave. The instructor turns to him and brings a finger up to his lips, making it clear that he wants Seven to keep out of it. Then Seven watches helpless as the instructor's hands swoop down like vicious talons and attack Tom's fingers, forcing them still, killing the music contained within the worm-like fingers. It hurts Seven to see it, but he says nothing—his cowardly heart—Tom wheezes out some air, Seven watching, trying to discount his feelings of guilt and remorse because he hasn't come to Tom's defense. He suffers a flush of curiously mixed emotion, wishing that his own feeling could somehow make the pain less for Tom, but knowing that it will not. He is all at once overwhelmed with a passionate longing to throw his arms around his charge.

Tom puts demands on both of them. *(You miss the point, Tom.)* But the instructor seems to be a man who knows how to make himself obeyed. *(In this house, you are my student, Tom.)* Physical force is not his only means. Why should he go easy on Tom? Why should things be any different for him? Tom should be treated like any other student. Tom has a head to learn and learn he will.

He has to endure a rehearsal of all he has done wrong over the past hour. He sits listening at the far corner of the bench, his body stiff, defenseless, unresisting, everything happening at once, his hands hovering above the keys like frightened birds.

Okay, now let me hear you try it.

And try it he does, Tom's hands slow and smooth, moving in such a way—soft, serious—as if to suggest that he now realizes he needs to curb his instincts and calm himself in the face of what he is up against if he ever hopes to play exactly how the instructor is determined to have him play. Seven shifts forward on the couch, uniformly, barely noticeable. He can see Tom's black mind working, searching, recalling, questioning.

The instructor gives Tom a smile, perhaps to lead him away from his unhappy thinking, but of course Tom can't see the smile.

Better, Tom, better.

The instructor's reasons for insisting that Tom play something a certain way are so written in stone he never bothers to set them out. But steadfastness is the one thing Tom has in abundance.

Seven observes it all with a sudden idleness—the possible danger of watching—a patience that comes from a routine hungering, a hearing beyond these failed notes nicking his ears. Listening to Tom with unhesitating faith. Tom's errors, his stammering and hesitation, somehow make him more striking, strangely heighten his endowment. (Glows.) Fragments of perfection Seven can believe in. Much still is possible, but he might be convinced—he is already convinced—to deem the continuous tapping on the keys some sort of private code between Tom and the instructor. And he is privy to it, this secret language, even if he doesn't understand it. The little his body enjoys in this moment he regards as a privilege, for God has granted Tom something withheld from him and Mr. Oliver and legions of others: music.

On another afternoon, Tom says, We want to sing.

Shimmering in the light from the window, the instructor begins singing in a language that Seven has never heard before. Seven goes cold, an unfamiliar thrill running up and down his body. He regards the instructor's tongue as if for the first time. He knows that mankind is an entity made up of tongues, tongues taking on names like German, French, Spanish, although the only tongues he's ever heard are nigger and Anglo-Saxon. And Indian. (Almost forgot.) Seven pictures these tongues as so many strands of leather attached to a whip handle, thin strips of hardened skin that might all have come from the same bull, reunited after death, or that might have come from many different bulls, a hodgepodge of hoof and horn. Just as a single tongue leaves the darkness of the mouth and produces words on contact with the air, the many-portioned whip whooshes forward and snaps out a word, nine strips say, all speaking the same word in nine different languages. *Snap!*

Seven has even heard that it is possible to trick your natural-born tongue into sounding foreign words. But this music instructor is the first man he has actually witnessed perform the feat. Little more than a hard-to-believe rumor before now. But it doesn't end there.

Seven witnesses something even more incredible. When the instructor finishes singing, Tom takes up the tune, singing it in the same foreign tongue while his native hands provide accompaniment at the piano. Seven sinks into serene amazement. (The instructor's eyes go wide for a moment.) Seven can feel his heart beating, slowly, steadily. Tom and the instructor shine in the fresh light, in the brilliance of this startling peace called music. Seven studies Tom's face for every trace of shifting emotion. He was right the entire time. Right indeed. In fact, he is quite sure that he detects a third sound lingering in the space between the sung note and the melody that accompanies it, some sound issuing forth from Tom's body—a wheezing, a humming, a cooing, a purring—an interaction of the vocal and respiratory musculature, which mix to form a third sound combining the two. As if Tom's tongue or lungs are stuck between one motion and another. Three sounds coming out of this one nigger body.

Tom never wants the lesson to end, the piano to cease. The instructor has to enforce a strict time frame.

I'll imagine you want to be getting back, the instructor says. He sees Seven and Tom to the door. He leans kindly toward them and expresses one final sentiment before he lets them leave. Guidance, he says. You are in need of guidance. Hard to say if he sounds glad or sorry or worried. Seven searches his face for the fun, for the teasing that might suggest he means something other than what he says. But he is also surprised by the note of sincerity in the instructor's voice. You have much to learn, the instructor says. How can Seven disagree?

Tom has developed the habit of throwing his hat onto the table in order to free his hands. Some days Seven will simply take the hat and put it in its proper place to spare himself the necessity of further struggle. Not today.

Tom, hang your hat on the knob beside the door, Seven says. Tom sits at the table with a look of relief spread across his face. Seven stands his ground. Tom, hang your hat on the knob beside the door. Tom gets up from the table and hangs his hat on the knob. Once he returns to the table, Seven dashes forward and fastens the inside bolt on the door. No one can get in or out without his express assistance. They sit at the table. Seven can hear the sound of his own breathing.

No one comes. No feet in the hall. No one knocks on the door. No one unlocks the door—or tries to anyway—and opens it wide. Tom accepts everything and smiles and is quiet. For everyone else Tom is absent from the world at this moment.

Do you like your instructor, Tom?

I like Mr. Howard. Seven, do you like your instructor?

What he witnessed earlier causes him to wonder about the countless bones supporting a tent of black skin and muscle, the blind blood blowing through. (The light inside which he sings.) Bone and blood and flesh shown to be remarkable. Mouth and teeth that can sit here and eat food and imbibe milk like any other any ordinary mouth and teeth, while knowing—trickery, deceit—that they are anything but ordinary. He thinks he can still hear the foreign words—he has yet to assign them a name—behind the voices coming from the neighbors' apartments mingled with many more familiar sounds. Who can hear any of it really?

Exciting flesh. Even if there is little for them to do but sit here in silence. They have fought or not fought their battle over the hat. They have eaten their supper. (The milk thick and sweet.) Nothing to do now but sit here and pass the seconds until Mr. Oliver arrives home. No telling how long he may be. No telling how long they've already been waiting. The mouth holds. The breath carries. He has lost track of time. (When did the room start stirring?) Fatigue comes on him with a rush. Careful or he may fall toward sleep out of sheer waiting. He keeps tossing his head to drive away drowsiness.

The best meat is sweet, Tom says.

Seven hears Tom but doesn't hear him.

The best bread comes from the flesh, Tom says.

Tom, what are you gabbering about? I dread hearing you go on like that.

The book speaks like a nigger, Tom says.

Seven doesn't have the slightest idea what Tom has in mind.

Jesus speaks like a nigger, Tom says. The Hebrews speak like niggers.

Seven doesn't know the source for this sudden religious outpouring, although it is not unusual for Tom to slap the mind awake with some sudden nonsensical statement.

The pharaoh speaks like a nigger. Moses speaks like a nigger. Adam speaks like a nigger too.

One day the music instructor has reason to leave Seven and Tom in the room alone. Seven asks Tom to exchange places with him on the couch so that he may seat himself at the piano. Moves his hands and head and feet the way he has seen Tom move but without actually touching the keys or pedals, a silent mimicry.

The firewood is stacked like a fragile shrine, ready to topple, rolling gods across the floor. Laboring hands, Tom takes great pleasure in handling the logs and kindling. Arranges some of them before him at the table, as if they are his true companions, neglected and vulnerable and misunderstood. Seven's understanding that the blind must first smell or touch a thing to know it.

Tom seems to be counting but loses track.

See this cricket in my neck, he says.

What can Seven do but service him? His fault that he allowed Tom to do something he shouldn't have. (He gives in here and there.) He goes over to his charge and begins to run his fingers over Tom's neck.

It's in two shoulders, Tom says.

Seven takes his hands from Tom's neck and moves them to his shoulders, to the afflicted spots, and massages the areas.

Damn it, Tom says. They're in my knees.

Seven massages his knees.

Frogs in my shoes, Tom says.

Seven removes Tom's shoes, the toes curled like toads ready to hop. He kneads and massages Tom's feet, only for the stiffness to return to Tom's neck. Tom's body appears to be breaking. Seven puts in a whole half hour or more of tending, of restoring and keeping together, scurrying about from this elbow to that heel, from that ear to this toe. Frogs, crickets, spiders. Tom only stops complaining once he has fallen asleep.

Massaging done, Seven settles into his seat, hoping to alleviate his out-of-jointness before Mr. Oliver's return. Just his luck that Mr. Oliver comes in—how did he undo the latch?—before he has gotten a breather. He steps into the middle of the room and looks around, blinking, seeing Seven but seeming not to actually recognize him, his eyes and face attesting to another hard day. He takes his chair, asks about the lessons. Seven gives him a full report, but Mr. Oliver says nothing. Is he pleased or isn't he?

Then Mr. Oliver says, Tomorrow, I should look in for myself. He hurries off to his room.

Nothing in their life is incidental. En route to the instructor's house each afternoon he finds time to stop the surrey and purchase the newspaper. No hurry. Plenty of time to get there. Plenty. No hurry at all. The air hangs unmoving over the streets so that the trees are gray like decaying flesh.

It looks like rain, Tom.

Rain fall and wet Becky Lawton.

Who is Becky Lawton?

Becky Lawton.

Yes, Tom.

Rainwater.

Seven lets it go. He likes to let things come out Tom's own way. No danger in that, even if he is perhaps too long accepting of it.

Inches separating them on the driver's platform, Seven in his place and Tom in his, two birds perched on a vibrating limb. Tom leans his shoulder into Seven. Seven shrinks back. But the second time he does it, Seven lets him. Tom requires touch. Touch settles him, a long easy ribbon of sound coming from his mouth.

Driving past the labor-loud fields Tom turns his head and cocks his face. A nigger is a fine instrument, he says.

Seven thinks about it some. Tom, how does it feel to be blind?

Some bread is better than no bread.

And how does it feel to be a nigger?

A nigger is a thing of no consequence.

Seven knows nothing about the part of town where the instructor lives. (A few half-remembered facts.) He makes it his business not to know. They ride through the streets, scattering wind, the surrey rolling them directly under the sun, Seven narrowing his eyes against one bright street after another under his Paul Morphy hat. Driving slowly to keep the dust off their clothes. Straight through the open eye Seven sees Howard's house. Here again. He parks the surrey and hitches the horse. Tom does not step down from the wagon.

Get out of the wagon, Seven says, muttering it softly, making sure to stay out of earshot, although the instructor's house is a good ten yards off.

Yesterday comes like today, Tom says. He gets out of the surrey. Seven is already thinking *Go* in his head, but Tom kneels down on all fours and starts feeling about in the dirt with his hands, like a person who has lost something.

Tom—

Looking, Tom says.

What?

Tom proceeds to crawl up under the horse. And there he remains, on all fours, his head directed toward the horse's belly, his tongue lolling.

Too stunned for words, Seven simply stands there looking, caught up in the wrong dream. Tom.

You'd better get back, Tom says. For what I'm doing there's light enough.

What are you doing?

Studying the niggers.

What niggers?

The only ones.

You don't understand, do you?

I understand, Tom says. Now you understand.

I understand, Seven says. Yes, he tells himself, he understands. Voice is the sight of the person who cannot see.

Seven feels himself yielding to Tom's way of thinking, the quick and instinctive compliance that comes when someone is shaken awake to uncertain surroundings. Recognition—plain sight—the holdout, slowing down that part of him that wants to give in. Long enough for the weight of mere witnessing to stop him altogether, cause him to disregard, to reverse his feelings. To look at Tom looking that way. This is his own hand posed to reach for Tom's hat, for his shirt, for his collar. No, don't touch him yet. Perhaps he should say something first. What are the correct words he needs to speak? If he understood him, he would know how to help him. *He* needs help. No force behind him but his own. Difficult to admit. Crying out could bring rescue, but it would also mean announcing his weakness as well. No way he can let that happen. He'll deny what is going on here should anybody happen to chance upon them. Much of what we see is not really what it looks like.

Just then the light brightens like a compromise. He stoops all the way down and speaks to Tom and Tom crawls out cat-quick from under the horse into the new sun, the dirt where he is kneeling reuniting behind him, as if it has never been disturbed. Seven uses his handkerchief to clean Tom as best he can. Business as usual.

Tom is changing. Everything about Tom is changing—voice, posture, expression. Is that what Mr. Oliver wants?

When he pens his history in the future, Perry Oliver will withhold one important fact, that it was the Music Professor who drafted the sworn proclamation attesting to the authenticity of Tom's genius, although his subscription was withheld, the words *W. P. Howard* never appearing on either the original statement or the various reproductions of it that Perry Oliver went on to have published in one newspaper after the next.

Dear Sir, The undersigned desire to express our thanks to you for the opportunity afforded them of hearing and seeing the wonderful performances of your protégé, the blind boy pianist, Tom. We find it impossible to account for these immense results upon any hypothesis growing out of the known laws of art and science.

In the numerous tests to which Tom was subjected in our presence, or by us, he invariably came off triumphant. Whether in deciding the pitch or component parts of chords the most difficult and dissonant; whether in repeating with correctness and precision any pieces, written or impromptu, played to him for the first and only time; whether in his improvisations, or performances of compositions by Thalberg, Gottschalk, Verdi and others: in fact, under every form of musical examination—and the experiments are too numerous to mention or enumerate—he showed a power and capacity ranking him among the most wonderful phenomena in musical history.

Accept, dear sir, the regards of your humble servants.

B. C. Cross	*Ross Necknor*
John M. Beck	*Carl Rose*
K. Blandner	*Paul Grace*
R. L. Stern	*J. A. Alfred*
Paul Swann	*Elijah George*
Samuel Harris	*Witherspoon Enright*
And several others.	

The signers—Perry Oliver had met all of them about town at one time or another during his dealings; and despite their rebuffs and refusals he would have made a conscious effort to be cordial on encountering them in the street, raising his hat to them had it been his custom to wear one—had received a flat fee of one hundred dollars each for their troubles and the Music Professor twice that amount. Any man is worth buying, for in Perry Oliver's eyes distinction is a thing wholly independent of social position. Several weeks earlier, he had asked Howard to approach every available music scientist in town and induce them to convene for the express purpose of listening to Tom so as to issue a notarized document of witness. The proposal—the very asking—would bring about the certainty of the Music Professor being in disgrace with his colleagues. No way around that. Although he should take some consolation in knowing that the one in a position to ask a favor holds greater power than the one who can only accept or decline, a fact that should thus enhance his prestige in the eyes of the world. (Perry Oliver feeling the need to extract this idea since he did not wish to exclude the possibility of a happy alternative.) Of course, his colleagues can like what they hear or not like it—the Music Professor has his own authority and his own views— but let's be clear, Perry Oliver needs them to endorse Tom, to recommend him to the public. *And when he had consulted with the people, he appointed singers unto the Lord, and that should praise the beauty of holiness, as they went out before the army, and to say, Praise the Lord; for his mercy endureth forever.* Money might help reassure them about their choice, help them arrive at a happy medium between their bestowing praise on a nigger and any slight reduction in their racial position in the world because of it. As well—turn it around—Tom's supporters might delight in the knowledge that they will take a mental share in Tom's rise to prominence, should that rise occur. (It will.) A dangling carrot: the prospect of fame being of far greater importance than the fear of ostracization, a dynamic that should gratify their self-esteem, at least in the short term. He removed fourteen hundred dollars in fresh notes from his wallet and held it out, choice hovering. The situation didn't merit much thinking, but the Music Professor made the thinking last as long as possible. Once Perry Oliver put the money in his hands, he pocketed it immediately.

He tells the Music Professor what he wants—this and that; some suggestions about the wording of the missive—guessing cleanly how far he will go. Now all he has to do is wait. The deference that he owes to Howard imposes on him the reciprocal obligation to do nothing that might render Howard less worthy of his colleagues' regard. (Empathy in recognizing that both the asking and the accepting will open doors of suffering.) Fortunately the Professor's colleagues had recourse to principles entirely in line with those that Perry Oliver intended (expected) them to adopt when the time came for them to form an estimate of Tom.

When Seven presented him with the letter several weeks later, Perry Oliver could not help but gaze at it with a blend of congratulation and irony. Now he can look forward to enjoying the fruits of the Music Professor's splendid connections. Not that he isn't grateful. Perry Oliver for weeks feeling bound to thank the Music Professor in person but as of yet unable to make the trip. Internally (to himself), he pleads the pressures of work. The moments steadily accumulate. Still so much to do before Tom's premiere.

Blind Tom. So it came to him. He does not waste time asking himself where it came from, but is only surprised at its slowness—he stood still, unable to move—at how the first word—language the material upon which we have to work—had been so slow in appearing, as were those that followed it. How he found that the thought *I must change his name* was already there, the idea having traced itself on his mind much earlier, somewhere or other, his mind heavy with its half-remembered weight. Only the words *Blind Tom* were missing, the initial forgotten thought (idea) coming back and passing between him and the image the name conjured up when he uttered the words

Blind Tom Exhibition out loud, listening to his own voice uttering the words as if they had come from someone else. How well he understands now that identity is not a disposition but an accomplishment. Tom today, Blind Tom in the by and by of history.

He hires a local printer to design a seal bearing an image in Tom's likeness, a sparsely detailed oval that finds Tom seated at the piano, the words *Blind Tom Exhibition* encircling him. Also has the printer produce several reams of watermarked stationery with the same image. From this point on all promotional documents he sends out in public or private will bear the inked-in oval, just as all business-related correspondence will be scripted on the letterhead. He's in control of what he does and what he wants. The difficulties—the lies, the put-downs, the accepting and accommodating, the laughter and complicity, the money spent or promised, the numerous rejections he has suffered in his efforts to secure a venue for Tom's debut—he has had up to now don't seem unfair to him any longer. His head is fully above the water, something definite bobbing into view, the surface part of the whole pattern that was once too far removed for him to bear any true conception of it, that he is only now beginning to see. (Perhaps he has always seen it?)

That afternoon a letter that he has been expecting for weeks arrives by courier. Return receipted to General Bethune, the letter is a deposition signed by a panel of medical experts, native and foreign, attesting to Tom's mental and physical makeup. *Between us we have arrived at a scientific evaluation of a Negro boy who goes under the name Tom, a slave boy who is approximately seven years of age and fraught with all of the handicaps of his race, but who can also demonstrate elevated and refined musical sensibility at the piano. He possesses the muscular ability to reproduce by hand and voice many of the finest selections from the European catalogue. This is in and of itself remarkable since the Negro's thought-organ generally is a lifeless and submissive receptacle with no power of specific reaction to anything challenging or demanding that might be introduced to it. So much so that the Negro's imitative abilities are usually little better than those of a parrot. Said fact, however, does not hold true for this Negro boy, Tom. What is even more incredible is that he is, in most respects, a far reduced physical representative of the Negro specimen, for his Maker has singled him out for direct burdening with a number of crippling afflictions— Blindness, Imbecility—ailments characterized by symptoms the full range of which a respectable member of the Anglo-Saxon language is both too chaste and too weak to describe in detail. It is material law that there exist points of reference the Caucasian and the Negro do not share and never will. Still, we, as men of science, shut our eyes to the known and accepted qualities and endowments of the Negro before we began our examination so that we would be fresh and unprejudiced in our deliberations. And we, one and all, agree that we are as perplexed now as we were before we began. We know of nothing out of the ordinary in this boy's upbringing, his parents being largely addicted to the culture of cotton. So we are left to ask—Is this Negro boy, Tom, the product of Nature or intentional design, and if the latter, whose? Medical science can draw no conclusions. In fact, this Negro slave, Tom, age seven, defies the laws of medical science.* Dr. Hollister is among the signers.

In this town, Culture manifests itself in a single structure, Hibernian Hall, a splendid neoclassical building, all sculptured stone and painted glass, with figures of the Greek (Roman?) gods carved in deep clefts hollowed out of the facade, summer light giving the hard pale muscles the color of flesh, and a smattering of green- or wine-colored bills positioned in such a way as to cause the viewer to lower his face from the celestial sights above and take in the terrestrial fact below, a gilded glassed-in cubicle where one may purchase tickets. The venue maintains a busy schedule hosting fund-raisers and temperance meetings, policemen's balls, fashion displays of the latest in clerical and mortuary designs, and soirees and barbecues put on by the rich. Perry Oliver finds a keen satisfaction in knowing that the operators rarely book an appearance that might be categorized as pure entertainment, niggers—minstrels—providing what little pure entertainment there is. So some might have expressed more than a bit of surprise to learn that it didn't take much convincing to get the operators to agree to put on an evening that differs radically from their usual fare, that Perry Oliver had completely won over Mr. Scowcroft, the venue's director, with a terse summary of Tom's history (supposed) and talents (actual), a booking fee of five dollars, an advance of another five, and promises of a full house, the director taken in by both the actual fact of the money and the supposed facts of Perry Oliver's promised words.

Perry Oliver signs the agreement and waiver, surprised that Scowcroft has given in so easily, that Scowcroft hasn't even requested an audition, the last thing he expected.

I hope you and your nigger will make them marvel, Scowcroft says, sounding quite sincere. Wind him up good.

Perry Oliver leaves Hibernian Hall, bearing away with him an acute awareness of his achievement and stunned by his sudden luck. (A date. A venue.) Everything falling into place. The biggest barriers are down. He is even further along than he had hoped. No longer that impoverished notion of chance. Can it really be this easy? He justifies himself to himself. A man moving at first with the force of idea purely. And now so much lies far behind. And still moving. Much ahead still. (Not as far perhaps.) The comprehensive gaze. "Blind Tom Exhibition" reduced for the first time to its true dimensions. The loneliness and emptiness of those short streets by which he returns home. Low-roofed houses spaced far apart, set in their appointed places, self-contained in misery and monotony. Cast in late summer light. Unsparing of his merriment, he purchases a freshly issued Paul Morphy medallion daguerreotype that he will present as a gift to Seven in celebration of Tom's (pending) premiere. Set in a wood frame, the daguerreotype is a clever series of images, an arrangement of ovals showing varied positions of the chess master's head against dark and light backgrounds. Eight small ovals circling a large one. A lunar cycle. A rising of planetary proportions.

He takes Tom into the tailor's shop. Needles in her mouth, the tailor measures Tom with ruler and string. A nigger woman sits at the sewing machine. Tom can hardly keep still, keep his arms outstretched, for listening to the sound, the click and clatter.

Mr. Oliver has decided on two designs. The first a collarless jacket with a row of white (bone) buttons down the front, breeches and stockings in accompaniment. The other an Eton jacket with coordinated vest and striped pants. Both jackets in black.

The tailor puts her fingers under Tom's shirt. Lifts one pants leg then the other. Squeezes his biceps. Kneads his chest. Touches his back, hands circling into the cotton. Tugs at elbow and sleeve. Looks at Seven in sober outrage. Can the nigger keep still?

This nigger can't keep still.

Keep your nigger still.

She can't quite fix his dimensions. Tries again. Now her every touch startles Tom.

They wander down one long aisle after another lined with shelves reaching all the way to the ceiling where logs of cloth are piled up. Huge spools of thread like squat trees down another corridor. *Now don't let that nigger go off and poke himself.* The sound of one sewing machine after another filling the high room.

Final fitting, Tom stands before the tailor to slip into his new clothes, test them for comfort, give and grab. The usual cursing complaints. The finished product is something to behold. Two fine suits, life glistening in each button.

Everything is moving. Silent, watchful, and mobile contentment. A sense that the thing he has been waiting for is about to happen. That all the limits he needs to exceed he can and will. Now, all he has to do is open up the channels of communication. Get the word out. Get people talking on the street. Seven begins to take Tom out each day in the surrey, canvassing the city. In this way, word of Tom's talents slowly circulates, drifting images half-developed half-finished, increasingly distorted as they pass from one mouth to the next, each witness diminishing or exaggerating the details in accordance with what his ears thought they heard and his eyes thought they saw, or as the independent heart and mind see fit. Truth often has to masquerade as falsehood to achieve its ends.

The patterns reverse. Now Perry Oliver stays home, while Seven and Tom venture out each day. Perry Oliver listening to them climb the stairs, setting their feet down softly, making an effort not to creak, stamping their shoes clean in the hall before they enter. Glad to be indoors after a long day.

Seven offers the silly suggestion of loading the piano onto a wagon. We'll stop and collect it from Mr. Oakley, he says in a loud and confident voice, as though there can be no doubt of Perry Oliver's answer. The idea takes firm hold of him—*we could rent a buckboard*—and Perry Oliver listens while Seven talks himself breathless, hoping the boy will realize on his own the absurdity of his idea. Seven is not lacking in self-assurance when a happy inspiration puts the right word in his mouth. They've paid for the piano but never collected it. (Where would they put it in this small apartment?) Seven believes that now's the time to make the most of it.

Seven gazes at Perry Oliver with a look of shy entreaty that gives him a touching air beneath his Paul Morphy hat. (More than Perry Oliver bargained for: Seven never takes the hat off. Would sleep in it if he could. Has tried to more than once.) Stuck in the middle of a sentence, Perry Oliver finally concedes. Let them think as one mind and act as one body. (A house divided against itself cannot stand.) His wishes and Mr. Oliver's form alloys of two instincts. Perry Oliver doesn't even see Seven as someone separate from him. What Perry Oliver expects of himself is what he expects of Seven. He is part of him and Perry Oliver requires that he give himself with the same completeness that Perry Oliver gives.

To instruct Seven in the proper method of negotiating a deal, Perry Oliver had told him the story of how he acquired the carriage. Several years ago he had purchased it at ten cents on the dollar from a destitute cotton farmer passing through town, headed west. *The bank foreclosed on my niggers. Hell, six months ago I had already lost half of what I owned when that cholera made them shit back to the earth all I fed them. If I had only done what my accountant had told me to do. Now this man, his advice was consistently good, told me to take out insurance on them, at least the pickneys. Never told me wrong. But a fool can't hear wisdom. At least I'd have a bit of something. Now look at me.*

They agreed on a price based upon the age and make of the carriage. Perry Oliver withdrew the exact number of bills from his pocket. But before laying out his money, he asked the farmer where he had come from and the man told him.

How far is that?

About two hundred miles, give or take. Mostly take.

Perry Oliver returned some of the bills to his purse and handed over the rest. The man was understandably confused. Perry Oliver explained that it was only right that he deduct a few dollars for two hundred miles of deterioration.

Along with bills and posters, Perry Oliver gives Seven a map, not knowing if he needs it. Seven seems to possess his own means of orientation. Seven and Tom patiently cross every ward of the city. The power of movement. Seven gains in being as he drives. The rush of things or their slow passage. Tom seems alert, smelling and listening, all of it interesting to him. His breathing even and careful. Curves and grades, major avenues streets and boulevards, dirt roads and gravel roads, beaten paths and those less beaten, logging trails and back roads. Mud on the wheels some days. Sheen on others. They put up bills on every clean and free space, bills printed on stiff paper that can withstand the weather. (Sight is never lost.) Out early, Seven rolls his sleep up as he drives, Tom seated beside him, sipping from a mug of tea laced with milk. He seems (almost) happy as the country-side spins by. They come out of the long silence for Tom to start singing abruptly, even before Seven draws the carriage to a stop. Tom sings on the busiest street corners and in any saloon, club, or watering hole that will allow them in, from the most fashionable to the least. Taking their meals where they can, whatever they can. Each evening, Perry Oliver hears them return, tired, not much strength, climbing the stairs very slowly, pausing for breath at each landing, or so it seems. Surprised him at first, as he has rarely seen either boy tired. Boundless energy. They take seats at the table and Seven begins to relate the tremendous happenings he (they) have witnessed, passionate and often confused and contradictory accounts full of detailed and persuasive description. Still enough there to allow Perry Oliver to reduce the material to an impassioned picture in his head, the story behind the story. A street-corner shyster dressed like an Oriental philosopher in turban and silk robes who hawks a broadside containing the "suppressed wisdom of the East." A doll that talks when you pull a hoop attached to a string coiled in its back. Two niggers playing chess under an oak tree. A large grassy square where dozens of preachers assemble to outsermon one another. Preaching done, they auction off their Bibles for charitable causes, pages blessed with holy water and angel's breath. One man of the cloth takes Seven aside and tells him, without any demonstration, that Tom's talent was preordered.

Preordained, Perry Oliver says.

No, sir. Preordered.

It is not so much the foolish wording that troubles Perry Oliver but the sentiment implied behind. The belief. Is Seven catching Religion? Happy to report, after that day Seven makes no further mention of the matter. How pleased Perry Oliver is.

Each return home revives the sense of possibility that he feels at the sight of a face whose details he has somewhat forgotten already since that morning.

How are you today, Tom?

I'm getting there.

The days stretching out in front of him, single and yet alternative. His room is dark and Perry Oliver stands at the window waiting for lights to appear in the sky. Summer wheels slowly toward its end, but it's not done with them yet. How much longer? He doesn't know if rain is falling or if leaves are crumbling or if the wind is breaking branches. The upcoming performance fills his mind so completely, an all-day, all-waking wideness, he can think of nothing else. So much catching up. So much to do. He will wake abruptly in the middle of the night—in sleep each man turns to a universe of his own—with the idea that he has some task to carry out, that some matter has slipped his attention, but without any understanding what it might be.

Tom is asleep, gentle weight against Seven's shoulder. An echo in his skin. Outside the moon is a giant lantern burning in black air. It's all the same to Tom, for he does not know how to distinguish time in his existence. Not so for his other. At night the road replays itself in his mind. The fine excitement he feels as they drive through the streets, and people gathering round to hear Tom sing. Even when they fail to draw a large crowd, he feels a curious charm with all the people moving steadily about, worldly contact. So this is what it means.

IF ANY MAN HAVE AN EAR,

» … «

let him hear the wonderful melodies of
BLIND TOM, *Musical Prodigy of the Age:*

» … «

a Plantation Negro Boy hailing from Savannah, a
wonderful chattel worth $2,500, with a decidedly
African-type face and every mark of idiocy, unlettered,
blind and awkward, and cursed with little of human nature,
but who yet has the amazing ability to both play and
improvise. He has been visited by
eminent Professors of Music, who have without exception,
proclaimed him the most wonderful Living Curiosity extant.
This boy, a perfect type of Negro, has never received
the advantage of Instruction, and though thoroughly
untaught
he manifests an intensity for the highest order of music,
mastering, after a few trials, the difficult compositions
of Beethoven, Bach, Mozart, Hertz, and others of equal
reputation. His memory for any air he has only heard once
is astonishing. Language can convey no adequate
conception of his Wonderful powers.—He must be seen
and heard, and will not fail to convince the most skeptical
that he is unapproachable on point of Musical Talent.

The citizens of C——are respectfully informed that
the above Lusus naturae will give a series
of his astonishing Musical Entertainments, at Hibernian
Hall, on the evening of SATURDAY, OCTOBER 24.

Book now. The last remaining seats will soon be sold.

**Admission Fifty cents, Children And
Servants Half Price**

The swiftness and ease with which Perry Oliver has accomplished these preparations give him a high he has never experienced before, possibly the peak point of fulfillment, causing him to wonder if and fear that the performance itself is destined to be a letdown. Worrying in the wood frame of his window, he tantalizes himself with varying mental pictures of its outcome.

Howard hands Perry Oliver a list of songs, a meager sampling of Tom's repertoire, nicely and brightly inked out. Only this limited sequence of selections—every concert must tell a story, beginning, middle, and end—that he has worked out for Tom's concert tomorrow night, including three encore pieces, should Tom need them. Perry Oliver raises the sheet to his face, muttering lines. The hall empty of people with the exception of Howard, Perry Oliver, Seven, and Tom. A single rehearsal because Perry Oliver wants it such. Isn't this simply a way for him to manage his panic, to try to clear up gaps in his understanding of the "Blind Tom Exhibition," notice what's missing? An opportunity for him to shop among a host of possible mistakes, mischances of mouth and body, miscalculations of time and energy? "The Manager of the Performance" curious to see if he has what it takes to carry him through a long evening. Who is aiding whom? Perry Oliver does an excellent job of pretending he knows what he is doing, no hesitation whatsoever. Indeed, he is showing presence of mind in asking Howard to be here now, exactly twenty-four hours before the scheduled concert, a single rehearsal. Reminding himself of his own power.

Howard answers whatever questions Perry Oliver puts to him, fresh anger and regret in his voice, trying his best to mask his feelings, and doing a lousy job of it. He is a man like any other. (If a prince be outraged, can his being a prince keep him from looking red and looking pale and grinding his teeth like a madman?) But Perry Oliver is the one who will benefit from his hard work with Tom. All Perry Oliver will have to do is call out the title of each song. *And now, ladies and gentlemen, Blind Tom will play for you* . . . Howard has received triple his lesson fee to come here today. The sight of Tom onstage had on first appearance aroused the exciting thought that Perry Oliver would ask him, Howard, to guide the audience through the performance. A dream that refused to leave him even as he began tuning the piano. He regrets that he won't be the one to introduce Tom to the public, to the world. (The planting and the cultivation are over. There remains but the harvest.) Perry Oliver has promised him free entry to the performance. No offense, he has already decided that he won't be in attendance, come what may. To listen would be already too late. But he likes the preparation, a chance to be wrapped up in the calm that comes over Tom whenever the boy is before a piano.

How's it going today, Tom?

Tom frowns.

Rhythm, tone, pitch—what can Perry Oliver say about these things with any intelligence or authority? The sole reason the Music Professor is here. Seven sits in the first row, a stand-in for the audience, watching and listening. Cheering and clapping. Extending the pause between songs with standing ovations. Tom seems distracted by Perry Oliver's voice, the way he speaks the song titles, how the words come out of his mouth. And his playing seems slow and instinctive. Nevertheless, it all goes smoothly, if Howard is to be believed.

Seven helps Tom down from the stage. Leans close and puts his mouth near the fleshy shell of Tom's ear. Nicely done, he says.

Tom rises earlier than usual the next morning and finds his way into the kitchen, seated at the table, head tilted at an angle, shoes laced and tied. Hands stalking the wood. Shoes turning circles above the floor. Seven goes over to him, sleep still clinging web-like to the corners of his eyes. Tom, he says. Are you feeling froggy today?

Tom says nothing.

Then hop.

Tom hops.

The road as bright as daylight in the unearthly glow.

Tom, are we all set about what you will play tonight?

Play what the day recommends, Tom says.

They got a late start, departed five minutes later than Perry Oliver had planned, Seven preoccupied with his newspaper at the table. Perry Oliver snatched it from his hands, startling the fingers, upsetting the Paul Morphy hat. Now he tosses the crumpled pages out the surrey window, white bats flapping against the dark.

Roam through the night in silence, the air sharp and clear, a felt exuberance although the streets are largely empty. They are following stars, leaving black earth under their wheels. The heavy scent of orchards and fields. Hibernian Hall rising out of the ground with a cold dingy glitter. Hurry inside. Don't keep us waiting.

Backstage, he hears voices, footsteps, doors opening and closing. How many of them are there? More than a hundred tickets purchased in advance, but it is conceivable that many more people will be in attendance. He watches a parade of types into the hall, some entering to the right, others to the left, white-gloved nigger ushers rushing back and forth, opening all the sturdy doors. He has no idea how many people the hall can actually seat, but the sight of all these well-dressed people, their admiration for Tom, fills him with a sense of disbelief, the promise of music and spectacle, something supernatural, drawing them out of their homes this evening.

He performs a rapid calculation and decides there must be four hundred or more ticket holders in the auditorium, only a handful of empty seats remaining. Why not have Seven run a head count? He can trust him to perform this matter. Simply hang back and wait, expectant. Stirrings, footsteps, murmurs, sighs, a hubbub of voices, little by little all the small and varied sounds of anticipation building up to the "Blind Tom Exhibition."

He has made all this happen, gathered all of these people in one place. Shocked to see the harmonious conciliation between his plans—his words: what he says, what he thinks, what he writes—and reality. One thing to imagine, another to witness it in actuality. Any number Seven brings him will be miraculous. Seven seems gratified, confirmed in his mission, even when he is lost from sight somewhere out there in those rambling currents of attendees.

Before he knows it (on an impulse) he finds himself walking out onto the stage. He doesn't think it necessary to ease into this all-changing moment. The chattering voices quiet down to a hush, but language is just what he needs now. Word defines the thing attached to it. Take the phrase *bare stage* and its many associations. He is what is bare. And so are they. Stripped down and innocent. The gaze is innocence itself aspiring to see the world in all its nakedness. The houselights go down, leaving nothing for the brain to watch but the musician (moving or still), nothing for the brain to hear but unblemished sound. Nothing stands between spectator and performer. Nothing can protect you (us) from direct confrontation. This erasure of solitude. The real advantage of this bare exchange lies in its flexibility. The spectrum of chance and possibility. No man-made script that can fully predict the outcome, that allows for easy escape. What is there. What we expect to be there. What could be there.

He looks up dazed into the span of air and ceiling that hangs above the stage. Looks out at all those he assumes are looking at him. Scrutinizing the silence. He has come to see faces, but he can't see anything for a number of seconds, a good minute or two, only glare, intense black streaks and gray shadows, so he stands dizzily where he is and waits for faces to appear, trying to regain his composure, too full for more, too astonished to speak. The only thing he can perceive for sure is Seven standing in the wings, large amounts of excitation pressing upon him, ready to bring Tom center stage anytime (once) the word is given. Is this an expression of surprise he notices on Tom's face? Knowledge? Acceptance? Tom aware, ready to assume his destiny. Blind Tom starts here.

He knows the exact moment to say something, to make his move. Now as good a time as any. So why doesn't he? Is it because he needs to see those he will address? Can't see them but can hear them, feel the contact in the air, all those bodies pressed together in the half light. From here they look transcendent. What a shock it'll be when the moment before him becomes brighter to his senses, the spectators slowly gaining volume, shape, characteristics, and features until they take on the full weight of existence. (How well blindness serves to protect Tom in this respect.) He might as well wait forever because he now understands that human eyes can't fully cancel out the blurry world created by this focused illumination, these stage lights burning full and unimpeded in the otherwise dark. *Good evening, ladies and gentlemen. Please allow me to introduce myself, Perry Oliver, Manager of the Performance.* He stops for a moment in something between alarm and vexation, realizing that he has prepared no formal introduction. Never even thought about it before now. This one oversight. And here the words are, tumbling out on his tongue. *You people of impeccable taste and understanding.* One word answered by another. *In the same hour came forth the fingers of a man's hand.* Feeling not quite connected to what he is saying—*Not in a thousand years would you imagine beautiful melodies flying out from the dark cave of this Negro's mouth*—although they are his words, his thoughts. Fearless despite the sense that the sentences can go one way or another, fail or achieve. Totally unscripted. He gets to say what he wants, a string of elaborate utterances and pronouncements—a *musical gem*—enjoying it now, as he finds, has always found, the theatrical instinct for disguise and transformation one of life's greatest pleasures. The audience can like it or not.

Only right that he should receive total credit for the affective force of his words, pulling Tom from the wings, positioning him at the piano, and eliciting his first round of applause from an audience even before the sounding of the first note. The hardest part over. Now he has only to take these few steps to this exact spot and introduce a song before disappearing from view behind the curtain where he stands sending searching glances at the sea of heads bobbing above all those chairs, distinguishing every fluid face in the audience. Seeing too their gestures and expressions. He knows what they are saying or not saying. All those thoughts joining and falling apart. The burden passed on to them now, as they sit listening, carried on the sound, hoping to grow accustomed to what they are hearing. Imagine all that has to happen, all that has to interconnect for the audience to be linked as one by the final number, applauding, each man or woman on his or her feet, before veering on their separate ways.

That night, Perry Oliver is careful to bury his face into the soft blind whiteness of his pillow, lest Seven hear him crying.

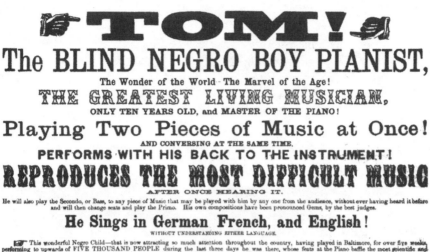

TOM!

The BLIND NEGRO BOY PIANIST,

The Wonder of the World--The Marvel of the Age!

THE GREATEST LIVING MUSICIAN,

ONLY TEN YEARS OLD, and MASTER OF THE PIANO!

Playing Two Pieces of Music at Once!

AND CONVERSING AT THE SAME TIME.

PERFORMS WITH HIS BACK TO THE INSTRUMENT!

REPRODUCES THE MOST DIFFICULT MUSIC

AFTER ONCE HEARING IT.

He will also play the Secondo, or Bass, to any piece of Music that may be played with him by any one from the audience, without ever having heard it before and will then change seats and play the Primo. His own compositions have been pronounced Gems, by the best judges.

He Sings in German French, and English!

WITHOUT UNDERSTANDING EITHER LANGUAGE.

☞ This wonderful Negro Child—that is now attracting so much attention throughout the country, having played in Baltimore, for over five weeks, performing to upwards of FIVE THOUSAND PEOPLE during the last three days he was there, whose feats at the Piano baffle the most scientific and learned men in the land—was blind from birth, has never had one moment's instruction, does not know a *flat* from a *sharp*, or the name of any key upon the instrument; yet he plays the most difficult Operatic pieces, without ever striking a false note, not only brilliantly and beautifully, but with all the taste, expression and feeling of the most distinguished artist.

AT EACH OF HIS ENTERTAINMENTS HE WILL GIVE

INIMITABLE IMITATIONS

Of THE DRUM and FIFE, RAIL-ROAD CARS, GUITAR, &c.

WILL ALSO PLAY FROM THE OPERAS OF

Norma, Linda, Lucrecia Borgia, Trovatore, Somnambula, La Fille du Regiment, &c.,

TOGETHER WITH

MARCHES, WALTZES POLKAS, FANTASIAS, CONCERTAS,

Variations on Celebrated Airs, &c., and will Sing several pieces.

A CARD—The boy Tom was born in Georgia, and is only ten years old, and being perfectly blind was caressed and petted, as all negro children are about a plantation in the South, and more particularly those afflicted with so terrible an infirmity as the loss of sight. But when the veil of darkness was drawn over his eyes, as if to make amends, for the infliction upon the poor Negro Boy, a flood of light was poured into his brain, mysteriously even through the darkened portals, and his mind became an Opera of Beauty, written by the hand of God in syllables of music, for the delight of the world. The development of his ability, which is startling the musical firmament, was a purely accidental. The boy being the pet of the family, had access to the parlor in which the Piano stood. The ladies in an adjoining apartment heard with surprise the instrument touched by no ordinary hand; entranced they listened to the thrilling melody, and hastening to know who could produce such exquisite music, found the little plantation negro Tom, scarcely able to reach the keys, fingering them with the skill of an accomplished artist. Can anything be more wonderful than the history of this gifted negro boy? It is worthy of special mark, too, that in all his wonderful improvisations he has never been known in any instance to be guilty of repetition or plagiarism. He is presented to the public as surpassing everything hitherto known to the world as a MUSICAL WONDER.

TOM will use the magnificent piano presented to him by Wm. Knabe & Co., of Baltimore.

OPINIONS OF THE PRESS.

Our readers are aware that we are not apt to be taken with "wonders." Generally speaking, we have found them to be unmitigated humbugs. The charlatanism of itinerant exhibitors has made us suspicious of nearly all pretensions in the way of the marvellous, and we have therefore been careful not to throw all ourselves to such Barnumisgs as are constantly obtruding themselves upon editorial notice in a city like Baltimore.

For more than a week past, however, there has been a series of musical performances at Carroll Hall, in this city, which have certainly exceeded in interest, of a particular kind, anything we ever before witnessed. The performer is an awkward country negro boy, of apparently ten or twelve years of age; tall, not slender, having rather an idiotic expression of countenance when not excited by music, a stutterer in his efforts at conversation, and has been totally blind from his birth. Altogether, the appearance of the child, as indicative of talent of any kind, is about as unpromising as might in any case be found after a day's search among our colored population. Yet "Blind Tom," as he is familiarly called, is, perhaps, as great a *living* wonder as there is in the world at the present day. If Paul Morphy is entitled to rank with the foremost men of the world, because he can do what no other living man can do, then "Blind Tom" is equally worthy of public admiration, for in music he as far excels, in some particulars, all other musical geniuses, as the celebrated chess player excels all others in the movements of the board.

But the reader is ready to inquire, what are the facts in this marvellous case? We believe them to be these: Born on a plantation in Georgia, nothing was known of this boy's peculiar musical faculty until he was about six or eight years of age. A piano in the house of his master had frequently arrested the child's attention, and it was noticed that any performance upon it affected him to singular enthusiasm. But, of course, a piano was very properly, as would be supposed, a forbidden object to a little blind negro boy's touch. At midnight, on a certain occasion, however, the occupants of the house were startled by the sound of the instrument. Who could be playing it at that hour? On descending to the parlor to ascertain the cause of this unexpected serenade, there was "Blind Tom," playing away in triumphant possession, successful at his first effort. He was performing an air of the class familiar to the negroes of the plantation. Of course this surprising event made "Tom" a hero. Like Lord Byron, *without* the waking up, he "found himself famous." It was soon discovered that such was his imitative power in music, that after hearing the most elaborate and difficult pieces performed a few times, he could reproduce them with an accuracy as minute as it was astounding. He has had no instruction from musical teachers, and does not even know the name of the different notes in the scale.

On Saturday last we had the satisfactory test of "Tom's" wonderful power of imitation. Repeated invitations had been given by Mr. Oliver, the gentleman to whom he belongs, to the effect that any gentleman or lady of the audience might play with "Tom" a duet, allowing four hands at the instrument, and although "Tom" might never have heard the piece, he would instantly play a correct accompaniment, and then changing seats with the principal, would reproduce the principal's part on the upper keys, no matter how long it might be. It happened that Mr. Otto Sutro was in the audience, a gentleman well known in this city as a musical teacher and composer, standing in the front rank of his profession. He walked to the platform, took his seat beside "Tom" and produced a brilliant melody, which, as the gentleman himself afterward informed us, was mainly an *improvisation*, so that "Tom" could not have heard it before. The boy went through it with courage and success. Had we not witnessed this feat, we could not have believed it possible.

Any piece heard by "Tom" seems to make the same impression on its brain that an object placed before a daguerrean instrument makes upon the plate which is to receive it. Once on his brain, it is soon at his finger ends. If the object before the daguerreotypist has defects upon it, the plate will show the defects. So, if the *time*, (for instance,) of the performer from whom "Tom" learns a piece is defective, the *time* for his reproduction will be correspondingly defective; and if the performer makes a false note in the piece, "Tom" will strike the same key precisely at the same place when he renders it, unless it is so discordant as to shock his nicer sense of harmony. This should be borne in mind by those who bring to "Tom's" performances the critical taste which they would exercise in noting the skill of one whose life had been given to musical science.

Now the whole case must be considered. See, here is a blind black boy, with all the peculiarities of his race, full of tricks and antics, clapping his hands in childish glee when the audience applauds, cutting all manner of monkey shines—now shrugging his shoulders, now grimacing grotesquely, now awkwardly gesticulating, and anon looking supremely silly, in the blank simplicity of his unsophisticated boyhood—a real unmitigated specimen of a little uncultivated corn-field or cotton-plantation negro, feeling himself quite out of place before a refined and intellectual audience—yet whose power over the instrument, when his fingers once has touched it, is such that holds multitudes in speechless wonder, and behind whose sightless balls is a storehouse of memory that carries apparently all the music he ever heard in his life. Not mere simple airs are they, but long and difficult compositions, requiring delicate skill of manipulation in expressive rendering. These are flung from his fingers with a strength and energy which show how perfectly the passion for music has the mastery of his whole being.

Whatever slight defects in *tone* some of the boy's imitations may exhibit, the *time* of his own compositions is faultless; for "Tom" is not simply a mocking bird. He can *improvise* with the public. He calls it the "Oliver Gallop," in compliment to his master. It is sprightly in movement, flashing with brilliance, and while it partakes somewhat of the negro peculiarity of melody, is so charmingly rendered, that it never fails to bring down the house in a perfect storm of applause. Prof. Stoddard, of this city, is preparing it for publication. By the way, it is quite evident that "Tom" relishes a little of the motion of the cane and heel among the spectators, quite as well as some older and graver persons, who occasionally are called upon to stand in the presence of the multitude.

The *fingering* of "Tom" is unique. It is itself a proof that he has had no teacher. A scientific performer won't crook his knuckles if he did not move his fingers with a more conventional and artistic grace. But "Tom" is the fingering of nature, and whatever the Professors may say, it is beautiful, because it is natural. That so slight a hand, with so singular and yet so certain a motion, should bring from the instrument such stirring

SONGS,

Sketch of the Life,

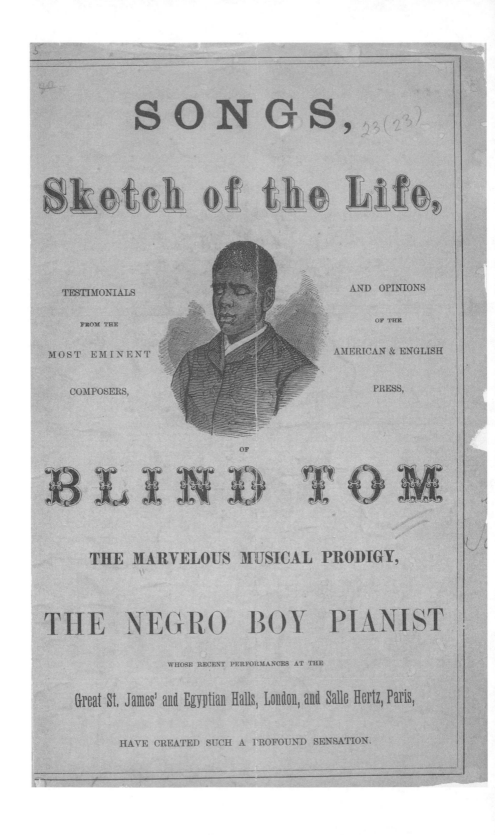

TESTIMONIALS

FROM THE

MOST EMINENT

COMPOSERS,

AND OPINIONS

OF THE

AMERICAN & ENGLISH

PRESS,

OF

BLIND TOM

THE MARVELOUS MUSICAL PRODIGY,

THE NEGRO BOY PIANIST

WHOSE RECENT PERFORMANCES AT THE

Great St. James' and Egyptian Halls, London, and Salle Hertz, Paris,

HAVE CREATED SUCH A PROFOUND SENSATION.

PROGRAMME.

SPECIAL NOTICE.

BLIND TOM can only play what he hears or improvises. Until about two years ago a list of pieces that Tom had heard was kept, numbering nearly 2,000. Unfortunately this catalogue was lost. Since that period he has heard perhaps 3,000 pieces, and his repertoire now numbers upwards of 5,000, entirely at his memory's disposal. From this extensive store Tom will introduce selections from BEETHOVEN, BACH, MENDELSSOHN, CHOPIN, THALBERG, GOTTSCHALK, and others; and also give his marvelous and amusing Imitations, Recitations, Anecdotes, &c., &c.

BLIND TOM'S CONCERTS.

PROGRAMME.

Classical Selections.

1. Sonata, "Pathetique" .... *Beethoven*
2.   "   "Pastorale" opus 28 .... "
3.   "   "Moonlight," 27 .... "
4. Andante .... *Mendelssohn*
5. Fugue in A minor .... *Bach*
6.   "   G minor .... "

7. Songs without Words .... *Mendelssohn*
8. "Wedding March" .... "
9. Concerto in G minor .... "
10. Gavotte in G minor .... *Bach*
11. "Funeral March" .... *Chopin*
12. "Moses in Egypt" .... *Rossini*

Piano Forte Solos.

13. "Trovatore," Chorus, Duet and Anvil
     Chorus .... *Verdi*
14. "Lucretia Borgia," Drinking Song
     (Fantasia) .... *Donizetti*
15. "Lucia de Lammermoor," .... "
16. "Cinderella" Non Piu Mesta .... *Rossini*
17. "Somnambula," Caprice .... *Bellini*
18. "Norma," Varieties .... "

19. "Faust," Tenor, Solo, Old Men's Song
     and Soldiers' Chorus .... *Gounod*
20. "Le Prophet" .... *Meyerbeer*
21. "Linda" .... "
22. "Dinora" .... *Meyerbeer*
23. "Bords du Rhine" .... "
24. "La Montagnarde" .... "
25. "Shells of the Ocean" .... "
26. "La Fille du Regiment" .... *Donizetti*

Fantasias and Caprices.

27. Fantasia, "Home, Sweet Home" .... *Thalberg*
28.   "   "Last Rose of Summer" ..... "
29.   "   "Lilly Dale," for left hand ... "
30.   "   "Ever of Thee," &c .... "
31.   "   "Carnival de Venice" .... "
32. Reverie. "Last Hope" .... *Gottschalk*
33. La Fontaine ....

34. "Whispering Winds" ....
35. "Caprice" .... *Liszt*
36. Fantasia, "Old Hundredth Psalm" ....
37. "Auld Lang Syne," and "Listen to the
     Mocking Bird," (Piano Forte Imi-
     tations of the Bird) .... *Hoffman*

Marches.

38. March, "Delta Kappa Epsilon .... *Pease*
39. "Grand March de Concert" .... *Wallace*
40. "Gen. Ripley's March" ....

41. "Amazon March" ....
42. "Masonic Grand March " ....

Imitations.

43. Imitations of the Music Box.
44.   "   "   Dutch Woman and Hand
     Organ.
45. Imitations of the Harp.
46.   "   "   Scotch Bag Pipes.
47.   "   "   Scotch Fiddler.

48. Imitations of the Church Organ.
49.   "   "   Guitar.
50.   "   "   Banjo.
51.   "   "   Douglas' Speech.
52.   "   "   Uncle Charlie.
53. Produces three Melodies at the same time.

Descriptive Music.

54. "Cascade" ....
55. The Rain Storm .... *Blind Tom*

56. The Battle of Manassas .... *Blind Tom*

Songs.

57. "Rocked in the Cradle of the Deep" ..
58. "Mother, dear Mother, I Still Think
     of Thee" ....
59. "The Old Sexton" ....
60. "The Ivy Green" ....
61. "Then You'll Remember Me" ....
62. "Scenes That are Brightest" ....

63. "When the Swallows Homeward Fly."
64. "Oh! Whisper What Thou Feelest" ..
65. "My Pretty Jane" ....
66. "Castles in the Air" ....
67. "Mary of Argyle" ....
68. "A Home by the Sea" ....
69. Byron's "Farewell to Tom Moore" ....

Parlor Selections.

70. Waltz in A flat .... *Chopin*
71. Waltz in E flat .... "
72. Waltz in D flat .... "
73. Tarantelle in A flat .... *Stephen Heller*
74. "Josephine Mazurka" .... *Heller*
75. "Polonaise .... *Weber*
76. Nuit Blanche .... *Stephen Heller*

77. Spring Dawn Mazurka .... *William Mason*
78. "Monastery Bells" ....
79. "California Polka" .... *Herz*
80. "Alboni Waltzes" .... *Schuloff*
81. "L'Esplanade" .... *Hoffman*
82. Anen Polka ....

Programme for the Evening to be Selected from the above.

BLIND TOM'S CONCERTS.

PROGRAMME.

Classical Selections.

1. Sonata "Pathétique"...............................*Beethoven*
2. " "Pastorale," Opus 28..................... "
3. " "Moonlight," 27........................... "
4. Andante...*Mendelssohn*
5. Fugue in A minor.................................*Bach*
6. " in G minor..................................... "
7. "Songs without Words".........................*Mendelssohn*
8. "Wedding March"............................... "
9. Concerto in G minor............................ "
10. Gavotte in G minor...............................*Bach*
11. "Funeral March" ....*Chopin*
12. "Moses in Egypt"................................*Rossini*

Piano-Forte Solos.

13. "Trovatore," Chorus, Duet, and Anvil Chorus......... *Verdi*
14. "Lucrezia Borgia," Drinking Song (Fantasia).......*Donizetti*
15. "Lucia di Lammermoor"........................... "
16. "Cinderella," Non Piu Meste......................*Rossini*
17. "Sonnambula," Caprice............................*Bellini*
18. "Norma," Varieties.............................. "
19. "Faust," Tenor Solo, Old Men's Song, and Soldiers' Chorus...*Gounod*
20. "Le Prophète"...................................*Meyerbeer*
21. "Linda"...
22. "Dinora".......................................*Meyerbeer*
23. "Bords du Rhine"................................
24. "La Montagnarde"................................
25. "Shells of the Ocean"...........................
26. "La Fille du Régiment".........................*Donizetti*

Fantasias and Caprices.

27. Fantasia, "Home, Sweet Home"...................*Thalberg*
28. " "Last Rose of Summer"................ "

29. Fantasia, " Lily Dale," for left hand.................*Thalberg*
30.   "   " Ever of Thee," &c......................   "
31.   "   " Carnival de Venise"....................   "
32. Reverie. " Last Hope "..............................*Gottschalk*
33. La Fontaine.......................................
34. " Whispering Winds "............................
35. " Caprice "..*Liszt*
36. Fantasia, " Old Hundredth Psalm "..................
37. " Auld Lang Syne," and " Listen to the Mocking-
         Bird " (Piano-Forte Imitations of the Bird)......*Hoffman*

Marches.

38. March, " Delta Kappa Epsilon ".......................*Pease*
39. " Grand March de Concert ".........................*Wallace*
40. " Gen. Ripley's March "............................
41. " Amazon March "..................................
42. " Masonic Grand March " ....

Imitations.

43. Imitations of the Music-Box.
44.   "   "   Dutch Woman and Hand-Organ.
45.   "   "   Harp.
46.   "   "   Scotch Bagpipes.
47.   "   "   Scotch Fiddler.
48.   "   "   Church Organ.
49.   "   "   Guitar.
50.   "   "   Banjo.
51.   "   "   Douglas's Speech.
52.   "   "   Uncle Charlie.
53. Produces three melodies at the same time.

Descriptive Music.

54. " Cascade "...
55. The Rain Storm...................................*Blind Tom*
56. The Battle of Manassas............................   "

Songs.

57. " Rocked in the Cradle of the Deep "...............
58. " Mother, dear Mother, I still think of Thee ".....
59. " The Old Sexton "................................
60. " The Ivy Green "................................
61. " Then you'll remember Me ".....................

62. "Scenes that are Brightest"..................... ...
63. "When the Swallows homeward fly"..............
64. "Oh ! whisper what Thou feelest"................
65. "My Pretty Jane ".................................
66. "Castles in the Air".............................
67. "Mary of Argyle".................................
68. "A Home by the Sea"............................
69. Byron's "Farewell to Tom Moore "...............

Parlor Selections.

70. Waltz in A flat..*Chopin*
71. Waltz in E flat..   "
72. Waltz in D flat..   "
73. Tarantelle in A flat............................*Stephen Heller*
74. "Josephine Mazurka"................................*Heller*
75. "Polonaise "..*Weber*
76. Nuit Blanche....................................*Stephen Heller*
77. Spring Dawn Mazurka.......................*William Mason*
78. "Monastery Bells ".............................
79. "California Polka " ....*Herz*
80. "Alboni Waltzes "....................................*Schuloff*
81. "L'Esplanade "..*Hoffman*
82. Anen Polka..

Programme for the evening to be selected from the preceding.

Voice of the Waves
(1856–1862)

"The feather flew, not because
of anything in itself but because
the air bore it along. This am I . . ."

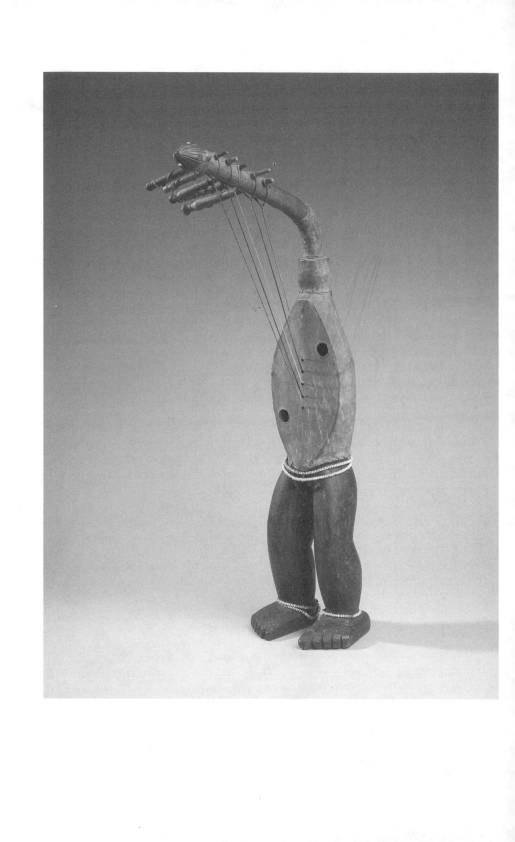

HE PLAYS "DIXIE" WITH HIS LEFT HAND IN THE KEY OF A, "Yankee Doodle" with the right in the key of E, and sings "The Girl I Left Behind Me" in the key of E.

He plays the *Moonlight Sonata* with his back to the piano and his hands inverted.

He plays a four-handed arrangement of Rossini's *Semiramide* with two hands.

He plays "Voices of the Waves" with his tongue and teeth, as if eating the ivory keys.

He plays "The Rain Storm" in a minor key with his bare feet, walking melody across the black keys.

He sings the song about his mother ("Mother, dear Mother, I Still Think of Thee"), and every woman in the audience starts crying.

And now, ladies and gentlemen, Blind Tom will perform for you one of his own compositions, the latest from his growing catalog. Feel honored, ladies and gentlemen, as your ears will be the first to hear this beautiful tune outside my own. It is titled, and I assure you that you'll see why, "Rattlesnake Charm." Speaking slowly to get it right.

You, Perry Oliver, the Manager of the Performance, call for a challenge from the audience. Who here in the house can make history by confounding Blind Tom? A man produces a composition of his own construction that he points out is some twenty pages in length. Please, sir, come to the stage. As soon as the challenger sets hands to his tune, Tom bends his head nearly to the floor and with one foot raised and stretched out behind him, begins to turn round and round upon the other foot, gaining speed as he spins, the entire figure agitated, rotating about itself on its own axis, performing implausible acrobatic contortions, in poses and expressions beyond the limits of the ridiculous and expressive. Now he begins to ornament the gyrations with spasmodic movements of the hands. He makes some members of the audience dizzy with his spinning. Some of the women cover their faces, or their husband's hands do it for them without their asking, but you don't think it odd. Tom looks like nothing more in the world than a man taking his daily exercise, strange gymnastics essential to his bodily health. Something strangely peaceful in the activity, Tom winding deeply into a private place, the eye of his own storm.

Tom ceases spinning about and seats himself at the piano. He plays back the melody note for note and in the exact rhythm, begins to play it again, seeming to inspect the melody first, run through it once as if to check it out before reshaping and revoicing it, weaving variations and building a continual stream of countermelody and changing textures, transposing the melody and harmony to another key, revealing all of the song's hidden permutations, one hand now active on the keyboard, the other fluttering in the air.

Another man in the audience takes to his feet and issues a different challenge, hoping to confound "the eighth wonder of the world." Rumor has it that Tom can recite certain passages from Plato, word for word. Does he know the fifth chapter of *The Republic*? Why indeed, you say. He does know it. And for the audience's additional pleasure, he will also recite chapters six and seven. So Tom does, reciting one chapter in Greek, the next chapter in Latin, and then the last in French, Tom's voice, the way it holds each person in the audience like a hand gripping a face, a kind of hypnosis. Now he gives—further amazement—an oratory in Japanese followed by in quick order selections from the Gospel according to Mark, several Articles of the Constitution—why stop there?—and the first chapters of Charles Dickens's *A Tale of Two Cities*, performing the pages in the exact voice of the master British novelist—*If it is too cold or wet I take shelter in the Café de la Régence and amuse myself watching people playing chess. Paris is the place in the world, and the Café de la Régence the place in Paris where this game is played best, and at Rey's the shrewd Legal, the crafty Philidor and the dependable Mayot sally forth to battle . . .*—saying what the day demands, his voice slow and measured, beautiful and powerful, all the intonations, syllables, and inflections exact, each member of the audience watching and listening with dark redolent attention, rapture, bodies stiff, listening with all their muscles.

Soon the lights come up, startling, each person like a puzzle piece in her/his seat collectively holding the light together. Applaud with everyone else. Impossible not to.

Light burning Tom into fame, into history.

The audience huddles near the orchestra pit, talking greedily, forming a tight arc around Tom, even as the navigator leads him backstage. Tom has no choice but to give himself up to the melee of greeting and compliments and handshaking. The needy who flock to Tom's dressing room like sick pilgrims, in a terrible hurry to touch or kiss Blind Tom's hands, forehead, neck, or cheek, to lay hands on his woolly scalp. Seated in a chair and moving as little as possible, Tom tucks his hands safely away into his lap and so doing keeps them out of view, hidden. For the most part, he remains silent in the face of their praise and pronouncements, their inquiries and entreaties, wincing at the smells of these strangers' colognes. Then the surgeons, doctors, and physicians, who politely or hurriedly wish to examine Tom and supply him the latest remedies and research. (No illness can be concealed from trained sight.) He barks out at those few who seem to agitate (annoy) him—the poking, probing, and prodding, medical fingers sounding his chest, tugging at his nose and ears, tapping his eyes as if testing an eggshell's firmness, prying his teeth apart; what it means to live in a body: maximum anatomical tension—but by and large he remains quiet and still. Nor does he perk up when the musical professionals inquire about some chord voicing or the tempo of a particular movement, or his feelings about the *Moonlight Sonata*, his own "The Battle of Manassas," or why such and such a composition is not in his program, or what songs did he love that he never sang? All those fussy unseen hands, all those heard or ignored or not understood voices. Tom in need of a good night's rest, two or three good nights, and something to fill his stomach and cool his mouth and tongue (hunkered at the table). *Lait.*

He sat on his stool a full half-yard distant from the piano, this awkward position making it necessary for him to stretch out his arms to their full negro length, like an ape clawing his food. His feet showed no better understanding of proper, keyboard posture; when not on the pedals, they twisted incessantly, rubbing into the stage floor like a boar snorting up a well-buried black truffle. When given a theme for improvisation, he would take some ludicrous posture, expressive of listening, but soon lowering the body and rising on one leg, spinning round and round, moving upon that improvised axis like a pirouette dancer, but indefinitely. The muddled notes went stumbling into dots. When he finished playing, he would applaud himself violently, kicking, pounding his hands together, and turning away to his master, the self-named "Manager of the Performance," for an approving pat on the head. All in all, his music was a conventional affair, uncomplicated in melody, rudimentary in harmony, exact in rhythm and pace, and basic in structure and form. Still, many carry on with the belief that this was the most remarkable performance ever witnessed in our city. A vaguely perceived hare is nevertheless a hare. Indeed, to the amateur ear, Blind Tom's "exhibition" would put to blush and shame many of our so-called "professors" of music.

—The Columbus Observer

The ship bellies into the harbor, faint birdsong sounding above. At last. He steps free of the deck, down the slanted plank, a sea-bleached wreck, a string of stirring bodies (passengers) behind him. (Pied Piper.) Always on the go, chasing an audience for Tom. Maps make the getting there look easy, foreshortening distance, the world small, flat, and manageable, a constellation of names—Chicago, Berlin, London, Boston, Memphis, Paris—laid out before him as prodigious as stars in the sky, names that bring together an elemental union between earth and flesh, ground and Blind Tom. So he draws up plans, his ideas bright forces quite apart from himself. He sees them rise, turn, spin, fall, as light as golden birds.

The taxis, hotels, and inns, the luggage damaged or lost, the saloons and restaurants. So much that can go wrong. Acts of man and God. Only when he sees multitudes rush in to take their seats inside a concert hall or auditorium does he unwind, thankful for the perfect alignment of events.

Days glide by like birds. Weeks ocean-wide. So much sky. (What is here must also be there.) Time measured by the number of seats filled, the number of tickets sold, his thoughts and speech full of facts. Like unnumbered pages the repetitions prevent him from counting the hours and the steps. Repetition. When the word is the same day after day, words like *travel, tour, recital, concert, performance.* Time does not change, it does not move, nor does his mind or his feet, even if they bear the illusion of coming and going, of getting to somewhere—perhaps not a place—important.

In Little Vicksburg, he sees a road adorned with the most magnificent carriages ever constructed. In Macon, he expresses his admiration for the brilliant uniforms of militiamen who pass before him. In Augustus—another city another recital. He flies through the minutes, feeling the draw of some vast venue opening up, all river, all ocean, all sky. Even before leaving one town or city for the next, he senses he has lost something he might have gained had he stayed longer. He steps on boat or train already thinking of home, the tour's end, and thinking beyond that to the next season. In his sleep he has to shake off thoughts of leave-taking, and when he is awake he feels firmly reassured at the sight of his locked suitcases, proof of future engagements. Nothing is as it used to be. His sense of the world is thrown off. Experience has set him in the firm belief that travel is a way of measuring where he is in his life. If things go smoothly his life is running as it should. However, if things go badly—trains off schedule, luggage lost, reckless or route-altering taxi drivers—his life is off course. But a tour throws even this sense of judgment out of whack. What he comes to desire is rest.

Tom, how do you like New York?
        I don't like it one bit. Too many fellow beings.

Like a line of ants, the would-be pianists and professors of music climb up to the stage and gather around the unguarded post-concert piano. The floorboards beneath them sponge sound back. First they examine the ivory keys with their eyes, the magic there. Now put their fingers where Blind Tom had put his hands, his warmth still there. Close their eyes, seeing and feeling the ghost of this man, handprints. Touching keys. Arguing from the man to the music.

Tom, do you like talking to us? the journalist asks.
        I am surrounded by friends, Tom says.
        Are you looking forward to your concert tonight?
        It will be better tomorrow. Tomorrow we will really begin.
        And why is that?
        It is the design of my head.
        Will you play "Moses in Egypt" tonight?
        I don't know what I can do. I promise nothing complete.
        Tom, how does a person stand up under all of the traveling you do?
        I am standing now.
        Do you ever suffer from fatigue?
        I could be bounded in a nutshell and count myself king of infinite space.

Hurry up. He coming.
        Voice that brings faces to the windows.
        Yall better hurry up.

Doors opening, pouring Negroes out into the afternoon, so many faces brown and beaming bright, cheeks swollen with pride. Oh happy day! Tom puts words into their mouths and movements into their bodies. In parade formation, they cross a Japanese bridge above a dark yellowish brown stream of open sewage into a field of flowers—gladioluses, petunias, tulips, chrysanthemums, and sunflowers—on the other side, and march on into the grove of Japanese cherry blossom trees in full bloom on the White House lawn.

There he is.

He looks bigger in person.

Praise be.

They look up at the sky to see if God is watching too.

Tom, would you like to say a few words to the people?

Yes, Tom says. I am Blind Tom, and so are you.

He sounds just like the Lord.

Praise be.

Tom walks right past President Buchanan, positions himself before the Chickering full grand piano, and starts to play. About the first song, the president's niece is heard to say, I never felt that song as I did just now. About the second song, a prominent senator in attendance will remember *majestic rivers winding over the floodplains,* while his wife will opine, Away flew the notes. Of the many journalists present, one will later sum up the recital this way: Music broke out on Blind Tom like the smallpox.

Even before the applause for his last song has ended (no encore), Tom makes his way over to the members of the Japanese delegation. Says, You don't understand our music.

Outside the White House, more journalists with their paper, pens, and questions. Tom, you're a big boy.

Yes. I'm a behemoth.

The photographer. His heavy plates, black scrim, flash. The camera he must carry tortoise-like on his back. He crawls inside the black scrim. The shutter falls, a puff of blinding smoke.

Tom says, A photograph is a mirror that remembers.
Where to now, Tom?
Tom is off to glory.

In the first place he will represent the Southern army leaving home to their favorite tune of "The Girl I Left Behind Me," which you will hear in the distance, growing louder and louder as they approach Manassas (the imitation of the drum and fife). He will represent the Grand Union Army leaving Washington City to the tune of "Dixie." You will recollect that their prisoners spoke of the fact that when the Grand Union Army left Washington, not only were their bands playing "Dixie," but their men were also singing it.

He will represent the eve of battle by a very soft sweet melody, then the clatter of arms and accoutrements, the war trumpet of Beauregard, which you will hear distinctly; and then McDowell's in the distance, like an echo at first. He will represent the firing of the cannons to "Yankee Doodle," the Marseilles Hymn, and "The Star-Spangled Banner." With "Dixie," you will hear the arrival of the train cars containing General Kirby's reinforcements, which you will all recollect was very valuable to General Beauregard upon that occasion after their arrival of which, as you will hear, the fighting will grow more severe (shouts and yells, and the imitation of horses, musketry, and death).

A tribute to genius, presented to Tom, the blind colored pianist, by Messrs Knabe & Co, Baltimore, Front Street Theater July 3, 186—

Testimonial:
I well remember in Charleston where a party of us had him with us on and off for two or three months, and a young lady sat down at the piano and began to play. Tom was at the dark end of the chamber, spinning upon his hands and heels, and mumbling to himself. He caught the sound of the instrument and stood for a mo-

ment still and upright. Then, like a wild animal, he made a dash and swooped down upon her. Terrified, the poor girl shrieked and ran, while the rest of us held him writhing and trembling with what seemed to be rage. "She stole my harmonies," he cried over and over, "she stole my harmonies." And never again did he allow her to come near him. If she were even in the room he knew it somehow and became restive and angry.

Attaining his zenith, the height of public regard, Blind Tom is a sun setting everything in the world ablaze, radiating excellent reviews, parades in his honor (the clamor, the sureness of gesture and step, the rousing speeches, the swells of fellow feeling), delighted and devoted concertgoers, invitations and entreaties from worthy personages and distinguished delegations who seek a private audience with this singular phenomenon of Nature (the decorum of Tom's hosts), the journalists who want to exchange a few words with him, and the many ordinary and cheerful well-wishers who go out of their way to simply catch a glimpse of Blind Tom in the flesh during those lapses and lulls when he is not onstage or otherwise on display. Open the gates of heaven, for everything in the world is either outside or inside Tom. Tom the everything in everything. Never before has Perry Oliver felt so recognized, so understood, so vindicated. Free.

So why then day after day this troubling disquiet that came upon him without warning several months ago—where were they then, in Seattle? Chicago? the war benefit in Charleston?—and that never seems to leave him? He sits up at night with his ledger of water-stiffened pages, trying to plan (order? predict?) the future in his clean penmanship, trying to escape the feeling that he is being carried helplessly toward some pitching instant.

That feeling even more so after he starts to notice three weeping women in black at every concert. Three weeping women dressed in black. Seated next to each other in the blue-black dark, tears flowing and mouths stunned open. Each woman assumes a distinct set to her body. The first with her face tilted to one side. The second woman holding the sides of her face. The third forehead gripped in the vise of her right hand. He watches their heaving bosoms without hearing their sobs, drowned out by the music perhaps. Sees them swallowing deep breaths then spilling the breaths out again. They become a familiar presence, concert after concert, city after city, three weeping women in black. They seem to have no idea that their gestures are extreme—bawling, wringing their hands, shouting meaningless phrases over and over. Do they assume that no one hears them? From the stage he searches out their countenances, trying to detect features around their expressions of penitence and grief. Strange remote faces. How old are they? Are they sisters of the Race? (This brutal looking into.) That's when he begins to notice that the faces actually change at each concert. Never the same three women, but always a set of three women in black, comely or ugly, young or old or of indeterminate age. Perhaps these women are all part of some union of the female sex a thousand members strong. Ten thousand. Besides their black garb, one fact holds true from concert to concert: although they are weeping he can see that their eyes are alive, registering and interpreting, taking in everything.

Then the night when red moon and red sun compete in the same sky above fog that rides low to the ground. He closes the curtains, canceling light, and starts fingering the keys in the dark. And he continues to finger them. An owl hoots in the ghosted air and he hoots back. In no one's name but his own let this long night end.

He dreams. Covered in dirt, the planters are hacking the earth with broad flat plates, no cutting edge. Their crops ground underground, down into the earth. What tool can reach them?

You just can't take him from me, Perry Oliver says. With no fair warning.

You will thank me for it, General Bethune says. The quicker you suffer, the sooner it ends. The General speaks slowly and fluidly, with great power. All the doors in the room are closed. (Every door tells a story.) And the Greek and Roman faces carved into the mantel near the ceiling look down on the conversation, Perry Oliver seated in a chair so tall that it rises three feet into the air behind him, General Bethune seated on the other side of him in a similar chair, chunks of ice sizzling (the sound) inside two squat square glasses filled with whiskey on the small round table between the two men, behind them a neatly bricked fireplace like a big wide yawning mouth ready to swallow them.

But, sir. Perry Oliver loosens the clasp joining the two ends of his string tie. All these years I put in. All those years.

And you prospered.

Yes, I have. Is that what this is about? You want more money, a percentage? That can easily be—

No.

Then what, sir? You are an honorable man, having spilled blood and directed others to spill blood, including their own.

Mr. Oliver, General Bethune says, no matter how self-activated, every man finds himself caught in the grip of forces that hold suzerainty over every vessel of his person and every aspect of his life, small to big. Despite his uniform—his medal-decorated chest, the heavy epaulets perched on his shoulders like upturned birds' nests, his sleeves thick with insignia, his legs leathered in black boots up to the knee—General Bethune is an ailing old man now it seems, beard and hair completely gray, a gaunt man now, hollows behind his jaw and beneath his eyes, his arms and legs thin, grotesque twigs, his hands brittle and weightless, bone on bone.

Perry Oliver speaks a reply, his voice quiet and serious, but his words seem to drop midair and plunge to the floor, exhausted, doomed.

I cannot put you before my family, Mr. Oliver.

Nor would I expect you to.

No, you wouldn't. But you are, Mr. Oliver. Do you see now? You are asking me to elevate you above my family. Understand, this is a family matter, not a matter of commerce.

I understand. But we helped the cause again and again.

We all did our part.

But we did more than most. More. And we can still—

Your country will recognize and thank you. You have my word and assurance. There is sadness then tenseness (worry, anger) on the General's face. A meager music hovers in the air (somewhere). The fireplace is trying to flame. In his gray suit General Bethune seems the focus of darkness in the room, under the ceiling repellent of light. Perry Oliver can't talk back to the other man's power.

But why now, just when—? Something has gone out of his voice.

You don't see it, do you, Mr. Oliver? But of course you do. The South will fall, no two ways about it. As a military man I can tell you that there is no chance for us to win this war. So what I am supposed to do: lose everything?

Perry Oliver removes his tie. Free now, unguarded, the tie coiled around his fist like a constrictive serpent. His tongue is equally constricted, trying to form words but curling up to the roof of his mouth and getting stuck on his teeth. So Seven knows at that moment that he has to speak for him, utter words that can save Mr. Oliver, save Tom, save himself. All he has to do is tell the General what he himself feels. That he is closer to Tom than to any person he has ever known. Tom sees what he sees, feels what he feels. Each of them is alone in the world. If he tells it just like that then the General will understand and let them be. All there is to it. As simple as that. Now if he can just say it, cover this gap of the silence with speech.

Now, look. I have nothing more to say. I have given you reasonable explanation for the termination of our contract. That is the only explanation I need give you. So let's get on with it.

No, Perry Oliver says.

What? General Bethune speaks a bit more savagely, his face unguarded about what it reveals, and Perry Oliver's mouth flinches. So stop me. There ain't a goddamn thing that a person like you could do ever to stop me. Not today. Not tomorrow. Not never. Now, remove yourself from my presence. Go buy a farm. Go build a factory, or go do anything else you want with your worthless life.

The General's words go deep and draw out Perry Oliver's history like a splinter in a finger. Seven is appalled. He vows: never (again) will he put himself in a position where he can so easily be humiliated, hurt, shamed, treated like a nigger.

On the train afterward—after it is done, Tom relinquished, Tom gone—Perry Oliver keeps his gaze directed on the coach window, looking out at the passing world with a vision smudged with grief. (Seven looking as he looks, looking through his eyes.) Looking through not-tears at houses and barns, hills and valleys, lakes and rivers (the South, Confederacy, Dixie), scrolling countryside, birds untroubled in the sky, sunlight fractured by the thin trunks of tilting trees. Seven tries to hold the thought of Tom in his mind. Then the train takes a bend, and he can see through the window one coach linked to the next like sausages. Where does one begin and the other end? All those months moving together, all those years gone. (So the earth moves to make time.) And thinking thus sees the past shrink to a black dot behind them, him and Perry Oliver.

Never forget. Never forgive.

The Celebration of the Living Who Reflect upon the Dead
(1867)

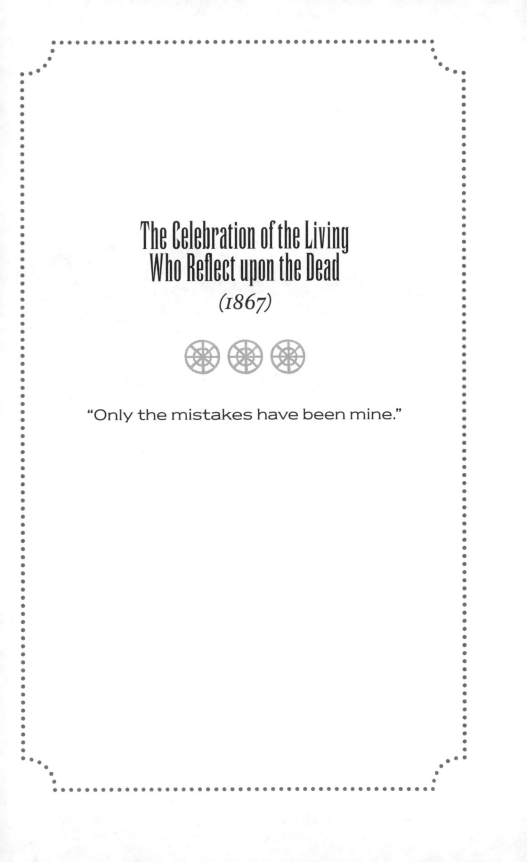

"Only the mistakes have been mine."

MANAGER OF THE PERFORMANCE. WHAT THEY CALL HIM, Seven. What he calls himself, although he has never felt easy with the term. Nothing unusual about the title, nothing striking or distinctive. The few or many he has known in his twenty-plus years of existence who've carried it, including Perry Oliver. And now him, Seven. (Mr. Seven to some.) Dreaming (still) out of that slow ship that carried him here to the city a many, oh a many months ago, years ago. Manager of the Performance. What it means: he must spend hours of negotiation in a room he won't be able to describe a minute after leaving it, this negotiation a slippery process of transforming the spoken into the written (a contract) through word and look, things said, things accepted or disputed through nods or shakes of the head, but mostly by what's unsaid, looking, listening, holding his ground, seeing down to the other man's base self, his breaking point, Seven's mouth curled slightly in dismissive disgust to give the impression that he is ready to walk out the door at any minute and do commerce with a rival across town or across the river. Hemmed in, but hemming in too, wearing the mask of civility while fighting against any moral urge (need) to be fair because that's what he is expected to do, and do it all for a banknote or two more or less. The hard sale. The soft coaxing. The planning and patience. The structure and discipline required to see a nine-month season through from start to finish, to frame a design and make it an actuality, to make words become music.

Juluster's voice floats out from some unseen place inside the apartment and echoes around Seven. The same phrase shouted over and over again, climbing each time into a higher more hysterical register, making Juluster sound abandoned, marooned, cast away where nobody can reach him. (Where is Vitalis?) Seven remembers (many many years ago) how he would let Tom talk until he ran out of words. That gift for gab he had, even if much of it was gibberish. Rambling. No wrong in that. Delight in the listening. The sound would slap into Seven's skin and once it had him, pull him into the flow—come along—and carry him off to a place where no one could reach him.

Now Seven hears Juluster wandering through rooms and halls, the sound of his feet dragging cautiously across the floor and his body bumping into walls and other solid objects, his breath repeating like a weapon. To judge by the sound of him—sighs, sucks of the teeth, grunts and moans and groans, curses, these expressions of puzzlement and frustration—he is getting more and more upset. Seven should do something. If there's anybody who can answer his needs, direct him to what he wants, that anybody is Seven. But Seven holds his tongue and comes back to the thing he knows. Here is his body, sitting in this chair, trembling and sweating, marinating in doubt in this city he has made his own. For better or worse Juluster is all he has, the closest approximation he has come across, and he must tolerate Juluster's petty annoyances. It happens very often that a man does something, that a man has something in him, and he does a thing again and again. So Seven must.

Seven needs Juluster. And everything that comes with that need. Each day is an achievement. Each day makes it harder to desist, to turn back, not that he has any intention of doing so. The greater the discouragement the keener he is to press on.

He lifts his gaze, surprised, because the air buzzes around a clean form that emerges into the day's expectations. The clear light keeps falling on Juluster—teetering tottering he has found his way into the room—on his shut eyes and hunched neck—what saddens him now?—shawling around his shoulders. He displays a forlornness resembling Seven's own. Still, it's hard to feel sorry for Juluster since Seven is forever aware of his agile body beneath all those well-tailored clothes, a body forced to bend in so many ways that eventually nothing comes naturally, Juluster's blankness offering nothing that links him with his other, Tom. He is Tom at the same time that he is too preposterous to be Tom. (Root distinction, difference: Juluster is a rare one, but he belongs. Tom never belonged. Tom never could belong. A challenge—what blind person isn't?—Juluster is both cooperative and independent in ways that Tom never was, never could be.) He looks somewhat like Tom. *A pure and simple brute, this negro with a narrow and sloped forehead, who bears in the middle section of his brain the signs of certain grossly powerful energies. The thinking faculties are poor or even null; therefore, he is possessed by his desire and also by his will, of an often terrible intensity.* (What does Tom look like now? Has the richness of his darkness faded from his skin?) And physical differences between Tom and his double can be put off to aging— who will remember anyway? The public has not seen Tom for more than five years—although Juluster is Tom's senior by a decade (more), having already reached thirty years of age. No. Even that is a lie. On his last birthday he achieved his Jesus year. But he still believes in his youthfulness. More importantly, he believes in the role that Seven has given him to play—game for the game—a role Seven mentally scripts moment by moment from memory—*lait*—selling the shadow to support the substance. Since Juluster is game for the game teach him his name. The body is a habit he can break. Even now his flesh quivers, every inch of it, the skin coming unhinged. He seems to be drifting out of himself, becoming other, becoming Blind Tom.

The Original Blind Tom. Seven says the name in a voice that doesn't sound like his own but rather like the voice of a magician, a sorcerer. (Repeated practice will cause the name to come naturally. So he must remain aware of his tongue. Correct it when it errs, when he says or thinks "Juluster" instead of Tom. So, around the clock, practice saying it. Tom. The Original Blind Tom. Tom. The Original Blind Tom. Until it becomes second nature.) The Original Blind Tom. In the sounds of the name he thinks he hears a way for returning Tom back to the world, back to himself. Each word a twin of itself, telling two stories at the same time, his and Tom's. *I have become a name.*

He gave his youth to Tom just as Tom gave his youth to Perry Oliver just as Seven expects Juluster and Vitalis to give their youth to him. Not quite boys, not quite men. (The flickering back and forth.) It's not just what Seven did but what Seven did not do that haunts him. (Juluster slips back into his skin.) Tom an extension of Perry Oliver in a way Seven could not be. (Craning his neck, Juluster hears something—Vitalis back from his errands or whatever the hell he has been up to?—and stumbles off to investigate.) Is that why he is here in the city, waiting to pick up where he left off? Is it because his mind has set wax-like around the first examples of industry and companionship that he accepted? Is this all a function of his waiting for that past to be resurrected, for Tom to come alive again? Funny almost, the way Tom flies back into Seven's mind and stays for as long as he wants. Blind Tom living in his blood. *You did not choose me, Tom said. It was I who chose you.*

Seven had expected some grand municipal structure manned by a hive of busying buzzing clerks. Instead he finds a shabby little affair, a single-level frame house in serious need of upkeep, set right where the road ends amid a weeded-over garden in what used to be the nigger part of town. The door is open, so he makes a point of entering first, his niggers behind him, the driver who likes to change his name every day—before they started out this morning he christened himself President Washington—followed by Juluster and Vitalis, the driver the oldest of the four, somewhere between middle age and death (visible under his broad-brimmed shadow-forming hat a patch of gray hair at each temple), and them not old, not young. The farther they go, the brighter it is, the more they can see, the interior of the house a cave full of light, illumination spilling out. A cannon shell or some other device of destruction had taken out an entire section of the house, leaving nothing behind but exposed beams and planks. Other signs of mayhem too: craters in the ceiling, walls bare and discolored in places where formerly a painting might have hung, and other walls stippled with projectile holes shaped like a cat's paw, a cat that can walk sideways across walls. (He has heard about the city's former troubles, about how all the niggers were either strung up and set ablaze or chased out during conscription.) In a confusion of setting each room they enter carries the pine smell of turpentine, evidence of recent cleaning.

Voices pull him to their source, two men hunched over a crude chessboard positioned between them, men who are not much older than himself but who have known war firsthand it would seem, as evidenced by the blue uniforms they wear. Then again perhaps the uniforms are castoffs, in this time of shortages—each day the newspapers' skinny columns worded with such claims—the city using whatever is at hand to clothe its officials. After all, the war has been done for almost three years now.

For several minutes the two guards trade insults, list all the wrongs that each has done to the other. Seven waits them out, listening to the ocean in the distance, the sound of all that wide water, audible even from here. A chandelier burns brightly overhead, releasing the sweet metal smell of kerosene into the air. Seven looking (watching), hearing (listening), smelling. Something reassuring about the rhythm of their crass curses and ridiculous threats.

I will eat your eyeballs with smelling salts.

I will wipe my ass with your balls.

A sound he hardly notices as he stands there waiting with the others but will miss he knows when it stops.

One guard (the black pieces) peers up from the board—why has it taken him so long to register Seven's presence?—giving Seven his countenance in full—his face looks almost flat, like a leaf—and finds Seven with his hard and shiny acorn-small eyes. Something alters in the air, but Seven affects to be completely unsurprised.

You have some business here? Those three can wait outside.

I am here on their behalf, Seven says. He hears his own voice beat back at him, bouncing off the ceiling and walls.

Registration?

Yes.

The soldier indicates with outstretched hand that Seven should take a seat, so Seven cramps down into the single chair placed before the long heavy table.

Then he remembers. I have some documents here—his hands are moving, searching through his many pockets. Hands that find, produce, and present a bundle of documents, with the Freedmen's Bureau insignia stamped in the wax seal that secures the fold in place. The guard takes the bundle, scraps away the wax seal with his fingertips, unfolds the bundle, and holds the stack of documents out at arm's length as if he is about to pronounce some decree. His head cants forward, eyes racing across paper—one, two, three—from top to bottom then he swivels his eyeballs—one, two, three—at each nigger in turn. Names?

Seven pronounces the name of each man, hearing himself slip into incoherence. The soldier repeats each name, drawling out the words in shameless confrontational mockery. Although it is English, the language Seven speaks to him still isn't his own. No way, because he knows that years of Perry Oliver's lessons in enunciation—he never spoke like a Southerner and expected the same of Seven—and years of traveling the known world with the Blind Tom Exhibition had permanently retooled his tongue, lathed and shaven the South out.

Listen to him, the other guard says. He does not lift his gaze from the chessboard. He sounds just like one of them contraband.

Haven't you noticed? He even smells like one of them. Pure shit.

Seven feels a length of wind penetrate the crown of his head directly from above, feels it begin to draw down through him in a straight line—his skull, neck, thorax—making a place inside, like a hook pushed through a worm. He had expected to encounter antagonism, even affront, small practical concessions, but sitting there, his race questioned, his manhood challenged, he undergoes a curious process of invalidation. He feels reticent, almost timid.

The soldier refolds the documents then holds the bundle before the slot of a four-foot-high, six-foot-square mahogany box, where it quickly disappears—swoosh—sucked inside like a thing preyed upon. Pulls a pen out from its fountain and holds it at the end farthest away from the stylus like a walking stick, an object foreign in his hands. They got to sign right here and right here. He points to the places on the passbook where the first must subscribe his name. Vitalis steps forward, signs his name, then issues Juluster a call. Juluster gropes his way forward and Vitalis moves his hand in place over the passbook. He subscribes his new name—Thomas Greene Wiggins—his hand wandering like a sleepwalker across the book. Now it is the driver's turn.

I don't know no letters, the driver says.

So Seven signs for him: *James Bethune.* Selling the shadow to support the substance.

The soldier starts to read the many pages of the city ordinance governing the use of the passbook—that the user must carry the passbook on his or her person at all times and present it upon request, that the passbook is not transferable to any other individual, that the city reserves the right to revoke the passbook should the user commit a criminal offense, that—Seven fastens on the one word that flies his thoughts to Tom: *criminal.* Yes, what happened to Tom was criminal. (The freshness of the time that was ours to live).

Have you committed to an understanding of the particulars of this statute?

The driver, Juluster, and Vitalis maintain a dumbfounded silence. Understanding thus, Seven answers for them. The guard instructs them to place left hands over hearts and raise their right hands. They do and he duly swears them in. Swearing done he stamps each leather-bound passbook, piles them onto the table like a deck of cards, and turns back to his game.

And that's all there is to it, although Seven still sits with expectations of some official closing to the interview. Closureless, he collects the passbooks and gets up from his chair to quit the office, leaving the colossal table to continue about its business.

The meeting has honed and sharpened Seven's senses. In the months (years?) that he has lived in the city he has come to know it in a way we can know few places—eyes opened, ready to believe anything—but the soldiers have shown him something he didn't know about how the city feels about its niggers, both the exiled repatriates (returned) and the new arrivals. Can't say how he feels about it one way or the other. (Niggers have always been okay in his book.) As long as no one gets in his way, as long as he can keep on keeping on with his business, building Tom, bringing Tom.

Before Seven can reach the door the driver swerves into the lead, putting it upon himself to be the first to reach their carriage, his business. For the first time Seven notices that the driver has a peculiar walk, stepping softly and delicately; looking at his feet, his hands, and the bend of his head, one might imagine that he was learning to dance the first figure of a quadrille. Arms and legs not quite working the way they should. He seems to be stumbling about in the way of the dead, but here is a man who doesn't seem capable of falling, of letting ground smack him in the face. The physical laws that govern the universe don't apply to him. He is keeping the planet in orbit. He can keep the sky up as easily as he can keep his broadbrimmed hat balanced on his head.

Once they reach their carriage, Seven sees that the horse has taken a healthy shit into the dirt, rich grassy smell, but the driver starts right in feeding it, the long black mouth and sideways moving teeth munching hay from his palm. The driver seizes Seven by the elbow and helps hoist him grunting (the muscular effort of it) into the cab. Does the same for Juluster, but leaves Vitalis to his own devices, no choice but to climb into the cab on his own. There seated next to the driver Seven hears thick pellets of shit thumping to the earth, one after another, builders laying a wall.

Go.

The driver kisses the horse's name fluently above the sound of the moving wheels as if speaking some pre-Babel tongue unknown to man. Seven lacks sufficient range of sight to take in the whole of Central Park. The park is so much, too much, for all of its durable beauty. The landscape changes with each intake of breath. Trees huddling, listening to their own leaves. Leaves sparkling with insects, branches glowing gray with squirrels. A black snake descending slow as molasses down the trunk of a tree. Not that the driver is moving much faster. Keeps them at a steady pace neither stroll nor trot. Nothing is hurrying him (them), just a vague threat that Seven feels hanging over him (them). Then a strange tree pops into view a number of yards ahead, the trunk rising smoothly for fifty feet or more above ground, far higher than any other in the park, before exploding outward in thick foliage-covered branches, a green cloud (leaves). The trunk as wide as a house. The tree vanishes when they turn a bend in the road but reappears after a second bend. Stands flickering, drawing him forward until he finds himself parallel to the trunk and beneath that green cloud that seems to promise access to heaven. A brown shape pokes through the branches thirty feet above. Takes Seven a minute to realize that it is a human face, viewed as clearly anything, a nigger face, a man, peering over the side of a colossal nest, a nest that is as wide and deep as a bathtub. Another brown face appears. And another. And still another. An entire family packed into the nest. Putting their heads around and between branches and twigs, their faces bursting with expressions. By what means did they come to perch in the tallest tree in the park and make it their home?

He knows that there are nigger camps all around them, niggers disenfranchised, destitute, desperate, dangerous, demanding—deeds in hand, those driven out of their homes during the draft riots want their homes back, or reparations in kind, *We demand the right to return*—but when he speaks to the driver or Juluster or Vitalis he tries to keep the panic out of his voice. The reports he's heard about the camps—calculated acts of robbery and murder, revenge enacted on anybody with a white face—have widened his sense of peril, of what can happen (to him). Human nature does not deliberately choose blood, at least not Negro human nature, but the war has driven some of these niggers crazy. He can taste fear on his teeth and on his tongue. The fear of being chanced upon, found out. They will just have to play it by ear, come what may, not that he thinks himself particularly brave. *Fear none of those things which thou shalt suffer.* (The driver's rifle positioned horizontally across his lap, crossbeam, cross.) Surely anyone who has been in a position to achieve something large would do the same. Indeed, he is afraid, but the violence, the hurt he knows exists but he doesn't see, can't keep him away.

They escape the park's green trap unmolested. Up ahead a pale rectangle, the illuminated trough of the horizon, pouring bright ocean out. He is thrown into astonishment. It makes a person hungry to travel in this light.

❀ ❀ ❀

They are bringing the dead. More each day. Carrying bodies. Growing coffins in the camps.

These Freedmen, Wire says. Arriving in the city mostly by foot. From that broken country. Frames of breath and skin. Their flesh a foot thick with diseases and afflictions. All parts of the body ready for death.

Wire speaks slowly, telling it deliberately, but without the least bit of hesitation, concern, regret. No shakes of the head. No frowns. Plain, matter-of-fact. A job like any other. Small work for a man his size. Even seated there in his chair Wire is a towering figure, his knees rising like andirons level with Tabbs's face, Tabbs staring into the blue cloth of Wire's trousers, as if he were holding a conversation with twins, left knee and right.

A messy line, Wire says. Crying and complaining all. Man, woman, child. Wire seated across from Tabbs black against white walls, dark skin and dark clothes, as if he is some foreign substance the wall has expelled. Hard to tell one from the next after a while.

Easy to go around in circles and waste what little time there is. Hard to say who is most deserving of your attention. Who you should see right now or an hour from now and who can safely be left for a day or two.

Tabbs cannot imagine Wire treating anybody with his big hands, how those hands can touch muscle and skin, explore mouths, necks, chests without giving pain, hands that are twice the size of his own, the knuckles high and sharp, shark fins.

Without the right measures, even the most benign injuries will consume. Best to clean the wound with kerosene to kill the lice and to keep the flies away. And you learn to treat in the way of war. Amputate first if you can keep the greater life intact. Give Death nothing else to feed on. Burn or bury what you cut off, what you saw away.

Tabbs sits there in silence, thoughts lost among the watery light and the sound of waves, experiencing the feel of liquid weight—the water, the glass in his hands, the hidden channels in his body—making no effort to hide his despair.

Wire tilts his own glass forward on his lap, aiming the rim at Tabbs, the bright wine inside threatening to spill over. Tell me, Tabbs. Tell me what it is you need to say.

Nothing, Tabbs says.

Nothing?

Nothing, he says. (The weight.) I can't get my head around it. I mean, for them to endure so much, endure until now. And to make it this far, all the way here. He shakes his head and keeps shaking it. Speaking into the darkness of the other man's face, not sure what sort of expression of bereavement Wire expects from him, not sure really what he is feeling just now.

Why it must play out thus?

Tabbs nods.

Why they should be cheated after having won?

Yes.

Wire swallows some of his drink. These times are no different from any other. You work around whatever these white devils give you, so as not to be led into their snares.

Yes, Tabbs says. But certainly it is not as bad as all that? I mean you can do something to contain it, to arrest the dying?

Wire stares back at him. You frighten me.

Tabbs sits across from Wire in the droning light, looking into the other man's eyes, clear eyes, trying to figure the flow of thought. So like Wire, a big man not big on coming to the point, too loud a gesture revealing his feelings and quality of character. If Tabbs needs to explain or excuse himself he can't. Wire is a man too often listened to, big in years—on this earth twice as long as Tabbs, fifty years or more—experience, wisdom.

Are we not one and the same? Wire asks. So you recognize that certain questions a true man of the Race will never ask.

No mistaking Wire's disappointment. Tabbs wants to get up from his chair right now and walk out of this room, a big circular room filled with Wire's furniture. Wire unable to relax in an ordinary chair, every chair in his home wide with long legs and a high back, throne-like. His home a dark haunting place full of stale evening light. Even the brightest rooms are dark.

It's terribly hard. In fact, the dangers multiply. More arrivals tomorrow. By mule. By sporadic horse. But I can't stay away. I have a certain affinity. I'm here with you now, but I'm thinking *there.*

Tabbs ventures to take a sip from the glass of sack he has been holding in his hands. The sea beyond the windows, outside the house, will float them through this silence. Wire seated in one monumental chair and Tabbs in another, across a table pointed with a decanter of wine. From this angle there seems little demarcation between house and sea, sea and house, as if the house is a cork bobbing in the ocean. A boat might come crashing through a window at any moment.

Every day we lose another surgeon or nurse. Why do they come at all? They work in silence. They pretend to hear and see and feel nothing. Wire's hand moves, starting the long trek to some remote part of his body. So many who wish to abscond. Perhaps I'm destined to be the last man standing. You don't just walk away from work like this. I will go to the camps tomorrow and the next day and the day after that, trying to pull death off these bodies. The weak have need of what is strong.

Wire brings the glass to his lips, his hair and beard barbered in a collusive manner making his beard look like a halter that has been slipped over his face. The end of the glass trembles as he drinks, his eyes wet and brilliant. He returns the glass to the hollow of his lap and takes his hand away, letting the glass rest, a shiny rising above cloth, crystal silo, liquid-drowned tower.

None of it stays with me. And none ever will. I'm used to trading in sin and rot.

He brings the glass to his mouth again, keeps it there for a time before returning it to his lap, the glass giving no evidence that it has been touched, the wine inside maintaining its previous level. The glass captures light in ways Tabbs thought not possible, glass as beautiful as water.

Doing what we do there you accept the limits of your power without thought about how much you can bear. You discover the limits of what you can feel.

Tabbs hears a donkey braying in the distance. A high congested honk followed by a low wheeze. Over and over again. He follows the sound in his mind. So many sounds he has yet to get used to here on the island of Edgemere. The call of a rooster in the morning. The shouts of fishermen. The familiar whine of the ocean. And sporadic calls, sharp and clear and far but unidentifiable.

Come see for yourself.

Tabbs eyes Wire warily, knowing not what to say, no time to lie, invent an excuse. I would welcome the chance, he says. How can he refuse? Wire's enthusiasm has to be indulged. People come to him for guidance. Put their lives in his hands. Besides, Tabbs will need to ask Wire for a money loan before he leaves this house tonight. He swallows some of his drink, hoping he has mollified Wire somewhat with his almost-promise.

How else can I convince you?

You don't need to convince me, Tabbs says. He knows the right words, the lie leaping from chin to chest, where it works its way back in. Does he sound convincing? He sees the look of doubt on Wire's face.

Would it that you accompany me tomorrow. Setting out before dawn. But you must take your own decision. None of your days are idle. Would it that I cause an interruption.

Would it, Tabbs says, but you can count on my joining you.

Tabbs looks into the face of the other man, waiting for him to say something, show some indication of what Tabbs's submission has earned him. But Wire says nothing, his face impassive. He lifts up the decanter from the table and refills his glass, pouring into the well of his lap, reaches across the table—this plane of smooth wood between them a silent road, a tongue stretched speechless—long arms forming a bridge over to Tabbs. He refills Tabbs's glass. Let me ask you something. He returns the decanter to the table and meets Tabbs's gaze. What compels you into your trade? You feel an obligation?

Yes, Tabbs says. Yes I do.

Concern for the greater?

Tabbs nods.

And so I ask you, what is the greater?

Tabbs hears the question.

I think I know you well enough by now and don't doubt in the least your convictions, but can you say that what you do is more important?

Plain words, the voice hard and clear, so certain of itself.

No, you cannot. So why aren't you there in the camps with me?

Tabbs feels his seat move back. Wire a big man and everything he does has force. A good ten feet away from him, but Tabbs feels the words catapult from Wire's mouth, like wind-flung gravel, knocking

Tabbs and his seat back. I would gladly put my services to use, he says, but I'm no surgeon.

What am I? Wire, expecting this response, leans forward, bringing his chest toward the rim of his lap-level glass, giving Tabbs the hard lines of his eyes, face, beard. Do you really believe that I am so without intelligence as to fail to recognize that you are not a surgeon?

Certainly not. If you will permit me—

What is it that you think I am?

Tabbs shapes words in his mind, tries them out, but can't get them past his lips.

Just what? Who do you see sitting here? A fool?

No, Doctor, Tabbs says.

Take your right measure. Take it.

Tabbs is looking away so as not to see and feel Wire's words. Wire is testing him, and Tabbs stares at Wire's large hands, trying to manage the silence under Wire's scrutinizing gaze, deflect the charge of moral authority. What Tabbs really wants to know, will Wire extend him the money he needs to carry on his efforts with Tom? Isn't that after all the reason why he had accepted Wire's invitation? Granted, Tabbs enjoys the comforts of Wire's home. All grace and courtesy, Wire supplies his visitors in a most satisfactory style, makes them eat and drink as much as possible, has a thousand stories for anyone who cares to listen, his polished manners rising from the room's armchair, his ease with people genuine, so too his concern, high-handed but always polite. They get along well. They hold similar opinions on many subjects. Tabbs is almost out of money and a free supper and good wine cannot easily be turned down. Who but Wire can supply him with a dose of funds? Should he ask Wire for a loan—

How much do you want?

As much as you can spare. More.

—Wire will set his crude conditions, no question of Tabbs coming to the camps the next day.

Is there any way around the camps, any way to delay his entry into those golden fields of Wire's hopes? He must walk into this trap of his own accord, the give he needs to get—*I'm obliged to come to the camps. You're obliged to pay*—an unhoped-for possibility.

Behind the scenes the Almighty is working things in our favor.

Yes, Tabbs says. Yes He is. He takes a quick breath, glad that Wire has mentioned God. Who knows, he, Tabbs, might at last say something embarrassing and true.

You must get used to the idea. *Earnestly contend for the faith which was delivered unto the saints.* But you don't believe.

It's just that I don't know where to commit myself. I don't know all that much about church.

Tabbs, you needn't worry. You are not welcome in my church.

Wire sits there, smiling—confident, male.

Then I'll stay away, Tabbs says, but only if you promise to preach my funeral. Otherwise bury me like a dog.

I would be happy to preach you and bury you. We all have thankless jobs to do.

Drowsing in the diminished light, Tabbs sits in an uncertain state, earnest, tired, something broken and floating inside his head. Despite hours of talk and drink, Wire looks surprisingly fresh, a full day of energy in his body.

So, you will tell. Are you not drawn to deep belief? Let's clear this matter up. What are your beliefs?

It seems to Tabbs that he has already answered the question.

I have my reasons for asking. When the Almighty calls me home, I will need something to report.

Please speak to our creator on my behalf, Tabbs says, that is, if you think I am deserving of a good word.

Many good words. Should it come to that. But am I capable?

Wire takes to his feet—the decanter is empty—an ending overly prolonged. Come now, it's time for you to go.

But through some force of inertia, Tabbs remains sitting, his mind commanding (pleading with?) his legs to perform their function.

Wire standing like a black wall before him, gazing. When limbs capitulate at last, Tabbs rises to leave, a painful weariness in all of his body, a thousand fists beating him. What derives from the accumulation of many monotonous hours. Nothing said that was not to be said. Nothing remaining unsaid. He has won the right to submit, to surrender. All he has to do is ask. Ask.

Here, Wire says. From somewhere in the darkness he produces a pouch of headache powder and offers it to Tabbs. Put that on your pain.

Tabbs is obliged to accept the pouch, round light weight in his hand, admitting to himself—so it is—that Wire knows the uncertainty that floats about inside his skull, however discreet he has been.

You prefer to leave here still suffering. What have I told you? Nothing is foul for those who win.

What can Tabbs say in response? He simply thanks the doctor-preacher. Wire had taken it upon himself to see Tom back to health when Tabbs and the boy first came to the island. (It had come to pass that the Bethune woman had for days or even weeks there in her lavish apartment allowed Tom to suffer from a breath- and flesh-stealing affliction.) He had put Tom in one of the upstairs rooms rather than admit him to the hospital for what he surely knew would be a slow and difficult convalescence and had assigned one of his nurses from the camps to sit all night at the boy's bedside, turning his head so that he would not strangle on his own vomit. Wire did not bother to set out his reasons for his generosity. *I am only too happy to do you this small service.* Why he had fresh clothes sent to the mother after her arrival on Edgemere. (Yes, that too.) Why he lent Tabbs the services of his driver and carriage. But Tabbs knew (felt, would learn) that it was more than just a pose. Tom for weeks reposed in a sea of white sheets like a black fish. Naked to the world. Skin dry and ashy, barely conscious, discharging rivers of urine. Tabbs and the nurse taking turns cooling down his body with water and chunks of ice. Wire would descend on the bed at set hours, pressing Tom's eyelids with his fingers, with a raised flaming lamp check the color of his patient's inner mouth, with palm measure the heat of Tom's body, put ear to the hollow of the rising falling chest.

What good medicines do you have, Doctor? Tom had asked.

Try this. Wire set a bottle of holy water on the bedside table and told Tom to drink all of it.

Do this for me, Tom said.

Yes, Wire said. You'll be happy to know that I have a piano downstairs. As soon as you are back on your feet.

You're the one all the time up in that church.

Wire stood looking at Tom, surprise glittering in his eyes. Yes. He laughed. I am of the cloth. How did you know?

Blind Tom doesn't play church music.

Released from Wire's care, Tom took a room in the Home and gave no further thought to the Doctor. But Tom's daily life remained of interest to Wire. No day went by without him dropping in to visit with the boy, entering the Home with his text- and appliance-heavy cloth satchel slung across his body, the instruments of his dual professions inside, not the least of which included hundreds of biblical verses stamped on leather and two leather-bound Bibles, the reason for the duplication unknown to Tabbs, nor clear the full purpose of their presence since Tabbs has never once seen Wire read from or even open either when giving a sermon or ministering to a patient, just weight in that bag he keeps slung across his body as he makes his rounds through the infirmary, all the happier to have Tabbs accompany him, should he wish to do so. Wire will pull a Bible from the satchel and keep it in one hand, moving from one tiny bed to the next, children weightless and inert. Wire full of knowledgeable satisfaction, perfectly comfortable in this world of dissipation, of retreating minds and withering skin, a bit fussy, scolding even, with the nurses and orderlies. As if to compensate for the failure of their hands, he brushes mentholated scent onto the sternums of his patients with the most tender strokes, especially those who are feverish—a remedy he had apparently never deemed appropriate for Tom—although nothing can hide his own smell after a day in the camps, the entire Home filled with the odor of cadaver, making it necessary to keep all the windows open for hours after he leaves.

One by one, the children will raise their faces in sensual curiosity, exploring the glassy green air. Wire can then bring it all to an end, having succeeded in putting off to the last possible moment any mention of Tom, Tom saved for last. He will enter the chapel to find Tom seated onstage at the piano. Enters quietly, without ceremony, no declaration, no announcement, but Tom removes his hands from the keys and places them in his lap, as if someone has blown a whistle, and he will resume playing only after Wire has left.

Is it so, a Chopin polonaise?

You know perfectly well.

He sits down on the bench next to Tom.

Should I remove my clothes, Doctor?

He defers to Tom, endeavors to be positive and polite.

We miss you at the house.

I don't know a thing about it.

Well, we do.

He tries some tentative touches of the keys, even as his words fall short.

Why do your fingers such injustice when I have a fine instrument that goes unused?

I don't want to live in a church.

You think that I live in a church?

Tom continues to refuse him. A Tom almost unknown to him.

You feel that?

What? What is it that you feel, Tom?

God just touched you.

Now he moves away, convinced perhaps that he has to do just that.

I'll see you tomorrow, Tom.

A lot of good it'll do you.

Wire gazes at Tabbs with a look of (he now realizes) mistrust. Still, he finds it in himself to smile at Tabbs as he prepares to leave the chapel. Says, his back to Tabbs, That boy is full of pranks. But Wire cannot not break himself of the habit, Tom an unvarying necessity. *I can have it brought from the house. No? You feel that's too much. Well, we'll just have to have this one tuned. Seeing there's no other way.* Tabbs attaches great importance to these visits and encourages Tom to open up to the Doctor. *Do him this one favor. He would be so pleased to see you.* But he can do nothing to persuade the boy.

Beyond thanking the Doctor, Tabbs has shown Wire nothing in return for his concern, persistence, kindness. (How can he really?) Small gestures are enough for him. (They must be.) The fact that Tabbs will visit Wire's church on a random Sunday or join him at his home for dinner.

Now, Wire says to him, Why go the way you came? Use some now.

Tabbs unloosens the drawstring of the pouch and rubs some headache powder on his forehead, then on his temples, a flurry of renegade particles flaking down onto his nose.

He is already on the point of passing into the foyer—things inside the room don't seem the same as they were earlier in the evening—when he hears Wire say, They've been telling me about the boy. My entire congregation. The entire island. These things get around.

The words (tossed at him) point to a truth that Wire has uncovered about Tabbs and Tom (and the mother too? Ruggles even?), a truth that he has chosen to withhold until this opportune moment when it will do the most damage. Truly hard luck. Tabbs cannot ask Wire (himself) what Wire knows—*What have you heard?*—without risking discovery—the arrangements he does not want to expose, the uncertain ubiquity of his hopes.

Is it really sensible what you've been doing?

Easy to read Wire now. Tabbs feels at once humble and guilty (humiliated) in Wire's presence. Now every vestige of control, of sense, of thought, goes out of him. How can he formulate his demand, knowing that it will seem feeble, undeserved, that anything he might say will seem suspect? He sees now that his plan has been nothing more than a misdirected outpouring of his energies. Wire had suspected (known) Tabbs's intentions before this evening, conspired to use an invitation to his home as a prophylactic against Tabbs's claims, thus freeing himself out of hand of any fraternal, moral, and practical obligations.

Even here at the door money lingers among Tabbs's hopes, comes back into the field of present and immediate possibilities—so much he needs—a final pass at the Doctor's purse will depend on a singular contingency: Tabbs will (he must) squeeze the request into the proper moral frame, an appeal on Tom's behalf—*You must do it for the boy. Only your money can save him*—which Wire can then either honor or deny, which Wire can't deny. *Your money, his salvation.* Tabbs sees a necessary connection between this prospective triumph and one cruel happening dating back to his (their, three) first days on Edgemere, an afternoon when he was in Wire's company, the two strolling about the little narrow streets of the island, sidestepping pancakes of donkey dung—*shit* Wire calls it—looking in on various shops, stopping for a time at the old square where men gathered around the big bleem tree to smoke pipes and arm-wrestle and play cards and chess—Wire never loses, game or challenge—indulging a coalition of views, then speaking (Wire) in the full presence of a crowd of children outside his donkey sanctuary (constructed a month after his expulsion from the city; *I saw the need;* the first on the island), the most attentive children perched high on the fence where the donkeys were penned—twelve beasts under his care; Wire had said their names—praying for child and donkey alike before moving on to a more salubrious district, the market, island center, Wire passing on handfuls of spare coins to the perfumed mongers, which they accepted with hands they wiped clean for Wire to take and kiss, exchanging jokes, inquiring (Wire) about their husbands, offspring, and other relations. That day they would never get far without someone stopping to greet them (Wire), Wire and Tabbs partaking of the generosity they were given.

When they reached the main jetty (east to the city), they saw before them a crowd circled three people deep, man woman child, heads lifting eyes catching, Wire looming above all, his place in their lives such that they began parting into two banks of bodies, affording him (them) unobstructed passage to the circle center where they discovered four fishermen, each positioned at one of the four cardinal points, their tired faces directed toward the ground at some object of interest there, a long tube-like form, not unlike a caterpillar in appearance, only too large to be that, massive—this something at their feet powerless it would seem, fixed to the wet ground it would seem, under the collective force of these fishermen, who eyed their captive menacingly, while the captive struggled against itself, splotched with eye-like spots of blood—red seeing through the skin—the promised life inside determined to break free, a butterfly imprisoned inside its own oppressive cocoon. Three of the four took up the unfortunate creature and tossed it into the hollow of their dhow with an explosive thud, leaving behind the man (West) closest to Wire. Disconsolate, embarrassed, he sought to establish the moral validity of their actions before Wire took them to task.

They had captured a thief, a man who had been stealing from everyone on the island for months. He (West) enumerated the terrible thefts the thief had committed. (Heads nodded.) The thief would go on stealing, unless they put an end to it now. (Uh huh's and You got that right's.) He had stumbled into their hands less than an hour ago after time and again steering clear of their most-watchful sentinels. They had bound him and brought him here. They beat him then stuffed and sealed him up in an unneeded sack with the stolen items they'd found in his possession and were now preparing to take him out and deposit him into a deep part of the ocean.

I see, Wire said. May I have a look at the thief?

They brought the sack forth, untied it, and roughly drew it free, exposing the thief who had been confined inside, now seated upright on the wet ground, short of breath, eyes closed (swollen shut?), nude, his whole body slick as if dipped in some red fluid. Tabbs had seen the thief about, a boy really, a new arrival like himself.

Wire continued looking at the thief. He couldn't look anywhere else for a long time. *Who shall deliver me from this body of death.*

Reverend. Sir. If you could—

Time's getting on, Wire said. He directed his face toward each fisherman in turn before his worried look settled once again on the thief. Gentlemen, I shouldn't delay you further, but I want to put your minds at ease. (Wire looking from the thief to the fishermen.) Want you to know that I fully understand what you are set on doing. You have the right to protect yourselves. Any man or beast who would rob you of your livelihood, who would snatch food from your mouth or the mouths of those you must feed, that man or beast is doing nothing less than trying to diminish your life, extinguish it little by little. Is this not murder by another name? How can such murder be tolerated? I am impressed. You're sensitive to have given this so much thought. Not that you require my approval. Certainly not. All will be well with you.

The fishermen looked one to the other, hiding their intimidation in the silence they stood in.

For we know what the Scriptures say. Turn the other cheek and suffer violence to the face, to the flesh and blood. But where does it say we must permit a strike to the stomach? Let him violate you if he must, but hunger you? Starve you? Burn your harvest? Carry off your crops? Poison your wells? I would love nothing better than to drown such a murderer myself, should I possess the authority. So wronged, I would drown my own son, give up my own father. But there is one fact you must consider. (Hear me out.) The flesh of a sinner is the Almighty's and He can do with it as He pleases. And that life contained within the flesh does not belong to you. Broach no claims on it. Wire raised the index fingers on both hands as if measuring some distance between them, the gesture nothing more perhaps than a strategic pause (space) that afforded him time to observe what the fishermen's expressions told him, time to register their hesitation and dismay. Protection is the province of man, Justice the province of God. Man has no claims on Justice. Understand that. Now, correct me if I'm wrong, but I've only heard Justice here today.

West started to stammer something, but the words faded in his mouth.

So how can I, a man of God, let you take from Him what is His? Who would be the greater criminal? Who would be the greater thieves? As much as I want to, I cannot.

The fishermen stood there without speaking, listening in what could only be described as attentive reverence.

This man has wronged you and wronged God. So give him his due. (What I can permit.) Let him work a thousand days to pay back what he has stolen from you. Or simply beat him, as you have. Beat him and banish him. Wire let the words stand for all to consider. And here is one more thing you might take into account. Should you decide to give him some of God's mercy, each of you might be blessed forever.

Were the men nodding? Were they smiling?

Wire took another look at the thief. Spoke to the fishermen while looking at the captive: You have already done enough. You would agree? Yes? Perhaps you haven't. Be certain. Beat him some more. Yes, beat him some more and be done with it.

The fishermen pummeled, punched, and kicked the thief with little energy or effort. The thief made no attempt to defend himself.

I'm glad to see that you're such reasonable men. Would it be too much to say that I am proud? Well, I am. Wire extended his hand, summoning each fisherman to come forward, which they did in turn. He spoke each man's name in a matter-of-fact way then proceeded to reach into his cloth satchel and pull out a scrap of leather verse, which he lifted high into the air above his head, like one feeding fish to a seal. The befuddled fishermen cupped both hands in front of them to receive (catch) the verses. Once the man before him received his verse, Wire stared into his face and recited it word for word in an unmistakably affectionate tone, all present awed by the demonstration, more awed in the repeating. On the face of it, either the performance or the blindly selected verses themselves spoke to the heart of each would-be killer, for one after the other they dropped their heads and seemed to feel real shame.

I'm sorry that I won't be filling your bellies or your fists today, Wire said. But if you visit the shop tomorrow I will see what I can do. Bring your Scriptures.

A promise he would certainly fulfill, although unclear what these men, accustomed to operating on the sea's moving surface, would need with any implements of stationary road travel that Wire could provide from King Jesus Carriage Parts, his *shop*. Unlikely that these men even owned donkeys.

Wire spoke to the thief. Take to your feet.

And the thief did in all of his nakedness. He made no effort to cover himself.

I should strike you too, Wire said. See what I've had to do. It's improper for me to stand here putting questions to these gentlemen with their friends and neighbors looking on.

The thief said that he was sorry, although clearly he was in pain and had difficulty speaking. And he said it again. Pain and all, he appeared happy, a bloody grin, if that's what it was.

You're sorry and yet you continue to be irreverent and disrespectful, standing here when you should be on your way.

I'll be, I wanna be, but I ain't got a goddamn thing.

What?

Said I ain't got a goddamn thing. Standing with his hands behind his back as if still fettered, his penis all that was free, on display, black signature of skin and bone.

Is that so? You expect me to reward you, for theft? For murder?

No, suh. Trying to draw a breath. I ain't asking for no damn re-ward. I jus need to get on up away from here. Get on up from this grave.

Wire looked at the thief as though he had said something im-mensely stupid. You're asking me to help you? He laughed awkwardly. Well, I see you expect me to take care of all of your complaints, a man able of body and mind.

I'd be much obliged to do something for you in return. Much.

Look at you. What can you do for me?

Taking Wire's answer as a refusal, the thief said nothing at first, then he was in distress, great distress, and insisted he go with Wire, a separate appeal in his expression.

Wire asked him what his name was. He said that he had no name he could give. Speech and body residing in some undefined space between gratitude and grief. The surf breaking behind him, dhows tossing and bobbing, and waves crawling toward shore like an army silent in ambush.

I haven't much patience. Wire made as though to leave.

You ain't got to worry bout me none. I swear on a stack. Left hand on Jesus. Right hand on God.

On hearing this, Wire approached the four fishermen. By then the four had boarded their dhow and were ready to set off to sea. Wire asked that they return to shore. (The hold he had over them.) It would be these men who would ferry the thief to the mainland, to the city. Talking quietly among themselves, it took doctor and fisher-men almost ten minutes to negotiate a price while the thief waited; someone gave him garments to cover his body; someone gave him a cloth to wipe his face; someone gave him a long draft of water; then he spat out blood. Relieved, he thanked Wire and thanked him again and again and went off with the men in subdued silence.

Wire and Tabbs took lunch at a café, never speaking a word about the event. (It was for Wire to speak first—*That's the way they do things here, why there are no criminals*—then Tabbs could respond accordingly.) Later it occurred to Tabbs that Wire was trying to impress on him something of the true nature of his work. He had saved men from murder. He had driven other men to kill. War his to declare, his to stop.

He can back Wire into a corner, force him to help, to give money. *If you can save a thief, a nameless thief . . .* So why does he stand here, hollow, posing? Why does he force himself to turn away from the words he would like to say and hear Wire say in return? Tabbs steps out into moon-begot shadows and light and starts for home with a reserve of animation and speed built up from hours of sitting, eating, drinking.

Blind Tom don't play no church music.
Too bad. The Almighty is the loser.

The boy would be waiting. He knew the boy would be waiting. He lacked nothing in punctuality. That's why *he* was here, wasn't it? Why he keeps coming every day, although for months the boy has been little more than a lumpen force. A few thick chords. A few loose melodies. Each sound coming out marvelously pronounced, shapely, smooth so that Tabbs feels the notes surge up his arms and enter his face and head, then sink into every nerve of his body, causing his muscles to uncoil, leaving a tingling satisfaction, a tease.

Let's go watch the blind nigger play.
You go.
I am. I ain't scared.
Go ahead then.
Nawl. I don't want to. You go.
Scared.
Nawl.

He chases the kids away, but he will catch their faces peeking in, hiding under the seats, crouching behind the curtains.

Mr. Tabbs, how come you don't like children? The little girl stared up into his face.

What would make you think a thing like that? Of course I like children. Don't let me hear you say that again.

The mother is on her knees, her head scarf knotted at the back of her neck, her knees squarely on the wet floor and her elbows and forearms covered with a white-brown mixture of suds and dirt. She looks up and catches him full in the face. A look that goes past him, dwelling, for a moment, on the chairs upturned on the table, the sconces and portraits on the walls, and the bucket filled with water and soap.

Mr. Tabbs.

He returns the greeting with a nod of his head.

He steps into the chapel, his eye catching the shape of the piano on the small stage, knowing that he will find the boy seated there, onstage, at his piano. He clears the room of children—

He crazy.

Nawl. They took his eyes out.

—and shuts the door. Calls the boy's name, causing the boy's shoulders to lift, startled. Tom had not heard Tabbs enter the room. He gets up from the bench, steps down from the stage, and takes a seat in the front row.

He's trying me, Tabbs thinks. I'm barely in the door and already he's trying me.

Should you go up? the boy asks.

We should go up.

You said it.

The boy moves sleepily toward the stage. Tabbs aids him up the few stairs, though Tabbs can't help feeling that the boy is helping him. The boy returning the embrace on his arm in such a way that he might have been the seeing one guiding the sightless Tabbs. Times when the boy allows Tabbs to embrace him. Parts of Tom's body mingle well with Tabbs. Times too few.

The boy goes through his routine. Fingers a passage, a slippery group of chords and notes, then he shoots up from his stool, clapping, congratulating himself, taking bows. Sits down and fingers another passage. More accolades. And so on. Months now and Tabbs has yet to hear him play a song from start to finish. A little of this, a little of that. Never a complete song. He can't pull those bits and pieces together. Or won't. Some failing of memory. Timidity. The melody crawling out of its shell only to, spooked, run back for cover.

And voices (sometimes) springing up from hidden places in the room, giggling and teasing.

See, I told you. That nigger can't play.

Wait till you hear him sing.

Then the mother will sweep onto the scene like a witch on a broom. And with the switch in her hand pointed forward like a divining rod, she will seek out the mannish boys in the room, draw the dirty intruders up from the floor like spurts of dark liquid—What yall doing in here?—and steer this black sea of orphans elsewhere. Get where you sposed to be.

Tom sits listening, but it's quiet now, more than quiet because the music is gone. The air charged, the hum of the chords still in the room. Tabbs tries to chart the inscrutable space surrounding the boy's body. Tries to imagine the story of this boy's hands and feet, speculating as to the brutal geography of slavery, a life in the South under the Bethunes, vile domestic terrain.

Tom, there's something I've been meaning to ask you. Tabbs listening to the song, listening long after it's gone. Do you wish to perform again?

I like being on top, the boy says.

Then what is it?

I want her. He stands up from his seat, aware of his own length, weight, and shape, as tall as Tabbs, but broader, thicker. The air rushes away. Tabbs wonders if the mother dresses him each morning. If she is the one who combs his hair and bathes him and keeps him clean and neat, who rubs glistening substances on his face.

You were about to tell me.

I'll leave you in peace, Mr. Tabbs.

But you were about to tell me.

Is she here? He stands there with his head upturned, noticeably swaying from side to side.

No.

I want her now.

So it goes. I want her now, he says, and sits back down on the bench, hands buried in his lap, and Tabbs will send for the mother, and in five minutes or ten the boy will stand straight up from his stool at the sound of her footsteps. They will go away together, she takes him away, and Tabbs throws the heavy canvas cloth over the piano and hopes that tomorrow will be better. So it has been.

She's not here, Tabbs says.

I want her now.

She had to go away.

Tom says nothing.

I'm sorry. I really am. But I'm here. I'll stay with you until she returns.

Tom says nothing to that, his silence more absolute than ever. So quiet and still (dressed in black, his jacket, shirt, and pants glossy like rinsed fruit) he might be a shiny appendage of his piano. Looked upon. An alien and disagreeable face. The eyelids thick and firmly fastened, impossible to crack. A face that had once, before the war, moved and enchanted Tabbs. Now no face at all. Inconceivable that this boy could be Blind Tom. Black, blind, of right age but nothing else. The Bethune woman had passed off an imposter, had proved to be a liar and a cheat like all the others who took the name Bethune.

The boy smiles. A careless amusement in that smile, gaiety at Tabbs's expense. He stands up. Sure enough, the mother is fixed in the door, watching her son with tender respect. (If that's what it is.) Now a deep breath activates him, making it unnecessary for her to come to the stage as she usually does. He goes to her, walking at his own pace, feeling his own time. The music following them out the door. Taken away. God knows where. Perhaps they go back together to the room they share here. Yes, she takes him away, again. Months and the boy's desire to see her has not lessened any. At first, those many months ago, Tabbs figured he would let it run its course, no need to cut it short. Go easy and let the two, mother and son, get re-acquainted, come to terms with the distances of time and geography, arrive at the place of knowing each other. And still, every day, today, I want to see her.

The silence fills his chest. Forms reflected in the eye-watering hues of the piano's surface. The entire island had come to watch the men unload the piano from the dhow, as if the piano were a sea monster that had chanced upon extinction in a fisherman's net.

Tabbs looks at his watch to see the time on it. The open case and calibrated face (metal eye and glass eye) watching him back, reading the hour on his visage. He closes the case and time collapses, sucked in.

The boy curls up in his piano, in himself. Waiting. Waiting *him* out.

The sound reaches him before he reaches the courtyard, tearing and shredding, pellets pinging against hard surfaces, girls seated around metal tubs, shucking ears of corn, emptying fingers of beans and peas, seventy girls or more arranged in groups of ten. All those learning hands. No surprise at his entry. Unnoticed or as unremarkable as those hills of discarded green skin rising up from the floor. Or he is only partially glimpsed passing through rows of freshly laundered clothes and sheets flapping flag-like on ropes suspended from one side of the courtyard to the other. Is it her he sees just up ahead beating dust from the pillowcases? Gone before he makes it there. Moving on, courtyard and clotheslines giving way to ceilings and walls, boys young and alive in rooms, speaking at once, taking stairs headlong at a gallop, leaping over couches and chairs. And now she is with them, laying down the law, her thick gold and silver bracelets rattling as she pushes and pulls the children. She can be heard going about her labors even when the eye catches no sight of her, bracelets clattering up and down her wrists and forearms. She crosses the room jauntily with a cluster of the smallest boys about her, ready to bring the older ones to order. Motioning at this one, shouting at that one. What did I tell you? Where my switch?

I need to speak to you a moment.

She stops and turns, releasing a movement of shadow. Mr. Tabbs.

Might I have a word?

Jus let me mind these children first.

I'll be in the church.

Set on a short walk to the church, he leaves the way he came, through the high wrought iron gate set inside the four-storied stone wall surrounding the Home, a wall ancient and crumbling but wide and strong, suitable for a castle or a fort. No clue who built it, when or why. His progress quickly stalls on a street where donkey buttocks block his passage, Tabbs caught behind a donkey train on a street so narrow you have to turn sideways to let another person or animal pass. The conductor carries a stick, beating it rhythmically against his own leg rather than against animal hide. Directs the train with a series of kissing sounds and whistles. One kiss means Go left. Another, Go right. This whistle, Straight ahead. That whistle, Step around that hole. Tabbs following along, a hoof a minute. These people and their donkeys. *A man without a donkey is a donkey.* Content to take life at a crawl. Why horses and carriages are rare here.

He wants answers. Something to go on. Unclear the source of the boy's despair. If he is cross or sad. Just what exactly? The boy had expressed no desire to see anyone other than her. *I want her.* He has no idea what the boy and the mother do together in their time alone. What the boy does with his day. She seems to be exactly the thing the Home requires. Works without complaint for the miserly salary the Home can provide. Makes no fuss over her own person or her own sufferings. She seems to like her work, and life here on Edgemere. Doesn't she owe this new life to him? Fact of the matter, she owes her new life to him. Edgemere. Salaried labor. Her son. Tabbs needs her to tell her son. Needs her to set the boy right, get inside his head and make him understand what they're doing. Who else better than her?

He had offered her a generous share of future earnings. (He had it on good word that the Blind Tom Exhibition took in better than twenty-five thousand dollars a year for the Bethunes, a sum he expected to meet and increase.) *For I know the plans I have for you, sayeth the Lord, plans for welfare and not for evil, to give you a future and a hope.* But she neither accepted nor declined the offer, only continued to sit with her hands in her lap, looking at the washtub hollow on the floor between them.

Tell me how much, he said.

You already said it good, she said.

So you're okay with the percentage? I can have papers drawn up.

I had enough of papers.

And that was that. Now he needs to know that Tom is still free to shaping, that all of him is within reach.

Turning the corner, the last mule in the train blinks him a big-eyed wink, proud of its balanced buttocks close enough for Tabbs to smell and touch, and thanking Tabbs for his patience, for hanging in stride after long deliberate stride, his shoes closely rhythmed with hooves, almost on beat. Passing the angular church the mule makes sure to lower its head and mumble a few respectful words.

> *Lord, do it*
> *Do it for me*
> *This is the cry of your children*
> *Please, Sir*
> *Do it for me*
> *Right now*

What is it that Tabbs hears? The choir (congregation) singing inside? Preaching, weeping, praying, hollering, testifying, grunting, groaning and moaning, and stomping feet. He passes under the prohibitive sign of warning above the church door. NO FISH ALLOWED.

Takes all of his wondering into the church, half-expecting to find Wire there.

If you read your Bible
You heard about the blind man who could not see.

But he is alone. Must have chased minister and congregation away, leaving only echoes. *Can I preach it like I feel it?* He takes a seat at the rear of the church, welcoming the hard pew beneath him, the creaking bulk of it. Closes his eyes and savors the privacy, the quiet emptiness, dozens of wooden pews like docked ships. Explaining it all to himself. Thinking about everything and nothing.

You should take your time with this one, Ruggles said.

Since when are you the man of caution?

I always look first.

I've looked, Tabbs said.

Nawl. You couldn have.

What am I missing?

What are you seeing?

A chance, Ruggles. A chance.

Shit. You already got that.

Ruggles, just come out and say it.

I thought I was.

Ruggles.

Okay. You're dealing with a white man.

I've never known anything white to scare you.

This ain't bout being scared. Everybody scared. But this ain't bout that.

Well, what's it about then? I can't change the fact that he white. Damn if I care.

You should care a little, a teeny bit. Cause his white skin ain't the only thing you got to worry bout. You want to hear the rest?

Are you gon say it?

The rest: You ain't half what he is.

. . .

He got everything to go along with that alabaster skin. Money to do his will. And men to boot. More and more of the same.

That's the story of this country.

And it'll be your story too.

He opens his eyes to discover her sitting on a pew at the front of the church, watching.

I ain't mean to wake you, she says.

No. I asked for you to come.

He waves her toward him.

She tries to rise, once, twice, three times, fumbling and weak, Tabbs refusing to accept such causality—*She is stalling for time*—primed to disbelieve, outraged. Then he sees that she is carrying something in her face, all of what she is. He speaks to her, softly but not softly enough. She sits down on the pew directly in front of him with unconscious ease and economy, like a section of wall slipping into an allotted place. He slides along the pew to angle a view of her face. Nothing of the son in the mother, the boy all black fire, dark sheen, while she bears the evidence of Anglo-Saxon blood—studding, rape. Her features indefinable, beholden to no eye, neither ugly nor pretty. Just. And ageless. He thinks of her as an old woman although she could as easily be thirty as fifty.

As if to further confound his pondering, she lowers her face, her line of sight directed at the floor, the same way she had sat beside him on the train up from the South, head fixed, silent (can't recall her saying a single word), never returning his gaze. He wonders now as he wondered then about her apparent timidity, to what degree actual, to what degree fabricated. Tabbs recognizes her dress as one of a handful Wire had given her, a length of fabric that in no way fits her form, but seems to stand away from her body and assume a shape of its own deciding, layers of air between material and skin. Preparing for their trip, Wire had guessed at her measurements, how what might best fit where, then had several fine dresses made for her.

I put on my speed, she says, talking at the floor. But chillen is a tribulation.

Well, you came when you could.

She says nothing to that. So he finds himself, reduced to her company once again, sitting quietly in the church, a space that he has decided to make his—should he lock the door?—for an hour or two before he sends her back to the Home. He muses about right and entitlement, about which of the two of them has claim to the church, Wire's domain, if only for an hour or two. Should he have asked first? *(Ask Wire. You should have asked him.)*

How do you find it here, on Edgemere?

I ain't never seen nothing like it.

Yes. And that's a good thing I hope.

Everybody so kind.

They just want to help. We all want to help.

. . .

We all feel so honored to have him here.

You did a good thing.

I'm only doing what I promised.

. . .

I hope you're finding some time for yourself. For you and your boy. He speaks into her profile, her skin smooth, her features firm, like a highly polished piece of wood.

Doin jus fine.

I can always talk to Ruggles if there's something else you need.

Mr. Ruggles, he so kind.

Yes. That's how we are. We all want to help, help you and Tom.

Thomas, she says.

Thomas, he says. Tongue corrected. Looking into that frozen face. You must feel special, so special because of the boy, Thomas.

I have him back.

Yes. But you know I've been worried. The boy has me deeply troubled. In fact, I've been praying, praying about the boy, Thomas.

The words turn her gaze directly into his face.

He hasn't been himself.

Thomas? Him? He new. He jus need some time.

Do you think that's what it is? I thought it might be something else.

He givin you some trouble.

Tabbs studies the fancy green-and-pink pattern of her silk shawl. Is it worry he hears in her voice?

Don't you worry about him. He got his own mind. Always did.

If you just try talking to him.

I can't see what good it would do.

We need to hurry this thing along. Isn't that what you want? You can have all that you couldn't before. And it will all be yours. No Bethunes to take. To steal and rob and cheat. Don't you want that?

You ain't got to yell, she says.

I'm not yelling, he says. Is she giving him some back talk? (What it is.) He feels like slapping her. (He has it in him. Knows this for a fact.) He could abandon the bad-tempered woman and simply walk out. But he brings himself to say, I'm sorry. I need your help.

She moves her hand and the loops of metal bangles go sliding and clanking from her wrist to her forearm then back again.

Now he has to sit here and put up with all her barbaric jewelry. Has he not been generous to her? Has he not given her back her son? A chance at a prosperous future?

I can only imagine what you two have suffered, he says. The Bethunes. For all those years. How you managed to tolerate them.

She wipes the sweat gathered at her eyebrows. I had my share of white folk. Before and since. I tolerate them jus fine.

I cannot help but sympathize with you, Mrs. Wiggins. *Greene Wiggins. With an* e. Through my dealings with the General I well know the nature of his character, the nature of that family, the whole line of them. If he keeps talking perhaps he can pull from her the responses he needs.

You know these woogies. They gave me misfortunes, misfortunes aplenty. They don't know no other way to act. You can't expect no different.

Tabbs nods.

But they did that one thing right.

What thing is that?

They gave my son a name.

He is on his way to Ruggles. Not that he has much choice in the matter, for his difficulties with the boy have persisted for almost a week (more time lost) after his useless conference with the mother. Best to see Ruggles.

Doing his best not to think of home, the city. His past lingers about him, a low humming in the ear, some memory trying to worm its way out. Many times since his return he has ferried to the city for one thing or another—interviews, appointments, arrangements—but he has never been able to summon enough will to venture to his old apartment in Black Town, afraid of what he might find there. White Pappa sitting in his chair. White baby sitting at his table eating out of his bowl and plate. White Mamma sleeping in his bed. Dreaming his history. A part of him there still, unfinished. He sees it but cannot hear it or remember its smells, tastes, and textures. No sounds or words carrying through time. His mind too full of present goals. The boy part of every thought, the boy even in his least ideas. Much is still unsettled, but he is borne in a single direction—the city, then the world.

Looking at all that water, you can't see the city, you never see it. You must trust that it is there. Perhaps Edgemere is drifting farther and farther away from the city into some dark unknown. He has devoted a great deal of thought to leaving the island, giving him and Tom the benefit of new surroundings. But he has already invested so much here, the preparations and negotiations. (Many waters crossed.) Why lose all that? Better to stay the course and push aside whatever stands in his way. He tells himself that the mother has honored her end of the bargain. Without her he doubts the boy would have progressed the little he has. Still, he has his own comfort to seek and his own situation to improve as he can. Give the stage back to Blind Tom and give Blind Tom back to the world, an interesting and worthy undertaking, highly becoming of his skills and powers. What better for him and the boy and the mother?

Just so happens he sees her in the market—speak of the devil—holding in each hand three chickens upside down by their three-toed feet, heads only inches above the earth (fantastic white-yellow brooms), their eyes round and blank as coins, oblivious to the slaughter awaiting them. He lingers among the fishmongers until he can no longer see her. Avoiding her he has chanced upon a heated argument between two women, their voices growing increasingly high above rows of fish lined up on identical wood boards, one accusing the other of thieving her money by means of a tiny hole bored into her bucket.

Edgemere seems the perfect place for the pull of superstition, the islanders at ease in their customs and habits. No white folks, alabasters, around to check them. Tabbs purchases a red snapper from each woman, but his coins fail to quell their dispute. They continue shouting, each woman standing up in anger from her bucket stool.

Outside the church Tabbs sees scores of children converge around Wire, their bodies weirdly frenzied. Father, they call. So much they want to tell him, their voices urgent and excited, speaking all at once, Wire trying to calm them, moving his hands and pulling first one tongue from the mix then another, temporary success, one voice barely waiting for another to finish. He lowers his torso bridge-like, making it possible for each child to kiss his cross, the big silver object attached to a lengthy thumb-thick loop of iron around his wide neck. It swings back and forth in the light, the shiniest metal Tabbs has ever seen, clanking like a cowbell. *You wear Jesus, Tom said.*

Tabbs can't help but notice Wire's ease with children. They don't fear his intimidating form but enjoy his company. They follow him into the church, a long singing chain.

Tabbs stands looking. Of course he is lost. Should he take the street on the left of the church or the one to the right?

Excuse me, sir. How do I get to Ruggles? No sooner said than corrected. People here know Ruggles by his Christian name, David, *Mr. David*. When he'd first returned after more than five years away, Tabbs had no clues to Ruggles's whereabouts, if he was dead or alive or if he had moved away, moved on. But he quickly discovered that on Edgemere *Mr. David* was a name in every mouth and ear. During the expulsion the island had taken Ruggles in with a thousand other exiles from the city, no questions asked. They provided him with a house and made him headmaster of the orphanage, an unlikely profession for the Ruggles Tabbs knew, a hard-nosed man loaded down with banknotes, a good twenty pounds or more distributed under his fine clothes and underwear, a man whose head was full of names, dates, places, and numbers, how much borrowed, how much paid. This Ruggles took his leisure at abolitionist parties, listened patiently while the runagate at the lectern narrated his horrible tribulations— ladies fainting, men vomiting in their handkerchiefs—and pleaded for donations toward the purchase of loved ones left behind, Ruggles unmoved, holding out for the post-testimonial food and spirits.

I won't put my hard-earned money into some slaver's coffers, Ruggles said. Rather I murder one or two of them instead.

By birth Ruggles's right leg was noticeably shorter than the left, every inch of his body twisted and swollen with his lopsidedness. He tried to mask (present?) his deformity as best he could beneath fine clothing and expertly stitched shoes—a big half moon of soft leather on each foot, always polished, black shine—walking with surety at his own unhurried pace. However, his vulnerable body and risky line of work brought him days filled with violence, legs and arms and pockets wracked with danger, he and Tabbs both accepting the brutal necessity of fending off some attacker or collecting a debt.

Nothing of his wealth survived the expulsion, ocean stripping him of suits shoes shirts and hats, dissolving the last of his banknotes, Edgemere restructuring the body itself, bringing about a change in dress and a change in personality (to the surface self at least), and creating in Mr. David a man decidedly different from his city counterpart, a man who finds everything in this life to his taste: the roosters, the donkeys, the narrow streets, the luring softness of sand and sea.

I was in the water. Dark. Cold. My lungs had no more life to give. I knew I would never make it across. Knew I would be carried under. I would be left to tell my last words and tales to the mud and eels. Anytime now. But I kept swimming and somehow I made it across. That's how it all started. Can't say if it took a week or a month. It happened so quietly and without my notice. One day I up and realized that my legs were now the same length.

These white devils had done a most wonderful thing. They had given me what God couldn't. I could never have broken free from their world on my own. They kicked me out the door.

Tabbs crosses the low hedge-lined and tottering and slippery narrow stone footpath that brings him to Ruggles's house, a little cradle of stone. *You should have seen it. A sight for sore eyes. Most of the windows gone, part of the roof, and all of the doors. They brought paint, plaster, and wood, and in two weeks the walls were white, the doors closed the way they should, the windows had shutters, the closets could be used, the floors no longer had holes in them, the roof and ceilings had been sealed. They brought beds and furniture and carried everything in and put each item where I told them. They started a fire in the stove. Stocked the pantry. Shit, wouldn't have surprised me none if they gave me a wife.*

Ruggles cracks his knuckles in the doorway, looking amusedly at Tabbs, eyes steady with their assured shine, stark wonder. The unexpected sight of Ruggles standing there as if by prior arrangement causes something to break inside Tabbs. He doesn't have the calmness of mind he thought, fearful of surrendering himself, Ruggles a master at balancing judgments, playing the devil's advocate, offputting, pushing around, cutting down. Tells himself that he must stick to his sense of right no matter what, that only his sense of right can decide it.

Tabbs directs the leaf-wrapped bundles of fish toward Ruggles, who accepts them with hands the color of dark soil, a good three shades darker than the rest of his body as if he is wearing gloves.

You want to fry these up?

No. They're for you.

Back inside Ruggles gives the parcels of fish to his housekeeper. The men take seats in the parlor, a small pleasant room sparkling and grand with the eye-filling sight of red vases in the wide tall windows, vases around which nude black figures pursue each other in an endless procession. The housekeeper hurries in with a whistling teakettle and a single cup on a saucer. She sets cup-saucer on a slim table between Tabbs and Ruggles. Starts to pour. The spout releases water so slowly it takes a good minute to fill the cup, Tabbs and Ruggles waiting for filling to be done and the woman to quit the room.

What's up, homeskillet?

You looking at it.

I'm looking at it? I know there got to be more to see.

Nothing to it. One day like any other.

Uh huh. How those women treatin you?

What women?

What women? The ones that's pretty as pee. You know how I like mine.

I know.

You run into a dry spell? Ruggles's smile is even coyer now. Better get you some of that pussy oil from Wire.

So we're going to sit here talking about pussy?

Homeskillet, you the one bringing me fish first thing in the morning. Sounds like a pussy problem to me.

I wanted to catch you before you left.

You could have caught me at the Home.

Tabbs looks at the steaming cup of tea he hasn't touched.

I don't know how you spend your days.

What's to know?

Lots. Starting with who you fuckin.

Dressed in a plain open-necked white shirt with black buttons and loose-fitting white pants encircled with a black leather belt, Ruggles sits with his left leg crossed over his right and his body inclined forward somewhat as if guarding his right side, a pose that seems to draw attention to his fit angles and lines while at the same time throwing his face in proud relief, a face exuding irrepressible vigor and excitement. His eyes do not smile when the mouth does, but his goatee moves with every facial expression like some adjustable ornament draped over his mouth. A lion's mane of hair roars from his head, black intensity although he is starting to gray at the temples and his hairline is retreating from his forehead, low tide. Still no mistaking the sense of youthful accord in his features. Ruggles looks not yet fifty but long past forty with teeth that shine white when he speaks or smiles. When they first met—twenty years ago? or was it more? less? far less, yes? *I was seven, give or take*—at the Zoological Society Ruggles must have been roughly the same age as Tabbs is now.

I'm not the only one out early. I saw Wire down by the church.

Probably saying his good-byes.

He's set for travel?

No, Ruggles says. He's leaving us. Leaving Edgemere. Moving back to the city.

Tabbs cannot prevent Ruggles from seeing his puzzled look.

You didn't know? He's been telling everyone for weeks.

Tabbs will say nothing about supping with Wire yesterday, about the camps and the amputations and the headache powder.

I tried to talk him out of it.

You should have saved your breath.

Don't hold it against him.

Shutters, lattices, and doors are all flung open to the rare breeze on this hot day, the room flushed with light as if the ceiling has been lifted away. Tabbs suffers a miserable feeling of inner and outer lightness. He watches Ruggles lift his teacup with those glove-dark hands, slurp it empty, and return it to the saucer.

It was getting cold, Ruggles says.

Ruggles was never one to let anything go to waste, finding use for stale bread and flat beer and wormy meat. The hard impact of his presence, his fierce determined eyes, sharp chin, flat weak nose, and scrotum-shaped head, turns Tabbs's mind to the Pygmy inside his bell-shaped cage, Tabbs a boy of seven or eight and the Pygmy no taller than him, a grown man withstanding with silent grim impersonality the food pelted at him. Each day Tabbs would sneak inside the Ape House and quietly make his way to the Pygmy cage. Succeed in eliciting (aggravating?) the patrons' disgust with made-up facts and chronicles about the Pygmy. As if by unspoken agreement with Tabbs, the Pygmy would act out with brazen savagery the peculiar traits of his species, gnashing his teeth, flailing his arms, gyrating his loin-clothed pelvis, and massaging his bare chest. Heedless of the bread, candy, cookies, apples, oranges, bananas, pears, and peanuts thrown into his cage until he took the offensive, his spit and piss driving patrons away. Tabbs would eat or pocket much of what had fallen short of the cage, what the Pygmy's short arms couldn't reach through the bars. One afternoon like so many before, Tabbs found himself in the company of a misshapen man who it would seem had not fled with the others. The Pygmy was aware of him too. The Pygmy began the first assault of many on the man, but the man only lowered his face, taking spit on the lapels of his jacket and the crown of his stovepipe hat, and urine wherever the directed streams found their mark. In this way the man endured fluids for a good quarter hour or more. The Pygmy ceased his attack for reasons only he knew and for several moments stood there in his cage gazing out at the spit-speckled man dripping from chest to shoes with piss. Then he turned away and sat down in a back area of his cage, relishing the first of his bananas. The man who had stood his ground calmly invited Tabbs to join him at his home for a well-cooked meal. Tabbs accepted without hesitation, and sometime later that night, after the man had taken a bath and changed his clothing, after both he and Tabbs had enjoyed a long rambling dinner, both belly-full, sometime during the course of that night—most of the details now are lost in Tabbs's memory—the man offered Tabbs employment. The following evening Tabbs went to work for Ruggles—that was the man's name—finding customers for Ruggles's black box, Tabbs quickly realizing an easy competence in the arts of procuring and persuading so that the line of entry to the black box on average would stretch twenty men deep. *Get them in, get them out.* The black box a place of pleasure but hardly a place of comfort, barely long and wide enough for one person to stretch out in, let alone two, the ceiling so low that you had to stoop at all times, and completely cut off from light. Still, men came one after the next, spilling in and out from opening to closing. Seeing how well Tabbs conducted this enterprise, Ruggles brought Tabbs along with him some years later when he went into lending.

I didn't think you wanted the tea. Ruggles imbibes his own cup of tea.

Of course I wanted it, Tabbs says. And I want it still. It is not the smallness of his beginnings he fears. Who he is now is whom he has chosen to become.

I'll have her bring another cup.

I was not. Now I am. Watching his own changing selves, malleable shapes lacking advantage of birth and education; resourceful and limitless and fearless. Beating the odds. Tabbs wondering whether there are any others like him and the Pygmy and Tom who have escaped the cages of their keepers and refused the roles held out to them. He sees the darkness inside his head filling with bananas and pears and apples. Hears peanuts clinking against the sides of his skull. Looks and sees a fresh steaming cup on the table. Takes it up with violent speed, sips forcefully, and returns it so loudly to the saucer he fears he has broken it.

Ruggles looks embarrassed, embarrassed for Tabbs. Ruggles has sunk back into the chair, into the softness of the cushions, his legs crossed easily in front of him. You might need still another, he says. And a fish. Smiling the words.

Hot fluid rushing inside him, Tabbs feels an ambiguous comfort. I need your influence with a certain matter.

Okay, Ruggles says. What?

It's the mother.

Tabbs observes the friendly uncertainty scattered across Ruggles's face. On second thought, Ruggles does not really look entirely like the Pygmy.

What about her?

I need you to send her away. Off the island. Just for a few days. Tabbs tries to say it as lightly as possible.

Ruggles continues to look at him. So now it comes out.

She commands his attention. I have to put an end to it, just long enough. I've tried talking to her. But how can I stop her from coming when he begs for her?

You can't.

No.

So put an end to it, all of it, for good.

What?

You've milked it for all you can.

And gotten what, Ruggles?

You found the boy.

And you think that's enough? Tabbs shakes his head. Can't believe I'm hearing you say that, Ruggles. Not you.

That's the experience, homeskillet. I tried to warn you. Hard head, soft behind.

Hell, I'm soft all over. But that ain't telling me much.

Dripping light, several swimmers outside seem to (semblance) climb in through the windows. Towel themselves dry with shadow.

You listening?

I'm listening.

Ruggles makes a gesture as if to say that anything he might add would be useless. He is displeased with the turn the conversation has taken and remains silent for a while staring at the floor. Tabbs hates feeling that Ruggles knows his mind, assumptions rooted in the certainties of their long history, Ruggles filling in the blanks about all that lay between Tabbs's first efforts before the war to free the boy from General Bethune to the freeing itself that leaf-strewn day last fall when Tabbs found *Mr. David* at the Home shortly after he and the mother had arrived together here on Edgemere. Knows too that correlated moment several weeks later when Tabbs returned from the city carrying the weightless boy in his arms.

I can't chance a week to see this through?

So see it through. You don't need me. You brought her here. You brought them both.

No, Ruggles. It must come from you. She will listen to you.

Ruggles looks up from the floor into Tabbs's face. He looks as if he wants to erase Tabbs with his gaze. Then I better leap to it, he says.

Tabbs says nothing in response. In a moment's concentrated rush, he realizes that he has insulted Ruggles, never his intention.

Where must I send her for your week? Say it and I'll obey.

Tabbs accepts the remark with good grace and continues to meet Ruggles's gaze, every tendon in his body throbbing, prepared for flight. The small room feels too full with them both, with them and the swimmers and the vases. Now the difficult task of restoring the equilibrium, but no apology is likely to impose its will on Ruggles. Strong-headed. Stubborn. A reconciliation best left for another day. Tabbs looks about the room with the sensuous approval of someone who knows it well. Draws up a name—*Wire*—that pinches his tongue.

Of course. Throw him in this too.

Tabbs lets the comment drip away, him here, Ruggles there, the separate curves of a parenthesis, space between them. She can help Wire settle in, he says.

Ruggles takes up the tea (cold now) and gives himself time to drink it in silence, dark hand strangling the white cup. Well, home-skillet. He balances the empty cup improbably on his knee. I'm glad you came for something important.

Tabbs starts back, the beauty of day and all the bright-colored dhows tethered in the harbor growing strong in him. Each hull tilts toward its neighbor, two conjoining in a clap. He catches himself beginning again the attempts at self-persuasion, self-justification. Doesn't relish the thought of punishing her, if that's what it is, punishing the boy. Putting another bit of separation between them. *What God join let no man tear asunder.* Not his intention. Never his intention. For he must do what she can't, restrained as she is by maternal attachments. No backing down. He never would have freed the boy from the Bethunes unless he had it inside to follow the idea wherever it took him. Remembers when the Bethune woman with a relaxed detached air took him into the stale dusty room where the boy was, a sight that raised in him a feeling of straightforward disgust. Skin and bones. Even the skin not fitting right, gone lax, like hand-me-down clothes three sizes too big. Something in him had wanted to kill the white woman, a familiar predatory self fully awakened. He pushed down the urge. Simply collected the boy as best he could and left the apartment, the glow of revenge lessening with each downward stair. He knew he had his work cut out for him, getting the boy back to health, that before all else. So much to recover, restore. But he told himself, I have the boy. Stalled, dragged back, I finally have the boy, Tom.

I want her.
  I'm sorry.
  Bring her to me.
  I'm sorry.
  And you'll bring her.
  That isn't possible.

But I've asked you.

She has left you. It's only me now.

You took her away.

I'm sorry. She has left—

The boy turns his face. You turn too and see her watching from the open door, fresh from slaughtering chickens, her hands and forearms lathered in feathers.

He feels a satisfaction that settles his mind: he is doing nothing time will not justify. What it will mean to give Blind Tom back to the world, back to the Race, and put the lie once and for all to the vicious claims for the Negro's lack of intellect and refinement, genius and culture—the collateral and collective gains of his personal campaign against the Bethunes.

The waves are soft and almost noiseless, starting from far out and breaking in long smooth lines at the shore. (Whatever the eye wants.) A bell rings faintly behind him. The shore swells under a confused sweep of voices, Tabbs pulled into the sight of her marshaling a herd of sea-bathing children, safety and sanity, her watertight garments overspilling with the noise of gold and silver bracelets.

The boy makes a brutal series of movements from the chair to the piano then back again. Sits down on top of the black lacquered surface, face angled toward the floor six feet below, forehead greasy with sweat, legs swinging. Is the boy conscious of him? He has said nothing since Tabbs came into the auditorium an hour ago, two. Has he really sat for this long simply looking at the boy from a comfortable distance, following with glassy attentiveness an agitated body scrambling from one side of the chapel to the other?

You can say if you like.

The boy's voice startles Tabbs. I've just been waiting here, waiting for you, he says.

To do it now.

Yes. Tabbs moves forward and takes a seat in the front row.

You like the bottom more?

He doesn't understand the boy's meaning.

Stay if you like. Wait and wait and wait.

Tabbs studies the coded mysteries, registering all the details of the boy's clothing and grooming.

The boy places his palms against his chest, a circular expanse of fingernails budding against light-colored cloth. Why did the noise go away?

Indeed, the Home is unusually quiet. No rush of whispers, scampering feet.

Where are the children? Where did they go?

I guess they've finally learned to stay out of your way. That's something.

Never enough of me.

I suppose not.

They miss me.

I'm sure they do. But don't worry. They can have you when we're done.

The boy begins rocking back and forth where he sits, arms rowing his torso into motion.

I thought you were about to play? The boy's torso snaps back and forth. Tabbs can't trust the boy's ability to stay perched. I never told you about the first time I saw you in concert many years ago. I can still remember the fine suit you were wearing and all the people who had come to hear you. How excited they were.

The boy rocks still, upright as before. They carried trees onto the stage.

Flowers, Tabbs says.

Round trees.

So you remember those times?

I live in this body.

You remember?

They kissed my hands.

You must have enjoyed it.

The boy says nothing.

Can you show me some of what you used to do?

You need to hear?

Yes, yes, I do.

Why?

Well, for one thing I'm now your manager.

The words don't have an impact on the boy's face. The boy's shoulders move once twice as if by their own accord.

How bout it? I would really like to hear you.

And you will pay.

Is it money that you want?

The boy says neither yes nor no but, Anything else?

You know there are thousands of people who will pay to hear you, Tom. Thousands.

I feel wonderful.

You should because you can have it all again, all and more, anytime you want.

One song on top of the other.

Yes.

Two niggers. Three.

Yes.

You will take me to all the places?

I will.

And bring the country.

Yes.

Tom leans forward, the piano supporting him in silence. I never had one like you.

That's right, Tom, you haven't. And I promise you it will be nothing like before. We're alike, you and I. Negroes.

The boy does not speak his thoughts. Tabbs can hear his deep breath, his scent wafting down from high, filling the room. Darkness gaining, light an unneeded thing. He hasn't asked for her. All this time and he hasn't asked once. That much at least. Progress.

Does it hurt? Tom asks.

Does what hurt?

Does it hurt to sit on your tail?

Dr. McCune cleans his medical instruments, dipping each object in a glass of red wine diluted with several drops of water.

You're the nigger doctor, Tom says.

Dr. McCune stops his preparations and stands over the seated Tom, considering the words. You remember me?

I remember you. Your hands smell like eyes.

Dr. McCune looks at his hands as if they belong to someone else. He holds them up and gives Tabbs a puzzled expression, but Tabbs stays where he is on the other side of the room, away from the Doctor and Tom, fearing that the Doctor expects him to sniff and offer an opinion. The Doctor requests soap and a fresh basin of water and washes his hands again, each finger receiving thorough and vigorous attention.

A nice nigger home below. I remember. Where are the others? I remember them.

Tabbs takes this as a pleasing fact, proving that Tom's powers of memory are still in place.

It's only me here today.

Hearing this, Tom lowers his head and remains mute long enough for Tabbs and the Doctor to lock concerned glances. You want to look down my throat. Take the nigger words out.

No, Tom, the Doctor says. I remember the nice people you lived with, Mr. and Mrs.—

I know her, Tom says.

When the examination is complete Tabbs and the Doctor retire to the smaller and more intimate anteroom. Here Tabbs feels that he can finally see the Doctor properly, comforting to let his gaze dwell on the other man's clothing and skin, the Doctor average in height but notable in presence and build, dark with long limbs, outfitted in blue military dress, a blue that dominates the eyes, welcome contrast to the plain humble discomfiture of the room's furnishings. A pistol on his belt, his bald head and face mounted cannon-like in his high collar, features strong, unashamed, broad nose, wide mouth, and bulky lips—Negro through and through. Gleaming mustache, gleaming skin, gleaming suit and boots—the shine of hard surface, armor. The only sign of vulnerability the black under his eyes, hanging bats.

His heart and lungs are strong, the Doctor says. Good circulation of blood. Decent musculature. A bit underweight but nothing to be concerned about. As for the condition of his eyes there's little I can say. The eyelids are completely sealed, which might be symptomatic, an indication that disease has set in.

You can find out?

Through surgery.

Another doctor who wants to cut, Tabbs thinks. He looks into the Doctor's face. You were his physician? He wants several questions out of the way before the Doctor leaves. The doors the Doctor's words can open.

Long long ago. Well, not that long really. Four years. Seems longer.

He seemed happy to see you.

The Doctor secures the latches on his bag as if this is enough of a response.

An old friend might be just the thing he needs, Tabbs says. He won't open up to me.

The Doctor cuts his eyes at Tabbs. Says, You know a hundred times what I know.

Tom is sitting on the bench with his hands extended high above the keys, as if warming them over a fire. We left the other place.

We'll be staying here from now on, Tabbs says. Quieter. More space. No one to bother you.

God man.

He no longer has use for the house. He wants us to have it, wants you to be comfortable.

The sickroom. Tom coughs, ribs heaving, his chest exploding with a second and third cough.

You can choose any room you like.

The children.

You can visit them.

Tom lowers his hands to his lap.

You'll like it here. Things will be much better. I promise. Tabbs sits down on the bench next to Tom. Some time before he speaks. You don't like me, Tom?

I like you, Mr. Tabbs.

Are you sure? Have I harmed you? Have I hurt your feelings in some way?

I like you, Mr. Tabbs.

Then what can it be, Tom? What can it be?

Tom's face brightens with some secret amusement.

What is it? Please tell me. You can tell me anything.

Three birds, Tom says.

What?

Three birds.

Tabbs turns his gaze to the window behind them, which frames a tree twenty yards away, large natural tallness, white fishing dhows docked twenty yards beyond it. Three pear-shaped birds occupy different branches of the tree, chirping singularly and collectively.

He hears Tom ask, You like the country?

Bedazzled, Tabbs looks at the boy, trying to think himself into the boy's face, seeing in it a large number of small traits that simply cannot be real. A face with a strange distinction all its own that the mother does not share.

You were there, Tom says.

Nothing familiar, nothing Tabbs can recognize. Unknown (undescribed) the boy's personality and his past. Nothing the Doctor could (would) tell. Had he the Bethune woman he might be able to interview her about some of the boy's desires and habits.

On the grass.

You want to go to the country? We'll take a trip. Just say the word. Tabbs is both drained of and filled with everything.

Tom says nothing.

I don't understand why you want to keep yourself from the world. Doesn't the piano give you enjoyment?

The keys are hard. Have you never touched them?

Only in folly.

If you try touching them.

Okay, so I'll touch them now. Tabbs places his fingers lightly on the keys, ivory widening to his touch.

Understand.

But I don't have your talent.

No. You are not Blind Tom. Tom stands up from the bench and bends over Tabbs. His mouth fits perfectly against Tabbs's ear. Speaks what the other hears.

A woman? That's what you want?

Take me to her.

Okay. I will take you.

Bring me her.

Do you understand? I will take you.

When can we go?

Anytime you want.

Tom lowers his head. You'd better go now, Mr. Tabbs, he says, circling the piano, in his own sphere of separation.

After all it has cost Tabbs to find the boy—the money, the miles, the years; *I've given up everything to follow you*—here the boy is, melting away, vanishing, again.

❈ ❈ ❈

The driver slowed the horse slowed the buggy to mouth the brass-numbered address of each house lined up along one side of the tree-lined street, mumbling the way Tabbs caught himself mumbling certain tentative ideas while he was in the middle of doing something else. The unpaved bumpy road so wide—sufficient space for four wagons to comfortably pass one another—that the high canopy of poplars had no chance of providing any protective shade for any person or vehicle unfortunate enough to be caught in the road. Facing the traveler on either side a baker's dozen of identical two-story houses with a good twenty feet of lawn separating one from the other, idyllic structures, peaceful, in all likelihood absent of human inhabitants given the wear and weathering. Barely breathing, the driver nodded his head, swung it from side to side, judiciously weighing the numbers. A single sidelong glance that he held as they advanced up the street. Tabbs leaning forward in his seat inside the black-hooded cab behind the driver, peering out from the cloth cave, mutely searching for the lawyer's house along with the driver, but itching to take a more active part. The driver angled in his field of vision. (Tabbs sees him still.) Infected with Tabbs's eagerness, he too was leaning forward, his upper body extended precariously over the wagon side, the shadows of horse and man blending on the road, seeing what he saw—nothing should escape his notice, nothing should happen unless he was there to capture it. But the driver seemed to grow visibly older each time he failed to identify the house. He could spell out letters, read some words, the most necessary ones, ones his profession required of him. Even though his mouth spewed out speech that didn't quite sound like the English language to Tabbs's ears, a world of difference between the word the driver saw and the way he vocalized it, a wide valley separating what he said and proper pronunciation, that is, the way Tabbs was accustomed to saying it and hearing it said where he came from and the many places he had traveled. With the exception of the victorious (Union) soldiers, nobody down here spoke in a way Tabbs fully understood upon first hearing.

Language loose around him. Where was it heading? (He still doesn't know, those strays with their stray speech.) Tabbs there in the shade of the cab, the driver fully out in the sun, a mile separating the two of them.

They had just driven for an hour (more) from the hotel where Tabbs was lodged. No small talk the entire way here, the driver occupied with keeping the horse at a steady gallop—perhaps he needed to concentrate on this one task, perhaps he had other needs—clicking hooves, his eyes shifting from the road to the fields to the sky, set on getting them to their destination even though he was not quite sure where it was, while Tabbs barely registered the world that existed outside the confines of the black cab, preoccupied, thinking of what to include in the story he might have to tell the lawyer. What if anything he had left out of the letter he was carrying. (What to remember. What not to.) He needed to act within a solid framework.

The driver had asked, Who you be needin? Tabbs had pretended not to hear. Later he will discover he need only have replied "Simon Coffin" and the driver would have quickly taken him there. Instead, he spoke the exact street address where he had written the lawyer two months earlier. Nothing secretive in his withholding of the name. No reason to have said more, to have acted otherwise. This driver already a relic of the past whatever the (deceptive surface) similarities between him and Tabbs. By Tabbs's estimation he and the driver were similar in age, give or take a few years, men of the same generation and men of the same flesh—the harmony of their hair, the harmony of their skin—descendants of the same vague African fathers—would to God every person walking the earth had certain knowledge of his genealogy—and yet they came from worlds wholly apart, nothing alike. A Northern city man who had never been to the South before now, having had no good reason to do so before now.

Once they reached the end of the street, the driver tugged the reins in such a way as to have the horse spin them a half circle onto the opposite side of the street headed back in the direction whence they had come. The horse snorted in acknowledgment—*All right, I can do this*—and they started the slow search, the driver leaning forward, numbers in his mouth. They soon arrived at the end of the street, the very point from which they had started out. The driver drew the horse to the side of road and pulled himself erect on the platform.

We ain't getting nowhere, the driver said. It sposed to be right in here somewheres but ain't nan sign. Best I dig it up for you. The driver speaking in a tender voice, comically unsuited to the circumstances. He hopped down from the platform, the most natural act in the world. A scarecrow stitched up in somebody's dark-colored hand-me-downs.

Wait, Tabbs said. Lacking the driver's speed and agility, he spun his body 180 degrees and began to work his way down from the cab—the driver did not offer to assist him—backward like a man descending a ladder, one foot then the other. He reached the running board, pushed his weight off, and took a short hop into the dirt. Stood there in the hot rough road carefully positioning his hat on his head, low enough on the brow to block the sun but not too low to block vision. Must see what he must see. Turned to face the driver and stood looking at him. The horse was still moving, wanted to go, stamping one hoof after the next into the red dirt.

Some houses yonder over that rise there. The driver nodded his head toward the opposite side of the plateau a hundred yards off where the forest began again. Where the road don't carry. Ain't nowhere else it can be. He took the reins and began wrapping them around a post.

No, Tabbs said. I can go.

It's pestering me now, the driver said. Clearly disappointed, at a loss, empty-handed, despite his best efforts. I knows where we be. Best I go.

No, Tabbs said.

The driver stood looking at Tabbs with the reins in his hands, the length of them forming a half loop from the dirt road to the horse's long mouth. His look a reproach to Tabbs's abruptness, possible rudeness. Tabbs stared right into the man's irises, clear living tissue, so that all else of him disappeared. The whole of the man in one (two), round windows, maps. An easy walk up the rise, the driver said. You needin directions from there? His voice was pleasant and measured, but his tone was less than welcoming.

No, Tabbs said. I can manage. He removed a smattering of coins from his leather pouch and paid the driver, adding a generous half-dollar tip.

The driver stared sullenly at the coins circling his palm as if they were some foreign and invasive growth, boils or pox, popping up from beneath the skin or embellishing it. He closed his fingers over the coins, a fist, not happy to take them. Slowly lifted his face toward Tabbs. How long you gon be? he asked. Eyes growing tighter, clearly irritated that after having driven this passenger two miles out he now had to wait.

I can't say. Tabbs quick to answer back, deliberately gruff even though the driver commanded respect. He started for the rise, stepping easily over the broken ground, his feet properly equipped with old sturdy water-repelling boots hardened with mud he had purchased from an alabaster native. Thirty paces out, he turned his head and looked back over his shoulder at the driver, the latter still standing in the same spot, resolutely holding the reins in one hand, the coins fisted in the other. Studying Tabbs, his gaze torn, wavering between one instinct and another. Wouldn't surprise Tabbs a bit if he found the man gone upon his return.

He started up the rise on a narrow footpath cutting through thick forest, his lungs working. This was the South.

Sometimes he could pick out the human arrangements with quick ease; other times he had to work to see them. Caught (glimpse) a man so thin, such a featherweight, that the slightest puff of wind lifted him a full six feet above the earth, sailed him along, and settled him somewhere else yards away. Tabbs dashed along rows of trees endangered (doomed) by so many varieties of birds, headed for an Anglo-Saxon native (no mistaking him) standing a few yards off. A small man hugging a small basket at his waist. No shoes, his tattered clothing revealing patches of skin not unlike the red dirt in color and texture, a man growing up out of the soil. He snatched up his head at Tabbs's approach, eyes bulging like two round marbles. Tabbs only went so close, leaving a strategic four feet between them.

Suh, you need one of these apples, the man said. He held out the small basket for Tabbs's inspection. Green crab apples. They never known a worm.

Tabbs took two of them and paid the man in the smallest denomination of coin he could produce from his leather pouch.

Thanks yese kindly, suh. He dropped his head forward until his chin touched his chest.

Tabbs came right out with it. Do you know where I might find Teaberry Lane?

Old or new?

Tabbs unaware until now that he had a choice. Old, he said, guessing.

Yonder. The man pointed to the other side of the plateau where the forest began, then pocketed his money and scurried away.

Tabbs took some enjoyment in seeing the alabaster this way, face flushed from exerting in the heat. Defeated and under constant watch, the Anglo-Saxon natives were no longer masters in their own homes. In fact, they were as unsure as he was, strangers in a new land under foreign occupation. (Crab apples in his pockets.) They had numerous crimes to answer for, crimes against his people. Not a day passed when he was not struck by a desire—his own stiffening rage—to take one of the hard alabaster faces and smash it into powder. A desire that always flitted nimbly through him and evaporated, overwhelmed by the reality of the cruel necessities of war. (The planters were all dead.) The phase of fear fast replacing the state of fury.

Looked ahead into the white band of the morning and continued across the red span of the plateau, brushing his hands free of red dirt, refusing to break his stride. Trod his way carefully past sweaty Negro women carrying baskets on their heads (they were perfectly beyond his reach), moving on to the opposite side of the plateau and into forest again. Started his descent, gravity pulling him into speed. Easy now or tumble down the rise. Land leveled out—running, slowing into normalcy—and he found himself upon another road that seemed to begin and end nowhere. Worked on steadying his breathing. Heaved like something had burst in his chest. He went the way all the traffic seemed to be headed. Careful about where he placed his feet. Mounds of animal droppings like golden stones in the sunlight. Cowbells followed one another into the distances of the afternoon. The shunt and pull of animals and vehicles. (Strange how the things of this world—horses, mules, oxen, dogs, donkeys—afford flight from it.) Mule-drawn two-wheeled carts and horse-drawn four-wheeled wagons stumbling along the plateau. Hard to believe that these skeletal animals were (once) living creatures. Hard to believe they simply hadn't upped and quit by now. All their drivers could do to navigate their vehicles through the ruddy ruts and puddles the rain had made—he recalled no rain—and maneuver around people who bothered neither to stop walking nor to move out the way. Had he found it? Was this road the elusive (Old) Teaberry Lane? Sitting very erect in their saddles, ten or twelve mounted soldiers—the victors, the conquerors—strode through on impressive stallions. Other soldiers walking behind them, meandering in loose formation, their rifles slung carelessly over their shoulders, their heavy boots sinking into the red mud.

What could he see in the spaces between the trees? Cemeteries in abundance. Fresh graves with plain wooden crosses to identify the occupants. (This country was growing the dead.) Would harvest a new generation from the old. Lesser life-forms hold little interest in the most recent of the dearly departed. Famished pigs (boars) and bearded goats grazed among the plots, while chickens flapped over the tombstones as if engaged in some athletic tournament.

Less than ten yards away, soldiers were mustering strays in a small muddy treeless break adjoining the road, grouping them into neat rows, only for the commanding officer to change his mind and mold them single file into a long crooked line extending well into the forest. The soldiers motioning and directing with their rifles, showing their irritation, their mounting disgust. The strays moving as one brown body, something large and hungry. Since his arrival in town ten days ago, no morning had passed that Tabbs had not seen them. They kept coming, a brown caravan. A brown sweaty stream, ill-smelling, off-putting to sight and nose—the strays, outfitted in rags, strips of torn cloth, feet shod in leftover leather or canvas, or no shoes at all. The little they owned—scalded pots and skillets, walking sticks, fishing poles, a coat or shawl here and there—in a jumble at their bare feet. The brutal stories he had heard fugitives tell back home on the podium or in the pub seemed so farfetched, much more so than even the most fantastic medieval romance or history. (The published narratives paled in comparison, no more unnerving or shocking than a good children's bedtime tale.) But seeing these people he could believe they actually lived this history. One thing he could say in favor of his Race: they are a rugged people. A state of being and becoming unknown to him. (And for that reason, better than him, at least in certain respects, nobler, more courageous.) To never have quite enough, hunger growing, satisfaction that never came (comes). Futures denied. They greedily fell (fall) upon every cup of milk offered them, each loaf of bread. Yearning. (Life piled on life.) They will not—even *now*—settle in his mind, his thoughts. Is it for them that he was here? To build a better day? (The soon-come day without the nigger.) Assured, for mankind always sets itself only such problems as it can solve. Looking closely, it will always be found that the task itself arises only when the material and practical conditions for its solution already exist or are in the process of formation.

Aware that he stood out for any casual observer who took the time to look, knew he was a foreigner, not from here. (I was not from there, the South.) Full of the sap and sense of life, he stood out, handsome tall well-made—he had engaged in hard labor with Ruggles and others when life had required it of him—always with the clearness of health in his face and vivacity in his eyes, and always neatly dressed, neither elegant nor flashy, but suitable and dignified. (Why in the estimate of a man do we prize him wrapped and muffled up in clothes?) Barely twenty-four years into this world but already a man of independent income—that is, he worked for no man other than himself—with expectations of much more. He had to put up a bold front. (Alabasters are a fact. What can you do with them?) Until a few weeks ago, as far as he was concerned, this small Southern town—not surprisingly, the Anglo-Saxon natives fancied it a city, one of their country's most important, the hub, the center; wrong here as they had (have) been wrong about so much else—didn't exist, and if it did, only as a word in a newspaper or a dot on a map. But now—what difference a day—he was caught, in the grip of this thing. (Going to see the lawyer, no turning back.) Moved along a muddy winding road in a country crossed with many such roads, sunken or stamped-in paths (nothing paved, engineered, constructed) surrounded by composed and watchful trees, endless branching. (What loomed on the other side of those darkened and charred trunks?) Clear and careful—feet on the ground, head out of the clouds—he looked for omens everywhere, fearing a chance medley of possibilities and occurrences. This was (is) the land that General Bethune had built, the land that General Bethune once walked. So let *him* walk it. Not really his normal fluid self though. Easy to understand his cautious gait—he actually counted each step, no false or sudden moves—his hesitation. Nervously anticipating, he tried to sense and scent prey. He sidestepped passersby even before they come into eyeshot. (No matter how broad the path, an alabaster must never give a Negro the right-of-way.) A habit he had developed since arriving in town.

Hard not to worry. Terrible things could happen like this: A Negro woman stands on the hot awningless platform not far from him waiting for the train, three children of various ages seeking shade in the folds of her ankle-length dress. From her appearance, hers and theirs, she can ill afford a ticket, but there she is, there they are. Her white bonnet glows like a halo in morning light. From somewhere—Tabbs still hasn't puzzled it complete—a white man runs up to her, lunges, and punches her in the face, reams of blood spilling red to the earth. A punch so sudden and wild that he loses his balance and almost tumbles to the ground. Solid, she doesn't buckle, only brings both shocked hands to her mouth, loose teeth spilling out between the joints of her fingers like lumps of sugar. The children cry. Almost instantly a soldier rushes up to the man, shoves the end of his rifle barrel between the man's eyes, and blows his brains red white and pink out the back of his head.

Tabbs recognized that he took a big chance traveling here, the soldiers, occupying army, the only force that stood between him and those who had lost the war. He had already escaped injury or death more than once: The natives yelled things at him, and the soldiers aimed their rifles and ordered them to move along. Everything he saw, has seen, bothered (bothers) him. Such squalor. Natives—men, women, and children—living in little crooked-planked cabins, ramshackle eyesores, alongside their few animals—hogs, cows, chickens, oxen, and goats, broken-down mules and horses—in unkempt filth. All the towns seemed run-down, the farmhouses had all been ruined, old windows replaced by new, or no windows at all.

Now on the plateau a soldier told him to hold up for a moment. Indeed, he had been stopped more than once his first two or three days in country, free passage since. Reasonable that they had grown accustomed to him. (He stood out. One of a kind.) He walked over to the soldier—a problem if a soldier had to walk over to you—and produced his pass, a quarter-folded sheet of paper, without hesitation. Fully three-quarters of the pass offered a poorly rendered drawing of his face—the right skin tone, the wrong features—with an official stamp in the corner, and a caption under it reading *Northern Negro*. He held out the pass for the soldier's scrutiny, and the soldier moved one hand across his body to clutch the strap shouldering his rifle then bent forward to peer closer—he did not take it, touch it—and measure with successive glances back and forth Tabbs's face against the drawing. How hard was he really looking? Barely studied it for five seconds. Satisfied, he drew back into his erect soldierly posture and emitted a short sentence in soldier's language—perhaps he said nothing at all—indicating that Tabbs was free to continue.

Tabbs noted a measure of difference in the way the soldiers treated him and the way they treated both strays and natives. When they weren't shouting orders or instructions they spoke like fops, barely deigning to articulate their words. But they accorded Tabbs a measure of respect usually reserved for white men of importance, a quality of treatment that he had experienced only on chance occasions. They even took the trouble to question his well-being and to warn him about places he should avoid and places he might see. *That bend has the best perch you'll ever taste. And the swimming ain't bad if you can learn the current.* He took it all in as if he was truly eager to learn and understand. Still, their facts caused him to wonder. Were they aiding him or manipulating him? Did they order him? Control him? And it was hard to say if he was obeying. He wanted to (needed to) follow his own orders (plans) so there was a good chance that at some point his will would (had to, must) collide with their wishes.

Many such thoughts flashed in him now—*foolish to come here*— but he did not dwell on them. Stubbornly avoided the details. Without the details everything is clear, inviolable. He had full clear hopes, as must any man who had come several hundred miles or more. General Bethune had (has) been cheated of what is rightfully his. That is why he was here. He had suffered setbacks before—what man hasn't?— but nothing of this nature or this magnitude, for up until this point in his life he had risen much unaided. (Credit the Pygmy. Credit

Ruggles.) Almost two months ago, before the war ended, he realized that the future held for him the absolute need to visit a prominent lawyer. He had written the lawyer seeking representation, and the lawyer had wired back a response for him to come. He had taken no one else into his confidence. In fact, he was sustained by the hope that that this lawyer, Simon Coffin, might be the one person in the entire country (nation?) who could aid him.

Old Teaberry Lane?

No, suh. This here ain't it, but gon and follow it up till you see the well.

Thank you.

Much obliged. The boy continued on, the brim of his hat wider than the entire circumference of his body, his snazzy grosgrain band less adornment and more necessary tool to keep the hat squeezed on his substanceless head. Equally if not more astonishing the boy had actually called him sir. *Suh.* For so many years—all his life, or at least since his first awareness of slavery—Tabbs had believed these natives were monsters, so it surprised him that even monsters can be polite. So many crimes to pay for, too many to count, but now that the war was done and the monsters tamed, he was willing to let bygones be bygones, if they were willing to do the same. Willing even to extend the hand of partnership—not to be mistaken for friendship, brotherhood—break bread, and work with these creatures. (Only the best need sign up.) Whatever it took to increase, multiply. (Indeed, was that not Lincoln's idea? *No one must expect me to take any part in hanging or killing of these men, even the worst of them. We must not open the gates and frighten them out of the country. Enough lives have been sacrificed; we must extinguish our resentments if we expect harmony and union.*) So Tabbs thought let's be rational and defer justice for now. (Blood should be left to cleanse itself.)

Tabbs found the well where the driver had said it would be, conveniently stationed where the road turned left and became Old Teaberry Lane. Strays raising and lowering bucket and rope to lean into and drink or lean away and wipe mouths dry. Another two dozen or more strays circling about the well or lingering within a few feet of it, many of them completely wet, as if they had just climbed up out of watery darkness to light dry surface. Like the banded boy, members of his own race addressed him as sir—*Morning, suh. Yes, suh. No, suh. Evening, suh.*—but never went further. Nothing more, even if he threw out some leading question or tidbit of talk. In fact, ten days running and not another member of his race had ever seemed to really notice him. Looked his way without seeing him, saw him without looking at him, as strays would later in the city. Not unlike their mode of interaction with any alabaster, whether native or foreigner.

Old Teaberry Lane turned—became another?—and Tabbs went down that way, the ground passing below him, dirt and clumps of grass giving way to his boots. The morning white from the heat, burning fierce and quick as a match. Light and heat ocean-deep. He wiped the sweat from his face, causing his hand to sting as if he had just dunked it into boiling water. Right then, he felt like giving it all up. He didn't know what put the thought in his head. (Still doesn't know.) He looked off into the forest. Plenty of nothing out there and plenty of everything. He thought he heard water running somewhere in the distance, the barest trickle, tried to calculate the source and how far he was from it and collided right into a black cape of flying insects, buzzing inside his nose and mouth. Head and hands worked to shake and jerk free, while tongue spat the mouth clean. He patted and checked his jacket pocket to be sure that he still had the letter he planned to present to the lawyer.

After his arrival in town he had spent a considerable part of each day at the desk in his hotel room writing a letter to Simon Coffin as he was (is) certain that he had left too much out of the first letter he had sent the lawyer almost two months ago. He wanted the new letter to be pure, no suppositions, all facts, and of the facts he separated the essentials from the nonessentials. Still, he couldn't help squeezing in the final remnants of ideas, plans, suppositions, even suggestions for possible remedies and courses of action. How is that for contradiction? Here he was, seeking out this lawyer, because he had already exhausted all other possibilities. *Who will open the doors I can't see?* Now see him on his way to the lawyer's office with the letter securely in his jacket pocket, having finished writing it to his satisfaction less than two hours ago.

He had drained himself of all that he did not need intellectually and emotionally for the sole purpose of this sit-down meeting with the esteemed Simon Coffin. Hoping for the best—Coffin would reveal General Bethune's whereabouts—prepared for the worst. To get the desired result, he was willing to push the lawyer—or anyone else—as far as he could.

He judged Coffin alone to be worthy of this knowledge. For thirty-five years or more (forty?) Coffin had been unquestionably among the most visible and influential men in the entire nation as an advocate for the Negro cause—no week passed without his name appearing a dozen times in the Negro journals—whether the bound or the free. A white Southerner whose circle of benevolence also extended to encompass many other scorned and abused groups—poor Anglo-Saxon natives, Catholics, German immigrants, abolitionists, and foreign visitors and travelers (including journalists). Known for both his bold pronouncements—*The cruelest man living could not sit at my feast unless he sat blindfolded*—and audacious tactics, this lawyer, more than any other man existing at that time, held the largest and most liberal view of the world, and was capable of devising the most practical and effective schemes in defense of these views. Coffin had even continued practicing his vocation through the course of the war without suffering arrest or any form of censorship or molestation. How explain that?

The road became what Tabbs normally would think of as a residential street. Small houses jammed together. Windows moving along as you advanced. Then the road rose (leapt) impossibly skyward where it carried him up to a section of modest three-story houses. One house was nothing like the others. How fortunate it stood where it did by itself between two oak trees on a little rise at one end of the street, trees broad and wide at the base like important men squatting before an audience of supplicants. A three-story gray structure with a sloped red-iron roof—the others were flat—the exterior rather old but pleasant, worse for wear, wood showing through the gray, streaked with longitudinal cracks, and heavy porch planks of bare wood and dust and dirt, having long given up color to a multitude of shoes and boots. The door was finely carved with a raised image of a fox and an eagle against a flat detailed field—tree, grass, pond, sunlight, wind—the eagle swooping down with beak opened threateningly, while the fox, head turned and teeth bared, leapt up to meet the challenge. Plenty of varnished wood between them, as if the animals had come to an agreement that they would only get so close. From the brass doorplate, Tabbs learned that Coffin's office was on the top floor.

Tabbs removed his hat, pinned it between his left elbow and hip, and entered a dimly lit hall floored in elegant tile. Though he was exhausted, he started up the mahogany stairs with force and energy, the wood squishing under his feet. The stairs seemed to have suffered the worst for the humidity, soft, the wood pressing in like cake, Tabbs cautious now, unsure if the steps might not give way altogether beneath him. At the third-floor landing he saw a door left partially open at one end of the hall, and headed for it. Found a mahogany door hinged into a frame made out of cedar, with a large stained glass window depicting a coat of arms fit into the door's upper half, and above it a brass plate engraved with the black-lettered name Simon Peter Levi Coffin IV, Esquire.

Tabbs leaned into the angle of opening and saw fifteen feet away Coffin seated bent over, gazing at some papers on his desk, pen in hand—the figure in everyday circumstances—late-morning sun entering the large room from two ample windows facing the street. Tabbs stood watching, took the time to observe, study what he could, unnoticed. This act of exclusive and privileged seeing both natural and possible because it was well-practiced, for Tabbs did (does) not view himself as one who was conditioned by—the system, the institution of—conventional intelligence. The room impressed the visitor as a place to conduct business just as it impressed the viewer as a place to exhibit a handful of choice artifacts. Scrolls hanging from the walls and a green (jade) vase mounted on a pedestal in one corner, a red (jade?) in another. Dozens of books neatly stacked near the fireplace. And papers of various sizes and description inserted in little wooden hold-alls nailed into every available space in the walls, papers that Tabbs assumed were legal files and correspondence, letters, memos, telegrams, and briefs relating to the countless cases Coffin had represented. He leaned back into the hall and tapped on the stained glass window to announce his presence.

Enter, please.

He did so unmolested. (How had he even made it this far? Reasonable to expect the lawyer to be under the protection of a personal armed guard, even his own small private band of protectors and defenders.) Face raised, the lawyer watched him enter. Stood up from his desk, smiling good-naturedly, an unmistakable man of modern height with a look of the world about him, broad shouldered and rather thickly proportioned around the waist but by no means portly or flabby (fat). He was dressed not only decently but stylishly—light (material and color) summer jacket, a linen shirt under a light-colored waistcoat, light-colored and loose-fitting trousers, and cordovan shoes from New Orleans. Tabbs saw—can see still, will never forget—in his whole impeccable figure something at once noble and ridiculous.

You must be Mr. Gross, the lawyer said with a puzzled look (so Tabbs thought).

Yes. I'm Tabbs Gross.

The lawyer leaned forward across his desk and extended his hand, and Tabbs leaned in and took it, catching the faint scent of sweet perfume.

Have a seat, Mr. Gross.

Tabbs sat down on one of two curved-back chairs positioned before the desk. Looked up and noticed a third window five feet behind and above the lawyer, lending just enough light to make visible dust drifting across the cedar panels that lined the roof.

The lawyer sat down. Well, Mr. Gross, it was good of you to come.

Sir, it was good of you to grant me an audience.

How else could we have it? Did you travel well?

Yes, sir.

I'm delighted to know that. Could I fetch you some water?

No, Tabbs said. He really wanted something to drink, his insides on fire.

Tea? Coffee? Lemon water?

I decline.

The lawyer was quiet for a few moments, maintaining his welcoming smile, a silence that gave Tabbs his first opportunity to really study the man sitting before him. With his somewhat wavy shoulder-length gray hair—waves tinged with blond streaks as if gilded, which shifted with a supple movement and brushed his shoulders when he turned or lowered or raised his head—his big-pored forehead, slanted eyelids (Mongolian fold?) that partly obscured his eyes and pupils, and heavy worm-thick lips, the lawyer looked entirely unlike himself in both the handful of well-known illustrations and caricatures—the lawyer swims the Atlantic Africa-bound with a pyramid of watermelon-eating slaves frolicking on his back—and the singular daguerreotype—that he had clearly sat for several decades earlier and that were so often reproduced in the newspapers. The way he leaned forward in his seat, his white jacket looked less like an article of clothing he wore and more like some independent object riding his back. A white impression of the kind of man he was (is), a man completely at ease here as he would be anywhere else in the known world, a tortoise-like man carrying his own white country on his back so that wherever he was he felt (and kept) quite comfortable and at home.

Tabbs (sneaky-eyed) spied the missive he had mailed two months earlier—he recognized his own handwriting—atop a pile of papers positioned exactly in line with the left desk corner edge. For some reason the desk, worn and sturdy, seemed out of order, although he couldn't quite put his finger on the why, the source of dissent.

I've looked over your letter, Mr. Gross. Coffin took up the document he had been reading—his hand reddish on the outside, brownish on the inside—and placed it on top of a stack of papers, then took the letter and moved it to the cleared space before him.

If I may, sir. I've taken the necessary move of adjusting it. Tabbs removed the new letter from his jacket pocket and placed it directly over the old, properly flat so that the lawyer might begin reading it. Please, sir. My apologies, but this letter before you now provides a detailed description of the case and is therefore a far more accurate accounting.

The lawyer said nothing at first, but continued to sit leaning forward in his chair, studying Tabbs, his eyes aglitter, avid but cautious, weighing the possibilities. Hard for Tabbs really to look the man directly in the eye, but he somehow did. *I did.* Finally, the lawyer said, Then I must, Mr. Gross. He lowered his line of sight to the letter and began reading it.

Tabbs waited quietly and patiently. No point to a missive if he had to explain it, although he was (is) far the better man at speaking than at writing.

While Coffin read, Tabbs studied the many file-jammed cubicles constructed into the walls. Each box carefully labeled by month, day, and year in bright ink. These files represented a preservation of history dating back more than thirty years. On the desk Tabbs noticed a plainly bound (cloth) Bible positioned along the right desk corner spine outward so that anyone who sat in either chair before the desk could not mistake the title.

Coffin took up both letters, one on top of the other, and placed them on top of a stack of papers. Tabbs adjusted his body in his seat, trying to snap his mind clean, and hoping Coffin—the lawyer lifted his gaze to Tabbs's face—couldn't see any trace of his impulses and speculations. Mr. Gross, Coffin said, there is much here, much that is concrete. The words surprised Tabbs. Some note in the lawyer's voice abiding with implication, the faint reverberation of secrets, facts withheld. Had he not spelled it all out in the new letter he had sweated over so?

I apologize for my handling of the pen, he said. Perhaps I wrote poorly. He sat awkwardly straight in the chair, like a man with his arms bound.

No, I would not say that.

You don't understand the nature of my dispute? He had to admit, his writing hand was (is) fluid but perhaps a bit abstract. Never a word written as a commoner might say it.

Of course I understand, Coffin said. Only a fool could mistake what you have set down here. He continued to look Tabbs in the face. Why did you come here? What are your true reasons?

He knew why he was here, but how could he admit it to the lawyer? I seek your representation. That is my true reason.

You hope to win a judgment against General Bethune?

With your help.

In what jurisdiction?

Sir, I trust you with all of the legal details.

Coffin studied Tabbs, reading his face as he had read the documents. And there's nothing else?

No, sir.

More silence. All right, so we can proceed with the case, as long as you understand what we are up against.

They set about reviewing the plain facts and the relevant dates of the case, a rough-and-ready conversion. Sure, he had written his side of it—*Everything set forth in these pages is substantially true and within the truth*—a twice-told tale, but perhaps his letter, one or both, differed in essential ways from the actual occurrence, from what he remembered (remembers) and what he said now. Best to acquaint Coffin with the whole of the monstrous wrong General Bethune has committed against him, from beginning to end and back again. As Tabbs spoke, the lawyer concentrated with all his might, frowning, like a dimly understanding devout listening to and pondering a sermon from the master, his hands continually moving across the desk as if he was engraving Tabbs's words into the oak surface.

You put forth the proposal. You entered into the agreement with conscious mind.

Yes, Tabbs said, aware that Coffin was not asking but telling, reporting, in condensed fashion.

And the contract?

Tabbs produced two documents—thrice folded to form a thick rectangle of paper—from his jacket pocket and held them out to the lawyer. (He did not place them on the desk.) Coffin did not take them right away, still and reluctant, giving Tabbs a doubtful (fearful?) look as if he didn't know what Tabbs was handing him.

As you'll see, sir, there are actually two. The one I drew up and the one that General Bethune had drawn up in addition.

Coffin spread the two contracts side by side before him on the desk, keeping the bent pages flat with the edges of his hands. Started reading them.

I signed one then the other, and he signed one then the other, and we spoke and shook hands, as gentlemen do, regardless of race, and I handed over the first installment.

Reading done, Coffin lifted both his face and hands, allowing the documents to fold half-open half-closed on the desk like bloom-shy flowers. He gave Tabbs an eye-scrunching look as if remembering what Tabbs had just told him, as if he had been present at the meeting but couldn't quite re-create the memory in his mind now. One thousand dollars.

Yes. With a promise of another four thousand, a promise that he never afforded me the opportunity to keep.

Five thousand dollars, Coffin said. An even better sum. More than most men could save in a lifetime or hope to save or dream of saving. His voice so resonant he seemed to be singing.

I have means.

You have a receipt?

Tabbs brought one hand to his pocket.

No, Mr. Gross. You may safeguard it for now. The hidden validity of the receipt seemed to bring about a physical change in Coffin, some ease in position, some relaxing of the shoulders. For the first time, he was leaning back in his chair, actually slouching. And after he reneged, you had no other communication?

I received—Tabbs started with that and knew he had faulted. He couldn't tell the lawyer the rest, couldn't tell Coffin that he had already gone to the Bethune estate. Had to and did think up something else to tell him. When I arrived here in town, he said, I received word that the Bethunes had left. It had been only a matter of speculation before. Thoughts and questions buzzing in the silent air. He could see the lawyer working to figure it out, to maneuver around the subterfuge and come face to face with the truth. So he added: The estate is completely vacant. So I was told. He realized that he had spoken incorrectly. In fact, the estate was not vacant. Far from it. Still, he saw no point in correcting himself. Enough damage done.

So you've actually driven out to Hundred Gates? The lawyer's jaw rose and fell with the words.

A certain uneasy remembrance flashed in Tabbs's mind. Hundred Gates. (The house enjoys the use of a big garden, surrounding it on all sides.) He had pushed the details out of conscious memory. (The gardens are full of flowers, none of which he can identify. What were his childhood names for startling grasses and other forms of curious or secret growth?) But he was pleased, for Coffin seemed to have set aside the idea of studying him more closely. Yes, he said, but only after I learned that it was vacant. (Not true. Anything but vacant.) He let the lawyer know that he had been out to Hundred Gates (trees like slender women) a half dozen times or more since his arrival in town more than a week ago. It never crossed my mind to impose my presence on you before our scheduled interview today. Then he paused—they were looking each other straight in the eye as custom and circumstance required (demanded)—not sure what he expected. Coffin was affected. Tabbs (years later) can still recall perfectly the rectangle of light that the sun cast through the windows, the pen leaning in the inkwell on the desk—a barren post minus its flag—and the slow way that the lawyer began to speak.

The Bethunes fled when so many others did, he said, his voice flat as he imparted the information. (He never said when. Months earlier or years?) He went on to inform Tabbs that upon his decision to meet with Tabbs—a decision he arrived at only after careful consideration—he had taken pains to investigate General Bethune's whereabouts and learned through his most trusted sources that the Bethunes had taken up new residence at an estate called Elway in Virginia, not far from the former capital. A recent purchase, he said. Quite recent. He moved his hand toward one corner of the desk as if he was about to produce the deed itself.

Not what Tabbs wanted to hear. Some time before he could will his tongue to move. Are you certain?

Yes.

Tabbs said nothing.

So it appears that General Bethune still has financial means.

But that isn't the end of it. (Bad news on top of bad news.) Coffin informed him that another party, one Perry Oliver—a name Tabbs recognized, *yes, the former manager, Tom's former manager*—had filed suit in the state of Virginia against General Bethune for reneging on a contract. The matter had been quickly settled upon the General's issuing this Mr. Oliver fifteen thousand dollars in cash, the sum total that the jilted manager had paid the General up front upon the original terms of their contract.

Fifteen thousand dollars?

Yes.

Tabbs said nothing.

I am sorry.

Tabbs sat quietly for some time with his disappointments, not sure what he should look at—the lawyer, the desk, the files, the tapestry, the windows.

Your case is irrecusable, Mr. Gross. Certainly the facts weigh in your favor. General Bethune willfully and negligently misled you. So the legal solution seems easy enough. A fair and impartial court, either judge or jury, should rule in your favor based on the documented evidence, the sheer logic of fact. Facts that, I might add, in this instance should amount to justice now that the war has been decided. But you understand that General Bethune remains a capable threat and can forestall a quick resolution. Coffin seemed completely immobile now, his body on pause, hold. Even as he spoke, the slanted flesh around his eyes—praying hands—remained stationary. Tabbs sensed that the light in the room had shifted, changed. For the first time he realized that Coffin's jacket was the exact color gray as the wall behind him. Found it necessary to watch closely to separate man from background.

Tabbs found it difficult to speak, his words hanging fruit, but out of reach. I've been cheated, he said. I've done all I can.

Of course, Coffin said. Of course. So this lawyer thinks he understands, knows Tabbs's troubles, as well as Tabbs's longings and aspirations; and as he took it all fully into heartfelt consideration he began to smile, not a cruel smile but one of pity. Mr. Gross, I offer no guarantee, but I believe a court should order General Bethune to square accounts and return the balance of your deposit, and also allow you some substantial monies to recuperate your legal costs and to compound reasonable interest. It may be that General Bethune will—

That won't do, Tabbs said.

Simon Coffin didn't say anything to this. I'm beginning to understand, he said. You seek revenge? Catch your thief in order to hang him.

No, sir.

Not that?

No, sir. Nothing of the sort. Tabbs said it as straight as he could, needing Coffin to believe that he could usefully influence Tabbs.

We're at peace now, Coffin said.

Peace? Tabbs thinks. *That's milk for the birds.*

Coffin leaned forward and inclined his fleshy face toward Tabbs, this lifting of the head suggestive of an immediate change in consciousness, all that was required for him to draw up a fresh thought and give—a redirecting of muscle and skin—Tabbs a look part smile, part smirk.

What's done is done, he went on. Nothing can change that. Keep your eyes on the prize, on the future, he said. Blind Tom once had a dazzling career, he said. Perhaps he will again.

Indeed he will, sir. (Indeed he will.)

But the boy is beyond your reach. Coffin paused, as if to let the words sink in. The General took advantage of you. You honestly believed that he would keep his word, that he would give up the boy.

Unclear if Coffin was asking or telling.

Yes.

What a funny turn of thought you have. The lawyer almost laughed. (Did he?) He shook his head, staring at Tabbs with a pitying look. Well, I foresee it possible that a mule might someday become a king.

Tabbs couldn't find a single word. What was there to say? Still, he didn't want a silence to develop, so he uttered a platitude. We take a respected man at his word.

And I'm sure you did just that, Mr. Gross. That makes you all the more the innocent. His eyes blinked beneath thick eyebrows that clung like gray slugs onto his face. Too much for Tabbs. Can any court or authority compel the General to produce the boy from hiding? the lawyer asked. By what means?

Tabbs stood up from his seat, walked over to one of the wide windows, and stood looking down at the street three stories below. The end of the morning presented a particular shade of color he witnessed for the first time. He turned and faced the lawyer, who was observing him with none of his former amusement.

Mr. Coffin, I am not naive. I was not weaned on babe's milk. I am here because I know that you are a man of intelligence and means.

Yes, I am.

Many of our citizens, the best and the worst, have sacrificed almost everything to secure the rights of my people.

And why do you report me this fact, Mr. Gross? The lawyer spoke in a quiet, unhurried tone. I am well aware of the recent course of history, as I'm sure you are fully aware of the far longer course, the many years, decades, I have spent offering fair and impartial representation for your maligned people.

Of course, sir. I am not accusing you.

You most certainly are, and in the worst way. With deceit and without forthrightness.

They talked like people close to last words. Tabbs could offer nothing in his defense.

As it is, Coffin said, I already face a dilemma. These days I am conflicted, tormented between two diametrically opposed callings. On the one hand, the longing for rest. And on the other, an acute awareness of our need to oppose human crime and human misery. With such serious decisions before me, what would compel me to entertain a flimsy claim? You choose to come before me with your own private cause.

No, sir.

Yes, Mr. Gross. Yes. Coffin sat watching and waiting for Tabbs's response—measuring his reaction?—and would not say another word until he got one.

Sir, I must respectfully inform you that you fail to understand why I am here. It is not a matter of my person. I come before you because no other man, Negro or Anglo-Saxon, stands a chance of aiding me in this cause. I stand before you at the price of a certain sacrifice of dignity, because dignity alone is the only worthy currency. There. He had said it. Now the lawyer understood (should) that this, at root and wing, was the substantive matter at hand.

He saw Coffin's eyes darken with kindness. Mr. Gross, I'm sure you are here on a pure impulse of the heart, but you must recognize that you are in an impossible position. General Bethune will never relinquish all that he believes is rightfully his.

Indeed, sir. He won't. I'm certain of it.

Coffin leaned back in his chair, thinking. Mr. Gross, I am often asked why I have never taken on a junior partner, an understudy to whom I might pass on all that I have studied, learned, and mastered over the years. Actually, I would very much like to do so. But I will tell you why I never will. No matter how much we attempt to speak to novices, indeed to all young people, they never take the trouble to retain what is most important.

Now, Tabbs felt that he was on his own, so utterly alone that nothing had transpired since he stepped through the door, that some other person from a very long time ago in a place very far away had seen and said and heard and felt.

I foresee a time in the future, one year from now, perhaps two or three, when you will be seated once again as you are now before another man of my profession. The lawyer turned his face and lowered his gaze to the desk. So, at your insistence, Mr. Gross, I will immediately begin considering our best course of action. I will have our complaint served on the General personally.

This was what Tabbs had journeyed here to hear. (Nothing less.)

Coffin knew General Bethune's hiding place. And Tabbs would kick in the safe house door, snatch off the roof, burrow into the General's secret hole underground.

Without looking at Tabbs—straight ahead, through the fully open door—the lawyer laid out two documents on his desk. I have here a letter of agreement in duplicate. You must sign both. Tabbs went over and signed each document with Coffin's pen. Signing done, he stood looking at the lawyer, who was (now) returning his gaze. And I will need a sum of two hundred dollars as a retainer for my services. I can give you a few days to acquire the money if you so need it.

Tabbs was already reaching for his wallet. (Thought twice. Should he or shouldn't he? Now's the time. Now isn't the time.) Produced a sheath of notes and laid one after another upon the desk. As he had earlier upon Tabbs's appearance, Coffin stood up from his desk and offered his hand. Tabbs took it for a brief sweaty meeting of palms.

If you will excuse me, Mr. Gross. I should begin my work.

Yes, sir. I don't wish to impose on your time, Tabbs said, but I kindly ask that you allow me to see you again after you have further reviewed the facts. Then I will leave town and return home.

Coffin stood looking at Tabbs, saying nothing for the longest time. Mr. Gross, you must know that there is no reason for you to remain in this city. Please leave at the earliest opportunity, today even. I assure you we will be in communication. In fact, you will find a wire awaiting you upon your return home.

That is so generous of you, sir. But you understand that I have come far. It will be a most difficult matter for me to return in my present unsettled state.

Coffin lifted his chin in skepticism. Mr. Gross, I should warn you, if you are thinking about—but he said no more, as if he already knew what Tabbs was thinking and didn't have the strength to offer any opposition. As you wish. At an hour best for you, kindly pay me a return visit on Friday.

Thank you, sir.

In the meantime, I urge caution, Mr. Gross. Coffin gave Tabbs an almost paternal look of concern. Take it upon yourself to be more circumspect.

You have my word.

I have your word.

You have my word.

He was gone too quickly. The day too hot and the road too quiet. He closed the door as much as he could—it was swollen, open as if this explained all, put motive to rest—hesitated in the hall and took his time about leaving the house—each stair a month, each landing a year—hoping the lawyer might call him back. Hard as he might try, he couldn't quite bury his mistrust. He would never entrust his livelihood, his survival, into the hands of a white person, an alabaster. How easy to see beneath the theatrical disguises of their faces, the secrets and riddles behind their words. Perhaps Coffin was deliberately leaving him up in the air about his intentions? Even if this was the case—he never found out—he had no choice but to trust the lawyer, although he, Tabbs Gross, wished there were some way he could bring the lawyer's true feelings to the surface. (Is it superabundance of heart or something else that makes him befriend, represent, and defend the—the great prediction, promise—last who shall someday be first?) As he slowly made his way downstairs, he realized that his reasons for being here, in this foreign land, were even remote to himself now. (A stranger.) How could he reveal to this white man, or any man for that matter, his purpose for his risky venture?

He started back for the hotel, determined not to show up in public again—I can take my meals in my room, I can have my meals delivered to my room, I need only leave my room to bathe—until Friday, two days from now. He would go about his day (that day and the next), thinking no more than usual. Understood that his decision to stay in town would involve (require, demand) two days of tense waiting. How would he manage it? (He still asks himself, *How did I manage it?*) His story already stretched too far. *Get this thing over with.*

❀ ❀ ❀

When did he first hear the name Blind Tom? 1859? 1860? 1861? Tabbs is not entirely sure. Tom was a regular topic of conversation on the Negro grapevine.

I would never pay a penny of my hard-earned salary to hear him, the well-dressed man said. This is the way of these alabasters, to present us in a bestial light.

You've got it all wrong, his companion said, casual dress, casual bearing. So what if the little blind nigger whirls around onstage. He's probably just taking him some exercise cause those candlefaces keep him cooped up all the time, under their thumbs.

Although total opposites in dress, the two men walked loose-limbed and carefree. What you got to say about it, Tabbs? Are you attending the concert?

Like other Negroes, Tabbs had thoughts about Blind Tom—was he aiding the Race or harming it?—

What are your feelings about the war, Tom?

I am not afraid of bullets. They fly so fast.

—but he couldn't come into words; whenever the subject came to his tongue he had difficulty speaking. His mind raced ahead.

Not a damn thing. Just like I thought.

Ah, don't be so hard on Tabbs. He's a real race man.

The men got a good laugh out of this statement. They continued on, Tabbs straining his ears trying to follow the argument as the voices faded with distance.

Tabbs had to admit, Blind Tom as a man, as a Negro man—well, he was still a boy, only thirteen years of age—was rather disappointing—

Tom, you keep up quite a schedule of travel. It would tax any man, young or old, Anglo-Saxon or Negro. Do you not get tired?

Be passersby.

—but his way with Bach, if one could believe the journals, was something to adore.

Indeed, hearing Blind Tom in actuality proved to be all he had hoped it would be, although he can no longer pinpoint the year when he first saw Tom in concert. He either doesn't know or doesn't care to know. (The years don't pass for nothing.) Only the concert itself remains firm in his memory. How would he describe it? Not unlike a body's first entry into the ocean, smitten, salt-tasting skin hungry for more, sea secrets. Feel it:

Fifteen minutes before the scheduled start of the performance the gold and white auditorium was quiet and still virtually empty, the highest boxes and the gallery dark, almost invisible, while the best boxes, draped with long-fringed pelmets and velvet railings on the ground floor and at stage left and stage right, were only dimly visible. A few Negro attendants stood about chatting in the dress circle and the stalls, lost among the red velvet armchairs under the half light of the tiny flames of the huge dimly glowing chandelier, and the great red patch of the curtain that Tabbs hid behind was plunged in shade. He waited patiently, his anger bending to anticipation. At nine o'clock, the scheduled start, the main doors to the auditorium opened, uniformed Negro attendants bustling in with tickets in hand, directing a train of couples in front or behind, Mr. and Mrs. Candleface done up in formal ballroom dress, buoyant (floating and flying) in ballooning skirts and expansive tails, who nested down in numbered seats and began sweeping the auditorium with a leisurely gaze. (Who's here? Who isn't?) Only after all the alabasters were seated did the attendants allow the Negro ticket holders to enter—a crush of bodies—the gallery (Coon Heaven), way up above just beneath the rotunda ceiling with its fresco of naked women flying about in blue sky and muscular gods pitched in battle. The Negroes scrambling and fighting over the best seats, a din that caused the alabasters below to crane their necks and catapult hard glances and hot curses in their direction. *Niggers!* Could the alabasters actually see the Negroes they damned and cursed? The Negroes were only momentarily ill at ease, refusing to let environs spoil a good time. They expected a festive event, necessary break from their everyday chaotic and hierarchichal world. Aware nonetheless that they were in public and hence were under inspection—all eyes watching, *all eyes on me*—each man representing all men, each woman all women. All would suffer shame and setback should any one step out of line. So put your best self on display. Mind your p's and q's. *Candlefaces!*

He heard the manager's voice, and carefully moved from his clandestine position behind the curtain. Took an innocent measure of the custodial closet before he stepped inside and closed the door three-quarters of the way. Confined so, he couldn't help but smell his own body sharp and fresh in the rank empty darkness, clean light splaying through the parted door.

Listen:

Here is the piano in semidarkness, plates of light, planks of darkness, black keys and white keys. Here is the boy seated at the piano, a Negro like yourself. The boy center stage before a packed house, and you quietly wedged inside a custodian's closet in clandestine repose—invisible, your stomach rumbles—with the door barely open, one long rectangle of vision, the boy there and you here, remote, far away—another time, another place—your eyes stinging with the effort to see over and around the broom and mop heads and handles, the buckets and pails and brushes and shovels and dustpans and hammers hanging from the walls, to look and cut through everything—one edge of the door frame, one edge of the stage curtain, the piano itself—separating you from the pianist a hundred feet away. Obscured, you think you catch a glimpse of his face behind the cantilevered slant of the raised polished lid. He brings his hands into position and begins the first selection, hands moving, casting a haze over his features, or perhaps it is the light shining down from the massive chandelier above—thousands of burning candles—that spins a web of glare that makes him so hard to see. You are skilled in fine general culture and know how to listen. Shut your eyes to skin and you are forced to admit that the performance is thoroughly in tune with the very best of European art, that the performer you are hearing is one of *them,* no doubt about it, a young virtuoso. He moves his body very little and has an odd way of bringing his lower lip up and letting it fall at short intervals, as a fish works its mouth while breathing. He seems to use only one foot, his right, in pedaling. And when he finishes the piece, he stands up from the stool, turns slightly toward the audience, and takes a quick bow. (Three seconds, four.) Then sits right back down on the stool and begins the next selection.

Ears pressed to air, you, Tabbs, stand for nearly an hour without words and listen, sound rushing in and piling up inside your head in copious abundance. His fingers tap the seconds into melodies, tick the chords into minutes—you stand for another hour—and you have the difficult task of maintaining your discipline, of somehow staying silent and inconspicuous. Dare not even shift your weight from one foot to the other. Aware of a certain pulsing. A tall man, you can cross the stage in five steps, erase time and distance, if you so choose. He pulls you toward him. Lightheaded, weak, you don't care. In this nowhere, you, Tabbs, feel yourself more solidly, no longer worrying about the mundane this or that. Something to behold.

It could have ended there—in a way it did—with the end of the concert. But signs—changing times, the war going badly for the South—flooded in. General Bethune took ill, the nature of his affliction a matter of speculation. *As it is, the slave owner and Confederate provocateur rarely travels, certainly never to set foot on free, Northern soil. Furthermore, he almost never traverses his own Southern climes with his shackled subjugate, young Tom, according that responsibility to the stage manager, Mr. Thomas Warhurst. Whatever his reasons for touring of late, he has apparently done so at considerable risk to his own health.* Tabbs hunkering down at his table with newspaper and a glass of wine as his imagination and hopes caused the air across from him to shape into the boy's hunched-over form, some timid insect with wings folded, lunging toward words, unable to suppress his impulse to higher efforts. Water plopped against the table, one drop, two, and another. A man setting out to war weeps.

For many years the outspoken Southerner's name, General James Neil Bethune, had been mixed up in the controversy over severance, minority rights, and expansion, no phase in that strange life that could not have graced the leaves of a medieval history or romance. From the fiery and impetuous young lieutenant who stole as his bride the daughter of a ruler-elect of the land—the Anglo-Saxon loves a soldier—to the cool and ambitious agitator of the platform and page, the podium and the press, who took upon himself the duty to voice his nation's cause—secession—before it was either a cause or a nation.

In Tabbs's reading of the man, General Bethune was less a product of his country and more an aberrant self-creation, a self-directed and sovereign nation of one.

A month after the concert, Tabbs found himself seated in a sun-bleached office, all nerves. (A Negro maid had led him down a long hall and put him before a desk. Led without speaking a single word. He had stood for a good ten minutes knocking on the door, under a hard hot wind flouncing the awning. The door finally drew open to a second Negro maid, a girl in her teens, blinking him into focus and understanding. Early morning and the girl already looked tired, gazing back at him as if looking through him for a quiet place to rest.) Morning light pouring through louvers, making white walls whiter. A legal text open on the desk, broken at the spine. A (third) Negro maid crawled on hands and knees about the floor, wiping and scrubbing, suds gathering and disappearing. Her pail came up, her rag went in, the water went out, her rag waved hither and thither, lingered to rub and massage, her knees and palms creaked forward or back. Tabbs flicked eyes over the delicacy of her thin legs, small frame and hands. Caught her face revealed under rows of bruises. Then the door flapped open and still another (fourth) Negro maid appeared. A narrow woman—a life spent in tiny kitchens and tinier outhouses—the light (bone?) buttons shining on her dark smock. She waved at him—come this way—without either entering or speaking. He removed his hat from his lap, got up from his seat, and followed her down the unlit hall. He had received a wire from General Bethune's lawyer, a Mr. Geryon, directing him to this location at this hour—no other instructions or information—but no signs so far of either the lawyer or General Bethune. Was General Bethune present? Would he actually appear? Important to make an imposing first impression, for General Bethune would know him without ever having first met him.

She stopped before an open door, pointed—in there—and he entered the room without hesitation, as if it was his right to be there. Whenever he considers it later—*now*—he finds it impossible to recollect what thought guided his first movement, unsure even if he had formulated any thoughts at the moment he entered the room. Remembers some force drawing him inside, not prompting but actually guiding his legs and hands and mouth. The room had no window—was it a pantry or closet?—and hence no source of natural light, but bright illumination radiated out from two tall thick candles burning on a small card table stationed in the center of the room, where General Bethune sat on the far side in a plain chair, staring blankly up at Tabbs. He gave no indication that Tabbs's fearless entry had disturbed or upset him, that it *(he)* was anything out of the ordinary.

He stood up from behind the table and extended his hand in offering. A man of medium height, perhaps slightly taller, in any case far shorter than Tabbs by several inches. And he appeared, despite rumors about ill health, to be quite fit, his body worked to the rhythms of regimented exercise, impressive for a man twenty years Tabbs's senior. A good-looking man on top of that—yes, admit it—with a full head of wavy back-combed hair, dark eyes, and nicely cut features. Tabbs stepped forward, this erasing of distance affording a closer examination that revealed that the General's face was beginning to show signs of (early) aging, the skin cracked in the places you might expect for a man in his midfifties rather than midforties.

Tabbs took the older man's warm hand into his own, and they shook firmly—which hand moved the other?—while General Bethune smiled in greeting. Tabbs forbade any smile to cross his lips, determined to show the other before him the coldness of profound, even deserved, respect. Their hands parted—who was the first to let go?— enough reason for Tabbs to casually take a seat in a second chair positioned before the table without General Bethune's invitation.

The next words out of General Bethune's mouth came in the form of a question. What has been the holdup? Excuse my asking, but why have you, sir, been so long in coming? I've been waiting here a good half hour or more. Completely cordial, expressing no rudeness or displeasure in his asking.

Took Tabbs a minute to respond. Sat gazing through wick-generated patterns bouncing off the table and gliding across General Bethune's face. He said that he actually had arrived several minutes before their appointed time. Then he realized that he had not checked his watch. (Couldn't do so now.) Nor did he know for sure how long he had actually sat waiting in the other room.

I regret to inform you, General Bethune said, that you are sadly mistaken about the hour.

Tabbs detected the scent of tobacco smoke, invisible fumes rushing into his nostrils. (Yes, someone had been smoking.) Calmly and without unnecessary words, he told as if giving a sworn deposition the circumstances leading up to their meeting today at what he knew to be the correct and agreed upon time. He wanted to be forceful and direct. Yet his words sounded cautious to his own ears.

I have listened, General Bethune said. I will henceforth consider the matter settled. You simply misunderstood. Let us leave it at that.

This caught Tabbs off guard. What should he say now? Review the facts again? Voice a complaint? Set this alabaster straight?

I understand you have a matter you need to present before me.

Yes. Tabbs wasted no time in outlining his proposition, making his intentions clear. General Bethune listened to it all with no change of expression.

You must have given this matter considerable pondering, he said.

Yes, I have.

You speak well.

Tabbs looked into the other's confidently upturned face, under its smooth sweep of hair. For whatever reason, everything apparently sat well with him. With this realization, Tabbs's face started to go tight. Difficult to keep his eyes open. Weighted under the fatigue of observation.

Then he saw something: General Bethune shifted slightly in his seat, an odd adjustment. And it occurred to him: something strange in General Bethune's physical makeup, although he couldn't say what exactly, couldn't put his finger on it. General Bethune wasn't (isn't) put together quite right.

But no matter how well you speak, what would possess me to give this matter serious consideration? I see no reason why I should.

Tabbs was pleased with the question, for he took it to mean that General Bethune would actually consider doing the impossible: entering into business with the darker other. Consider it, sir, Tabbs said, for one primary reason. The war may end tomorrow or the day after, next month or next year or two years from now. We know not the hour. But one thing is certain. *You* will lose.

General Bethune didn't flinch. By all indication, you are right, Mr. Gross. If I understand you correctly, you wish to rescue Tom. But Tom is already free.

No, Tabbs says, quite the contrary. This is not a moral matter, but an industrial one. I see an opportunity. More likely than not, other men will soon approach you, perhaps some already have.

Ah, General Bethune said, the early bird.

Yes.

And why shouldn't I wait for one of the latecomers?

I will best any offer.

I already possess money. I own industry. Discretion outweighs all else.

Tabbs contemplated this some, needed to see what was back of it. You would claim to understand better than myself a person of my own blood?

General Bethune did not answer right away. Sat watching Tabbs, his face betraying no emotions. Perhaps you are right, Mr. Gross. Tom might best be served by another Negro. Even so, must that Negro be *you?* What I see before me is merely another boy. He had intentionally or unintentionally spoken with signs of growing dislike—the moment Tabbs had, perhaps at his deepest self, hoped for, an insult that would justify a full venting of his anger.

Your kind always knows what's best for us, Tabbs sneered. I suppose what I require is the blood of experience on my conscience to become the equal of you.

Understand something, Mr. Gross. You are clever and strong, but you will never be the equal of me.

Tabbs idled in his seat, hot air slowly escaping from his lungs.

How could a son best a father? But your equality or lack thereof is not why you are here today. You seek Tom. I would sorely regret sitting in unfair judgment of your youth. For that reason, I need you to make clear to me what logic would justify my putting Tom in your hands. I have no intentions of insulting you, Mr. Gross, but I must express my belief that at your age you can hardly answer for your own self.

Tabbs held back hard air, fists clutched. Could he save himself? All lost in his mind. He decidedly had not wanted anything outrageous to happen, anything to go over the line, the more especially at his provocation, but it had. As I said earlier, sir. I seek opportunity.

You well understand this. As a military man, you are accustomed to leading. And in your present role, retired from military service, you remain one of the leaders of your country, perhaps more now than before.

Yes, General Bethune said. I am a leader. But I am no longer a leader of men but one of thought. That is why I publish.

Indeed, Tabbs said. You would agree that thoughts are easily led?

I would. Still, Mr. Gross, you have failed to fully satisfy my conscience. Surely you have considered the possibility that his own kin should want possession of him?

Yes, sir, I have. And I will back down if they so request. But I ask careful possession of him until such request be put forth.

General Bethune was quiet for a time studying Tabbs carefully. What time frame do you have in mind?

I am willing to pay you one thousand dollars now, sir, at this very moment.

I see. And how did a youth, a man such as yourself, a Negro, come into such a sum?

Respectfully, sir, is my history of concern in this matter?

You are correct. Winged light flew across the General's face. And what about the balance?

My investors will provide me with the balance after you sign and notarize the contract. Then we will expect immediate delivery of Tom into my charge.

General Bethune fidgeted in his seat. So you have investors?

These grimaces brought to light that Tabbs had the white man where he wanted him, that he held the black upper hand. Yes, sir. I can supply you with a list. He needed General Bethune to believe that he was not alone in this venture, as a white man neither respects nor fears a singular Negro.

Perhaps it is more pertinent at this time for you to produce a contract.

Tabbs removed the contract from his jacket pocket and smoothed it flat on the table. (Any who should read it will find it carefully worded.) From the other pocket he removed a stack of banknotes, two leather cords wrapped around either end to keep it neatly formed.

General Bethune did not move or give any indication that he noticed either the money or the document. Only continued to look at Tabbs.

The money is completely sorted, Tabbs said.

I trust that it is, General Bethune said. Still, you understand that my attorney-at-law will need to review the contract. He did not touch the document. Nor did he touch or count the money.

I would expect nothing less. You will find the money is all there.

I shall sign in receipt.

I have no such receipt for you to sign, Tabbs said.

Room flickering, General Bethune looked surprised. You elect no receipt?

No, Tabbs said. He knew full well that the money was a calculated risk, small bait for the larger catch. I know you as a man of your word, however much I might disagree with certain views you express and certain causes you champion.

So you know me. You needn't worry. I will present this contract before my attorney-at-law today and you should expect a speedy reply. May we both wish that this contract meets with Mr. Geryon's exacting standards.

I so wish. Tabbs could barely contain himself, remain seated. I will wire word to my partners that you have accepted the terms of our agreement and plan to subscribe yourself to the contract upon your finding it suitable.

You have my permission to do so. General Bethune extended his hand out to Tabbs. Why did the gesture surprise him? Was it because he had not expected to glide through the negotiations? And certainly not in a single day. Deals are never so easy, unless one party already feels at a disadvantage, defeated. He hooked his hand into the General's—brown to pink—and gave it a firm tug before letting go, leaving the other to feel like the fish lucky enough to yank free of a captor's hook whatever blood and flesh loss.

Found himself moving down the dark hall and encountering on his way to the front door one after another the three (four?) black maids. Seeing the women made him think, How did we get from there to here? Only now had history made it possible for him to give flesh to an abiding logic of thought. The world he could (can) make—you possess a thing only when you build it with your own two hands—if he accepted the challenges and risks. Chance speaking. Hands measuring and shaping.

He threw the door wide and stepped out into the street, expectant, both where he wanted and needed to be. The Tabbs who spoke to General Bethune would soon disappear, the Tabbs-to-be carrying this fact in his mind as if it had always been there, a name he could slip out of anytime he chose to. He fluttered through the city, gaze rising and dipping, catching and losing a hundred faces.

A week later, one maid let him through a door, another led him in darkness halfway down a long hall, and a third took him the rest of the way. She turned (pointed?)—*in there*—and she was gone, returning—to light?—down the same blind corridor whose dark length would understandably dissuade most. Everyone quiet and still and looking up at him from their respective places at the table, as if caught off guard. He managed to stumble forward into an empty chair at the table and sat down before he was invited to do so. Taking the liberty, liberties. Carrying the room. This pretense at certainty and confidence mostly for himself, caught off guard too—admit this much—forgetting for a minute what had brought him here.

Mr. Gross.

General Bethune was speaking. He sat opposite Tabbs on the other side of the table, leaning slightly to one side as if favoring a damaged limb. I'm glad that you could join us. Allow me to offer you a refreshment. What will you have? Tea? Coffee? Lemon water? General

Bethune lifted one hand from the table and raised it to his side, like one about to take an oath.

Took Tabbs a second to realize that his other was prepared to summon a servant into action. For the first time he noticed a black woman standing in a far corner of the room, a good thirty feet away, as if caught in the distance of another life. She was fashionably clothed in a black dress with maline cuffs and trim, her torso wrapped in a shawl of yellow and red challis. Her face spiteful and impudent, like something trained and caged, ready to pounce upon him should she be so commanded. Then again, perhaps he was judging her appearance, reading her looks, incorrectly.

Thank you for your kind offer, Tabbs said. I respectfully decline. I am not in need.

Should we proceed then? General Bethune returned his hand to the table. Tabbs was already growing tired of seeing him, of hearing his voice. Couldn't wait to be done with it all. Kindly allow me to introduce you to the other gentlemen you see before you. The man seated beside him he introduced—he gestured—as Dr. Hollister, a medical specialist who guarded over Tom's health. Seated next to him—General Bethune gestured—was, at last, Mr. Geryon, General Bethune's *attorney-at-law*. (That peculiar phrase.) The two men seated on Tabbs's side of the table: Mr. Warhurst, Tom's stage manager, a well-dressed man with black distant eyes who took the trouble to smile at Tabbs—Tabbs in midlumbering with his hat, hidden hands (beneath the table) straightening it, then moving it to his other knee, crushing it—and a curious-looking man of the cloth—*our pastor,* General Bethune called him—Reverend H. D. Frye. Blunt and inexpressive, he appeared to be still in his teens, possibly younger. His clothes fit him poorly, oversized, his body a small concern among the folds. All the men in the room received Tabbs nicely enough. After this initial introduction, General Bethune and Mr. Geryon dominated the talking, words upon words, Warhurst and the two men seated alongside Tabbs never a single utterance, Tabbs continually aware of the silent weight of their watching, the gaze of one (Warhurst) unreadable, that of another (Dr. Hollister) curious, and that of the last (Reverend Frye) resentful. Of course, General Bethune did not introduce the woman, presumably his servant or the servant of one of the other white men. Tabbs was prompted to ask—*And who is she?* or *Madame, your name would be?*—but he couldn't risk making a mistake. Intent on acting in concert with what he believed might least offend.

Excuse me for asking, Mr. Gross, General Bethune said. Might you have some idea how much longer we must be detained? I assume your legal counsel will arrive shortly.

My attorney will not be joining us today, Tabbs said.

General Bethune peered into Tabbs's eyes defiantly, a look that also seemed to hold some strange uneasiness.

Is all in order? Mr. Geryon asked. Today, we truly wish to arrive at terms agreeable to all involved if so possible.

I have already submitted the contract for your review, Tabbs said. I am perfectly capable of attending to any required modifications.

His words silenced both General Bethune and the lawyer, the men at once transparent (stunned) and impossible to entirely see through, completely still, for a time, as if unable to move. Then Mr. Geryon spoke. Even if that is the case, Mr. Gross, is there some reason why your esquire cannot be present today? In your favor, we can adjourn until a later date.

My attorney believes me perfectly and fully capable of handling any negotiation.

Mr. Gross, certainly you are aware that—

Let us proceed, General Bethune said, leaning forward on the table, hands cupped.

I have carefully reviewed your contract and weighed its fairness, the lawyer said. I have so counseled my party, General Bethune, to subscribe, pending your willingness to sign an agreement I have drawn up. The lawyer's hand disappeared under the table, resurfaced with a leather satchel, which the lawyer promptly laid flat on the table and opened, pulling a sheaf of papers, several pages thick, from inside. The lawyer slid—how small his hands seemed bringing the words, whatever they were—the bundle toward Tabbs, until letters pushed into sight, a document titled "bill-of-sale agreement."

Mr. Gross, the lawyer said, his voice high and tight, we see the need for two substantially similar, if not exact, versions of a contract, *your* contract, so that the exchange will be legally binding in both nations.

Tabbs considered this some.

Shall we review it together?

Yes, Tabbs said. Keeping the bottom edge touching the table, he took up the bundle and inclined it, propped for reading.

The lawyer took up a second copy of the contract positioned on top of his leather satchel, fit his bifocals onto his face, and with extreme readiness began to read it aloud, paraphrasing clauses where he felt the legal language was difficult, pointing to certain lines with his fingers as if to something too difficult (hidden) to see. Granted, perhaps Tabbs didn't understand all of what was written there, a foreign language, Greek to his skin, but he made the effort, fully listening and taking in the lawyer's abbreviations and clarifications point by point, seeking to understand it here in the moment—no time later—checking that understanding for validity, pursuing further to see if this validity served him, then persuading himself to accept it or reject it—well, in the end, he rejected nothing—before he privately arrived at a final decision to embrace the proposed terms.

So this is what we ask, Mr. Gross, the lawyer said. I hope I have been sufficiently clear.

Yes, Tabbs said.

We can give some time alone for a second reviewing.

That won't be necessary, Tabbs said. I am prepared to sign. He feared nothing. *I feared nothing.* Some weeks later he would realize that he should have. *I should have.*

His words hummed in white silence above their heads. With all the eyes in the room turned on him—*all eyes on me*—he felt in himself a complete and triumphant assurance. He needed more and he would find it here, right in this room, among these men. With no hesitation, only fresh clean movement—he will inhabit the free spaces—he removed a precounted wad of crisp banknotes and counted out two thousand dollars in notes of large denomination on the table, then with one edge of his hand slid croupier-like the stack of notes across the table to General Bethune. No one moved. No one said anything. Then a sudden shift of delicate forms (skin, paper, leather, and other solids): the lawyer, moving, speaking.

Now, if you gentlemen would be good enough to sign. General Bethune, it is only right that you should subscribe yourself first. The lawyer repositioned the stack of banknotes just enough to make room for the contract and the bill of sale, then offered General Bethune a fine-bladed pen. General Bethune took the pen, signed one (Tabbs's) and its duplicate then signed the other (his) and its duplicate. Joy caged in his throat, Tabbs could hardly believe what he saw. (He paused to breathe.) It was as he wanted it.

And now you, Mr. Gross.

Tabbs accepted the pen and signed all four documents as quickly as he could. Then he looked up. The banknotes remained on the table.

Congratulations to you both, gentlemen.

General Bethune extended his hand out to Tabbs across the table. Tabbs accepted it—a touch he would decline—with his own, and they shook, as men should, but they did not simply shake once or twice and cease. General Bethune continued to move Tabbs's hand—a fish trying to free itself, no luck this time—with his firm fearless grip, strong bones, pressing so hard that Tabbs felt the blood drain from his fingertips. Only then did he let go, release the other.

One difficulty remains, the lawyer said. That of settling on a pattern and date for the transfer of Tom into your custody, Mr. Gross.

Allow me to put forth a schedule, General Bethune said. He spoke for ten minutes without pause, providing a thorough explanation for why he would need a full week to hand over Tom—Tom must finish out his schedule; the professionals (Warhurst, Dr. Hollister, Reverend Frye) will need time to elucidate it all to the boy; the boy should be granted a final gathering with his kin—even as Tom was only a short distance, a few minutes away, presently in town for a concert. Tabbs took this verbiage to be a measure of the General's own seriousness. Or so he felt he must (wanted to, did) interpret it. (How else understand it?) Then too, the General's facts appeared reasonable. Perhaps General Bethune was a better man than Tabbs thought, better than himself in many ways.

One week from today, here at my office, and shall we say at this very same hour? the lawyer asked. Mr. Gross, are you in agreement with such designation as the appointed date?

I am, Tabbs said.

We fend accord.

Should we drink a toast? General Bethune asked.

Yes.

General Bethune nodded at the servant standing in the corner, who hurried over to a small cupboard at the opposite back corner of the room, her scarf zipping behind her like a black flag. She lifted up a silver tray holding a crystal decanter and several crystal glasses, and carried the tray over to the table. With one hand steadily holding the tray, she proceeded to pour and set down before each man a glass of whiskey, working her way around the table from General Bethune to Tabbs. General Bethune raised his glass, the other men following his lead, and all drank a toast.

The liquor warmed and brightened Tabbs like a light that wouldn't stop going through him.

I hope you are pleased, Mr. Gross.

Yes, sir.

Just like that, only the two of them, Tabbs and the General, were in the room, a bare exchange, the other men invisible even as they were physically present.

I hope I have not disappointed you, General Bethune said, a man in mourning fumbling for words. At first I suffered resentment. However, I quickly realized that I should have no reason to be upset with you, for you are only performing your perceived duty to that world which you believe in and that you believe to be true. I fully understand your motives. Why then is it I feel the lesser man in this transaction?

Tabbs knows now but did not know then the duplicitous courtesy with which General Bethune was speaking to him. In his vanity, he had lost sight of danger, the trap already set.

Sir, Tabbs said, if anyone is the lesser, it is me. Why not say it, throw the General a bone or two? Tabbs had much ahead. What more could the General ask for, require? He should count his blessings, reaping gain for all these years to the benefit of no one—it helped no one—other than himself. Tabbs powerless to correct this man's past even if he wanted to. When he quits the room the lights will gutter out. From now on the world will remember General James Neil Bethune as a man who could have but did not and will come to know Tabbs Gross as a man of vision and will who did.

On the appointed day, he rushed out into the street, the city solid and real about him, daylight twisting in his eyes. Hurrying to meet the moment when he would board a ferry and cross waters to Tom. With Tom—*Blind Tom*—his story would (will) begin in earnest.

Tom, why do you play Bach?

I prefer to live by that which I know.

In only a few short hours. Hurrying to meet that moment—I will be early, count on it—because they had kept him waiting, the promised delivery deferred, pushed back until today. Two days since he had answered a caller at his door, opened it—the bolt loud, the hinges louder—to find the lawyer, Mr. Geryon, standing there leather satchel in hand. Stunned at this unexpected arrival, all he could do to exchange the most obligatory greetings and gestures. The lawyer had

stepped inside after waiting patiently for Tabbs (stunned) to make
the offer, removed his hat, and sat himself in the first seat he came
upon, then proceeded to remove a sealed envelope from his satchel
and hand it to Tabbs, who took it, confused, his frame of mind all the
worse because he was still thinking about, pondering, certain facts
and speculations he had just been reading about in the newspaper.
Tom—*across the river*—had finished his extended run at the town hall.
Naturally, the journal had given high marks to Tom's closing recital
at town hall—the Negro press can't hymn his praises enough—but it
also issued more reports (rumors) about a continuing and steady decline in General Bethune's physical well-being and the vanquishing of
his professional and financial holdings, the cause for the latter: every
dollar earned from both the General's press and Tom's concerts and
publications went into the Confederate war chest. Tabbs had already
grown numb to such pronouncements. What truly caught his interest
was the photograph accompanying the story. Tom seated on a stool at
his piano with the General posed behind him, one hand in paternal
rest on the boy's shoulder. In the photograph General Bethune did not
come across as a man on his last leg, a man who was suffering daily
ruin and facing an early grave. He still possessed that big-eyed look
of desire, hunger, and expectation that Tabbs recollected from their
two meetings. When had they sat for the photograph? How recently?

Hands in flight, the lawyer took it upon himself to explain the
letter, reciting it word by word, and inserting comments and clarifications and meaningful pauses as he saw fit. General Bethune seeks
an additional two days and a small change of venue for the transfer.
Tabbs sat gazing at the lawyer, unable to speak for a time. As much
as he tried to avoid wrongful thoughts, his first inclination was to
reject the request out of sheer defiance, tit for tat. Then he thought he
should practice caution, the sooner to get on, two days part and par-
cel of his transformation, of making anew. Clearly General Bethune
had his own fears. Otherwise why had he elected to conduct private
business in a public space?

Despite the early start, he arrived at the meeting place thirty minutes late for reasons that he was hard put to explain, but that he now believes were a foreboding of bad things to come. The restaurant was empty as far as he could tell. He took a seat at a table offering an unobstructed view of the door, a Negro waiter motionless at his dais, looking at Tabbs but pretending not to. Tabbs felt safer in the open air of the street. Not for anything did he want to be surprised. The restaurant was a continuous row of windows on three sides, glass glinting out onto impressive views of the town, beach, and river. Easy looking out, easy looking in. A glass crib thrust into sight. Came the thought that he was positioned perfectly for a sharpshooter's bullet.

He checked his watch. The time was all wrong. Surely his watch was malfunctioning. He returned it to his pocket. But the clock fixed to the wall behind the waiter (watching) confirmed the hour. And no sign of General Bethune. Had he come and gone?

Mr. Geryon walked in, leather satchel swinging at his side. The waiter rushed forward to greet him, but the lawyer brushed past him, walked over to the table where Tabbs sat—the waiter backed away, as if from contagion, scurried return to his dais—and, without a word, seated himself on the other side, quietly positioning his worn satchel on the immaculate white cloth covering the table, draped over the sides.

Mr. Gross, he said. You are not the man you say you are. His face down-tilted toward the satchel, avoiding Tabbs's eyes. Speaking words into leather. You will be arrested.

What the lawyer said, no mistaking it. Tabbs could hardly keep his eyes open. The moment demanded some kind of gesture, but what could he do with his body?

No, you don't want to go to jail. The lawyer shot Tabbs a glance, flickering his fingers irritably against the table. He opened his satchel and pulled from it a crisp stack of banknotes, held together with Tabbs's distinctive leather ties at both ends. You have violated our trust, he said, speaking to the leather again, and in so doing have annulled all contractual claims. He placed the bound notes before Tabbs. Here is a sum total of one thousand dollars, your original deposit, plus the cost of rail passage.

Tabbs out on a limb, past words.

The balance of your monies will remain in our possession, pending calculation of penalties, investigative costs, and matters of forfeiture.

The lawyer said nothing else. Enough said. Simply closed his briefcase and departed. Some time before Tabbs could do the same. See his startled angle of retreat from the restaurant, from the hotel, earth streaming away under his feet, a thick swarm of indistinct sounds pursuing him.

Some of what Tabbs did in his life for the next few days after that meeting is lost to him now. What he sees is himself leaning back into the darkness of a hallway and patiently waiting outside a receiving room after one of Tom's concerts, listening to the invisible chatter of voices inside the room. Emboldened, he was intent on confronting General Bethune. How had he arrived at that decision in the face of the General's threats of arrest and imprisonment? Perhaps his presence there was the sum total of his intelligence, his shrewdness, his astuteness, his courage, a man daunted by nothing. Perhaps it was precisely the time for gallant gestures. One after another the supplicants began to leave the room. Counting, Tabbs entered the room only after the last had exited.

General Bethune looked up from the table where he was seated and saw Tabbs standing, contained in a pocket of light, his appearance now, there, no different in purpose from the previous one only days before. Went rigid with surprise, unbelief. He was trapped. What is this man, this Tabbs Gross, not capable of?

Tabbs took a seat at the table within touching distance of his adversary. The General gave him a look of mild approach, then he and the General glared at each other across the silence.

I will never cease in knowing you, General Bethune said. Your history increases each day. You have murdered men. You have pandered women. You have befouled children.

From far away the thunder of a noisy sonata reached Tabbs: Tom's encore. Feelings are ridiculous in such moments. He must not speak. Would he really be foolish enough to report his most private feelings to a white man?

General Bethune pushed both hands into his pockets, pulled free two fistfuls of banknotes. Tossed the crumpled notes onto the table, patted his pockets for more. Annoyed, as if cornered into donating charity.

Tabbs looked at the banknotes, no intention of picking them up, cast-off leprous skin. Understanding the other's restraint, General Bethune swept the notes off the table and right into Tabbs's lap. Already Tabbs knew: he would never see the General again. He never has.

For weeks after he did not leave his house, welcoming no callers—*Ruggles, Ruggles*—in his increasing dismay, forgetful of the most ordinary matters, eating (strings of onions, loaves of bread), bathing, cleaning his teeth, washing and combing his hair, shaving, passing urine, moving his bowels, instinct equating, mind skipping off, sunk in his memories of that terrible moment, playing scenes, what he could have said, what he could have done. Signs, gifts, wonders. The trick in the hand. From dawn to rocking close of day. Thinking small, thinking big, he greeted each morning with many tongues. *What must I do to be saved?* Sickness when there was nothing else. Sickness that made him (feel) capable of anything. (What might strong hands do?)

So one day, once he had retrieved enough of himself, he packed his bags—*Fill up your horn with oil and be on your way*—put on good clothes to go out into the street, and set out—he served notice to no one, *Ruggles, Ruggles*—following the Blind Tom Exhibition from town to town—maps make the getting there look easy—engagement to engagement, one month, then the next through the raucous scrambled world of dark streets dark rivers dark halls. Tunnels, blackness he would (will) never come out of. Iron wheels pulling in and iron wheels pulling out. The muffled strain. The jarring chord. The running smoke and heat. The whoosh and hissing. The melting in his legs. The hot puddle between his thighs. The black ink flying at angles across paper. Advertisements. Certificates of purchase. Bills of sale. A surfeit of work. The blood-stained gate. Beat by the hammer. Beat by the fist. Prodded and pushed. Nothing had the color he would expect. Always in pursuit but sometimes falling behind schedule or, worse, losing the trail altogether until he chanced upon another lead. Knocking on a door and stepping through that door held open for him. Checking in. Checking out. Stale and alone in a country busted apart. Not another summer. Please, not another fall. Then the Union instituted a war lottery (draft) and the city exploded, fire surging like a red sea, smoke in the wide sky and hot things going up and coming down that Tabbs, trailing Tom (always, because the boy was all that mattered to him), could see in his imaginings from a thousand miles away. The planters down South driven in, underground, and Tom and Warhurst and the Bethunes dropped from public view. What now? Knew he must set out again—comfort in motion, hope—but to where, what the port of call? How would he fish up Tom out of a deep dark unknown?

For the next three years (almost), he lived with his anxious ear pushed up against the world, traveled—no end to it—from one city to another across the North tracking any mention of Blind Tom—Tabbs time and again clutching his ever-hopeful ticket of passage—some supposed sighting of him here, some supposed recital he was to give there. Rumor, all rumor. His dream deferred. Biding time until the war ended.

※ ※ ※

And so it was that the war ended, and he found himself deep in the enemy's country, determined to unearth Tom. See him thus: exhausted and bewildered, he walked right into the hotel restaurant without taking the time to wash up first and settled on a table. Sat right down, knotted his napkin around his neck, took up utensils crafted from pure silver, and waited, the rattle of a hungry body in a room that smelled of salted cooking grease. Little astonishments going off all over the restaurant. What remarkable things these chefs could do with cowpeas, peanuts, greens, rice, cabbage, and potatoes, Tabbs partial to the food here—rib eye, roast, tenderloin—taking all of his meals here each day—*You shall eat the fruits of this world*—morning, noon, and night, although to sit down to a meal with the other guests was to dissemble, Tabbs dining dumbly, rolling wine in his mouth, even when the guests, all men, all alabasters, all Northerners, would sit down at his table and try to make small talk, engage him in conversation above the soft clattering of plates, the scratching of silverware on porcelain, and the clinking of glasses, trying to gain a sense of Tabbs's feelings about the war and the reconstruction of the South, taking his hand in greeting, the hard power of their granite grips crushing his skin.

Tabbs sat thinking into the day, into the moment.

Why would he do this to me?

Because he can, Ruggles said. Because you're a nigger.

He made up his mind to add that to the account he was determined to settle with the General, a promise that surfaced spontaneously into consciousness while he sat over his dinner engineering the fried fish (whole) on his plate with knife and fork.

Get yo grits right.

He looked up from his plate and saw Mrs. Birdoff frowning instructions, her sculpted eyebrows arched and sharp like Oriental temples, each eyelash black and hard and separate.

You got to mix em.

He shoveled his fork into the pool of grits on his plate and performed some vigorous stirring.

Mrs. Birdoff looked at him for a long time without a word, no movement in her eyes. You ain't never ate none befo. I can see that. Her surprise uncovered a set of fine white teeth.

Just what does she want him to mix?

You know what you eatin?

Fish, he said.

Crappie, she said.

He looked at her.

You just gon and eat. Don't worry bout how it sound.

You have to put the worm on the hook, Ruggles said. Go ahead. Hook it through. Why am I telling you twice?

It's greasy.

Get it between your fingers.

I don't think I can touch it good.

You want me to do it? Is that what you're telling me? You want me to do it?

Mrs. Birdoff gave him a wide sweep of the hand, a blessing. Bless the hominy, bless the crappie, bless the greens, bless the beans, bless the sack, and bless whatever else I've forgotten. She left, gathering her deliberate walk about her as she went.

Several hours later, he found himself entrenched along the perimeter of General Bethune's estate. Light flowed in a smooth reflection that outlined the shadow of the trees whose branches and leaves closed rank around him. Hid him. He could watch the house from here, so he did, watched and waited. No way he would (could) fully abide by Coffin's restrictions. *Keep to the hotel, Mr. Gross. Stay away from Hundred Gates.* Let Coffin do his part. As for himself, he could submit and observe, decide and execute, all at the same time, torn away from the usual incongruous questioning, his mind free, clear, and quick. He viewed the General's house as the empty shape of a heaven he coveted and had been promised, that he longed to enter once and for all. Nothing protecting it, only this single iron gate that opened at his touch, no fence. He walked right through the garden all the way to the porch without encountering another soul. Squinted in at the window, trying to see beyond morning glare and his own reflection shiny on the glass pane.

A Negress appeared in the doorway. You again, she said. I already told you. He ain't here.

She frowned. Muttered under her breath. Should he stay or go? Where is he?

We livin here now.

When did he leave?

Now she greeted him like any caller. She offered him a cup of tea—she did not say hot or cold—as if she knew that he was (is) a tea drinker. Then he understood: she was trying to trick him into revealing his true nature, man or ghost.

And you're sure he's not here? These planters' mansions have all sorts of box rooms, hidden passages, and unexpected staircases. So he had heard.

Come see for yoself.

He stepped through the doorway. Looked once or twice, here and there.

I got to get back to my work. She looked at Tabbs sideways.

Where did he go?

I ain't ask him.

It fell to Tabbs to guess. (Light suddenly more clear.) Now he was sure—uncertain before—that she had been the woman present at the meeting with General Bethune years earlier, standing quietly in the corner, wearing a black dress with maline trim. (What is she wearing today?)

He sold the house.

Don't you see us livin here? Ain't no coming back.

She seemed to be out of breath, hauling pots, washing dishes, wringing laundry.

He left nothing behind.

Nothing, she said.

She has turned her back on servitude. Elevated herself in the world. He could enforce his presence. Speak to her openly and honestly. She would embrace him instead of exclude, absolve instead of condemn.

What you see? she said.

A perfect translucent silence fell over the house. He felt oddly at home. (The piano in the hall.) He would like to move but couldn't. Didn't know whether it was his mind not speaking loudly enough to his limbs or whether these limbs had grown treacherously stiff, or something else, another foreign force making him stay put.

Did he leave anything for me? A letter? A message?

I'm sposed to give you this, she said.

What?

She shut the door in his face.

Back at the hotel, he heard music coming from somewhere on an upper floor—no, from somewhere downstairs, in the parlor, filling every room and corner with song, disembodied scales and tones quite like nothing he had heard before. Drawn in, squeezing into bodies and furniture populated with dead bottles no one had bothered to remove.

He saw a face that bore a connection to him, Dr. Hollister standing by the fireplace on the other side of the room, his head bent with listening. The blunt impact of the man. Feeling flowed in. The Doctor saw Tabbs but did not appear in the least bit surprised. Tabbs saw the Doctor's mouth move, but the words were lost on him. The Doctor came slowly over with long sad strides—moving to the music perhaps? Tabbs couldn't say.

He greeted Tabbs like an old acquaintance, shaking hands with him in a friendly way. So you remember me? I ain't think you would. Turned back to the music. You ever heard anything that good?

The musicians were seated in the layered shadows of Mrs. Birdoff's ruffles and skirts, Mrs. Birdoff standing wide behind them, above them, like a shady tree. She looked across at Tabbs and Dr. Hollister, her eyes as surprised as Tabbs's. Looked away.

We'll be all alone in the garden, Dr. Hollister said.

We can stay right here, Tabbs said. He didn't look at the Doctor, acted as if he could not be thinking about anything in the world, his thoughts sliding across the strings of a violin, a banjo plucked and pulled.

So you stay. But you got to leave sometime.

The words sinking beneath the music.

Another chord. Another exchange between the instruments. But the Doctor wasn't talking, talking that talk. Tabbs saw some of the men (listening, dancing) pull their faces from the music to watch the Doctor leave the room, nodding and smiling, all courtesy and respect. Tabbs followed. What else could he do, having resigned himself to capture, a spy in the enemy's country, no matter who had won the war, who was in charge. Six beats behind the Doctor, he felt a renewal of everything he could suffer from ugliness and stupidity.

They struck out to the garden and followed a solitary side path speckled with blue moonlight, walking neither fast nor slow, without hurry or hesitation, space between their bodies, Tabbs put on edge.

Dr. Hollister curved his face back to hook a glance at Tabbs. You look like a man who wants to run.

Maybe I should.

That's why I came. The General and I, we're worried about you.

I should thank you.

My agreeable duty. We want you safe.

Tricks upon tricks, Tabbs said, speaking to the back of the Doctor's head. He was on performance, standing on his head and hands, turning somersaults. You even look like the General.

A man can't change what he is. He is my cognate.

The night hummed with the rasping sounds of insects. Everywhere in the garden, naked marble women glowed white from under the foliage. What was one supposed to feel here? *Their eyes are upon me, and I am not.*

But you know more about him than I do. So there ain't nothing I can give you. He looked back at Tabbs, showing his strong white teeth.

Sooner quiet than say too much, Tabbs said nothing, a silence that did not reside on the surface of his lips but in the mouth. The world is always half someone else's, never one's own, never Tabbs's. He wished he possessed his own private language that could represent him speak him be him.

You talkin bout how I look. I don't see him walking here with you. Why don't you go ask him for it? Go on out there to Hundred Gates, if you ain't already been.

(The wrought iron gate.) (The carefully arranged grounds with fine shrubs and vines and graveled walks bordered with flowers.) (The waveless sheet of the pond.) (The marble fireplace inside the great hall.)

I'm all you got.

He continued to follow the Doctor, the sweep of hair, the hunch of shoulders, the squat wall of back, nothing of the Doctor's legs visible in the dark, only this floating faceless torso.

Certain things a man ain't gon give up, can't give up, even if that thing be his owning the flesh of another man. I absolve myself of such claims. When all this mess started I set mine loose, every one of them, one hundred and twenty-four mouths that I gave food, upkeep, clothing, a roof and walls, year after year, settling their vexations and celebrations and all matters in between. They belong to themselves now. And where are they? Roaming about, confused, hungry, dead.

I just want the boy.

So does he.

What?

They went into the grass, no longer solid path beneath his feet but soft earth, his shoes pressing down with each step. Any time now, he would sink, disappear, sucked in.

You mean to tell me you ain't figured that out by now? He ain't got him.

Tabbs said nothing, bursts of facts illuminating the night with the fireflies. Some way off he could see Mrs. Birdoff and her help heaping crates into a cellar.

Ruggles: a long pull on a fish hooked deep. Raising the fish from water, still alive (thrashing) at the end of the hook. What about the worm?

Who did you think I was talking about? *Thomas.*

He wanted to stop walking but couldn't.

Do you know where the boy is?

What I know don't matter. Go bargain with his mother. You can bargain with her. She has a right to what's hers.

I already spoke to her.

Speak to her again, Dr. Hollister said.

The Doctor stopped walking and turned to face Tabbs, Tabbs almost stumbling into him. He watched Tabbs for a moment, the edges of his mouth working. Maybe I got you wrong.

Bearing no grudge and hardly any sorrow, Tabbs breathed in the smell of the Doctor's cologne. He had all he needed, a chance to undo what had (has) been done, a possibility, plan of action that could not have suited him better if he had designed it himself.

Take them in there, Tabbs said.

Master boss, President Lincoln said, we can do it right here. Right here in front of her so she can see.

President Lincoln didn't move, lingered staring at the Bethune daughters in one long unbroken moment, his rifle at his chest, the barrel close to his nose as if he were sniffing it. (Tabbs disliked the driver's casual handling of the rifle, but what could he say?) The Bethune daughters remained standing where they were, each girl with a distinct look of terror on her face, each girl planted in a cone-shaped dress, their slim torsos tapering off to constrictive bonnets, slim nothings, three long-stemmed flowers. And Tom's mother with garments in kind, similar but apart, her face placid, undisturbed, riding above the driver's words.

Just take them in the other room.

You ain't got to worry. Only us here. Ain't nobody gon know. President Lincoln saying what he is, what he wants.

Tabbs needed to talk, needed to penetrate the driver's focus, keep his hands from doing the thinking. I just need to talk to her. Nothing else. He said it without panic or force, calm, trying to bring the driver back to himself.

So you gon and talk while I take care of this.

I need them.

The driver paused in his offer to look at Tabbs. You ain't got to do it. Not nwan one. I'll do it. I'll do it all.

I don't need you to do my work. Tabbs tried to sound capable, tried to create the picture that what had drawn them together was something greater than money, the dollar he had given in exchange for the driver's services, the dollar he might give tomorrow.

But you gon stop me? Why? They ain't nothing but woogies.

I know what they are.

Then you know. All them years, master boss. The driver looking at the daughters again, his eyes wet, moving. All the hurt these woogies put on me, years they put on me, put me through.

But I need to talk to them. How will I talk to them? The dead can't talk.

Okay, master boss. I ain't gon get in yo way. You go on and talk. Talk. Then just say the word.

Tabbs was relieved. Lucky him. He hadn't the will to talk sense to the driver. The driver nodded a command, and the daughters herded into the other room, the white buttons on their shoes moving under the smooth expanse of their skirts, their hands linked like paper dolls, President Lincoln behind them, the long barrel of his rifle fisted in his right hand like a walking stick. He firmly shut the door.

Tabbs heard himself say to her, He won't hurt them.

The woman watched him sternly.

But I need to ask you something and I need you to tell me the truth.

I know some truth.

Tabbs looked into her face for some time. Miss Bethune—

Wiggins, she said. Greene Wiggins. With the *e*. That's who I be.

He wondered by master or marriage? The Wiggins. The *e*. Her words said to him, I'm other, I'm not a Bethune.

Miss Wiggins—

You looking for him, Thomas.

I'm looking for your son.

Thomas.

You are free. You both are.

Proclaimed, she said. Proclaimed.

He thought about it. The Bethunes cannot stand in the way of maternal bond. So why are you here? He has no hold on you.

He gave me the girls. I got them to tend to.

They are his daughters, not yours.

I know what's mine. All mine gone, she said. Niggers always gon have cause to call on a woogie. Ain't nothing come from us, and ain't nothing gon end with us.

What have they done with your son? Where are they keeping him?

He livin up north with that Yankee woman, the one who marry Massa Sharpe. Her words rose to the ceiling, stayed put for a few breaths before they started their descent, settled on his face and shoulders. *Our child you have returned to us. My child you have returned home.*

All this time, Tabbs said. All this time. He shook his head. He been right there in my face. In the city. Back at home. He laughed. He shook his head some more.

She asked, How did you let yourself get mixed up with General Toon? I never known him to have no dealings with our kind. With niggers.

Gold and Rose
(1868–1869)

"My song will stand."

I'LL BRING HIM BACK TO THE HOME TOMORROW, TABBS SAYS. He is far, far away, the floor between him and Ruggles like a shimmering lake of sunlight. He doesn't know what work he will do once he leaves the island. Only this: he has settled this matter of Tom once and for all. After all else, now the boy himself is the great impediment to his aim, Tom the final impasse that can't be moved. No remedy to his loss. The sooner he's done with the boy, the better. Anything but surrender to Edgemere. Anything but getting stuck here. Once he's gone, the island will shrink to a tarnished coin that he might lift and carry in his pocket.

He expects Ruggles to speak but he doesn't. Because Ruggles's response is silence, he assumes Ruggles is waiting to hear more. You might as well send for her, Tabbs says. Send for anybody you like. Damn him. Damn her. The boy can stay here and give concerts to piss-poor orphans.

How did this all start?

I'm losing track of things.

Has he asked for her?

He hasn't asked for her, Tabbs says. He hasn't asked for a goddamn thing.

Ruggles listens, sitting not quite straight in his chair, his back to a window, sits quietly, watching Tabbs, Tabbs trying to put a name to the look on Ruggles's face.

Happy now? You got what you wanted.

Ruggles continues to look at Tabbs.

I never had a chance, Tabbs says. His face falls. Something not right about both of them. Maybe he's what they always said he is, an idiot. And she ain't much better. Who knows? Maybe we're just not like them. We've been free from the start. He leaves in what is essential, takes out what is not.

You and I, homeskillet, we ain't like nobody. Never have been. Never will be.

That's some comfort, Ruggles. Some comfort.

They say nothing for a time. Then:

Well, I should give you a fitting good-bye.

Or bury me.

You ain't ready for that. You got some years ahead.

Tabbs draws his breath but says nothing.

You ain't got to go back among them.

Tabbs forces himself to look directly at Ruggles. I can't stay here.

You want to go back. You still seeking their approval, their praise.

I hate them as much as you do. They use us any way they like then throw us away.

Then why go?

You expect me to stay here, on this island filled with donkey shit?

Take some time. Get yo head right.

What's to think about? I tried to give her something. He got what he wanted and left nothing for me.

And what did you get her to give up to come here?

I brought her here.

A husband.

She had nothing.

Children.

Ruggles—

Siblings.

I took nothing from her. I gave her back what the Bethunes took away, her son. And look how they repay me. I'm the only one losing here.

You paid what she couldn't.

Somewhere beyond his consciousness, his thoughts are racing, unformed, disconnected. He trusts these surroundings. He can relax in the midst of this conversation, this running series of ruminations, let his eyes close and give in to his tiredness, his body unbearably heavy, drained. Needs to close his eyes, try to collect himself. Dissolving, parts of him drifting away. Haven't they discussed all this before? What's being remembered, confirmed, denied?

Him secure in his own awareness, Ruggles asking him to open out to accept this place.

Tabbs!

He looks at Ruggles, tired of everything.

You sitting there feeling sorry for yoself, thinking yo luck ran out. You can't even see what's happened. He put one over on you. He ensnared you. The boy was the bait. You couldn't resist.

But I was the one. He didn't know me. I made the offer. Drew up the contract. Me, Ruggles, me.

Don't matter. He had you.

Why would he go through the trouble? For what? Just to get my money?

They never need reasons, Ruggles says. Ain't you figured that out by now?

Ruggles was like that. Everything he said was a certainty in his mind, and he expected you to see it that way too.

We can't be among them.

So you think this is what the boy deserves, Edgemere?

I ain't say that, Ruggles says. Don't matter what he deserve. Nothing you can do about that now.

Tell me something I don't know.

But the boy ain't got to be the end.

Tell me. Tabbs saying anything rather than sit in ungracious silence.

Forget all that. Bygones.

Forget? Damn, Ruggles. What's happened to you? They took everything from you, everything you had, everything you worked for.

None of that was mine anyway. I only thought it was. But them alabasters had claim to it. All of it. You can't be king in somebody else's castle. No way they gon let that happen.

Well, Ruggles. You go on and be king.

I'm glad they took it.

Wish I could say the same.

Your three thousand. Ruggles says it with slight disgust, his lips working against the words.

You don't know what it cost me.

Take them into the other room.

Ruggles gives him a strange look of anger. And you don't know what it cost me, living among them.

Maybe I don't, but one way or the other you'll keep sitting there flapping your mouth about it.

Ruggles snaps to his feet like a fish yanked from water. He unbuttons his trousers.

So, what, you're going to piss on me now?

Ruggles lets his trousers drop to his ankles, a cloth puddle. Tabbs is thinking, Did they take that from him?

Ruggles raises his shirt ends to reveal his shaved groin, his long even thighs. To Tabbs's eyes, the sight is a relief. Go on, Ruggles says. Get you an eyeful. See?

Tabbs neither confirms nor denies. But he can plainly see that Ruggles's deformed leg is deformed no longer. How could this be?

Take your measure, so there's no doubt.

What?

Measure them. Measure each and see if they match. You can't dispute numbers.

I ain't got to do that. Pull your pants up.

You sure?

Ruggles.

Ruggles secures his trousers in place. Resumes his seat.

You really think you need to prove that to me?

Seem like I do.

He finds it impossible to answer. Without words. *I must not surrender to Edgemere.*

Wire told me that it was a sign I should give myself over to the church. That the Almighty had been good enough to take pause and go back and correct what He had created. And what about the many

He hasn't corrected? I asked him. I can't speak for them, he said. Far more the mistakes of man than the imperfections that can be attributed to God's hand. But we ain't talkin bout God, homeskillet. God ain't play no part in it. These alabasters made the man you see here.

Tabbs feels the focused tension of violence beneath the words.

My house burned to the ground. My friends dead. Had I a firearm I would have killed the first alabaster I saw—man, woman, or child. Truth is, maybe I did kill one or two. Maybe I even spent my rifle to the last bullet. Hate carried heavy in my heart. I can still feel it, feel it now even as we speak. But I ain't got no reason to hate them anymore, do I?

Some hours later, he finds himself alone once again with Tom. The boy holds the glass of milk up to his ear as if listening to it, a seashell, the sound of ocean. Brings the glass around to his lips and makes quick work of the contents. Sets the glass down on the table and sits with both hands on the table. It's not as flat as it feels, he says.

What, Tom?

Water.

His statement is like many things he says, demanding (deserving) no reply. Now he sniffs the air, smelling water, ocean, Edgemere.

You want something? What would you like?

Lait, he says.

You are tired? You wish to rest?

You'll give me the drink.

A drink? I have tea, sweet water. Even wine.

Lait. Hot or cold. You know, the honey from cows.

More milk?

Yes.

Tabbs fills the glass, both hands carry milk to mouth, then one ear listening to the glass.

I'm going to take you back. He might as well say it.

Across the water.

No, Tom. To the Home, the orphanage.

Across the water. He sips the milk.

I'm trying to understand, Tom. Is it that you don't like me?

You brought me here.

Yes, Tom. Yes I did. So why? I only wanted a chance. Why give white men that chance and not one of your own?

Tom neither moves nor speaks. He is misinterpreting the boy's behavior, assuming he knows—*this*—what he wants. Then: You gave him money?

Yes.

These. Tom holds his hands up and wiggles his fingers. And you bought tickets when you heard me?

Yes.

And you heard me sing too?

So you remember?

Yes.

How amazing it must have been, playing for all those people.

You want to know?

Yes.

I can show you.

Okay.

They walk to the piano. After some time:

It's not as hard as I thought, Tabbs says.

Your hands are easy.

For the first time the boy appears in good spirits. I would like to learn more, but I don't want to take you away from your own work.

Don't try.

Would you like me to send for an instructor?

I can teach you.

Not for me, Tom. For you.

I'll teach you.

The piano shines, animated in late afternoon. Tom plays with a powerful joy, a melody played too fast or too slow. It's got things that shouldn't be in there, foreign tones, melodies taking wrong turns, bass notes darkening passages that should be clear, chords with so many notes they cancel any understanding, foot hand allowing chords to resonate and invade where they shouldn't, a deliberate display of excess, of error, of noise, Tom having his way, one side of the floor rising, the other falling, a rocking, storm-tossed sea. Time assumes the shape it should. Tom where Tabbs wants him, taking a song from start to finish. Tom, Tabbs, and piano at a point of decision, agreement.

Tabbs sits forward in his chair, interpreting a new toughness in the boy's face.

Wire walks in, walks into his house and finds them there, trespassers occupying space that belongs to him. So you're here? Unfleshed speech against the mute surface of the furniture, Tom quiet at the piano, chin high as if straining to hear, Tabbs trying to puzzle together words and phrases, his head heavy, his body cold. What can he say with the freakishly tall preacher standing there, his right to stand on his shiny floor under yellow light hanging from the ceiling? Ruggles must have summoned him, and the mother too, not that it matters now. Mother or no mother, Tom will return to the stage.

Wire looks around. Nothing out of the ordinary. It's no accident you are here, he says. The Almighty has impeccable timing.

I only thought to—

Stay. The sheep has heard your voice. He must follow. Wire shifts direction, moves to another side of the room, a walking tree, strange to watch. The Almighty spoke to me and told me to treat you like a son. (Noah had three.) He wants you, us, our race, to prosper. That's why you couldn't walk away.

As if I had a choice, Tabbs thinks.

Expectation is a cord that binds.

Wake me, Tom says. Wire beside him now, putting a hand on his shoulder.

See, isn't my piano everything I said it was?

A promise, Tom says.

More than that. The Almighty has blessed you so that you can bless others.

> *You can't preach like Peter*
> *You can't preach like Paul*
> *One thing you can say*
> *Our Lord Jesus died for us all*

Tabbs holds still, pressed against the chair. I don't feel so blessed. He surprises himself, his willingness to speak aloud his feelings to the preacher. Less surprising the unspoken distinction he makes in his head—not blessed but deserving, deserving what's rightfully his.

But you are.

Always one more thing to say, Tabbs thinks.

You will lay hands on a million people. Wire is soothing the boy's shoulders.

The boy sings,

> *One two*
> *Buckle my shoe*
> *Three four*
> *Open the floor*

Yes, Tom, yes. Smiling, touching the boy's shoulders. If the Bible is silent, we should be silent. If the Bible talks, we should shout a clarion call.

Tabbs can think of nothing to say. The ease of the preacher's assurance almost annoys him.

You have come far, and you still have far to go. What you are willing to walk away from, leave behind, determines what the Almighty will bring to you. The abundance.

You brought her? Tom asks.

Wire takes a beat to consider the boy's face. I'm sorry, son. She should be here, right now, with you, but she stayed behind, in the city.

Tabbs hears. The words assume a shape in him.

Yes, the city woman.

Wire presses both hands into Tom's shoulders as if he is trying to keep the boy seated on the piano bench. We were in the camps, as regular as rain. Doing our work. Then one day, she just up and—it's just some misunderstanding. What else could it be? Wire's face holds some reticent knowledge that seals him off from Tabbs and Tom, some harmful (damaging) facts.

And you don't know where?

I know. She is out there. In the city. Somewhere.

Tom's face goes wild.

We will find her.

We can go across the water, Tom says.

That's just what we'll do, Tabbs says. Believe it if you want, he thinks.

Yes, we will find your mother. She wants to be with you.

Always mother, Tom says.

Wire walks about the room in his high-shine shoes, looking everywhere at once with his three heads. How have I ended up back here, again?

❀ ❀ ❀

Wire watches the slow stirrings of the chapel come to life. Swears that he has been in this scene before, with these very men, positioned about the pews as they are. A dream. A presentiment even. (Sight is anticipatory sense.) Did he dream it last night? Is he dreaming it now? Were it not for the smell (burning trees, gunpowder, blood) he might doubt the reality of what he is seeing and hearing.

Drinkwater is speaking in a loud insistent voice, his throat wild with words, words undoing words, his mouth open so wide that Wire can see his small teeth. His body appears tense with a terrible effort of will to remain standing where he is, clutching his hat in his hand like a messenger sent on an errand. He no longer has the aura of someone exceptional, with his troubled disposition, his overexcitement, and his shoddy appearance, his skin and clothes speckled with mud and soot.

The five soldiers scattered around him in various poses of disheveled collapse chime in where they think necessary with expressions of incredible assurance—*uh huh* and *that's right* and *yeah* and *you know it*—and constantly nod their heads, small movements of spasmodic affirmation (and shock) as if Wire, Double, and the other deacons are not impressed by Drinkwater's account of murder and tragedy, the stark facts of the city's offensive against them in Central Park, which has claimed the lives of all the men in their unit except those present. Double sits motionless on a pew in front of them, his manner extraordinarily composed as always, head bowed, one hand clutching his chin. Wire can feel the Deacon thinking, his mind fidgeting with the future. The Deacon has strong ideas—more than once Wire has thought about telling him so—but he is also reserve personified, never the first to speak, never a loud word, a man so at a remove listening and observing that his silence seems to cancel out his presence altogether, a man so purely inward and oriented toward the duties of his church that he enlarges the world around him by an erasure of self, occupying (filling) space but without taking space away from other things around him. Sometimes Wire will sit and think about how he wishes he knew more about the Deacon's life.

After a long introduction containing many unusual words, Drinkwater's second-in-command, dark and solidly built, his ears too big, picks up the story in minute detail, going beyond the bare facts—life making its extensions—narrating entire conversations, throwing himself into the attitudes of the participants, changing the expression of his face and voice like a professional actor. As Wire listens, his thoughts blow backward, the stench of donkey dung, the troughs filled with donated rations, the creaky dhows, the unkempt tents, the barefoot vendors, the half-naked children sporting in the glare of the noonday sun—all a background to thoughts and feelings not easily gauged, never completely assayed.

Christ bought us with his blood. The words come from his mouth, but they are not his words, his mouth. *Whoever drinks from my mouth will become like me. I myself shall become that person.* Everything in the room pulls into silence, time broken around them. The dancing light from the kerosene lamps assume shapes that give everything in the room an oddly broken impression. Light he does not trust. Such terrible darkness.

Do not unduly bear the burden of your fallen brethren, Double says. He doesn't speak loudly, but his voice carries and everyone listens. For unless Jehovah has raised you up in this thing you will be worn down by the opposition of men and devils.

Heat cleaves to every object in the church like a low fever. Wire feels the grip of weariness, both drained and filled.

The search for a homeland has always been at the center of our chronicles. And so the years go by.

Double's expansive words seem to push at the walls of the chapel, make them fly apart and come together again.

Truth crushed to the earth shall rise again, he says. The same indignation that cleared the temple once will clear it again. Brothers, await that day. In the meantime, say nothing, do nothing. It is enough that all of us are here now. When the time comes, the Lord will give us the words to speak. Scarcely moving in the darkness, he unsnaps the button on his left shoe, removes the shoe, then unsnaps the button on the right shoe and removes it. He cups his hands together and from knee to toe slides his left silk stocking free from his leg and foot. Repeats this process with his right stocking. Then he just sits for a while looking at the other men in the room, his bare feet contoured like two red-brown mushrooms. Wire gathers vaguely that he wants them to follow his example, but it takes the soldiers a full minute or two to catch on. Drinkwater sits down on the pew and his men follow his lead, taking places in his proximity, shoulder to shoulder, where they proceed to remove their soiled boots and socks. Many ideas taking shape in his head, Wire is the last man in the room to partake in the brotherhood of bare feet.

Double takes up a pitcher and pours water into a basin. He kneels before Drinkwater and carefully lifts the lieutenant's foot as if it were a delicate bird, pours water over it, and massages it clean. He returns the clean foot to the floor then lifts up the other foot smoothly and easily and effortlessly, pours water and cleans away the mud and dirt. He passes a freshly filled pitcher and a newly emptied basin to Drinkwater's second-in-command, who kneels down before the soldier to his left. Amid the somber circulation, the sound of pouring and rinsing, Wire cannot shake the feeling that they are being spied on, shadows watching them from the corners, and even through the high windows, darkness looking in; he is certain of it. And yet they continue pouring and rinsing, Wire secretly glad that, true to form, Double had brought into being this evocative ritual—ribbons of water—for these soldiers requiring answers, consolation (some at least) in knowing that the Deacon has succeeded (momentarily?) where he, Wire, had not the fortitude, resolve, and presence of mind to try.

And this feeling deepens as Double slides from water back into words, his voice a low grunting accompaniment.

I was in a wilderness sort of place, all full of rocks and brushes, when I saw a serpent raise its head of an old man with a long white beard, gazing at me, wishful like, just as if he were going to speak to me, and then two other heads rose up beside him, younger than he—

The hands on Wire's feet are pleasing to the touch.

—and as I stood looking at them and wondering what they could want with me, a great crowd of men rushed in and struck down the younger heads and then the head of the old man, still looking at me so wishful. This is a dream I have had again and again and could not interpret it until now.

Charity looks around the austere room where Wire works on his sermons—*Brethren, I have taken off my shoes and on this consecrated ground adored the God and Father of our ancestors. You've been crowned with victory. There is a king in each of you*—looks at the bed, the table, shelves of books, sketches on the walls, and the shiny white sheets of paper that occupy his hard narrow desk like felled birds. No easy time of it. His robe stiff tight on his shoulders like feathers mashed in place. He shifts his bulk from time to time. She waits in silence, the room hot, airless, can feel the urgency flowing from him in waves. Wouldn't surprise her any if he rips the sermon into skinny strips and tosses the wasted words out the window. Nothing a preacher can't do. He puts down his stylus, shakes his head, looks up at the sagging ceiling—God pressing in—shielding his eyes as he does so. Seems to have forgotten that another person, her, Charity Greene Wiggins, is in the room with him. But then he looks at her, and for a moment his eyes look almost compassionate. Try again. He shuffles the papers, moves them about on the desk, piecing together a new nest where his tired hands can perch. Looks at her absently, eager to get back to his sermon. So she'll just keep standing here, awaiting some sudden surprise of light, color, or motion. Not much longer now. He takes a sip of chocolate tea, lukewarm now, returns cup to saucer. Primed, he stuffs a black plug of tobacco in his mouth and chews his annoyance away. Spits brown puddles of tobacco juice right onto the floor.

She remembers moments of the recent past that already seem distant, long ago:

Why did you go? Thomas asked.
I ain't go nowhere.
You been.
They took you, took you away.
You say.
He gave you to them.
He put his arms on the table. Still arms, slack face.
You understand? They took you away from me.
But here now.

··· 495 ···

Yes. Here. Together . . . . Don't you miss me?
Got no words.
Why? They took you. A nigger ain't go no say.
You want to play. Play. I'll hear you.
She started to hum a song, low in her throat.
Don't ever touch me like that again, he said.

She blows out the quotidian candles, readies the kerosene lamps, and carries them lit by the latches, two to a hand, into the small sitting room where the Vigilance Committee, twelve deacons from as many churches, come with weekly reports about trials, tribulations, and triumphs. (She does not give as much thought as she might to what the men actually speak about.) Looking at the men, she thinks about how the black children of Israel are like a speckled bird in their many shades of skin. She serves them decanters of sack, kettles of soma, and goblets of Medusa for those who want their eyes to roll back in their head. Bowls of goobers and pecans, apple and pear preserves on little rafts of hard bread, and flat cakes of ground meat smothered in sweet red sauce. Reverend Wire is brightly attired in blue robe with a line of silver buttons shining—she keeps button polishers in the pantry— from his throat down to his shoes. All of the men at the table wear robes of the same color if not similar in fit and construction.

Using only the tips of his fingers, Deacon Double lifts a newspaper from the table, the newspaper some vile unclean thing. Brothers, this is what they write about us. He lowers his eyes and reads from the newspaper. Negroes at every turn. Their presence is undesirable among us. They should be confined to large tracts of unimproved land on the outskirts of the city, where they can build up colonies of their own and where their transportation and hygiene and nourishment and other problems will not inflict injustice and disgust on worthy citizens.

A little breeze reels through the white curtains and suddenly the entire room feels different.

Double raises his line of sight from the newspaper and makes a point of catching the gaze of every man in the room. It would be nice to be able to say a miracle had happened, he says. But it hasn't. We know these alabasters, know that their hearts and hands are capable of anything. Knowing what we do, it is the duty of every man here, men of God, to provide himself and his congregants with arms and ammunition. I myself have at least one rifle and at least enough projectiles to make it useful.

Wire says, At this moment of revolution, when our country needs the blessing of Almighty God and the strong arms of her children, this is not the time for us to solemnly enact injustice. In duty to our country and in duty to God, I plead against any such thing. We must be against wrong in its original shape and in all its brood of prejudice and error.

No blood is to be shed except in self-defense, Deacon Double says. One hand goes into the sleeve of his robe and reappears holding a rolled leather map. He unrolls it and spreads it flat on the table before the other men, turned so that they may easily view it, paperweights pinning down the corners. Bends his bulky body over the map and begins moving his hand freely above the leather.

She set the glass before him. Milk will pass right through a haint, a white puddle on the floor. Best she find out. Maybe that Mr. Tabbs ain't all he promised. Good chance of that, with his fancy clothes, proud hat, and that silver tongue. Made-up nigger thinking he other, better. I can give you your son.

He stuck his tongue out like a snake and let the tip of it touch the milk, his lips far away, keeping safe distance. He set the glass down, milk intact.

Who thirsty, he said. And then: You are just a weak worm of the earth.

The strays in Central Park have multiplied. At least double yesterday's number grouped around the well, sweaty and haggard.

> *I can't stay behind, my Lord*
> *I can't stay behind*

Swaying like vile flowers, dirty mushrooms, in their wide-brimmed hats. A steady drift of them dressed in rags, some of the women in cast-off soldier's coats, both blue and gray, men and women alike carrying their households on their backs (dirty sacks, splintery crates) and heads (baskets, bundles), arms toting tubs, kettles, and pots, animals too, pigs and roosters and chickens, their rickety children and gaunt mules, their porkers, goats, lambs, and dogs trailing behind them. A common sight: a swollen belly leading the rest of the body like a big stubborn eye.

The nurses work with dignified speed. Sun boiling, moisture and sweat hanging in the air. She can't quite keep up, her hands like a den of aggravated snakes, the green veins beneath the skin pulsing and writhing in the heat.

A nurse he calls me. I ain't never done that, I said. And I'm dry. No milk. I ain't no nurse.

The church touches her hands. This is the abiding nature of the place. Always there. Once she settles down on the bed her day stops, her body crumpling inside her sweat-heavy dress. She tries to pay it no mind. Won't bother to take it off. Can't. Exhausted beyond wanting company, she lies still and tries to empty herself, empty herself of all that water out there, all that ocean she had crossed to get to Edgemere, and had crossed again (back) to get to here, the city, to this room in this church. She has a room in the church, small, but the bed is perfect for sleeping. Not too soft, not too hard, and plenty of pillows to cushion her head just right. Cracks in the drapes let in random patches of light. She lays bare her worries and tallies her setbacks. Thinking a long time before she falls asleep.

She awakes, the room ablaze with light. Drags herself up out of dreams, works the knots in her body out, doing all she can to turn away from sleep into morning. For yet another day she will have to get up, leave this room, and go back among those people to save herself.

Now that she and Reverend Wire are here, in the camp, nurses dressed in white descend from the topmost branches of the trees like a lost flock of birds. Tall trees that brush the light in, brush the shade out.

Her senses come alive. She breathes in the smell of strays, mouthful by mouthful, struggling for air. Every glance a landscape, too much for the eyes to take in. The broken, the blood, the pain. But the Reverend touches them all. His hand on each person's shoulder carries absolute certainty. He issues a string of authoritative commands to the other nurses. *A nurse he calls me.* She wraps bandages, cleans wounds, snaps bones in place, wanting nothing of the skin. Cloth boiled clean spinning in speeding circles around a head, an elbow, or a waist. Spinning herself, a dull throbbing in her temple. *A nurse.* Why has she consented to such contact?

Trapped in their own collapsing bodies, the strays take their time getting from one place to another, brittle-shelled turtles. The oldest and most weathered of the bunch don't seem able to get about at all, planted at a spot along the road or under a shady tree. Even sitting such, they seem to suffer from erethism of their digits and limbs, and twitching and tics of eyes and face. The Reverend tries to look them in the face, in the eye, when he talks to them, but they get all respectful, hold their elbows and study their feet. Every now and then he swings his face toward heaven, either seeking guidance or receiving approval.

They drool nonsense sounds to each other, Charity dizzy with listening, nigger talk that even she can't understand.

Blouse open, the thin fan of bones wafting heat through wet skin, the moist pressing air cool for a moment, until the next breath. She picks and plucks determinedly at gray desiccated flesh, uncovering the dirty buried life, lifting it to the surface. Plugs up holes where existence can escape. No two bodies alike. All the bodies alike. For weeks now since they sent her from the Home to the city, she has gone out each day and tried to see the city through Wire's eyes and with Wire's words. How impossible. Too much. Too much. She follows this perfectly aligned road, putting her feet down in those overlooked spots speckled with brown and green, feeling twigs break under her shoes—the sound at least—walking on bones. On her way. By and by, finds herself far from the camps, on the out-reaches of what she knows, unfamiliar streets. Moves through the streets (never stumbles) with these thoughts on her mind. Many people about. Black men in blue and varying shades of blue and gray. (She is looking for color.) She sees ship sails sticking up out of the water like amputated wings, and boats that look like dis-embodied feet kicking the water.

We have to board the ferry, Mr. Tabbs said.

What fo? I ain't lost nothing over there.

Thomas was there, on the island, surrounded by all that water. What had happened to the Thomas of old that she can still picture, still feel? *Don't ever touch me like that again.*

She walks through the streets and tells herself, *I cannot bear stay-ing in this city any longer.* But she is alone with only her labor in the camps and the church chores. She has no other bed, no other place to go back to. Elsewhere in her head. (Which way to turn?)

A hand snakes out and touches her then someone grabs her by the shoulder from behind. She jumps with fear, heart beating. Even before she turns around, her head goes into an accelerated and fever-ish deliberation, picturing several possible scenarios and how she will attack or defend and extricate herself. Someone calls a name, and she turns at the call, but she has turned in error, wrong person wrong name. A mistake that won't let her go, that gets her thinking. All those faces out there. People everywhere. A gathering around her. No one knows her, knows her name. She can get lost. Disappear. Charity Greene Wiggins no longer.

She breathes the warm night air, people inhaling her breath and she inhaling theirs. One of them now. Stray. Contraband. Refugee. Free.

Song of the Shank
(1869)

"I didn't think screaming
was part of music."

We are pleased to have with us in the recital arena a singular Negro virtuoso during this era which has been largely defined by virtuoso-frenzy. This sable personage is none other than Blind Tom, who has returned to the stage after an absence of five years or more, a murky period with much still unknown, unasked, and unanswered since we the public and the press had no clue as to his whereabouts or his well-being for half a decade. Notwithstanding these facts, his talents were on full display last night as of the days of old. He is all the musician of a Liszt and Rubinstein. Indeed, it goes without saying, his technique is superb. We expect nothing less of a virtuoso. Both hands share complete equality, the interaction and rivalry between them being a constant source of new inventions. Let us celebrate the return of the most famous musician, indeed the most famous celebrity, in the world, who now tours under the name Original Blind Tom to distinguish himself from the many imposters.

I have a new song.

No new songs.

Let me play it for you.

No new songs, Seven says. Do I have to tell you why? He does not have to tell Juluster why. Of late Juluster has been running his mouth too much:

I am ignorant of my Father's reason for choosing the piano as the instrument on which I am to illustrate my wondrous gift. My dear mother told me, she said, My son, the Heavenly Father gave you certain gifts in exchange for depriving you of sight.

Tom, the journalist said, that is such a beautiful song about your dear mammy. She must be so proud of you.

Mother is a jewel, Tom said. Father is a mirror.

My dear mother, do you know what else she told me? My son, she said, you had not long been from my belly when I received a sign. A rock dove set down on the rafters above where you lay and shat down on your forehead. From that moment on I knew you were destined for greatness.

And this:

"The Rain Storm" received its title because in the opening statement of the composition, I tried to give the feeling of something coming down—descending octaves—and then overflowing. In a way, it's musically analogous to rain. I wasn't, however, thinking specifically of a flood, but rather of an overflow of something. In a way, I suppose the original impetus for this piece came from my first years of being taught the Holy Bible in Sunday school and of hearing about deluges, good old Noah and the ark and all that. Of course, I wrote the piece at a very young age when I still accompanied my good mother to church almost every Sunday and when we attended Bible study together several hours before service began. With one thing or another, I am no longer afforded the chance to attend church all that often. So, now, at my present age, I certainly would approach the song differently. I would even give it a different title, "Deluge," or something like that. Have I said too much?

Yes, Seven thought. You have said too damn much. Let him do the talking. Who knows Tom better than he does? The person he invokes when he thinks of Tom is accurate to the inch. He has memorized Tom's measurements, knows all of Tom's dimensions, the space between Tom's fingers and toes and teeth. Knows. They had that between them. Not for nothing has he taken pains to come to this city where Tom gave his last concert and where he is thought to have died and may have died, probably did die. To the consternation or delight of many, he, Seven, will resurrect Blind Tom right here in the city. *Do this in memory of me.* What he can do for Tom. What he owes Tom is beyond action and expression. Tom has given his life a size and shape that no man can diminish. Tom would want this, he tells himself. Tom wants this. Tom wants this for me.

And how does it feel to be a nigger, Tom?

A nigger is a thing of no consequence.

Mr. Seven? Juluster says.

Yes. Seven leans in to hear the question.

A blind man walks into a fishmonger's shop. Do you know what he says?

What?

Oh, beg pardon, ladies.

Will Seven laugh?

Mr. Seven?

Yes.

You want to hear another one?

As many as you have.

There was this cross-eyed planter who confounded his niggers to no end because they could never tell what or where he was looking. (Give me blindness any day over that.) He would say, Nigger, bend down and bring me that, and four or five niggers would bend down. Or, Nigger, what's your name again? And ten or twelve niggers would answer. Mary, Martha, Matthew, Michael.

And there they are, the three weeping women in black, clustered together in one of the first rows, their faces veiled. Seven sees them but refuses to believe what he sees. Could these be the same weeping women in black from his days with Perry Oliver and Tom? *Are these those? Vitalis asked.*

In the days and weeks that follow, his thoughts seem stuck, he feels paralyzed by the sense that Time is repeating itself, three weeping women in black entering the order and comfort of his life concert after concert. He wonders about their appearance again and again, and even as he hears a voice call out to him in the noisy solitude backstage after one recital.

Sir, the woman says, do you know me? She is encased in a black dress from throat to ankle.

He is asking himself the same question, unless the answer he is looking for is hidden in the next question she throws at him.

Where have we met?

I don't believe I've had the pleasure before now.

Sir, we've had the pleasure.

Her thin frame seems more substantial, seems to possess more flesh than what's there, under its assured bearing. She stares at him with the impassiveness of a sculpted form. Her face etched with weathered lines that are not at all unpleasant, but (somehow) patterned and elegant. Her gaze is frank and unsparing.

Well, ma'm, that cherished encounter I seem to have forgotten.

Sir, the woman says, you are an imposter. You and your blind nigger both. She is a thin lady and she is out of breath. I *know* Blind Tom, and that ain't him.

Ma'm, I can assure you—

The real Blind Tom was of the lowest Guinea type. Your boy is clearly an amalgamation.

Ma'm, I will be happy to refund your ticket. But nothing he says can do the work of either convincing or dismissing her.

He collects Tom and Vitalis, the accusation pushing him into the vivid dark.

Who she? Vitalis asks.

The crazy old bitch, Seven says out loud, speaking mostly to himself. Thinking: She does not believe. She sees right through me.

Juluster holds his hand straight out. Wire—the name the tall nigger preacher had given—reaches and takes it and Juluster tries to give it the same painful grip that he gives everyone, but the preacher's hand is large enough to grip a watermelon. Blind Tom, Juluster says. Eighth wonder of the world.

Pleased to make your acquaintance, the nigger preacher says. He releases Juluster's hand.

Likewise, Juluster says.

His hair angrily askew (so much, too much), Vitalis stands next to Juluster looking up at the preacher in astonishment. Nature has afforded this Wire radical proportions, a very Hercules in stature, seven feet in height and nearly as wide as two men, a man too wide and too tall to squeeze his way through the average portal. And the black robe he wears, splayed out in front and behind winglike, intensifies his colossal proportions.

I watched and listened tonight and after watching and listening, after what I saw and heard tonight, I had to bring myself here before you. The preacher's voice is needlessly loud, as if he is addressing an audience. Judging by the wrinkles on his face, the preacher is over sixty years old, a bad sign. The old like to talk.

They will have to suffer the inconvenience (no way around it), but Seven hopes that the preacher will avoid beating around the bush and simply hurry into the purpose of his visit—a donation for his church? He wants to pray with Blind Tom? Bless Blind Tom? Have Blind Tom bless him?—the sooner the better.

You've done a fine job—speaking to Seven now. The preacher lets his gaze drift over Seven.

And Seven stumbles in his thinking. Thank you. Trying to smile, the words carrying with their own insistence since Seven has no idea what the preacher means. And now he notices a faint but deep forest smell coming from somewhere inside the gallery, a wood and leaf and soil scent, green and brown against the marble floor and smooth granite walls.

Bemused, the preacher gazes steadily at Seven. But sometimes another is chosen in preference who by all rights should not even be considered your equal.

The meaning and importance of the words escape him, but Seven feels (detects) something in the preacher's vocabulary that is rallied against him. Just who is this nigger preacher anyway?

Still, to your credit your illusions and confidences and deceptions are of sufficient approximation to confidence most people, especially those least in the know.

It's up to him now to talk this nigger preacher out of whatever it is he thinks he believes. Reverend—

Your present condition comes as no disclosure. We have to know what we want from the start. Already as children we have to be clear in our minds what it is we want, want to have, have to have.

Reverend, perhaps we could visit your church? Seven sees the old woman in the oil canvas behind the preacher, her hands stiff on her lap, the skin pale, the hurtful rheumatic veins—life as it is. Given the vagueness of this black body, this Blind Tom, surely the preacher is only drawing upon all he can remember or guess.

Out the mouths of babes, the preacher says. Do you really think so little of me?

It is hot inside the hallway and quiet, the air full of thoughts and things to say. Seven stares into the preacher's impassive face. Gives the signal for Vitalis to take Juluster down to the driver and the carriage, but Vitalis does not move, only looks at Seven as if he has never seen him before. Stands there looking like a damn fool, with that tear-shaped rush of hair rising skyward from his forehead, six inches tall at the tip. Then Wire smiles as if to encourage Vitalis to follow Seven's instructions. He touches Vitalis's back, quick firm pats. Vitalis and Juluster hurry purposefully ahead. Juluster, his movement constrained by the weight of Vitalis, accelerates to escape his navigator, and they disappear from sight, leaving Seven and the preacher staring across confrontational space.

Now Wire starts to walk away too, huge and lumbering, a black moving wall, and Seven sets off after him through the grandest structure in the city, all pristine neoclassical stone with an interlacing arcade. A marble labyrinth of stairways and galleries, gangways and corridors, pillars and porches, halls and dead ends.

I see no reason why you can't revive the name of Blind Tom on every tongue in the civilized world, Wire says, for the replica in your charge is no person of ordinary means. He is an extraordinary talent, the genuine article. Perhaps the spirit anointed him in this purpose. So I ask you, is it for me to stand in your way?

Words vie in Seven's mouth. No, he says. But you want something.

They exit the building and come down the wide grand staircase situated like a series of descending bridges between two stone lions, the memory of roar and kill long drained from mouth and claws. Walk past a little booth at the foot of the staircase, where earlier that evening hundreds had purchased tickets. Seven's body acts without him.

Yes, I do.

Here it comes, Seven tells himself. He is leaning toward the idea that this preacher will take him for all he can.

In the receding light, crowds of people walk in small groups by the sea, some of them holding hands. All of their movements seem identical, the same pace, the same stride, arms swinging. A dream. If anyone knows if Tom is alive or dead, this preacher does. He is sure of it. He feels powerless against this unforeseen enemy. The preacher's mind remains against them, against him and "Tom." Nothing good can come out of their time together.

And you will want to know that I seek nothing for myself since my private needs are few. However, the needs of my collective are wide-ranging and extensive, and will require means of both a material and an immaterial nature, in the present moment as well as long term.

It is more than Seven expected, too much. No two ways about it, he must lie to earn the preacher's trust and to win himself more time to devise a true course of action.

But already I am at fault in assuming that our goals are not at cross-purposes. Ignorant of your character, I should not pretend to understand your motives behind this venture let alone assume that we can arrive at a meeting of the minds.

The sun coming through the branches of the trees makes the sidewalk look reddish, like a river.

I will do all I can, Seven says.

The big nigger preacher looks down at him with eyes the size of plums. No, Wire says. You will do more than that. You will do whatever I tell you to do.

Seven hears the words like something coming from very far away, from the top of a hill or mountain. Thinks: Things can change in a day. Beneath history is another history we've made without even knowing it. Blind Tom is a name that he can no longer claim, a name that perhaps no one can claim or that everyone can claim. A million Blind Toms.

Later, he will think that this nigger preacher was worth killing.

❀ ❀ ❀

Tabbs crumples paper to encourage the flame. Getting to what he wants will be slow going and mostly smoke. How many weeks has he been laid up in bed now? Can't say for sure, only knows that he was already coming down with something serious, something severely debilitating on that day right before the start of winter when Wire came to visit him, made him sit down, then spoke to him with utter directness about an imposter Wire had chanced upon several days earlier, a prevaricator going under the stage name the Original Blind Tom. Tabbs no longer recalls Wire's exact words, but can still feel the way the words worked into his chest and moved up into his throat and face. Although the preacher's visage (eyes, mouth, jaw) was distorted with outrage, Tabbs did not let Wire know what he was feeling—*so that's it, I've finally lost, it's over now*—his straining body sealed tight so that no sound or movement could escape. They sat quietly for some time in a semblance of mourning and reflection until Wire took to his feet. Tabbs saw Wire to the door and managed to remain standing until the preacher left. Then days of sickness. Fever. Chills. Thirst. Delirium.

His mind freezes on the image of Tom coming to his aid with a circle of hands and comforting words, Tabbs growing in the shade of the other male's nursing presence. Tom so particular in his touch, Tom so familiar, so pleasing. Just when Tabbs's recovery had appeared complete, he was seized by another fever. So he dragged his wretched body back to the safety of this bed where sleep eludes him.

Sometimes smoke rising from the kerosene lamp fools him, mirages created by light and heat, the city's reach into his memory mapped along whatever streets he can name. Looking out through the giant glassy eye of window from his supine position on the bed, he cannot see the city. No city. No sun. Only the sky's dull palette of gray with ocean beneath it. A dhow passes, the captain swinging the tiller from one gunwale to the other, the man looking for all the world like someone sitting in the bowels of some oceanic monster. Another man passes in the street atop his donkey, the animal's movements at once awkward and perfectly poised in the cold. And whatever other sights distract Tabbs's eye in drift. Such is life on Edgemere. A practical people, a sober people. They make allowances, make way with whatever measly means they have at their disposal. No crying or complaining. So why not remain here? Remain here on the island and make Edgemere home.

That's Christmas out there, he hears Tom say.

Not for long, Tabbs says. He turns his head to see Tom standing outlined before his tired eyes, his facial movements and expressions giving a distraught impression, his shirt so dingy that it looks less like a shirt and more like milk spilled across his chest. His frock coat repulsive with its dark patches. Repulsive his whole delicate figure.

Take me to her.

Will you shut up about it.

I want to see her.

You will.

I want—

All right, you'll get there.

Need makes us hungry, cold, afraid. (The air rolled in dirty winter wind and light.) We can only imagine what is absent. (Nothing completed, nothing attained.) Winter chill curls in around the door as Ruggles enters. Tabbs props himself up in bed. Was this his tragedy? So late in the game he is still condemned to make that effort of adaptation that he has always made, play the outward role, sometimes without being conscious of it.

Ruggles doesn't bother to take off his hat or coat. He looks about the room as if his eyes want to glimpse nothing else. So you're still under the weather. He shakes his head. God grant everybody such a life. He pulls up a chair, letting the legs scrape across the floor, and sits down with a grim concentrated expression. Cocks his misshapen hat.

If I could get out of this bed.

You can. All of this over some imposter? You're just throwing dust up in the air after the fact. Ruggles looks at him with anger, face full of passion.

It is snowing now, snow whirling nimbly over the street, falling thick through the brittle air, and settling on the grassless ground, startling white against the gray day.

Let it go. Ain't that what I been telling you all along?

Guess I never heard. Why don't you tell me again?

Sides, this Original Blind Tom has little life left to live.

Is that so? His little life seems fine to me.

Think of a three-legged cow. The deformity is only interesting at first. Nobody wants to look at that same three-legged cow a third and a fourth and a fifth time.

Thanks, Ruggles. That helps.

Now they simply sit like members of the audience waiting for the next act. Comes the news that Ruggles has just been appointed postmaster.

Why are you always bragging on your gifts? The words are hard and icy in Tabbs's mouth.

Me? Homeskillet, have you ever heard me brag?

All the time.

Tell him, Tom.

Tom's face shows bewilderment (fright). A slight exhalation, lips pursed to air.

Damn it, Ruggles. Now you gon get him started.

What did I do?

What did I do?

Why don't we just get going?

Damn your meeting. I can use your meeting like spit in my face.

But you're still going to bring yo sorry ass.

Like a new set of balls.

Sorry motherfucker.

An hour after dusk the men of the Vigilance Committee come in silence, emerging from darkness, walking toward the slim triangle of Wire's church, Resurrection African Christian Episcopal (RACE). Inside the church they move in noise and light. Tabbs sees Wire near the front of the church, busy greeting the deacons. He waves and Wire raises his hand and continues what he is doing. Tabbs follows the men to the row of pews at the front of the church, where a circle of kerosene lamps casts yellow light, the whole room aglow with objects, fresh and bright and distinct, but the ceiling beams above them hardly visible. One after the next, the men come up in a breezy manner, shake him by the hand, and ask him how things are. You better now?

How can he tell them about what he really feels? That something has settled in him after all those weeks in bed. That he is able to settle easily enough into the way of life here on Edgemere. That he feels utterly alone whenever he is in the city, alabasters consuming him with their cold bitter eyes. He endures their finger pointing, their verbal insults, their angry bodies brushing against him, comes to expect it (the stable framework of the body and the mind), accepts the position of one scorned as if it were proper and natural. Tells himself, They think I'm a foreigner, a stray. Me. And this is my city. My city.

The soldiers—brown rifles and white hands—are supposed to watch over the strays, keep them orderly, keep them safe. Can it be they are responsible for the fact that he is still breathing? Soldiers and their weapons everywhere in the city, weapons shining clean.

He feels transparent, all those eyes looking through him. So he feels thankful whenever he leaves the city to return to Edgemere. Letting the island further inside him the longer he remains here. He is immensely comfortable on Edgemere; his time here, this year, month, however many months or days it's been, have brought a feeling of protection he has never experienced before. Saturated in blackness.

The soldiers are leaving the city. The city is sending them away.

Nawl.

They are.

How you know?

I'm telling you.

The news is an occasion for some emotion—sighs, gasps, utterances, and expressions of disbelief.

We knew that, knew that they wouldn't stay forever.

And now is the time.

A people cannot be redeemed by military victory, Wire says, but only by the spiritual and moral rebirth of the individual and the nation.

Amen, Deacon Double says. He is the only man standing in the room, his appointed duty to see to it that every member of the committee has what he needs, whether it's a glass of water or something more stringent like Medusa, a plain wafer or a blessed slice of bread. He is clearly a mongrel, two bloods mixing in his buttermilk-colored skin. However, brother, I can hardly see this as good news. For without the sword, covenants are but words and of no strength to secure and protect a man.

Protect Africans. The refugees.

Are you afraid? Ruggles asks. We will protect the refugees. We will protect ourselves. Why should another protect us?

Go protect them, Tabbs wants to say. Has Edgemere taken possession of him for good? He cannot leave. He does not want to leave. He must not leave. Let the soldiers leave.

Speak, brother, Deacon Double says.

Neither borrowers nor lenders be, Ruggles says. We must either stand on our own two feet or start wearing garments unbefitting a manly race. Ruggles stands up now and begins pacing. He needs to move his arms to be more forceful. God said to Moses, "I am that I am," or more exactly, "I shall be that I shall be." Each race sees from its own standpoint a different side of God. The Hebrews could not serve God in the land of the Egyptians, nor can the Negro under the Anglo-Saxon. He can only serve *man* here on Edgemere.

How did we get to God? Wire asks.

Ruggles looks at him. Well, brother, ain't this a church?

Just go carefully, that's all I'm saying. Go carefully.

Brother, what are you saying?

A lot of people say things with they mouth, Ruggles says. I'm not one for a lot of talk.

Indeed, Double says. What the whole body does is more eloquent than lips.

So what are you saying?

Tabbs knows that he will never forget a word or gesture of Ruggles's tonight.

What am I saying? Ruggles says. Here is what I am saying. Every man in this room was forced from his home. Everyone here. Each one of us. Ruggles looks at each member of the committee in turn—Wire, Tabbs, Drinkwater and his soldiers, Double and the other deacons. Tabbs sees something in Ruggles that he will never fully reach.

What you supposing we do?

Yes, brother. What? The Deacon waits for an answer. We have arms, we have ammunition, safeguarded right here in this very church.

That's right, Drinkwater says.

Now, don't go too far, Wire says. In battle men see things they thought they'd kept hidden.

They do, Double says. They do.

Each day brings word of mass graves of strays sprouting up all across the city, mutilated corpses rising knee deep out of the earth with the abrupt arrival of spring, and half-fleshed corpses floating in pits filled with rainwater, fat unwholesome frogs perched atop muddy torsos and water moccasins swimming in and out of organs and skin. Stories splinter in all directions, the hurt Tabbs doesn't see far away. Black bodies burned. Black bodies hanging from trees and telegraph poles. Africans pulled off random streetcars and mobbed to death. Bloated black bodies floating in canals, rivers, and ponds. Blood in every eye. Such stories become commonplace. Tabbs bears these facts with equanimity, nothing so barbarous that the human mind cannot accept it. He lives in a silence with noise and conversation all around him. Air thick with event. Hard to keep up with it all. Many times Tabbs will hear running footsteps, yells of fear and excitement, everybody around him trying to get to the bottom of some new tragedy, loud donkeys filling in the spaces between words. Delivered out of nothing, strays flee the city for Edgemere, the city's African population expelled again. Ferries heavy with hundreds of the expulsed, their hulls low in the water. Uprooted. Exiled. Displaced. *The land grows weary of her inhabitants.* Pulled continually into their orbit, Tabbs struggles to gain a footing in the changing daily life of the island. Lives, giving his entire attention to thoughts that on the one hand grow more vague day by day and, on the other, grow more precise and unambiguous.

The strays want to forget, erase the bad old days of hunger, desire, and desperation spiriting them across the ocean to this island, dazed by their own movement, sagging, dragging. Most have no experience with money. They work hard for very little, for less than they should. And they are cheated of what they earn. The bony women with big butts always seem to be pregnant. The stunted children seem wallowed in ignorance, cunning, play, and slovenliness. Strays display their impoverishment and degradation to anyone who cares to see. Every stray he meets is named Lincoln. His life is no longer a single story but part of theirs. Tabbs Lincoln.

Tabbs wants to say to them, Tell me what it was like. (Why do you just look at me instead of telling me about your sadness?) But he rarely speaks to them—stilted and confused; downcast and dejected; their inaccurate but splendid words—content to observe them from a distance. How can he open himself to arms that will not embrace? How heal wounds that do not bleed?

Fair to say that Tabbs does not sense any changes in his own physical condition or wish for anything to be different. The world is what it is. He has to force himself to be gentle with this frailty he finds himself in the midst of.

Uncertain of clear boundaries, the exiles put up makeshift shelters in the main square, old canvas tents and burlap lean-tos flapping under the walnut trees. Their children steal from stores and grow bold enough to sneak into kitchens while their parents are out fishing or peddling firewood. And their famished dogs begin to seek out and kill chickens and goats, tearing out the throats of younger animals, and doing enough bodily harm to the larger—donkey, sheep, cow—a plug bitten out of a calf or flank, an eye lost, an ear ripped away—to make them unusable. That's when feelings turn completely against them. Black-robed members of the Vigilance Committee shoot their dogs on sight, and tear down their ugly shelters, row after row.

Comes the day when Tabbs sees from a distance four heads set in a stationary circle around the fountain in the main square, long faces, long necks. Horses shaped out of stone. He expects water to spill from the mouths of these horses until he sees one head dip, muzzle sinking into the water. Closer, the horses prove to be strays kneeling in the grass under arrest, hands tied behind their backs at the wrist with lengths of rope. Confined to the reach of their bodies. The single deacon guarding them letting them rest some coolness back into their bodies, jabbing the air this way and that with his finger. Fountains are not for human consumption, he tells them. Each stray turns his face toward Tabbs in embarrassment, while the Deacon lifts his head and nods at Tabbs in silence.

Some get sick from tainted food and cloudy water. Die.

In this overexcited atmosphere Tabbs is content most days to let the hours in Wire's house pass without any disruption. Other days he attends meetings with the Vigilance Committee.

Look at these poor bastards, he says.

They stretch forth their hands, Wire says. And we stretch forth ours.

You might as well appeal against the thunderstorm as against these terrible but necessary hardships, Deacon Double says.

They need light and instruction, Ruggles says. So either give it to them, or let them all starve.

I thought you were going to protect them, Tabbs wants to say.

It'll take them time to learn, Wire says. Them chains is hard on a man. Hard.

Amen.

Many a morning as Tabbs drifts into town he notices Deacon Double moving with a look of reserve and obstinacy on his face. Though he walks with his head down, many locals will recognize him and stop to greet him, and he will glance up and smile a reply as he hurries on with the swiftness of a man who feels both humiliation and danger in recognition. He is as tall as Tabbs but thick and strong, muscled up perfectly, his threatening frame always amenable in immaculate dress, his eyes—a fleeting exchange of glances—his most noticeably attractive feature, green. The pace of those days was such that Tabbs was never able to talk to him at length, in any intimacy. He would do so today. He sees the Deacon approaching, ready to enter his office. As he unlocks the door, he turns his face toward Tabbs but not his body. He knows that I don't like him, Tabbs tells himself. He knows that I think he is a son of a bitch. They greet one another.

I'm surprised to see you here, the Deacon says, something unnaturally deliberate in the way he utters the words.

Have a moment?

A questioning look.

He swallows dry breath, strays itching in his memory. They enter the Deacon's office. Tabbs strives to get his bearings, for every time he visits the deacon's office he finds that the positions of the furniture and decorations have changed. He swears that this is an actual physical fact—like some bizarre variation of musical chairs—and not simply a failing of memory explained by his few visits and the separation of time between each. He'll make a mental map and later sketch on paper what he remembers seeing, then will use the actual drawn map to verify his suspicions upon his next visit.

He decides to be direct. I don't know who's in charge.

We all are. The committee.

Tabbs is absolved. He goes to the meetings not simply because he has time to kill or because he wants to study their beliefs, but because he wants to be there when they step back into the world of order.

You don't approve?

No, it's not that. I'm just trying to get my bearings. Tabbs sees Double clearly on the other side of the table, his handsome features, green eyes, the startling colors of his shirt. Double indicates that Tabbs should sit and he does, but Double remains standing.

Do you pray?

He takes in a grand vista of bookcases that reach the ceiling, three walls, a tall line of rifles inside each case, a fence of armaments. A window set in the front wall, where Double stands in morning light, pistols on the long table between them. Tabbs knows there is intimacy in what he is seeing. I do, but perhaps not enough.

Yes. You must ask yourself, Why did God give us this situation?

He can smell soaps on the other man's body.

And you should know the answer without any doubt. Divine power operates far beyond the limitations of what my human awareness can grasp or my five senses can detect. His voice is exact, crystal clear. If we live and move and have our being in Him, God also lives and moves and has His being in us. Double plants and unplants his feet until they are perfectly poised. That's why we must pray. "Whatever you ask for in prayer with faith, you will receive." Matthew 21:22. What I know is not based on what I see.

I am not unaware of your point of view.

But I can see that my words fall on deaf ears.

I don't see any need for fomenting violence.

Double waves the suggestion away. We are fomenting nothing. Mr. Gross, if I set before you a cup of hot water and a portion of tea, would you call it a cup of tea?

I must place the hot water to the tea.

Exactly.

Tabbs watches Double, understanding what kind of God is behind his stare.

What an opportunity we all have now, Mr. Gross. The war has given us a new world. We can turn the page and begin afresh. The work to be done is not to be a reproduction of what we see in the Anglo-Saxon's country. It is not to be a healing up of an old sore, but the unfolding of a new bud, an evolution, the development of a new side of God's character and a new phase of humanity. As in every form of the inorganic universe we see some noble variation of God's thought and beauty, so in each separate man, in each separate race, something of the absolute is incarnated. For the special work of each race the prophets arise among the people themselves.

Prophets? Tabbs sees in Double's gaze something of that amused expression with which General Bethune had observed him many years ago.

Yes, prophets must do what they are required to do. You see, Mr. Gross, the great sin of that institution called Slavery is that it fostered the need for a greater sin called Emancipation that tricks the unknowing into the belief that any of us, African or Anglo-Saxon, are free. Man can never be free. At birth, he is firmly tied to his mother through the umbilical cord. And even death does not free him, for his Maker then claims what is rightfully His and assumes charge of his soul.

Tabbs listens to it all and tries to think through it, hearing (suspecting) something unsaid, that all of this talk about prophets and freedom is, in the end, about Tom.

We are all bond and must do as we are so scripted to do. Indeed, these Freedmen can't remain idle, loitering about, seeking handouts, falling into wells. Or all of us here on Edgemere will fall. Jesus came into the world not to condemn. He came to save that which was lost. We are saving the world for the Ethiopian. And we are prepared to move heaven and earth. *Conquer the waste places.*

He feels comfortable (admit it) sitting here, listening to Double, gathering his own perspective, but does that he mean he should display his true thoughts before Double in this sparse room with one window and two chairs, pistols on the table and rifles on the walls? No. He should remain silent, refuse communication and hold his feelings within himself, so that Double will know him only as he wants Double to know him.

There are those who would condemn both you and me for the things we have tried to achieve. But I can hold my head high.

Tabbs holds his head high.

In the evening, Ruggles invariably makes an appearance, three or four evenings a week calling on him at Wire's house. They take seats in the garden, tender evening light falling across the foliage. Share the bottle of sack that Ruggles brings. Ruggles is usually tired after a day's work and not in the mood for conversation. He will talk only vaguely concerning his day—his affections and irritations— sometimes with rude familiarity. Tabbs appreciates his coming, for there is additional post to be delivered, additional criminals to be had, vigilance to be maintained, but Ruggles chooses to be here with him. Of those things they cannot speak of they simply say nothing. A measure of how far they've come.

Take me to her.

Mr. Tabbs is away. Two come and get him, struggling from side to side.
Tom, we thought you would like to help us this Sunday.
No church music.
You can play whatever you like.
No church. Legs dragging.
Outside light gallops over his body. The church is cool. The organ has a powerful sound, waves rising and falling.
Reverend Pastor speaks to him. Thank you for coming today, Tom.
Jesus rose.
Yes he did.
He can smell burning in different parts of the church. God is the Lord of both light and darkness.
Then he goes on greeting people in the church. I see you two are still without child.
It is in the works, the husband says.
All that opens the womb is mine, he says.
The deacons do the devotion. Then it is Reverend Pastor's time to speak.
The Almighty is good. I don't think you heard me, the Almighty is good.
Yes.
He allowed us to get up this morning. I been sick for the past three Sundays. But He lifted my head off my pillow today. Yall gon help me?
Yes!
I say, He lifted my head off my pillow today. He made sure I got out of bed this morning. Cause he knew that I had to be with yall today.
Uh huh.

Said, I had to be with yall today.

That's right.

It's Easter Sunday. And the good Lord has brought us someone special today. His parallel is not to be found the world over, nor in any time of which the records are known. He reigns forever in an outlandish wayside temple of his own, full of bright dreams and visions. Brothers and sisters, the Original Blind Tom.

The two men pull Tom up into the air, three men standing on six feet. He hears the congregation, animal noises. They explode into applause. He takes his bows, one and another and another.

I thank the Almighty for allowing me to be here today to witness this miracle.

The two pull him back down, sitting on six feet. Then he tells the two, There ain't no original.

You are the original.

You see, brothers and sisters, the days of miracles are not yet done.

Preach it!

You all gon help me this Easter Sunday?

Yes!

Take the original out of my name.

Said, yall gon help me this Sunday?

Yes!

We serve a mighty God. I do believe I have some witnesses in the house?

Yes.

He gave His only son so that we might be free from death. His only son. And He gave us all gifts. That's something you got to understand, the Almighty gave us all gifts. And what was Jesus's gift? Jesus came here to die. And in so dying He opened the cage and made us all free.

Tom.

Jesus Christ, the redeemer of man, the center of the universe and of history. His gift was He cheated death. Only Christ's tomb is empty.

Amen.

Tom.

Now if Christ preached that He rose from the dead, how say some among you that there is no resurrection of the dead? But if there be no resurrection of the dead, then is Christ not risen? And if Christ is not risen, then our preaching is vain, and your faith is vain. Yea, and we are found false witnesses of God, because we have testified of God that He raised up Christ, whom He raised not up, if so be that the dead rise not. For if the dead rise not, then is not Christ raised? And if Christ be not raised, your faith is vain; ye are yet in your sins. Then, they also which are fallen asleep in Christ are perished. If in this life only, we have hope in Christ, we are of all men most miserable.

You ready to sing?

No church music.

Okay.

Don't go doubting Jesus's gift.

No!

The Almighty gave each of us a gift. We need to know what our gifts are. And we need to put our gifts to use for God and the church.

Two deep breaths.

Some Sundays I can't wait to get here to church. The sisters look good, they smell good, and what they cook is good. Everything is good.

Tell it.

You must have the audacity of hope. Lord, your church often seems like a boat about to sink, a boat taking in water on every side. In Your fields we see more weeds than wheat. And the soiled garments of Your church throw us into confusion. Yet, we got to remember something. It is ourselves who have soiled the garments.

Preach!

We put holes in the boat.

Yes!

We failed to plant the seeds!

Ready?

We can't go out and change the world until we're right. He took some breaths. I wish some of you wouldn't sing in church.

Ha!

And I wish some of you wouldn't cook. You got to know what your gifts are.

He lets the organ move about the room. And they start in on a hymn. Then it gets quiet again.

You got to know what your gifts are. You got to put your gifts to use for the church and the nation. And you got to get right.

The organ speaks.

There's a reason that Blind Tim is here in the church this morning. He ain't here just to sing. Some of you think that. "When is he gon shut up so Tom can sing and play us some piano?"

Laughter.

The time has come for us to forget and cast behind us our hero worship and adoration of other races, and to start out immediately to create and emulate heroes of our own. We must canonize our own saints, create our own martyrs, and elevate to positions of fame and honor Ethiopian men and women who have made their distinct contributions to our racial history.

But I think I said enough. The Almighty has been fortunate enough to bless us with the presence of one of our heroes, the Original Blind Tom.

The congregation applauds. Before Tom can take his bows the two walk him on legs to the front and sit him at the piano. He doesn't touch the keys, just feels the wood beneath his hands. He feels the wood for a long time.

Play! Play! Play!

The whole church shouting to the roof, but he keeps feeling the wood. Then Reverend Pastor speaks something and the two walk him on legs to receive the wafer of bread. He takes the thin wafer onto his thick tongue. Take, eat. This is my body.

Be quiet, Reverend Pastor says, grinding the words through his teeth.

They put the cold cup to his mouth.

This is my blood. Drink.

I am one of the greatest men that ever walked the earth.

I'm sure you are. Now drink.

I overcame the earth.

Mouth quiet.

They put the cold cup to his lips, and he sips from the chalice filled with blood.

The tasteless water of souls.

What did you say?

The tasteless water of souls.

Then the two take him away and sit him. Then the Reverend Pastor. Words fall from his mouth. Ends his sermon with, Become. New or old, become. Citizen or Freedman, become. Change is the only constant. Become. Don't die. Multiply.

Let us pray.

Two men (the same two?) take him outside after his mouth settles down. He says it, word for word. My gift is the peace which I leave unto you. Whoever drinks from my mouth will become like me. I myself shall become that person. He says it again. And again and again.

Two take him back to the house. Still saying it. Mr. Tabbs isn't there.

Stay here, one says, until your tongue gets better.

I didn't afford you prayerful consideration, Wire says. I should have sought your permission first, I will admit that. A revolting expression flamed on his face. I'm actually glad he doesn't play Christian music. Over the years I have given enough to substantiate my claim of precedence for the Almighty's natural laws and their marvelous, even incomprehensible working, over any so-called supernatural endowment.

Big sparse drops of rain patter on the window.

But they already have their Tom, Tabbs says. Haven't you heard? He doesn't try to hide the sarcasm in his voice.

We are a peculiar people, prone to prayer on the one hand, and superstition on the other.

How do we put an end to this? You have to put an end to it. Speak to Double.

Double is of different stock. He was born in a white womb.

Can it be that he and Wire are feeling the same ache?

The rain stops. There is a smell of donkeys and some other very sweet scent. He can see the stones of the gate, the trees by the window, the dark sea. He feels that everything is looking at him and waiting.

Yes, things have gotten out of hand. But can you blame us for trying? The essential things in history begin with small convinced communities. So, the church begins with the twelve Apostles. From these small numbers came a radiation of joy in the world.

But it's *your* church, Wire. Why are you giving them, these deacons, this Vigilance Committee, Double—why are you giving them all the power?

Every church in the South, every church in the city, every church in the nation, indeed every church on earth, must, by and by, become nothing but the church and renounce all other aims that are incompatible with the principles of the church. Our only enemy is sin.

But it's your church.

I know. At least I thought I did. But God has become an exile to Himself. I want to believe that we can save these Freedmen. *Lifting as we climb.* I want to believe that we can save all of us. But Satan has made his way into our temple through some crack in the roof or some open window.

Urchins shelter in the lee of a crudely constructed command post, while their cohorts taunt and tease the horses, hitched to posts or braced to wagons along the main street, attempting to blacken hooves with their rags and brushes. The horses jerk in their traces.

Their loud overjoyed laughter.

Jay-bird sittin on a swingin limb
Winked at me and I winked at him
Up with a rock and struck him on the chin
God damn yer soul, don't wink again

One blacker screams at a cohort, I ain't tellin, Magellan, then jumps out of reach before the other can connect with a lunging punch. These shoe blackers—audacious, fearless, and self-contained. (Mischief always holds the seeds of further disruption and destruction.) Only yesterday Tabbs had declined their barefoot offers with a quick dismissive wave. Blackers with no shoes themselves. Now one points at him with perfunctory disdain. He sees a second's brow rise and the corners of his lips fall. The boy who approached Tabbs yesterday seems more relaxed today, the look of panic gone (disappeared) from his face, replaced by a flat hurt look. Tabbs somewhat ashamed of his refusal. He should show the urchin some kindness. The boy looks Tabbs's way, sees that they know each other. He smiles, the sound of sea waves coming at him clearly from the right, but the latter turns his face away, a quiet face, without any of yesterday's irritation.

Tabbs feels he should amend, pay off this small debt. (No, he is not under sway of doing good deeds, nor the motive of unattributable guilt, the erasing of daily sins. Only wants to make penance for yesterday.) Though he believes that begging is undignified, he pulls a dollar from his pocket, silver big and round, and quickly presses it into the boy's hand. I don't need the blacking, he says. Share it among you. Only upon his taking his seat at home thirty minutes later does it occur to him that a few coins would have been sufficient, both to feed and to teach the greater lesson.

Holy bejesus, the boy says.

Hot damn.

Hey, what you got?

Half-change.

A case quarter.

Yall niggers don't know nothing. That's a dollar bill.

Gon buy my way into heaven.

Black-robed deacons approach. The coin-wealthy boy pops alive, sees them, and dashes off. Shiners and dancers alike, a few of his cohorts notice his hasty departure, turn to see the why, and off they swoop. Then the remainder of the group—slow learners—catch wind and rush off at breakneck speed.

Take me to her.

I sent her away. And she hasn't come back. I'm sorry. I sent her to the city.

I can find her if you take me off the water.

Tabbs almost laughs.

Where we were living before.

What.

With the piano.

You're asking about the Bethune woman?

Bring me to her.

Is that who you mean? Tabbs understands. Tom wants the Bethune woman.

Take me to her.

Tabbs sees three girls, strays, contraband, dressed in black, seated out in the open, light rising up from under them as if they are sitting on top of blankets of sunlight. As he passes them, a woman comes over to take him by the elbow to halt him. She speaks but he understands nothing of what she is saying in her irritable quick patter.

Flying their rags at the end of broom handles like the standards of an impoverished army, the shoe blackers shuck and jive. Juba it up, clapping and singing.

> One mornin Massa ready to head out the door
> And gon away
> He went to git his coat

But neither hat nor coat was there
For colored gal, she had swallowed up both
Then took her nap in the chair
Massa took her to the tailor shop
To have her mouth made small
Colored gal took in one breath
And swallowed ole Massa, tailor and all

They exhibit many steps strokes lifts without breaking the measure of the music, with high-pitched shouts of *A show for your money, a shine for the show.*

Clutching something in his fist, the coin-rich boy holds aloof from the rest in the shadows of a tree. He notices Tabbs—the businesslike usage in his steady gaze—and comes over to him.

Good day, suh.

Good day.

You not from round here?

No, I'm not.

I ain't either.

He gives Tabbs an expression that says, *We got that in common.*

I'm in need of employment, the boy says.

I would like to help, but I don't have any work for you.

The boy silently closes his eyes and does not say a word more, as if stricken blind and dumb.

Urchins tussle. Pitch rocks and stones. Spill blood and bones.

Put your ear to a tombstone and hear the sound of the dead trying to rise. An aphorism that Wire has heard time and again here on Edgemere. But these newly dead have had no stones fashioned for them, only raw fresh graves, one black mound after the next like the shiny backs of so many beetles against the red horizon where a low-hanging sun turns the ocean into a rippled sheet of metal, throwing the shadows of the dhows lining the shore against the sky like so many black nests. None have sailed today, or will sail tomorrow, or take to the ocean the day after that, and many more days perhaps, not now, not after this.

He stands surveying the widening prospect of the island, children and mules rapidly coming and going in a rattle of speech and chatter between the bodies of the dozens upon dozens of mourners assembled here waiting for Wire to speak. Everything they do is considered, unhurried. He tilts his head as though to shake water out of his ear. He has an accounting to give, but quiet is knotted into his body, already wearied by what he will have to say, tired beyond bearing by all the events that have led to this moment. Wire already hurrying away from the thought before it becomes solid enough to take a grip and summon other thoughts that he has safely penned away . . .

Then he hears Double speak. God has three rings: of birth, of death, and of the resurrection of the dead.

It is Wire's place to speak, his ordained right, as Double well knows, so in addressing the crowd before Wire has a chance to, Double has supplanted Wire's authority, no two ways about it.

But the alabaster has only one, Double says. Death. Their actions have made clear that they will no longer permit us to fish these waters that we have always fished, and in so doing, they mean to starve us.

Motherfuck them, Ruggles says. Motherfuck every stinking alabaster that some white bitch shat out of her stinking womb.

You cannot qualify war in harsher terms than this, Double says. War is cruelty, and you cannot refine it.

They have numbers, Wire says.

And so do we, even if our numbers are less. Let one man be ten. Be careful.

Brothers, I ask you, is it wrong to ignore the arms and the ammunition that God has entrusted to us? The church can order them to be removed, but nay. Rather let the church hang like Christ on the cross over these boxes of arms and ammunition until the boxes are used.

Be careful. Think it through. Every man here had better do that. Wire looks at each man in the room.

Injustice is on the throne, Double says.

Shit, Ruggles says. You ain't said nothing.

They're shitting on us.

They can't help it. It's in their nature. All a woogie knows.

Walking all over us. Shitting on us.

I ain't never been nobody's slave. And ain't gon be.

Can't they jus leave us be?

You're talking willful destruction, Tabbs says.

They're killing us one way or the other. If we must die . . .

Walking all over us. Shitting on us.

They don't know no other way.

Be careful.

Advances only a few yards when he sees the band of shoe blackers, all of them, the youngest and the oldest, fully seated on the ground outside a stone gate. Resting. No, not resting, more as if they are all waiting for something, expecting something. Whispering, nodding, grinning. One urchin looks up and sees Tabbs, then they all begin exchanging excited winks. The last to notice, the coin-rich waif turns his head and falls silent under Tabbs's gaze. The unmoving darkness of his eyes. He does not look away. Tabbs can see him watching, preparing himself.

Sir? The boy stands up. Tabbs thinks twice about acknowledging the waif. He should just continue on, walk right past him and wash his hands once and for all. So why doesn't he? For no conscious reason, he decides to go over to the boy, neither curious nor suspicious, and having (seeing) nothing to lose, nothing to gain.

The boy holds out his hand, then opens it to reveal the coin Tabbs gave him yesterday glinting with sweat in his palm. It's okay if I come to your hotel room with you, he says.

What?

It's okay if I come to your hotel room with you.

This boy—Tabbs had not asked his name—with his flushed face, shining eyes, and poorly obedient tongue. He takes Tabbs with his other hand, the hot little dirty coinless one, this final action—Tabbs thinking, I will never see him again, I never saw him again.

In the ocean air his thoughts play. Strangely peaceful here, the water glowing and rippling, and light hanging in the sky like trailing silk. The night cooler than you might imagine, out in the open like this, all those stars freezing above.

An ungodly man diggeth up evil, and in his lips there is a burning fire. So is the tongue among them, that it defileth the whole body and setteth on fire the course of nature. Double is quick and alive, full of energy and expectation, his movements strong and excessive as he strolls back and forth along the water's edge, which is like the spine of some colossal animal, strolls before the men assembled one and all in white robes along the shoreline, the men perfectly calm and relaxed in their garments as if these robes are simply another feature of this landscape, shawls of sea fog. He is part, one of those white-robed men, and he stands waiting and watching and hearing the low buzz of the other men breathing alongside him.

I was there at the beginning, Double says. I remember the cold hold where together we were held in shackles and wallowed in filth and stewed in disease and pondered the worth of life and the finality of death as the chains rang and echoed and the ship creaked.

And when we spoke out, they tried to remove us from speech and exile us to silence.

The Deacon puts one hand on Drinkwater's shoulder and exerts downward force until Drinkwater drops into the wet sand, porous beach dented around his knees.

And he has to consider his own weight, all of that sinking softness beneath him, wet and black and full of shapes.

In a barely audible voice Double asks Drinkwater to open his mouth. Drinkwater opens his mouth. (Small teeth.)

O sons of Israel who feed upon suffering and who must quench your thirst in tears, your bondage shall not endure much longer, for there is something in us that cannot be outside us and thus will be after us though indeed it hath no history what it was before us, and cannot tell how it entered into us.

Double's left hand arrows into the opposing sleeve of his robe then angles free. The glinting object he now clutches in his hand he holds out for all to see, a glass vial filled with red liquid and secured with a bone (ivory?) cap carved in the likeness of a fish. Even from a distance of several feet in the fading light, he can see that the cap is so finely and intricately detailed that one might mistake the cap for an actual fish shrunken into miniature.

Behold. Consecrated blood.

Double unscrews the cap and allows one drop of consecrated blood to spill onto Drinkwater's tongue then three additional drops to plop onto Drinkwater's forehead.

Do not mourn. Each of us is a celebrant here. In the times to come we shall know each other by bloodstains.

Double moves on to the next man, who kneels down before the Deacon and opens his mouth without the Deacon having to first instruct him.

The path of the righteous man is beset on all sides by the inequities of the selfish and the tyranny of evil men. Blessed is he who in the name of charity and goodwill shepherds the weak through the valley of darkness, for he is truly his brother's keeper and the finder of lost children. And so stand with us, poised at the entrance to our suffering. Leap for our islands, our towns, our cities. Leap for our seaborne ships.

No one comes in, Tabbs says. And you don't go out.

Yes, suh. The top end of his black boots rise well above his knees, like strange appendages, new growth, the boy's body rising plant-like out of each leather sleeve. (Boots full of sound. Whenever he walks, his footsteps are hollow in sound as if there are hidden cellars under the floorboards beneath him.) And the shank, a sharp shiny addition to the belt around his hips, with its long wooden handle and equally long blade, also seems too large for this boy.

Do you understand?

Yes, suh.

Tom is beside them before Tabbs notices his presence. I got stories to tell, he says.

The way I feel this morning we might witness a miracle today. Double looks at the Bible on the dais, gets momentarily lost in admiring contemplation of the pages, then turns his gaze back to the congregation. Sermonizing, he keeps one hand on the Good Book. Are you all with me?

Yes!

I thought so.

Excited laughter and exchanges from the congregation.

I'm gon say something that yall don't want to hear today.

Uh oh.

We are not worthy of this island, Double says. I don't think yall heard me. I said, we are not worthy of this island.

Silence.

Our work has been slow, but it has been certain and unfailing. And our enemy steps in and puts an end to it. Unworthy I say. Because the enemy told all of us to leave. Did they not? They shot us. They poisoned us. They burned us. They took what rightfully belongs to us. Did they not? And what do we do in return? Nothing.

Double shakes his head.

They drove us out of our homes in the city, not once, but twice. And they will drive us from our homes here, on Edgemere, if we let them. Are we to build homes in the sea? I think not. But we seem willing to simply stand by and let the enemy do to us whatever they desire. Do you mean to tell me that you gon jus let the enemy edge you into the grave?

Once again, Double shakes his head.

Do those words hurt? I hope they do. God's words should cut deeply. If you ever been cut, you know that you remember the knife forever.

Speak, brother!

If you haven't been cut, you forget. God's words should make you worse. Before you get better you have to feel sick. I'm gon make you all feel worse today.

Preach.

Double's black robe is adorned with two red crosses on the front. A day of red. Red cloth draped across the black wooden Jesus affixed to the crucifix on the stage behind the dais.

You wronged, buked and scorned, outraged, heartbroken, bruised, bleeding, and God-fearing people. Double drew his free hand against his glistening forehead and continued. I love all of the streets of Edgemere, and all of the alleys. Every inch of our island. And every man, woman, and child. Every cow and chicken and donkey. Each of the powers of the soul has a different luminosity here, a different coloring, a different richness, a different profundity, a different clarity and a different mystery from that which it has in other lands. Only upon this soil can our nation exist. His eyes radiating in their intensity some message to supplement his words.

And our enemy is taking it all away. And you gon jus sit by and let them. Why oh why? His face is trapped in a smile so sick-looking that many are embarrassed into looking away.

O God why has Thou cast us off? Remember Thy congregation. Lift up Thy feet unto the perpetual desolations. Thine enemies roar in our midst. They said in their hearts, "Let us destroy them together." O God, how long shall the adversary reproach? How long?

The words squeeze to a close like a carriage drawing to a creaky stop. Double brings both hands to his throat, with his thumbs pressing into his Adam's apple. And he begins pushing up on his face at the chin as if he can lift his head from his neck. He falls backward to the floor headfirst, hands still at his throat, and starts thrashing about, arms wailing, face moving in a circle windmill-like. Wire is quickly at his side trying to bring an end to the seizure with a medical hand. But Double's energy is such that he rolls around in the dirt on the floor, clutching his throat, rolls over and over, one direction and another, until he comes to rest on his left side, kicking his legs like a fallen horse.

He gives up that position and remains flat on his back. Shut eyes, gnashing of teeth. Then his head cranes back, pushing up the temple of his throat, words gurgling there. Soon all twelve deacons surround Double, closing him off from view, Ruggles roaming the periphery trying to keep others away. Give him some air! Step back! Give him some air to breathe. The hum coming from Double's body gradually approaches understandable sound. Wire and the others continue to minister to him, although Tabbs cannot see their actual movements.

Then the deacons get to their feet one after the next, grouped in two rows like parted water, six deacons here and Wire and the other six deacons there. That is when Tabbs sees a second Double emerge from the right side of the first, one man on the floor become two. Both men sitting up slowly then both getting into a kneeling position before standing fully upright. One Double falls down, two Doubles get up. Two Doubles. Tabbs looks intently, trying to clarify what he sees. His own eyes must express amazement first, denial second, and then acceptance. Two Doubles. They take to the podiums at either end of the stage. Audible expressions of awe and disbelief from the congregation. Indeed, it is Double, same skin, same hair, same teeth, same black robe with two red crosses dirty in the same places. Wire tries to take one Double by the hand, but both Doubles wave him away.

You see. I was slain in the spirit. But I arose. See me now. Double on the left and Double on the right, both speaking at once.

Yea, I tell you, if we die, it will be but a temporary farewell to this earth. Let me assure you that we will rise up some day from the ashes and come again. The two Doubles are looking at the congregation as if they are staring at something behind them, something that they can see only by looking through them. The dark places of the earth are full of the habitations of cruelty. Arise, O God. Forget not Thine enemies, for the tumult of those that rise up against Thee increaseth continually. Double's tone is flat, so hostile that it lacks even the warmth of anger. Help us rain flesh upon them as dust.

Members of the congregation begin to fall to their knees in awe.

And let them eat, and be well filled, and die while the poisoned meat is yet within their mouths. Help us. *We are become a reproach to our neighbors, a scorn and derision to them that are round about us.*

Preach.

Turn us again, O God, and cause Thy face to shine; and we shall be saved. And render unto our neighbors sevenfold into their bosom their reproach. But fornication and all uncleanliness or covetousness, let it not be once among you. Each Double points a finger at the congregation. Neither filthiness nor foolish talking nor jesting. And be not drunk with wine. No whoremonger, nor unclean person, nor covetous man who is an idolater hath any inheritance in the kingdom. Let no man deceive you with vain words. And have no fellowship with the unfruitful works of darkness.

Go away, Satan!

Walk as children of light.

Satan!

Hold not Thy peace, O God, and be not still. For, lo, Thine enemies make a tumult. They hate Thee. Thine enemy places his mother, sister, wife, and daughter on a platform up among the stars, then this enemy gets a thousand swords, rifles, and cannons and decrees death to him who seeks to drag them down.

Tabbs tells himself, I will take Tom and leave. I must take Tom away from this place, from Edgemere, from the city. Tom and me gone by morning.

Underground (Return)
(1869)

"The closer I'm drawn to God,
the more things on earth
lose their color and taste."

SOMETHING IS SUCKING ELIZA IN, SUCKING HER INTO THIS country landscape, Eliza a city lady who holds a fit against the country but who now feels absolutely secure here. Go wherever you please. Look at whatever you please. Solace and delight in the honey-colored bales of hay dotting the landscape, the sacks of feed, the bushels of peanuts and firewood lining the road. Surroundings so rich she has to select senses.

She walks until the landscape slurs into darkness. And once it is dark she is inside the house in ten minutes. She can sit down, rest her tired soul, and let her hungry body fill itself. Night around her continues to be alive, her body porous to every noise, scent, and taste. The lovely swallowing of thick night air as it carves around her brain, cutting away any thoughts or memories she doesn't want, leaving her with nothing but her lean anonymity. Glad to be cut off from the city. Not the slightest clue about what is going on there. Her final appalling days there enough.

Perhaps the events should not have proved as stunning as they did, however suddenly they came. One miscellaneous night she heard wild thunder and knew that people were going to die. Then in the days that followed, sky noises, abrupt light, and fires glowing in her windows like fireflies painted the complete details of scenes that she did not need to see, mobs hunting and hounding the way only white blood can, Eliza not quite believing that it was happening again.

Tom, how did you escape the mob?

Tom said, I went up in a chariot of fire.

She knows that she cannot return to the city. She is uneasy at the thought that this stay in the country is a return to a kind of beginning, a push back. (Sharpe. Tom.) She tries to shove away from the thought, but it stays suspended in her brain. What is she saying good-bye to?

You did not choose me. It was I who chose you.

She flames a lamp. Light pushes its way about the corners of the disintegrating roof. It had once been a nice house, with soft timber selected for the beauty of its grains. Now the house carries a faint odor of dampness. The beams in the ceiling look old and insecure, little monsters chewing up the wood from inside. She feels calm in a strange distracted way. Lingering in this wayside place where new emotions enter her. Thinking (what else?) about black days and nights in the city where she would wake early each morning, the pain in her head on again.

What she wanted was something not far from herself, but she would not want to think her feelings out. Back home in the city, even before the violence, she would be overcome by such a sense of aimlessness and futility that she would venture out, purely in order to preserve an illusion of purpose, and walk about the streets with no particular destination in mind. In this way she got to see the city in her own good time. The streets always curiously empty, no explanation for it, unless—perhaps—half the population spent every day drowsing the hottest part of the day indoors. Only those few but serious faces returning her gaze. In the faces she would sense some terrible knowledge shared. Then one day she saw a man who looked like a beardless General Bethune walking freely about, crutches circling him, like a man rowing a boat on dry land. Peeking into the man's silent face, she convinced herself that it was someone else entirely. That was when she knew she had to get out of the city, alone there in her apartment, no Sharpe, no Tom, only the piano. Convinced herself that she had to go to the house in the country, for the outside world in the city had become so painful for her that she could no longer stand to be in it. And then the violence came.

Walking around the house she sees only lifeless objects. She is the only crazily alive thing in the house. She will always stand outside, against herself, searching for that something inside that can break down her despair. (Why?) Daylight remembrance of words said and events that happened far apart, now no longer separate but pushed into each other. (Bath. *Lait*.) Her days will be filled with more broken things. Any reason she should think differently? This is what she has. *This is what I have.*

Some nights when she sleeps, the long day behind her, she hears Tom speaking inside her, speaking in a voice that does not sound like the one she remembers—but why does it sound familiar?—and speaking words she doesn't remember him saying. She does not resist. Indeed, she lets it happen, forgetting who she is for a time to become him. Sleeps on serenely. No one has heard these words, it seems, but her, a rare luxury:

The doors spring open. The people enter. The music flies up. Breath stops. I am what I am. A what and a who.

Go down belowdecks then climb back up top into sunlight and noise. Look, Blind Tom! What seeing is.

They choose me. I cannot choose them. What seeing is. A hand touches my shoulder. A voice comes into my ear. Each person is a surprise.

People see me. Even when I cannot feel them. (Will you look after him? Please look after him. Please walk him back to the house. See to it that he doesn't fall. See to it that he puts on the white suit.) *I must be spoken to or touched. I must speak or move. Draw water. Drawing with hands. What is "deep"? How high is "above"? How much space is "wide"?* Even there thy left hand shall lead me and thy right hand shall hold me. *What is "tall" or "short"? "Ugly" or "beautiful"? Measure. What seeing is. Hot and cold I understand. Hungry and tired. Sleep and awake. They always think I am asleep. What seeing is.*

When I sit down the world stands up. Tom, the man says to me. How does it make you feel to know that all these people are here for you?

The horses go galloping across the keys. The men pop up from the small spaces between one key and the next. Trenches. Where silence lives. The soft space. The men rush for the edge where they will fall off and die.

Tom, the man says. What do you know about the Battle of Manassas?

The cannons roll along too, positioned for firing. I had hot metal in my mouth, under my tongue, and I spoke it.

I skip to one short key after the next. Toss notes into the air that the world may see and catch. The running men are blown down at the sound. I stand up and take my bow, and the seats stand up with me, hands and voices coming at me.

Yes, I've brought them all here. I've brought them all here. With the long and the short keys. Water running down my face.

The General cuts across the floor with his stabbing canes, a man walking on knives, shanks.

At church one Sunday, the General slapped a planter. How it happened:

Boy, what brings you to church today? the planter speaking to me.

Me speaking back: Many of the first will be last and become a single one.

The planter laughed. Said: That's why God protects children, niggers, and the crazy.

And that's when the General's hand found skin. Watch yo mouth, the General said. Don't you ever mock anything that belongs to me.

That must be hard to do, the man said.

No, I said. I like to find things. I am a natural finder of things, I said, words in my mouth. Running through rain. Rain running through me.

Blind Tom?

Ain't no Tom here.

Me against the floor, against ground. Words like hard, firm, solid. *Words like* pain. *The stabbing canes move the ground along so that the world walks when they walk.*

Eyes put light in the dark. The face is the place from which the voice comes.

Why do you sing like that?

A person puts all of his body into his voice.
I hear the rain sounding upon the fence, clattering on roofs, and on
nests where the birds take baths.

Words like shallow *and* deep. Hot *and* cold. *I walk wet-footed to the table.*
Lait.
She pours. At my mouth it enters me in a rush.
She pours when I say it again.

Hardly had she settled in her armchair at the window overlooking
the garden when she hears a knock on the door. Her skin tingles in
quiet panic. Back in the days of the Blind Tom Exhibition the journalists would always speak rapidly, a thousand words a minute, so
Sharpe would have to be diligent in answering their questions, making an effort to speak slowly and clearly in complete sentences. But
what can her tongue do? Moreover, what reason does she have to believe that the caller is an innocent, only an annoying and innocuous
newspaperman wielding words and not a brutal intruder? How long
has it been since a journalist has come calling? Since anyone has?

She doesn't have to answer. Just keep sitting here, a secret. The
pure vulnerability of an open body. Another knock. So the caller
knows she's here. She stands up from her chair, rising with a reluctance that ascends right up to her head. The doorknob mushrooms into
her hand. A nigger woman appears in the doorway and stands there
looking collected and very intent. Tom's mother. (Who else?) Eliza
feels a heavy uneasiness. Something has happened to this woman's son
and his mother is here to see that Eliza answers for it. Payback.

Mrs. Bethune.

She has seen the woman only once before. Then like now she is
not bothered by their unalikeness, Tom and his mother. Indeed, they
look nothing alike, but unseeing and sighted are two separate catego-
ries of existence. The blind look only like themselves.

The mother steps into the house and two niggers follow her,

three intact shapes, Tom himself (Glory!) and one she doesn't recognize, a mere boy. She is steady under his gaze.

Mrs. Bethune.

What does she feel upon seeing Tom? (Glory!)

The Negress releases her head from the bonnet, rubs the color out of her face, and becomes someone else, half woman, half deception. Tabbs Gross.

You.

I brought him, Tom says.

Then they say nothing for a time, wordless knowledge. The room seems composed of impossible red and yellow hues. And it seems terribly strange to her that she should meet this man now with no anger at all, something quite different in her feelings. This new emotion, whatever it is, sternly demands that she pay no attention to him, pretend nothing has happened—*I'm here to take the boy to his mother*—no interest or shock, that they share no history. He seems to walk about the room, triumphant, looking and touching, his presence physical and insistent, her attention taken by his sex-changing stunt, a man fluted in a beautiful dress standing in the middle of her room. Then he goes over to examine the piano. Now Tom starts to move. For some time he strides about the room with the unnamed Negro boy following him like a clumsy devoted animal.

She and Tom let their hands touch. Mr. Gross keeps a respectful distance, his eyes changed with reduced feeling. He seems nervous, even afraid. Then he is speaking, light bright words flying and chirping like birds in the room, busy with claims and proclamations. Here he is talking about the piano. She would have expected Tom to come upon the piano first.

To where? Where will we go?

South.

Why on earth hadn't she thought of that? Suddenly she is glad to have them here in the country with her, her buried senses unearthed. Remembering (what else?) the beautiful boy in boots—Sharpe—the black leather long and lean. And now Mr. Gross in a dress with boots of his own, dress cupping their length. He is saying something that she can't hear. She smiles at him, wanting to get over the fact that he had accused her before, that he had taken Tom away from her at a time when she could no longer tolerate the boy's presence, but he had done it in such a way to imply neglect and cruelty on her part. (She could say to him, *I was here when no one else was.*) And Tom. (Glory!) Tom who manages to veer away from the boy shadowing him and is now holding her at the elbow, hugging her, touching her hair, Eliza aware of the boy's protective eyes taking in this moment. Indeed, she is going places that she does not understand. Fine by her. She can't remain here.

❀ ❀ ❀

Tom sits on the floor, his legs spread and his head hanging from his neck like a heavy flower.

Tabbs squeezes into the last of the petticoats. The dress will come next, cotton smothering his strength, putting male and female together to deny the one and to lie about the other. He had removed shirt, pants, undergarments—layers of events and incidents, taking on new layers, a determined creature, his face immaculately shaved, smooth to the touch, not a trace of hair. And with color at his mouth and cheeks, his face brightly exaggerated by rouge, he actually looks like a woman, a Negress. Now, a touch of perfume. Then the head scarf, the final touch. Earlier, he felt like a chicken standing there naked in the room, sunlight like hot wax unfeathering him. Through no fault of his own he has to relinquish this part of his self, conceal his sex, for the sake of practicality and safety, the closest he can come to a kind of invisibility. Figures the alabasters probably won't attack him if they think he is a woman. Hopefully, the orphan's youth will be protection enough for him. (Women and children.)

I got to dress up too? the boy asks.

No need. The boy is so thin that his clothes seem to have made an effort to fit as close as possible to his body so as not to miss his ghostly proportion of skin and bone.

Mr. Tabbs.

You can't call me that. Once we're out there, no misters.

Okay, Mr. Tabbs. The boy goes on looking at Tabbs, nodding at some private thought.

You just remember to keep an eye on Tom.

You ain't got to worry about me. I done worked as a navigator befo.

He will set out again. He must set out again. He sets out again— his choices are his choices—for a country estate on the murky outskirts of the city (the geometry of moving from here to there). His motives for traveling are justifiable. *Fill up your horn with oil and be on your way.* He will find the Bethune woman, his duty to press on, but his brain runs in the wrong direction, trying to push down, unable to push down, one grisly thought that speeds repeatedly through his head: What if she is gone for good? How then will he get Tom to budge?

Earlier all evening he kept discovering himself stilled, unable to think. Now he must go directly toward what he fears.

They move in thick blinks of travel to the main jetty. *It will cost you to get there.* He will have to negotiate with a captain the price of passage to the city—Yes, ma'm. No, ma'm, five for you each—a cost too much, but he pays it. Eyes flashing beneath his cap, the captain takes Tabbs with one hand at his elbow and the other in the small of his back and helps him down into the slightly wobbling dhow. The boy leads Tom. Four in a dhow, wind smacking the sail, waves thrusting up. The captain proves to be a good ferryman, maneuvering against the strong currents. The dhow seems to glide along of itself, the water awake and rushing now that they've decided to take their chances, facing into the wind, feeling the wind, grateful (Tabbs) in fact for the cool salty blowing and flapping, all of the colors you can think of sparkling on the surface of the water, a shock of bouncing brightness, only this flashing substance lying between them and land on the other side, the final crossing. The captain speaks to them calmly in a condescending language, but there is no energy in Tabbs to be angry or insulted. The captain offers them oranges and bananas, which Tom and the boy accept. Eating done, they toss the rinds and peels into the ocean, the captain unspeaking, occupied with the close focus of sea, his hands working in silent rhythm, his eyes glazed with concentration. For the rest of the hour Tabbs watches the captain's mannerisms along with the (unavoidable) shifting of the sea, Tabbs remotely enjoying the ride, forgetting. Then the ocean changes, starts to break open. The dhow rocks and dips, wood creaking, the sound of nails freeing themselves, water splashing up over the sides, splashing over them, and Tabbs starts to rue the moment, panic in the boy's face, the boy scooting from one side of the dhow to the other and back again in an effort to avoid the water. Quit that now. Water, get away from me. Now I said quit. I ain't playin. He reaches as if to grab his knife, until he realizes that it will do little good to cut the water, a thing that can't be killed. Tom tries to brush and shoo the water away from his person. Tabbs feels dizzy, sick, stupid. Have they come this far, land just up ahead, only for the dhow to disintegrate beneath them, right under their feet, for them all to sink into a place of forgetting, nothingness? For his part Tabbs displays not the least bit of panic—too late for that—hands stiff and calm, keeps his knees parallel to each other beneath his dress, while light bounces off his scarf, tries to remain as calm as the seated captain. Tom stands fully upright, shoulders squared and chin high, in self-assured defiance of the swaying, hands outstretched to balance himself, knowing without the others' saying that they (Tabbs) are afraid, that all is not well. With gracious ease the captain works the rudder this way and that and regains control of the craft, careful to give Tabbs a look of amends. Or is it something else? Hands moving, he draws the dhow parallel to the quay. Then he just sits there, looking at them, waiting for them to quit his dhow. He does not try to hide his dismay, making it clear that he will not assist them. To his credit, the boy (wobbly) regains his composure enough to climb the stone stairs twenty feet to the pier with Tom directly behind him.

They walk without hurrying, long slow breaths, although the streets are full of alabasters, alabasters who watch three Negroes go by, the only three, a Negress, a boy, and a blind nigger, Tabbs tense with uncertainty. The air carries to his ear sounds that have no understood meaning. Every window in the city unshut, shades lifted, curtains open. He should shrink down into himself, go back, but he cannot. Despite the heavy petticoats he feels light in his low-cut boots. The boy steers Tom away from any obstacle in his path with a slight tug of the sleeve. Tabbs realizes that they have set a course for the train station, Tom leading the way, walking more sprightly than he and the boy. Who is he that he can do this? Blind Tom can do anything.

They move in silence, everything suddenly heavy and slowed down, until they reach the train station, shade-filled and muted in color. A strict stillness. Alabasters, their curious watching of Tabbs, Tom, and the boy. Tabbs purchases three fares. (He catches a waver in the eyes in front of him, the alabaster caged inside the ticket booth.) And they take a bench, sit down, and wait, Tom between Tabbs and the boy.

We're going to her, Tom says.

Tabbs's hand on his shoulder to quiet him, a tenderness.

The room is so still that Tabbs hears no sounds until he thinks of listening for them, hearing calls of "nigger" and "blind." The station towering over them so they feel they are within a deep iron well. The roof and walls rattle and shake whenever a locomotive leaves or enters the station. Caged and aging light in this echoing vault. There is no wish in him to step away from this place.

Tabbs breathes in the forbidden atmosphere. Eyes everywhere. Has his secret been found out? He feels manically awake. Tom blind and the boy eyes wide open, swallowing everything, shank glinting in his boot. Tabbs continues to sit locating himself. Not their train.

Two or three more trains are called out. He lets the calls seep into him. The boy's head is bent down, his lips moving, as if speaking with someone. He opens his eyes when Tabbs touches him on the shoulder.

Finally, they hear the call.

Train, Tom says. And already he is up and walking toward the platform, the boy shambling after him. Once again, Tom is leading them—to the proper car. (Blind Tom. Half man, half amazing.) They walk the stretch of the station to reach their compartment, from front to rear, open air on either side of them, Tabbs aware of every sound as the alabasters come and go. What he wants in his life now seems a huge thing.

Tom pulls himself up into the car and clatters about the almost empty compartment. The boy slides alongside of him and directs him to a seat. Tabbs sits directly behind the two of them, attached instantly to the sounds of the train. The alternatives that surround them. Not too late to turn back. But he understands the complications of removal. This is his whole life right here. No turning back. Soon they are pulling out of the station. Too late to turn back.

Fire up the engine, Tom says. You will see her.

Who?

Her.

Pulling into speed, above clattering wheels. Motion simultaneous around him. Tabbs nestles back into his seat, watching the boy, his face young and lean and dark, his eyes bright. Encased in the slow-rocking compartment. The train sweeps unhesitatingly into a tunnel, deep space around him. He sees his reflection in dark glass—some woman—and is shuddering in the darkness. This is when it will happen, he thinks, in the impersonality of darkness. But the train comes into daylight, his eyes inches away from the window, receiving the moments of brightly lit trees, water left behind, the city left behind, the train stirring its way up into the light, passing small towns.

For some time—an hour or more?—Tabbs sits in the slow-rocking compartment and tries to lose touch with the world around him, looking with hope at the boy's and Tom's faces every now and again. Then the conductor calls out their station, and Tom rises up out of his seat. Debarked, Tom resumes his frantic push for the Bethune woman's country house. Spills forward without hesitation, his legs running ahead of his speed-shaken body.

The thrill and terror that get knocked into Tabbs when he sees the house. He wants to say something but can't, opening and closing his mouth as he takes in the full aspect of the sight blooming up before them, as they draw the house closer to them. The grounds are a jungle. Grass overgrown. Tangles of vines climbing up to the roof so it appears the house has grown hair. Wind banging and loosening a roof tile, trying to unpeel it. And Tom is already banging on the door, the boy twenty feet behind him, unsure what to do next, watching Tabbs, who nods to acknowledge that everything is all right.

Tom, let me.

With Tabbs's concerned hand on his shoulder, Tom steps back to allow Tabbs access to the door.

He sees her face, unbelieving, baffled. Startled, she backs away. He simply walks into the waiting silence behind her, the politest entry he can make. Enters into stunning emptiness. A room that holds nothing of interest except for a settee and a few chairs made soft by embroidered pillows and antimacassars ready to soak up pomade. The room bright and hot, sun streaming in, revealing all the dust in the air. Tom and the boy follow, and he watches pure surprise (fear) slide into her face. His hands work quickly, removing the dark head covering and the bright coloring from his face, no more need to hide and deny.

You.

The whole of her person shaped now into an accusation that drives her confusion into him. There is no wish in him to be here.

She stares at Tom long and with so much concentration, like a person taking a farewell look. She looks exhausted, face and body drawn out. Tom takes her hand and holds it, caressing it. He moves closer toward her, bringing his excitement. She does not seem able to say anything. Tabbs watches them with far-off curiosity, and so watching, feels himself receding from the scene.

The room appears to have suffered a flood sometime recently, the walls mildewed with dampness and ocher in color, a far wall taken up by the large pattern of a watermark seeping through from another world, spreading in the shape of stupendous buttocks, the windowsills and the wainscot deeply outlined by dark liquid. Thin white curtains like a thin glaze of water across the windows—light free, light that is not blocked out by the huge oak looming in view outside the window behind Eliza and Tom and extending upward out of sight, a good ten feet above the house itself.

He takes a seat, as dusty as it is. Something new—a kind of fascination, vitality—has entered her manner, a mischievous glitter in her eyes. She looks at him and smiles, waiting for something. Tom is holding her hands and pressing them with a desperate intensity. Tabbs sees her troubled look, but she turns her head away. He casts his gaze over to the piano, tempted to rise to his feet and go over to it. Instead he looks around in amazement at all the dirty things in the room, dismayed. That is a beautiful instrument, he says.

She glances doubtfully at the piano and laughs self-consciously. Tom touching her hair. But why are you here?

We're here for you.

Me.

You.

She does not push him to answer any more questions.

We have to leave.

She just watches him.

It's the only way, the only way we can be safe. We can go to the South where the soldiers can protect us. Our only guarantee of protection.

I'm not going anywhere with you.

Eliza, Tom says. Miss Eliza. Stroking her hair.

The boy standing by the door in speechless astonishment, something loosed in him at the sight—disdain, desire, resentment, a yearning for identification. For his part, Tabbs resents the boy's squeamishness but says nothing.

You're asking me to pack up my belongings.

No need.

But then I'll have nothing.

I'm not the one asking.

Her head slightly inclined in the attitude of someone who is hard of hearing. Tom leaves her side, his movements quiet as the night, and while the Bethune woman, Eliza, stands considering, Tom circles the room, once, twice, stopping before the piano on the third pass; he rounds it once, twice. A pageant of odors invades Tabbs's senses, mildew and much else. No way he can (will) leave this room without her. He is ready to say more, but what more can he say? What does she want him to say? Unwilling to let go, he can only hope that she will press him for details, a reasonable explanation. That she will share her worries.

Tom kneels down on all fours and crawls under the piano. Then he tries to grunt upright into a standing position, tries to lift the piano, hoist it onto his back.

❀ ❀ ❀

Take me home. Tom speaks over his shoulder to Tabbs. Tom is sitting rather solidly, not a care in the world, Eliza seated beside him, Tabbs and the boy—all seriousness—in the seat behind them, the compartment empty except for the four of them, together, a solitary quartet. Take me home. I don't want no trouble. No thirty pieces of silver.

Okay, Tom. Okay. Thinking, Please cease your babbling. A woman again, Tabbs had secured his scarf and applied ample portions of Eliza's face powder and rouge before they set out, his head abuzz with the task before them. So far so good, although the journey here was not without challenges, Tabbs reliving the moment when Eliza encountered the startled expression on the face of the station clerk; not until they were almost upon him did he notice them, the ancient alabaster awakened by this odd pairing of a white woman with three Negro traveling companions. Tabbs was glad she had done the speaking to the station clerk since his voice was wanting in firmness, its quality unsteady. But his troubles weren't over. The entire time in the station, he stared in dumbfounded frustration at Tom hanging about the woman, cooing, wanting to tell her something. Doors cracked open in Tabbs's head, releasing a fresh fit of panic. No way of knowing what trouble Tom might bring forth, the havoc he might cause.

Tom and Eliza engage in a whispered conference, while Tabbs sits watching the boy in appreciative quietness and listening to his halty breathing. Side by side, he and the boy are nearly touching. He wants to make conversation. The boy's lips move. If they manage to formulate the faintest of sounds, Tabbs doesn't hear what they say. Tabbs requests that the boy repeat himself. Listens with all his body, searching for clues, but the boy is having difficulty getting his words out, his eyes feverishly active, fear the source of his discomfiture. Now Tabbs starts to worry again too, fresh unease, not that he had ever stopped. They will need to change trains in the city.

Tabbs speaks to him, and the boy lifts his shoulders in a meaningless way, his brown eyes rippling with sun, which rises and falls inside them. When he is praised, his eyes light up with a glow of their own, red suffusing his cheeks. The afternoon sun starts to lose its harsher edge. Late afternoon light. The city calls out to them, Tom playful still, full of rejoicing.

Tom. Tabbs touches him on the shoulder.

Eliza and Tom are the first to detrain when they reach the station, Tabbs and the boy behind them. He steps down to the platform, his feet wobbly. They amble on, cautious, looking (and listening) this way and that—Tom in his gangling posture, as clumsy in his bodily movements as a child taking his first walk, a body of mixed messages—before venturing on to their southbound locomotive. They are the last to board. The train snags into motion, pulling out of the station. They weave toward the sleeping cars against the violent rattle of the train.

They walk a gauntlet, successive rows of nigger-seeking faces lifting in concert. Tabbs feels a storm gathering inside his head, a spinning turbulence that sets his whole body atremble, his eyes going far beyond what is visible, starting to water, blurred sight. Against his expectations, they reach their assigned compartment and slip into their berths. Anxious, time is transferred from one station to another with the swiftness of a thought. Now the city looks very far away out the window, and he feels achingly free of everything in it. Can it really be this easy? He fidgets in his berth. As he sees the city through the glass a smart hurt imposes itself on his mind. Something is eluding him, but what?

The boy is a need evocative of other necessities. His once terrified face loosens into a bemused grin when their eyes meet, traces of dried sweat marking the boundaries of his brow and chin. Still, there is a glimpse of self-doubt in his physical posture. Small, a pygmy to Tabbs's manly stature. Tabbs sees him shift restlessly in his berth. What can he do to help?

He tells the boy something about the science of locomotion, about engines, pistons and pulleys, steam and tracks. He hopes in speaking this way he isn't causing a greater shock than the boy has already suffered. He feels the words go into the boy, but the boy remains silent, his features sporting a specter of worry. Stations drone by.

Train, station, train. Train, station, train. Train, station, train. A sameness of place, sound, and motion. After a while it no longer seems to him that he is trying to put space and distance behind him or shorten space and distance ahead, but that he and the train are now hanging suspended in pure time like a single thread of spiderweb. Going nowhere and fleeing from nothing. A hypnotic steadiness (seeing) of trees and towns and solitude. Eliza and Tom speak amicably. He and the boy should too, but the boy sits quietly, an expression at once fierce, wild, and tender.

I thought—Tabbs begins, but he does not say it, disappointed in his own failed and spent flesh.

Something releases in the air. Alabasters enter the compartment. Tabbs feels a constriction in his chest, a muscle withdrawing to some empty space within. Warily, the alabasters (four of them) begin making their way toward Tabbs and his party, moving slowly, closing in. Soon they are close enough for Tabbs to take in the expressions on their faces, faces registering a type of disbelief more akin to caution (fear). The figures identical, the same, in dress. *We all dressed in Memphis cotton, Ruggles said.* They cast their slow heavy-lidded glances upon Eliza, Tabbs, Tom, and the boy in turn, surrendering to the sight.

How you all doing?

Eliza speaks a reply.

Where you heading?

She tells him.

Is that right? . . . These niggers are with you? . . . You don't say? That one here, she sure is a peculiar-looking one.

Yeah. What's your name, auntie?

She can't talk, Eliza says.

One blind nigger and one mute one. Trust my eyes. And what's this one's affliction?

I'm jus a nigger, the boy says.

I can see that.

The four alabasters continue to stand before them, their expressions eager, puzzled, and wild. Tabbs begins to tremble. *To have made it this far.* From the way that their features scramble he can tell that they are tense but undecided, as if waiting for a higher authority to instruct them. For a while the four alabasters continue to do nothing but stand there in wordless confrontation, staring with a peculiar blankness. Now all he can do is to continue to sit, weighing a thousand expedients, stippled shadows ever present, moving across his lap. Now he hears a humming cadence. Tom's lips are amurmur with faint sounds. Talking to himself? Singing? Then Tom starts to string together phrases, a disjointed discourse. The alabasters turn their eyes toward Tom.

What's that?

Tom speaks sings discourses on and on.

I could swear that he's—

He's just an imbecile, Lucky. Can't you see that?

Yeah, Lucky. Leave the nigger be.

Still the words of this man's cohorts do nothing to lessen his sober intent gaze, the air full of Tom's voice, a hysterical music, roaring saliva bellowing above their heads, building in volume and intensity until ears hurt.

Lord Jesus!

The alabasters back out of the compartment. Tom continues to shout scream his gibberish.

Tom, Tabbs says.

No stopping him.

Tom!

You hear that nigger?

Yeah, I heard him. Son of a bitch.

The air falls still.

On my mother's life.

The four alabasters enter the car again.

They've come for you, Tom says. You could not put it off forever.

And Tabbs hears the startled shout, There, that one there! and he feels monstrously exposed, breaking out of the limits of his body. Hurrying forward, the deceived snatch the scarf off his head and hurl it into the air, a red moth, the furious flutter of things undone.

Station!

Needing to feel superior to his attackers, Tabbs stands straight up to his full height—

See, what I tell you?

That nigger son of a bitch.

—but when the first blow comes he recoils back into his seat. He fights the air, his heartbeats coming in little waves of acceleration, knowing that he is going to fail, and he slows his body down until he is breathing with infinitesimal care while some fragment of his attention thinks soberly about the facts. A refusal to put his life in the hands of these others. If he holds his breath will he disappear? Held breath decreasing his weight and whatever space he takes up. He becomes quite still, sitting with unbreathing rigidity, listening to the sound of his held breath until he spills his air out all at once in a noisy rush. He does not even feel the boot. One minute he is in his berth, the next prone in the aisle, feeling his eye, the side of his face, his mouth, his nose, his entire head, the slow painful pounding of the blood.

You damn nigger bastard!

Someone stooping over him with the coldest eyes he has ever seen.

He hears, *You did not choose me. It was I who chose you.*

More hands touch him with savage interest. He hears the sound of his body being pummeled, the shock of blows about his head, and it angers him, their determination to handle him as if they own him, have a right to his flesh. He hears now the sound of his fists on flesh, hard muscles, skin, and bone shocking against his fists. Back on his feet as quick as he can be, sealed in by bodies—still four? or more now? the compartment filled with alabasters, every fucking alabaster who has ever lived and some who haven't even been born yet—receiving their weight and laying his own on them.

He hears Tom say, Fire up that engine! then hears Eliza say something, her voice calm and sensible, without panic. Hears someone else say, You let him call you that? Sees the boy's hand move in a lazy arc and one alabaster bring both hands to his throat, as if choking himself, a vise grip, streams of blood spurting through his fingers despite the liquid-stamping pressure he applies. The alabaster goes down with a gurgling sound.

The boy moves the shank in furious desperation at his attackers. A second falls, and a third, and a fourth. Then someone seizes his shank-wielding hand, while another jumps in to afflict damage. Hellfire, the boy says. They got me. Screaming even as he is lifted out of his berth, sound swarming into the marrow of Tabbs's consciousness, weeping and shouting and wild talk. Tabbs feels himself being lifted, too, kicking, squirming and squiggling like a hook-baited worm but going wherever they carry him. The nerve. Off the train now. The bitching nerve of these godless people. Damn every one of them. Above ground, he sees alabasters, some of the locals, staring alert down the street or seated on benches, porches, and stoops, pulled tidily into themselves. A few smile approvingly. Tossed into the gravel and the dirt. He does not move at first because he cannot. A small shower of stones falls around him. A few hit him. Then they are on him again, fists and feet.

He half pushes and half flings an alabaster off of him, and his feet flee beneath him. In the shouting and running he has no time to stop and see what damage he has suffered. (He tastes blood.) No time. He twists quickly left, shrinks his body to push it through a hole cut in a hedge, then comes upon uneven ground running across patches of dry grass, his head light, his mouth dry, his saliva thick and bitter, sound building and breaking inside him. But the noise behind him is loud and wilder now. Looking back over his shoulder, he sees that the first of his pursuers is near. Run even if he can think of nothing to give him safety, no hiding place.

The ground erupts. Planters unearthed. Up from a hidden seam in the blackness. Their garments shining clean. They spit dirt free from their mouths. Lick and restore luster to their boots. Both time and anti-time. All he can dream and then some—foot stretching into yard, yard stretching into furlong, furlong stretching into mile, mile stretching into league, a line of bodies that extends to the horizon. (Does the world really reach that far?) A future promising that it can hold far more than the past could ever hope to. A world to get lost in.

Minutes slip through his hands, and hours fail to raise his feet. Where you going to run to? Why not escape down the path that lies in the direction you were heading, south? Paths stretching in all directions, hidden inevitabilities. Yet and always yet.

He blinks words. Can't help but hear the faint rumbling behind his eyes, some unseen whole taking shape.

And he thinks, I've lost him. I've finally lost him. No earthly way he can bear the loss, not now, not ever.

Although she had been living in a third-floor apartment at 6 Gracie Square for a decade or more, none of her neighbors knew her name or knew where she was from. No designation either family or Christian was ever put on her postal box or doorplate. And the neighbors say she never answered the bell and that her groceries were left in the basket set for that purpose outside her door. Moreover, although up to twenty families resided alongside her in this unpretentious five-story red-brick apartment building located on a quiet cobblestoned street with thick-trunked trees perfectly spaced and aligned as if on parade, the fact that a blind Negro was living in her apartment with her was known only in humor and disgust. Indeed, her neighbors considered her barbarous in electing to live with a Negro, even if they were too well bred and polite to tell her so.

Sightings of the Negro were few and far between. Last summer, several of the neighbors saw the woman lead him to a closed carriage, and the same neighbors witnessed them return in their carriage at summer's end.

On several occasions, the superintendent was summoned to her apartment for maintenance or repairs, but he never saw the blind Negro, only heard him moving around in a far chamber. Saddled with the tools of his trade, the superintendent would go about his work, while the Negro's mistress—thin, tall, angular—watched him openly and frankly in her plain velvet blouse and ordinary skirt, her face creased into a look of distrust. One time when he was perform-ing some odd job, the superintendent heard the Negro throwing a tantrum somewhere in the apartment and claims that the Negro's mistress grew ashamed and blushed.

Some claim that the woman almost never entered the Negro's room since he detested human contact. However, whenever he let her enter, she would take the opportunity to clean what she could and wipe dust from the chair, the bureau, and the bedposts with slow quiet movements of her bare fingers. While she cleaned, he would stand silently at the window with his back turned to her and his afflicted arm stiff at his side.

The neighbors say that for the entire decade that the woman lived at 6 Gracie Square, they had become accustomed to hearing piano music coming from her apartment at all hours of the day and night. They would be in the middle of one activity or another when the music would suddenly begin, and they would listen attentively and respectfully, a disciplined and discriminating audience, even as they carried on with whatever they had been doing.

Then one day, several people passing on foot along the street heard big windows unlock with a clang above them and looked up to see the Negro plunge out onto the balcony and lean over the railing with his head cocked at some sound. After a minute or two, he went back inside. The big windows shut, and he was seen no more that day, or any other day that anyone can remember. But once he was back inside the apartment, they recall hearing piano music, a tune that none of them recognized. Soon thereafter, the music stopped. And no one ever heard it again.

May 31, 2013
Zanzibar

Acknowledgments

Here, I wish to acknowledge some of the people who uplifted me in more ways than one during the many years it took me to write this novel. Thanks and praise to Myrtle Jones, Binyavanga Wainaina, Lore Segal, Joe Cuomo, David Mills, Reginald Young, Bayo Ojikutu, Duriel Harris, Jacqueline Johnson, Randy Levin, Tucker Hyde, Steven Varni, and Terese Svoboda—dear friends who I trust with my life.

Special thanks to Robert Polito, Michael Anania, Beatriz Badikian, Elizabeth Borque, Fernando Ruiz Lorenzo, Doreen Baingana, Wanjiru June Wainaina, Ed Pavlic, Calvin Baker, Junot Díaz, Edwidge Danticat, Caryl Phillips, Grandmaster Masese, Zanele Ndolvu, Tyehimba Jess, Sandra Goodridge, Fran Gordon, Pamela Fletcher, Randolyn Zinn, Scott Dahlie, Grant Jones, Dr. Brenda Greene, Dr. Patricia Jabbeh Wesley, Mohammed Naseehu Ali, Malaika Adero, Mikhail Iossel, Ramon Garcia, Josephine Ishmon, Kitso Kgaboesele, Matthew Sharpe, Laura Pegram, Josip Novakovich, Jennifer Baker, Sherwin Bitsui, Aleksandar Hemon, Ishmael Reed, Colin Channer, Paula Kling, Elisheba Hagg-Stevens, Shalini Gidoomal, Suhaila Cross, Aldon Nielsen, and Chimamanda Ngozi Adichie for their love, support, and encouragement.

Special thanks to Martin Donoff, Rene Steinke, David Daniel, and the entire Fairleigh Dickinson crew.

I am grateful for the guidance of my elders, fathers by another name, for the wisdom in their words and ways: John Wideman, Sterling Plumpp, Quincy Troupe, Arthur Flowers, David Henderson, Keorapetse Kgositsile, and Stanley Crouch.

Thanks to my agent Cynthia Cannell and all the good folk at Graywolf Press, especially Fiona McCrae and Ethan Nosowsky, for their book smarts.

Thanks to Creative Capital, the Dorothy L. and Lewis B. Cullman Center for Scholars and Writers at the New York Public Library, the Whiting Foundation, the Ernest J. Gaines Foundation, and the Norman Mailer Center for their patronage.

A very special thanks to my wonderful kids, Elijah, Jewel, and James, who are a daily source of joy and inspiration and who make me eternally proud. And to the source, my mother, Alice Allen, who taught me how to keep on keeping on and how to make a way out of no way.

Last, this novel would not be possible without the music of the usual suspects (Jimi, Miles, Bob Marley, Trane, Bird, Muddy, and Mahalia), but also the music of some recent discoveries, namely Oumou Sangare (the world's greatest singer), Soriba Kouyate, Ayub Ogada, Cesaria Evora, Dawda Jobareth, Miriam Makeba, Richard Bona, Tool, and last but not least Blind Tom, whose life and music transformed me. The circle shall not be broken. Into light, into history . . .

Illustration & Epigraph Credits

Carved Door in Darkness (page 4) is from Sally Price & Richard Price, *Maroon Arts*, Beacon Press, 1999 (*Les arts des Marrons*, Vents d'ailleurs, 2005). Reproduced with permission.

Ancient Dhow (page 100) reproduced courtesy of Robert Barnett Photography.

"Path of a Hunted Bird" (page 158) is from *African Fractals*; reproduced courtesy of Ron Eglash.

Blind Tom and Lerche (page 218) is from *Ladies Home Journal*, September 1898.

Harp (page 350), MO.0.0.30371, is from the collection of RMCA Tervuren; photo by J. Van de Vyver, RMCA Tervuren. Reproduced with permission.

Newspaper advertisement (page 341) is from the National Archives and Records Administration.

Concert Program cover, special note, and overview (pages 342–344) are from the Library of Congress, Daniel A. P. Murray pamphlet collection, ML417.B3 M3.

Concert Program (pages 345–347) is from *Music and Some Highly Musical People* by James M. Trotter, Boston: Lee and Shepard, 1878.

Dominican Abbey, Ibadan (page 366) reproduced courtesy of Victor Ehikhamenor.

Harmonograph (page 482) created using www.subblue.com/projects /harmonograph.

Long Exposure of Ocean Waves at the Beach (page 504) by Joyce Vincent; reproduced courtesy 123RF.

Carved Door in Light (page 542) from Sally Price & Richard Price, *Maroon Arts*, Beacon Press, 1999 (*Les arts des Marrons*, Vents d'ailleurs, 2005).

The first epigraph is from an unattributed source, the second is an Ewe proverb, and the others are by Frédéric Chopin, Muddy Waters, Hildegard von Bingen, Malcolm X, Skip James, Abbey Lincoln, and Muhummad Ali, respectively.

JEFFERY RENARD ALLEN is the author of two collections of poetry, *Stellar Places* (Moyer Bell, 2007) and *Harbors and Spirits* (Moyer Bell, 1999); a story collection, *Holding Pattern* (Graywolf, 2008); and the widely celebrated novel *Rails Under My Back* (Farrar, Straus and Giroux, 2000), which won the *Chicago Tribune*'s Heartland Prize for Fiction. His other awards include a Whiting Writers' Award, a support grant from Creative Capital, and the Charles Angoff Award for fiction from the *Literary Review*. He has been a fellow at the Dorothy L. and Lewis B. Cullman Center for Scholars and Writers at the New York Public Library.

His essays, reviews, fiction, and poetry have appeared in numerous periodicals and anthologies, including the *Chicago Tribune, Poets & Writers, TriQuarterly, Ploughshares, BOMB, Hambone, StoryQuarterly, Callaloo, Other Voices, Black Renaissance Noire, 110 Stories: New York Writes after September 11*, and *Homeground: A Guide to the American Landscape*.

Allen was born in Chicago. He holds a PhD in English (creative writing) from the University of Illinois at Chicago and is currently professor of English at Queens College of the City University of New York, an instructor in the graduate writing program at the New School, and an instructor in the low-residency MFA writing program at Fairleigh Dickinson University. He has also taught for Cave Canem; in the Summer Literary Seminars program in St. Petersburg, Russia, and Nairobi, Kenya; for the Farafina Trust Creative Writing Workshop in Lagos, Nigeria; for the VONA/Voices Workshop; and in the writing program at Columbia University. He is the fiction director for the Norman Mailer Center's Writers Colony, and is also the founder and director of the Pan African Literary Forum, a nonprofit organization that supports and aids writers on the African continent. Allen lives in the Bronx, New York.

Book design by Ann Sudmeier. Composition by BookMobile Design & Digital Publisher Services, Minneapolis, Minnesota. Manufactured by Edwards Brothers Malloy on acid-free, 100 percent postconsumer wastepaper.